VAMPIRES AT MIDNIGHT

THE COMPLETE TRILOGY

M.P. STARKWEATHER

I want to dedicate this book to my two biggest fans, my husband Josh and my son Thom, who will probably never read any of my books. Thanks for pushing me to chase my dream. I love you both to the moon and back.

<h1 style="text-align:center">Acknowledgments</h1>

I would like to thank:

My author besties, who encourage me to keep writing, even when it's hard;

My amazing PA, Gwen, who is my twinsie;

My Alpha Team who tries hard to keep me on track;

My Editing Team who does their best to make sure my books make sense and have as few typos as possible;

My Cover Artist, Ravin DeMarco, who's responsible for the gorgeous images on the front of this book

and My ARC Team, who catch some of the things the rest of us miss.

BLOOD MOON

VAMPIRES AT MIDNIGHT
BOOK ONE

M.P. STARKWEATHER

Chapter 1

Delilah

"What the hell do you think you're doing?"

I whipped my head around at the harsh voice. It was dark, and I couldn't see his face. "I... I was..." I let go of the lock and stood up. The hulking figure stomped toward me, backing me up against the cold steel bars of the cage.

"You were trying to steal from me?" His accent was strange, and I couldn't place it. Thinking was impossible when a six-foot-three hunk of a man was pressed up against me. Now that I could see his face, I struggled to keep from being entranced by his warm brown eyes. The crying that had been coming from the cage behind me stopped as soon as he was near. The room went silent.

"I don't steal. I was trying to free them. They shouldn't be in cages." I hoped that I sounded braver than I was. My heart threatened to jump out of my chest. If my hands hadn't been pinned to the bars at my sides, they would have been shaking. As attractive as this man was, he was terrifying too. Every instinct in me screamed to run.

"They are exactly where they're supposed to be. It is not your place to release them." His breath was warm on my ear. He stepped back momentarily to look me up and down. I tried not to squirm under his scrutiny.

"What do you mean, they're exactly where they're supposed to be? You can't keep people in cages. It's against the law," I tried to sound tougher than I felt. The thumping of my heart was going so fast, I thought I might pass out.

"I can do whatever I want. Your laws can't touch me," he responded. His accent was sexy but definitely out of place. I wondered if he was a dignitary from another country. They seemed to get away with nearly anything. That would explain his attitude about 'my laws' that couldn't touch him. Then he turned and yelled in the direction of my uncle's office before trapping me again, this time with my hands between us. "Vinny! Get in here! I caught someone trying to break into the cages."

A minute or so later, Uncle Vinny appeared. He had a baseball bat on his shoulder and a 'don't fuck with me' look on his face. For a moment, I thought I was safe. "What's all this racket about someone breaking in?" He spoke as he walked. When he saw me, his expression changed. "Delilah, I told you to stay out front. The backroom is off-limits. You know that. Go back to the bar."

I nodded and breathed a sigh of relief, then I tried to move to obey my uncle's request, but my captor had other plans. He leaned forward and took a deep breath. If I didn't know better, I'd swear he was sniffing me. This whole situation kept getting stranger. "Let me go. I need to go back to the bar." I pushed against his chest, but he didn't budge.

"I'm sorry, Mr. Maxwell. It won't happen again. She's my niece and tends the bar." Uncle Vinny tried to reason with the gorgeous slab of man, but he growled in response. "Delilah, go."

"You don't give the orders here, Vinny. I do. It's my bar now. She'll do what I say." He looked down at me, and I shuddered. "Unless you'd rather be locked up?"

I opened my mouth to object, but nothing came out. I managed to shake my head. Uncle Vinny stepped forward, curling his fists around the bat like he was going to attack the guy physically. Mr. Maxwell turned away from me, and a whimper escaped my lips. My body felt ice-cold from his absence.

"Let her go. My family was not part of the deal. You got the bar and the operation. Delilah isn't a part of that." My uncle didn't back down easily. I covered my face with my hands as I waited for this to come to blows.

Mr. Maxwell leaned down and got in Vinny's face. "You will not disobey me."

Uncle Vinny relaxed. "You're right, she must obey. I'm sorry, sir. What would you like me to do with her?" He sounded so defeated. I'd never seen or heard him like this. My uncle wasn't a large man anyway, but now he looked even smaller.

"Lock her up until she decides to cooperate." Feeling confident that Vinny would obey him, Mr. Maxwell looked over his shoulder at me, then walked out of the room.

After he left, I turned back to the cage and started trying to break the lock again. Uncle Vinny grabbed my arm and turned me around. "You have to stop. You heard Mr. Maxwell. I have to lock you up. Come on." He grabbed my arm and started dragging me toward an empty cage on the other side of the room.

"Wait, Uncle Vinny. What are you doing? You can't just let this guy boss you around. Midnight is your bar! Kick him out!" I tried to reason with my uncle, but I could tell from his face that it wasn't working. It was almost like Mr. Maxwell had hypnotized him. That was crazy, right? His eyes were glazed over and he didn't respond to my pleas. I fought against him until I broke his hold, then crossed the room quickly. Before I could leave, he started coming toward me with the bat on his shoulder again.

"You can't do this. You're my uncle. You can't lock me up like this. It's illegal!" I tried to plead with him, but he didn't waver from his mission. It was as if he was being controlled somehow. He shoved me into the cold, metal box and locked the door. "Uncle Vinny, please. I won't tell anyone about what you've been selling back here. Don't do this," I begged him, but his stare was vacant, and he turned to leave. I still wasn't sure what exactly he'd been selling, although it was becoming apparent it was some sort of human trafficking ring. But why?

He stopped at the door and faced me again. "You have to learn to obey, Delilah, if you want to survive. I tried to keep you out of this; I really did. Why didn't you just listen?" He shook his head and walked out.

Adrenaline was still coursing through me after Uncle Vinny left. I paced the cage, then I turned to the occupant of the cell next to mine. "How long have you been here? Do you know what they want?"

A blank stare was the only response I got. It didn't matter which person I tried to talk to; none of them would respond. The crying woman had stopped and now wore the same blank stare as the others. If only I could figure out why they were locked up, maybe I could find a way to free us all.

I tried to talk to the woman who had been crying. "Can you tell me why you are here?" It didn't make sense to me. She'd been crying earlier, yet now she refused to make a sound.

She looked at me blankly, with the same stare that Uncle Vinny had before he'd left. She didn't even seem to hear me. I turned to another woman in a cage nearby. She had the same look on her face; all of them wore the same vacant expression that my uncle had. What was going on here?

"Please, I just want to understand. What is happening here?" I begged her to answer.

"Do not talk to them," Uncle Vinny scolded from the doorway.

"Did he send you back to torment me?" I asked with tears in my eyes. He ignored my snarky comment and walked into the room, stopping in front of my cage.

"They are here because they signed a contract. This is a part of the contract they signed. That is all I can tell you. They are not permitted to speak to anyone, not even me. Please don't make things worse for them by trying to get them to talk to you."

Uncle Vinny's words were quiet and deliberate. The blank stare was gone, but was replaced with smoldering anger. I knew that look because I'd received it every time that I had done something wrong as a child. I knew from the look on his face that I wouldn't be getting out of here tonight.

After he left, I pounded on the bars, pulling, pushing, hitting—anything to break free. I couldn't give up. I needed to get out of here.

I wondered how long it would be before I could convince my uncle to let me out. What if I was forced into whatever had happened to these other women?

My mind raced through all the possible scenarios. Were they being sold into slavery? Were they victims of a sex trafficking ring? What if they had been kidnapped from their homes? Or could they be mail order brides? There were so many crazy options that could be possible.

Once my hands were battered and bloodied, I had to admit defeat. I hated myself for it, but I couldn't stop the tears from falling as I sat there in that cage, feeling completely alone.

I spent the next three days in that cage, locked up like a dog who had bitten its owner. I should have been happy that I was being fed, but the whole thing made me angry. Tear stained and bloody, I begged and pleaded with Uncle Vinny every time he came in, but it did no good.

"Please, Uncle Vinny, just let me out of here." I knew it was useless, but I had to try. He shook his head and left again after dropping a small tray of food through the bars. A few minutes later, he dropped off a first aid kit so I could clean and bandage my wounds.

Over the time I spent in the cage, I watched as each of the women who were locked in the cells around me were taken. One by one, my uncle came in and opened a door. Each time, the woman inside nodded at him and walked meekly to the door. He led them out without a word, and I never saw them again.

I couldn't figure out what Mr. Maxwell wanted with the women in the cages, and the more I thought, the worse my ideas became. I didn't want to become someone's slave, whether sexual or manual labor.

As I ate on the third day, alone since the last woman had been taken out, I let my imagination wander. I'd heard of a cult that hunted people for sport. Maybe that's what Mr. Maxwell was after.

Finally, when I'd almost accepted that this was my life now, he came in.

"Have you decided to cooperate, then?" He walked over to my cage and stared down at me. I had no choice but to look up at him.

"Cooperate with what, exactly?" I hoped that I sounded braver than I felt. There was something dangerous about this man.

"With the hostile takeover of the bar, of course. What did you think I meant?" His accent washed over me like a warm cup of cocoa on a cold night. I shivered. "Are you cold, Myshka?"

I looked around the room, trying to figure out if he was still talking to me. "My name's Delilah. I don't know who this Myshka is. Will you just let me out of here?" I knew from what little Uncle Vinny would tell me that I was walking a fine line with this man. If he thought I was being disrespectful, he could leave me here, or worse. One by one, I'd seen all the women taken from their cages and not returned. I was sure she didn't get released.

"You are Myshka. It means little mouse. You didn't answer my question. Have you decided to cooperate?" He unlocked the cage and motioned for me to crawl out. Part of me wanted to stay where I knew he couldn't reach me, but the rest of me craved to be close to him.

I scampered out of the cage before he could change his mind. Mr. Maxwell grabbed my arm and helped me up. "There now, isn't that better?" I was pressed up against the bars of the cage with him trapping me, just like when we'd met a few days ago.

I couldn't respond, so I nodded. There was something captivating about his scent. He smelled citrusy but with a touch of something metallic that I couldn't quite place. I shook my head to clear my thoughts, then realized that I was still picturing his lips on mine. My heart would not stop racing. What was it about him that drew me in?

"Provided you are not planning to do anything stupid, I am willing to let you resume your bartending job for now." He reached a hand up and tucked a lock of my dark hair behind my ear. I had expected to recoil from his touch, but I found myself leaning closer.

"What do you mean, for now?" I was skeptical that he was going to pretend that nothing had happened here.

"I have other plans for you, Myshka. You'll see in time." He smiled at me and gestured toward the door. I started to walk out in front of him. "You will be measured for your new uniform tomorrow. Today you will go upstairs, take a shower, and relax."

"I don't live upstairs, though," I mused, trying not to be disrespectful.

"You do now." He handed me a keyring with a single key on it. The keychain held the logo for his company.

I followed him to the stairs. How long had this takeover been planned? Did Uncle Vinny know and not tell me? What exactly did Mr. Maxwell have planned for me? And why was I suddenly so anxious to find out?

CHAPTER 2

Viktor

I KNEW THAT VINNY's family was off-limits according to our agreement. It was the only thing he'd requested when I'd forced the deal on him. I generally had no interest in humans since I was turned, except for blood donations. Vinny was lucky I hadn't sent them both away when I took over.

For me, it wasn't about the money. I had everything I needed. I wanted to cut off the supply to Strain and the other vampire factions. If they were forced to depend on me for their survival, I would be able to control their unsavory actions.

I hadn't planned on walking into the backroom to find Vinny's niece trying to release my blood slaves. It was blatantly apparent that she had no idea what was going on. I was shocked that her uncle hadn't told her about the dangers of messing with vampires and their food supply, but I guessed that wasn't the kind of thing most humans had to worry about.

Even if she'd managed to open the cages, none of the women inside would have tried to escape. They had already traded their lives for the protection of their children. It was a small price to pay for the protection of Maxwell Incorporated.

The gangs in our city were dangerous and had no issues with destroying homes or families to get what they wanted. My company was in a position to protect people from having their children stolen in the night and forced to join these gangs. The police dealt with the vandalism and drugs, but they couldn't stop the kidnappings.

With the vampire factions getting in on kidnapping people for blood, it was becoming more difficult to keep our existence a secret. Of course, there were people who knew about us and helped us hide things from the public. My plans included forming a council to regulate vamp behavior. I wanted a vamp specific police force to keep the violence against humans in check.

I remember when I got wind that Vinny had been kidnapping women to sell as blood slaves. He'd been my supplier for years, but I had never thought to ask him where he was getting the blood. The moment I found out, I set my team to work on the hostile takeover. Luckily for me, Midnight was on the verge of bankruptcy, even with Vinny's blood trade. I couldn't figure out what he'd done with all the money he was bringing in. The numbers didn't add up.

I wondered if he had a secret stash somewhere or an offshore account that no one knew about. I wasn't going to ask him, since he caved to the takeover so easily. It didn't really matter; I would get my way and move forward with my plans. Midnight was the first step.

My mind wandered back to Delilah. Her scent did things to me that I hadn't felt in decades and it wasn't just her blood. I couldn't remember the last time a woman had affected me that way. If I hadn't snarled at Vinny to lock her up, I might have drained her. Any other day, I would have snapped Vinny in half for the way he spoke to me. But I understood the urge to protect family. Everything I've done was to save mine, even when I failed.

I had to walk away to keep from acting on my other desires as well. Delilah was the sexiest woman I'd seen in ages. I tried to avoid romantic entanglements to protect my business, but I felt as if I was being tempted simply by standing near her. I needed to get myself under control or I would risk losing everything.

Since purchasing Midnight from Vinny, I spent most of my time going over the books in the office. If I took a break, I tried to avoid being near Delilah, although she made it difficult.

The first day after she was released from the cage, she insisted that we meet to discuss the changes I was planning to make. It seemed as though her freedom had sparked her anger. I was relieved that she wasn't as meek as I had first thought. It pained me to think she would simply agree and go along with anything I ordered. Once she was in my office with the door closed, Delilah screamed at me for ten minutes about locking her up and expecting her to cooperate now. It was obvious that she had no idea who I was, or even what I was. No human dared to speak to a vampire the way she did. It was actually refreshing. I couldn't allow it to continue, but I couldn't react in my usual way. Her ignorance would save her life today.

As angry as she was about me having her locked up, she loved the bar more. The moment I realized how important Midnight was to her, I knew that I had a way to control her. I made her an offer for employment, and she jumped at it.

I was certain there was more to her reasoning than she admitted. That was as important to me as her anger. Neither mattered in the big picture. I knew she would stay angry for a while, and I was fine with that. I needed her to stay away from me.

By the end of our meeting, I was holding my breath so her scent didn't make me do something we would both regret.

A week later, I called Vinny into the office to set some boundaries. I knew he was angry with me for locking her up, but I didn't care. He had to learn his place. He needed to keep her busy and away from me.

"Yeah, boss? You wanted to see me?" He poked his head in the door and waited to be invited inside.

"I did. Please come in and have a seat. We need to talk about these books and your niece." I gestured toward a chair.

Vinny looked around awkwardly before taking his seat. I had redecorated the entire office to suit my style. There was no trace of the disorganized mess he'd left me with.

In place of the sports memorabilia, I brought some sleek, modern art. I preferred the finer things in life and I wasn't afraid to spend money to get what I wanted. The antiques and artwork in the office were more expensive than the building itself had been.

I reviewed the loose papers that were everywhere, then scanned them into the computer and destroyed the physical copies. I even went so far as to have my own safe installed in the wall without Vinny's knowledge.

I had the smoke-stained walls scrubbed and repainted eggshell white as the perfect canvas to showcase my art and collectibles. There was no way I would hang a Picasso on those nasty walls. I noticed Vinny checking out the changes when he entered, but didn't bother to mention it.

I wasn't one of those vamps who thought they were better than the humans simply because I was turned. However, I knew I was better than Vinny because he was a trash person. I was planning to see if we could fix that.

"What can I do for you?" he asked, clearly not aware that there was a problem.

"Who handled your books before the takeover?" I asked, leaning forward and forcing him to look me in the eyes.

"I did. I know I'm not very good at it, but I didn't have anyone else." He tried to look away but was captivated by my eyes. The weasel seemed desperate for me to believe his lies.

"Ms. Stone isn't skilled enough to manage the books?" It seemed he didn't give her enough credit.

"She's just a kid. She has all these fancy ideas of how to liven things up and bring in more business. I couldn't give her the books. If I did, she'd start making changes. Besides, she had no idea about the blood trade," he sputtered.

"I see. So it was better to run it into the ground than to let your niece help you? Well, there will be a lot of changes soon. You'd better get on board with them, or I'll have no choice but to get rid of you." I knew that threatening him wouldn't keep me away from Delilah, but his admission that he didn't want to let her have any creative freedom struck a nerve.

"I can do that. Whatever you want, I'll make it happen." Vinny was almost too agreeable. It annoyed me, but at least I knew that he was planning to let me make the decisions. That may or may not have been because of some threats that were made during our negotiations earlier in the week. Or it may have had something to do with the compulsion I used to force him to lock Delilah up with my blood slaves.

"Good. I want you to understand that you work for me now. I'm sending out new pricing schedules as well, so be ready for some pushback. You've kept things the same for far too long. Our product is worth more than you've been charging." I didn't bother showing him the new invoices. I wanted to see how he would take being cut out of the decisions.

"Okay. I'll be ready for it. If someone has a problem, should I tell them about the change in ownership, and redirect their questions to you?"

"If they get irate about it, yes. Otherwise, just tell them that prices went up. As long as it's not an issue, I'm not going to make it one." I stood up to signal him that our meeting was over.

"Um, sir?" He stood, but didn't leave. "You said that you needed to talk to me about Delilah. Is something wrong?"

"Oh, that. I wanted to let you know that she will be the bar manager by the end of the month. If you have a problem with that, you can collect your last check and be on your way." It wasn't what I'd wanted to say, but his attitude toward her earlier had pissed me off. I had needed to tell him that he needed to keep her busy when I was in the bar, so I didn't have to be around her. There was something about his attitude toward her that made me change my mind.

"No problem, sir. She'll make a great manager." He walked out of the room quickly, as if he was afraid that I might eat him. To be fair, the thought had crossed my mind. I was sure he'd heard the rumors that I did just that during my last hostile takeover. I didn't, but that didn't stop people from talking. I mean, you kill one guy for disagreeing with you, and suddenly you're a murderer. The idea of it was ridiculous. I just wanted to ensure cooperation. Plus, that guy was a dick. None of that mattered now. That was twenty years ago.

I had already decided that Vinny wouldn't be trustworthy, and his attitude toward Delilah had cemented that feeling. I would have to double check everything he handled until Vinny realized that I wouldn't put up with him half-assing things. I wanted to throttle him for nearly bankrupting the bar. I could remember a time when it was popular and wanted to get it back to that.

I had been a regular patron of Midnight before I'd been turned. It had been the best karaoke spot in town. Then Vinny took over and focused more on his back-room dealings than in running the bar.

That meant chancing another run-in with Delilah. As much as I wanted to avoid her, I wanted Midnight to succeed, and that would take sacrifice.

CHAPTER 3

Delilah

THE NEXT FEW DAYS were a blur while I adjusted to my new boss. I shouldn't have let myself forgive him for having me locked up, but somehow I did, or I tried to anyway. There was something almost magnetic about him. I wanted to be near him. If I were being honest with myself, I would admit that I was seriously attracted to him. I wasn't ready for that realization yet, though.

Each day was spent trying to ride out the roller coaster that had become my emotions. I was so angry about him locking me up, but I was so intensely attracted to him as well. Part of me hated that Uncle Vinny had let him in on whatever was going on in the backroom. My uncle still refused to let me in on his secrets.

I wanted to beat them both with Uncle Vinny's bat and force them to tell me everything. I even stormed into Mr. Maxwell's office and spent a long while yelling at him about everything. It didn't get me anywhere, but I felt better afterward.

Although I was conflicted, I wanted Mr. Maxwell to take me seriously so that he would listen when I presented my ideas. Midnight had been my home for as long as I could remember. It didn't matter if I hated the new owner, I couldn't force myself to walk away. I hoped that somehow, I would be able to come up with enough money to buy the bar from him.

So, I would bide my time, pretending to be a good little worker bee until I figured out how to stage a coup and steal my bar back from him. I spent my days saying, "yes, sir," and my nights crying in the shower. I needed to get my emotions in check. I went from angry to sad to aroused way too quickly.

I wanted him to take me—anywhere. Maybe I was just horny and should give Ted a call. I wasn't really interested in him, but I knew he'd be willing. Nah, it really wouldn't be the same. I guess I'd just keep drooling over my boss.

"Please, call me Viktor. We will be working closely together. There is no need to be so formal," he insisted again.

"I'm sorry. I can't get used to calling you by your first name. It's a respect thing, I guess." I couldn't tell him that Viktor was far too sexy of a name for a boss and that I'd been fantasizing all day about sighing his name while he did naughty things to me.

"When our adjustment period is over, I want to start teaching you how to handle the books. I'd like to promote you to the manager at some point. You seem to have a good head for business." His compliments made me weak.

Every time he told me that I did a good job, or handled a demanding customer well, I imagined him calling me into his office and bending me over the desk. It was surprising how many times in the past couple of days I'd had that same fantasy.

I got the impression that he was avoiding me after our initial meeting. That was basically confirmed when I ran into him in the stockroom.

I walked in to find him doing inventory, which was unexpected, since I knew my uncle had already done the counts. He jumped when the door swung closed, and I cleared my throat.

"Oh, Mr. Maxwell, I didn't realize you were doing inventory yourself. I thought Uncle Vinny was taking care of that for you." I needed bottles of scotch and tequila to restock the bar. Wasn't it just my luck that was exactly what he was standing in front of?

"Ah, Ms. Stone. I'll be out of your way in a moment. Some of Vinny's counts were off, and I needed to confirm those suspicions before I spoke with him about it," he explained, looking from his paperwork to the shelves and back.

"I'm sure he didn't do it on purpose, though. He's usually very thorough." I hated lying but felt like I needed to defend my uncle.

"I think we both know that's not true. I respect your need to protect your family. There's nothing more important, you know. Don't worry, I'm not going to fire him. I just have to explain that I expect things to be done a certain way and if he can't handle it, I'll have to demote him to janitor." Viktor smirked, and I couldn't tell if he was being serious or not.

"Oh. He wouldn't like that at all. He's not exactly the cleaning type," I responded.

"Well, there are far worse fates that could befall him," Viktor smirked as if imagining something worse than cleaning the bar.

My hands were sweating, and I was terrified to even think of what he might mean. I attempted to change the subject. "I just need to get bottles to restock. Will that mess up your count?" I walked over by the shelf he was in front of and gestured toward what I had come for.

Viktor took a step backward to put some space between us. *So, I wasn't imagining his avoidance.* I never was one to back down, so I took another step toward him, caging him between two racks of bottles. "I think you're avoiding me, but I can't figure out why," I challenged, moving close enough that our chests were almost touching. I still wasn't sure why I cared. It was better for me if he hated me. Then I could stay mad at him over locking me up the way he had. But for some reason, I just couldn't leave well enough alone.

I looked up at him and could tell he was uncomfortable. "I'm not sure what you're talking about. I've been swamped, as have you. If there is something you need to discuss, you can make an appointment."

"I guess I must have misinterpreted your body language, then. It seemed like you were trying to get away from me." Part of me was baiting him to gauge his reaction.

It worked because he stepped closer, turning the tables and cornering me against the shelf. "Does this seem like I'm avoiding you?" he growled, using his arms to keep me from moving away.

I stared up at him for a minute, neither of us blinking. My throat was dry. The moment our eyes met, I completely forgot why I'd come into the backroom. His eyes dropped as I licked my lips and swallowed hard. I had to force my eyes away from him. I shouldn't be having these desires about my boss, much less a man who would dare to lock me in a cage. My heart was pounding so hard. What was wrong with me? I couldn't bring myself to look at him again.

Viktor tilted my head up to look him in the eye, and he captured my lips with his. I wrapped my arms around his back and held on. He put one hand on my lower back, the other on my neck, and pulled me closer.

He deepened the kiss and I pressed myself closer to him. I could feel his erection growing. I rubbed against it, encouraging him. When he realized what I was doing, he started to grind against me.

Just when things were getting heated, he pulled away from me completely. "I shouldn't have done that. It was inappropriate. Please excuse me."

Before I could object, he was gone. I stood there, mouth open, staring at the door. *What the fuck had just happened?* Did I just make out with my boss after he kept me in a cage for three days then ignored me? *Get yourself together, Delilah. You can't be throwing yourself at him like that.*

After berating myself for causing that situation, I headed back to the bar with the tequila and scotch long forgotten.

CHAPTER 4

Viktor

I KNEW THAT I shouldn't have bolted after I kissed Delilah. To be fair, I shouldn't have kissed her either. I wanted to do so much more, but somehow, I managed to stop myself just before I lost control. I should have set clear boundaries and explained to her why this wouldn't work. But I couldn't.

That kiss had me mesmerized. I wanted so much more from her, even though I had no right to ask. I knew the blood lust was coming on, so I had to stop. I can't let that happen again. I don't drink from the vein. Not anymore. I must stay away from her. It's torture either way. I might as well protect her while I suffer. I couldn't pinpoint exactly what it was about Delilah that drew me to her. She was strong and opinionated but still wore her heart on her sleeve. That had to be why she reminded me so much of my love.

The last time I ran into a woman who reminded me of my deceased wife was nearly three decades ago, right after Kat's death. I still remembered her face when she realized what I was. I couldn't control myself back then and drained her. I refused to let that happen again.

I hadn't bitten anyone since that day. Instead, I prefer to drink from a bag or a coffee mug. That was, after all, why we had donors. It was the entire reason for the contracts and explained the women who had been locked up in the backroom. Of course, Vinny's methods are a lot different than my own. There would be no more women in cages. The cages were being relocated and contracts were being rewritten.

I'd come so far since I was turned. It took every moment of the past thirty years to learn the level of control I have now. Along with that control came respect from my community and fear from those who would think to disrespect me.

Control didn't equal weakness. I wasn't afraid to get violent if a situation called for it. But I preferred to negotiate first and use fists as a last resort whenever possible.

Any time one of us has shown restraint, it was only a matter of time before he lost it and went on a spree. I am convinced that everyone is waiting for me to slip up. It wasn't going to happen. Not if I could help it.

For a moment, I allowed my mind to wander back to the early days after my transition. It was all a blur of bodies, blood, and sex. I spent a lot of time making up for all of it. I couldn't go back now.

I had to find a distraction, something to keep me away from her. That should be easy, since the bar was days away from going under. If I hadn't stepped in and bought it from Vinny, he would have had to close.

It would take a lot of work to get it renovated and reopened. I had a vision of what Midnight could be, and I suspected that it aligned closely with Delilah's ideas. That would be the biggest challenge. I needed to find a way to work with her while not being around her. I knew that would never happen, though. No matter how much I wanted to stay away from her, I couldn't. My body craved to be near her.

I definitely shouldn't be sitting in my locked office daydreaming about that kiss, imagining that she's on her knees in front of me, pleasuring me with her mouth. I absolutely shouldn't be stroking myself while that image is plastered in my mind. That wasn't going to help matters at all, but it was my current situation.

I didn't usually behave like a schoolboy with a crush, but there was something about this woman. Her kiss sent me over the edge. I hadn't been this out of control since before I was turned.

I wanted her. It was rare for me to not get what I wanted. This time I was the one denying myself, though. The thought crossed my mind as I came, then cleaned myself up so no one would know what I had just done.

Once I got my thoughts under control, I went back to reviewing the files that Vinny had kept pertaining to the business. With the backing of Maxwell Industries, we could get the blood supply much cheaper and with less hassle than Vinny had. There would be no reason to kidnap women or keep them in cages. That alone was one of the main reasons I forced him into this deal. I disapproved of his methods. There was a better way to do things.

I could simply offer their families protection in exchange for their donations. It didn't even have to mean trading their lives. I planned to exchange weekly offerings for security instead of the way Vinny had things set up. It made more sense in the long run. We would expand collection to include any human over the age of eighteen. Those who didn't need protection would be compensated with jobs or other means.

I had charts and binders full of business plans explaining the compensation levels. If a human wanted to terminate his or her life, we had a plan for that. Their family or preferred charity would be compensated for their donation. There would be required medical exams and psychological tests to make sure they had made the right decision.

Since human diseases didn't affect us, we didn't have to worry about if someone who donated was sick. If they were going to die anyway, they could negotiate for a termination. If there was a medical way that we could help them, there would be a donation plan to accommodate that as well.

I had been testing it out slowly within my own corporation for months before deciding to purchase the operation at Midnight. We had seen the project work. People volunteered for it, and a few even applied for the termination plan. With my extensive research, I was sure the program was ready to be rolled out to the public. My company didn't have the connections that Vinny did at Midnight, though. Somehow he'd managed to make friends with a few members of each gang in the city. My guess was that he was doing favors and trading more than just blood. This area was known for the Vipers, who in turn were known for their cocaine. It was another primary reason I decided to acquire the bar. I wasn't about to let Midnight be a part of any drug operation. Taking over would allow me to streamline the blood donation process while stopping any other dealings Vinny had been a part of.

It was a revolutionary plan. I was convinced it would work and increase our supply for decades to come. I knew that the guys at Strain wouldn't like it because it would keep them from having their hunts and make it unacceptable to kill donors. I would fight that war when it came to me, though.

It seemed that more humans were learning about us every day. It wouldn't be long before they all knew. I wondered if we would be the monsters under their beds when the news broke. The few humans who knew about vampires right now felt safer being tied to one of the corporations. We had the ability to keep the gangs at bay and prevent anyone from being drained.

I was deep in thought when the phone rang, pulling me back to the present. I was surprised to hear Jones on the other end. "What is it?"

"We got Blaze and the Vipers pinned down. Do you want us to take them out? Or just bring him in?" Jones was supposed to observe and report back.

"If you can bring him in without issues, do that. If you have issues, take them all out." I hated giving that order, but I also couldn't have the Vipers contaminating my city any longer. I had planned to make their leader, Blaze, an offer that included a generous pay off to take his operation to another state. If his guys made trouble for mine, killing them all would be the only other solution to the problem.

I didn't wait for a response before disconnecting the call. Knowing that the Vipers may be out for revenge if things went south, I decided to check on Delilah again. I wasn't going to risk her life if I could help it.

CHAPTER 5

Eli

"Excuse me, Mr. Strain, the invoice for this month came from Midnight. You're gonna wanna take a look at this," Francine poked her head into my office without warning. I hated random interruptions. The look on her face told me that she disapproved of my attire. I was the boss, so I didn't care about the dress code. I was more comfortable in jeans and a t-shirt, so that's what I wore. The look I shot her changed her expression to embarrassment rather than judgement.

"I told you before, Frannie, just pay the thing and keep the records. I don't need to see every little change." I struggled to keep the annoyance from my voice, but it seemed as if this girl couldn't understand. This was the third bill she had brought me this month to discuss increases. I didn't want to see every statement that came in—that was why I hired a finance department.

"I know, Mr. Strain, and I'm sorry, but this one's different. It's not just a ten or twenty percent increase. It has to be a mistake. I need you to approve it if you want me to pay the bill. This one'll take two signatures to pass at the bank," she explained. That piqued my interest.

"Two signatures? It's that much more? That has to be a mistake." I raised an eyebrow and waited for her to hand me the paperwork. I glanced over the documents and growled. I felt my fangs drop and click into place. "That cowardly, sniveling, son of a bitch can't get away with this. I have half a mind to go down there and rip his head off."

Frannie cringed at my reaction. I could tell she wasn't familiar with how my business dealings were handled. She was a newer vampire and had only been with us for a few months, and things had run pretty smoothly for the past couple of years. It had taken a long time to straighten out the mess Kat left. I shook my head at the thought. I couldn't afford to get lost in memories right now. I had to deal with Vinny.

"It's okay, Frannie, I'll take care of this. You can get back to work now. And take a two-hour lunch today, okay?" I turned back to my desk and set the invoice down before facing her again. She hadn't moved. "Was there something else?" I asked impatiently.

"I need the invoice to pay it, sir." Her words barely squeaked out.

"I'll take care of it. Go back to your office and get back to work. Don't worry about this invoice. Got it?" My tone could have been softer, but I was pissed that Vinny was trying to pull a fast one.

She nodded meekly and practically ran from the room. I sent her supervisor an email letting her know that Frannie was approved for a long lunch, but left out the reason. Jenna knew well enough that if I sent an email like that, someone saw something upsetting. Besides, I was the boss. I didn't have to explain my decisions to anyone.

I turned my attention back to the bill from Midnight. I scanned it for any inconsistencies. It wasn't faked. Vinny was actually trying to bill me double for the same shipment as last month. Why? If I hadn't lost my temper in front of Frannie, I could have asked if there were any other papers with the invoice. Maybe he had included an explanation. Now it was too late. Frannie looked as if she would pee herself if she had to be in my office for a moment longer. I had to send her back to work, or risk her flipping out and deciding to sue.

I wasn't about to let that happen, any more than I was going to let Vinny get away with billing me double.

I always did whatever it took to keep things in line. I was known for being a caring and supportive boss. There were moments, like today, when I lost my temper, but I made sure to go out of my way to make up for it. And I tried daily to do better than I did the day before.

In the beginning, I didn't care who I was rude to or who was scared of me. I was a tyrant and I knew it. But I was also heartbroken after finding out that the man I had considered my brother had betrayed me. He was the reason my sister was dead. I needed to put that out of my mind. I couldn't risk settling back into old habits. I needed to focus on today. This is what was necessary.

I tried to go back to my own work and let the invoice settle to the back of my mind. I had to review the applications today and decide who got to join our corporation as a newly transformed vampire. It was more difficult than it sounded. My mind wandered to the structure of our arrangement with the government.

The city was split into four zones, and each one was run by a vampire held corporation. Each of those company heads was responsible for reviewing applications and keeping their people in line. Essentially each company was a coven, a family. I was the leader of mine. I took that job more seriously than some. At this point, I didn't even know who the other two heads were. I was so focused on taking down Maxwell Industries that nothing else mattered. My company was set up in a way that I could be hands off most of the time.

My guys knew to keep an eye on the gang activity. If anything seemed off, or a family was in danger, they would let me know. It seemed as if the humans were discovering our world slowly. As long as I continued to offer protection to them, they would keep my secret. In exchange, I gave several of them jobs across my part of town and my guys protected them from the scumbag gangs that I couldn't seem to get rid of.

Once they found out about vampires, some people begged to be changed. They thought that vamps had it easier than humans. Not everyone knew about us for obvious reasons, and I wanted to keep it that way. There were some humans who had genuine reasons for requesting the change, like a terminal illness. Those requests were usually granted with minimal red tape.

The greedy ones were denied. Then if they tried to expose us, they were relocated and had their minds wiped. It was standard procedure, even though vamps didn't exactly have a system of laws like humans did. Most were loyal to the vampire who turned them, or to their coven. The ones who weren't usually had a good reason.

My sire had been killed a few years after I was turned. Because of his sacrifice, I was able to take over as leader. Fortunately, that wasn't like the movies had portrayed it. Vampires' life forces weren't connected or linked, although some did have psychic gifts and could speak across those types of bonds. Most of those gifts were just an enhancement of human ability.

I was a small child when I realized that I could sense what others were feeling. My mother was excited to have an empath for her son. She used my ability to her advantage as often as she could while I was still living with her. She was a con artist and liked to trick people out of their money. I hated it, but had to stay until I was old enough to make it on my own. If I helped her, I got rewarded. If I refused, I suffered.

My sister Kat had been the lucky one. Our grandmother had been ill when we were young and our mother refused to take care of her. Because Kat had no gifts, she was forced to stay with Grams and be her caretaker. It wasn't a glamorous childhood, but I envied her for it.

My gift became enhanced once I was turned. If I wanted, I could read the feelings of each person in this building and tell you which ones belonged to which person without leaving my office. I could even push feelings into others if I tried hard enough. Most of the time I preferred not to do that. When I did use that part of my gift, it was usually to calm someone down.

I'd prefer to let people have their own free will. I lived by the thought that if I didn't want it done to me, I wasn't going to do it to someone else. Or I tried to, at least. There were always moments when a man had to show someone that he meant business or risk losing everything. And sometimes that meant I had to kill. To protect everything, to keep the family I had built safe.

I'd worked too hard all these years to get to where I was to let someone like Vinny take advantage of it. I knew that I couldn't just bust in there and attack him, though. No matter how badly I wanted to pound his face in, I needed to calm down.

I locked my office and headed down to the gym that was located in the basement. I would take out some aggression before I went to see him. It wouldn't do to lose my temper and alienate my supplier.

After I changed into my tank, shorts, and sneakers, I put my earbuds in and blasted my favorite music. There was nothing quite like rock from the 1980s and 1990s. I knew every word to every song, not that I'd be singing any of it, at least not when other people were around.

I started with the free weights. I did some curls and squats, then turned my attention to the wall. I'd had a climbing wall installed when I purchased the building. The basement was two levels high and had been reinforced just so I could have this particular feature.

Most people used a harness when they climbed, but I preferred to take a risk. I knew that even if I fell from the top, it wouldn't kill me. I knew because I had dropped from the top on more than one occasion. It never took long to heal, so there wasn't much risk. I liked the thrill of it, too. And with the accelerated healing that vamps had, I wouldn't even be down for long if something did happen.

Climbing relaxed me. It gave me time to clear my mind and focus on something besides the issue with Vinny. There was more to that situation than I was seeing. I knew it. None of that mattered while I was scaling the wall. The only thing that I cared about in that moment was where I'd find my next hand and foot holds.

I made it to the top quickly, then turned my focus to climbing back down. The gym was pretty deserted this time of day, so I didn't have to worry about anyone bothering me or getting in my way. I took a deep breath when my feet finally hit the floor.

After my workout, I felt calmer. I showered and dressed to go see Vinny at Midnight. If he was that hard up for money, maybe I could convince him to finally sell the bar to me.

CHAPTER 6

Delilah

MY IMAGINATION WAS WANDERING while I was getting the bar ready for the lunch rush, if you could even call it that. I knew it wouldn't be busy, but I loved this bar. It had been my home for more than half my life. I couldn't give up on it now. Not when it actually had a chance. I hoped that I could convince Mr. Maxwell to give my ideas a shot. After what had happened with Uncle Vinny when I made my presentation, I wasn't sure. Maybe he was right. Maybe my thoughts weren't good.

But maybe if people believed that Viktor could make a difference, they'd start showing up. I mean, he seemed really scary when we met, but now, there was something about him that drew me to him. He could be exceedingly charming when he wanted. If I wasn't careful, I might lose my heart.

Even though Uncle Vinny had objected, I sang as I cleaned and prepped the bar. Yesterday I overheard our new boss tell him to 'let the girl be' when my uncle said he would make me stop. Apparently, I had at least one fan.

Our regulars kept trying to get me in front of the mic, but sadly, I had to explain to them that Uncle Vinny wouldn't let me perform, even if it was just karaoke. The song that had been dancing through my head started to play on the radio and I sang along. There was something about Monsters by All Time Low that made me think of my new boss. As if I hadn't already been obsessing over him, especially after our encounter.

I couldn't believe that I'd made out with my boss in the stockroom. It was the wildest thing that I had ever done. Things had been a little awkward between us since then, but at least I knew he was interested. It wasn't just my imagination. I didn't have to wonder,

I just had to decide if it was worth pursuing. With his reaction to me, I was confident I could have him if I tried.

I shook the thought from my head as the bell indicated the door had been opened. I looked up just in time to see a tall, tanned man with blonde hair storm inside, and the song died on my lips. He was a tempting mix of anger and sex appeal. I wondered who he was.

Viktor was always in a suit; this guy was wearing a snug pair of jeans and a rock band t-shirt that left little to the imagination. The only thing they seemed to share was the pissed off expression of a man who was used to getting his way, and the fact that both of them dripped sexuality. I didn't understand why, but it looked highly sexy on both of them. Part of me wanted to bite him and see if he was real. I blushed at the thought as he walked up to me.

"Where is Vinny? He'd better get out here and explain this invoice, or I'll find him myself." The tall man growled, and I jumped. I could tell that he was barely holding his temper and I didn't want to see what would happen if it got out of control.

"I'll go get him," I offered, turning toward the stockroom where Uncle Vinny had been re-doing inventory. Viktor hadn't been thrilled about the counts being wrong, so he was making my uncle recount everything, which was amusing because I knew that Viktor had already redone inventory.

Hmm, it seemed that this guy hadn't gotten the memo about the change of ownership. Or maybe he was here to discuss Uncle Vinny's more personal business. I wasn't sure if Viktor had taken over everything or if it was just the bar.

"Uncle Vinny? There's an angry guy out here who wants to talk to you about an invoice. You might want to see if you can calm him down. He seems like he might get violent."

Vinny looked up at me and nodded. "That has to be Strain. I figured he'd be in when he got the bill. I'll take care of it. Get back to lunch prep."

I nodded and followed him out of the stockroom. It didn't seem like the situation was any of my business, but I couldn't help listening in as I stocked and cleaned the bar. From the look on my uncle's face when he responded, I was confident that this had to do with the backroom dealings. I was also convinced that those were illegal, and nothing my uncle or new boss could say would change my mind. Sadly, that made both of the hunks a little less sexy. I wasn't a fan of the things that went on in the backroom. I might feel differently about it if someone would let me in on the secrets. Maybe it's not as bad as my imagination thinks.

I watched the man who had raised me approach the much larger, much angrier man with very little apprehension. I couldn't imagine walking up to someone twice my size without feeling intimidated. The man my uncle had referred to as Strain was taller than Maxwell. He had to be at least six-foot-five. It was evident that he worked out. Even more so as he flexed while my uncle walked closer to him. Uncle Vinny looked tiny at five-foot-two in comparison.

"Mr. Strain, it's nice to see you. I hear you have something to discuss with me. Let's have a seat and talk this out." As usual, Uncle Vinny turned on his sleazy charm to convince the angry man to give him a chance to fix whatever the problem was. He ran a hand over his greasy black hair before he gestured to a nearby table, flashing his best used car salesman smile.

The look on the large man's face terrified me for my uncle. I had to hand it to Uncle Vinny, he didn't seem rattled by the looming threat. The only hint I had that he was nervous was the way he kept running his hand through his greasy hair.

"I'm not taking a seat. I'm not going anywhere. I'm not leaving this spot until you give me an explanation for this!" He shoved an invoice at my uncle, and I tried to restrain myself from leaning over the bar to see what it said.

"This is your invoice. You get one every month. It tells you how much you have to pay for services rendered. Everything is clearly itemized. I'm not sure what more of an explanation you want." Uncle Vinny's demeanor had suddenly changed. His tone was sarcastic, bordering rude. I had never seen my uncle speak to a customer this way. He was bracing for an attack. I couldn't tell if Mr. Strain had noticed. Why would Uncle Vinny expect one of his business associates to physically attack him? It didn't make sense. That wasn't how business worked.

Strain stepped closer and grabbed Uncle Vinny by the shirt, lifting him off the floor. "Look, you little worm, I'm not paying double for the same shipment I get every month. I'll take my business elsewhere if I have to."

"My apologies, Mr. Strain. I no longer have any control over prices. Midnight has been sold to Maxwell Industries. You'll have to discuss pricing with Viktor Maxwell." To his credit, my uncle seemed relaxed and calm under the threat of harm from Strain. My heart was racing and I was terrified to move. Strain's face turned red and for a moment I thought his eyes may bulge out.

"What? You sold the bar to that asshole instead of me?" Strain screamed as he threw Uncle Vinny across the room. There was a loud crack as my uncle slammed into one of the exposed beams in the center of the bar. I was frozen in place as fear took over. This man I was just fantasizing about had tossed my uncle across the room as if he were a rag doll.

Then Strain took two steps, reached across the bar, and dragged me to him, gripping my arm hard. "Then I'm taking this one as compensation. Tell your boss that I won't pay double. If he doesn't revert the prices, I'll be back for another one next month." He turned to leave before my uncle could respond.

"Let go of me!" I yelled at him while fighting pointlessly as he dragged me toward the door. There was no way for me to escape. I wondered how much more my heart could take before it gave out. It was thumping so hard.

There was a whir of movement, and suddenly Viktor was standing in front of Strain, blocking his way to the door. I don't know how he got from the back of the building to the entrance so quickly. It wasn't humanly possible. Then Viktor's fist collided with Strain's jaw. It threw him off balance enough that I was able to wrench my arm free and dive behind the bar. I couldn't stop myself from peeking at the fight. They were like feral animals, trying to rip each other apart. As I watched, hiding behind the corner of the bar, I started to shiver. I was freezing, my teeth chattering, as I watched the scene play out before me.

There was a flash of red in Viktor's eyes, and I swore that his teeth looked different, longer somehow, when he growled at Strain. They kept going around in circles so it was hard to keep up. Then Strain was facing me, and I saw a similar flash of red, and what looked like fangs extending from his teeth. What the hell was going on here? Terrified, I ducked back behind the bar and started crawling toward the backroom.

It took everything in me not to run to Uncle Vinny, but I knew that if I did, I'd be in the middle of these two hunks trying to kill each other. It didn't matter how attractive they were if I got killed in the middle of their fight. And with my growing suspicions, I was certain they'd kill me if I interfered.

I stopped to watch as Viktor lifted Strain over his head and threw him, barely missing Uncle Vinny. There was something incredibly sexy about that show of strength. Strain didn't stay down, jumping back up to launch himself at Viktor again. Mmm, I'd like to be in the middle of that hot, hunky, man sandwich. *What is wrong with me? I should not be having sexual fantasies while I watch two grown men try to kill each other.* I couldn't tear my eyes away as they beat each other. How much more could either of them take?

Wait, are they biting each other? This is really strange. Could they be—? I stopped the thought before it could form. There was no way. Those were just stories, fairy tales, legends, designed to keep young women inside at night. It wasn't possible. Vampires weren't real. Right?

I didn't have time to overthink that, as Strain soared through the air again, landing only a few feet from where I was hiding. I imagined Viktor using that strength to subdue me while he had his way with me. *What is with me being attracted to psychotic behavior lately? Never mind, I'll have to figure that out later. Now I have to get somewhere safe.*

Instinct kicked in and I scrambled backward, trying not to get Strain's attention. Unfortunately, it didn't work. He latched onto my arm again and tried to drag me with him. "I told you that you belong to me now. We're leaving."

His deep growl was terrifying, and I hoped that Viktor wouldn't step aside and let him take me. Of course, I'd only known him for a little while, so I had no idea what he would do. Strain's hand was large and covered most of my bicep. His thick fingers dug into my skin, and I was certain there would be a bruise in the shape of his handprint there tomorrow. If I lived that long. Of course, if he squeezed a little harder, I was sure my arm would snap in half. Any of these scenarios were terrifying.

Out of nowhere, a machete came down on his arm, inches from mine, severing the hand that gripped me. Once removed from its arm, the hand loosened its grip on me and fell to the floor. I screamed and tried to run for the backroom as Strain's blood spattered on me. I slipped in the growing puddle but didn't let it stop me from getting as far away from him as I could.

No matter how many times I hit the ground, I kept crawling, running, sliding as far away as I could, as quickly as I could. When I ducked in the backroom, I closed and locked the door, then leaned against it. I hoped that the heavy door combined with the lock would keep everyone out. The shaking got worse as terror took over.

I didn't know how to process what just happened. With an injury like that, it wouldn't take long for a man to bleed out. Viktor had just killed this man because he had objected to his bill. Or because he tried to take me, I really wasn't sure. What was he being billed for, exactly? Was Strain a buyer for the women who were in the backroom? If he was, what did he do with them?

It didn't make sense, and my mind couldn't wrap around the strangeness of the situation. What would I tell the cops when they came? How would this all be explained? If this was about the nefarious backroom dealings, would the cops even be involved? Was I an accessory to murder? I started to hyperventilate, then a strange sensation came over me and everything just stopped.

I sat there as shock took over, covered in a dead man's blood, and stared off into space. A wave of calm washed over me. I should have been more upset, but I wasn't. As attracted as I had been to the blonde man called Strain, I was relieved that Viktor had done it. Did that make me a monster? Did I even care?

CHAPTER 7

Viktor

ONCE I KNEW THAT Delilah was safely in the backroom, I was able to entirely focus on Strain. I was shocked that he thought he could come into my bar and lay claim to any of my employees.

Who was I kidding? I wouldn't have reacted that way if he had claimed Vinny, or anyone else on the staff. It was only because he claimed her. I would have let him take all of the others, including Vinny. No one will touch Delilah. She's mine. The thought sprung up out of nowhere, although I'd been feeling it since I met her. There's something about her that makes me feel protective, like a feral animal defending his mate.

I can't let thoughts like that get to me. We aren't together. We can't be. She doesn't know who I really am—what I really am. There's no way she could ever love a monster like me. And even if she did, I hadn't been this possessive since I lost my wife. That thought brought even more rage.

I punched Strain in the face again, knocking out one of his fangs. By the time I was done, I'd have to remodel the entire place to get his blood off everything. I didn't care. He had to learn that he couldn't just come in and lay claim to things that were mine. I knew I should push that thought away, but the more I let it linger, the stronger I felt.

Had I been wrong all these years? I thought caring for people who weren't family made a person weak. Maybe it was the opposite and caring for Delilah was giving me the strength to finally demolish Strain.

I didn't stop pounding my fists into his face until Vinny grabbed my arm. I was surprised to see him up and moving after the position he'd been in when I came into the bar. Horror showed on his face when I turned to him. I must have looked like a mess, but I didn't care. I was kneeling on top of a barely conscious Strain in a growing pool of blood. We both knew it wouldn't kill him.

"Mr. Maxwell? Are you okay? I think he's had enough. Do you want me to call someone to pick him up?" Vinny offered, stepping away from me.

No, I want to kill him for having the nerve to touch Delilah, I thought. But I knew better than to express that thought. There may not have been actual laws that applied to us vampires, but there were certain courtesies that each coven followed. This would not be considered an acceptable reason to kill another vampire, and it wasn't worth giving up my own life for revenge.

"Yes, that would be good, Vinny. Then call the clean-up crew and close the bar for as long as it takes to remove any evidence of this happening, but put his hand in a jar in my office. I'm going to make sure Delilah wasn't injured. I don't want anything else to upset her. Call my cell if you need anything."

I didn't wait for a response, instead turning toward the backroom. Vinny knew what was expected. We'd talked at length about his new responsibilities before we finalized the paperwork, and I had reminded him several times since everything was settled. I trusted him to do his job, and he trusted me to protect his family from people like Strain. Now I had to see if I'd held up my end of the bargain.

I paused at the door. I knew it would be locked and could hear her breathing, so she was alive at least. From the sound of it, she was leaning against the door and was in shock. I tapped gingerly on the reinforced steel before calling out. My finger on the metal echoed. She didn't budge. I took a moment to wipe some of the blood off my face and hands. I didn't want to terrify her more when I convinced her to let me in.

"Myshka? It's me, Viktor. Are you okay? Please open the door so I can see if you are injured." I tried to keep my voice steady, but I was terrified that Strain had managed to seriously injure her before I could get there. I held my breath for a moment while I waited for my words to register with her.

There was a slow scuffling noise, and the lock clicked. I turned the knob slowly and pushed the heavy door open just enough for me to slip through before closing and locking it back. I assumed she would feel safer that way.

I wasn't prepared for what I saw when I turned toward her. She was covered in blood. There was no way to tell if it was hers or Strain's. I could feel the tears threatening to fall.

"Myshka, please look at me. Are you injured?" I stepped closer, but she stepped back as if she was scared. She kept staring past me. "It's okay. Everything is taken care of now. He can't hurt you anymore. Will you let me see if you're hurt?"

I took another small step forward, and she didn't move. Her eyes were focused on the door behind me. I walked the rest of the way to her and started wiping the blood from her face and arms. There were no cuts or scratches, and thank the gods, there were no bite marks. It was hard to get the blood off of her when I had just as much on myself, even with the quick wipe down I'd had outside the door.

If Strain had bitten her, I would have walked away, removed his heart, and ripped his head off before his men could retrieve him. Delilah appeared to be fine, but was definitely in shock.

"Will you come upstairs with me to get cleaned up? We can take the back way, so you don't have to see the mess out front," I offered, speaking softly and keeping my eyes on her face.

Her expression never changed, but she nodded slightly and let me lead her toward the stairs. I probably should have taken Delilah to her own room to clean up and change, but I wanted to make sure she was safe. We walked up the back stairs to my apartment on the second floor. I'd had it explicitly remodeled to give me access to the bar while maintaining privacy.

Delilah didn't say a word as we walked. I stopped her outside my door and pulled out my key. A moment later, we were inside, and I led her through the master bedroom to the master bath. The bloody footprints would be hell to get out of the beige carpet, but that was a problem for later.

She didn't object as I removed her phone and keys from her pockets, then took off her shoes. Her clothes were ruined, but I could replace them. I needed to get the blood off her and make sure she wasn't injured.

I turned the shower on to let it warm up, then guided her through the glass door. She stood just inside the door as if she couldn't move. I had hoped she could take care of herself once I had her in place.

I kicked off my shoes and jacket, emptied my pockets, and entered the shower behind her. She only stepped forward when I placed my hand on her back and gently pushed her.

Once the water was running over Delilah, I realized how hard Strain had grabbed her arm to drag her away. The skin was turning purple already in the shape of his giant mitt. I hated that he'd marked her. Without thinking, I leaned down and kissed the mark. "I'm so sorry this happened, Myshka."

Something about that action made Delilah turn toward me. Her expression changed, and the tears started to fall. She reached for me and clung as if her life depended on it.

"I was so scared," she whispered, "is he dead?"

"No, but he won't bother you again. It will take him a while to recover, but I think he got the message," I reassured her, then kissed her forehead.

I don't know what I was thinking. That was too personal. As if being in the shower in an embrace with her wasn't? "I'm sorry, I shouldn't—" Before I could finish my apology, her lips were on mine.

The kiss was hot, greedy, and sexual. It was so much more than I'd imagined the moment we met. Her tongue danced with mine, and I could feel my arousal begin to grow between us. I tried to pull away from her, but she wrapped her arms around my neck and held me tightly, refusing to allow even an inch of space between us.

I kissed her as if she were a bottle of water and I was dying of thirst. Her moans of pleasure had me pulling her closer. Without realizing it, I'd backed us up against the shower wall. I pulled back for a moment to let her breathe. I didn't want her to feel caged in.

I wasn't trying to seduce her, at least not yet. But I wouldn't turn her away either.

CHAPTER 8

Delilah

I HAD FOLLOWED MR. Maxwell up to his room willingly, too much in shock to think about any possible outcomes. One moment I was standing in the shower with my clothes on, staring at the wall, the next everything hit me and I desperately needed to cling to something positive.

The closest thing was Viktor's mouth. It amused me how I had refused to call him Viktor, even after he insisted, until the moment our lips met. I was sure that I would never call him Mr. Maxwell again. I knew that kissing my new boss was a bad idea, but at that moment, I wanted nothing more than to be at his mercy.

He tried to pull away so I wouldn't know how aroused he was. I didn't let him. I wanted him so badly I couldn't stand it. Bad idea or not, my clothes were coming off. I could tell from his erection that he wanted me too. When he backed me against the shower wall, I knew that I'd convinced him.

I started unbuttoning his shirt and slipped it off of him. His broad shoulders were accentuated by his undershirt. I had to get that out of the way so I could look at him. Viktor leaned forward and kissed me again while my fingers found the end of his shirt, then pulled it up and over his head.

I leaned against the wall and looked at his chest. Of course, he had a perfect six-pack. I was getting wet just thinking about getting him out of his pants. I reached for the button, but he grabbed my hand and stopped me.

Viktor put his other hand on my cheek. "Are you sure you want to do this, Myshka? You've just been through something traumatic. I don't want you to regret this decision." He was giving me a way out. I smiled.

"I'm sure. We're both adults. I need this as much as you do," I responded before capturing his lips with mine again.

He groaned and fisted his hand in my hair, exposing my neck. Then I shivered as he trailed kisses from my chin to my shoulder. I was desperate to get rid of every article of clothing that was still between us.

I leaned back and as if he understood, Viktor peeled my wet tank top off. He groaned at the sight of my lace bra. I wondered what his reaction would be to the matching thong.

I reached for his waistband again, and he grabbed my hand. "You first," he growled. I licked my lips and nodded.

I unbuttoned my jeans before I realized just how hard it was going to be to peel them off in a sexy way since they were soaked.

I almost fell, then Viktor caught me. I started laughing uncontrollably. He was shocked and didn't understand. "What's so funny?"

"This. We're soaking wet and trying to get naked. The whole thing is hilarious. My jeans are stuck to me. I'm sure yours are too," I explained between giggles. I gestured to his dress pants as I spoke. Viktor growled playfully. I was relieved that my laughter hadn't killed the mood.

Viktor chuckled, then pulled me close for another kiss. A moment later, he ripped my jeans off me. After watching him fight with Strain, it didn't surprise me that he was able to do it.

What surprised me was that every time he looked at the dark purple handprint on my arm, sadness crossed his hazel eyes. He leaned down and kissed the bruise again before running his tongue up my arm to my ear.

He took a step back to take his pants off, and I caught him staring at me. I should have felt self-conscious, but instead, I felt sexier than I ever have. There was something about the way he was looking at me that made me wonder if this was more than just sex to him. It couldn't be, right? We'd known each other for such a short time.

My ability to think left me when he dropped his boxer briefs. I could tell through his clothes that he was huge, but wow. I stood there staring for longer than I should have.

Viktor grabbed me and pulled me close for another kiss. His tongue was trying to dominate mine, and I hadn't decided how I felt about that yet. I didn't usually like letting someone else control me. But this seemed less about possession and more about pleasure.

He unfastened my bra and it fell to the floor where he kicked it out of the way before ripping my thong off my body as if it had offended him.

He kissed me again while his hands explored my body. His caress lit a fire in me while giving me the chills. He found my damp center and took control. I threw my head back and screamed at my orgasm.

He growled as I grabbed his engorged member and stroked. Before I could do anything else, he picked me up. The next thing I knew, my back was against the wall and my legs were wrapped around his hips. If I had any doubts, this would be the last moment to object. I could feel my heart racing in anticipation.

I rolled my hips, rubbing myself against him. Viktor groaned. He stroked my clit with his erection before entering me. He thrust into me more gently than I'd expected, taking his time as if he was memorizing every inch of me.

He kissed me again and pinched my nipples, causing another shock wave of orgasmic pleasure to rock through me. I couldn't take the leisurely pace anymore. I started quickly lifting and lowering myself, until Viktor took my cue. He began to pound me faster.

I came hard and fast, screaming his name. His eyes turned red again and I heard a click. I felt my heart pound faster. I couldn't deny the truth. I was terrified, but curious. He tried to turn away and I stopped him. "It's okay. I figured it out earlier. You don't have to hide from me."

I put my hand on his cheek and turned his face back toward mine. He definitely looked intimidating, but to be fair, I'd never seen a vampire up close and personal before. I leaned forward and kissed him.

"I want to taste you," he sighed as he continued thrusting.

Without a word, I pulled my hair over my shoulder, exposing my neck. He looked at me nervously, "Are you sure?"

I nodded. "I trust you."

"That's probably a mistake."

He kissed me gently, then turned his attention to my offered neck. I felt him cum at the exact moment his fangs punctured my skin. He sucked for a moment, then pulled me close.

"You taste amazing; even better than I expected," he whispered. It should have been weird, but I took it as a compliment.

I ducked my head under the spray to wet my hair. It would probably take a while to get all the blood out of it. When I reached for the shampoo, Viktor grabbed it and scrubbed my hair for me, taking care to get every bit of blood washed away. He was so gentle and thorough.

Once my hair was clean, he combed the conditioner through it. I didn't know how to react to being taken care of this way. No one had ever been this attentive. The last time someone else had washed my hair for me was when I was six, before my mom had run off for the first time.

I tensed at the memory, but Viktor lathered soap on a loofah and started rubbing me down with it. Between the citrusy scent of his soap and his massaging hands, I had no way to hold onto the stress the memory had caused.

I marveled at how long the water had stayed warm, barely noting that as soon as I was clean, Viktor rushed to get out of the bathroom. I carefully rinsed the conditioner from my hair as I combed through it to remove tangles. As I stood there, alone in my boss' shower, I realized the full weight of what I'd just done. *Was this a mistake?*

CHAPTER 9

Viktor

I HADN'T MEANT TO let things go so far with Delilah, at least not yet. Something about her reminded me too much of Kat, and I needed to be sure I could keep the two separate in my head.

After we finished, I took my time helping her clean up, then quickly washed myself, stepping from the shower before she had finished rinsing the conditioner from her hair. I was angry with myself for taking advantage of her that way. At the same time, she didn't seem bothered by it.

I dressed quickly, then grabbed a gray t-shirt and a pair of shorts from my workout gear for Delilah to wear until I took her back to her apartment. I knew they would be big on her, but it was better than walking around naked. I wanted to make sure her arm wasn't broken. The handprint was almost black when I walked out of the room.

I knew that I could heal her if she would drink some of my blood, but I didn't think she was ready for that conversation yet. Most humans freaked out when they found out that vampires were real. Delilah Stone was unlike anyone else I had ever known, but I still didn't think she would be willing to blindly trust me about drinking vampire blood.

Just the thought of Strain's hands on her pushed me to the limits of control. I put my fist through the wall before I realized what I was doing.

At that moment, Delilah came out of the bathroom wrapped in a towel. "Are you okay? You left pretty suddenly." She stopped talking as my fist went through the drywall.

"Oh, Myshka. I'm sorry, I didn't hear you there. I was getting you some clothes to wear," my response sounded lame in my head, but I wasn't sure what to say to her.

"Did the wall make you angry?" Her attempt at humor was not lost on me, but I didn't respond. It irritated me that she chided me like a small child who had misbehaved. I handed her the clothes, then went into the kitchen to give her some privacy to get dressed. If I had stayed, I wouldn't have been able to resist taking her again. I already knew that had been a colossal mistake, one I couldn't let happen again.

It wouldn't be easy to distance myself from her, but I had to try. I couldn't let what had happened to Kat happen to anyone else.

I needed to talk to her and explain things, but I didn't know how. I feared that I was already too attached. While I waited for her to get dressed, I poured myself a cup of blood from the fridge. I would think better if I could get the taste of her off my mind. I crinkled my nose at the smell of it, and grimaced at the taste. My fears were confirmed. Nothing would ever taste as good as she did. I would have to get used to it.

While I drank the bland sustenance my body required, I let my mind wander back to Kat. I'd managed to block out most of my memories since she left. That wasn't exactly what had happened.

She was the love of my life. We'd met before either of us was turned. Our love story was a whirlwind. We were married within weeks of meeting. Her family had hated me at first, but eventually started to come around.

Her brother and I had become close friends. I considered Eli to be my own brother. Things were going so well for our family.

Then Strain Industries came into the picture. I knew they were led by vampires, but back then, vamps couldn't be out in society the way we are now. Shawn Strain was the puppet master, and had humans doing his dirty work. He helped Eli to get away from his mother, who was a controlling bitch. Shawn even "adopted" Eli and let him change his name to become the heir to the company.

Then Shawn managed to convince Kat that she should come work for him. To be fair, he's the reason I am what I am today. What should have been a simple secretarial job changed so quickly. Kat ended up being promoted to human relations, dealing with the interactions between humans and vampires within Strain's company.

While she was working for him, there was an explosion at one of his buildings. There had been an anonymous tip called in, but the bomb squad couldn't get there in time. My heart shattered.

There were no bodies recovered that day, but dozens had been killed. The explosive used burned hotter than anything the police had ever seen.

Kat had been declared dead a year after the explosion. I'd spent that year searching for any evidence that she was still alive. I refused to let them complete the paperwork that would admit she wasn't coming back until I was sure. I died inside when I couldn't find her. I finally had to admit she was dead. When the paperwork was finished, I sought out someone to help me rid myself of my humanity.

I built my corporation on the idea that someday Shawn Strain would pay. It was his fault that Kat had died. I'd come to blows with Eli when he defended his patriarch. I lost everything that day.

I made my fortune on stocks and trading, then branched out into other areas. Maxwell Incorporated owned banks, restaurants, bars, movie, television, and photography studios, and almost any other type of business a person could imagine. I had more money than I would ever need.

It was never enough, though. I wanted revenge. I wanted Strain to pay. I wanted to take his entire operation down. That's why I bought Midnight. I knew it was where his blood supply came from, and that doubling the price would piss him off. What I didn't expect was for Kat—I mean Delilah—to get caught in the middle of it.

CHAPTER 10

Delilah

I COULD TELL THAT Viktor needed a minute alone, although I wasn't sure what he was upset about. Maybe I misread his interest in me. There was no point in worrying about it now; what's done was done. If it was a mistake, we would deal with it and move on.

Mama always told me that you can't change the past, and you can't let the past dictate the future. I wished she had been able to take her own advice, but I understood how hard life was after Daddy left. He had been the love of her life. When he disappeared one day without warning, she lost her mind.

Everything changed that day. She was convinced that someone had taken him. Her days were filled with conspiracy theories that consumed her sanity. From the time I was six until I turned fifteen, she was gone for weeks at a time, searching for him. After a while, she ran out of money and came home. Once she wore Uncle Vinny down again, he would give her money to leave.

Things changed when I was fifteen, though. My uncle didn't know that I had heard about their arrangement. I was good at hiding back then. I knew that she had asked him for money again. Mom had been home for six weeks, which was a record. Uncle Vinny told her he wasn't giving her any more money at all. She would have to work and save if she wanted to run off again.

That night I'd been bussing tables at Midnight while Mom tended the bar. She was mad at her brother for not giving her the money to run off after my dad, and yelled at him about having a fifteen-year-old bus tables in a bar.

They fought and he ended up offering her a rather large sum of money to sign her rights as my mother over to him. It didn't seem strange to me that he'd already had the

37

paperwork drawn up. I always suspected that he had planned it. He was protecting me from her.

I cried silently when she agreed and signed the paper without even reading it. My heart was broken at that moment and nothing would ever fix it. The pain of her betrayal was so much worse than Dad leaving. I shouldn't have been surprised by her actions though.

After she came home that night and lied to me about not leaving anymore, I woke up to find her gone. My uncle took care of me like he always had, and neither of us mentioned that she didn't come back this time. He had to know that I'd overheard their deal, but he never said it. He gave me a permanent job, put me through school, and was the best father figure he could be.

I let my thoughts wander as I paced the room, looking at the decorations Viktor had chosen. There were photos on the desk and the dresser of him with a woman. She was beautiful with long blond hair and blue eyes. I fought off a twinge of jealousy. How could I feel jealous of her without knowing who she was? Because she was standing so close to Viktor, of course.

"I will escort you to your apartment now, if you'd like," he said when he came back into the room.

"Sure," I replied as I picked up the photo. "I'm sorry for being nosey, but who's this woman in these photos with you?"

His eyes glazed over for a second, and I thought I'd said something wrong. "That is Katarina, my wife." He stepped over next to me and took the picture from my hands, carefully placing it back where it had been.

"Your wife? Why didn't you tell me you were married? We just—" I couldn't believe I'd just committed adultery. It wasn't something I'd ever planned to do.

"It is a long story, but nothing you need to concern yourself with. Kat has been gone for a long time now." There was a sadness in his tone that made me regret asking.

"Oh, I see. I think I can find the way to my apartment on my own. Thanks, for everything." I turned and headed toward the door, stopping with my hand on the knob. "You know, I didn't expect anything from you. This was a one-time thing. A mistake that needs to be forgotten."

"I agree. Please let me know if you need anything. Today has been a traumatic experience. Take tomorrow off." His tone was cold and detached. He sounded so differently than he had earlier in the shower. The heat of passion had been replaced by frigid nonchalance.

I nodded and walked out the door before the tears had a chance to fall. I wasn't lying when I said I didn't expect anything from him. I guess that's not entirely true. I had expected him to be honest. My anger was ebbing through me, fighting the hurt and sadness at Viktor's dishonesty.

When I got back to my apartment, I slammed the door, locked it, and collapsed on the floor. I leaned against the door and cried until there were no tears. I told myself that it was because Mr. Strain had manhandled me, but I was pretty sure that wasn't the whole truth.

I hated that I had already started to fall for Viktor. I mean, not that long ago, he had me locked in a cage. Then today, I seduced him before finding out he's married. I wasn't going to let myself dwell on that anymore tonight.

At least I had a day to figure out how to face him at work. I knew that I should eat something, but I hadn't been to the store in a while. I was planning to grab something downstairs during my shift, but I was pretty sure Viktor had closed the bar.

Viktor. Mmm. I remembered the feeling of his hands on my skin. I could still feel his lips on mine. So much for not dwelling. I guess if I couldn't eat, I'd just take another shower.

The shower didn't help. I was still trying to process the fact that not only had I just slept with my married boss, but he was a vampire. How is this possible?

Vampires are real. I should be more shocked than I am. It makes perfect sense. I never could quite figure out what Uncle Vinny was selling that kept the bar out of bankruptcy. It has to be blood, or slaves—blood slaves maybe? I knew it couldn't be drugs. He'd threatened to kick my dad out on more than one occasion for being high, so I didn't expect my uncle to put up with that. It was nice to know that he'd draw the line somewhere. I had hoped that he wasn't kidnapping those women he'd had locked up, but there was no way to know without asking.

Maybe a jog would help me to relax. I decided to head to the park a few blocks down. It had a great path for runners. As I walked toward the park, I couldn't shake the feeling that I was being followed.

I stopped and looked behind me. The street wasn't empty, but it didn't look as if anyone was paying any attention to me, even in my skimpy running gear. I was probably paranoid from the fight between Viktor and Strain.

Just thinking about it made me shiver. I didn't want to run into that guy again. It was difficult to believe that someone that was so handsome could be that dangerous. I'd seen it with my own eyes, though.

The paranoid feeling of being watched stayed with me even when I got to the path. A quick glance over my shoulder made me stop in my tracks. I swear there was a guy in a dark hoodie following me. *Come on, Delilah, get it together. Maybe he just prefers to run in his sweatshirt. You've seen plenty of people like that.*

Just as I talked myself out of my suspicions, someone grabbed me from behind and pulled me into the darkness of the trees that surrounded the path.

"I don't have any money." I braced myself for the reaction to my statement.

"It's a good thing I'm not after your money, then, isn't it?" A deep growl followed the words. The hoodie was pulled down low and his face was obscured by shadows. The only thing I could see were his eyes. They were red, like I'd seen Viktor's and Strain's change when they fought.

I'd taken several self-defense classes over the years, but at the moment, I couldn't remember what to do. Being attacked by a vampire was a lot different than fighting off a would-be thief.

"What do you want?" Maybe if I could keep him talking, I would come up with a way to escape.

"You'll see," was the response. I heard a faint click, but still couldn't see anything but the blood red eyes staring at me. I was going to be a meal for this monster, and there was nothing I could do about it. He had me pinned to a tree. I tried to squirm, but all that did was scratch my backside. He growled again, and I was confident it was from the scent of my blood.

Out of nowhere, he released me as he was thrown backward. I looked around to see who had saved me, but there was no one nearby. The vampire who attacked me was lying on the jogging path. It didn't look like he was even breathing. Although to be fair, I had no idea if vampires needed to breathe.

I walked over to check it out. I didn't want to get closer to him, but I also didn't want him to attack me the moment I turned my back. I crept slowly to close the space between us. He wasn't moving. I stopped a foot away. No breath. No movement. I leaned down to check for a pulse when a voice whispered in my ear.

"*Run,*" was all I heard. I sprinted toward Midnight. It was a miracle I wasn't hit by a car or arrested for jaywalking, but I didn't stop until I was inside the front door of the bar that I'd always considered to be my home.

"Are you okay, kiddo?" Uncle Vinny asked from behind me.

I jumped and squealed, then turned toward him. "You scared me."

"Your back looks horrible. Did you fall?" He was pushing for answers that I didn't want to give.

"I'm fine. Just an accident on my run." I hurried up the stairs to avoid more questions. I needed to get cleaned up before Viktor saw the scratches. With what he did to Mr. Strain, I wouldn't put it past him to hunt down the asshole who'd attacked me.

It didn't make sense, but I knew it was true. Even if he was married, there was a part of him that wanted me. I knew that he would do anything to protect me, no matter how upset I was with him.

Chapter 11

Viktor

I COULDN'T KEEP PUNISHING myself for past mistakes. I'd made so many, and was sure that I would make more before the end. I had to find a way to forgive myself for failing Kat, and to make it up to Delilah. I felt like I'd used her, and I hated myself for it. Did I? Or did she use me to forget temporarily about what had just happened to her?

I probably should have told her that Kat is dead, so she didn't feel like a whore for fucking a married man. I just couldn't bring myself to say the words. Maybe it would make her want to stay away from me if she thought I was still married. That would be safer for her anyway.

I couldn't put the business on hold, so I had to pull myself together. After all, I'd given her the day off today. Maybe we'd be able to pretend like nothing had happened. With any luck, she would hate me now and we could resume our employer-employee relationship.

Every time I told myself that, I flashed back to the shower. I would never forget her legs wrapped around me, or the look on her face when she climaxed. I couldn't get the feeling of being inside her out of my head.

Stop! This is torture. I need to stop thinking about Delilah and her tight—no, I have to focus on work. I won't get anything done if I let myself get distracted.

I decided to start with Strain. He had to be dealt with sooner or later. I wondered how pissed he would be at losing his hand. I'd made sure that it was hidden when his men picked him up so he couldn't have it reattached. It was petty, but he deserved a reminder to keep his hands off things that were mine.

That line of thinking was dangerously close to circling back to last night with Delilah. I had to do something besides thinking of her. I locked myself in the office and picked up the phone. I shouldn't have called him and I knew it. I would push his buttons and he would reciprocate with mine until we were fighting again.

I dialed the phone anyway. When his secretary answered, I was respectful and charming. She transferred me immediately. I almost felt bad for her having to deal with his wrath after.

"This is Strain, what can I do for you?" The voice that answered was pleasant. That seemed strange to me.

"You can start by sending an official apology letter to my employee that you injured," I said gruffly.

"*Maxwell*, you son of a bitch. You're lucky I didn't have you arrested for assault. Where is my hand, anyway?" I was already getting under his skin.

"In a trophy case where it will be displayed to warn others not to try to take what doesn't belong to them," I retorted.

"What do you want? I should come after you for this," he was pissed and yelling now.

"I just told you, I want an apology for the girl you hurt while trying to kidnap her from my bar. You could have easily broken her arm and you know it. And I want you to pay your bill with no further complaints. In the future if you have an issue with your bill, I want you to object in writing through the proper channels instead of coming down to the bar and throwing a fit," I explained calmly. I knew that being condescending to him was a bad idea, but I couldn't help myself.

"You bastard. If you think for a second that I'm just going to roll over and let you double the fees, you've lost your mind. You want a war, you'll get one." I knew he wasn't one for empty threats, and suspected that this was what he'd had in mind since he found out I was the one who'd taken over.

"I'm not the one making threats, *Strain*." I tried to remain calm, but he was testing my patience.

"You know you can't overcharge like this without some sort of compensation. Give me the girl, and we'll call it even for now." He growled, edging closer to becoming unhinged.

I couldn't believe that he thought I would just agree to hand her over. "No. I won't give you anyone as compensation. There's nothing to compensate for. You can either pay my fees or get your supply somewhere else."

"You're willing to start a war for some blood bag? What is she to you, anyway?" He snarled at me through the phone, and I was glad that I wasn't close enough to remove his other hand. I wanted to rip off his head. I paused for a moment to regain my composure. When I responded, I made sure to speak clearly and without emotion.

"She is one of my employees. You are the one who constantly wants to go to war. If that's what you need, then nothing I offer will stop you." I decided to cut my losses and hang up on him, before I said something that would have him headed my way. I needed to plan for anything he could throw at me. I slammed the phone down, then started pacing the office.

Strain was big on explosives, so I would have to increase security. I would need to make sure a detail kept an eye on Delilah. I hated that I couldn't tell her what was going on, but she just found out about vampires yesterday. Could I really expect her to understand a decades old rivalry that had turned bloody and was about to go to war?

I made the necessary calls to put the increased security in place. Then I went out and relieved Vinny from behind the bar. I sent him to clean the whole area while I tended to the few customers we had. I needed to gauge the interest in changes, and there was no better way than to interact with the customers.

CHAPTER 12

Eli

VIK'S CALL HAD PUT me in a foul mood, worse than when he'd sliced off my hand and knocked out one of my fangs. Although with that, he may have done me a favor. Now I would have an excuse to try out our newest prosthetics. If they worked correctly, I'd be stronger and faster than I was before. It would be almost like connecting directly to the computer. And we'd been working on genetic advances that would allow me to regrow the fang within a few days. It wasn't like I would go hungry, but I wouldn't be able to feed in the manner I preferred.

Mike from my tech department had handled the new hand fitting personally at three in the morning. I didn't usually bother my team after hours, so they knew if I called it was significant. Even more so if it was Scott who called. He assembled the medical team and met me at the lab. There was no way I was taking that mess to my house. I ended up staying here last night and was in the office early. If it hadn't been for Viktor, I wouldn't have been here for his call. That dick would have to pay.

I hadn't planned to take a blood slave when I'd gone to Midnight. I was going to negotiate with Vinny and get the invoice straightened out. I saw red when he said he'd sold the bar to Maxwell. I had been pressuring Vinny for years to sell the bar to me. I couldn't believe he would betray me like that, selling to my biggest competition.

I had grabbed the girl as a matter of convenience. I didn't plan to keep her. I just wanted to make a point. Her scent caught my attention. I figured I'd just missed a meal. I didn't even get a good look at her until after Vik attacked me. But once I saw her face, my resolve to take her was renewed. Something in her eyes pulled at me. I needed to know who she was and I was determined to find out. I wasn't trying to hurt her, but I couldn't stop myself. I had been so close to losing control.

I could feel her sense of panic grow as the situation escalated. I knew that I shouldn't have grabbed her so hard, but I wanted her to come with me. After Vik severed my hand, I felt the girl start to freak out from another room. I pushed everything I had into calming her and letting shock take over so she didn't end up with a heart attack or stroke from the excitement. Her heart had been racing so fast. Something about her had grabbed me in a way that I decided she was more important. Even after losing my hand, I didn't want to see her upset or hurt. That had been what allowed Vik to defeat me. If I hadn't been preoccupied with calming the girl down, I could have finally taken him out. Or at least that was what I would tell myself.

Maybe I would make it a point to get to know her. I wondered if she would even consider giving me a chance. If she did, it would soothe my curiosity. It also had the bonus of pissing Vik off. Perhaps an apology *was* in order. I didn't usually behave that way. Generally, if I did, I would apologize. It only made sense. There was something about that man that brought out the ugly in me. I arranged for flowers to be delivered the next day. I wouldn't want him to think he'd won. I made sure to include a card that would definitely get a rise out of him.

Once all of that was settled, I called Joe in acquisitions. We needed a game plan to combat Maxwell Incorporated doubling our supply cost. I wanted to hit him where it hurt. "Joe, this is Strain. Gather your team and come to the conference room." I paused to allow him to respond.

"Now, sir?" His voice was higher than usual. I must have caught him off guard.

"Yes, now. We're having an emergency meeting. Bring everything you have on the supply chain." I dropped the phone onto its base and sat back in my chair.

I was the CEO and owner of my company, but no one would ever suspect it unless they knew. I refused to wear suits, no matter who I was dealing with. I was the exact opposite of Vik and my mentor. Shawn had been a good man, but he leaned toward the old ways. Our rules were updated when I took over.

My employees were encouraged to be themselves. If that meant blue hair, visible tattoos and piercings on the Human Resources Manager, then so be it. Amber was way too qualified for me to hold her personal choices against her.

Everyone on my payroll was treated with that respect, and because of it, no one tried to take advantage, or very few did, at least. My company was also one of the few that was vampire owned that had humans on the payroll. Only a few in the inner circle knew who they were actually working for. Others just assumed I was some eccentric rich guy who hated suits. Not that being a vampire had anything to do with my decisions. I was still the same as I had been before the transformation. Mostly. I just needed an implant to be in the sun now, and drank blood. Neither of those things was a big deal.

It amused me that Viktor's company had been the one to come up with the implant idea, but mine had perfected it. I was able to create a small device that provided an internal UV shield to vampires. The ultrasonic pulses it emitted were low wave enough to be virtually unnoticable while altering a vampire's skin cells to allow the sunlight to bounce right off. It was almost like having tinted windows on my skin, but without anyone being able to tell. The team I was about to meet with had been instrumental in the development of the device, so I was certain they'd find the answers I was looking for.

I grabbed my laptop and tablet, checked my pocket for my cell, then headed to the conference room. To be fair, we had dozens of conference rooms. Some people might have had to ask which one I meant. But Joe knew which one I preferred and had his team waiting patiently when I arrived.

"Okay, there's no point in sugar coating this—Midnight was bought out by Maxwell Inc. Vik's taking point. He's doubling our supply cost. We need alternatives. All feasible ideas will be considered," I explained, "so get to work."

The team started brainstorming while I busied myself setting up my laptop and connecting to the projector. I was hoping someone would come up with a good idea, and fast.

"Mr. Strain, I'm not sure there's anything we can do. He has the market cornered for supply. It's not like we can boycott or do without." Joe said after three hours of brainstorming.

An intern raised his hand. I gestured and he spoke. "We went over every option before we settled on Midnight's operation, sir. If there had been something else, we would have found it." He looked apologetic, so I nodded. The kid wasn't wrong. The only other option was to ask for volunteers and that meant outing vamps to the humans. I wasn't ready for that yet.

His team had gone over every possible solution and with each, someone had a logical reason why it wouldn't work. I was stuck paying whatever Vik charged. Unless I found a way to make him change his mind. The only other option was to move my entire operation to another city. The cost of that was prohibitive, but I told the team to keep running numbers. I didn't want to move, but if it was the only way, I'd have to consider it. Maybe it wouldn't be so bad if the girl went with me.

"Keep working on everything, and keep me updated. We can dismiss the meeting for now. You've all worked so hard this afternoon, take the rest of the day off. If you come up with any new ideas, let me know. Sometimes taking a break helps. Besides, I have some things to take care of," I announced to the room before picking up my laptop and tablet. I walked out into the hall and headed back toward my office.

I wanted to scream and throw things, but I knew that wouldn't solve anything. I should go back to the gym and work out this rage, but I didn't want to let go of it yet. Damn you, Vik. We used to be brothers and now I wanted to ring his neck. Thinking about him led me back to thinking about her. I needed to know her name at least.

I settled in at my desk after locking the door and closing the blinds. No one would dare to disturb me—they all knew better. Unless my door was open, no one came in. I opened my laptop and started searching. If she worked at Midnight, there would be employment reports. It shouldn't be too hard to find out who she was.

Delilah Stone. Twenty minutes later, her name was on my tongue. I found her social media accounts and her credit history quickly enough and discovered that Delilah Stone had nearly perfect credit. She had an apartment a couple of blocks from the bar. Apparently, she'd worked there since she turned eighteen, although the look of the records was that she was there a few years before that. I wondered what made Vinny hire an underage girl. I couldn't prove it, but I was confident with a little more digging I'd have exactly what I needed to take Vinny down if needed. The whole thing seemed a little creepy. I hoped there was nothing shady going on there.

I wasn't able to find anything about her family. It was like she didn't exist until she made it to Midnight. That was strange. I would have to do more digging. Something was pulling me toward this woman. I needed to know why.

I set up a program to keep searching, digging through her records to find anything that would tell me who she was, who her family was. She couldn't have just popped into existence at the age of fifteen. That wasn't possible. There had to be a birth record somewhere. If it existed, I would find it.

Once I was satisfied that the search would run on its own, I packed up and went home. There was no reason to babysit the program. I decided to spend a few hours in the pool this evening swimming laps.

CHAPTER 13

Delilah

A DAY OFF WAS just what I'd needed to get my head straight. I had spent the day mourning poor choices and berating myself for what I had allowed—hell, encouraged, to happen. I was done pining for Viktor. He was a married man after all, and not one with good morals. Hopefully his wife was understanding. I would hate to have to explain what had happened. Surely, she knew about his womanizing ways. With thoughts of Mrs. Maxwell in my head, I started my day as usual, by going downstairs and stocking the bar.

Viktor must have had Uncle Vinny run my shift yesterday, because the place was a mess. I had to clean everything before I could stock. And we were out of almost everything. It must have been a busy night. I didn't mind the extra work, though. It kept me too busy to wonder what could have been between us.

While I was bringing out new bottles, Uncle Vinny came to find me. "Thanks for covering for me yesterday," I offered.

"You're welcome, even though I didn't have a choice. Besides, Mr. Maxwell took the bar for a couple of hours. Anyway, you have a delivery," he said, pointing to the bar.

I looked over and sitting on the bar was the biggest bunch of wildflowers I'd ever seen. It was a gorgeous bouquet, full of daisies, roses, dahlias, and carnations, along with a few others I didn't recognize. The colors were bright and cheery like a summer day.

I instantly thought Viktor felt terrible about lying to me and was trying to make it up to me. I wasn't sure if I would accept his offer or not. I turned to Uncle Vinny, "Have you met Mr. Maxwell's wife?"

He shook his head. "She's been dead for a long time. Why would you ask about her now?" He kept shaking his head and mumbling to himself as he walked away.

48

That must have been why Viktor got so upset. I had no idea she'd passed away, and there I was prodding at old wounds. No wonder he got angry. I needed to compose myself and apologize.

I leaned over and smelled the flowers first, noticing the card tucked in the middle. I pulled it out and read: *I believe we started off on the wrong foot. Please accept my apologies. Allow me to make it up to you over dinner this weekend. I'll pick you up at 8.* It wasn't signed, but who else could it be from?

Viktor wanted to take me on a date to apologize for the misunderstanding. One of the most powerful men in the country was interested in me. This was exciting, and not because of his money. I couldn't wait for a replay of our night together.

The note completely distracted me from finding him to apologize. I started cleaning and stocking the bar again, dancing around and humming like a teenager with a crush. It was ridiculous, but I was the only one here, so it didn't matter.

A little while later, I heard a throat clear behind me. My dancing and humming stopped. I slowly turned around to find Viktor staring at me as if I'd grown a second head.

"I'm glad to see you're feeling cheery today, Delilah, but I'm not sure those dance moves are appropriate for work." His tone was cold and detached, as if he hadn't sent me flowers and asked for a date. My thoughts swam around my head. Maybe he's trying to keep it low key so no one finds out? That would be a good reason to not sign the card.

"I'm sorry, Mr. Maxwell," I said, blushing at his comment and forcing myself to use his formal name.

"I've told you, please call me Viktor. I see someone has an admirer. Those are lovely flowers." He walked over and smelled them.

"Yes, they are. Thank you. I'm looking forward to our date," I replied.

Viktor looked at me, obviously confused. "What date?"

"Wait, you didn't send the flowers?" I couldn't stop myself from asking.

"Why would I send you flowers?" He seemed as confused as I felt.

"To apologize for the misunderstanding the other night, I thought." Shit, if he didn't send them, then who did?

"Wasn't there a card?" He looked around in the bouquet.

"It's right here," I said, pulling it from my pocket and handing it to him. "I really thought they were from you. Who else would they be from?"

He took the card from me and read it silently. His face got red, as if he was getting pissed. I couldn't imagine who would have sent me flowers to get to Viktor. It didn't make any sense.

"I know who these are from, and you will absolutely not be going on that date," he ordered sternly.

"Wait a minute," I responded, "I'm a grown woman, and I can go on a date if I choose to. We aren't together. You don't get to decide that for me."

"You don't even know who sent these to you, do you?" He retorted.

"No, but you don't either. You just think you do." I knew I was being hateful, but I couldn't stop myself at this point. I didn't like being backed into a corner, and I was determined that I would go on this date, no matter who it was with, just because Viktor had told me not to.

"Strain sent them. The guy who tried to kidnap you the other night. Now he wants to take you to dinner. No doubt a ruse to get you away from me where he can kidnap you without interruption this time." He seemed so sure of himself.

"Why wouldn't he sign the card, then?" My voice trembled, and I couldn't stop the shiver that ran down my spine. I didn't want to be anywhere near the neanderthal who'd thought he could claim me because he wasn't happy with his supply cost. It didn't matter how gorgeous he was.

"So you'd be curious and go on the date. Once he got you away from here, you'd have been his for the taking. You're not going. End of discussion." Viktor turned to leave.

"You can't tell me what to do." I stood my ground, like a petulant child, even when he turned and walked over to me. He kept coming toward me, backing me up against the bar. I could feel my heart beating faster. I should have been scared of him, but I was excited. I desperately wanted him to show me why I shouldn't go. I wanted him to throw me over his shoulder and take me upstairs. No matter how bad of an idea it was. I knew that I would wait as long as it took to get him into my bed.

"I just did. You will not go out with Strain. He is dangerous and cannot be trusted. I will do whatever it takes to prevent him from kidnapping you, but you have to cooperate." He looked down at me as he placed his hands on either side of my waist, blocking me against the bar.

"Exactly what are you going to do, then?" I knew that I shouldn't push him, but I couldn't help myself. I bit my bottom lip as I waited for his response. For whatever reason, I trusted him. My mind knew it was a bad idea, but my heart didn't care.

Viktor leaned down and captured my lips with his. I wasn't ready for him to kiss me again. I gasped, then moaned and relaxed into it. His hands moved around my waist and pulled me closer as I wrapped my arms around his neck.

Maybe I wouldn't be waiting too long for a replay of the other night after all. His tongue coaxed my lips apart and he deepened the kiss. I fisted my hand in his dark hair as I relished the feeling of his day-old beard on my skin. Just when I'd started to get used to the idea of giving him another chance, he pulled away.

"Whatever it takes," he said, then turned and walked away.

CHAPTER 14

Viktor

I SHOULDN'T HAVE KISSED her. I knew it; she knew it. But I did it anyway, just to shut her up. And I didn't want to stop. I wanted to throw her over my shoulder and carry her upstairs. I needed to lock her up so she couldn't be taken from me. I wasn't about to let her go anywhere with Strain, no matter what he was promising. I had told him to apologize, but not like this. I knew he was up to something. I couldn't lose her.

I wouldn't put it past him to attempt kidnapping Delilah again. I had hoped that losing his hand would convince him to stay away. I'd have to keep a close eye on her. So much for staying away.

For the rest of the day I avoided going into the bar and taking a chance of running into her. I couldn't face her after that kiss. I knew I wouldn't be able to control myself.

The next morning, I gave up that thought and I tasked myself with finding reasons to be in the bar instead of my office. I had no idea when Strain would show up again, or how many more 'gifts' he would send to convince her to go out with him. I suspected that Delilah knew what I was doing, but she didn't say anything.

After my third trip, she stopped me. "You'd be better off just getting your laptop and working out here. You'd get more done." She turned and walked away without looking back. Delilah was right, I should have just brought the laptop out here in the first place. It would have been less noticeable. Being the boss gave me the freedom to work anywhere on the property that I chose.

"What are you talking about? I'm getting plenty of work done," I tried desperately to cover, even though she had figured me out.

"Look, I get that you're worried about that Strain guy. And I understand that you two have some sort of feud going on or whatever. You don't have to hover. I'm a big girl and I can take care of myself," Delilah tried to act tough, but I got the impression that she liked me hanging out.

"You don't know him the way I do. He's dangerous," I tried to explain, but she cut me off.

"I bet he'd tell me the same thing about you," she quipped before walking away. I followed her, trying to reason with her stubborn ass.

"You don't know all the things he's done. Please, Delilah, just stop for a minute and listen to me." I reached out and grabbed her arm without thinking. She winced as my fingers brushed the still bruised bicep that was covered by her uniform shirt. "I'm sorry." I pulled my hand back, feeling guilty that I'd hurt her.

"It's okay. I couldn't stand to look at it anymore, so I thought covering it up would help. Not so much." She gave me a small smile. Delilah pulled the sleeve of her shirt up to show that the mark was still there.

"But it's not okay. This is just one small example of what he's capable of. I've known him for a long time, and the only things he brings are death and destruction. Please promise me you won't go out with him." I hated how close I was to begging her, but if that's what it took to keep her safe, I would do it.

"If you're that hung up on it, then tell me why. I won't just do what you tell me to because you say so. I haven't known you long enough to give you that much control." She stared at me expectantly.

I wanted to tell her; I just wasn't sure how. Kat's story wasn't easy for me, and I didn't want it to sour what we might have. Wow, I didn't realize that I was actually considering a relationship with Delilah. I told myself I wouldn't let that happen. Oh, the lies we tell ourselves.

"Delilah, I want to tell you, I do. I just don't know where to begin. It's not an easy story to tell. Can't you just trust me?" I knew that I owed her more than that, if for no other reason than the fact that I didn't tell her my wife was dead. I had hoped that keeping that from her would convince Delilah to stay away from me. It seems that Vinny had a big mouth, though. I'd have to take care of that later.

"Does it have something to do with your wife? I'm sorry; I know it's none of my business. Uncle Vinny told me that something happened to her, and I felt awful about bringing it up the other night." Her sympathy tore at my heart.

I nodded. "It's his fault that she's gone." Tears started to form in my eyes, and I blinked to keep them from falling.

"It's Uncle Vinny's fault? No, that doesn't make sense." She paused before speaking again. "It's Strain's fault that she's gone." Her realization was a stab in the heart.

"I don't think I can talk about it right now. Please, promise me you won't go out with Strain, and I'll tell you the whole story after we close up tonight."

She looked at me as if she was trying to tell if I was lying to her or not. Just when I thought she was going to tell me to go to hell, she nodded. "Okay, it's a deal. I won't go anywhere with Strain, and you'll tell me what happened."

"Thank you. I promise that I will keep you safe. Nothing will happen to you while I'm here," I vowed. I knew it was dangerous to make such promises, but I wanted to keep this one. I needed to be sure she would be safe. "We can have dinner in my apartment while we talk if you'd like."

"That sounds good. I have to get back to work. My boss will be pissed that I'm talking instead of working," she joked before turning and walking back to the bar. I laughed at her joke, but still felt as if something was going to happen with Strain.

"I'm certain your boss is a very handsome and understanding man," I quipped back.

I grabbed my laptop from the office and took a seat in a booth near the door. I was in just the right spot to not be seen from the door, while being able to see everything.

I kept an eye on her as she worked, bussing tables, cleaning, and taking care of the handful of customers we had. As I opened my laptop, I brought up her plans for Midnight. Vinny had kept them even though he refused to consider any of them. She had good ideas. What she suggested could triple business, but he wasn't interested just because she was a kid.

If we updated the decor and equipment, we could have live music three nights a week and still keep our karaoke status the other four nights. The whole karaoke schtick pained me, but I could tell that Delilah loved it. She was constantly dancing around and singing along with the music while she prepared to open or after the bar closed. I couldn't figure out why she wasn't ever on stage until Vinny had mentioned telling her to shut up. I told him to leave her alone. She was a far better singer than some of those who tried.

Fortunately for me, it was too early for the amateur singing crowd to be in today. There had only been a few people who showed interest in singing in the past week. Vinny assured me that the weekends were much busier, but I wasn't sure I believed him.

CHAPTER 15

Delilah

I COULDN'T FIGURE VIKTOR out. He was hot then cold, interested then not. When he kissed me, the passion was red hot, but then he hid from me for days at a time.

I'd known him for a little while, and still couldn't figure out if he was interested or not. I think the only reason he kissed me today was to keep me from going to dinner with Strain.

To be honest, I was seriously disappointed when I found out Viktor wasn't the one who'd sent me the flowers. I didn't want to go anywhere with the guy who'd tried to kidnap me. I just refused to let Viktor think he could tell me what to do.

I knew that being stubborn about it could get me in trouble. I wasn't actually going to go through with it. But I was going to play it off like I was going to go to dinner with Strain.

Then he kissed me! What the hell is that all about? Now we're going to have dinner? So in a way, because of the flowers, I get to have dinner with Viktor. I was starting to get nervous about it. Especially since he insisted on sitting in the bar and keeping an eye on me. He thought I didn't know what he was doing, but that's only because I didn't feel like arguing about it again.

He jumped when the phone rang, trying to cover it up by walking past the bar to his office. I answered as usual, prepared to give our business hours or search for someone's spouse who should have been home by now.

"Did you like the flowers?" A smooth voice whispered the words. Panic started to set in. *Strain.*

"What do you want?" I asked, trying to calm my racing heart. His face filled my mind and my heart picked up again, for different reasons this time.

"To make sure you got the flowers. I know your boss, and well, he can be a dick. I sent flowers as an apology. I wanted to make sure he didn't throw them out." The response was strange, as if we were old friends instead of strangers.

"I got the flowers. Thank you. They're beautiful." I glanced around the room for Viktor as I spoke. I wondered how he would react if he knew who had called me.

"So you'll forgive me? I'll do anything." The hint of laughter in his voice was incredibly sexy. It made me want to agree.

"I'll consider it." I began, smiling at the prospect of him trying to make it up to me. Suddenly the line went dead. I looked down at the receiver in my hand and turned to the base hanging on the wall. Viktor's hand was on it. I hadn't seen or heard him walk up behind me.

"Why'd you do that?" I asked, shocked that he'd hung up without knowing who I was speaking to.

"I know it was him. I won't let him manipulate you. Besides, we're getting busy." My face flushed with his words before I realized he was talking about the bar.

"Oh, right. I'll get back to work." There was nothing else to say. As I served drinks and cleared tables, I now had two men—vampires—on my mind instead of just the one. I was still angry that Viktor was trying to control me, but at the same time, I was still a little scared of Strain.

The night life hadn't been as wild for the past five years as it was when I first started working at Midnight. Because of that, Viktor had been closing the place up around eleven every night. If it cleared out earlier, he usually had us close down to keep from wasting time and energy. 'There's no point in paying you to be bored,' he would say.

I couldn't explain it, but business had picked up tonight. I knew it would die down again before midnight, and I was thrilled. I was anxious to have a quiet evening with Viktor and talk.

When midnight came and went with the bar still packed, my mood soured. I spent the rest of the night tending bar and taking care of customers. I loved this place, but I was definitely disappointed about the change in plans. Viktor gave me an apologetic look as he moved from the bar to his office. I guess he figured I was safe as long as there were this many people around. Midnight's hot streak lasted for a few days, then business died again.

After a couple of days with the bar being mostly empty, I approached Viktor. He'd started hanging out in the bar more as business died down. "Are you really going to make changes to the bar, or are you just using it as a front the way Uncle Vinny did?" I knew that I shouldn't have been so blunt, but I wanted to know. He raised an eyebrow at me and I continued. "I don't know the details of the back room operation, but I've seen enough to know it's not exactly on the up and up."

"Well, I can't address those allegations, but you're welcome to check out this proposal I'm reading if you're interested in my plans for the bar," he gestured toward his laptop and motioned for me to take a seat next to him. It was silly to think that he would just tell me about what he and Uncle Vinny had been up to.

"Can't. The boss is around, and wouldn't like it if I was spending too much time with one customer. Speaking of which, do you want a drink or a sandwich, or something?" I had to keep my distance, or I was afraid I'd end up in his lap. That would be bad.

"I'm sure your boss wouldn't mind you taking a break. You might be surprised at how generous and kind he is when you get to know him." Viktor tried not to laugh at his own ridiculous comment, but he failed. I think my grimace may have factored into that, but I can't be sure.

"I guess a minute couldn't hurt," I said as I slid into the booth beside him. His laptop was open and he gestured to it again, as if he wanted me to look at what he'd been studying. "That's my proposal! Did Uncle Vinny give you that?" I was shocked that he seemed to be taking my ideas more seriously than my uncle had.

"It's excellent. I'll have to change a few things so that the Maxwell logo works with it; like the color scheme, but other than that, I think it's perfect. You obviously spent a lot of time on it." His kind words made me blush, and I found myself leaning closer to him.

"I should get back to work. It looks like my last table just left. I don't know if we'll get anyone else tonight." I stood up, but before I could walk away, Viktor put his hand on my arm.

"Why don't you close up early? We can go across town to dinner. I know a quiet little spot," he smiled as he spoke, and my heart melted. "I feel bad that our plan got cancelled the other night and I'd like to make it up to you."

Without hesitation, I replied, "That sounds great. I can have everything done and be ready in an hour." I looked at my watch, shocked that it was only seven. "Are you sure you want to close this early?"

He nodded. "I am. It's one night, and business is really slow anyway. The rebranding and remodeling will make up for it, I promise."

"Okay, I'd better get busy then." I turned and walked away. As I started bussing the now empty tables, I heard Viktor on the phone. He made a reservation, then called someone else. A few minutes later, Uncle Vinny showed up and practically pushed me out the door.

"Go get ready for dinner. I've got this." He took the rag from my hand and continued cleaning the bar.

"Are you sure?" I asked as I removed my apron and strolled toward the stairs. He knew that it was a rhetorical question and didn't bother to respond.

"I'll pick you up in an hour. Take your time," Viktor called as I walked away from the bar.

I ran up the stairs and into my apartment. Once inside, I did a little happy dance, then ran to my closet. Viktor hadn't said what kind of restaurant we'd be going to, so I had no idea what to wear.

I took a quick shower and opted for simple black pants and a red sweater. Paired with my red flats, I thought it was cute and practical. Hopefully it was dressy enough for whatever Viktor had in mind. It was hard to tell what to expect from a man who never wore anything besides a suit.

I laid out a dress just in case I needed to change quickly when he came up to get me. Then I focused on my hair and make-up. I wanted to look my best, even though this probably wasn't a date. *Oh, shit! Is this a date? I have no idea.* I'd managed to talk myself into being nervous. Great. Just what I needed, to be more awkward than I usually am. I couldn't help but laugh as I applied my cosmetics and scrunched my wavy hair.

CHAPTER 16

Viktor

AFTER SETTING VINNY UP to close the bar, I waited for Delilah to go upstairs before I returned my laptop to the office, locked it, and headed up to my own apartment to get ready. Changing our plans to go out instead of spending time in either of our apartments was a last-minute decision. I knew that if I had her alone, I would take her to my bed again. I needed something to keep me from devouring her.

I knew that taking her to Starlight would be a risk as well. I hadn't been there with anyone since Kat. I was sure that Mary had started to gossip about my reservation the moment she hung up the phone. Did I care? I wasn't sure that I did. I liked Delilah, and a part of me wanted to see where this would go.

I knew I could never let things get serious though. I had to protect her from Strain. That had to be my top priority. To be honest, I would have closed the bar early anyway as a way to keep that scumbag away from her. Just knowing that Strain was planning to take my Delilah out on a date made my skin crawl.

I knew that he would never admit his part in Kat's death, just as well as I knew he'd never forgive me for taking his sister away from him.

While I was changing, I realized that I hadn't given Delilah any indication of what type of restaurant we'd be heading to. I hoped that it didn't cause her any anxiety, as I was sure she would change clothes for the occasion. I decided that casual would be the best bet, so I opted for black pants and a white button up shirt. Starlight was a five-star restaurant, but it wasn't black tie.

When I was done, I headed down my stairs and up the other side to Delilah's apartment. I was a few minutes early, but I didn't mind waiting if she wasn't ready. I knocked and was shocked when the door opened almost immediately.

She looked amazing. "Wow, you're stunning. I wasn't sure if you would be ready yet."

"Thanks. With Uncle Vinny taking care of closing, I didn't need as much time as I thought. I hope this outfit is OK for wherever we're going," she smirked at me as she looked me up and down.

"It's perfect. We should go." I held the door while she grabbed her phone and keys.

The drive to the restaurant was awkward and tense. Neither of us knew what to say.

"Tell me a little about yourself," she said after a long period of silence.

"What would you like to know? I promised to tell you about Kat, but that will be better told at the restaurant, without so many distractions." I tried to focus on the road instead of her scent. She smelled of cotton candy, something I hadn't indulged in since I'd been transformed.

"How long have you been a vampire? What was it like to change? Do you ever regret it?" She paused to take a breath. "I'm sorry, none of that is any of my business. I honestly had no idea that vampires were real until the other day. I have so many questions." I caught her blush out of the corner of my eye before she ducked her head.

"It's okay. I had no idea until just a few weeks before I was turned, which was a long time ago—nearly thirty-five years. The change itself wasn't bad after the initial pain of death. I don't regret the choice, but sometimes I do regret the circumstances that led to it." I knew that all of this would come out at dinner, but I wasn't ready to talk about Kat yet.

"What about you? Tell me something about yourself that no one else knows," I prompted in an effort to change the subject.

"In addition to my business classes, I took acting and singing lessons. I kept pestering Uncle Vinny to let me sing, but he refused. *Employees can't participate in karaoke—it's not good for business,*" she mocked Vinny when she quoted him. It didn't surprise me that he refused to let any of her talents shine. He was a selfish dick, who only cared about himself. That was the same character flaw that allowed me to purchase Midnight from him at a loss.

"Really? You can sing? I hadn't noticed. We'll have to get you on stage at Midnight for a debut. Maybe I'll have you entertain instead of tending the bar. If you're any good, that is," I smirked at her. She must have decided to let me act as if I hadn't heard her singing while she worked, and I was okay with that. I was confident that she would be a great performer, even without lessons.

"Are you serious? You'd let me sing at Midnight? Wow, I really should have had a more open mind about you taking over the bar," she paused, then continued. "But you know, part of that was your fault. You were the one who made Uncle Vinny lock me in that cage. I have questions about that too."

"He didn't want to lock you up. He fought with me about it, but I didn't give him a choice. It's a vampire skill that most can't master. I happen to be proficient in most vampire skills that others can't seem to figure out," I glanced at her as I spoke.

I took a chance and laced my fingers with hers. "I am sorry about that. I'll be honest with you. I don't know how to handle myself around you. Your scent is almost too much. I shouldn't have had him lock you up, but it was the only way I could protect you from me until I could get myself under control. I hope you'll forgive me."

She turned to look out the window, pulling her hand from mine, and spoke softly. If my hearing wasn't enhanced, I might have missed her comment. "I wanted so badly to hate you, but I can't. I don't like that you made that decision, but I think I understand now why you did it. And you saved my life the other night. If I'm being honest, I don't know how to handle myself around you either."

I chuckled, and she turned toward me. "You heard that? How?" I glanced over again and she was staring at me.

"Enhanced hearing. I'm glad to know I'm not the only one struggling here."

She took a few minutes to process what she'd learned as I pulled up to the valet station at Starlight. Her eyes opened wider when she realized where we were.

"You got reservations at Starlight last minute? How? Do you know the owner?" Delilah asked me accusingly.

I nodded. "I do, actually."

"Wait, you own it, don't you?" She accused me as if I had lied to her about it.

"I do. That makes it easier to get a last-minute reservation. You should have heard Mary's shock when I called to get a table for two. I'm sure you'll be the talk of the town tomorrow." I laughed. I hoped that knowing people would be talking about her wouldn't make her regret agreeing to dinner.

"Then we should definitely give them something to talk about," she said as I escorted her to the door. She seemed excited by the prospect of being the center of the local gossip. Once we were inside, Delilah waited until she saw Mary walking up to seat us, then leaned into me and pressed her lips to mine.

I was caught off guard and my usual composure was gone. I groaned and pulled her close, deepening the kiss. I only stopped when I heard Mary clear her throat. *Well, that's one way to make sure everyone knows we were here.*

"Fantastic to see you sir, and your lady friend. I have your usual table ready. Please follow me." Mary kept her expression neutral, though I could hear that her heart beat faster with anticipation. She would spend the rest of the night telling anyone who would listen about the boss's indiscretion.

Once we were seated, Mary handed us menus and walked away. Our server took drink orders and left us alone.

"This place is amazing," Delilah gushed.

"Thank you. I'm hoping to elevate Midnight to these standards with your help," I replied, watching her cheeks turn pink.

CHAPTER 17

Eli

I WONDERED IF DELILAH would be surprised when she saw me walk up to Midnight to pick her up. Since I'd already sent her flowers, I brought a box of fancy chocolates. I had hoped that she would agree to go to dinner with me even though I had scared her. I knew that I had taken things too far, but I couldn't stop myself once Vik showed up. I needed to make up for it. I needed to get to know her. Dinner would be the start of that.

I knew there was a chance she wouldn't go with me. That was why I had sent the flowers early and called a few times before I showed up. She seemed intrigued by me, so I was hopeful she would go out with me. Unless Vik had already claimed her.

He had always been able to get under my skin, no matter how hard I tried to ignore him. Vik was the reason I'd gone into half of the business ventures I'd attempted in the past thirty years or so. I wanted so badly to take him down. So far, I was about half way there. I'd beaten him in several areas locally, and was working on the international market. But if he held the majority of the blood supply, there was no way I'd ever truly beat him.

There had to be a way to fix things with him. There was no point in all the fighting. It seemed silly to keep going after each other instead of simply competing the way we used to. Everything changed when Kat died. Vik couldn't let go, instead insisting that it was my fault or Shawn's. It didn't matter that neither of us had set the explosives, she shouldn't have been there. I agreed with him on that one.

Maybe Delilah would have some ideas on how we could manage a truce. It was worth a shot. I was so sick of constantly feeling like I had to go after him. Even if I couldn't beat him, there should have been enough of the city for us to live comfortably. It wasn't like the competition always had to be deadly.

I'd gotten lost in my random thoughts of war and peace. I caught myself walking past Midnight, not realizing because it was so dark inside. The bar should still be open. This is strange. I tried the door, but it was locked. *Maxwell.* That dick had closed down because he knew I was coming.

Oh well, I knew where Delilah lived. I'd just walk there and pick her up. I turned the corner and walked up to the building that had been listed on her credit report. I knew that I was borderline stalking her, but I couldn't help myself. There was something about this girl that was pulling me to her, and it wasn't just to get back at Maxwell.

I walked up to the door just as a dark-haired guy was leaving. He held the door for me to enter. "Thanks, man."

He nodded, barely giving me a second glance, "No problem." I would have to talk to Delilah about the lax security in her building. It wasn't safe for the residents to let just anyone in without knowing where they were going or who they were. I could have been a serial killer for all this guy knew.

I walked up the stairs to the apartment and knocked. *What if she gets upset that I was this forward about our date?* I shrugged the worry off. I would explain that I'd found out where she lived because I wanted to apologize in person. No big deal.

I knocked on the door, but there was no answer. I tried again, and the neighbor to the left opened her door. "Delilah moved out. I don't know where she went, but if you need some company, I'm available." The woman was wearing a barely there red negligee and a matching see-through robe with red high heels.

"Thank you for the offer, but I'll have to pass." I raced out of the building without giving the woman another thought.

She moved out? Damn you, Vik. This had to be him. I guess I should be flattered that he remembered how tech savvy I am, but I was more pissed that he'd ruined my plans. I'd show that bastard. I stormed down the stairs and out the door. The rage was taking over, and I hoped that I didn't do anything too crazy. I vaguely remembered sending a text before everything went black.

Once the rage took over, I only caught bits of what I'd done, like flashes of a dream. My body was moving on its own and I had no idea what I was doing. All I knew was that I was on a mission to ruin Vik. Flashes of bright light, broken glass. The smell of alcohol and busted cinder blocks assaulted me. I didn't feel any pain. Just as I caught the scent of blood, someone was pulling me away. I tried to fight, but must have been drugged.

I woke up hours later in my own bed, filthy and groggy, but alone. The images came in waves as I showered and went back to bed. Maybe I would figure out what I had done tomorrow. This day had been enough of a shit show for now. With any luck, the team would have good news in the morning.

My last conscious thought before I passed out was of Delilah. I hated that our date had been taken from me. I vowed that I would get even. No matter what.

CHAPTER 18

Delilah

THE RESTAURANT WAS GORGEOUS. I'd never been inside because the waiting list was years long. It was hard to believe that I was not only here, but with the owner. Life seemed surreal sometimes.

"I can't believe I'm here right now. This menu is crazy. I have no idea what to order," I admitted, feeling a little out of place.

Viktor must have picked up on my discomfort, because he leaned forward and put his hand on my wrist. "You simply order whatever sounds good to you right now. Let's start with drinks. I'll be getting my usual, which wouldn't interest you, but I can help you decide if you'd like," he offered, and somehow I knew that his usual would involve drinking blood in some form.

In a way, it was nice to know that the vampire population was being taken care of. Just thinking about them hunting humans made my insides feel wobbly. He hadn't told me a lot about how their feedings worked, but there had been enough to know that I was safe with him.

It didn't matter to me anyway, there was something about Viktor that kept pulling me toward him. I didn't think I could resist him if I wanted to. And if I were being honest with myself, I didn't want to.

He helped me choose a glass of wine, an appetizer, and an entree, then insisted that I have the creme brulee for dessert. I wondered how he knew it was my favorite, but didn't mention it. Once our food had been ordered, the waitress didn't come around for a while.

"You were planning to explain things to me, right?" I asked, trying to steer the conversation back to what we'd discussed in the car.

"Yes, I told you that I would explain about my wife." He paused and looked at his hands.

"If you're not ready to tell me, it's OK. I understand. I just want to get to know you better. Whatever you want to share is fine." I figured there was no reason to ruin a night out if he needed more time.

"Thank you, but I gave my word, and that's the one thing I try to keep. It's not easy for me to talk about Kat, but I think that knowing will help you understand why I'm so against you going anywhere with Strain." Viktor paused and looked into my eyes.

"I'd like to understand," I responded, trying not to get lost in the way the light reflected in his eyes, making them more golden than brown.

"Kat and I met as she was finishing law school. I had just completed my Masters in Business, and we ran into each other at a coffee shop near campus." He looked off into the distance as he spoke, as if he was lost in another time.

"She was beautiful, but what got to me was how kind she was to everyone. We had coffee that day, then went on a date the next night. After that, we were inseparable. At least until I learned her dark family secret."

Viktor stopped talking for a moment as the waitress brought our appetizers and refilled our drinks. When she walked away, he continued.

"A few weeks after we started dating, I realized that her brother was constantly calling her. He wanted to know where she was and who she was with all the time. It was pretty annoying, but Kat always defended him. *'Eli's a good guy. He just worries,'* she would say. He paused and looked at me again. I could tell that this was hard for him.

"It's his fault she's dead. His men set the bomb that killed her. I can't let that happen to you," he blurted suddenly.

"Wait, are you saying that Strain was your wife's brother?" I had to have misinterpreted what he was saying. It made no sense. Those two hated each other. They couldn't be family, could they?

Viktor nodded solemnly. "He was her older brother. I struggled with how close they were, and it nearly drove us apart for a while. After a few years, he and I became friends. Then she went to work for his boss, and she was killed in an explosion. I lost my mind when I lost Kat. It was hard. Sometimes it still is."

"I'm so sorry. I don't understand, though. Why would he have his men blow up his own sister?" I knew that it was a bad idea to ask, but I couldn't help it.

"Because she was pregnant with my child, and he couldn't stand the thought of her being with me. Their relationship was the only thing Kat and I ever fought about. Everything else was easy." He paused again and looked at me. "After the bombing, when I lost it, I sought out some shady people. That was when I became this."

"Why?" I couldn't stop the question.

"So I would be strong enough for revenge. I'd lost everything. There was no reason to live. I had planned to offer my life as a sacrifice, but the vampire I went to had other plans. He convinced me that revenge was a better path. I was young and stupid. I had just lost my family, and I wasn't thinking straight."

I tried to understand what he'd been going through. I couldn't imagine being in that situation. Having everything you'd ever wanted, then having it taken away like that would be devastating. I didn't know what to say, so I just nodded, and he continued.

"Once I had transitioned, I began to amass my own wealth. As a human, I had access to my family's money, but I needed more if I wanted to take Strain down. My mentor helped me set everything up, and my parents loaned me a large sum of money as a nest egg. I didn't think that they would understand my need for revenge, but I was wrong. They wanted Strain to pay for what he'd done to their grandchild." Viktor raked his hand across his face and into his hair. I could tell that this story was taking a toll on him.

"So you've spent all this time gathering the resources to get back at Strain for taking your family from you. I get it. I'm sorry that this happened to you; to your family." I knew that there was nothing I could say to make it better. A tear ran down my cheek. We sat in silence for a bit. I didn't know what else to say, and it was clear that he had no desire to talk about it anymore.

After an awkwardly long pause, I let him change the subject back to discussing the bar. Midnight could be a lucrative business if it was taken care of. Viktor agreed with most of my ideas, and suggested that I work with him on the design. I was thrilled. Our food came, and I got caught up in the scents and tastes. Conversation lulled, but it wasn't uncomfortable.

The food was every bit as good as it had been rumored to be. I ate every bite, moaning as if I were having sex. I tried to control myself, but I couldn't. Viktor didn't seem to mind. He just sat there, drinking from a coffee mug and watching me.

I had so many questions, but it didn't seem fair to throw all of them at him in one night. I wanted to know everything about him and about vampires. Maybe I would make a list and ask a few at a time over a couple of weeks or so. I almost asked him if that would be okay, but something stopped me. Instead, we finished dinner in awkward silence. Well, after I finished with my foodgasm.

CHAPTER 19

Viktor

I FELT GUILTY FOR telling Delilah about what happened with Kat. I knew that it was vital for her to understand why a part of me would always be off limits, but it seemed as if she were too sympathetic about the whole thing. I didn't want her to feel bad for me. I wanted her to understand. The look in her eyes was almost too much for me. I couldn't take the pity.

I could tell that there was more that she wanted to know, but she didn't ask about anything. I didn't want to push, so I let it go. Perhaps we would talk about it later.

We headed back to Midnight, as it was getting late. When I pulled up to the bar, I concentrated on parking and didn't even glance at the building. Delilah's gasp caught my attention.

"What's wrong?" I asked, putting the car in park. I turned and looked at her. She was staring out the window and tears were streaming down her face.

"Myshka, what is it?" I turned her head to meet my eyes.

"Midnight, it—it's ruined," she sobbed.

At this point, I looked past her to the building. It had been trashed. Glass littered the sidewalk where every pane had been shattered.. The door had been ripped off the hinges and lay on the sidewalk a few feet from the entrance. The sign had been torn from the front of the building, and was nowhere to be seen.

I needed to check it out but didn't feel safe leaving Delilah in the car alone. I was almost convinced that Strain was behind this and didn't want to risk her being kidnapped. A snap decision had me taking her along to check the damage.

"Come with me, do not leave my side. Promise me." I rounded the car and opened her door, taking her hand protectively. I couldn't let him have her.

She nodded and gripped my hand hard. "Who would do this? Why? I don't understand," she was still crying. I understood her pain. Midnight had been her home for the past twenty years.

"I have an idea of who is responsible, but I'd rather find proof first. I need you to trust me. Can you do that? Will you do as I ask without questions?" I forced her to look at me again.

Delilah nodded. "What do you want me to do?"

"We're going inside to survey the damage. I have hidden cameras everywhere. I should be able to get to the feed. You need to stay focused and be aware of anything around you. The people responsible could be anywhere. Stay close to me." I hated ordering her around, but keeping her safe was more important than proving that I wasn't a chauvinist pig.

Delilah followed me inside, carefully stepping over bricks that had been dislodged from the wall. The inside was as bad as the outside. I had expected it to look worse. From her gasp, I gathered Delilah hadn't considered that someone would have destroyed the interior too.

Every table was broken in half. Every chair, barstool, and bench had been busted up. There were no bottles left untouched. Everything that could be broken was. Glass from broken liquor bottles and glassware was everywhere. It would take weeks and a small fortune to rebuild. At this point, it would make more sense to demolish the building and sell the lot. One look at Delilah's face, and that thought was out the window. It didn't matter how long it took or what it cost; I would fix this. For her.

We managed to get to my office. The door had been ripped off its hinges as well. "Stay quiet and stay close." I kept my voice low, listening for any movement. So far, I'd heard nothing since we pulled up in front. The anxious beat of Delilah's heart made her fear evident. We crept into my office and over to the far wall where the safe was hidden. It looked like that was the only thing in the building that might not have been touched. This room was as trashed as the bar had been. The computer was destroyed, the monitor busted, and the phone was in pieces.

I could feel her body pressed against mine as I dealt with the wall panel. In another situation, I would have pinned her against the wall and had my way with her. There would be time for that later. I needed the security feed. I refocused my efforts on removing the panel and opening the safe.

The computer housed inside had an external hard drive to record security footage. I was able to remove it, slip the drive in my pocket, and grab the other valuables from the safe. There wasn't much, but I had put a few things in there for safe keeping.

"OK, we're going back the way we came. We'll take the car and go to my place." I'd been staying above the bar, but I had a condo across town.

There was a muffled noise before she could respond. It came from the backroom. Fear spread across her face as she gripped my arm harder. I pulled her close and pressed my lips to hers. This wasn't the time to worry about sending the wrong signal. She needed comfort, needed to calm down before something else happened. I felt her relax against my body as I let my tongue assault hers. When I pulled away, she seemed much calmer and more focused.

"Stay behind me. We're going to check it out." I led the way, keeping one hand behind me on her arm. It didn't matter, since she was still pressed against my back as if she was scared to let there be any space between us.

As terrified as she was, I had to admit, it felt nice to be the one protecting her. Part of me wished that we could stay like this forever. Her blind trust would get her hurt or killed though. I didn't even trust myself as much as she trusted me.

C H A P T E R   20

Delilah

I followed Viktor so closely that every time he stopped, I ran into his back. I couldn't help it; I was terrified. Someone had broken into my home and destroyed everything they could. What if this noise was the person who'd done all of this? What if they'd waited for us to get back?

Even though I hadn't known him for very long, I trusted Viktor with my life. If he hadn't been here with me, I would have already run away. Anxiety was taking over, and I could feel it clawing at me. I wanted to hide somewhere, but I knew that I couldn't.

His kiss in the office had relaxed me for a little while, but staying here in what used to be my home was bringing it all back quickly. I needed to run. I had nowhere to go, but I needed to get away from here soon. I wasn't sure how much more I could take. My heart broke again with every room we walked through.

As we crept along, I tried to ignore the trickle of cold sweat that ran down my back. Viktor stopped short in front of the door to the backroom—the only door in the place that hadn't been ripped off, and I ran into him again. I wrapped my arms around him from behind to calm myself for a moment. He squeezed my hand before nudging me to release him. Once I let go, he stepped forward into the stock room. I only let an inch of space live between us. I was too terrified to get any further away.

"Vinny, is that you?" Viktor whispered, gesturing toward something on the floor. The room had been ransacked, bottles were busted, shelves were turned on their sides. The sickening smell of all the different types of alcohol mixed together made my stomach turn. My eyes followed his hand, but I couldn't make out the figure. The only thing I could see was the broken glass and the puddles of liquid.

Viktor silently urged me to follow him as we moved closer. After a few more steps, I was able to make out a body on the floor. "Uncle Vinny!" I cried before Viktor turned and clamped his hand over my mouth.

"Shhh," he warned before removing his hand, "we don't know what or who's here. Let's see if we can get him out quietly."

I nodded, then I stepped back against the wall, making sure that I could see everything around me while Viktor moved rubble off Uncle Vinny. It was the most space that had been between us since we'd entered the decimated building. He scooped the unconscious man up as if he weighed nothing, then gestured to me to head toward the door. Without hesitation, I followed him as he carried my uncle. I said a silent prayer that the man who'd raised me would survive, though I wasn't sure if it was possible at this point.

We moved almost silently, keeping against the wall and stopping at every noise. As soon as we slipped out the door, the ceiling collapsed. Viktor grabbed me and ran across the street. I'd never moved so quickly before. I was shocked that he could move so fast while carrying Uncle Vinny and me.

"Are you okay?" He asked as he placed me back on my feet. My head spun from the quick relocation.

"I think so," I replied, "but what about him?" I gestured to my uncle, who was still unconscious.

"He's breathing, but his heartbeat is irregular," Viktor replied. "We should get him to a hospital."

He placed Uncle Vinny in the backseat of the car, then opened my door. "Thanks." I wanted to say so much more. He'd just risked his life to save my uncle. I didn't know how I would ever repay him. I had no idea how we would pay for the hospital, especially with Midnight destroyed, but I would do whatever it took to get my uncle the best care possible.

The drive to the hospital was a blur. I was caught up in what could have happened if I'd been home when the break-in occurred. Viktor made a call to the hospital, and a stretcher was waiting for us outside the dimly lit emergency entrance. After the nurses settled Uncle Vinny onto it and strapped him down, Viktor nudged me toward the entrance.

I thought we were going to fill out some paperwork for my uncle. Instead, I found myself being escorted to a room and being checked out by a doctor. "I wasn't even inside when any of it happened," I protested, "I'm fine, really."

Viktor shook his head. "Physically, maybe, but you've been through a traumatic event. I need to make sure that you're not in shock."

It was touching that he cared enough to make sure I wasn't hurt. While I was talking to the doctor, Viktor excused himself. Of course, Dr. Harper had to ask if I was being abused at home. I laughed.

"I have to ask," he replied.

"Other than my home being destroyed for no logical reason while I was out tonight, I've never been close to being abused," I countered. My parents weren't around enough to abuse me and my uncle had always kept me at arms' length.

As the doctor finished up his examination, Viktor returned. "Is she okay, Doc?" he asked, and I felt my cheeks get warm.

Dr. Harper nodded. "She may have a mild case of shock, but she's still pretty feisty. You can take her home whenever you're ready."

"What about Uncle Vinny?" I asked, ignoring the fact that I had nowhere to go.

The doctor checked his phone before replying. "He's stable, but still unconscious. We're still assessing his injuries. Don't worry. We'll take good care of him." The doctor didn't seem worried, but I couldn't help it. My uncle had taken care of me for a long time. I couldn't bear the thought that something had happened to him.

"It's fine. I have his room number. We can come back and see him in the morning. Come on, Delilah, let's get you home," Viktor gently grabbed my arm and led me from the room.

"I don't have a home anymore. I gave up my apartment to live above Midnight. Now it's destroyed." Tears fell as I walked with Viktor to his car.

"Don't worry about that. I have a place for us. We'll get it all fixed. Whoever did it doesn't realize that they did us a favor. After the police report is filed and the insurance adjuster checks the place out, we'll rebuild it exactly the way we wanted. To top it off, the insurance will cover all of it. Win-win," he claimed as he buckled my seatbelt, then his own.

"Tell that to Uncle Vinny," I snarled before turning to stare out the window. Viktor didn't respond.

I must have dozed off while Viktor maneuvered the car through the city streets. When the car came to an abrupt stop, I woke up groggy. "Where are we?"

"This is home for now," he replied.

Chapter 21

Viktor

I was relieved when Delilah fell asleep in the car on the way to the cabin. Trust wasn't an issue, but she was in shock, and I didn't want her to freak out more by seeing where we were going. Her nap would give me time to explain before we headed back to the hospital tomorrow.

I loved the little cabin so much that I couldn't bear to sell it after Kat died. She had never even seen it. I bought it for us when I found out she was pregnant. I wanted us to have a place outside of the city to raise the little one. Even after that dream was destroyed, I held on to the cabin.

Delilah was awake when I rounded the car to get her. I opened her door and held out a hand to help her out. "Welcome home, Myshka."

I should have been more cautious about it, but I wanted her in my home. At the moment, I wasn't concerned with the future or what I was risking. I had to keep her safe. That was all that mattered.

She squinted in the darkness, apparently not seeing the cabin. It was easy to forget that she didn't have the same enhanced senses that I did. Since she couldn't see it, I put my arm around her and escorted her toward the front door. Delilah stumbled on the steps, and I scooped her up, carrying her the last few feet to the door. I disabled the security system until we were inside.

I turned on a lamp inside the door so Delilah wouldn't be in the dark. I didn't need the light, but somehow I remembered that she might feel better if she could see. I reactivated the security system and turned to her.

"Let's get you to your room," I offered. She winced. "What's wrong? Where does it hurt?" I scooped her up and ran to the couch, where I carefully dropped her to the soft cushions.

"I'm fine. I just can't handle the thought of being alone right now. I'm worried about Uncle Vinny, and I'm scared." Her lips quivered as she spoke, and I could feel her heart start to race.

"What can I do?" I hated feeling helpless, but I knew that I couldn't leave her alone right now.

"Let me stay with you. Just be near me. Please."

I couldn't refuse her simple plea. I wanted to be near her as much as she needed me to stay close. "I need to watch the video feed. Are you up for that?"

Her wince told me that she wasn't. I nodded, shrugging out of my jacket. I moved the thumb drive of the security feed from my jacket to my pants pocket. I would watch it after she fell asleep. It didn't matter, as I was certain I knew what I would see. Only a vampire could have done that much damage to the bar in such a short amount of time. Strain had made the next move. No doubt it was because Delilah spurned his advance.

I relived the feeling of relief that I'd felt when she agreed to have dinner with me instead of insisting on going with him. I knew that I had almost screwed everything up by pushing her away. I wouldn't let that happen again. I couldn't keep letting my mistakes with Kat influence any potential future I could have.

I sat down on the couch with Delilah and encouraged her to lean on me. "I can deal with the security feed later. You need to rest." I put my arm around her as she laid her head on my chest and wrapped an arm around my waist.

"Thank you. For everything." The words were a whisper before she finally gave in and fell asleep. I leaned down and kissed the top of her head, then pulled the thumb drive out of my pocket, along with an adapter and my phone.

She didn't budge the whole time I was digging things out of my pocket. Since I was convinced she was asleep, I hooked the drive up to my phone and played the video.

What I saw did not surprise me. I knew it had been Strain or his men who destroyed Midnight. From the video, I could see that he did all of the damage himself.

He walked up to the door like a man possessed. Strain started pounding on the door until it cracked under the pressure.

Once he was inside, he tore through the place, breaking anything that got in his way. I switched from the external cameras to the internal and continued to watch.

Strain made a show of breaking every bottle in the bar while screaming at the cameras. He knew that I would be watching. The whole thing was for show. He knew that it was pointless to damage property. That could be easily repaired.

I watched as he continued to destroy everything that Delilah and her uncle had worked so hard to create. It broke my heart. The moment Strain found Vinny was difficult to watch. It looked as if there was no way the human could have survived the attack. His doctors had assured me that he would make a full recovery, but maybe that had been because I told them I was paying for everything.

Delilah's shocked gasp told me that she'd woken up at some point during the video. She had watched Strain beat her uncle nearly to death. The good news was that it didn't look like Strain had bitten Vinny. I wasn't sure how much comfort that would be to her.

"I'm sorry. I didn't realize you were awake," I tried to apologize, knowing it would never be enough for the trauma I'd just allowed to happen.

She shook her head without lifting it from my chest. "It's not your fault. I could have looked away. I wanted to know what he did. That man is a monster." She started to cry and buried her face in my shirt.

I smoothed down her dark hair, letting her cry it out. If she thought Strain was a monster, perhaps she would have the same feeling about me if she knew everything that I'd been responsible for during this feud.

CHAPTER 22

Delilah

VIKTOR GOT QUIET, TOO quiet. I wondered what he was thinking. *Did it upset him that I'd called Strain a monster? Did he think it was because the man who'd almost killed my uncle was a vampire, like him?*

I tilted my head up to look at him. His expression was serious, and he wouldn't make eye contact. Apparently my comment had gotten to him. I refused to apologize. Strain was a monster. Nothing anyone could say would change my mind on that.

I put my hand on Viktor's face and turned it, forcing him to look at me. "This isn't your fault," I said.

He didn't respond, but I could tell from the look in his eyes that he still blamed himself. I scooted up a bit until I was sitting closer to him. I put my hand back on his face, pulling him closer to me. I pressed my lips to his and kissed Viktor as if my life depended on it. He returned my passion with his own.

I had no idea if what I was feeling was real, or if it was just because of everything that had happened since I met him. At the moment, I didn't care either way. I wanted him. I wanted him to want me. The rest of the world didn't matter; neither did the future. We had this moment.

I kissed him again, taking control and climbing onto his lap. Our tongues tangled, then I trailed kisses down his cheek and nipped at his neck.

He growled, pulling me back to his mouth. His hands roamed down my back and grabbed my ass while his tongue battled with mine for dominance. I unbuttoned his shirt and peeled it off his shoulders.

75

He grabbed my sweater and pulled it over my head, letting it fall to the floor. "You are so gorgeous," he breathed before trailing kisses from my neck to my shoulders and back.

I ground against his growing erection, begging without words for this to continue. Viktor's hands ran up my body from my ass to my shoulders before sliding around to knead at my breasts through my lacy bra.

I reached between us to free him from the restraints of his pants. Then I slid down onto the floor and licked him from base to tip before taking his erection into my mouth. He groaned and fisted his hands in my hair.

Suddenly Viktor pushed me away, grabbing my hands with his. "We should get some rest. It's late, and you'll want to see your uncle in the morning."

His rejection stung. With tears in my eyes, I nodded, then sat up. I didn't want to be alone, but I couldn't handle being that close to him anymore. I refused to sit there and let him watch me cry. And I wouldn't beg him to sleep with me. I got up and walked toward the door he had indicated would be my room.

Without a glance behind me, I opened the door and walked through. As soon as the door was closed, the tears started to fall. I slid down onto the floor with my back against the closed door. I felt so isolated, so alone. I had nothing left. My family was gone, and had been for a long time. On top of that, my home had just been destroyed.

I still had Uncle Vinny and I knew that Midnight could be rebuilt, but I didn't understand Viktor. One minute he seemed to care for me; the next he was pushing me away. I couldn't let myself get caught up in something that toxic.

Maybe I should just call Anna and go stay with her. I was certain my friend would let me sleep on her couch if I needed to while things got sorted out and I found a new place. I would need a new job too, because there was no way I'd be able to work for Viktor with the way he was treating me. I would never know where I stood with him.

I wondered what had broken him so badly that he couldn't talk about his feelings. How horrible it must be to push people away instead of letting them in. I started to cry harder at that thought.

I knew that I wouldn't sleep anymore, even though it was the middle of the night. Every time I closed my eyes, I saw what was left of the only place I'd ever considered home. It broke my heart to see the bar destroyed. Most people would claim it was fate; the push I needed to leave town. Maybe they were right. Leaving would be easier without Midnight to keep me here.

I needed to come up with a plan. There were decisions to be made. I needed to double check my bank accounts and see just how much I had saved. I hadn't planned to live at Midnight forever, but I had always felt like that was my home. But maybe, just maybe, it was time for a fresh start.

A few minutes later, I managed to fall into a fitful sleep. I was assaulted by nightmares until I awoke with a start.

CHAPTER 23

Viktor

I DIDN'T WANT TO push Delilah away, but I hadn't eaten in hours and didn't think I could control myself with her. The more aroused I became, the worse the hunger was. I knew if I didn't stop what was happening, I would be putting her at risk. I needed her away from me. I had to keep her safe.

After she shut herself in her room, I could hear her crying. It took every ounce of self-control not to break down the door and scoop her up in my arms. I wanted nothing more than to go back in time and not push her away.

I shot a text to Jones and instructed him to bring some blood bags, food, and other necessities to the cabin. He was the only one I trusted with the location.

Even though it was four in the morning, it would only take him a couple of hours to get everything together. I was certain I could avoid Delilah until then.

I double-checked the locks and alarm system. Jones had access to both, so I didn't have to watch for him. After I was satisfied that Delilah would be safe, I retired to my room. When I turned on the light, I was assaulted by the scent of Kat's perfume.

How her belongings kept her scent all this time is beyond me. She never stepped foot in the cabin, but this room, in particular, smells as if she's right here with me. Right after her death, I couldn't function. Everything was too much. Even now, there were days when I didn't think I could go on. Then I met Delilah and for the first time, I felt like there was hope for the future.

I knew the cases of vampires having children with humans were rare, but it was possible. Could I allow myself to think she would want that? Would I refuse her if she did? I shook the thoughts away. I needed to rest so I could figure out what to do about Strain.

I had already emailed my insurance agent and sent him the video of the break-in, claiming not to know who it was that had destroyed my property. We had an understanding. He knew about vampires but kept it quiet, and in exchange, my corporation only purchased insurance from him. There were moments when it seemed strange to me that we weren't fully exposed.

Distracted by my memories, I decided to take a shower. I knew that Delilah would be safe since the alarm system was on, and Jones was the only person besides myself who had the codes. I didn't bother to lock my bedroom door, because I didn't think it was necessary.

The hot water felt good against my cool skin. I heard the door open but wasn't concerned, as I assumed it was Jones arriving early with the supplies I'd requested. I finished my shower, wrapped a towel around my waist, and walked into the bedroom.

And ran right into a very bewildered Delilah. "Oh, I'm sorry. I shouldn't have come in, but you didn't answer when I knocked. I thought maybe you were sleeping. I'm so sorry. I'll go," she rambled.

I grabbed her arm gently to keep her from running off. "It's okay. No need to apologize. What's wrong? Did something happen?" I looked her up and down, forgetting about the fact that I was standing there barely covered.

She shook her head. "I had a bad dream and got scared by myself. I wanted to see if I could stay with you. I know we had a misunderstanding earlier, but I promise I'll behave myself. I understand that you're not interested that way." The fear across her face floored me. I'd never seen her shaken up this badly. This was worse than when Strain had tried to kidnap her.

I didn't know how to respond to her accusation that I wasn't interested. If anything, I was too interested. "Of course you can stay in my room tonight. Jones will be here in a little while with some food and clothes. Why don't you lie down and rest until he arrives?" I gestured toward the bed.

"Thank you. Everything you've done for me tonight has been amazing. I don't even know why you're trying to take care of me." She looked at the floor. I knew that she was embarrassed about crying in front of me, but I wasn't going to let her feel bad for needing help.

I lifted her chin so her eyes met mine. Her eyes were an entrancing shade of hazel; brown with hints of green and amber. Tears glistening in them nearly broke me. I knew that kissing her was a bad idea, but I couldn't stop myself. I pulled her closer and pressed my lips to hers.

She wrapped her arms around me, and for the first time since I realized she was in my bedroom, I remembered that only a thin towel hung between us. I might not have noticed if it hadn't been for my reaction to her being so close.

I scooped her up and carried her to my bed. I knew that I should stop myself, but I couldn't. I kissed her again as I eased her down on the bed. Just as she shrugged out of her sweater, I heard the door close.

"We have company," I sighed as I pushed up from the bed. I grabbed a pair of pants and shrugged on a shirt. "Stay here, I'll take care of it."

CHAPTER 24

Delilah

IF VIKTOR'S FRIEND HADN'T arrived, I was pretty sure we'd have had sex again. As much as I wanted him, it was probably better that we'd been interrupted, especially after his rejection of me earlier. I couldn't get past the nagging feeling that he was hiding something from me.

There was something about the way he'd pushed me away earlier that didn't sit well. Maybe I was reading too much into the situation. I wondered if the only reason he wanted me was because Strain did as well. It wasn't like I could just ask him. The last time I had tried to question his actions, I ended up locked in a cage for three days. And I still slept with Viktor the first chance I had. Wow, there was something really wrong with me. I decided to push that thought away. I would deal with that later.

After he left the room, I pulled my sweater back on. My phone vibrated, distracting me from trying to listen to the conversation happening in the other room.

Be careful who you trust.

I didn't recognize the number. Who would be texting me at four in the morning?

Who is this? I replied. I knew it was a bad idea, but I couldn't help it. I wanted to know who this was and what they were trying to warn me about.

You didn't show up for our date.

Oh, shit. I sat up in the bed, suddenly tense.

Strain, I didn't agree to a date. Why did you destroy the bar?

I waited a few minutes for the answer, wondering what was keeping Viktor.

He deserved worse. I don't know what kind of lies he's telling you about me, but if you want the truth, I'm happy to meet you somewhere to talk. And please call me Eli.

80

How did Strain—Eli— get my number? What could Viktor have done to make destroying my home simply collateral damage? I wanted to ask, but feared the answers I'd get.

I'm not going anywhere with you, especially after you almost killed my uncle.

I was fighting tears again.

Vinny's your uncle? I had no idea. I'm sorry. He got in my way. I wasn't there to hurt him. I wanted to get back at Maxwell.

I laughed to myself as I read his response. Did Strain think he could convince me that he wasn't dangerous?

Yes, he's my uncle. He practically raised me at Midnight. And you destroyed my home. Please leave me alone. I don't want anything to do with you, or the crazy war you're waging against Viktor.

I knew that I should just stop replying to the messages, but I couldn't help myself. There was something about Strain that pulled me toward him as much as Viktor did.

When you realize that he's lying to you, I'll be there to pick up the pieces.

What was wrong with this guy? He was seriously persistent. And how did we get from him trying to kidnap me to claiming that he's the only one who can tell me the truth?

Why should I trust you? It probably wasn't smart to bait him. I should stop responding.

Because I know where you are. If I wanted to hurt you, I could be at the cabin in ten minutes. Is that a good enough reason?

When I didn't answer, he stopped texting. I knew that I should tell Viktor about the messages, but a part of me wondered if Strain was telling me the truth. Or if he actually knew what Viktor was hiding from me.

I knew from my date with Viktor that the two men had a complicated past. It had to hurt to know that your brother-in-law had killed his own sister to keep you apart. I wasn't sure how I would handle that.

I shifted my attention to the conversation between Viktor and his friend. I had no idea if the men were actually friends, but that sounded better in my head than anything else I could come up with.

"Are you sure?" Viktor asked him, with an angry edge to his voice.

"Yeah, Mr. Maxwell. The reports are all over the news about the bar being destroyed. It looks like they're blaming the Harris gang for it."

"Harris knows better. Besides, I have the tapes. I know it was Strain. What about Vinny? Is he awake yet? I want to talk to him first," Viktor growled. It was as if the edge on his voice was getting sharper the more irritated he got.

"Not yet, but I'll let you know the second I hear something, Boss."

"Jones, I've told you not to call me that."

"Sorry, Sir. Do you need anything else? If not, I'll get back to my patrol."

"This should be good. Thank you for getting everything so quickly." It sounded like the edge was finally wearing off Viktor's tone. I wondered why he'd gotten so upset about some random gang being blamed for the destruction. I also didn't understand why he hadn't planned to turn the video over to the police.

I took a couple of deep breaths to calm myself. I suspected that Viktor would know if I was faking sleep, but after that conversation with Strain, I wasn't sure what to do. Pretending to sleep until I actually could seemed like a good enough plan. I curled up in the bed and closed my eyes. I hoped that when Viktor came back, he decided not to push the issue. I wasn't ready to tell him that I'd talked to Strain yet.

CHAPTER 25

Viktor

It didn't surprise me that Strain had decided to find a scapegoat for the damage at the bar. What surprised me was that he'd talked Harris into going along with it. He was supposed to be one of my allies. I wondered what Strain had used as leverage to sway his loyalty. There would be time to find out tomorrow.

I crept back into my room quietly. I'd heard Delilah settle into the bed a few minutes ago. As much as I wanted her, I knew that she needed to sleep more. There would be time for our passion later. Unless I talked myself out of it and pushed her away again. I shrugged out of my clothes, pulling on a pair of boxer briefs. Then I crawled carefully into my bed so I didn't disturb her.

I suspected that she wasn't actually sleeping, but didn't want to push her. I was worried that she'd been listening at the door when Jones was here. I half expected her to barge in and start yelling at me while I was giving him instructions. I need to have everything in place to go after Strain. I also needed some time to get used to her scent. Even after downing a full blood bag, it still called to me like a siren song. I wanted to drink from her more than I had ever wanted anything before.

I also needed Jones to set up a meeting with Harris. I had to get to the bottom of this. I wasn't sure how I would get away and still keep Delilah safe. The situation was getting out of hand.

I managed to get a couple more hours of sleep and woke up with Delilah wrapped around me. It took every ounce of control not to flip her over and have my way with her. But we needed to get back to the hospital and see what Vinny had to say. It was already eight in the morning, and I didn't want to waste the day.

I sent a text to Jones and discovered that Vinny was still unconscious. There was no point in going to the hospital until he woke. Yet there was no way I could stay in bed with Delilah and not have sex with her.

"Myshka, it's time to get up. We have to check on your uncle," I whispered in her ear. I already knew what the hospital would say, but I wanted Delilah to hear it for herself.

Delilah woke up with a start, jumping at the sound of my voice. She looked confused as if she had forgotten where she was. I wrapped my arms around her and held on tight.

"It's okay, Myshka. You're safe. There are clean clothes in your room if you'd like to shower." I spoke softly as I released my hold on her. "We'll call the hospital before we decide to go. If Vinny is still unconscious or they are running tests, we can relax here for a while."

Delilah rubbed her face and nodded. Realization spread across her face with my words. "Thank you."

While she showered, I prepared a quick breakfast for us, knowing that there was no reason to rush. Jones had assured me that Vinny was stable and still sleeping. From his report, I was certain he was still in his hiding place.

I poured myself a cup of coffee, then mixed in the fresh blood Jones had delivered. Delilah found me on the porch watching the fog burn off the city.

"I didn't think vampires could be out in the sun," she marveled.

"We can't. At least not for long, and not in direct sunlight. The shade on the porch keeps me protected enough." There was no reason to explain the implant yet. That would be a conversation for another day. I had so much to tell her. I wasn't sure when or where to start. Part of me wanted to shield and protect her, but the rest of me wanted to share every detail.

I turned to look at her. I had guessed her sizes perfectly. Delilah looked sexy as hell in the blood-red sleeveless top and blue jeans. I wanted to ask her if she liked the lingerie, but decided it might be inappropriate. Perhaps with a little luck, I'd get to see it later. What was I thinking? I'd been trying to put space between us, and now I was wondering if I would get to see her underwear? I felt as if I were losing my mind. I couldn't help it, there was just something so enticing about her.

"You look refreshed. Did you eat?" I turned the conversation away from details about myself. I didn't like to divulge my weaknesses to anyone. I refuse to make it easier for those who want to hurt me.

Delilah nodded. "I'm ready whenever you are." With that, I dialed the hospital and asked for the nurses' station for her to check on Vinny.

"Oh, okay. Thank you." Her response sounded defeated. I felt badly for her because I already knew what she'd been told.

"Are we ready to go, then?" I asked, waiting to see if she would insist on a visit anyway.

"No. We're not going today. He's still unconscious. They are running more tests to see how extensive his injuries are. They said it'll be a day or two before we can see him." Delilah hung her head as the tears started to fall.

I pulled her into my arms and held her while she cried. I knew that she was worried about her uncle. I suspected that their relationship was closer to that of a parent and child, but I didn't want to hurt her more by asking.

For the next few days, I tried to keep her distracted while maintaining my distance. It was nearly impossible. Somehow I managed to avoid having sex with her again even though my entire body burned for it. I was being eaten alive by my desire. Just when I'd reached my breaking point, the phone rang.

"Yes?" I snapped. It was the trauma nurse calling with an update. Vinny was waking up. "We'll be there shortly."

"What is it?" Delilah started to panic, thinking the worst.

"He's waking up. We can go see him now. Are you ready?" We'd been up for a couple of hours and had been watching sitcoms on tv since breakfast. Delilah nodded and grabbed her jacket without saying anything. She seemed more quiet than usual on the trip, but I thought that she was worried about her uncle. He seemed to be important to her. I wondered again about her parents, but for some reason, that subject felt like it was off limits.

CHAPTER 26

Delilah

THE DRIVE TO THE hospital was brutal. Neither of us spoke. I think Viktor was trying not to remind me of what I had seen on the security feed from Midnight being destroyed. I was trying to forget how I'd made a fool of myself by trying to sleep with him again. You'd think I would learn to stop throwing myself at him like that, no matter how many mixed signals he sent.

I had no desire to go back to the hospital, but I did want to see Uncle Vinny. I hated watching the video of what happened to him. The memory of it haunted me, especially after Strain's messages. I should probably tell Viktor about that, too.

I felt guilty for not telling him about Eli's messages. Of course, there was no proof that Eli was going to kidnap me. He flat out told me that he wasn't. And he knew where we were but didn't make a move. It wasn't like Viktor and I were in a relationship, either. I had no idea what we were exactly.

Part of me wanted to tell him. I wanted to see what he would say in response to Eli's claims that he hadn't been honest with me. Another part of me wanted to forget the whole thing and focus on healing my heart from Victor's rejections.

I turned to face him as he drove to the hospital. "Are you okay?" He met my gaze.

"Yeah. Just nervous I guess," I responded. I had been about to tell him about Eli texting me, but I couldn't make the words come out.

Something stopped me every time I considered it. Maybe Strain was telling the truth. I had a nagging feeling that Eli was being more honest with me than Viktor was. I had no idea why. Maybe there was more to Viktor than he was sharing. In the end, I decided to wait and see what happened next.

We arrived at the hospital in record time and were escorted to Uncle Vinny's private room with no issues. I wondered again how he would pay for all of this. It wasn't like the bar had been making enough money for either of us to have healthcare.

I steeled myself at the door before entering. I wasn't sure I could face my uncle knowing what he'd been through. He hated sympathy, and I was certain that would be written all over my face.

"Are you feeling all right?" Viktor's voice behind me pulled me from my thoughts.

"Honestly, I'm on the verge of a panic attack. I just don't think I can go in there yet. I need to use the ladies' room. I'll be right back." I rushed down the hall after making my excuse, half expecting Viktor to follow me. He'd been extremely clingy since Strain had tried to apologize. Maybe that was part of the cover-up, a way to keep his secrets. It's not like I could ask him without telling him that Strain had messaged me. Still, I was surprised he let me go alone to the bathroom.

I turned left at the end of the hall and ran right into a brick wall. "Ow," I said as I looked up and met a familiar face, blue eyes staring at me smugly. Not a brick wall. Strain.

"Just the person I wanted to see," he replied, refusing to give me any space.

I tried to back up, but his arms were around me before I could move. His large hand covered my mouth to prevent a scream. I grabbed at it and pulled until he let me speak. "Please let me go. Viktor is right around the corner. All I have to do is yell and he'll be here." I hoped that was true anyway. After everything that's happened, I wasn't sure if he would protect me or not.

"Shh, love, we're just going to talk. I won't hurt you." He looked down at my arm as he spoke. His eyes seemed drawn to the deep purple mark he had left on me. For a moment it looked as if he felt bad for the bruise that still marked me. The handprint was dark and showed through the thin blouse I wore.

Strain picked me up and took me inside a janitor's closet. The space was so small that I was pinned to the wall with his hulking form pressed up against me. My mind screamed danger, but my body enjoyed every second of the contact. My heart raced the same way it had when I'd met Viktor for the first time.

"What do you want? You said that you weren't coming after me." My voice came out breathy and tinged with desire. I wished so badly that I could sound tough just once when I was dealing with these men.

Strain brushed his blond hair from his eyes and bit his lip. "I had to see you. I had to know that you believed me, that you trust me." He leaned closer and sniffed my hair. "I can smell him on you even now. It drives me crazy that I couldn't get you out of there."

I pushed against his chest to no avail. His pecs were like solid rock and didn't budge. "You almost broke my arm. It didn't seem like you were the one who was trying to save me."

"Sometimes I don't know my own strength, love. I promise I'll make it up to you." His stare was unnerving. I found myself leaning closer to him, staring at his lips as he spoke. I wondered what he would taste like. His scent was like chocolate mixed with fresh brewed coffee, and it set me off in the best way.

"You said you wanted to talk, so talk, Strain." I tried to sound bitchy, but it didn't work. I sounded whiney instead and it pissed me off. I wanted to ask about his hand, but was scared it would make him angry.

"Please, call me Eli. I do want to talk, but there isn't enough time now. Maxwell will come looking for you if you don't go back to him quickly enough. Trust me, you don't want to see what he does when he gets angry," he said with a hint of sorrow in his tone.

"Do you really hate him because he married your sister? Is she the only reason you're interested in me?"

Eli's blue eyes met mine again. "Is that what he told you? Can he be that stupid? He really doesn't know, does he? I thought he was smarter than that." He spoke half to himself as if he forgot I was there for a moment.

I had no idea what he was talking about, and he seemed to realize it. All I could do was shake my head.

"First of all, she has nothing to do with my interest in you. I don't know how to explain it, but I'm drawn to you. I know you feel it too." He paused and cocked an eyebrow at me as if daring me to deny it, then continued.

"Second, Vik is the reason Kat's dead. He'll never admit his part in all of it, though." He pressed closer to me, and I could feel his erection fighting against his jeans. "But enough about that. It's not important; you are."

Before I could come up with an excuse to get away, his hands were in my hair and his lips were on mine. There was no stopping the moan that escaped me. I knew it was a bad idea, but I wrapped my arms around him and deepened the kiss. His tongue tangled with mine as I rubbed myself against his growing bulge. If I didn't stop this, I would end up having sex with him in this janitor's closet. I wasn't sure that I wanted to stop.

My mind and body were at war with each other. I knew that kissing Eli would cause problems with Viktor. There would be no way to keep him from finding out. It really was too bad they didn't get along. I could picture the three of us having a lot of fun together. But my body was excited about being so close to Eli. To be fair, Viktor had made it clear that he really wasn't interested in anything from me, so there was nothing stopping me. I just had no idea how I would explain it if he found out.

Eli's hands moved from my waist to my neck, then grazed the sides of my breasts as he moved them down to grab my ass. I moaned again and gave up fighting it. I was all in for whatever happened next.

I wasn't ready for Eli to step away from me, but he did it anyway. "You have to go now. I suggest a quick trip to the bathroom to straighten yourself up before you head back to Maxwell." Eli's words stung, as if he wanted me to feel guilty for trusting Viktor.

I couldn't speak. I had no idea what I would have said anyway. Instead I nodded and turned to go. I felt as if I'd been rejected by both of them in less than twenty-four hours. That had to be a record. Somebody call Guinness. I want my reward.

He must have sensed my frustration. A smile crossed his face as he spoke. "Don't worry, love, I'll message you later. We'll have another meet up soon, I promise." Eli winked at me, and I felt my face get warm. It surprised me that I wanted him to keep that promise. I was curious to see what would happen if there were no interruptions.

I opened the door a crack and looked down the hall to make sure the coast was clear before stepping out, then jogged down to the ladies' room. I spent a few minutes calming myself by splashing water on my face before I headed back down the hall to Uncle Vinny's room.

I tried to come up with a good excuse for taking so long, but the best I could come up with was that the closest bathroom had been closed for cleaning and that I'd had to use another one. It was a lame excuse and I really hoped that he didn't ask. I wasn't good at lying and didn't like doing it. I didn't want to see Viktor's reaction if he suspected that I was being deceitful.

CHAPTER 27

Eli

It took every ounce of self control to let Delilah walk away from me. I could tell that she wanted me, even if she didn't want to admit it. The feeling was mutual. I knew I would be suffering from our meeting for a while. Having her pinned to the wall in a janitor's closet wasn't my idea of romance, but I wanted her so badly, I'd almost given in to that desire. I imagined pinning her to the wall and pounding into her while she screamed my name. That would have drawn attention, though, so I restrained myself.

I still couldn't remember exactly what I had done when I blacked out. It bothered me, even though I couldn't change it now. Delilah accused me of destroying the bar. Could I have done that? I don't know. I was capable, but would my anger have pushed me that far? It didn't matter now, what's done was done. If she claimed to have watched video footage of me doing it, then I must have. It was just another thing I had to make up for with her. I really screwed this one up. It would take forever to fix it, but I was definitely planning to try, if she would let me.

Still, I was impressed with how loyal she was to Maxwell, even though she tried to hide it. I should have figured she was sleeping with him too. Well, it wouldn't be the first time we'd shared a partner. I laughed at the thought. If only he knew. Maybe I'd record our next visit and make sure he got a copy.

The thought amused me, but I knew better. If I did that, it would be like putting a bullseye on Delilah's back. I didn't want him to hurt her. I just wanted him to know that we were sharing. I could imagine his face when he found out.

I knew that I would have to hide until Maxwell left or risk having to fight him in the hospital. I may be a dick, but I'm not enough of one to risk innocent people getting hurt

90

in the crossfire. I had better things to do than fighting with him anyway. Like taking care of what Delilah had started.

I locked the closet door to ensure that no one interrupted me. Then I pulled my aching cock from my jeans and stroked it. I imagined Delilah's mouth on me. I couldn't wait to get her alone again. I wanted to taste her so bad that I could barely control myself. I got lost in my thoughts of her while stroking myself. I wanted it to be her touching me, but that would have to wait.

It didn't take long to finish because of how on edge kissing her had made me. I cleaned myself up and listened at the door. It was almost too quiet.

I checked my phone, looking at the video feed of the hospital. I knew that hacking into it would be the only way I would be guaranteed a moment alone with Delilah. I wondered if she had told him, or if she would.

I laughed out loud at the thought of his face when she admitted she was with me in this closet. The whole situation was ridiculous. I should just move on. There was no reason for me to chase after Delilah. Yet there was something about her that kept pulling me toward her. Like an invisible magnetic force drawing us together. I couldn't explain it. I couldn't fight it. To be honest, I didn't want to fight it. I wanted to embrace it—the situation and her. I wanted to tie Maxwell up and make him watch while I fucked her until she screamed my name.

Movement on the video feed caught my attention. Maxwell was leaving and Delilah was going with him. Well, either she kept our secret, or he was going to use her as bait. I guess I'd find out later which was the case.

I waited until they'd cleared the building to leave the closet and exit through the back of the hospital, opposite of the way they had gone. There was no point in taking a chance of him turning around for something and running into me.

CHAPTER 28

Viktor

"Look, Vinny, I just need to know what Strain said to you while he was pounding your face in. That's all." I struggled to keep my cool. I'd had to ask him more times than I wanted, and still couldn't get a straight answer from him.

"I know, Boss, I'm trying. It's hard to remember. The whole thing is a blur." Vinny rubbed his hand over his face and looked out the window. I knew he was lying, but there was no way to prove it. Strain must have threatened him. That was the only explanation.

"Vinny, don't worry about it. He can't get to you in here. I have guys watching your room to make sure you're taken care of." Maybe with a little reassurance, he'd come around and tell me everything.

"What about Delilah? Is she OK?" Terror crossed his face, and then I understood. Strain had threatened his family.

I had been just about to dig in his brain with compulsion to see what he was keeping from me when I heard Delilah coming down the hall. I knew there was no way to get the truth from him without her seeing. There were still things she didn't know about me, and I intended to keep it that way.

"She's fine. She will be in momentarily. I told her I needed to talk to you first. When she gets here, you aren't going to tell her anything, right? She doesn't need to be any more scared than she already is. Understood?" I towered over the small man in his hospital bed. Was it horrible of me to intimidate someone who'd almost been beaten to death? Yes. Would I do it again? Absolutely, if it was necessary.

Vinny nodded just as the door opened and Delilah walked in. She was flustered, but I couldn't tell if it was from being at the hospital or if something had happened.

"Sorry, I didn't mean to take so long," she apologized as she walked past me to her uncle. A strange scent wafted in the air as she passed by. It must have been the soap in the bathroom. There was something familiar about it. Something I just couldn't quite place.

"I have some business to take care of, so I will leave the two of you to visit. I'll be back in about thirty minutes to pick you up, Myshka." I waited for her to nod in response and left the room.

They didn't need me interrupting their family business. Besides, I needed to talk to Jones. I shot him a text when I walked into the hall.

Where are you? I'll meet you.

He responded, *third door to the left.*

I walked down the hall and opened the third door on the left. "This is a nice set up. How did you get by with bringing surveillance equipment in here?"

Jones laughed. "They don't even know I'm here. I charmed the desk nurse to put the room out of order for a week while repairs were made. She has everyone convinced that there's a water leak in here. No one bothered to check it out for themselves."

I nodded. "Good. Has anyone been in to see Vinny?"

"No one has been to visit him except you and the girl. But I don't think he's the one you need to be worried about. Look at this." He turned on the video and tilted the screen toward me.

I watched as Delilah headed down the hall toward the bathroom. She ran into someone and was whisked into a janitor's closet. It happened so quickly that the camera barely caught the movement. "That has to be Strain. How did he get in here? Our guys were supposed to be keeping an eye out for him."

"I know. I'm reaching out to them now. I suspect one or more won't respond, then we'll know who he took out." Jones was typing away on his phone while I continued to watch the video feed.

"Why didn't she tell me about this? Did he threaten her too? I have to get to the bottom of this." I paced the room as I debated if I should just ask her. If he'd charmed her, she might not remember. If he'd compelled her, she might not be able to tell me. That meant I would have to wait and see if she said anything on the way home. I didn't want to scare her more than she already was. I had meant that when I said it to Vinny. I wanted to protect her.

CHAPTER 29

Delilah

AFTER VIKTOR LEFT, I felt like I could relax a little. I sat down in the chair next to my uncle and looked at him. The bruising on his face and chest was bad, but the casts on his arms and legs looked worse. I worried that his injuries were more extensive than he let on. Viktor had been the one talking to the doctor, so I wasn't really sure how badly Uncle Vinny was hurt.

"How are you feeling today?" I asked gently. I hoped that Viktor hadn't upset him by asking questions about what had happened.

"Eh, I'm okay, kiddo. What about you? Did he hurt you?" Uncle Vinny looked scared like he wanted to tell me something but couldn't.

"Who, Viktor? He wouldn't hurt me. He gave me a room at his cabin outside the city. Why?" I stared at my uncle, willing him to answer my question.

He shook his head. "I just have to be sure. I promised your Ma that I'd take care of you. I don't want to let either of you down." It was a rare moment of actual emotion from him, and it caught me off guard. My uncle, whom I'd looked up to since I was little, looked so small and broken in the hospital bed with the wires and tubes coming out of him. He wasn't a large man, but this was painful to see.

"He was a perfect gentleman. You have nothing to worry about." It felt strange to comfort him, especially when I wasn't sure if there was something to worry about or not. At the moment, all I knew was that two sexy, rich vampires were interested in me, and I wasn't sure how to choose between them. I couldn't tell either of them about my attraction to the other, although Eli seemed to already know and appeared more interested in sharing than I suspected Viktor would.

94

As if my thoughts had called him back, Viktor walked into the room in a rush. "We need to leave. Now." He looked angry. Oh, no. Could he have discovered that I'd been with Eli? Shit, how was I going to cover that up? Should I even try?

I leaned over and kissed Uncle Vinny's cheek. "I'll see you soon." The look on his face said that he didn't believe me. I hoped I wasn't promising something I couldn't deliver.

"OK, let's go." I walked past Viktor without looking at him and headed down the hall to the exit.

He followed quickly, grabbing my arm to stop me. "I want you to tell me what that was about."

"First of all, let go of my arm. Second, I have no idea what you're talking about. You said we needed to go. I figured there was a reason that you would tell me once we were out of the room," I countered. I hoped that I appeared more brave than I felt. My insides were quivering. I wasn't sure if I was scared that he'd be angry about Eli kissing me, or if I was worried that Viktor wouldn't want me anymore.

"What happened when you went to the bathroom? You were gone for a long time." Viktor was trying to cover his anger with curiosity.

"I went to the bathroom and hid, trying to talk myself into going to see Uncle Vinny. I didn't want to see my uncle that way. I hate hospitals." I turned to walk away, but he stopped me again.

This time he pulled me close and wrapped his arms around me. "Viktor, let go. People are staring." I tried to wiggle free but only managed to rub myself against his growing erection.

"Let them watch. Or are you afraid your boyfriend will see us together?" My glance shot up to meet his and I knew that somehow he'd discovered that I'd met up with Eli. A split second decision had me lying to cover it up.

"I don't have a boyfriend and I'm not worried about anything. You're the one who keeps pushing me away." I turned my head as if I wasn't interested in looking at him anymore.

His arms went slack for a moment, then pulled me against him harder. I turned back to speak, and his lips were on mine. Instinctively, my arms wound themselves around his neck and I deepened the kiss. There was no way I would be able to say no to either of these two men. But how could I have both? It seemed odd to me that I was fantasizing about a threesome while Viktor was kissing me, but hey, he couldn't read my mind, right?

Hot passion enveloped me as his tongue tangled with mine. It was as if he wanted to claim me, to mark me as his, using only his mouth.

Suddenly he pulled away from me and started walking toward the exit. I was breathless and in shock. What the hell? Suddenly he's acting like he didn't just make out with me in the lobby of the hospital. I jogged to catch up to him.

"Oh, good. You've decided to come with me. We have lots to do today." He opened the passenger door for me while he spoke. I slipped into the seat and had the seatbelt fastened before he climbed in.

"What was that about?" I asked as he started the car and raced out of the parking lot.

"Just staking my claim. Do you have a problem with it?" He glanced at me sideways as he sped through the streets.

"I—I'm not sure what to say. You want to be with me? Or you don't want anyone else to have me?" I waited a moment for an answer but he didn't even acknowledge my questions. "Where are we going?" I figured changing the subject would be better than having this particular conversation.

"We're meeting the contractor at Midnight to begin the repairs. After that, I'm taking you home and going to have a meeting with the man responsible for all of this." His tone gave nothing away. It was obvious he wanted to kill Eli, and while I was angry about the bar being destroyed, there was no reason to continue the cycle of violence.

"Do you have to meet with him?" I tried to make myself sound scared, and it worked, probably because I was terrified. What if Eli told him about our kiss?

"You seem upset, Myshka. Is everything OK?" Viktor's smirk told me that he would push me to see if I would tell him. Well, he didn't know just how stubborn I was.

"I just don't like the idea of you going to meet with him. Look what he did to the bar; to Uncle Vinny. What would I do if he did that to you?" I didn't have to will the tears to well up in my eyes. At that moment I realized that I wasn't just worried about Viktor, though. I would be equally upset if Viktor did something to Eli. I was terrified that they would hurt each other.

"He's not going to hurt me. Trust me." The confidence in his voice was borderline arrogance.

"How can you be so sure?" I knew the moment the words were out that I shouldn't have said it.

The car stopped abruptly, and Viktor leaned over, putting his face inches from mine. "Because I have what he wants, and he'll never get it if he tries to harm me."

Terror spread across my face. I hadn't considered that Viktor would try to use me as an object to negotiate with. Then it hit me. I have no idea how these vampires view humans. Was I just a meal? A plaything? Would he trade me away if it meant Eli would leave him alone?

I couldn't stop the tears from falling at the realization that perhaps neither of them cared about me the way I thought. I unfastened my seatbelt and dove out of the car before Viktor could grab me. At least I knew this part of the city and had friends nearby.

CHAPTER 30

Viktor

I KNEW THAT BAITING Delilah was a bad idea, but I couldn't help myself. I wanted to know if Strain had charmed her. From the changes in her heartbeat, it seemed she was hiding something from me. That meant that she knew exactly what transpired at their meeting.

Her reaction at my meeting with him surprised me, though. It seemed as if she genuinely cared about me, and perhaps him. This could be a problem.

Why did Delilah dive from the car and run off? I hadn't anticipated her jumping out of a moving vehicle to get away from me. I wondered if that meant she had lost interest. Wouldn't I have sensed that? She must have felt overwhelmed.

Now I would have to postpone my meetings and hunt her down. Or maybe I would keep my meetings and let her calm down. Perhaps making her wonder for a while would be good for her. And some space would be good for me.

I dialed my phone and Jones answered.

"Sir? Is everything okay?" He knew that I wouldn't call unless there was an issue. I would usually wait for him to check in.

"There is a small issue. Delilah has run off down Third Street. I'm certain she has friends in the city, though I don't know who. I need you to find her and make sure Strain's men don't get to her until I'm done with my business for the day. Report her location to me and I'll pick her up later."

"Got it." Jones hung up without waiting for more information. He was good at his job and knew he would be compensated for his time.

Ten minutes later, I pulled up in front of what used to be Midnight. The contractor was there waiting.

"You must be Mike. It's good to finally meet you," I said as I offered my hand. Mike took it and shook heartily. The human was short and stocky. His years of working outdoors had weathered his face, making him appear older than his file indicated.

"Yeah, Viktor? It's great to meet you. I hate that your property was destroyed, but I'm glad to have the work. I've been checking it out while I waited for you. I don't think it will be as bad as you explained." He walked closer to the building and I followed.

"You think you can rebuild it?" I already knew that he could. There was a reason I'd called him. He was well known in the city for doing historically accurate repairs and remodels.

"I can. I mean, there's some structural damage from whatever blew up here, but I can do it. The job won't be cheap, though. I took a look at the proposal you sent over. Those are some high end materials." Mike seemed hesitant to agree to the designs I sent him.

"Well, if you're not comfortable with the design, I could always get someone else to finish after you rebuild the structure," I offered, knowing that the statement would make him more determined to get the job done and stay under budget. Besides, I already knew that I would pay whatever it took to bring Delilah's designs to life. It would be worth it to see her face when she realized that Midnight was hers. I hadn't told anyone that I planned to sign it over to her once it was repaired. Vinny would be pissed. It was going to be fantastic.

"Oh, no, that wasn't what I meant. It's going to be hard to stay under budget with these materials, that's all. I can definitely make it happen though." It was as if my words flipped a switch in him and confidence took over.

"Good. Was there anything else you needed from me? I have an extremely busy day, and would like to get to my next meeting." I hated brushing him off, but I needed to get to Strain before he had a chance to come after Delilah again.

"I think we're set. You want construction to start today, right? What do you want me to do with the personal effects we find in the rubble?" There were clearly things in the building that had meant something to Delilah, and I intended to replace everything that was damaged.

"Yes, start today. Keep those things aside for me to examine. There were some valuable things in my apartment and office, and I'm sure the other tenant had personal mementos as well. I'd like to salvage whatever we can." Mike nodded, and I turned to walk away. It was a relief to lean on my psychology studies instead of resorting to charm every time someone didn't do what I wanted. The contractor was easy enough to read and manipulate.

Now to track Strain down and have a few words with him. He would leave Delilah alone one way or another. I wasn't about to let her go. I dialed his office, hoping I could convince them to tell me where he was.

"Look, he's going to want to talk to me. Please, just call him and tell him Viktor Maxwell wants a meeting. I'll even be generous and let him pick the location. He can call me with the details himself. Thank you."

I hung up the phone and decided to start looking for Delilah myself. I trusted Jones, but since he hadn't gotten back with me yet, I was certain he wasn't able to locate her.

I headed back to Second Street, determined to track her down. It had been decades since I'd had to use any of my tracking skills. I opted to park the car near one of the restaurants that I owned on that end of town and continue on foot. She couldn't have gone far, right?

Since she jumped out at Third Street, I would start at Second and see if there was any indication of which way she went. Tracking had always been Strain's strong suit, but with any luck, I would figure out where she had gone before one of his men got to her.

CHAPTER 31

Delilah

AFTER JUMPING OUT OF Viktor's car, I ran to Anna's house. We'd been best friends growing up. I hadn't seen her in months, but knew that she still lived in the same apartment on Ninth Street. For the first few blocks, I ran like I was being chased. I kept looking behind myself to see if Viktor had decided to follow me.

I couldn't say how many people I knocked over while I was racing down the street. I honestly didn't care at that point. I needed to get away. Once I was sure he wasn't behind me, I slowed down. I needed time to think.

My emotions were threatening to take over, and I didn't want to be sitting on the side of the road crying. What would I do if Eli killed Viktor? Or if Viktor killed Eli? The pain of those thoughts was too much for me. I couldn't take it. It might have been easier to explain the whole thing to Viktor and talk him out of his meeting, but I was terrified. Not of him, but of his reaction. What if he didn't want me anymore when he found out that I wanted them both?

My phone vibrated. One glance showed a text. I ignored it because I assumed it was Viktor. I couldn't deal with him right now. He was being controlling and overbearing.

With tears falling, I made it to Anna's building. I buzzed her apartment, but it looked like she wasn't home. Great. Now I would have to find somewhere to hide. It wasn't like I could just call Viktor to pick me up. He was probably so angry. This was a mess.

When I unlocked my phone to text Anna, I realized that the text was from Eli, not Viktor. *Are you okay?*

I shook my head. I wasn't, and I knew that I probably wouldn't ever be again. *I'm not. Had a fight with Viktor. How did you know?*

Then I shot Anna a quick text. *Hey, I know it's been a while, but I'm outside your building. When will you be home?* I waited a minute for her response.

I'm at work until 8. You okay? I can leave now if you need me. I laughed as tears filled my eyes.

I'm fine. I had the afternoon off and just wanted to see you. Don't leave work. I'll get with you later. I was a horrible friend, and I knew it. Work had gotten in the way and I didn't even realize it until I needed something. I promised myself I'd do better.

I sat down on her step and gave in to the tears that were trying to fall. I had no idea what to do. Just then, my phone went off.

Where are you? Why did you run off like that? I knew without looking that it was from Viktor.

I needed some time to think. You're mad, aren't you? I braced myself for the answer, but nothing came for a few minutes. When my phone vibrated again, the message was from Eli.

Are you with him right now? That was a strange question.

Actually, no. I think he's angry with me. I ran off to think, and now I'm sitting here alone. I wasn't sure if it was a good idea to tell Eli or not, but for some reason I trusted him.

Where? I'm coming to pick you up. Why was it that I wanted to tell Eli where I was, but not Viktor? Because Viktor was being a dick, that's why. Ugh. I knew that if I went anywhere with Eli I would be making things worse, but all I wanted was for someone to hold me and tell me everything would be fine. Viktor wasn't exactly going to do that. Which meant I had no choice but to follow my heart.

I'm on Ninth, near the park. I'll meet you there. My heart was pounding at the chance to see him again and keep him from meeting with Viktor. What was I so afraid of? Would Viktor really hurt Eli? I was pretty sure I already knew the answer to that.

Be there in five. Black Porsche.

I walked over to the park and waited for Eli. He showed up in less than five minutes. I slipped into the car and as I buckled my seatbelt, I looked out the window just in time to see Viktor walking down the other end of the street. He turned the radio down as I entered the car.

"Please don't fight with him. Can we just go? I need some time away," I begged, not realizing that Eli had no idea what had happened with Viktor.

"He can't see you. My windows are tinted so dark no one can see inside. If you don't want to go with him, you don't have to. You can stay with me," Eli offered.

"I don't know. I just can't be around him right now, and I would rather you not be either," I replied.

"That's enough for me, love. Hold on," he said as he squealed tires and sped down the street. I covered my eyes because I thought for sure we were going to die in a fiery crash before we got to our destination. Eli's laughter was music to my ears when he realized that I was basically curled up in a ball braced for impact.

"Sorry, I'll slow down. We're almost there, anyway. You wanna tell me what you and Vik were fighting about?" He looked at me as he pulled the car into a garage and parked. Just as I was about to answer, his phone rang.

"Yeah, this is Strain. What's up?" He listened for a minute before responding. "Oh, really? He thinks I'll drop everything for an unscheduled meeting. What a dick."

He paused, then, "No, Marcy, don't worry about it. I'll take care of the problem. You did exactly what I asked of you. Thank you."

When he hung up the phone, he turned to me. "Your boyfriend is causing some issues for me with my staff. He called and harassed my secretary trying to set up a last-minute meeting with me today. You wanna tell me what that's all about?" His blue eyes burned into me.

"He wants you to leave me alone. I'm afraid he'll kill you. Please don't meet with him." Tears started to fall, and I could tell from Eli's face, he wasn't happy about it. He reached over and wiped the tears from my cheek, then leaned in and kissed me gently.

"I'm not scared of him. You know that, right? But if you want me to stay away from him, I will. Only because you asked. I don't want to do anything else to hurt you. Trust me, I have my reminder of what happens if I do." He gestured to his hand, which looked perfectly normal.

"I don't understand what you mean." I scrunched up my face and tried to see what he was motioning to.

"Oh, I forgot. This thing looks almost real." He grinned, then popped the hand off his wrist. I couldn't help myself and gasped at it. I had somehow forgotten all about Viktor slicing off his hand for trying to take me from him. He quickly secured it before turning back to me. "I'm sorry, love. Let's go inside and talk. We'll figure out what to do about Vik, then I can take you home if you want."

The whole thing was so ridiculous that I laughed. We climbed out of the sports car, then he walked around and put his arm across my shoulders. "What's so funny?"

"I don't have a home. You destroyed it. I have a room that Viktor gave me, but as pissed as he has to be by now, I may not have anywhere to go." Even though I was laughing, I was pissed, embarrassed, and hurt. It was all too much to process.

"Oh. I hadn't thought of that. I really am sorry. I had no idea you lived above the bar. I just lost my temper when he swept you away from me." Pain showed in his blue eyes.

"Maybe the three of us should talk together. I just don't know how to make that happen without the two of you trying to kill each other over me," I admitted. "I don't want to be the cause of a war."

"I'm not going to do anything you don't want me to, but I will defend myself if he attacks. Other than that, I'm open to a discussion. Does that mean you're ready to choose?" Eli leaned in close and pressed his lips to mine. I couldn't help myself. I turned toward him and jumped into his arms.

He pressed me against a pillar in the garage and kissed me as if his life depended on it. I wrapped my legs around his waist. His lips left mine and trailed down my neck, stopping for a moment when he reached my pulse point. I knew what he was considering, but didn't fight or push him away. I knew that he could lose control and drain me, but I didn't care. I wanted his lips on me; I wanted him to taste me. I wanted him to fuck me.

I pulled my hair out of the way and gave him better access. I heard his fangs click as they descended. It was exciting and terrifying. "I need you to say it. I won't drink if you don't." His voice was raspy and full of need.

"Bite me," I breathed. This could very well be the worst decision I'd ever made. In this position, there was no way I could get free if he did lose control. He kissed me again, making me dizzy with desire. I should have been worried about what I had just agreed to. Instead of panicking, I leaned into him as his teeth penetrated my skin. The feeling was orgasmic, and I moaned.

A moment later, I was standing there on my own, holding the pillar to keep myself upright. My head reeled from being dropped as he disappeared. "Eli? What happened?" I whispered, looking around for him.

CHAPTER 32

Viktor

AFTER SEARCHING FOR MORE than an hour, I had given up temporarily and returned to my car. I was just about to call Jones when my phone started to ring. *Strain.* I knew he wouldn't be able to resist calling me, especially with the message I'd left.

"It's about time you called. I had almost given up on civilized communication." I barked at him, still pissed that he had managed to get past my guys and into the hospital without me knowing.

"Shut up and listen. I'm done with this stupid fight. We need to talk. Now." Strain was out of breath and sounded upset. Interesting. I wondered what had him spooked. He was enough like me that I knew he didn't scare easily.

"Where?" I wasn't even going to respond to his disrespectful tone. I could deal with that when we met.

"I own a warehouse at the pier. Meet me there in twenty minutes. Come alone. No weapons." He hung up the phone without waiting for a response.

I knew the exact place he spoke of, as I had my men casing it. I suspected that they were using it to smuggle contraband into the city, but couldn't prove it.

I shot a message to Jones letting him know where I was going. He knew that if I didn't check in within an hour of the meeting time, he was to gather his team and come after me. Jones responded that he still hadn't been able to track Delilah down.

My next message was to her. *Are you okay? I've been looking everywhere for you. I'm getting worried.*

She didn't respond right away, and I wasn't about to beg her to talk to me. "Fuck it, you want to be childish, go ahead." I knew it was immature of me to feel that way, but she'd hurt my feelings by running off. Not that I would ever tell her that such feelings exist.

I climbed in the car and sped through the city. I stopped at my office to pick up some packages I'd had delivered.

"Oh, Mr. Maxwell! I didn't expect you to come in today." Liz was at her desk, exactly as she should be, fielding phone calls and dealing with visitors.

"Just a quick pop in to pick up some deliveries. I trust everything came as promised?" I knew Liz wouldn't be able to resist opening the packages and looking through everything. That was one of the reasons I'd ordered a silk scarf for her. She was already wearing it, which made the question moot.

"Yes, sir. Everything on the list was accounted for. Thank you so much for the gift. It was totally unnecessary." She played with the scarf as she spoke. I was pleased that she seemed to like it. "The rest is boxed up right here."

I carefully picked up the box and carried it back to my car. It was a struggle to get it in the trunk, but I managed. I had hoped that Delilah would be excited about the new wardrobe. At this point, I wasn't sure if I would ever even find her. Maybe if I did, she would accept the gifts as an apology.

I drove to the pier slower than I had ever driven before. I felt like a man who was headed to his execution for a crime he didn't commit. There was a time when I thought of Eli as a brother. Then his boss started coming after Kat, and it all fell apart.

As much as I hated him, I respected him for what he'd built. His corporation was the only one in the state that came close to competing with mine. I knew that was intentional on his part. If he hadn't created it that way, I probably would have changed mine to compete with him.

It seemed as if we would always be rivals. First for Kat's attention, then in business, and now for Delilah's affection. If she remained terrified of him, I would win. However, if he got her alone, he might just be able to charm her and convince her that I'm the bad guy. I had to do whatever it took to keep that from happening.

I checked my watch as I put the car in park. I knew I was early, but I planned it that way. I wanted to see him pull in and gauge if he'd stood by his own request to come alone.

The black Porsche that pulled in and parked on the other side of the lot looked familiar. It only took a moment to remember where I'd seen it. That was the car that sped away while I was walking down Ninth Street looking for Delilah.

My heart started to race. What if he'd called me here to tell me that he'd won? If he had managed to kidnap her from right under my nose, I wasn't sure what I would do. I swung my head from side to side, searching the area for hidden guards. It appeared that the area was empty, but that didn't mean anything. Strain's men were almost as good as mine at hiding.

Panic set in as Strain climbed out of the fancy sports car, then walked around to the passenger side to help someone else out of the car. I took a defensive stance and prepared to flee if needed. I wasn't above running away from an unfair fight.

CHAPTER 33

Eli

It didn't surprise me to see Vik already at the meeting location when we arrived. I turned to Delilah. I could feel the fear coming off of her in waves. But there was more. She had so many emotions that I wasn't sure if she could even sort them out.

"Are you sure about this?" I asked her before climbing out of the car.

"No, but I have to do it. The three of us have to talk. There has to be a non-violent end to this war you two are having. I can't be the thing that stands between you," she replied.

"Love, there is so much between Vik and myself. Trust me, it's not all over you. But even if it was, is that so bad? We both want you. It's your decision. You get to call the shots here. You decide." I could tell from her face that my response wasn't what she wanted to hear. I wasn't sure what she wanted. It was so hard to interpret all of her emotions right now.

Sometimes being an empath was helpful. Sometimes it was confusing. It's hard to be with someone intimately and not read their emotions. I tried to block it all out, but everything she was feeling was so strong that I couldn't.

I climbed out of the car and walked around. Vik eyed me suspiciously. I didn't blame him. I told him no weapons and no backup. I wondered if he had actually listened. I guess we'd find out in a moment.

I opened Delilah's door and she grabbed my arm to steady herself. It was like she was drowning and I was her lifeline. I loved that feeling and hoped that this negotiation didn't go south. I wanted to be part of her life. I was willing to negotiate. I would give my rival whatever he wanted in return.

106

I looked down at Delilah, urging her to step forward. There was no point in being here if we weren't going to talk. In order to do that, we needed to be much closer than fifty feet away. I didn't think any of us really wanted to yell about our feelings today.

Since she didn't let go of my arm, getting her to move was easier if I just started walking. She hesitated for a second, then scrambled to keep up with me. I walked slowly, like a man who was headed toward the executioner. Or at least that's how it felt.

Delilah's emotions were so jumbled that I wasn't sure what was about to happen. She was happy to see Vik, but was terrified of him at the same time. I sensed similar feelings about me. I understood why she was scared of me. I would spend forever trying to make that up to her. That mistake has haunted me lately. I didn't want to ever make her feel that way again.

Every instinct in me said to grab her and run. There was no way he would give her the freedom to choose, unless he was certain she would choose him. And I planned to do whatever it took to be with her. Even if that meant sharing. Whatever she wanted was fine with me.

I put my hand on top of hers, patting gently. I could feel her fear growing the closer we got to Vik. I tried to push calm into her, but I didn't think it was working. She was shaking and I was afraid that she would break down.

Part of me wanted to carry her the rest of the way, but with the glare Vik had on his face, I didn't think that would be in our best interest.

Why did this situation have to be so complicated? I wanted Delilah, and I could tell she wanted me too. Why couldn't life ever be that simple? She just had to want him too. It was ridiculous, but I was all in. What Delilah wanted, Delilah would get. I would make sure of it.

CHAPTER 34

Delilah

Eli running away from me after drinking my blood had made things weird between us for a bit. Then he explained that he'd done it so that we could arrange a meeting with Viktor. Eli was going to give me a safe space to make my choice. A choice that I couldn't make, no matter how much they wanted me to.

I didn't know how to tell him that I couldn't choose. Of course he expected me to pick him, and Viktor would be the same. This was a nightmare. My heart raced as Eli opened my door. This was the moment of truth. Could I tell these men that I cared for both of them? Was there a way that this would work?

Judging from Viktor's reaction when he saw me, I would guess not. Tears welled up in my eyes. This was going to get bloody. I turned to Eli and gripped his arm harder. "Please, I can't do this."

He grabbed my hand and squeezed. "Yes, you can. You just tell us what you want. It's easy. You have my word that we will both accept your decision with no drama. okay?" He kissed my knuckles and I heard Viktor gasp. I wasn't as confident as Eli about this plan.

"Get your hands off her, Strain." The anger in Viktor's tone was like a slap in the face.

Eli looked at me, as if asking what I wanted. I shook my head slightly and gripped his hand harder. "Only if she tells me to, Maxwell."

"Delilah, come over here," Viktor softened his tone slightly, but it still came across like he was scolding a naughty child.

I shook my head slightly again, and Eli stepped in front of me. "You can't force her into whatever it is you're trying to do here. If you're not going to let her talk, then I'm going to take her away."

My body started to shake. I didn't want them to fight. It was why I hadn't asked the two of them to talk to me together. Eli had insisted that it would be fine. This wasn't going to end well, I could feel it.

"Myshka, please. Come over here and let me make sure that you're okay." There was a sad edge to his voice that made me want to obey. Eli looked over his shoulder at me.

"I won't let him leave with you unless that's what you want. Say the word and we're out of here, love." I could tell that Eli was barely controlling himself. I gave him a little nod and he released my hand.

I was still shaking all over as I tried to walk the few feet between the two men. The closer I got to Viktor, the more uncontrollable the shaking was. I started to feel lightheaded and my legs got weak. Just as I started to collapse, two sets of arms caught me.

"Are you okay, love?" Eli whispered just as Viktor said, "It's okay, Myshka. I've got you." They both stared at me for a moment, then seemed to realize how close they were to each other.

I wasn't sure which one of them growled first, but the other joined in. I braced myself for the fight I knew was coming, but nothing happened. "I'm fine, really. I need a minute. I just need to sit down." Before I had even finished the sentence, Eli stripped off his jacket and eased me down on it.

"Take a minute and just focus on breathing. I want to talk to him," Eli began, then continued when I made a face, "I promise, love, no funny business."

Viktor looked at me, then looked at Eli. "I'm not leaving her alone here."

Eli nodded. "We're not going far. Just a few steps away."

Viktor nodded. "I'm right here if you need me." Then he turned back to Eli. They took a few steps away from me, although neither looked happy about it.

A few hushed words were exchanged, then things got heated. "Why are you always like this?" Viktor yelled, leaning closer to Eli's face.

Eli's response was much quieter, but I still managed to hear his words. "Probably because you always want to be in control. She wants us both. If you don't believe me, ask her. If she's not too terrified of you, she'll admit it. If she is, you'll know from the racing of her heart."

Viktor glared at Eli, then lowered his voice. I barely heard his question. "Did she tell you that?"

Eli shook his head. "She didn't have to."

I didn't have to ask what Eli had told Viktor to upset him. I was certain that Eli figured out that I was attracted to them both. Now they were going to make me choose. And I had no idea how to do that. I hadn't spent much time with either of them. There was no way to know which one would be better for me.

I sighed out of frustration and they both turned to look at me. "You might as well come back over here. I know what you're talking about."

Eli looked from my face to Viktor and nodded before coming to sit next to me on the ground. Viktor made a face as if sitting on the ground was beneath him, and Eli laughed. "You always were a pretty boy."

I couldn't help chuckling at Eli teasing Viktor. I knew they had been friends. Was there a way they could get back to those feelings?

Viktor growled again and sat on the opposite side of me. Now I was stuck in the middle. It didn't bother me as much as I thought it would.

"Well? What exactly is it you think we were talking about?" Viktor began while reaching for my hand. I let him take it, and I started tracing my thumb on his.

"You want me to choose," I said, threading my fingers through Eli's. My eyes were filled with tears, and there was nowhere for me to hide from their stares.

"But you don't want to, do you, love?" Eli said with a smirk. If looks could kill, Viktor's eyes would have shot daggers at him.

"I don't know how to." I had to tell them. I couldn't be scared anymore. "We've been through a lot in such a short time. But as crazy as it sounds, I like you both, and I don't want to choose between you. I wish I could have you both. I know it's ridiculous to even suggest something like this. I'm sorry."

I tried to pull my hands back, but neither vampire would let go. I looked from Eli to Viktor, confused at their lack of reaction to what I had said. I expected another fight to break out.

"I typically don't like to share, but for you, I might make an exception, love." Eli winked at me and laughed at the thought. Viktor scowled at him.

"I'm not sure that I can do that," Viktor replied, not letting go of my hand. His jaw was clenched and he seemed to be holding himself back.

"See, love? He's already taking himself out of the equation. Problem solved." Eli's joke made Viktor growl again, and I heard the soft click of fangs.

"Please don't start fighting. The three of us have to figure this out. I feel like I'm being ripped in half. It hurts," I couldn't stop the tears from falling.

At that moment, I learned just how powerful tears were. Eli stood up and pulled me into his arms, and Viktor wiped my cheeks with his thumbs. In a moment, they went from debating killing each other to taking care of me. It was touching and confusing.

"I don't know what's going on here, but I can't choose. When I think about it, I feel as if my heart is being ripped in half. The two of you will have to decide." I whispered the words as tears continued to fall.

Eli held me for a few minutes more, then suddenly I was in Viktor's arms. It startled me and I looked around. Eli was still standing close enough to touch me, but he was giving Viktor a moment. I couldn't believe the completely selfless gesture.

"Well, Vik, what are we gonna do about this?" I looked up again to see Eli staring at Viktor. There was no animosity left, only the question standing between them.

"Well, Strain, I guess that's up to our girl, isn't it?" Viktor replied through gritted teeth.

I could feel the tears coming again. Before I could say anything, Eli stepped closer and pulled both Viktor and me into a bear hug.

"It's not going to be easy, Myshka, but I'm willing to try if it makes you happy." Viktor said, shoving Eli away.

"Agreed. It's been a long feud, and we'll probably still do stuff to annoy each other, but I think we can make it work. For you, love."

It was strange to see them agree on something. I wasn't sure how this would work and had a ton of questions.

"We're not going to worry about any of the details right now, love. It'll be fine; don't worry," Eli assured me.

"Well, there is one decision you'll have to make today, Myshka," Viktor cut in.

My eyes widened in terror. "There is?" I could feel my heart start racing. I thought the panic was over, but here it was again.

"Where are you staying tonight?" Viktor winked and grinned at me. My expression made Eli laugh.

"Oh. I don't know. I didn't expect you two to get along or to agree to share, honestly," I admitted.

CHAPTER 35

Viktor

I NEVER WOULD HAVE expected Delilah's decision to be made by a game of rock, paper, scissors. The whimsy of Strain's suggestion made her laugh, so I agreed. He even took it pretty well when I won.

"So we'll meet tomorrow to start looking for a place where the three of us can stay and have more privacy than our existing options," I suggested. I hoped that by agreeing easily, I could manipulate Delilah into choosing me over Eli.

"Can you have the apartments above Midnight remodeled to work for the three of us?" Delilah asked with hope in her tone. She was certainly attached to that bar.

"Of course we can, love. Three bedrooms, three bathrooms, a kitchen, and a common area. I'll draw it up today and send it to Vik," Strain offered, turning to me. "Then you can send it to your contractor. And I'll take care of the extra cost. I'm sure changing the plans now will put you over budget."

I laughed, but it wasn't an amused sound. I was pissed. "Well, it's your fault we have to rebuild the bar anyway. You should have to pay it all."

"Wait a minute, pal. I understand that you're upset about the bar, but weren't you going to gut it and remodel the whole thing anyway? I just saved you from paying a demo crew." Strain grinned. Even I had to admit he was a handsome man.

"He's not wrong, Viktor. Besides, he's willing to forgive you for cutting off his hand," Delilah interjected.

I winced. "I guess I should apologize for that."

Strain shook his head. "Not at all. I mean, yeah, I would have preferred that it never happened, or that you'd returned it so I could've had it reattached. But I understand why you did it. I hurt Delilah and you were protecting her. I'm still pissed at you, but I can set it aside if you can."

Agreeing to a relationship that included Strain was a stretch for me. There was something about Delilah that made me think that maybe it could work. Only if I couldn't persuade her otherwise.

"Since you guys are being friendly, I have a request," Delilah began.

"Anything for you, love," Strain responded.

I was a bit more skeptical. "What is it?" I didn't want to agree to something I wasn't interested in, like a threesome with my archnemesis.

"Would you two please stop saying each other's names with such disgust. It's making me crazy." Delilah sighed in exasperation.

"Sure, love, we can do that." There he went again, agreeing to things for me. It was annoying, but he wasn't wrong.

"Agreed. I think we can be civil toward each other." Although I wondered if I could come up with a nickname to drive him crazy. I'd have to think about that later.

"See, no problem." He held out his hand to shake mine, signaling he was good with the truce. I shook it a little harder than I should have.

"Good. Thank you. I guess we should head home, then." Delilah looked at me cautiously before closing the space between herself and Eli. Then he looked at me just before he kissed her. Were they asking permission? This entire situation is strange to say the least.

I couldn't stop the growl that escaped me at their embrace. But I didn't bother to look away. Instead I watched the way Delilah reacted to his kiss, to the feel of him against her. What made me fiercely jealous turned me on as well. For a moment, I could actually picture the three of us together. Could it really work, though?

I pushed the thought away as they finished saying good night. There would be plenty of time to explore that interest later. For now, we needed dinner and rest. Tomorrow would be the beginning of our new challenges.

CHAPTER 36

Eli

I THOUGHT I HAD him when I challenged Viktor to rock, paper, scissors to decide who Delilah would go home with. How could I forget how good he is at anticipating what people will do? I wouldn't make that mistake again.

Having the night to myself did give me a chance to get a few things in order before Delilah started staying with me. I didn't really mind the idea of sharing, so long as I knew the other guy. Vik and I went way back, and even though I wanted to ring his neck most of the time, I knew he wouldn't go back on his word.

He promised to make things work with the three of us and I knew that meant he'd do anything he could to keep that promise. I'd seen him kill to keep promises to Kat. I knew that he'd do it again if needed.

It was strange for me to see him with Delilah. I knew that my sister died a long time ago and it wasn't fair to expect him to stop living his life because she was gone. I would definitely need some time to adjust to seeing him with someone else. Especially when that someone else was mine as well.

I couldn't wait to get Delilah alone. There were so many things I wanted to do to her. I wanted to know everything about her. Would she like the same things I did? Would she be interested in getting kinky? It was fun and torturous to think about it.

My mind raced as I headed back home. I knew that I had reports to go over and emails to return. My day was far from over. Being the boss had advantages, though. I loved that I could take off as soon as Delilah texted me to pick her up. It didn't matter when I got my work done, as long as I completed it or passed it along to someone else, though that rarely happened.

Working while distracted wasn't getting me anywhere. I had read the same report three times and it still didn't make sense. It looked as if there were some shortages in the warehouses nearest the east side of the city. Would someone really be stupid enough to steal from me? I responded to the email with some follow up questions and decided that I would drive down to check it out myself. I texted and asked Scott to meet me at the docks.

"Whoever it was had to have known the codes, sir. There's no way they would have gotten in so easily without them." Scott was convinced that it was an inside job. He may have been right.

"That gives me plenty to think about. Thanks for meeting me here. Let's take a look at where things were taken from, shall we?" I followed as Scott led me to the different bays within the warehouse. The items that had been stolen seemed random at best. I knew there was a connection, even if I didn't see it yet. It was a puzzle and I knew that I would figure it out.

Once we'd reviewed every area, I sent Scott home and headed back to my place. The sun was rising and I needed rest. I planned to discuss this with Viktor in the evening. I needed to find out if he'd had any issues with his warehouses being broken into. I made note of it before dropping into bed and passing out.

When I woke, the sun was setting. I felt as if I hadn't slept at all. It was a fitful rest at best. I showered, wrapped myself in a towel, and grabbed a blood bag before settling in on the couch. I turned on the news and pulled my laptop onto my lap to check my email.

The first email I opened had me calling Scott again. "What's going on at the docks now?" I started as soon as he answered.

"We're not really sure. The alarms just started going off and it looks like there might be a fire. I'm on my way there now. Do you want me to pick you up?" He offered.

"Thanks, but I'll meet you there. I need to take care of a couple of things first. It should be about an hour." I didn't wait for his response before hanging up the call and dialing Viktor.

"*Strain*? What do you want?" He snapped at me the moment he answered. I heard Delilah get after him in the background, then his tone changed and he said, "I'm sorry, *Eli*. Do you need something?"

"Yeah, there's something going on down at the docks. I wondered if you've had any problems lately with your properties." I figured I would start there, then see where it led.

"I've not been told of any. I assume if there were any issues, Jones would keep me apprised. What kind of problems are you having?" I actually had to give Viktor credit, he seemed genuinely concerned. I wondered if it was because Delilah was there, or if he was as sick of our feud as I was.

"Someone broke into one of the warehouses a few days ago and stole random items. Tonight, someone tripped the alarm and may have set a fire at the same warehouse." I explained.

"We should go check it out. Do you want to pick me up? I'm at Midnight right now." He was offering to help me, with no strings attached. It was a strange feeling, but I liked it.

"I can swing by and pick you up, sure. Bring Delilah, too. It'll be safer for her to be with both of us. I feel like there's more going on here than we're aware of right now." I said, standing and walking to my bedroom to get dressed. "Be ready in ten minutes."

I disconnected the call and dressed quickly. I was outside the bar within seven minutes. I hated waiting, but because I had told them ten minutes, I wasn't going to press the issue. I didn't have to wait long before Viktor was strolling out the front door, holding it open for Delilah.

She climbed into the back seat and Viktor took the passenger seat next to me. It was definitely a tense situation and I wondered if I had interrupted something with my call. "I'm sorry for bothering you during your time with Delilah." I figured an apology might smooth things over.

"It's fine," he responded. "What do you think is going on at this warehouse? You have to have a theory."

I nodded. "The things that were stolen seemed random, but when you look at all of it together and include a few incidents I originally thought were unrelated, it looks like they're gathering equipment to start making Powder." I glanced at Viktor. Powder was an extremely potent drug that vampires used to get high, since human drugs didn't process the same way after the change.

"That's a serious accusation. Any ideas of who's behind it?" He glanced at Delilah, who appeared to be lost. There was no time to explain it all to her right now. We'd have to take care of that after we checked out the damage. I shook my head in response and he understood that we'd talk about it later.

We pulled up to the warehouse at the same time the police arrived. I knew it was serious if Scott had involved the authorities. An officer walked over as we climbed out of the car.

"Excuse me, sir, this is an active crime scene. You're going to have to leave." the officer said as he approached.

I growled in reflex and Viktor grabbed my arm. "Officer, my associate is the owner of this building. An incident was reported and we've come to check things out. You're doing a great job, but you need to let us through."

The officer nodded and gestured for us to continue. "I'll never get over how you do that," I whispered to Viktor as we approached the building.

He shrugged and kept walking. Delilah had snaked an arm through his and mine. It was a little awkward and I would definitely be answering questions about this later, but I would worry about that when it happened.

She let go of my arm when Scott walked up. For some reason, she seemed to shrink back and try to hide under Viktor's arm. I wasn't sure if it was Scott or if the awkwardness of our situation finally sank in. I'd have to remember to ask her about it later.

"You called the cops? How bad is it?" I started before Scott held up a hand to stop me.

He gestured for me to follow him, moving away from Viktor and Delilah. "There's a body, sir. And it looks like they were murdered right here."

"Why would you call the police for that?" It seemed odd to me that he would have contacted the authorities when we had a department specifically for cleaning up this type of mess.

"The stiff is the mayor's kid. I didn't think we could exactly take care of this one ourselves. He was obviously high when it happened. The M.E. said as much when she examined the body. Even with the kid being an adult, I thought it would be better to let the mayor have closure. I'm sorry if that was the wrong call, sir." Scott looked at me apologetically.

"Not at all. If it had been a homeless person or someone without a family, it would have been different. At least we all have alibis for tonight. They always suspect the property owner first. What can you tell me about what happened?" I listened intently as Scott explained what he'd learned from the police investigators and the security feed.

There wasn't much to go on. It looked as if the kid had broken into the warehouse and got jumped by someone else with the same idea. I agreed it was a matter for the cops to handle.

After explaining the whole thing to Viktor, we headed back to Midnight. The repairs were coming along slowly, but the place was inhabitable. He had the plans hanging on the wall behind the bar. I couldn't resist taking a quick look as we walked past.

I wasn't offended that Vik hadn't used the plans I drew up. I knew he was stubborn. But I had a few ideas of how to improve on his design and made a mental note to draw up the changes. I wondered if he would lend me a copy of the plans. *This isn't the time, Elijah John. Let it go for now.*

CHAPTER 37

Delilah

WITH THE PLANS FOR Midnight clearly lined up and being executed beautifully, Viktor had agreed that we could all move into the apartment upstairs before the downstairs was completed. I didn't think it was really fair to call it an apartment, but nothing else really fit. The entire second floor had been remodeled into a four bedroom, four and a half bathroom condo. The common area was beautiful, with a beige sectional that made an extended U in the middle of the space. We each had our own bedroom and bathroom attached for privacy. This was designed to ensure that I couldn't be forced into anything I didn't want. I had my own bedroom with a lock on the door. And there was an extra bedroom for storage or whatever.

At my suggestion, Viktor even had two different studies put in. One where he could take care of Maxwell Industries and one where Eli could focus on Strain Corp.

Eli wasn't too excited about staying there with construction going on during the day, so he had only been staying in his room on the weekends when the crew had been off. It messed up our schedule, but I was determined to make it work. If it was my time with Eli, I would just go to him at his place. If we had an argument, I could either take a bus back home or call Viktor to pick me up. It didn't happen very often.

With the issue at the warehouse, we'd all ended up back at Midnight. I wanted to ask a ton of questions about the whole thing, but I already knew that neither Eli nor Viktor would tell me what was going on. I tossed my shoes in my room and came back to catch the end of a hushed conversation.

"Technically your time with her starts at midnight, but if you want to chase down leads on this, I'm happy to entertain our girl a little longer," Viktor whispered. I did my best to keep my expression neutral. I didn't want them to know that I could hear everything they were saying. But I knew that Eli wouldn't be pleasant company if he was distracted, so I let them talk.

"That's probably a good idea for a while. I need to see what I can find out. Give me a couple of hours," Eli replied in a hushed tone.

"If I didn't know better, I'd think you two were up to something," I said loudly as I walked over and flopped onto the couch.

"Not at all, love. Just figuring out the best place to start looking for answers. I'm going to get some work done. You can hang out with Vik if you want, or you can wait for me." Eli looked at me expectantly. I wasn't sure what he wanted me to say.

"I'll let Viktor entertain me for a bit, but don't waste all of our time," I warned teasingly.

Eli walked over and kissed me hard before walking away. He went into his room and closed the door. If I hadn't heard their conversation, I might think that he was upset with me and trying to pawn me off.

Viktor walked over to me and wrapped his arms around me. "So what shall we do while you wait for Eli?" He licked his bottom lip and my knees got weak.

"I have some ideas. Come with me." I grabbed his hand and led him to his room, leaving my room between us and Eli. It wasn't fair for him to hear what was about to happen if he was too preoccupied to participate.

Once the door was closed, I grabbed Viktor's hand and pulled him toward the bed. He cooperated to see what I was doing. I backed him up against the edge and gave him a little shove. He sat down on the edge of the bed and watched as I started to strip. I took my sweater off and my leggings, then stood in front of him in my matching blue lace bra and thong.

He groaned and reached for me. I stepped back, shaking my head. "Not yet." He nodded and put his hands back on the bed. I grabbed his shirt and started unbuttoning it. He was clearly impatient and tried to help until I slapped his hands away.

I removed his shirt and undershirt, then his pants. I wondered if I would ever see him in anything but dress clothes. He was always wearing a button down and slacks. It was sexy, but I preferred him naked. There was something primal about the way he was looking at me, as if he wanted to devour me.

I returned his look, admiring his chiseled body as he sat on the edge of the bed in nothing but his boxer briefs that did nothing to hide his enormous hard on. I stepped closer and he didn't move. He had finally accepted that I was in control right now.

I grabbed the waistband of his boxer briefs and slid them down. He growled as I released his erection, allowing my still covered breasts to glide against it. I looked up at him quickly before taking him into my mouth. I was certain there was no way I'd get it all in. He was just too big. But I was determined to try. Especially since the last time I had offered, he'd turned me away. That rejection still stung. I was determined to make him regret it.

He groaned as his cock entered my mouth again. I could tell he was having trouble holding back. I wouldn't have much time before he decided to take over and pound me. I continued sucking him, then stopped to tease him with my tongue. I was trying to push him over the edge, but his stubborn need to be in control kept him from giving in.

Viktor growled at me again before flipping me onto the bed and climbing on top of me. Before he could even get my undies off, the door flew open and Eli barged in. I wouldn't have minded, but the look on his face killed Viktor's erection.

I had no idea what had just happened, but suddenly Viktor was getting dressed and following Eli into the other room. When I was alone in my room, I let out a sigh of frustration. "What the fuck just happened?"

It looked like the guys were going to be hiding the details of what had happened at the docks from me as much as possible. They didn't think I could handle being involved in a murder investigation. I didn't want to know everything, but I wanted to feel included.

CHAPTER 38

Eli

I hated interrupting Delilah's time with Viktor, even if I was jealous that it wasn't me with her. I wouldn't have, but I needed him to see what I had found.

I managed to discover proof that the mayor's son, who'd been killed, had been involved in the robberies at both my company and Vik's. It seemed as if he was working for someone, though, and the trail just dead ended. I needed another set of eyes on the data.

"What the fuck just happened?" Delilah asked as we walked away, leaving her on Vik's bed by herself. She would probably be mad at both of us for this.

"You know I wouldn't have interrupted if it wasn't important," I offered, ignoring Delilah's irritation.

"I am aware. I do think you could have waited a few more minutes, though. I hadn't yet had the chance to take care of our girl," he countered.

I winced at his statement. Yeah, she was going to be really angry at me for that. I'd worry about it once we'd figured out this puzzle.

I showed him the data I'd been trying to figure out. "Any ideas on what this could mean?" I had been over it every way I could think of, and nothing made sense.

"The relevant information seems to just stop. That usually means someone has gone to great lengths to hide what's really happening," Vik seemed irritated, but this time it wasn't with me. "But that doesn't necessarily mean they're making Powder."

"Why else would Bill steal these specific things? There's nothing else that makes sense. And it's not like he's the mastermind behind it." I was irate about the fact that the kid had to be working for someone else. It was the only thing that made any sense.

"So follow the money. You've been chasing the kid. Switch it up and follow his source. Figure out who's paying him and you'll have our next step." Vik's calm statement made me realize that he was right. I had been looking at it all wrong.

Vik and I chased down the money trail where Bill had been paid. It was funneled through so many umbrella corps it was hard to tell where we were headed. "I can get the source, but with all of these shell corps it's going to take time."

After a few hours, I felt like I was getting nowhere. Vik had gone off to take care of some business Jones had called him about. I decided a break was in order. I walked into the common area. The renovations were coming along nicely. There were still a few things I thought could be improved on, but I would bring that up later.

I walked into the kitchen and checked the fridge. Of course, Vik would have blood bags. I wondered if Delilah cared that they were in the same fridge as her food. Even though I preferred mine warm and directly from a willing source, beggars couldn't be choosers, as the saying goes. I knew that if I didn't feed soon, I'd risk going after Delilah. I didn't want that to happen.

I drained the bag, then made sure to rinse it and put it in the recycling bin under the sink. If I were going to live forever, I might as well try to save the planet too.

I sensed her before her scent wafted over to me. Delilah. In an instant, my cock was hard and throbbing. For a split second, I felt guilty for interrupting Vik earlier before he could take care of Delilah. That thought was replaced with all the things I wanted to do to her, and I growled as I turned to face her.

I had expected her to jump or be scared. Instead she laughed at me. "Why are you laughing?" I tried to sound stern, but my voice was laced with need.

"That was the cutest thing I've ever seen. I don't think Viktor has ever rinsed out a blood bag for recycling before. It was sweet," she countered.

"Oh, love, I am anything but sweet. You'll see," I remarked as I scooped her up and took her to the couch. She shook her head.

"What? Did I hurt you?" I started checking her over as we sat on the couch. She laughed again.

"I'm fine. But we won't get any privacy here. We should go to my room."

I cocked an eyebrow at her to ask if she was serious. She nodded and took my hand, practically dragging me to her room. The ground rules had been pretty clear, neither Vik nor I was allowed to enter her room without permission unless she was in danger. We took that very seriously.

I let her lead the way until she closed the door behind us. Then I backed her up against the wall and captured her lips with mine. Delilah wrapped her arms around me and fisted her hands in my hair. I growled against her lips and slipped my tongue in her mouth.

I already felt like I was going to explode and we'd only kissed. I needed to get myself under control or I would be finished before we even got started. I pulled her to me and turned around backing her toward the bed. When we got to the edge, I gave her a playful shove. I loved the shocked look on her face.

She scooted back away from the edge and I followed her, caging her in again. I pulled her sweater over her head and stared in awe at her for a moment before pulling her leggings off too.

I groaned. "You know what those lacy little matching sets do to me."

Delilah smirked in response. I knew that I would find her wet and ready, but I wasn't done teasing her yet. I climbed on top of her and hovered just out of reach. She strained to reach my lips, but I didn't give in yet. She growled at me and flopped back on the bed, obviously deciding to let me have my way with her.

I leaned down and kissed her very gently. Then I planted gentle kisses down her cheek and started to nuzzle her neck. I wouldn't allow myself to kiss her there because I wasn't sure I could stop myself from biting her. I wouldn't risk hurting Delilah no matter how badly I wanted to taste her again.

I turned my attention to her perky breasts that were currently trapped in the nearly see through lace of her bra. I desperately needed to correct that. I started by kissing her shoulder, then trailing kisses all around the edge of the offensive article before I ripped it off her and took a nipple into my mouth.

Delilah gasped in surprise before moaning at the sensation of my mouth on her. I trailed kisses between her breasts as I worked my way to the other nipple. By the time I was ready to move onto the next part of her body, she was writhing and trying to rub herself on my hard on for release.

"Now, now, that's no way to be. The party will be over before it starts," I teased as I moved lower, kissing my way from her breasts to her waistband. Delilah arched her hips and I slid her panties off, tossing them across the room. I wanted nothing more than to bury myself balls deep in her hot, wet pussy.

But I still felt bad about interrupting her and Vik earlier, so this was all about her. I would make up for the interruption before I even considered my own needs. I licked her stomach and winked at her before letting my hand travel lower. I watched her reaction as my fingers found her moist center. I had planned to see how many times I could make her cum, but this seemed like it might be too easy.

I turned my attention to her apex, licking her before taking her most sensitive nub into my mouth and sucking. When she gasped, I released it, then flicked it with my tongue. Her moans cheered me on, and I kept licking and sucking her clit until she screamed my name. Then I slid two fingers inside of her and worked to find that special spot that would send her over the edge. The whole time, I kept my tongue working—back and forth, side to side, small circles, big circles.

Every orgasm she had was punctuated with her gasps and moans of pleasure. I kept going until I thought I would explode just from being in such close contact with her.

I pulled my jeans off and positioned myself above her, ready to plunge inside. The door swung open and Vik barged in. "What is it? Can't you see we're a little busy here?" I barked at him without moving.

"I got a lead on the Powder lab. I thought you'd want to know," he growled back.

I guess I got a taste of what I'd done to him earlier, because my dick was no longer standing at attention. I groaned and pulled my jeans back on.

"We have to take care of this. Are you okay?" I asked Delilah before tossing her the sweater and leggings I'd peeled off of her a few minutes prior.

"I'll manage. I feel bad for the two of you, though." She seemed sincere, but at the same time, amused. She didn't make a move to get dressed or get up as Vik and I left her room.

CHAPTER 39

Delilah

THE IDEA THAT THESE two powerful vampires would agree to share me was a shock. There was no way this could end well. They would be at each other's throats in no time. I decided to just enjoy the ride until the whole thing blew up. There was no way I would be able to decide between them.

After a few strange days of splitting my time between the two of them, Viktor and Eli agreed on a slight redesign for the living area above Midnight that would allow each of us private space, while letting us be close. They had already pretty much split up the space, but finally agreed on the specifics of it. I had lost everything in the destruction of the original building, so it didn't matter to me what they did.

The next three weeks were a blur. With rebuilding Midnight along with Viktor and Eli's side project looking into thefts at their companies, there was no time for setting ground rules. I did manage to get my guys to agree on a schedule, but that didn't seem to be helping.

The spatting had already started, and I knew it was just a matter of time before things went south. Every time Eli and I got close to sleeping together, Viktor would find a way to interrupt. Because of that, Eli made sure to return the favor. I was pretty sure the three of us were miserable, and I only had the two of them to blame.

Like today, I had a couple of hours alone with Eli at his condo, and he was so distracted with his rivalry that he barely even noticed I was here. I started rubbing his shoulders, but he shrugged me off because he was working on his plan to get back at Viktor.

"Can't that wait? We only get a couple of hours, and you've wasted half of it already. I have to get back to work at Midnight soon," I snapped at him. We were preparing for the grand opening next week, since most of the big construction had been completed.

Eli grumbled his response and I began to wonder if I wasn't just some random pawn in this battle. Lately it seemed like neither of them was as interested in me as they were in one-upping each other.

Their rivalry had even gotten worse in their business. Viktor was obsessed with making Midnight the most successful karaoke bar in the city. Eli's jealousy had him remodeling his bar, Dusk, across town and trying to compete.

"Seriously, you two promised. I can't take this fighting all the time." It probably wasn't a good idea to scold Eli at lunch, but I couldn't get him to come within fifty feet of Viktor. I had wanted to yell at them both together.

"I'm not fighting. I'm defending. There's a difference," Eli replied.

"No, you're instigating. You don't have to make your bar compete with Midnight. You have Viktor beat in the fashion industry. Can't you let him have the bar scene?" I was trying to split things up so both companies could be profitable, but it was hard.

"I could, if you made it worth my sacrifice." Eli wiggled his eyebrows suggestively.

"I'd be happy to, if the two of you would leave each other alone long enough for any of us to have some alone time." I never knew that blue balls were a thing women could get, but I had a serious case.

Before I realized what had happened, Eli scooped me up and dropped me into his Porsche. "Where are we going?"

"To have some alone time," he said, speeding down the street.

"But we were just alone inside and today is supposed to be Viktor's turn. What happened to following the schedule?" I elbowed him in the ribs as he drove.

"Just call him and tell him I'll have you back in an hour. He can have an hour of my time tomorrow. I want to show you something," he pleaded.

I couldn't resist his sexy pout, so I pulled out my phone. Before I could dial, it rang.

"I was just about to call you," I said before an outraged Viktor cut me off.

"You're with that lying son of a bitch, aren't you?" He growled the words at me, letting the accusation hang in the air as I tried to figure out what he was talking about.

"Eli is taking me for a quick drive. We'll be back in an hour. You'll still get your full time, don't worry." I thought it would be comforting to him.

"After what he's just done, I don't ever want to see him again. Or you for that matter. I should have known the two of you were playing me. Just like he did all those years ago. I never wanted to admit that what people were saying was true, but I guess we have the proof now, don't we?" Viktor kept rambling, so I put the call on speaker.

I turned to Eli, "What's he talking about?"

Eli shrugged, but slowed the car. "Vik? What's going on? What are you talking about?"

"You! You did this. I can't believe I trusted you and you betrayed me. How could you? I'll kill you. You'd better hide, because I'm coming for you." Viktor was sounding more unhinged by the moment.

"Viktor? How can Eli or I answer your questions if we don't know what you're talking about? Did something happen with the renovations?" I was starting to get worried. Apparently I wasn't the only one. Eli had turned the car around and headed back to Midnight. "Are you at the bar?"

"Where else would I be? Especially after your boy-toy blew up my penthouse and main office. I have no place else to go now. Everything is gone." Viktor had stopped yelling and his voice got quieter until he whispered the last bit.

"What do you mean, everything is gone? Someone blew up your properties?" Eli leaned closer to the phone as he spoke, hitting the gas to return to the bar faster.

"You should know. It was your signature bombs that did it. I can't believe that I trusted you. We were going to be brothers again. How could you do this?" He sounded defeated, and I started to worry that he might do something rash.

"Viktor, we are on our way. Please wait for me to get there. Don't do anything. Promise?" I begged, motioning for Eli to drive faster. It seemed like we would never get home. The phone went dead as he hung up on me.

"Eli, I'm scared," I admitted.

He nodded and pressed the gas, "Me too, love. Hold on."

We flew through the city streets toward home. I hoped we wouldn't be too late.

Eli pulled his phone out and made a call. "Dave. I need you to find out who was behind that bombing. Yeah, the truce is still in place. No attacks on Maxwell or his men."

He listened for a moment, then responded. "I mean it. No matter what they do, you take them down non-violently or you deal with me. Understood?" Eli hung up the phone without waiting for an answer.

We pulled up to Midnight, and I was out of the car before Eli could swing it into a parking space. I ran to the door, but it was locked. Of course, I didn't have my keys. "Eli, the door is locked. Hurry!"

I could see movement inside, but Eli had stopped to take a call next to the car. "What the hell? Come on, he needs us!" I ran back to him.

A deafening roar stole my hearing and knocked me on top of Eli, who was thrown onto the ground. I turned toward the bar. I didn't see how anyone could have survived that. Where my home had been, there was now just a pile of rubble.

I stared at it as the tears fell. I'd fought so hard with my mom to stay here.

"I know it's a bar, Mom. But it's more than that. I don't know how to explain it. This is the one place that feels like home." I remembered begging her to leave me there while she chased after my father. And now it was gone. Again. Only this time, I lost Viktor too.

I felt hands on my shoulders, but didn't turn. Eli walked around me, looking for injuries. I think he was talking, but I couldn't hear anything. I didn't care if I was hurt. The pain in my heart was enough to cover it all up. He picked me up and carried me away from the mess that had been mine. I didn't fight. I couldn't. There was nothing left to fight for.

CHAPTER 40

Viktor

How could I have been so stupid? I actually let down my guard and started to trust Eli. That bastard. I should have known that everything he said to Delilah was a lie.

Why would he wait until things were going so smoothly to blow my properties up? Unless his goal was to kill me in one of the explosions. Which he might have accomplished if it hadn't been for the renovations at Midnight.

Being stuck in a pile of what had been a bar wasn't fun, especially when it was the middle of the day and the sun was out. Normally my implant would help, but I had the distinct feeling that it was crushed beneath the stone that was keeping me from getting up.

Even though I told Delilah I didn't want to see her again, this wasn't what I'd had in mind. I wanted her to choose me. To tell me that she understood now why I hated Eli, and that she wanted to be with me. I wanted her to show up and profess her love for me, while Eli watched, devastated.

I could tell that someone was already digging in the rubble, but it may take hours for them to find me. Isn't it just my luck that the building falls on top of me, but somehow the sun still manages to shine directly in my location? Wait—could that have been planned?

I couldn't get to my phone, and it was apparent that whoever was digging didn't hear my pleas for help. My throat was so dry that I couldn't yell anymore. All I could do now was wait. There was no way I was going to let this kill me. Eli wouldn't get the satisfaction. Besides, I would have to plot the perfect revenge.

I hated stooping to his level, but the bastard deserved it after what he'd done. Blowing up my penthouse and my main office building downtown was one thing, but destroying the one building that Delilah loved? That was taking it too far. Why would he do that?

Logically, I knew that he couldn't be the one behind it. My emotions were running wild with the threat of bursting in flames bearing down on me. I could hear the rescue team getting closer. Part of me hoped that they were too late. After this much trauma, I would need to feed. I didn't want to drain an innocent. There would be no stopping me if that happened.

I could hear the sirens closing in. That meant it wasn't rescue workers clearing the debris. My head was spinning and I couldn't figure out why that thought was important. Unless I was imagining that someone was here. I tried to call out again, but couldn't make a sound with my parched throat.

The sunlight was searing my flesh but there was no escape. This would be my end. I was going to lose my immortal life because of petty jealousy and a stupid feud that had gone on for far too long. If only Eli were here right now. Perhaps we would be able to mend fences in time for me to die with less weight on my shoulders.

I could feel the tears running down my face from the pain. Everything was spinning. The world kept getting blindingly bright then going completely dark. I began to ponder where I was going to end up. I'd done a lot of dark things during my time here. I wondered if there really was a higher power that I would have to answer to for my crimes.

I had nothing left to fight with. The pain was eating me alive. Suddenly my body felt weightless, as if I were floating in the air. I saw images flash in front of me. It was impossible to tell what was real and what was caused by the pain of death. The last image I saw before everything went dark was Delilah over Eli's shoulder. She looked scared and his expression reminded me of a man who was heading out for revenge. I wondered what it meant as the darkness took me.

Bright lights brought me out of the inky blackness of my accepted fate. I blinked a few times to orient myself, but I didn't recognize the room I was in. How did I get here? I tried to lift my head to get a better look, but I couldn't move. The ceiling was white and the walls were a pale shade of blue. It was familiar and alien at the same time.

I tried to speak but there was no sound. Since I couldn't lift my head, I tried to turn it to the side. Still nothing. I closed my eyes in defeat. It was no use. Even if I was still alive, I was paralyzed somehow. I would never get out of here.

The quiet clop of shoes on the tiled floor caught my attention. As much as I wanted to see who was here, I kept my eyes closed. I wasn't sure who had me or why I couldn't move. I needed to assess the situation further before I revealed that I was awake.

"Hmm, I could have sworn from the readings that he was awake. Oh, well. It can't hurt to let you sit with him. Just don't mess with any of the machines this time." I didn't recognize the voice, but she was stern.

"I won't let Eli touch anything, Nurse Jacobs. I promise." There was a lightness in Delilah's tone. How could they both be here? And a nurse? Was I in a hospital?

I heard the door close before anyone spoke again.

"Are you sure this is the best place for him? Aren't they going to wonder what's going on when he's magically healed in a few days?" Delilah spoke quietly.

"It's fine. They don't need to know. You just have to keep the nurse occupied later so I can give him more blood. It would be easier if they'd listened to me and given him a transfusion, but nobody wants to cooperate." Eli sounded concerned, not at all like someone who'd just tried to have me killed.

"I still don't understand why I can't give him my blood," Delilah sounded jealous. Maybe I misjudged the two of them. But if Eli didn't blow up Midnight, then who did?

"Love, I've explained this. He nearly died. I wasn't even sure that we could revive him after I dug him out. Didn't you see his reaction to your blood on the way to the hospital?"

"We want him to fight for his life, right? Let's give him something to fight for." I heard a scuffle, then the warm sensation of something flowing into my mouth. It was sweet but familiar, like the nectar of the gods. I wanted to drink it forever, to let myself drown in its flavor.

Eli's voice rang in my ear. "You're killing her. Stop. Now!"

I released Delilah's arm and sat up. Eli had moved her away from me and bit himself to feed her. She was disoriented enough to go along with it, even if she didn't fully understand what was happening. Vampire blood would heal the wound and replenish the nutrients she lost in sharing with me.

"What happened?" My voice was raspy to my ears. Although Delilah's blood was helping to heal me, it still felt as if a building had fallen on me.

Chapter 41

Delilah

"Viktor! You're awake!" She turned and slapped Eli before running to my side. "I told you it would work."

"I don't—" his voice gave out.

"It's okay, brother, just rest. I'll explain it the best I can." Eli's words stopped Viktor from trying to argue. I'd never heard them speak so gently to each other before. Something about it felt familiar, though.

"Someone framed me for the explosions at your properties. After you spoke with us, we turned around and came back to Midnight. I wanted to help you figure out who was responsible. Our men are following leads as we speak. It took a couple of days to get yours to listen to me, but I think I made a decent case." Eli paused, looking at me.

"He didn't hurt anyone. We convinced Jones to help talk the rest into helping. I didn't think you'd get mad," I interjected. It was nice to see that my blood worked better than the bags we'd been sneaking in for him. Viktor looked as if he was starting to feel better, even if half of his face was charred so badly that it may never heal.

Eli nodded and continued. "We pulled up just before the bar exploded. I took Delilah back to the car, then I ran back to find you. By the time I got to you, you were severely burned and barely alive. You were mumbling at the gods to take you already. I can only imagine the pain you were in. I carried you to my car and Delilah insisted on giving you her blood. You went a little crazy at the first drop, and I had to knock you out. I won't apologize. I was keeping our girl safe. You'd have done the same." He lifted his prosthetic hand and raised an eyebrow.

131

Viktor nodded and wiped a tear from his eye. His movements were slow and his grimace gripped my heart. I hated seeing him in pain. I would let him drain me if it meant he didn't have to hurt anymore.

"Why would someone have planted bombs at three of your properties? And what would make you think that Eli had done it?" I was terrified to ask, but felt like I needed the answer.

"Someone framed me, because I've done this before," Eli responded, "but you have to believe me. This time it wasn't me. I had no desire to hurt you, Vik. Yes, I wanted to compete, but that was all in good fun. Who wouldn't want to look good in front of our girl?"

Viktor looked as if he was considering Eli's words. It was so hard to tell what he was thinking. I hated that he couldn't speak.

"Maybe I should give him more blood. It's healing him, just not fast enough."

Eli grabbed me before I could cut myself again. I looked at Viktor. He was staring off into space as if he couldn't even hear us. I struggled against Eli to no avail. I knew I couldn't defeat him physically, but thought that maybe I could outsmart him. He seemed to anticipate my thoughts and countered every move I made. There was no way I was going to be able to give Viktor more blood without getting Eli to agree to it.

I mean, yeah, it might have been a little impulsive to slit my wrist over Viktor's mouth. Why couldn't Eli see that it worked? Wasn't that the important thing?

"You can't sacrifice yourself to fix him. He's healing. Right now he needs to rest," Eli spoke softly, as if Viktor wouldn't hear him. I struggled against his hold, but Viktor cleared his throat.

"He's right. I need rest. I'll be fine, Myshka. Let Eli take you home for now. You can come back to see me tomorrow." Viktor couldn't hide the pain, but at least his eyes weren't filled with anger at Eli anymore.

"But we have to figure out who did this so we can take them out." Both men looked at me as if I'd grown an extra head. "What? I thought you'd be glad I jumped on the bandwagon."

"Take her home. Distract her. Please. I'll be fine," Viktor spoke to Eli as if I wasn't even there. What the hell was it with these two? They were allowed to want revenge, but the moment I suggested it, I'm wrong. It didn't make sense.

Eli let go of me and walked over to Viktor. It was strange to see him lying there. He looked so small compared to the hulk of a man standing over him. I pretended not to see Eli slip him a new cell phone. His had been destroyed, but Eli's tech guy had been able to move everything over to a new one. We had agreed that Viktor didn't need his phone right now, but I guess with him sending us away, it made sense. At least I would be able to check on him later.

I waited until Eli stepped back to run over and hug Viktor. It was all I could do to not climb in his lap. I needed to be close to him. I didn't want to leave, but it seemed like he would be safe here. I kissed him gently before turning to leave. "We'll be back first thing in the morning."

He nodded, then leaned back on the pillows as if he were going back to sleep. I knew better. He would wait until I was out of ear shot, then he'd be on the phone with Jones arranging his own revenge. We walked out of the room and I zoned out.

Eli nudged me, "Love? Are you listening to anything I'm saying?"

"Of course I am. Why?" I raised my eyebrow at him.

"Because I asked where you wanted to go for dinner and you said, 'Yeah, that sounds great.' So tell me what's wrong. Vik is fine. Don't worry." He slipped an arm around me as we walked down the hall.

"I don't want to be left out of your revenge plans. We're a family now, which means I'm involved, even if you two don't want me to be."

CHAPTER 42

Eli

I COULDN'T BELIEVE DELILAH'S reaction to me calling her out. She wanted to be involved in any revenge planning. We didn't even know who we needed to go after, and our girl was stepping in, making her intentions known. My heart swelled with pride. I was worried she might not take too well to the more violent side of things, but this gave me hope.

"You think we're planning revenge?" I asked in a teasing tone.

She nodded. "I do. And I'm going to be involved. You two will not keep things from me. Understood?"

"What makes you think you can handle it?" I asked.

She glared at me. "Either you include me or I go after whoever hurt Viktor myself. Do you want to argue about it, or would you rather just cooperate?"

For being so much smaller than me, she really was determined. Honestly, I was a little scared of her already. It was so hot. I wanted to rip her clothes off right here in the hospital and fuck her brains out. What can I say? Crazy turns me on.

"I'm not arguing. As far as I'm concerned, you're in. But we have to figure out who we need to go after first. So just take it down a notch, Killer."

Delilah chuckled at the new nickname. Her amusement made me laugh too. It was nice to know that we didn't have to be serious all the time. She growled at having to wait, but nodded.

"Fine, I'll wait. I don't like it, but I guess I can't cut a bitch if I don't know who I'm going after. I'm just glad he knows you weren't really involved." Her response made me laugh again. I pulled her in for a hug and tickled her until she squirmed away, squealing.

Some of the nurses started to stare. We were causing a commotion. I decided that we needed to tone it down, making a mental note of her ticklish spots for later.

"What if we check on your uncle while we're here? You can pop in and see how he's doing before we go find food." I knew that I wouldn't go in with her, since I'd been the one to put him in this position. I still had to find a way to make it up to him. I was certain he wouldn't accept an apology, even if I still didn't remember hurting him.

My face must have been wrinkled in concern. Delilah stopped walking and stared at me. "What?" I asked, stopping next to her.

"He'll forgive you. I did. Don't worry about it, okay?" It was as if she'd somehow sensed my emotions. Leave it to Delilah to try and make me feel better when I had all but killed her uncle. The situation was ridiculous.

I pulled her to me for a kiss. "How do you always know what to say to make me feel better?" I kissed her again before she could respond.

A moment later, she pushed against my chest. "I could tell when you suggested that I go see him that you were still feeling guilty. I know that's not going to go away, but I also know that he will forgive you. It's going to take time."

As usual, Delilah knew exactly how to make me feel better. I knew the guilt wasn't going anywhere, but I didn't have to focus on it right now either.

I walked with her to the elevator and we headed toward her uncle's room. We approached the nurse's station and Delilah walked away to discuss her uncle with his nurse. I stayed a few feet away, but could still hear the whole conversation because of my enhanced hearing. Vinny was doing better. They were expecting a full recovery. The nurse had given Delilah clearance to visit, but warned her not to push him too much or upset him. That ruled out me going in with her, which was fine by me. I would wait outside until she was done, then take her home.

CHAPTER 43

Viktor

I'd been relieved when Eli slipped me a new phone, especially after I realized that he'd somehow transferred all the info from the broken one. He certainly had a way with technology. The moment Delilah was out the door, I called Jones.

"I heard you were giving Strain some crap about ordering you guys around," I said when he answered.

"Boss? You're okay? Yeah, we gave him a hard time, but then I listened to him and convinced the others to cooperate. We won't do anything that goes against you, though."

"I know, Jones. Have you found anything useful yet?" I knew the answer before I asked, but I had to start somewhere.

"Nothing yet. The alliance with Strain has been helpful, though. He gave us access to his surveillance system that runs on all his properties. If he had anything to do with the bombing, we'll know soon." Jones seemed determined to blame everything on Strain. That was probably my fault, as I regularly used that particular scapegoat.

"I don't think it's him. Keep looking, let me know what you find." I hung up the call and slid the phone behind me just as the nurse came in. There was something about her that I didn't trust.

"Oh, good! I'm glad to see you're awake. And you seem to be healing nicely. That'll make transport easier." Her perky tone didn't sit well.

"Where am I being moved to?" I asked while trying to get her to look at me.

"Recovery. Don't worry. We'll take good care of you." She refused to make eye contact, so I was fairly certain she was lying to me. I needed her to look me in the eyes so I could charm the truth out of her.

"I'm feeling a bit woozy. I think the cut on my head is bleeding again." I spoke softly to sell the lightheaded bit. She walked closer and I was able to grab her. She looked at me in horror, but wasn't able to look away.

"Who are you working for? Where am I being moved to?" I spoke slowly and carefully. She would be forced to answer, since I was charming her.

"I don't even know. I'm only supposed to knock you out so they can transport you." The monotone response sent chills down my spine. I wasn't sure that I could escape on my own. I was still weak and healing.

I hated myself for it, but given the choice between her life and mine, there was no other way. I sank my fangs into the nurse's neck and drank my fill. Bloodlust took over and I felt her body go slack as I drained her. A few minutes later, I started ripping the wires and tubes out of my arm and off my chest. My strength had returned, even if my skin wasn't fully healed from the burns.

I got up and searched the room for my clothes. Of course they were ruined in the explosion. I grabbed the phone and my dead nurse's access badge. I would have to sneak out of here and find something to wear. If I was right, I would need to get away from the hospital before I called Eli.

There was no way I was dragging him into this until I knew for sure. I crept down the hall to the supply closet where I found scrubs that fit.

With half of my face burned and no sun block implant, I needed something to cover up before I ventured outside. That task was more difficult, though the scrubs helped. Before I could find the employee lounge, an alarm sounded. I knew that meant someone had found my nurse's body.

I ducked into a patient's room when I heard footsteps pounding behind me. The guy in the bed looked about my size. He must have been in a coma to sleep through the chaos going on around him. That was fortunate for me, because I was able to steal his hoodie. I pulled it on, leaving the hood up and jogged out of the room.

If I got caught, this would be the end for me. There was a reason why most of humanity still didn't know about our existence. I had broken rule number one. Never leave a body with evidence where it could be found. It was too late for me to worry about that now. I slipped into the crowd and continued down the corridor toward the exit. I paused for a moment when I saw the armed guard at the door.

I knew I could overpower him, but it made more sense to keep my disguise intact if I could. I boldly walked up to him. "I need to check the parking lot. Someone said they saw the guy run outside before the lockdown started."

The guard looked at me and nodded, moving so I could leave. I jogged outside like a man on a mission. Now what? It wasn't like I could call Eli and wait here for him to pick me up. I darted between cars, looking for one that was unlocked and had no security system.

I got lucky near the exit and found an unattended motorcycle. I looked around nervously before I decided to take it. Just as I managed to get it hotwired, there was a commotion behind me. My best guess was that the guard realized his mistake in letting me through the door. I laughed to myself as I sped off. I needed to find somewhere safe to hide and let Delilah know what had happened.

By the time the sun set, my hands were burnt as badly as my face. I'd been riding around for hours, searching for somewhere safe to hide from whoever it was that seemed to be after me. I ultimately decided to risk going to the cabin. At least if I made it there, I would have a change of clothes and a meal before I had to run again.

CHAPTER 44

Delilah

I DIDN'T WANT TO leave Viktor alone in the hospital. Eli must have sensed my hesitation, so he insisted I visit Uncle Vinny before we left. He looked better the last time I saw him, but still had no idea where he would go when he finally got discharged. I didn't want to explain the current situation, so I made Eli wait outside when I went in. It wasn't like he was begging to see my uncle anyway, with the guilt he felt over being responsible for Uncle Vinny's injuries. I totally understood.

"Are you feeling better today?" I asked as I entered the room. It was strange that he didn't answer, especially since he was sitting up in his chair. He seemed to be staring out the window.

I crossed the room, still talking. "The nurse said you were healing nicely. She didn't say you were out of bed, though." I walked around the chair and froze. I couldn't speak. I felt like I couldn't breathe. "Eli. Eli, please." I whispered the words, but he was by my side in an instant. I felt as if my legs couldn't hold me up. Before I collapsed, I felt his strong arms clutching me to his chest.

"Oh, love. It's okay, I've got you. There's nothing we can do for him now. No, look at me; stay focused on me," he ordered, then turned me away from the gruesome scene. Someone had murdered my uncle. His throat had been slit and his face was frozen in a horrified scream. It was strange that there was no blood, though.

"Eli, we need to get Viktor. It's not safe here," I begged him to go back with me, but he shook his head.

"Vik will be fine. He'll get out and come to us. We need to go. Come on, love. You're going to walk out as if nothing happened. You just had a lovely visit with your uncle who is healing nicely from his accident. We can talk about it once we're in the car, okay?" He spoke softly, but I knew he wasn't asking. I had to do what he said. I nodded and tried to wipe the horrified look from my face as we exited the room.

There were so many questions running through my head. Who would have killed Uncle Vinny? Why? There was nothing to be gained from his death. What had he done to deserve this? I knew that my guys would do everything they could to find out who'd killed my only family. That didn't make it any less painful. I did my best to walk out calmly with Eli. Once we made it to the door, he picked me up and carried me to the car.

Only when the doors were locked and we were speeding down the road did he finally speak. "That was a hit. I have no idea who ordered it, but a vamp did it. He was drained before his throat was slit. That's why there was no blood."

I couldn't focus enough to answer. It shouldn't surprise me that there were vampire hit men, but it did. I still couldn't figure out why.

"I promised not to hide things. You need to know what we're up against. Someone wanted him dead."

My words came in a whisper. "But who? Why?"

I glanced at Eli, who mirrored my pain back at me. "I don't know, love. But I will find out, and they will pay."

I sat there as Eli drove and the shock took over. A few minutes later, I found my voice. "What about Viktor?"

"He'll be fine," Eli responded, too quickly.

"What aren't you telling me?" I turned toward him, but he avoided eye contact. "Eli! You promised."

"We need to get out of the city. I'm not sure where we can go and be safe." He was deflecting and I wanted answers.

"Tell me or I'm jumping out of the car," I threatened. He looked at me, trying to judge if I was serious. I reached for the door handle and he sighed.

"The style of that hit reminded me of something I saw a few years ago. It was how Vik's men would take out a target. I don't know why he would do that to your uncle, but it looks like he's responsible." He still wouldn't look me in the eye, but it didn't matter because I turned away myself.

How could Viktor do this? Why would he have Uncle Vinny killed? Eli had to be mistaken. There was no way Viktor would do this.

I shook my head but didn't speak. It couldn't be true, could it? As much as I didn't want to believe it, I knew that Eli had no reason to lie. Unless all of this had been a lie and he was trying to undermine my relationship with Viktor. I needed some time to think. "Where are we going, then?" I asked without turning to face Eli.

He hesitated before answering. "Vik isn't the only one with a secret home outside the city. I have a small house out in the woods a few miles past the city line. We'll go there and figure out how to get Vik back." It should have been touching that he wanted to help Viktor, but with the revelation that one of my guys could have killed my uncle, I wasn't sure that's what I wanted.

"Shit! I totally forgot. You gave Viktor his new phone. Do you think it's safe to text him?" I didn't bother to pretend that I didn't know.

"You saw that, huh?" Eli winced at the realization that he wasn't as slick as he'd thought.

"Yeah, I did. But it gives us a way to find out if he was the one who did it or if he knows anything about it," I could barely bring myself to say the words out loud. I pulled my phone from my pocket and texted Viktor.

We need to talk. I knew it was somewhat ominous, but I had no idea how to ask him if he'd killed my uncle. I didn't know how to process the thought that the man I was falling for could be so cold as to kill my only remaining family. I mean, my mom was probably out there somewhere, but she'd been chasing my dad for so long. I was certain that by now she'd forgotten all about me.

With that realization came the tears. I hadn't broken down when I found his body, or when Eli had all but accused Viktor of murder. But now, sitting here in the car thinking about how Uncle Vinny had been the one person who was always there for me, I couldn't hold back. Every scraped knee, broken heart, aced test—he was the one who'd helped me through everything and celebrated with me when I'd done things I didn't think I could. And now he was gone. The whole thing seemed so unreal.

I picked up my phone again and sent another text. I knew it was pointless, because I hadn't heard from her in the past ten years, but I sent it anyway. *Hey, Mom, just wanted to let you know that I'm okay. A lot has happened in the past few weeks. The bar was destroyed, and Uncle Vinny passed away. I'm sorry to tell you this way, but I don't know if this is even your number anymore.*

I didn't expect a response. The last time I had tried calling, the voicemail was full and no one had called back. I knew that most likely something had happened to her, but even that thought didn't hit me as hard as Uncle Vinny's death.

"What did he say?" Eli asked as he turned down an unmarked road.

"Nothing yet. I hope he's okay," I replied, wishing we hadn't left the hospital.

CHAPTER 45

Eli

I WASN'T SURE WHY Viktor hadn't answered Delilah's text, but I knew that she would be obsessed with going back to make sure he was okay. I needed to distract her.

I knew that trying to work with Viktor's guys would be tough, since he still thought I was behind the explosion. I mean, I get it. I love blowing shit up. It's my thing. But Vik's thing was draining humans then slitting their throats to cover it up. That didn't mean that I automatically thought he killed Vinny. Maybe for a minute. What mattered right now was that I knew he didn't do it.

Maybe one of his guys went rogue. Or maybe one of us has a mole who's been working for whoever was doing these bombings. That would explain how they were able to duplicate our specific signatures so easily.

I sent Scott a text and explained my theory. I had him start looking into everyone at Maxwell Industries. I would research my company myself. I had no indication that Scott couldn't be trusted, but in this situation, it was better to handle the delicate stuff alone.

How did we get here? Earlier today I was planning to seduce Delilah, and now I'm sitting in front of a computer setup reviewing every single employee's financial records and social media to search for a mole. This was definitely the craziest day.

I started with Scott, since he was the closest to me and had the most security clearance. I didn't want to believe that he could be compromised, but I couldn't afford to take any chances.

I spent the next hour combing through Scott's background. I checked every transaction, every post, every purchase. All I learned was that Scott donated half of his salary to cancer research in his grandmother's name. He posted pictures of his cat and shared video game updates. There was nothing even remotely related to work. He didn't even list his employer on any of his social media. He had to be the most loyal employee I'd ever had.

I moved onto the next name on my list and continued searching for several hours. I thought that Delilah was watching TV, so her voice next to me was startling.

"You need to eat. I'm not sure exactly what you're looking at here, but it can wait." She turned my face to look at her and brushed the hair over her shoulder. Her exposed neck called to me. I knew that I couldn't bite her, though. Drinking from the vein was my preferred feeding method, but I didn't trust myself not to hurt Delilah.

I shook my head and turned back to the computer. "I'll get a bag in a little while. I need to focus on this."

She grabbed my face and turned it toward her again. "You're taking a break. Now." She shoved me back from the desk and pulled me by both hands. I guess it was her turn to distract me.

I followed her over to the couch where she shoved me down and climbed on my lap. We had started kissing when my phone rang.

"Leave it. Unless it's Viktor, there's no reason to answer," she ordered.

I glanced at the screen. Scott. I had to answer, even if it made Delilah mad. I shrugged apologetically as I pulled the phone closer and answered. "What did you find?"

"There are a few people who are questionable. I'm not through everything, but I figured you'd want to see the ones I've weeded out so far." Scott had been with me since he'd been turned six years ago, and he knew exactly how I ran things.

"Send it all over. I'll get to it in just a bit." My tone was dismissive and I knew it. But it was hard to be focused with Delilah grinding on my lap. She must have decided that torturing me while I was on the phone was the perfect punishment.

"Um, boss?" Scott's tone had changed and seemed apprehensive.

"What is it?" I wasn't used to him sounding scared or nervous around me, even when I'd blown up at people.

"I know you have to check all of us out too, and that you'll want to do it yourself. I just wanted you to know that I understand. I hope you don't find anything though. I hate to think that any of our guys could be involved in whatever this is." Since I knew that he wasn't involved, I could relate to his feelings. I didn't want it to be any of our guys either.

"Chances are, someone will be guilty of something. It's only a matter of time before we figure out which people are involved. Keep working." I disconnected the call without saying goodbye.

Delilah was glaring at me when I hung up the phone. "I know, but it was important. Scott may have a lead on whoever is responsible for blowing up Midnight." Delilah froze. Her glare softened a bit and tears filled her eyes.

"It was my home, and now it's gone. Why would anyone do that?" She started to break down, but I pulled her close and kissed her.

"We will figure it out. And we'll rebuild. I promise. Even if I have to buy the building from Vik and do it myself." I knew the promise was easier said than done, but I was determined to get rid of any reason our girl had to be sad. I couldn't handle the tears. I knew that I would do anything to keep her from crying, even happy tears.

"Can we call the contractor and get him started?" Delilah had pulled up the number in her phone. "I'm sure Viktor won't mind. If he ever answers his phone, we can tell him."

I nodded and she dialed the contractor. He was a nice enough guy and didn't mind that we'd given him the okay to restart construction instead of Vik. Especially when I had explained that I would be doubling the budget. He'd been in the neighborhood when the building had gone down and knew that Vik was inside.

"Yes, he's fine. Resting and recovering," I lied. "I've already let him know that we're going ahead with the renovations and construction to rebuild. He's on board, but with everything he's been through, we thought it would be best for me to take over for a while."

Convincing the human to gather his crew and start rebuilding Midnight again hadn't been as difficult as I had expected. Perhaps Vik had said something to him when we'd agreed to share Delilah. It didn't matter now. All that mattered was making sure Delilah was safe. I felt like her concern for Vik was rubbing off on me. I was starting to worry about his safety too.

At this point, I knew that she was right. I needed a break and so did she. I decided to take her for a drive. We got in the car and drove toward the city.

"So, food?" I asked, opening the car door for Delilah to climb in.

"Surprise me," she said with a wink. My dick twitched at the innuendo. If she wasn't careful, we'd end up back at my place with nothing to eat at all.

Every time we'd tried to be intimate, Vik had found a reason to interrupt. It was like he was paying me back for the one time I barged in on them. It didn't matter that I'd apologized, so I decided if he could do it, so could I. I was dying to be inside her. If only the rest of the world would go away for a while.

Because of my rivalry with Vik, whenever she and I had alone time, I made sure Delilah was taken care of first. I knew that most likely I wouldn't get to finish, but that was fine. There were some things that were worth waiting for, and Delilah was one of them. Once all of this mess with Midnight and the Powder operation was taken care of, there would be plenty of time for Delilah and me to get physical.

Since she'd opted for dinner to be a surprise, I decided to show her my favorite taco joint. It was less of a restaurant and more of a food truck that parked near my headquarters three times a week. I may or may not have paid them five grand a month with free parking for the privilege. The tacos were that good.

"Delgado's Tacos? That doesn't seem sketchy at all," Delilah teased as I parked the car and opened her door.

"Don't dis Delgado. He's the best," I defended my favorite food truck fiercely.

"Wait, can you eat tacos? I thought you had certain dietary restrictions," she said. Delilah was obviously trying to be subtle about her curiosities. That was a good thing, since we were on a public street, and not in a vampire part of the city.

"I'm not allergic to them. It's complicated, but I can explain more when we get home." I hoped that she would understand that I didn't want to discuss it in the open.

She nodded. "So what's good?" We were standing in front of the truck looking at the menu.

"Everything. Do you trust me?" I couldn't resist asking and a wicked smirk crossed my face.

"With my life," she responded simply, with the most serious expression I'd ever seen on her face.

I turned to the order window just as Delgado poked his head out. "Hey, Eli! I haven't seen you in a while. I thought something had happened. I can see now that you've just been busy with your lady," he said as a large smile crossed his face.

"I had no idea that you knew the guy personally," Delilah whispered.

I leaned closer to her and whispered back, "I know everyone, love." Then I turned to Delgado. "Sorry, man. Did they give you any trouble?" When he shook his head, I continued, "Can we get my usual, but make it a double and throw in a dessert?"

"Anything for you, Boss." Delgado smiled at Delilah and retreated back into the truck to make my order.

"Did he just call you 'boss'?" Delilah cocked an eyebrow at me.

"He did, but this truck is one of the few things I want to own that I can't convince the owner to make a deal about. We have an arrangement that keeps me in tacos and makes things easier for him to follow his dream. It's not a big deal," I assured her.

"I feel like I'm learning more about you by being out in the city than I have by talking to you," she laughed.

"I'm sure Vik helps people out too," I tried to defend myself. I couldn't have her thinking I was weak.

"I don't think he does. But he did pay for all of Uncle Vinny's expenses at the hospital, so who knows? The two of you are a mystery," she responded.

A few minutes later, with tacos to spare, we were headed back to the safe house. "So you really can eat regular food?" Delilah asked as soon as we were in the car.

I laughed. "Yes, we can. Some vamps only drink blood. Personally, I like food too much not to eat it. I still need blood to survive, but the food doesn't hurt anything."

"Hmm, that's interesting. Does it taste different now?" I was impressed that I'd found a way to distract her without even trying.

"Everything is more crisp. Flavors are more potent. It's the same with our vision and hearing. Sense of smell. The change enhances everything. Why do you ask? Are you thinking about joining team vamp?" I had meant it as a joke but one look at her face told me that she might actually be considering it.

"I don't know. Maybe?" Her response was quiet, as if she was still thinking about how it would change her life.

"Wait a minute. I was joking. We're not turning you. If you want to discuss it later when Vik is with us, we can, but for now, let's just drop that thought all together." I didn't want her to try and talk me into turning her without finding out what Vik thought of it.

I had to admit, the thought of Delilah becoming a vampire just to be with us for eternity was an appealing one. Maybe I could talk Vik into it. I had to push the thought away as I drove us back to the safe house.

CHAPTER 46

Viktor

I DITCHED THE BIKE in the woods just outside of the city and hiked to the cabin. It was a three mile walk and by the time I arrived, I almost missed the fact that someone else was there. I crept around back. There had to be a way to see who it was without giving away my position.

My security feed! Of course! Time to see how well Eli did duplicating my phone after all. When I finally pulled it from my pocket, I realized that I had missed a text from Delilah hours ago. She was probably worried about me. I would have to call her the moment I knew it was safe.

I searched for the security app on my phone and logged into it. From there I was able to get a real-time video showing what was happening inside my cabin. I decided it would be safer to climb a tree and hide while I figured out my next step. I walked silently through the trees until I found just the right one to climb. I needed to be far enough away from the house to not be seen, but close enough that I was still on the wi-fi so I could keep the video going.

Climbing wasn't easy with the damage to my hands from the sun. I would have to arrange another UV implant as soon as possible. Once I made it up into the tree far enough to be sure I wouldn't be seen from the ground, I pulled my phone out and opened the app again.

As I switched from room to room throughout the cabin, I saw that every room had been tossed. I realized that whoever this was seemed to be looking for something. If I could figure out what they were looking for, I would know who had sent them. There was no way to do that without tipping them off to my position.

All I could do was watch as the hooded figures trashed my cabin, the one place I'd managed to keep secret from nearly everyone. There was no way an enemy could know about it. Unless—was that what Delilah needed to talk to me about? Had she told Eli about the cabin? Why would he have saved my life if he were going to send his minions to trash my home? None of it made any sense.

Unless it was all a plot to fool me into trusting him so I would let my guard down. If that was the case, what were they looking for? What did I have that Eli would want bad enough to attempt murder?

I let my imagination wander as I watched the three thugs destroy my cabin. I might as well text Delilah back and see what she wanted.

We need to talk? That sounds ominous.

A moment after I sent the text, one of the thugs stopped and pulled out a phone. I couldn't zoom in enough to see what they were doing, but it looked as if they were texting. What a strange coincidence.

I got Delilah's response as the thug pocketed their phone. *Are you still at the hospital? We heard the alarms. Eli said it's not safe there.*

Curious, I dialed her number. The thug pulled the phone out again, drug the ski mask off her head and tousled her dark curls. She answered the phone just as I heard Delilah's voice.

"Viktor? Is that you?"

I hung up, shocked that Delilah would be involved in destroying my home. I had nowhere to go, and no one to help me, since my men had all been instructed to follow Eli. I rubbed my eyes and looked again. *That's not Delilah.* My eyes were playing tricks on me. It had to be the lack of blood. It was so hard to stay focused. My mind was playing tricks on me. I had to get away from here. I put my phone away and scrambled deeper into the woods. There was a cave a couple of miles further. It was obscured and no one knew about it. I could hide there until I was certain these people had finished searching my cabin.

If I'd been stronger, I would have barged in and demanded answers. I knew that running was a cowardly move, but I was more interested in self-preservation at the moment. I could feel my phone vibrating in my pocket. There was no time to stop and answer now. I could hear movement behind me. The footsteps seemed to be getting closer. Only a few feet to go, but it felt like an eternity to get there.

I ducked inside the mouth of the cave and held my breath as two of the masked figures crept past. They had obviously been tracking me. I was lucky to have made it. I wondered how long my luck would hold.

When I was sure they'd moved on, I pulled out my phone and headed a little deeper in the cave. I didn't want to get so far away from the entrance that I couldn't see the path outside, but wanted to hide in the shadows.

When I pulled my phone out again, I had six missed calls. Five were from Delilah, and one was from Eli. It seemed strange to me that they would call as they were trying to hunt me down. At this point, I was too tired to focus on why that seemed odd.

My burns weren't healing as quickly as I wanted. I would have to deal with that before I'd be able to sleep. I put my phone away and crept back to the opening of the cave. I heard a rustling and prepared for an attack. I took a deep breath and realized that the person hunting me was human. And I was hungry.

I waited a beat, then dove out the opening and tackled the thug who was walking past. I punched him hard enough to knock the guy unconscious, then dragged him back into the cave. I made sure no one was following me, then pulled the limp body further into the cave.

Once we were a safe distance inside, I sat down on the dirt with my meal. It didn't matter to me that this was a person with a family. It should have, but right now, survival was key. I had to eat to survive. In my mind, it was him or me. I wasn't ready to give up yet. I drained him, making sure not to spill a drop, then shoved him off to the back wall of the cave.

As my burns healed, the pain of self-loathing took their place. I spent my entire after life fighting against vampires who did what I had just done. I just became the monster I was trying to defeat.

CHAPTER 47

Delilah

"I CAN'T BELIEVE HE called and hung up. What is going on?" I ranted at Eli, even though I knew he didn't have any more answers than I did.

"I've got Jones trying to track him, but the signal keeps cutting out. We'll find him. At least we know he made it out of the hospital before things got crazy," Eli offered. We'd been watching the news since Jones texted about the hospital being on lockdown.

"Do you think he was responsible for those murders? He couldn't have done it, right?" I was certain Eli was getting tired of me asking the same questions, but I needed some reassurance that this wasn't Viktor.

Eli shook his head and shrugged. "I'm not sure. Trust me, I don't want to believe it either, but he's done things like this before. The only way to find out is to find him." He turned back to his phone. He must be talking to Jones again.

I pulled my phone out of my hoodie pocket and texted Viktor again.

Please answer me. I need to know that you're okay. I've been trying to call.

He didn't answer right away, so I put the phone back in my pocket. There was no sense in getting worked up about something that may or may not be true. Either way, I had to help him. To do that, I had to find him. I wasn't getting anywhere by sending texts or calling. I would have to let Jones do his job.

I looked up to find Eli staring at me. "What?" I asked, suddenly feeling self-conscious.

He chuckled, "You're sexy when you're worried." Eli licked his bottom lip and nodded for me to come closer.

I slid into his lap and snuggled into his arms. I knew he was going to try to take my mind off Viktor. I wasn't convinced that he'd be able to do it.

150

"Why don't we watch some TV and relax a bit?" Eli turned on a movie and pulled me closer.

I tried to focus on the screen, but ended up staring off into space. A few minutes later, I felt Eli's lips on my neck. He must have realized that his distraction tactic wasn't working. I pretended to be focused on the movie, wondering how far he would take things to get my attention.

His lips moved from my neck to my ear. It was all I could do to pretend not to notice. When my toes started to curl, he stopped. I didn't dare turn my head to see why. It seemed funny that I was nervous about finally having sex with him. We'd come close to this point a few times, but then Viktor would find a reason to barge in or call. There was little chance of that happening tonight.

I knew that if I was uncomfortable, I just had to say something and Eli would stop teasing me. Maybe that's what he thought was going on. I wanted to tease him, though.

I stretched, grinding my bottom against his erection. I had no idea how these two guys always seemed in control when they were sporting boners all the time. I pulled my hoodie over my head and dropped it on the couch beside us.

The sight of my lace tank and lack of bra seemed to set him off. So much for always being in control. Eli growled before grabbing me and flipping me around to straddle him on the couch. I started grinding against him again and he pulled me closer. I kissed him as if I were absorbing his essence into me. I couldn't get enough. His tongue tangled with mine until I knew I was dripping.

He moved down my neck to my collarbone, then ripped my tank down the middle to free my breasts. I gasped in protest but it didn't stop him. Eli took his time kissing and licking every inch as if he were memorizing my body. He wrapped his arms around me and cupped my ass while he teased my nipples.

I pulled his shirt over his head and tossed it away, running my hands down his back and chest. I started kissing and nibbling on his neck, easing him back against the cushion. After I left my mark on his tanned skin, I caught his lips with mine again. While I kissed him, I unfastened his belt and jeans.

I slid off his lap and tugged his pants and boxer briefs off. I didn't give him a chance to argue about wanting to please me first. I grabbed his engorged member and licked from base to tip. He moaned and gave up any fight he might have been considering. I stroked him while teasing with licks and nips until he couldn't stand it.

"Let me take care of you," he begged as his breath hitched.

I smirked, "Make me." I wrapped my lips around his erection and bobbed up and down, deep throating him. Eli's groans turned me on so much that I knew if I didn't get him inside me, I would be done before we even started.

He must have sensed that because he pulled me onto his lap and ripped my shorts off. "Hey!" I objected, but that didn't stop him from tearing my panties as he removed them too.

He thrust into me with no mercy, obviously planning to go rough. I wondered how he knew I would love that. Eli worked me up and down his shaft, then flipped me around backward.

I slowed him down until he couldn't take the teasing anymore. He flipped me onto the floor on my stomach and pounded me from behind until I was screaming his name.

Once we were both sated, Eli carried me to the shower. "You get cleaned up while I make you something to eat. I'll shower after." It seemed odd that he didn't want to join me, but other than us having sex, he'd acted odd all day.

I turned on the water before he left, but didn't get in yet. I crept to the door and listened. Sure enough, I heard rustling in the kitchen. Eli was making me something to eat. I listened for a moment longer and heard his voice.

"Have you found him yet?" Eli asked. He must have been on the phone, because I couldn't hear the other side of the conversation.

"Absolutely not. Keep looking. And make sure you have the blood bags and the sedative. You'll need both to bring him in. He doesn't trust anyone." Eli's words echoed in my head. I knew that if I stood here listening to his conversation, I would reveal myself. I turned and went back to the shower, not bothering to shut the bathroom door. I didn't want to make it obvious that I'd been spying.

CHAPTER 48

Viktor

I WASN'T SURE HOW long I sat there, staring out into the darkness of the cave after I fed. At some point, I realized that the guy I had drained probably had a cell phone that could be tracked to my exact location, so I dug through his pockets until I found it. I turned it off and slid it into my pocket. I'd search through it when I was safe.

The numbness spread through my body at what I had done. The bloodlust was the one part that I hated about myself since my transition. I never wanted to be out of control, and that was the one thing I struggled with daily. Yet somehow I had let myself drain two humans in one day. And I wanted more. I had to get the craving under control.

It was the biggest thing that Eli and I argued about. He didn't understand why I didn't want to drink from the vein. I didn't understand his blatant disregard for human life. It made so much more sense to take donations and let the humans live to produce more blood for us.

"None of that matters right now. Why am I beating myself up for this?" I said the words aloud, but they came out barely more than a whisper. If I were being honest with myself, I knew why I was so worried about it. What would happen when Delilah found out that I'd killed someone by draining their blood? I knew that this guy would have tried to kill me if he'd been given the chance, and the nurse had been working for someone who wanted me weakened. But who?

If I didn't know better, I'd swear that Eli's mentor was behind it. He'd been killed shortly after Eli and I had both been turned, though. Which was not long after Kat's death. Eli was to blame for so much of my pain.

How did I agree to share Delilah with the man who'd taken everything from me? I tried to backtrack through the decisions that had led me here, but I couldn't figure out what it was about her that made me agree that having part of her would be better than none.

I still felt that way, even now. I longed to be close to her, even for a moment. I hadn't been this attached to anyone since I lost Kat. Honestly, I knew that my initial attraction to Delilah had been completely physical. She was gorgeous. What little time I'd spent with her showed me there was so much more to Delilah than just her looks.

I knew from the moment I met her that I wouldn't be able to deny her anything for long. If she wanted to be with me and still wanted Eli, I wasn't going to argue. And that was what she decided. It wouldn't stop me from trying to convince her to drop him for me. So why was I sitting here in this cave having a pity party?

Delilah would understand that I'd done what I needed to in order to survive. It wasn't like I was going to hide it from her. I planned to tell her exactly what it had taken to get back to her. She had to understand. Right?

There was only one way to find out. I pulled my phone from my pocket. I had to hand it to Eli, this new phone had an amazing battery. I watched a couple of hours of surveillance video, and the battery was still almost full. I turned on the screen and winced. Seventeen missed calls and nearly twice as many texts.

Most of the calls had been Delilah, although there were a few from Eli, and a couple from Jones. The calls didn't surprise me, but the fact that half the texts were from Eli did. I expected Delilah to freak out when I disappeared. I hadn't considered that Eli would object to having her all to himself.

Where are you? D is so worried. I can't keep her occupied. You need to call or text her.

That was the last text he sent, two hours ago. I hadn't realized how long I sat there. I walked to the cave entrance carefully, listening for footfalls in the forest around me. I didn't hear anything, so I poked my head out and looked around. The sun would set soon. Once it did, I could sneak into the house and get a change of clothes and the keys to my car in the garage.

Well, there was no use putting it off. I typed out a quick response to Eli and slinked back into the cave to wait for darkness.

Has she been with you the whole time since you left the hospital? I need answers. Nearly got taken from the hospital, then again after getting out. Let D know that I'm okay. Where can I meet you when it gets dark?

I settled back into the spot where I had spent most of my day. I turned the cameras back on, searching for the people who'd ransacked my cabin. It looked as if they were gone. Did they give up on their ally so easily?

Eli's response vibrated in my pocket. *Of course she has been with me since we left you. I haven't left her alone for a minute. Why? What happened?*

His response made me think that I'd imagined the coincidence that led me to believe Delilah was part of this break in. Why would she do that? There was no reason to think she would ever be a part of that sort of thing. I must have been hallucinating from my injuries. Or was it just someone who looked a lot like her?

I was on guard as I crept through the trees to the back of the cabin. They shouldn't have been able to access it because of the security system. Jones and I were the only ones who knew the codes. I knew he would never betray me. Would he? I had spent millions protecting his family after his transition.

From the outside, the only trace of their presence was that the alarm wasn't set and the doors were unlocked. I walked inside slowly, expecting an ambush. After going through every room, I knew I was alone. I quickly changed the security codes and turned the system on before going to shower and change clothes.

I packed a bag for myself and another with the things I'd purchased for Delilah. She hadn't even seen half of it. I cautiously carried the bags to the car, locked it and went back inside the cabin. I needed to clear the safes before I left. I knew that I probably wouldn't be coming back here.

The hidden safe in Delilah's room hadn't been touched. I gathered the cash, jewels, and other valuables from it and settled them carefully into a suitcase before heading to my room. I knew that my safe had been tampered with, but that one didn't have anything truly valuable in it.

As suspected, the main safe had been emptied and reclosed. I hadn't considered that they would find the hidden safe in my room so easily. It looked as if nothing there had been touched. I was shocked to find it empty when I got it opened.

"Damn. Now I have to figure out who did this," I grumbled to myself as I packed another bag with the rest of my belongings, deciding to leave Kat's stuff behind. I did another pass of Delilah's room to make sure I didn't miss anything, then headed to the car.

Once I was in the driver's seat, I checked my phone. When I hadn't responded to his text earlier, Eli had gone ahead and texted me an address across town. I knew it was one of his properties. I would meet him there and we'd figure this out. Or I would discover that he was behind it all and we'd fight to the death. Either way there would be some sort of closure to this.

CHAPTER 49

Delilah

AFTER MY SHOWER, I put on my leggings and one of Eli's shirts. Most of my clothes had been at Midnight when it was blown up, so my choices were limited. Where Viktor would have given me a button up dress shirt, Eli gave me a vintage concert tee. I had heard of Metallica, but I wasn't much into classic rock.

He told me about the concerts and played some of their music. It was good but didn't take my mind off Viktor. Eli's phone went off and I looked at him expectantly. He read the text twice before responding.

"Who was it? Did they find him?" I was worried that something bad had happened.

"It was him. I'm supposed to tell you that he's okay but I'll let you see for yourself when he gets here," Eli responded without looking up from his phone.

"There's something else, isn't there?" I felt like things were never going to get back to normal for us.

"He wants to meet somewhere. I think he's trying to decide if he can trust me. I want to meet him alone, then bring him back here. Are you good with that?" From his tone, it didn't seem like I really had a choice.

Instead of arguing, I nodded. "Bring him back safely," I begged. I knew there was no way Eli would let me go with him. I needed a distraction so that I could hide in his car. Luckily, his phone rang while he was getting ready to leave.

"I'm going to lie down," I fibbed, kissing him on the cheek, then turning toward the bedroom when he answered his phone. He nodded and walked into the kitchen. I only had a few minutes to sneak downstairs and hide in the car. I grabbed a small blanket, locked and quietly closed the bedroom door, and tiptoed out the door.

I have no idea how I managed to get into the backseat and cover myself up before I heard Eli shutting the door and starting the car. I expected him to throw the blanket off me and yell at any moment. Fortunately for me, Eli loved listening to loud classic rock music when he drove his car. As soon as the radio started, I knew I was safe.

I resisted the urge to peek out from the blanket. I wanted to know where we were going but didn't want Eli to take me back to the hideout. It was a better bet to stay hidden until we got to where he was meeting Viktor. Once both of my guys realized I was there, I knew neither of them would send me away.

Suddenly the music stopped. My heart stopped with it. I was about to be busted. How would I talk my way out of this one? I relaxed briefly when I heard Viktor's voice come through the speakers.

"Where are you? I can't stay hidden very well here. The city is busy tonight." Viktor sounded annoyed, but not hurt like he was the last time I'd seen him.

"On my way. Delilah locked me out of the bedroom and refused to say goodbye. She was pissed that I told her she had to stay behind. You wanna explain exactly why you told me to leave her at the safe house?" Eli's annoyance matched Viktor's. I almost laughed at how pissed they'd both be when I popped out of the backseat.

"It's not safe for her. We need to discuss what happened at the hospital. She doesn't need to hear that." Viktor's voice softened a bit. My heart swelled with his need to protect me.

"Did you do it?" Eli asked simply and I assumed that he knew what Viktor wanted to discuss.

"I did what I had to in order to escape. I'll explain it all to Delilah when I see her."

"You'll have to explain it to me as well. It makes no sense. Why would you kill someone whose life you saved? Why would you pay his hospital bill in full if you were only going to end his life?" Eli sounded as confused as I felt.

"What are you talking about? Did something happen to Vinny?" Now Viktor sounded confused. "I think we must be having two different conversations here."

"You didn't kill him?" Eli asked, pausing before continuing, "Because whoever did it used your signature. They drained the body, then slit the throat, removing the bite marks."

"Fuck. No, I didn't kill him. I killed the nurse so I could escape. I thought that's what you were talking about. I didn't want to do it, but she came in throwing around the idea that someone had paid her to prep me for transport. They were going to knock me out and move me somewhere."

I winced at the reminder of how my uncle had died. No, he hadn't died. He'd been murdered. I knew it couldn't have been Viktor, but I felt a wave of relief wash over me when Viktor said he wasn't responsible for Uncle Vinny's death. I guess there was still a part of me that didn't fully trust him. How could I with all the things he was hiding from me?

At this point, I felt as if I were suffocating under the blanket. It didn't matter how mad they got, I couldn't stay hidden for another moment.

Just as I was about to throw the blanket off, the car went spinning. I looked up to see Eli lying on the pavement a few feet away from the car. Before I could call out to him a pair of strong hands clamped down on my arms and pulled me from the wreckage.

My vision blurred. I felt the scratching of rope as it was wound around my hands and feet. Then I watched as someone attacked Eli. I tried to move but couldn't. All I could do was lie there and watch as this man fought with my love. I tried to scream, only to realize that a cloth had been tied around my mouth.

I watched as two more men came from the shadows and joined the first one, all three attacking Eli. He seemed to be holding his own, but I wasn't sure he could keep fighting. I was terrified for him and for me. He didn't even know I was in the car.

Why hadn't I listened to him when he said it was safer to stay at the house while he picked Viktor up? I was certain they'd both be pissed that I'd rebelled against his command. At this point, I would happily take any punishment from both of them if only I could find a way out of these ropes.

"It's pointless to fight. You'll only get yourself killed before your time." A gravely voice crept into my ear. Hot breath on my neck made me cringe. I knew that if Viktor or Eli knew that I was here, they would save me. There had to be a way to let them know.

I watched as the three men attacking Eli wore him down. His movements were getting slower and they were landing more punches. I wasn't sure how much more he could take I tried to pull my cell from my pocket but one of my captors was paying attention. He jerked it from my hand and crushed it before throwing it. Defeat washed over me.

Just when I thought it was too late, a blur of movement came from the shadows and started helping Eli. It had to be Viktor. Hope filled my heart but only lasted a moment. Once the man who'd tied me up realized that the other three were losing, the tailgate of the truck was slammed closed and the truck started flying down the street.

One of the men who'd been fighting Eli jumped into the bed with me. I cringed at his touch, even though he was keeping me from banging my head on the cold metal as the truck sped away. I silently prayed that Eli and Viktor would find my phone and somehow find me.

I tried to focus on the buildings we passed and which direction we turned. If I knew where I was, I could plan my escape. There had to be a way. After a couple of turns, the guy holding me must have realized what I was doing. He took off his bandana and wrapped it over my eyes. "We can't have you spying now, can we?" The words came out as a growl and I wondered how long it would be before he bit me. If my own guys had trouble resisting me, I knew that a stranger wouldn't be able to.

I slammed against the cold metal as the truck screeched to a halt. The man who'd been holding onto me grunted, then lifted me up and jumped from the truck. I wondered where we were and what they had planned for me. My heart raced as my imagination poured through every crime documentary I'd ever seen. If I survived this, I swore to myself I'd start reading more and avoid crime shows.

I didn't try to fight since I was tied up and gagged anyway. I let myself go limp as he carried me, and the bandana that was covering my eyes fell to the ground. I wanted him to think that I had passed out from fear. I carefully turned my head and took in details of the building he carried me into. If I had a chance to escape, I had to know where I was and how to get out.

CHAPTER 50

Viktor

I PULLED UP TO the meeting area, expecting to find Eli waiting for me. Instead, I found a trap. At least now I knew who I was dealing with. I just had to find out why. It didn't matter at the moment; I had to help Eli. There were three guys attacking him and he didn't seem to be able to defeat them.

I rushed over, jumping on the tallest one. I kicked him in the stomach and turned to throw another off of Eli. I wanted to ask if Delilah was safe, but he'd assured me she was staying behind. It was one less thing to worry about. These guys were fighting dirty. I shot a look at the truck that seemed to be hovering just far enough away that I couldn't tell who was in it.

"Eli! Behind you!" I called as one of the men rushed him with a bat. My warning was enough to have him spinning and grabbing the asshole by the throat. I knew that we had a small window to defeat them before they called for backup. These were my guys after all. The betrayal hit like a ton of bricks. What could have convinced them to work against me? I needed answers.

"Vik, look out!" Eli yelled.

I turned my head in time to see the third guy coming at me with a hunting knife. Without Eli's warning, he would have taken my heart. I spent the next few moments reevaluating my choice in friends as I fought off a familiar face. I knew this guy. Jones introduced us on his first day with the company. *What the fuck was his name?* Corey, Kyle, Jeff? It didn't matter because I was about to rip his heart out for betraying me. I knew if they defeated us, they would hunt Delilah down next. Protecting her gave me just enough determination to kill this bastard.

The moment I spent trying to remember his name was all he needed to stab me. I refocused the moment the blade penetrated my side. As many times as I'd been in fights before, I knew that he'd missed my vital organs. Not that it mattered much, since the only way to kill me was to remove my head or heart. Blood trickled down my side as I adjusted my stance. I knew this guy wouldn't give up until one of us was dead for good. I was determined it wouldn't be me.

He tried to slice me with the knife, but I grabbed his hand and knocked him to the ground. I stood on his chest and pulled his arm off. I knew the injury wouldn't kill him because he was one of us. He was a vampire, fighting other vampires. I threw his arm a few feet away and bent down to pick up the knife with one foot still holding him in place.

I glanced around for Eli, who had the second man subdued. The third had run off. I wasn't going to worry about that right now, or the fact that the truck had also left. I needed to end this so Eli and I could get back to Delilah. I clutched the knife in my hand and leaned down. "Who are you working for?"

He shook his head, refusing to answer. He wouldn't betray his boss, but it didn't matter. I was certain it was Jones.

I stared the asshole in his eyes as I shoved my hand into his chest and pulled out his heart. "This ends now." I turned to check on Eli.

He was on the ground several feet away from me. Blood covered him and the corpse lying next to him. I wasn't sure if any of it was his blood or not. I rushed over to help him to his feet. "How badly are you hurt?" I asked as I gently lifted him off his feet. I would carry him to the car if I had to.

It would be a mirror image of the last bar fight we had before Kat died. She was working long hours and Eli had been tasked with keeping me occupied so I wouldn't show up at the office again. Of course, his idea of keeping me busy was a night out drinking. He hit on the bartender's girlfriend and we had to fight our way out of it. That day, he had carried me to the car and bandaged my wounds. Today, I would do that for him.

"Broken ribs, concussion, shattered wrist. I'm fine. Are you hurt?" He seemed concerned. His actions during the fight proved that he had my back. I never thought a woman would bring us back together after one tore us apart. I realized at that moment just how much I had missed my friend.

I shook my head, thinking about the blood trailing down my side. It had slowed to a trickle. "Nothing serious. What happened?"

"I pulled up to wait for you, and that truck hit me. The one guy got out and we started fighting. My head was spinning so badly that I couldn't take him out before two of his friends joined." Eli gestured to the man I had killed.

"The other one got away. We'll find them. And whoever they're working for." I reassured him as I half carried him to my car.

I followed his directions back to his safe house, not bothering to tell him yet that I know who ordered this attack. I needed to know who our traitor was really working for. Honestly, I needed a few minutes to wrap my head around the betrayal from my most trusted employee. I had started to suspect that something was going on with him, but it was still hard to believe Jones would have attacked Eli and me like this. He had to be the one behind the explosions as well.

Eli must have tapped into my emotions, because he gave me the time to process without pushing me to discuss it. Part of me hurt over how much had come between us. There was a time when the man sitting next to me was my best friend, my brother.

Kat. That was what had pushed us away. Shawn's obsession and my jealousy had wedged between Eli and myself until there was nothing left of the bond we'd shared. I knew that I would always hate Shawn for what had happened, but I was starting to see that maybe Eli wasn't the one to blame.

I needed to push the sentimental thoughts away and figure out exactly what I needed to do. I needed a plan. I was so focused that I didn't hear what Eli was saying.

"What?" I glanced at him.

"I said, there's something you're not telling me." Eli was staring at me intently as if he were memorizing my every move.

"Oh, that. Just trying to wrap my head around it all. And I don't have proof yet. But I think those guys were all recruited to my company by the same person." I replied, stealing another glance at him as I drove.

Eli nodded, then leaned back against the seat. I didn't need to be an empath to know that he was in pain. He needed a blood bag and time to heal. I hoped we'd get it. It seemed as if Jones was one step ahead of us.

I parked the car where Eli instructed and helped him inside the safe house. The bedroom door was still closed, and when I tried the knob, it was locked. "I guess she must be mad at both of us."

Eli nodded, sinking onto the couch. "There's a key in the kitchen." Once he'd explained to me where to find the supplies, I went off to get them.

I figured I'd give her some time to cool off before I barged in on her. Maybe she was sleeping. Besides, I needed to take care of Eli. I gathered a blood bag from the fridge and the first aid kit from under the sink. With our accelerated healing, I didn't think we'd need much from it, but it was a good thing to have.

After tending to Eli's injuries and allowing him to look at my own, we decided that Delilah had enough time to herself. Eli unlocked the bedroom and cautiously walked inside.

"Shit," he muttered before slamming his fist through the wall.

I ran into the room and looked around. It was empty. "Where is she?" From the look of the room, there hadn't been a struggle, so wherever she'd gone, it had been willingly.

"She must have taken off after I went to get you. Unless—" I could hear the panic welling up in his voice as he raced to his computer set up in the other room.

"Unless what?" I prodded, following him.

"Damnit. I knew I shouldn't have left her alone here. She snuck out while I was on the phone. She must have been in the car when that truck hit me. Someone took her." Eli was barely containing his anger. He pointed to the video feed on the screen. Delilah climbed in the back seat of the car less than a minute before Eli walked out of the safe house.

"This is bad." I started to explain. Since I knew who had her, but didn't know why, it was worse than bad. My imagination ran wild. Images of Delilah being tortured felt like being stabbed in the heart. I wouldn't be able to live with myself if something happened to her. I couldn't go through that again. Not like what had happened to Kat.

"I know," Eli responded. He seemed to understand my feelings, but I wasn't certain he knew how much danger she was in.

"No, you don't. Jones has her. He trained those thugs that attacked you. I'm certain of it. I have no idea how we'll find him or who he's really working for, though." I fought against the hopelessness that threatened to take over.

Then a thought occurred to me. I had taken a phone from the guy I'd killed at my cabin. I pulled it out and handed it to Eli. "Unless this has some clues on it."

Eli took the phone and studied it, not giving away his thoughts. Eli was the best when it came to technology. With him, there is still hope. We will find Delilah. There is no other option. Jones will pay.

CHAPTER 51

Eli

THE PHONE VIK HANDED me was encrypted, which was expected. The encryption wasn't as difficult to break as I had expected, but what I found on the phone once I was in horrified me.

"Where did you get this?" I asked Vik, staring at him.

"From one of the guys who broke into my cabin. I told you that." He seemed annoyed that I had asked for clarification.

"Okay, but how? I'm sure he didn't just hand it over," I prodded, wanting more information.

"I was waiting to tell Delilah first, but I killed him. To survive. I wasn't healing from my injuries and hadn't eaten in hours. I drained him, then stole his phone." Vik's face looked grim. He was a firm believer in never killing a blood source.

"That must have been a difficult choice to make," I replied. His face said that he was shocked at my response. "You know I'm not as pro-life as you are. You did what you had to in order to survive. Trust me, it's fine."

"I doubt Delilah will think so," he countered, lowering his head.

I shook my head at him. "You came back to her. She'll accept that you did what you had to, and it'll be okay. She's more understanding than you give her credit for. When we find her, she can tell you herself."

"Thank you for the kind words. Why did you want to know how I got the phone?" Vik asked, changing the subject back.

I turned away from the computer screen to face him. "It looks like the guy you killed was pretty high up in this organization. It seems odd to me that he was breaking into your house instead of sending people who were below him to do it."

"So you're thinking what I'm thinking?" He looked me in the eyes, and we said in unison, "The Vipers."

"Yeah, but why would they come after Delilah?" I showed him the data I had been collecting since before we had agreed to share Delilah. It was extensive research showing overlaps in specific crimes against both his company and mine.

"Well, from my research, I've found that they picked up Vinny's method of blood sourcing. They've been kidnapping women and selling them to the highest bidder. They've also been arrested recently for selling drugs—both human and vampire." I paused and knew that Vik understood. If they had taken Delilah, it was to sell her to the highest bidder as a blood or sex slave.

Then I continued, "It all seems to be connected. I think the Powder operation is theirs too. I'm not sure if you knew it, but back in the day, they were the biggest drug runners in the city." Understanding crossed his face at my admission.

Vik nodded. "I had heard some of that, but didn't realize how big their operation was. What do they want with Delilah, though?"

I laughed grimly. "Who knows? Maybe it was a random attack, or maybe they're after something bigger and need her to bargain with us. Maybe someone just wants revenge." I hung my head, feeling as defeated as Vik looked.

"Are the Vipers working with vampires now? I thought they were an anti-vamp organization." Vik's question acknowledged my fears. The men who had attacked me were vampires, and they were working for whoever had taken Delilah. There had to be a clue somewhere.

"I didn't think so, but they must be. Something caused this change. We have to find out what it was. Then maybe we'll get a clue about Delilah."

I typed new information into the search windows and had the traffic cams looking for Viper members. If we could pinpoint their headquarters, we could find Delilah. Vik paced the floor as if he was weighing something.

"They took her, brother. There's no reason to sit here and try to figure out the why of it. Besides, our feud is done. Delilah has chosen both of us. It's our job to protect her. Let's find the Vipers and take care of this threat." Vik sat down in one of the office chairs I had in front of the computers.

"Agreed. Delilah is the most important thing. Oh, I nearly forgot," I started, watching him carefully while I spoke. "Delilah and I called your contractor and convinced him to start rebuilding Midnight again. I approved the overage in the budget. Before you object, I'm paying half. For Delilah. I know now isn't the time, but I don't want you to think we're keeping anything from you."

He nodded, wiping a tear from his eye. I'd forgotten how sentimental he was. I told D that he would do anything for her, and I was right. He wouldn't object to a partnership on the bar.

"Partners, then?" He offered his hand with the question. I shook it willingly.

"We can work on the contract once all of this is settled." I offered and he nodded in acceptance.

"Now let's find those bitches," he snarled.

I turned back to the keyboard and continued my search. An email in German caught my attention, and I scowled at the screen. Scott only sent emails in his native tongue when he wanted to be sure I knew it was urgent and private. I read through the email twice before responding. I instructed him to keep an eye on the situation and report back as soon as he had more.

"What's that one about?" Vik asked, trying to read the email from Scott over my shoulder.

"It's nothing. Just business stuff. Don't worry about it." I tried to brush it off.

"You seem awfully upset for it to be just business stuff." Vik accused.

I still needed a location and confirmation that Jones was working with the Vipers. I didn't want to accuse Vik's right-hand man without proof.

"Maybe we should head back to the accident site and see if there are any clues?" I suggested, trying to keep Vik from asking about the message that had me distracted.

"Did that email say something about the wreck being involved?" Vik wasn't that easy to distract after all.

"No, it wasn't about that. I just figured that if D had been in my car when the truck hit it, maybe there's some clue as to which direction they took her." I stood and grabbed my keys, hoping he'd follow me and stop asking questions.

"Fine, but I'm not going to let this go. That email was something important. You're going to tell me." Vik was persistent, but I was determined not to tell him about my suspicions without proof.

CHAPTER 52

Viktor

I COULDN'T TELL WHAT had Eli so irritated. He refused to tell me, so we argued. I thought for a moment he was going to hit me to avoid telling me anything. I knew that wouldn't solve anything, so I decided to find a way around it.

He tried to distract me with the idea of going back to the accident site, but I wasn't giving in that easily. I would keep prodding until he told me what I wanted to know.

"I just want to know what you saw on the monitor that upset you," I said again, waiting for him to finally answer.

"It's nothing. Don't worry about it. My guys will take care of it," he responded, avoiding the question.

"You're lucky I can't read German. Otherwise, I would know what it said myself. I don't know why you must be so stubborn. I'm only trying to help," I growled.

"Look—" he started to reply, but his phone rang. "I have to take this." He answered the phone and walked toward the kitchen. I could still hear him, but he was far enough away that I couldn't hear the person who'd called.

"What did you find?" Eli barked into the phone. He waited a moment while he received a report. A grimace tightened his face and he growled. "That's what I was afraid of."

He paused again while the other person talked. "No, just observe and report. Send me the location. I'll take care of the rest. And for the love of your mother, stay hidden. Do not let them catch you spying. I don't need to lose anyone else tonight. Got it?" He was harsh but the words came out as concerned.

After he hung up, I walked over to him. "Care to share?"

He shrugged and walked back to the computer set up. He punched some keys and the screens changed again. Eli appeared to have gone back to whatever had annoyed him before.

"Are you seriously not going to tell me anything? I thought we were past this. Do you really not trust me at all?" It was hard to keep the hurt out of my voice. I knew that our truce was tenuous, but I thought we were past the worst of the mistrust.

"Look, one of my guys saw something suspicious and he's checking it out. Once I have proof, I'll share it with you. Until then, I don't want to start shit where there's no cause." Eli looked up from the keyboard and looked at me. I could have sworn there was a tear in the corner of his eye.

"So I was right," I muttered, turning away from him.

Why would Jones betray me like this? What had I possibly done to turn him against me? How did I not see it sooner? Was I too trusting of him?

"Damn you, Jones. You son of a bitch. After everything I did for you." I growled to myself, not caring that Eli could hear everything I had just said.

"Wait, you knew? Why didn't you say anything?" Eli asked, still staring at me.

"I didn't know for sure, but I do now. He was the only other person who had my security system codes to the cabin. And he was only one of two besides me who knew about the cabin at all. Now will you tell me what your guy found?" I asked, taking a seat on the couch. I suddenly felt drained.

"I can, if you can get your guys at the precinct to give me access to the cameras around the city," Eli said with a wink. Great, we've turned to blackmail as a way of communication. At this point, I didn't care as long as we were communicating.

I made the call, and within minutes, Eli had police clearance without the use of my gift. I was shocked that his idea worked. But I guess when you can follow the idea of "ask and ye shall receive" literally because of compulsion, it shouldn't be that surprising.

"Okay, your access is in the works. Now tell me what you have on Jones," I growled.

"He's at one of my warehouses right now on the docks with a group of masked thugs. They've broken in and are stealing crates of supplies. Things they'll need to make Powder." Eli looked at me to gauge my reaction.

"That son of a bitch. Well, I guess now we know that we were right about someone being in on it. And about the Powder being connected." I paced the floor, trying to figure out what I could do to help Eli with this part. I got a text from my police contact. "You should have access now."

Once he was tapped into the cams, he could see everything he needed to search for the Vipers and Jones. We needed to keep tabs on them if we were going to find Delilah and bring her home safely.

"I've got something," Eli said, drawing me out of my thoughts.

"What is it?" I asked as I closed the distance between us.

"So your guy gave me DMV access too, which was strange, because you didn't ask him for it. I won't question it, but it did allow me to find a car registered to Phantom Corp.

But why would the Phantoms be working with the Vipers? They're enemies." Eli directed my attention to the screen so I could see for myself.

"I don't know. They've always competed for drug sales in the area. I never thought they'd team up. Especially with the Phantoms being more hidden. The Vipers are known for selling drugs out in the open." I was certain Eli already knew about it, but it helped to get everything out in the open.

"Yes, and most of the Vipers have been arrested on multiple occasions. But the Phantoms usually target upscale parties and private events. Do you think they've combined forces, or are the Phantoms using the Vipers so they have a fall guy?" Eli's speculation made me think. Then I noticed something odd.

"Either way, this is bad. It looks like they own most of the east side of the city. How did we miss this?" I wondered aloud.

"We were so busy fighting each other that we didn't stop to worry about who was controlling the other quadrants," he replied.

"I think it would be a good idea to discover and seek out the head of the west quadrant to broker an alliance before they do." I was even more worried for Delilah now that we had an idea of what we were up against. When something makes the two biggest rival gangs decide to team up, there's a bigger problem than we realized.

"I'm on it," Eli paused before continuing, "We'll find her, Vik. If Jones is responsible, my guys will be able to give us a location soon. They're following him now."

So all I could do was sit and wait. "We should go back to where the fight was. Maybe there are some clues to find Delilah." I insisted.

Eli nodded. "We need to check the traffic cams and see what we're up against first. We need to know what kind of situation we'll be walking into. I don't want to walk into another trap."

I wanted to argue that there was no time, but my phone rang. It was Jones. "It's him. What should I do?" I asked Eli, turning the phone so he could see the display.

"Act like you don't know he's behind it. Just play along with whatever he says." Eli suggested.

Nodding, I answered the call. "Jones. What's going on?" I tried to keep the panic out of my voice and pretend everything was normal.

"If you want her back, you have to find her. It won't be easy. If I find her first, she's dead." I knew Jones well enough to picture him running his hand through his sandy blond hair as he spoke. His dark brown eyes glinting with hate, as I had seen multiple times before. I had never been scared of him before, but that was when he was on my side.

I took a breath, my hands shaking at the thoughts going through my head. He wouldn't hesitate to kill Delilah, especially if he thought it would hurt me.

"What are you talking about?" I tried to stall him and get more information, but he disconnected the call.

"Eli, we have to go. Now. They've hidden her somewhere in the city. If we don't find her, he's going to kill her." We were both moving toward his car before the words left my mouth.

CHAPTER 53

Delilah

I watched carefully as I was carried inside a building. I couldn't help but notice the giant snake that had been tagged on the side of it. I wondered if that meant I had been taken by one of the local gangs. It didn't make sense. I had no money or power. Why would they want me?

Once I was inside, I saw the crates that had been stolen from Eli's warehouse. There were crates with Viktor's logo on them as well. I knew if my guys found me, they'd discover who'd been stealing from them too. I tried to hang as limply as I could from the asshole's shoulder as he carried me through the large front room and into a smaller room behind a set of double doors.

I was dropped onto a thin cot inside a cage before the man kicked me and walked away. I didn't make a sound, and I didn't move. The pain in my stomach had tears running down my face, but I refused to give him the satisfaction of seeing me cry. I guess he knew I was awake the whole time.

I could hear talking but couldn't tell where it was coming from. I strained to hear the conversation.

"Yeah, she's in the cage." The man who'd carried me from the truck spoke in a growl.

"What about Strain and Maxwell?" The voice was familiar, but I couldn't quite place where I had heard it.

"They killed two of our best. I barely got away. They were seriously injured, though. I can send a team to recover the bodies."

The familiar voice growled, "No. You will take care of it yourself. If Strain and Maxwell aren't dead, it's your head. I will not have them coming after me here. Go."

I sat up a little and strained to look around. I was terrified to stand up. I knew that if I wanted any chance of escape, I needed to know where the exits were and how to get this lock open.

As I was studying the lock, I heard sounds of a struggle and imagined that the familiar voice had shoved asshole, making his shoes scrape on the concrete. His steps echoed as he jogged toward the door. I rubbed my hands over my face, wiping away the tears. I was terrified before. Learning how powerful these guys are made it worse.

Eli and Viktor were seriously injured? I wondered if they had managed to get away. I still had no idea where I was or why I had been taken. Instead of giving in to the fear that was trying to take hold of me, I decided to focus on my surroundings. I needed to remember how Eli taught me to relax.

"Focus on five things you can see," he had told me when I started having panic attacks after Uncle Vinny was killed. "List them in your head or out loud." I pictured his blue eyes and that piece of blond hair that always dropped down to cover them. I would reach up and brush it away. Thinking of him helped.

Okay, I can do this. Five things I can see, four things I can smell. I took a deep breath and looked around, sitting up. I wasn't brave enough to stand up. That might draw too much attention. *No, wait—that's not right. Five things I can see, four I can touch, three I can hear, two I can smell, and one I can taste.* I could hear Eli's words in my head.

Five things I could see—three guards with guns hanging around the door, two other cages that are empty, windows along one wall, a table with four chairs in the middle of the room, and a ratty rug on the floor opposite the windows. I wasn't sure if any of it was important, but it did help to calm my mind.

Next, I needed to list four things I could touch. I noticed the bars of the cage, the concrete beneath my feet, the thin cot I sat on, and the musty blanket lying on the cot.

Then three things I can hear. What did I hear? Those two guys had stopped fighting. I listened closer for a moment. I heard footsteps—probably the guards patroling the exits. There was something else. What was that sound? It could be a generator. I focused more, pushing everything else away. It was definitely a generator, and I could hear a truck idling outside. That meant I was near an outer wall.

Two things I could smell. This was more difficult. The scents here all seemed to mingle together. I tried anyway and managed to notice stale coffee, and something I couldn't quite figure out. The unknown scent was sweet but metallic, almost like blood. That thought made my heart race again. What if they'd brought me here to drain me? What if I was going to be their dinner?

That thought freaked me out so much that I couldn't remember the rest of the calming steps Eli had showed me. My mind refused to stop showing me every bad thing it could come up with that might happen to me.

A man came to my cage and opened the door. I didn't move. I knew I couldn't escape yet. I had no idea where I was or which direction to go if I tried.

"Come on. It's time to go." He spoke quietly, almost as if he didn't want to do this. When I didn't move immediately, he gestured toward the door where the guards with guns had turned their attention toward me. I nodded and stood to follow him.

When I got to the door, he put a black cloth sack over my head so I couldn't see. I knew it was pointless to ask why. He didn't want me to see where we were going or where I was.

He shoved me along until I felt the cool breeze blowing on my skin. We were outside. Where was he taking me? My heart started racing again, but I was too scared to speak. The man kept shoving me, making me walk forward, then grabbing my arm and turning me in the direction he wanted me to go.

He pushed me into a car. "Stay here," he ordered. I heard a door close, then another opened and closed. I guessed he got into the driver's seat because the car started to move. I wasn't sure how long or how far we drove, but when the car stopped, I heard a door open and slam. Fear froze me to the seat. I clutched the cool leather and prayed that Vik and Eli would find me. It was the only thing keeping me from sobbing.

The door next to me opened and the bag was taken off my head. I took an automatic deep breath of air, searching the world around me.

"Go inside and sit away from the window. If Strain or Maxwell finds you first, you lose. They will be killed." His gruff words terrified me. He was tall and lanky but I could tell he was stronger than he looked. His dark hair was greasy and he smelled of stale coffee and cigarettes.

"What if they don't find me first?" I asked, my voice shaking. He didn't answer, instead shoving me toward the door of a deli.

My heart raced as I walked inside. I glanced around the room for someone who could help me. I had no idea if any of these people were vampires or had the resources to fight against the men who'd taken me. The faces were a blur against the tears in my eyes. I knew that even if I did exactly what I was told, my guys weren't safe. Which meant I wasn't safe. I fought against the terror taking hold of me.

As instructed, I had taken a seat at a small table that was near the windows without being right in front of them, with my back to the door in case Eli or Viktor managed to drive past. I didn't doubt their ability to hunt me down for a moment. I knew I didn't have much time to figure this out. There was a commotion behind me, and I turned to glance over my shoulder. *What is Jones doing here?*

I almost held up a hand to wave when I saw the gun in his hand. *Did Viktor send him to find me?* Wouldn't that be just like Viktor to send his right-hand man to hunt me down for running off? Did he and Eli think I ran away? I sank lower in my chair, trying to hide. Hopefully he would just leave if he didn't see me. That idea was lost when he started shooting. I stood up and turned toward him.

"Hey, it's okay. I'm right here," I said, thinking that somehow him shooting up this deli was because he was searching for me. Jones turned his attention toward me and snarled. He hadn't been looking for me after all. Or maybe he had. Something told me that I should have stayed hidden.

"I guess Petey decided to make things easy for me." He bared his fangs and pulled the trigger. I didn't have any time to even think of moving out of the way. The bullet impacted and I felt it tear through my stomach. It burned like I was on fire, and I collapsed to the ground. The pain was unbearable. I screamed.

Suddenly it was as if everything around me was going in slow motion. I pressed my hands to my bleeding stomach and tried to look around the room. I heard the faint clicking of fangs extending and realized that most of the patrons here had to be vampires. I couldn't see any way that I would survive this. I wondered if Viktor knew that Jones wasn't loyal. That was a strange thought to have after being shot. I got shot. The room started to spin, and I dropped to the floor on my knees.

I tried to stay awake and focus on everyone around me, but it was impossible. The room was spinning, and everything was moving so slowly. I felt myself falling but couldn't stop it. I could hear voices but couldn't tell what they were saying. I knew that I was losing too much blood and if I didn't make it to a hospital soon, I wouldn't make it.

I thought about Viktor and Eli as I lay there, on the floor of a deli on the west side, bleeding to death. They had no idea where I was or that I'd been shot. Viktor had no idea that Jones had gone rogue. Or did he? Had Viktor sent the man to find me? Was this what he'd wanted? The thoughts swam through my head as I bounced in and out of consciousness.

I barely felt it as a strong pair of arms scooped me up and carried me from the deli. I couldn't really feel anything at all. The voices weren't familiar but encouraged me to stay with them. The broad chest I was pressed against was solid and comforting. The thumping heart against my ear calmed me. I felt a hand gently caress my face and wipe tears from my eyes. The pain wasn't as bad now.

I wondered if that meant I wasn't injured as badly as I had thought, or if it meant that I was dying. *Hmm, so this is what death feels like.* Either way, I was glad for the reprieve from the burning. I thought the strong arms placed me in a car, but I couldn't be sure. All I knew was that suddenly the broad, strong chest I was leaning against was replaced with the supple leather of a vehicle of some sort.

Nothing about what was happening to me was familiar. I tried to focus enough to see who was driving but couldn't. I thought I saw a pair of green eyes peek at me through a mane of red curls, but then the car hit a bump and the world went black.

CHAPTER 54

Eli

LETTING VIKTOR DRIVE HAD been a mistake. He treated my Porsche as if it were a sedan, barely hitting sixty on the city street. I wondered when he lost his edge. When I finally got the car's computer to work, I shouted directions at him, and he took them at a sluggish pace.

As pissed as I was about his driving, I knew it was most likely because he was worried about Delilah. I was terrified that something had happened to her. Especially if the Vipers and Phantoms were both working with Jones. It would be nearly impossible to keep Delilah safe from the psycho bitches. That wouldn't stop us from trying.

"Take a right here," I ordered, hoping that Vik could make the turn without wrecking my car.

"Got it," he responded, turning down the street and gunning it. This was more like it.

"Okay, you'll have to slow down after the next intersection. Scott said they're on that block. That means she's close," I explained. I was already searching the street for signs of her. Some of the buildings were tagged as Viper hangouts. Others had the more subtle mark of the Phantoms. It seemed as if this part of the city was overrun with gang activity.

I heard gunshots and yelled at Vik. "There! Pull over!" I spotted chaos at a local deli. Vik pulled over and we both jumped out, running toward the deli. There seemed to be some sort of commotion going on. People were running away and screaming.

"Is that Jones?" I pointed to the man who was fleeing the scene. Vik nodded and raced off after him, leaving me to search for Delilah. She was close, I could smell her.

Something was wrong. If she was close enough for me to smell, I should have been able to sense her emotions too. I stopped for a second to focus. Nothing. But her scent was still there. I walked into the deli, where chaos seemed to have taken over.

There were gunshot victims all over the place. I followed Delilah's scent to a table near the front window. Then I saw it.

The puddle of blood on the floor was the source of her scent. I knew it before I dropped to my knees next to the blood and dipped a finger into it. I licked the maroon goo from my finger and shivered. It was hers. She must have been shot. But where was her body? There was no way she lived through losing this much blood.

I glanced around the room, but no one was even paying attention to me. The police hadn't arrived, and neither had emergency services. Whoever had taken her might have done it to save her life. None of the people here were coherent enough to interrogate.

I struggled to fight the tears that wanted to fall. I had vowed to protect her, and I had failed. Delilah was gone because of me. There was no way to go back and fix this. But maybe there was a chance she was still alive. I had to hold out hope.

I growled and tore out of the deli, chasing after Vik. If Jones knew where Delilah was, we needed him alive. I ran up to see Jones on top of Vik, about to stab him in the heart. I grabbed him from behind, restraining him to my chest.

Before I could speak, Vik was on his feet and thrusting his hand in our enemy's chest. When he pulled his hand away, I dropped Jones' lifeless body at Vik's feet. A wave of jealousy hit me. I had wanted to kill the bastard.

"I wish I'd been the one to do it, but I'm glad it was you." I pointed to his hand and cocked an eyebrow at him. It was covered in blood and held a red, nearly softball sized blob that dripped onto the floor. The same red stained his suit and dripped from his hand. This guy was a little psycho after all. I was impressed.

Covered in Jones' blood, his eyes wild with adrenaline, Vik didn't seem to hear anything I had said. "Where's Delilah?" He looked around, sniffing the air as I had done.

"Gone. I only found her blood." I responded. I knew he was in shock, but I needed him to focus.

"What? I don't understand." He looked at the bloody organ in his hand.

"She's gone," I repeated. "Not dead—maybe, but not here. It looks like she was injured. Probably shot by Jones, from the way things look. Someone must have taken her to the hospital. We'll check them out and let the ERs know that we're her family and that she's missing. They'll call us if she comes in." I filled him in as I guided him back to the car.

I climbed into the driver's seat of the Porsche as Vik got in the passenger's side, still holding Jones' heart.

"Are you keeping that?" I asked as I started the car.

"Damn straight I am. That fucker tried to kill our girl. She's gonna have this as a souvenir. Now we must find her," he responded. He didn't even need proof that Jones had done it. Honestly, neither did I.

"I just hope it's not too late," I said as we sped away.

CHAPTER 55

Delilah

EPILOGUE

As I lay in the backseat of the car, feeling my life fade away, I took in my surroundings. If this was the end, I would remember my guys and notice every detail.

The interior of the car was gray, the leather seat was cold against my skin. It was slick from the blood I'd been losing steadily since getting shot.

I faintly remembered an arm in front of my face. "Drink, a chroí. It'll help." Drink what? From his arm? I opened my mouth to ask, but the arm was on my lips before I could speak.

I felt something dripping into my mouth. It tasted sweet and metallic. Blood. My guys had mentioned that vampire blood could heal humans. But why was this stranger trying to help me?

I passed out again as the darkness took me under. I knew I was getting close to the end. The vampire blood hadn't worked.

I imagined Eli and Viktor being with me, comforting me in my final moments. I pictured Viktor's stern expression when he didn't get his way, and Eli's teasing grin when he was messing with Viktor. I knew they'd had problems, but I was certain that losing me would bring them back together. At least I could take comfort in them not being alone after I was gone.

I pictured what our life could have been like if I hadn't been shot. Happiness would have been great. Pain shot through me again and I opened my eyes.

Staring back at me was a gorgeous man with red hair and green eyes. He must have been an angel. He smiled at me sadly as he spoke. "I'm sorry, mo chroí. You're not going to make it." His fangs clicked as the world went black again.

BLOOD LOST

VAMPIRES AT MIDNIGHT
BOOK TWO

M.P. STARKWEATHER

Chapter 1

Declan

I punched the dashboard, leaving a fist-sized dent. *Damnit, Dec, get your shit to-gether.* I knew that berating myself would do no good. Neither would destroying my car. Besides, I'd have to bribe Kayden to fix the damage I'd already done. I didn't have time to worry about that now. Once she was safe, I could deal with all of it if that was even possible. If Steph could save her. I kept playing the scene from the deli in my head.

I should have taken Jones out the moment he stepped inside. Everyone knew Maxwell Industries' second in command. For the past year or so, he had been different somehow. I hadn't been around him a lot, but something had changed. I didn't trust him. I wanted to talk to Viktor about it, but something came up every time we scheduled a meeting. I began to wonder if he was avoiding me. Hell, he probably didn't even get my messages.

And Eli Strain was just as bad. Seven canceled meetings. His people blamed some personal issues he was having. At least they gave me that much of a reason. Viktor's people just canceled. I finally gave up on getting a meeting with either of them. I had wanted to form an alliance and get their help cleaning up the city. It seemed they weren't too concerned with that.

I wasn't even sure if they knew I had taken over the west side of the city. I didn't blame either of them. The bombings had taken a toll on everyone. It seemed like there wasn't a safe neighborhood. Besides, getting the gangs under control had been my priority. My anonymity helped with that but seemed to get in the way of making broader plans.

But when Jones had walked in, I was caught up staring at the pretty little dark-haired girl. She looked terrified, and I tried to figure out what had her so spooked. I would have

181

thought she was waiting for someone, but she kept glancing at the door as if she was terrified someone would find her. What was she hiding from? Or who?

I didn't even see the gun until it was too late. I smelled her blood before I realized that the pop I had heard was a gun being fired. Of course, I had to scoop her up and try to save her. There was no other option. I had no idea who she was, but her scent was enticing. It was all I could do to drop her into the back seat of my SUV and force myself into the driver's seat. I wanted to taste her so badly. I felt my fangs click into place the moment her blood spilled.

I trusted my guys to hunt the errand boy from Maxwell Industries down for causing chaos in my zone. He wouldn't last long out there. Now I just had to focus on saving this girl. There was no way I was going to let her die. Not on my watch. Once that was taken care of, I would talk with Viktor. He needed to know that this type of behavior would not be tolerated. Part of me was jealous that my guys would get to end the prick who'd hurt my girl. *What the fuck am I thinking? I don't even know her, but I'm staking a claim? She might not even survive. If she does, she might not want me.*

I growled as I drove toward my base. I slowed down once to try to heal her myself. Maybe if I had acted sooner, it would have worked. I couldn't get her to drink my blood. What little made it in her mouth spilled out on the seat when I hit a bump. Then she lost consciousness again. That was when I'd called my team. I had medics on standby, and they were prepared for anything. It pained me to hand her over to them. I wanted to be with her.

"Dec, we'll do what we can. It looks bad," Stephanie said as Matt carried the girl back to the operating room.

"Let me know if she gets worse," I barked. The moment they walked away, I started pacing the floor. What options did I have if they couldn't get the bullet out and stop the bleeding? There may not be another way. Could I really be considering this? Without giving her a choice? It seemed almost cruel how selfish I was being. And for what? I didn't even know who she was.

I heard the alarms from the operating room and raced in, my instincts taking over. "What's going on?" I heard myself say as I reached for the unconscious girl, gripping her hand in mine. Steph should have screamed at me for entering her sterile field. The fact that she didn't say a word when she saw me told me what was happening before she had a chance to speak. The girl wasn't going to make it. She was going to die. Unless I turned her. Almost as an afterthought, she spoke.

"She's coding. I don't think we got to her in time. She's lost too much blood. I'm sorry," Stephanie was shoving Matt out of my way. It was as if she knew what was about to happen and didn't want to stop me.

"What's he doing?" Matt asked, trying to get around Steph to stop me. She shook her head and pushed him against the wall. "He can't do this. We have laws for a reason." Before he could talk me out of it, Steph clamped her hand over his mouth.

I pulled the dying girl to my chest, taking in a deep breath of her scent. This wasn't a decision to be made lightly, but there was no time to debate the pros and cons or even consider what she would want. If I were going to save her, it had to be now. My eyes met Stephanie's, and she nodded slightly, encouraging me. My fangs clicked into place once again, and I bit down on the soft skin of the girl's neck.

It had been a long time since I'd tried to transform anyone. But it was like riding a bike. I felt my venom flow into her as I tasted the sweetness of her blood on my tongue. By the time I released her, I could feel both Matt and Stephanie's eyes boring into me. I realized that I had held her to me for longer than I should have. Fortunately, she had already been getting a transfusion, so there was little chance of me making things worse. I gently placed the girl back on the bed, avoiding their eyes. I wiped the blood from my mouth, adjusted my boner, and walked out of the room without another word.

I stormed through the waiting area and locked myself in the bathroom. I knew that Stephanie would let me know if it had worked. And that they would keep the girl sedated until I was ready for her to wake up if she survived. If she survived. There was a chance her body would reject the change. If hers didn't, we would have a lot to deal with.

A newly turned vamp would have to adjust to the hunger, or blood lust would take over. She would need guidance the same as I needed answers. I hoped that saving her wasn't a mistake. I was on the verge of losing control the moment my fangs touched her. And now, here I was jerking off in the hospital bathroom because I had tasted this girl. Talk about losing control. Once I settled myself, I hunted Stephanie down. I was sure I didn't want the lecture I would get when this was over. What I'd done was reckless. What's worse was that I would do it again, without hesitation. That idea scared me.

"How is she?" I asked, unable to meet her eyes. I was surprised that the lecture didn't come.

She touched my arm to make me look at her. The kindness in her blue eyes shocked me. I was confident that my lack of control would be a problem. "She's going to be fine. I have her sedated but can bring her out in the morning. You can sit with her if you'd like. I know you won't be leaving anytime soon." Stephanie pointed me toward a private recovery room, where the patient appeared to be resting comfortably even with the restraints.

"Her wound?" I couldn't bear to look. She walked past me and lifted the hospital gown. The girl's stomach looked as if she'd never been shot.

"As I said, she's going to be fine, physically. Mentally might be different, but we'll find out tomorrow." Stephanie gestured to a recliner that had probably been brought in just for me.

"Did I do the right thing?" I hated that the girl didn't have a choice in this, almost as much as I would hate myself for ending her if she didn't want the hassles of her new life. I stared at my best friend, waiting for her to tell me that I was the monster I feared becoming.

"We'll find out soon enough. Don't beat yourself up over this, Dec. You saved her life." Stephanie turned and walked out, leaving me alone with the newly turned vamp.

I pulled the chair closer to the bed then sat in it. "What am I going to do about you? It seems you've already gotten under my skin. And I don't even know your name." I knew the dangers of getting attached, but there was something about this girl that drew me in.

Even in her unconscious state, I was pulled to her in a way that I couldn't explain. In my mind, I had already started referring to her as *mo chroí*, which meant my heart. I didn't even know her name, but I felt like this girl was a part of me.

When I thought she was dying, I felt like I couldn't breathe. It was like the world was imploding. I wasn't one for poetry, but I finally understood all the broody, depressing stuff that Stephanie had shared with me over the years. I felt as if my existence would end if this girl died. I was anxious for her to wake up, so I could learn her name and make sure that she didn't hate me for the selfish thing I had done.

I watched her sleep, wallowing in the guilt of what I'd done, yet knowing that if I had it all to do again, I wouldn't change any of it. I would do anything to protect her and prove I was good enough for her.

CHAPTER 2

Eli

IT WAS HARD ENOUGH keeping myself in control after Delilah disappeared, much less chasing after Viktor and trying to stop him from killing everyone who didn't give him answers. I raced after him as he returned to the deli again to question witnesses. I caught up with him at the car and somehow convinced him to let me drive.

"I don't know why you think the same people who were there the night she was shot will be there again. It doesn't make sense. The deli is probably closed for repairs anyway." I knew it was ridiculous to indulge him, but I wasn't about to let him drive anywhere in his condition.

Vik hadn't showered or shaved since Delilah disappeared. He was getting more erratic and frantic in his need to search. "Someone saw what happened. We just have to find them so we can find her."

"Maybe if you had let me question Jones before you killed him, we'd know where she went." It wasn't fair to blame him, but I couldn't help it. Neither of us had stopped since that night. We had barely fed, and there had been no time for sleep. We were on edge, and it was only a matter of time before we were fighting again.

"You think I don't know that now? I'm not an idiot. I should have been calmer that night. And now she's gone. We have to find her." His guilt squeezed at his insides, and I had to put up another mental block to avoid absorbing his emotions.

I parked the car in front of the deli, and Vik got out before I even turned it off. By the time I made it inside, he had a small man with a name tag claiming he was the manager up against the wall, holding him a couple of inches off the floor. "Vik, let him go. I'm sure if he knows anything, he'll tell us." I encouraged as I put my hand on his arm. He slowly lowered the human to his feet.

When Vik removed his fingers from the man's throat, I raised an eyebrow. He shivered and shook his head. "I told you already. I don't know her or anything about her. I saw her that night. There were so many people in here. I don't know what happened." I could taste his fear and Vik's rage. I knew that this would be the end for the human if I didn't step in.

I turned to Vik, placing myself in front of the man. "You see? He doesn't know where she is. Let's keep looking." I tried to escort him out of the deli, but Vik wouldn't budge.

"No. He knows something. Someone in here knows something! I'm going to make them talk." Vik was losing it fast. It was as if he'd stopped trying to control the anger and was instead channeling it to make himself feel stronger. I wished that was the answer but knew it would get us nowhere.

I gestured for the man to get out of the way, and he took off running to the back. If this didn't work, I'd be paying to rebuild the deli. I'd have to find out who owned it. I took a breath, then raised my prosthetic fist and punched Vik in the side of the head. He turned to look at me as the pain registered, then fell to the floor unconscious.

I dug a bill from my pocket and dropped it on the counter. "For your troubles." I nodded at the man as I slung Vik over my shoulder and carried him out to the car. I zip-tied his hands together and tossed him in the backseat. I couldn't take a chance that he'd wake up and want to fight while I was driving. This was all becoming too much. I headed back to my office to see any new leads. My receptionist looked at me funny when I walked past with Vik tossed over my shoulder, but I shook my head, and she didn't ask. I dropped him on the couch, cut the zip tie off his wrists, and sat at my computer. While he was knocked out, I reviewed leads that my team had been running down.

It was strange for me to be the one in control while Vik went psycho. I was not too fond of it, but it was necessary. I had learned a lot about power since Vik, and I had our falling out. Sadly, things were more manageable when we lost Kat. At least we had a body to bury. We knew that she was dead.

With Delilah, we had searched non-stop for three days before I gave in to exhaustion today. Vik was ready to go again as soon as he woke up.

"We need to be out there searching for her." He was insistent. I sensed his desperation, probably because I felt it too. We needed to find her. "She's out there, alone and scared."

"Look, just take a break. We'll relax for a minute. Get something to eat, then come at it with fresh eyes." We'd been at each other's throats since this began. I needed a minute to refocus. I had lost track of how many fistfights we'd had over the past three days. My emotions were out of control, and I knew I wouldn't be any help if I didn't figure out how to reign it in. I couldn't find the words to tell Vik that, though.

"I don't want a break. I want Delilah. She needs us. How can you give up on her so easily? Are you that weak?" Vik stomped back and forth across the floor in my office while he yelled at me. He tossed out the insult as he marched toward me.

I took a deep breath and tried to cage the violence that was building inside of me. "I'm not giving up. I know that she needs us. We're still looking. I have my best guys on it. If they find any clues, we'll be the ones following up. Just take a minute to rest. You're no good to her if you've worked yourself into a frenzy," I tried reasoning with him. There was very little chance that this conversation wouldn't end in Vik and I trying to kill each other again.

"It's not enough. We need to find her now. There's no time to relax or take a break." I could tell from his tone that he was feeling helpless. I had to block his emotions, or we'd kill each other. He was so angry with me right now. "It's like you don't even care. Was she just some conquest to you?" His words struck a nerve, and my wall fell.

My fist struck his jaw, and he flew backward into the wall. Logically, I knew Vik wasn't the enemy, but with my own emotions on edge and his thrown on top, I was going to rip his head off his shoulders. Vik pulled himself out of the wall I had slammed him into, leaving a hole. He rushed me and landed a punch. I felt my nose break again as blood poured from it.

Rage took over, and I grabbed him by the throat, lifting him from the ground. I knew that I would kill him if I didn't stop myself. Would I be able to face Delilah if I did? That thought alone prevented me from completely crushing his windpipe. I lowered him to the floor, still holding him by his throat. Vik gasped for air and tried to get my prosthetic hand to release him.

"Are you finished?" I waited for his response before I let him go. He still couldn't speak, but he nodded. I opened my fingers, and Vik fell to his knees.

He stood and punched the wall a moment later, leaving a fist-sized hole next to the last one from an hour ago. "I know. I can't help it. I need to find her. We don't know what Jones did with her."

"And beating holes in my office is helping you find out?" I knew I shouldn't bait him, but honestly, I was as pissed as he was. And him punching holes in my office wasn't helping my mood. A part of me blamed him for not realizing that Jones was working against him, and another blamed him for not giving me the chance to question the traitor about what had happened. I understood the desire to rip the man's heart out when we realized that he'd shot Delilah. I just wished I had been the one to do it.

Vik stopped and stared at me for a moment, obviously realizing how close I was coming to losing control again. "I'm sorry. You know I'll pay for it. I'm not used to feeling so helpless." His voice was soft and sad. I'd never heard him sound so lost.

The raw emotion in his voice broke me. I crossed the room and pulled him into my arms. It was an awkward hug that we both needed. Neither of us wanted to let go, trying to hold on to our girl by holding each other. A knock at the door had us jumping away from each other.

"Come in," I called as Vik stepped away and straightened his suit. I could have sworn he wiped his eyes, but he turned to look out the window, so I couldn't be sure.

One of the interns, whose name I couldn't remember, walked in with a folder. He looked around the room at the damage and gulped. "I was asked to bring you this, Sir." He handed the folder over and walked out of my office, not waiting for a reply.

"What is it?" Vik walked over to the desk, where I had just opened the folder. There were pages of transcribed interviews inside. Each page had notes detailing a sighting of Delilah. I knew better than to take it at face value, but Vik and I would have to check them all out just to be sure.

"Leads. We'll have to check each one out to see if any of them lead to Delilah," I replied, grabbing my keys from the desk as I closed the folder and walked toward the door. I didn't have to ask Vik to follow; I knew he was as ready to get back out on the streets as I was.

CHAPTER 3

Delilah

I STARTED TO PULL myself from the darkness. A strange feeling grabbed me. I'm not sure what it was—pain, hunger, thirst—some sort of craving and the desperation to feed it. I can't feel my heartbeat, and it scares me. I tried to move, but the darkness wouldn't let go. I was trapped. Panic took over, and I cried out, only to find my voice muted by the inky black. What happened to me? Where was I? Did I die?

I lost the battle once more as the darkness pulled me under. Images started flashing through my mind. People, places, what seemed like important events, but I couldn't figure out who they were or why they felt important. Blue eyes, brown eyes, my name on their lips, but I couldn't understand what was being said. None of it made sense.

Another flash, and I saw a man with a gun before a sharp pain hit me. My shirt turned crimson just above my waistband and the crippling pain seared through me again. I remembered this moment. I'd been shot. But why? Who was that man? I had no idea what I could have done to deserve being shot like that. Oh, no. I was dying. There was so much blood. There's no way I could survive that. This was what dying felt like. My throat felt so dry.

Wait—who do those green eyes belong to? It didn't matter that I couldn't remember. Somewhere deep inside came a growl in response to the images. *Mine.* The growl came each time I saw those eyes. But how were they all mine? Three sets of eyes, three different colors, three different faces. Yet I had claimed them all.

The man with green eyes had tried to save me. His red hair tumbled down in his face when he picked me up. It looked so soft; I wanted to run my fingers through it. He carried me to his car and drove away. I could still feel the cool leather against my damp skin. I shivered at the memory of the cold sweat that had drenched me as I lay on the floor of the diner waiting to die. The green-eyed man had tried to give me something, his arm, I think, and he kept saying, "Drink, mo chroí." I had no idea what *mo chroí* meant, although it seemed like he was trying to help me. I tried to do what he commanded, but my body wouldn't cooperate. Something metallic touched my tongue just before I passed out. It tasted strange yet familiar. A warm feeling spread through me, and I wondered if I would survive. It was short-lived, with the pain returning moments later. I knew that I had to fight.

Each time I fought my way out, I felt the darkness drag me back. Something felt different this time. I looked down at my hand, and someone was holding it. His long red hair covered his face, but somehow I knew he was mine, even though I couldn't see his eyes. I felt it inside me. I wanted to wake him, to look into his eyes and ask who I was. Before I had a chance, that craving hit again. I wanted something. No, I needed it. But what was the thing I was craving? What would satiate this need burning inside of me? I wasn't sure, but I could smell it. I needed to follow the smell. I felt almost feral in my need to find where the odor was coming from. It was intoxicating and drew me out of bed I'd been lying in. Something was wrong. I couldn't get up. I was groggy, and the room started to spin.

I tried to scream again, but the darkness swallowed me whole. I fought against myself, trying to wake up. I needed to get out of this bed before I lost myself. The more I tried to pull myself out of the dark, the more I realized that something was wrong. I didn't want to die. I wanted to go home. Where was home? Who was I? I tried to search through my few memories to figure it out.

I should be in pain. My stomach should be on fire like it was right after I got shot. I'm not ready to die. I prayed that something would happen to save me. Suddenly, I walked through a dense fog, trying to find my way back. Something was hiding in the mist. I got the feeling it was dark, something sinister that wanted to claim me. I ran into a man with dark hair who grabbed me. I tugged out of his grip and sprinted. I heard him call after me and wondered what it meant. "Myshka." While I was looking over my shoulder to see if he followed, I slammed into something dense. I felt arms around me again and whipped my head around. Somehow I knew the blue eyes I was staring into. "I've got you, Love."

"Who are you? Who am I?" I tried to ask, but he faded along with the fog. I was standing in front of a door. Would this door take me back? As I thought the question, a dark red substance started to run from the top of the door. Instinctively, I stepped forward and touched it. Sticky, thick liquid coated my fingertips. It smelled familiar, like the metallic substance the green-eyed man had wanted me to drink. But he had put his arm against my lips. It didn't make sense. He couldn't have been holding something if it was his arm against my mouth. Unless...had he tried to make me...drink his blood?

The thought shook me, and I took a step backward. Was that blood coating the door? I felt as if I were going crazy at this point. Dying was a strange experience; nothing at all like books and movies had described it. I didn't feel any pain, but my mind was so scattered. I was lost and disconnected. "I might as well get this over with," I said aloud as I stepped up to the door and gripped the handle, letting the blood coat my hand. I turned the knob, wondering if the door would be locked. It opened freely, and I walked through.

A bright light stole my vision for a moment. I repeatedly blinked to clear my eyes. I felt strange again, like that craving from before was back. I could smell the thing I desired, and it had me sitting up to follow it. As I sat up, I realized that I hadn't been dreaming of a red-haired man who held my hand while I slept. He was sitting right beside me with his head lying on his arm and his other hand holding mine. I hated to wake him, but I wouldn't be able to get up unless he moved. And I needed to get up. I had to find that smell. It was a desperate yearning that I couldn't argue with.

"Excuse me," I whispered, leaning down toward his ear. The man's head popped up, and I moved my face to avoid having my nose broken. "I'm sorry, I didn't mean to scare you."

"Mo chroí, you're awake. How do you feel?" He pulled out his phone and typed something without letting go of my hand. Then he lifted his face, so his eyes met mine. I had seen those eyes before. Those were the eyes in my dream. My soul screamed, *Mine.*

"I need to get up. There's something over there. I don't know how to explain, but I need it. Please, will you help me?" I decided to keep my claim to myself for now. I had no idea who this man was, much less who I was. It would be good to have those answers before telling people that they belong to me now. The thought of that made me laugh, and the man looked at me with his head cocked sideways.

"Someone will bring what you need. Before they get here, we need to talk." His dancing green eyes turned dark. I could tell this would be serious.

"What is it?" I braced for whatever horrible news he could have to share.

"You were shot, and you were dying," he began, pausing to see my reaction. "I did what was necessary to save you. I hope you don't hate me for it."

"What did you do? I feel fine except for this tingling in my throat and the weird craving." I had no idea what he was trying to imply. Had he donated a kidney or something?

"That tingling and craving are connected. You need to feed to complete the transition. Steph is bringing some blood now."

"Blood? I need to feed to complete the transition. What does that mean?" I could feel the fear gripping my chest, but my heart wasn't racing. It was as if my body remained calm while my mind panicked.

"It means I've turned you into a vampire. There was no other way to save your life. I'm sorry. I would have preferred giving you a choice in the matter, but you were dying." He sounded as if his remorse was eating him alive.

This man saved my life. I leaned forward as I pulled his hand, encouraging him to come closer. He hesitated, then did what I had silently requested. When he was close enough, I wrapped my free hand around his neck and pulled him to me, pressing my lips to his. I kissed him as if I owed him my life because I did. The moment our lips touched, my mind screamed my claim on him at me again.

He pulled away gently and brushed a dark curl from my face. "I don't even know your name."

"That makes two of us," I admitted before flopping back on the bed. I felt so strange. I was exhausted, but at the same time, I felt stronger than I had ever been. My vision was crisper, and I could smell things that I had never noticed before. Something inside of me felt right—as if this was what I was meant to be.

Before he could respond to my admission, the door swung open, and a woman walked in. She was short and thin. Her light brown hair was cut in a spiky pixie that brought out the green and brown in her hazel eyes. "I think you might want this," she said and handed me a bag with a straw poking out of it. I stared at the blood bag in my hand. It didn't take any encouragement for me to bring the straw to my lips and drain it.

"I brought a second one, just in case. Here, Dec; I'll let you handle it. I'm sure our patient is feeling a little weird about people watching her eat." The woman's smile was kind, and I liked her immediately.

"Thanks, Steph," the man responded as she left. He turned to me and handed over the second bag, then watched as I gulped it down too. "Slow down a little. You're going to feel like you need more when you finish that one. It's normal. We'll work through it."

I stopped when half the bag was gone. "How much do I need? Is there not enough? Who are you? Where am I?" The questions fell out of me in a rush. I felt out of control again, and this time it wasn't because of the craving. He looked at me and smiled.

He held out his right hand and waited for me to put mine in it. "I'm Declan Roarke, and you're at my home. There's plenty of blood, don't worry. Generally, two bags will keep the craving under control for a day or so in a newly turned vamp."

CHAPTER 4

Viktor

I wasn't handling Delilah's disappearance well. I felt as if I were losing my mind more and more the longer she was away. I knew that there would be another bloodbath, like when I was first turned if I didn't pull myself together. I couldn't let that happen again. I'd been able to cover up my involvement and kept that secret hidden all these years. I couldn't go through that again. I needed to find Delilah. That was the only way I would genuinely regain control.

Eli had been playing peacekeeper for the past few days. I had no idea how he managed it. Our roles would have been reversed in the past, with me trying to reign him in. There had been so many times in our human days when he'd gone entirely psycho to protect his family, and I had been the one to clean up the mess. I wondered if he understood me better since taking on my usual job in our relationship.

I wanted to rip him in half when he stopped me from killing that guy at the deli. I needed answers. I knew that the only way to make people talk to us was to scare them into it. If I had killed that guy, someone else would have told us what we'd wanted to know. Instead, Eli knocked me out and dragged me back to his office.

Our next lead had us going to the East side of the city. I wasn't convinced that we would find anything useful in Phantom territory, but I went along. What else was I going to do? I refused to sit around and wait to find out who had Delilah.

While Eli drove, I contacted the contractor to check on his progress with Midnight. I needed to make sure the rebuild was on schedule. We'd been set for the grand opening just before the bombing. After, the entire building had to be torn down and completely rebuilt. I trusted Mike to keep his crew on task, but I wanted an update.

Before I could dial Mike's number, my phone rang. "Jane? Is something wrong?" I hoped that Jones' replacement had good news. It wasn't likely, but I had her assemble a team to comb my part of town, looking for clues about Delilah's disappearance.

"Mr. Maxwell, we haven't found any sign of her yet," she began. I didn't get a chance to ask why she'd called when she continued speaking. "I found something down by the docks, though. I thought I'd run it by you and see what you want to do about it."

"What is it?" I didn't have the heart to tell her that I really didn't care. Without Delilah, nothing else mattered.

"We found a portable Powder operation, Sir. It was abandoned, but we ran samples anyway to ensure we knew what we were dealing with. The Powder is poisoned. If it gets distributed, we'll have a lot of dead vamps on our hands." She seemed concerned, and I knew I should probably do something about it.

"Let me discuss it with my partner, and I'll get back to you. If you find anything else, call me immediately." I disconnected the phone and stared out the car window. Why should I care if a bunch of addict vamps died because of their drug of choice? Well, if they were citizens of my zone, I should care. At the moment, I didn't. I stared out the window, ignoring Eli's attempts to get me to talk. I saw a girl with long dark curls turn a corner. "Eli! Turn here. I just saw her walking down 5th!"

"What? Are you sure?" He asked but turned to follow my directions anyway. "I don't see her. Which way?" We had sped down the empty half of the street, then Eli slammed on the breaks to crawl past the crowd.

"I don't see her now." I punched the dash. Was I hallucinating again? Would this be like when I swore I saw Delilah destroying my home at the cabin? Of course, it wasn't her. This probably wasn't either. I felt my sanity slip away a little more. I couldn't tell Eli that I had imagined it. He would lock me up, and I'd never find her.

"It's okay, Vik. We'll keep looking. What was that call about?" Leave it to Eli to change the subject to calm me down.

"Jane said something about poisoned Powder being manufactured at the docks. If it gets out, a lot of vampires will die." I couldn't believe my tone. I had made the statement so matter-of-factly as if it didn't matter that people were in danger.

Eli stopped the car and pulled out his phone. I didn't have to ask if he was sending an email to Scott with Jane's contact info. He would have them coordinate their efforts and assign a team to deal with the Powder issue. At this point, I felt like Eli was running my corporation as well as his own. The longer we sat there, the more guilt ate at my insides. "We need to find her. We aren't doing enough. There has to be something we're missing."

"Vik, we're doing everything we can. People have to rest. You can't expect everyone to go for this many days straight without a break. It's not healthy." Eli tried to calm me down again, but I wasn't interested.

"If you're not worried about her, then maybe I should do this on my own." It wasn't a fair statement, but I didn't care. I was pissed enough at myself to take it out on Eli or anyone else who tried to get in my way.

Eli growled at me, and I knew I had hit a nerve. He leaned toward me and grabbed my shirt, pulling me closer until our faces were inches apart. "Don't you ever tell me that I don't care about Delilah or that I'm not worried about her. She's all I ever think about. You should know that better than anyone. I'm not going to defend myself to you. We're going back to the office to regroup. If you're not interested in doing anything helpful, you can get out and walk home."

I stared at him in disbelief. I knew that he cared for Delilah as much as I did. And I knew that he was doing his best to find her. I was so mad at myself for everything that I didn't care who else I hurt. It was as if I needed someone else to hurt as badly as I did. I could see now that I had accomplished it with Eli. I wasn't sure if I should go with him or be alone for a while. It didn't seem like we were any closer to finding Delilah either way.

He didn't wait for my decision, tearing through the streets toward Strain Industries' main office building. I hated to admit that Eli was right. We needed a break. I couldn't tell him that I finally understood what he meant. I'd always had trouble admitting when I was wrong. Instead, I waited for him to stop the car at his office.

"You go ahead and take a break. I'm going back to Maxwell Industries to run down some leads on my own. I'll let you know if I find anything." I got out of the car and headed toward my own before he could respond. I knew it wasn't fair, but I couldn't admit that I needed some alone time. I was terrified that I would lose control if I let myself dwell on Delilah being gone without doing something about it.

I headed back to my office, making sure to turn down the street where I thought I had seen Delilah earlier. I crawled down that stretch of road three times before giving up. Once I was back at my office, I locked myself in and collapsed on my couch.

I'd been so exhausted that I passed out as soon as my head hit. Sleep was fitful, though, as I was plagued by nightmares of Delilah being killed. I walked into the deli in time to see Jones pull the trigger and shoot her in my dreams. I tried to save her, but no one could see or hear me. I dropped to my knees and picked up her limp body. Why wasn't anyone trying to help? I could only hold her as she bled out on the floor. I knew it was a dream because her body hadn't been there when Eli and I arrived. But my heart shattered as I watched my love die.

I woke with a start, sitting up on the couch. The nightmare dazed me, and I stared blankly around the room, looking for her. I shook the haze from my vision, forcing myself to push the dream away. I knew that what I had seen wasn't how she ended. She was out there somewhere. I could feel her. I had to find her.

I couldn't do it alone. I needed Eli's help, which meant I had to apologize. Delilah had brought us back together just for me to push him away again the moment there was trouble. I hoped she wouldn't be too disappointed in me. I dialed the phone with a heavy heart.

"Eli? We should talk."

Twenty minutes later, he was standing on my doorstep. I took a good look at him as I opened the door. My old friend had bags under his eyes and was paler than I had ever seen him. I knew that part of his stress was my fault. Like when Kat died, I blamed him instead of seeing my involvement in the situation. I pulled him into my arms and hugged Eli tightly, letting the tears I had been holding back fall freely. If we were going to save our girl, we needed to work together and trust each other. I'm not sure exactly when I decided that Delilah truly needed us both, but I knew that I would no longer try to change her mind about Eli. If we could get her back, that is.

If she was gone, I knew that Eli and I would burn down the city to make sure the people Jones was working with paid for it. We had to figure out who they were and what they wanted. Then we'd find her or get answers. Either way, this would be over.

CHAPTER 5

Declan

RELIEF WASHED OVER ME that the girl wasn't upset at being turned into a vampire. There were a lot of humans who would have been pissed and preferred death in the way I do. When she kissed me, it caught me off guard. I wasn't sure how to react. Then she admitted that she didn't even know her own name. There was no way to tell if that was because I had turned her or if she'd had amnesia before she'd been shot.

I couldn't continue to make out with her when neither of us knew who she was. When I pulled away from her kiss, the look on her face nearly melted me. It wasn't fair to her for us to get involved if she had someone else. And with her beauty, it would be difficult to believe she was single. For my peace of mind, I needed to wait until she at least knew who she was before I decided to make a move on her. I wanted her so badly I almost couldn't stop myself. But she needed me to help her through the transition. To do that, I needed to remain in control. I wasn't sure how long I'd last, but I was certainly going to try. Besides, maybe I would get lucky, and she would decide she wanted me instead of whoever she'd been with before.

Okay, Dec, you can't dwell on what could be. This girl needed me to help her survive. After all, I was responsible for her now. "What if we focus on something else for a while and see if you remember anything without trying too hard?" I flipped on the stereo and let the music play low enough to talk still but loud enough that we could hear it. Music was my comfort, which was why there were stereos in every hospital room. It was important to me, and I played it anytime I could. Her face lit up as if she recognized the song.

Watching her finally sense something she remembered made me smile. She hopped up and danced around the room, singing along with the music. The transformation was almost as intense as her change from dying human to vampire. I almost panicked when she stopped suddenly and stared at me. "What's wrong?" I was at her side in less than a heartbeat. She threw her arms around me and kissed me again.

"Declan! I remember!" She pulled me close and pressed her lips to mine. When she pulled away, she bounced up and down with excitement. "My name. I remember my name! It's Delilah." I smiled at her revelation as her face fell.

"What is it, Delilah?" Her name felt strange on my lips. I'd been thinking of her as my heart since I found her. "Can you tell me, Mo chroí?"

"I can't remember anything else. No last name, not where I'm from or who my family is."

The tears in her eyes tore through me to my soul. She stopped for a second, then looked up at me. "What is it that you called me?"

"Mo chroí?" I asked, even though I knew what she meant and what she would ask next. I wondered what her reaction would be. "It means my heart." I pulled her into my arms and held her, unsure if she would be upset by the pet name.

"Oh. It's beautiful." Pink crossed her cheeks, and she turned her head away from me. I wanted to go back to the moment when she kissed me. Every part of me longed to pull her close and keep her safe while taking my time pleasuring every inch of her body. I wanted to ask why she'd turned away, but I was terrified that I had crossed a line. I'd never been brave enough to call a girl that before. I'd been thinking it, and somehow, it just slipped out.

"Are you sure we didn't know each other before?" She turned her face back to mine, her lips a whisper away. Her brown eyes looked almost amber since the change. I fought the urge to pull her close and kiss her again. She didn't give me a choice, backing away for a moment before wrapping her arms around my neck and jumping on me. Her lips were on mine just as her legs closed around my waist. I was lost the moment her lips touched mine. No matter if it was wrong or not, I couldn't deny her. I would take whatever she offered and give her anything she wanted. This was dangerous, I knew, but I couldn't stop myself. I would burn the world down just to see her smile.

"What about your family?" I couldn't stop myself from asking. It didn't matter how badly I wanted her; I wouldn't take advantage of the situation.

"Well, I'm a vampire now. It's probably better if they think that I'm dead. Unless vampires live in the open, and that's just something I've forgotten too?" Pain seized her expression while she waited for my response.

"No, you could never tell them what you are. You're right; it's probably better if they think you're dead. Unfortunately, you can't remember your last name. We could leak a news story about your body being found so they would have closure." I kept trying to come up with a way to help her.

I tapped a button on the stereo remote to change the song. Distracted, I glanced at my hand for a moment. The remote had the Strain Industries logo on it. That by itself wasn't an epiphany; Strain was the biggest manufacturer of stereos and computers in the country. A grin spread across my face as I realized that there might be a way to help Delilah after all. Eli Strain was well known for being a tech genius. There was no doubt in my mind that he could help me find out who Delilah was so her family could have closure.

I picked her up and twirled her around to the music. Her laughter lifted my spirits almost as much as the idea had. I couldn't tell her yet because I didn't want to get her hopes up if there was nothing he could do. I would schedule a meeting and discuss it with him as soon as he was available.

"Why don't we get out of here? We can get you settled into your own apartment, and you won't feel so much like you're trapped." I figured she would get restless being cooped up in the hospital wing of my headquarters.

Delilah looked up at me, and her smile faded. "I guess it would be too much to think I could stay with you." I never wanted to see that look on her face again. It was as if she had confessed her love, and I had turned her away. My heart hurt. She started to pull away from me, but I tightened my grip.

"If that's what will make you comfortable, of course, you can stay with me. You'll have your own room, though, in case you want privacy or need time alone. Given the situation, that's probably a better idea than turning you loose as a new vamp." My suggestion was a hit. Delilah started dancing around again, and her smile returned. I was thrilled that she felt comfortable with me but still wondered if I was making a mistake.

I left Delilah in the hospital room to find Stephanie. I knew she would try to talk me out of it, but my mind was made up. I found Steph in her office. "Hey, Steph, can we talk?"

She gestured to the empty chair across from her desk. I closed the door before sitting down. "You're making a mistake." The words came out of her before I could explain what I was thinking.

"What makes you so certain you know what I'm thinking?" I cocked an eyebrow at her and smiled. The stoic look I got in return was an indication that she knew me way too well. "And just why shouldn't I let her stay with me? She seems scared. She will for sure need supervision. It's a win-win situation."

Steph smirked. "I knew it. You're already in love with her. It's clouding your judgment. Dec, you have to think about what's best for the whole community, not just yourself. It's a bad idea." She paused to look at me. "That said, if this is your choice, I'll stand by you. Be aware, when it all goes tits up, I will be the first to say I told you so."

"Delilah will be thrilled. I appreciate your support, and I expect nothing less from you, my friend." I stood up to walk to the door. I knew that she was busy, and I didn't want to keep Delilah waiting.

"Wait, Delilah? Is that her name? Did she finally remember who she is? I need to get in there and run some tests." Steph stood up and rushed around the desk. I turned to face her while blocking her exit. "Get out of my way, Dec."

I shook my head. "No. No tests. Give her time to settle in; then, you can ask if she wants to be subjected to all of that. And if she says no, you'll accept it and leave her alone about it. Understood?" The look I gave her would have withered nearly anyone else. Steph stood her ground. She wasn't afraid of me.

"Fine," she sighed. "I'll wait. But I'm going on record here. This is a mistake, and you will regret it." Steph turned and stomped back behind her desk before flopping in her chair. She was pissed at me and wanted to make sure that I knew it.

"Noted." I turned and walked out the door, making sure to close it carefully. She had been on the verge of pushing me too far, but I refused to take it out on her. I knew that Steph wanted to help. She had a habit of going too far too fast, and I didn't want that to upset Delilah.

On my way back to the hospital room where my girl was currently staying, I pulled out my phone and called Strain Industries. I knew it was a long shot to get a meeting with Eli Strain, but if anyone could help me, it was him. After his secretary promised to deliver my message, I hung up the phone and returned to Delilah's room. I was disappointed that I didn't have more good news for her, but I hoped that moving her into my apartment would be enough.

CHAPTER 6

Delilah

I WAS TORN. I wanted to know about who I was and about the life I was giving up by becoming a vampire. But there was a part of me that felt like I should just leave it alone and move on. Nothing good could come from digging into my human life. That man shot me, after all. I had to have done something to make him want to kill me. Maybe I was a horrible person. What if I stole from him or worse, what if I had hurt him or his family? Would I be able to live with the truth of my past? I let the music play after Declan left, hoping that new memories would surface. With each new song, I got flashes of memories. One tune reminded me of a tall, dark-haired man who had made my knees weak when he'd kissed me. Another brought up an image of making out with a hot blonde guy. There was nothing concrete, and I had no reason to think these images would help me. Since I didn't get anything but singular images, I considered it a fail. At first, I was disappointed that it didn't seem to work, then I was relieved.

If I remembered, would I be giving up whatever this is between Declan and myself? I had no way to know yet, but I didn't want to discount this attraction. It didn't matter to me if I had been married before. That life was over. This one would be different. I would have to learn who I was and figure out who I wanted to be. Right now, I wanted to be his. I just had to find a way to make it happen.

While I was considering my options, Declan came back into my room. I wasn't sure where he'd gone, but there had been a spring in his step. He seemed like a pretty light-hearted guy. So far, I'd had fun spending time with him. "You look like you just got away with something."

Dec looked at me, and his smile faltered for just a moment as if he was pondering my comment. "Maybe I did. I managed to get Steph to release you into my care. You can come home with me in a few days and get settled in. I'll make sure you have everything you need before I go back to work."

I couldn't contain my joy at hearing that he was going to let me stay with him. I ran and launched myself into his arms, pressing my lips to his. The way he stiffened at my touch made me aware that he wouldn't be instantly comfortable with me being affectionate. But the fact that he wrapped his arms around me and deepened the kiss after only a moment told me that he wanted to give in to the feelings we both seemed to be having. With us living together, it would only be a matter of time. I just had to find a way to speed things up.

I spent the next few days thinking about my past and my future. They passed slowly, torturing me that I was stuck in the hospital alone, even if Dec did come to visit.

I wondered how much of myself was the same as before the incident and how much had changed. Was human Delilah a patient person? Was she a prude? Would she have thrown herself at a stranger? I may never know. It didn't matter anyway. I decided that I liked who I was now and would fight to keep it that way.

I knew that today was the day I would get to leave. As soon as he walked in the door, I threw myself into Declan's arms and pressed my lips to his. When I finally tore myself away from him, Dec looked disappointed.

"Can we go now?" His disappointment melted at my smile. Dec nodded and turned to a cabinet I hadn't noticed before. Inside was a stack of clothes.

"These should fit. I'll show you around my place; then, later, I can take you out to get some new clothes." A new apartment and shopping? I was hooked on this guy already! I couldn't believe how generous he was. It made me wonder if all vampires were this way or if he simply felt guilty about turning me. It didn't take a psychologist to see that he was worried about his actions. I figured it would be up to me to ensure he didn't regret anything.

I took the offered clothes and started getting dressed. I probably should have been more self-conscious than I was, but from what Stephanie had told me when I woke up, Declan had helped cut my ruined clothes off before she attempted surgery. It wasn't like he hadn't already seen me naked. The blush across his cheeks and how quickly he turned his back to me would have embarrassed me if I hadn't already known his role in the events that brought us to this moment. "Sorry, I just got excited about getting out of here." I laughed at his reaction.

"It's no problem. I don't want to make you uncomfortable. I want you to feel at home here with me—with us, I mean." He tripped over the statement as if he was trying to avoid expressing his true feelings for me. I wondered if he was as invested in me as I already was in him. I didn't know anything about him except that he was kind and caring and that he seemed to be in charge around here.

Once I had the sweatshirt, leggings, and tennis shoes on, I wrapped my arms around Dec from behind. "I'm perfectly comfortable with you. Now let's get out of here." He took my hand and led me from the hospital room. The hallway was long and wide, similar to a regular hospital, but something about it was different. It was hard to put my finger on it, but something was off. I caught Dec staring at me with an amused look on his face. "What?" I asked, suddenly feeling nervous.

"It used to be a military compound, and now it's a hospital specifically for vamps. We're just outside the city limits. I figured you were wondering where we are." I nodded at his response, shocked that he had nearly read my mind. I wondered if it was a talent he had or if the look on my face had given away my thoughts. "We're going back into the city now. Steph will come to my place to check on you later. You'll need to make sure you don't roll down the car's window and that you only get in or out once we're inside the garage. The sunlight will hurt. A lot. At least until we get you an implant."

Declan's info dump was a lot to process. "An implant? What does that have to do with sunlight?" I was confused and hoped there wasn't some extensive scientific explanation behind it.

"Strain Industries makes an implant for vampires that protects us from sunlight while allowing us to walk outside in it. I'm not sure how it works; I just know that it does. Most of us have one. Since you don't, you'll have to take extra precautions against burning. That's why we got you a sweatshirt and leggings instead of a t-shirt and shorts. More skin coverage is a good thing."

I winked at him and grinned suggestively. "Are you sure about that?" The look on his face was priceless, and I couldn't contain my laughter. "You know I was teasing. I understood what you meant. Sun protection is more important than fashion anyway, at least I would think so for vamps." The words felt strange to say. I was a vampire. I still needed to learn so much about myself, both from my past as a human and from my present as a vampire. I followed Declan out the doors into the garage, where his SUV was waiting.

He opened the door, closed it immediately, and pulled me back toward the building. "What's wrong?" I asked as I struggled against his grip on my arms. He had gone pale and was shaking. I managed to shrug out of his hold, then took his face in my hands. "Take a deep breath, then tell me what happened just now."

Dec was on the verge of hyperventilating. His eyes stared past me to his car, but he didn't seem to be focused on anything. "Declan! Look at me. Now breathe in. Good, now out. One more, that's it. Now tell me what spooked you." He shook his head as if to clear it, making his auburn curls dance in front of his eyes, then pulled me close and pressed his lips to mine.

"I thought you were going to die. I was so scared." His voice was a whisper against my lips. Chills spread across my skin with his admission.

"But you saved me. I'm not dead—well, I mean—I'm still here. Right here, with you. What happened when you opened the door?" He stared at me with his deep green eyes, and it was almost as if I could read his mind. "The blood. That was the car you brought me here in, wasn't it? And you haven't had it cleaned yet. Crap. I get it now. It's okay, Dec. I'm right here. I'm not going anywhere. Can we get another car?" The tears filling his eyes broke my heart. How could this man care so much about a stranger? Even though it may have seemed strange, I felt it too. It was as if we were connected, tied to each other, without even knowing it.

I wrapped my arms around his waist and pulled him into a tight hug. I'm not sure how long we stood there, just holding each other before he finally moved. Declan lifted my chin, so our eyes met. "I'm sorry. I was so caught up with making sure you survived that I forgot about the car. I'll get Steph to drop us off and have someone pick it up to be cleaned. Are you okay?"

I nodded and embraced him again. His reaction to me being shot was so intense that I wasn't sure how to handle it. He cared for me a lot already. Would that change if I recovered my memories? Would either of us like the person I had been?

CHAPTER 7

Declan

AFTER A QUICK TEXT, Steph drove us back to my place. I was amazed that she didn't scold me for forgetting the mess in my SUV. The three of us being cramped in her sports car was punishment enough, but I never put it past her to rub something in. I expected her to decide that she needed to come in with us to chaperone, but again, she surprised me by saying goodnight before we left the car. I could tell that she was already nearly as attached to Delilah as I was. If this went sideways, I would have to hear about it from her for decades. I made a silent promise to protect Delilah's heart as if it were my own. Now I had to find a way to keep it.

Once we were inside, I noticed that Delilah had gotten quiet. Since the music at the hospital had seemed to help her remember things, I decided to turn some on and see if that would help her mood. I wasn't sure what kind of music she preferred, so I left it on the alternative stuff I usually listened to. If she remembered that she liked something different, I would change it. After I showed her around the apartment, I took her to the room that would be hers. Delilah's eyes went wide when she saw the king-sized four-poster bed in the middle of the room. "This is gorgeous!" She exclaimed as she ran her hands over the dark-stained walnut.

"Thank you. I had fun carving and building it." This piece had taken me two whole years to get just the way I wanted it. I had intended to save it for the woman I would marry. When I laid eyes on Delilah, I knew that I had made it for her.

"You made this? It's amazing! I can't believe you made it yourself. You're so talented." She gushed as she ran her hands over the intricately carved posts and wandered around the bed. I stood there watching her enjoy my handiwork with the biggest smile on my face. I knew it was a nice piece, but I didn't expect anyone to react the way she did. "So is that your job, or just a hobby? The wood stuff."

"It started as a hobby; then I decided I hated the corporate world and made it my job. I do okay with it, even though I didn't escape the business sector because of it." I laughed while she tried to figure out what I meant. "I make custom sculptures and furniture for clients, most of whom are business people who want something fancy for their offices."

Delilah looked impressed. I wondered what she had done as a career before all of this happened. As if she had somehow heard my thought, her smile fell. She looked up at me with tears forming. "Will I ever remember? I know it's only been a little while, but there's so much about myself that I don't know." I pulled her into my arms and held her tightly.

"It's okay. Steph said that you might remember everything or nothing. There's no way to know for sure. It won't happen instantly, though. Please don't be so hard on yourself over this. We'll figure it out. You're a blank slate now; you can be whoever you want." I tried to resist, but her lips were calling to me. I leaned down and pressed mine to hers. I wanted to comfort her, but more than that, I needed to claim her. It would be easier if she didn't get her memories back. Delilah's remembering could cause more complications than we would already be dealing with. If my phone hadn't interrupted us, I doubt I would have been able to restrain myself.

"Sorry, it's work. I have to take this." I sighed as I answered. "Yeah, Carol, what's up?" I knew it had to be important for her to have called me. She knew that I was dealing with a situation.

"Well, Mr. Roarke, there are two gentlemen who just showed up here *without an appointment.* They're insisting that they see you immediately." I could picture her face as she shot venom at the intruders.

"Who are they? What do they want?" I asked without thinking. There was no way I would leave Delilah alone here, so it didn't matter who wanted to meet with me. They would have to make an appointment.

"Mr. Maxwell and Mr. Strain, sir. They refuse to tell me what they want. I'm too old to be of any use to them." She snarled. I felt terrible for the poor bastards. Carol was a force to be reckoned with, especially if you showed up without an appointment. I doubted that either of them had told her she was too old, but the lack of an explanation for the emergency meeting would have set her off.

"See if you can get them scheduled for next week, please. I'll be out of the office for the rest of the week. I'm taking care of some personal business." I knew that I would have to call Carol later and explain, or she would hunt me down to get answers. I never took time off. But I had never turned anyone before, and I felt responsible for Delilah.

"Will do, sir. I'm sorry to have bothered you while you were occupied. Have a great evening." Carol's southern drawl dripped with sweetness, and I knew that Viktor and Eli were in for it. She would undoubtedly get them scheduled, but she would also read them the riot act about showing respect and calling ahead. She might even lay into them about all the canceled meetings I had tried to set up with each of them previously. I chuckled to myself as I hung up the call.

"Do you need to deal with that?" Delilah asked. I turned back to find her lying on the bed. She looked more relaxed than I had ever seen her. I'd only really known her for a few hours, but she had been preoccupied with remembering her past for most of that.

I shook my head. "No, Carol can handle it. I'm all yours. I mean, I'm here to take care of you. I didn't mean I belong to you or anything creepy like that." I paused and ran my fingers through my hair. "I'm trying to say that I'm here to help you settle in and adjust to your new life. I'm sorry I wasn't able to explain that better." Her laughter was music to my ears, and I felt a smile spread across my face. "Are you making fun of me?"

Delilah's eyes grew wide, and her laughter faded. She looked at me in mock horror. "I would never!" I had to hand it to her, she almost had me convinced, but then she lost her control and doubled over with the giggles. Her lightness eased my embarrassment, and I tackled her on the bed. I tickled her until she begged me to stop. "Dec, I can't take any more. Please." We were both out of breath but more relaxed than we had been.

CHAPTER 8

Delilah

I KNEW THAT SOMETHING was bothering Dec, even if he wouldn't tell me what that weird call was all about. I loved how he got flustered when he said he didn't need to leave. He's all mine; damn right you are. I didn't even care what he'd implied with it. I was more than ready to get to know him better in every way. My soul craved to claim him. Who was I kidding? I knew that I had already claimed him. I just didn't have the guts to tell him as much. I might have been more forward if I knew anything about my past. I hoped that the memories would keep coming, but they had all but stopped since we got to his condo.

Besides my first name, I could only remember a bar and two sets of eyes. I couldn't see their faces clearly, but I knew that they belonged to me just like Declan did. It sounded ridiculous in my head. There was no way three guys would agree to all be in a relationship with me. Yet somehow, I felt that it was meant to be. I just had to find the other two and convince the three of them that there was enough of me to go around.

Declan's voice brought me out of my thoughts. "Are you all right, mo chroí? You've been staring out into space for a while now. I don't think you heard anything I've said." His grin argued with the concern in his eyes. I knew that watching me try to remember was hard on him.

"I'm fine. I was just thinking, that's all. Trying to figure out who I was and who I am now." I didn't dare tell him the details of what I was thinking. That thought would probably scare him off immediately. So, I changed the subject. "I have some questions about being a vampire, if that's okay." I knew that he would answer whatever I asked. For some reason, I completely trusted him already. It felt strange—as if I had never done that before.

His smile faded, and concern took over his entire face. "Are you thirsty? I have blood bags in the fridge. I'll go get you one." I grabbed his arm and pulled him closer so he couldn't leave. I was stronger than I expected, and he ended up on top of me, pushing me over. I stretched up and pressed my lips to his, silencing his worry. For a moment, he kissed me back, fisting his hands in my dark curls. Then as if he'd been bitten, he jumped off me and sat up. "Delilah, we can't do this. We don't know anything about your past. What if you're married?"

"I appreciate the concern, Dec, but honestly, my human life is over. What will it take to convince you that I want this? It doesn't matter to me that there may have been someone else before. You and Stephanie both said there was no way to return to my human life, so why worry about it? Unless you don't want me, and you are afraid of hurting my feelings?" I stared into his emerald eyes, daring him to tell me that he wasn't holding back his desires. I knew he couldn't do it.

"That's not it," he said, shaking his head. "Of course, I want you. But you need closure. You need to know who you are or who you were. Then we can move forward. It's the right thing to do." As soon as he said it, I vowed that I would break his resolve. I would find a way to seduce him and make him see that he wanted me as badly as I wanted him. I leaned forward, pressing my lips to his again. He didn't try to stop me, but his hesitation was apparent. He meant what he'd said. I realized that this would be more difficult than I had imagined.

Declan's lack of enthusiasm had me pulling away from him. I knew what I wanted, but I couldn't force it. "Do you want to show me around the rest of your apartment? Or the city? Maybe getting out of here would help me remember." If I were going to seduce him, I would have to work slowly. He wasn't going to jump into bed with me. Today proved that. Relief relaxed him in a way that words could never have.

"We can go out if you have another blood bag first. Since you like the music so much, I'll show you the club that's around the corner. They have karaoke almost every night. Steph loves it." His smile lit up the room, and I knew that I wanted to see it forever. I nodded in agreement as I followed him to the kitchen. "I want you to feel comfortable here. I need you to understand how dangerous it is for a newly turned vampire to be exploring the city alone, especially one who doesn't remember her human life." Dec handed me a blood bag with a straw, and I started to sip.

"I need you to promise me you'll let Steph or me know when you're going out. I would prefer that you take one of us with you, but I understand if you feel like you need some alone time. I just want you to be safe." Concern coated his words. I knew that he wasn't trying to control me; he was genuinely worried about my safety. I wondered if it had more to do with the possibility of me remembering than the idea of me getting into trouble.

"I like that idea. I feel safe with you, and Steph seems nice. But if we're going out," I paused and gestured at my sweatshirt and leggings, "is there anything else for me to wear?"

"You should check your closet. I had Steph arrange a few things for you until I can take you shopping. We weren't sure what you'd like, so there's a little bit of everything." He kissed me on the cheek then walked away. I was hurt that he left me standing there for a second, then I realized that he was showing me trust. I had a choice to stay here where I felt safe or leave by myself. I finished the blood bag and headed to my room to check out the closet.

I thought he'd been kidding when he said there was a little bit of everything. He wasn't. There were shorts, jeans, bibbed overalls, dress slacks, dresses, t-shirts, sweaters, and nearly anything else I could imagine. I had no idea what my style had been like before, but I was determined to make Declan want me. What better way to do that than a little red dress? I found a lot more than clothes in the attached bathroom. It was as if Dec and Steph had anticipated any style decision I could have made and stocked the entire room accordingly. I was showered, dressed, and ready to go within an hour. I left my dark curls free and wore simple makeup, letting the curve-hugging red satin remain the star of my look.

I wondered how the club would be since I had no ID. Hell, I had no idea how old I was or when I was born. Worry began to consume me until Declan walked into the room. One look at him, and I couldn't concentrate on anything else. It was obvious the feeling was mutual. "You look amazing," he breathed before crossing the room to take me in his arms. For a moment, all was right with the world. After a brief hug, he seemed to remember his self-set boundaries and pulled away.

"You clean up pretty good yourself." I didn't hide my stare as I looked him up and down hungrily. He was gorgeous, even if he didn't seem to realize it. For a second, I let myself imagine what sex with him would be like. Would he be bossy and dominating, or would he prefer to be more submissive? I couldn't wait to find out.

CHAPTER 9

Viktor

AFTER MAKING UP WITH Eli, I stopped and really looked at him for once. The dark circles under his eyes had grown since we lost her. He was exhausted and nearing his breaking point. For some reason, that did more to reign me in than any of his words. I told him we could take the night off. I knew it was a lie when I said it. I'm pretty sure he did too. I couldn't help feeling like something was wrong. We needed to find her now. If Eli couldn't help, I would do it myself, and I wouldn't give him shit about it this time. Maybe if I had realized how this was wearing him down, we'd be closer to finding her. We had spent days searching with no real clues. The city was big but not big enough for no trace of her. I went back to the deli on the west side. I planned to start there and work my way around the area.

I didn't expect to end up at a club that reminded me a lot of what I wanted Midnight to become. I couldn't help being drawn inside, telling myself that perhaps I would find Delilah there. I knew better. I was simply trying to feel closer to her by surrounding myself with memories. The outside was dark, with all the windows covered. I wondered if there was more to that than just the fact it was a nightclub.

The inside was beautiful. The purples and blues mixed perfectly to compliment the decor. The lighting was dim but on point for dancing. The place was packed, and it seemed like everyone was waiting for their turn at karaoke. The clientele here seemed to have more musical talent than Midnight had seen. The dark-skinned vixen at the microphone belted out a song of misery that matched my mood. Maybe taking a small break would be good for me too. I took an open seat at the bar, ordered a drink, and turned back to watch the performers. Over the past few days, I had begun to see Delilah

211

everywhere. It came as no surprise when I thought I saw her walk in with a red-haired vampire that I didn't recognize.

"It's not her. I'm seeing things again," I whispered to myself as I watched them cross the room to a table near the front. Undoubtedly, it was just a girl who somewhat resembled my lost love. There was no way this could be my Delilah, my Myshka. Even if she'd survived being shot, which was unlikely, she wouldn't be healed enough to pour herself into the red dress her doppelganger was wearing. I couldn't tear my eyes away from her, even though I knew my imagination was playing tricks on me. If I had a soul, it would have been screaming for her. This girl looked so much like Myshka that I almost called Eli. I shook the thought from my head and turned my attention back to the stage. The golden-voiced woman had just finished her song, and a new entertainer would be taking the stage in a moment. The crowd cheered for her as if they'd come only to see her performance. I clapped along with them but stopped suddenly when I saw who was taking the stage.

The girl in red. She was going to sing. Myshka had always wanted to sing, but Vinny found ways to keep her from it. He said it was for her protection, but I knew better. It was to keep her from realizing that she had talent. If she had more confidence, she would have left him long before Midnight had been blown up. I wondered what taking over the bar would have been like if she hadn't been there. I shook the thoughts from my head again and focused on the beauty standing shyly on stage. The red-haired man had walked on stage with her and took the microphone from the host. "Okay, okay, settle down," he began as he looked around the room. "This is my friend, Delilah, and she would like to sing for you all tonight. Be nice." His warning was pointed at a table in the front row where some ladies in tight dresses had already begun to snicker. I turned to the bartender who was standing behind me.

"Did he say, Delilah?"

"Yeah, why, you know her?" The large man eyed me suspiciously.

"Maybe. Who is that guy with her?" I knew that the question could get me punched or worse, but I was desperate to know if that was her.

"Declan Roarke. He owns this place and most of this area of the city. If you want to know anything else, I suggest taking it up with him." Before I could say anything else, the guy glared at me and walked away. From experience, I knew that he would tell his boss about me. If this operation were anything like mine, I'd probably get my ass kicked before the night was over.

I decided to stay a while longer and see if I could talk to Delilah after she sang. Maybe Declan would step away, or she would go to the ladies' room, and I would have a chance. I needed to make sure it was her and figure out how to save her. There was no way Delilah would just leave Eli and me. She had to be here as a prisoner. I kept an eye out for security while waiting for her to start singing.

The instant her sweet voice hit my ears, I started to cry. I knew this was my Delilah. How was she here? How was she fully healed? Why couldn't I smell her anymore? I had so many questions. I knew that I should call Eli, but I wanted to see if I could be alone with her first. As she finished singing, I wiped my eyes, laid money on the bar to pay for my drink and the information, and walked toward the bathrooms. I planned to wait in the shadows to corner her. I needed to talk to Delilah. I needed answers.

Luckily, I didn't have to wait long for her to walk by. I didn't expect her to be escorted by another woman. I would have to try something else. "Girl! You didn't tell me you could sing! And I'm impressed with how much control you're showing. Most baby vamps would have already attacked half the club by now."

'Baby vamp'? What did that woman mean by that? Had Delilah been turned? Was it her choice, or did someone decide for her? Now I had even more questions than before. I was too caught up in the ramifications of what Delilah's friend had said that I wasn't paying attention to anything else. I didn't see the right hook until it was too late.

I woke up in my car, a few blocks away from the club. Groaning, I looked in the rearview mirror. The bruises and broken bones would heal, but until they did, I would have a constant reminder to be more careful when I was looking for information. I shot Eli a text letting him know I was coming to talk to him. Delilah was alive, and I knew just how to find her.

CHAPTER 10

Eli

"Slow down, Vik. You're not making any sense." I repeated the exact phrase I'd said a dozen times since Viktor Maxwell showed up on my doorstep claiming to have found our girl. "You went to a club and had a few drinks, then suddenly Delilah showed up with another guy? She wasn't even injured, and she sang karaoke? That sounds crazy."

"You're forgetting that the guy owns the club and that his henchmen beat me up for asking questions." Vik took a deep breath and gestured to the bruises covering his face. His jacket was ripped, and his dress shirt was torn open. Someone had pounded on him. I had no idea why, though.

"I would love just to take you at your word, Vik, but you've been seeing her everywhere. It's just not possible for her to be healed already from a gunshot wound that bad. She lost a lot of blood. Maybe it was just someone who looked like her." It had to be. There was no way Delilah was in perfect health this soon after being shot. Unless the rest of Vik's ramblings were right, and Delilah had been turned into a vampire. "You said the woman who was with them called her 'baby vamp,' right?"

"Yeah, and the guy is Declan Roarke, the same guy we tried to see, but he was 'busy.' I'll bet he was busy with our girl." Vik's thoughts strangely made sense, but I couldn't believe it. Jealousy poured off him and seeped into me through our empathy bond. I hated that I let him influence my feelings that way.

"Why would he turn her? She never told us that she knew any other vampires. Delilah didn't even know what we were until we showed her. Why wouldn't she have asked for one of us?" I mused, hurt that our girl could have abandoned us like this. I sat down at my computer and pulled up every file I had found on the man who held the west quadrant of the city. There wasn't much to discover. He'd taken power recently, and no one had been able to dig anything up other than a list of businesses he owned and who his top security personnel was. "This guy is practically a ghost. Except for the fact that he owns several businesses in that zone, he doesn't exist digitally." It seemed odd to me for someone to be off the radar like that.

"Not everyone likes tech the way you do, Eli. I'd rather know why she was with him. Jones kidnapped her. Maybe he brainwashed her too. Or maybe she was in on it. She could have been working with him and just stringing us along. I bet they both were working for that Roarke guy. We have to meet with him." Vik sounded crazy, but there was no way to know unless we met with Declan. Or ran into him in public and made him talk to us.

"What if we go clubbing tonight? We could check the place out and see if Delilah is there. If we can corner one or both of them, we'll find out what's going on. It can't be as bad as you think, Vik. There's no way she could pretend to feel the things she projected at me. Something else is going on here." I despised being the voice of reason, but Vik left me no choice. Since he'd gone off the conspiracy theory ledge, I had to play devil's advocate and argue the opposite of whatever he said. All I wanted was Delilah back in my arms. And to punch the person responsible for taking her from us. If that turned out to be Declan Roarke, so be it.

Vik wasn't thrilled with my idea. After all, we had no idea if Declan and the girl who could be Delilah would be there tonight. I was reasonably confident they wouldn't still be there now, and I knew that it would be impossible to keep Vik away if they were. He was out for blood, especially after being attacked by Declan's men. I figured there would be no harm in slipping him a sleeping pill. He needed rest, and I needed time to prepare for finding our girl. "Here, drink this," I coaxed as I handed him the mug of blood with the pill's contents in it. He eyed me curiously but took the mug from me. Vik didn't break eye contact as he brought the cup to his lips and drank gingerly. He must have decided that I wasn't trying to poison him because he drained the cup and settled back on my couch. The sleeping pill was fast-acting which had him passed out a moment after the realization that he'd been drugged hit him.

I should have felt bad about drugging my best friend, but I didn't. When it came to Delilah, I didn't regret anything except not keeping her safe from Jones. I vowed to spend eternity making up for it and ensuring that Vik did as well. We may have spent decades as enemies, but I can't ignore how important he is to Delilah. I checked Vik to make sure he was sleeping soundly before heading down to the pool. I needed a workout to clear my mind and prepare for tonight.

A few hours later, Vik and I were headed to the club he'd told me about. I had heard of Nightwalkers before, but I wasn't much into the karaoke scene, even if I had briefly tried to set up a bar to compete with Midnight. Crimson Mist didn't last long as a karaoke bar but did much better once I started hosting live bands.

My eyes met hers the moment we entered the bar. There was no doubt this was Delilah, our Delilah, but something was different. I couldn't smell her the way I had before. Her emotions were there but seemed more confused and intense than I'd ever felt from her.

My mind knew I should stay back and watch from across the bar, but my body craved to be near her. I barely registered Vik being stopped by security. I shot him a glance before I continued to follow the pull toward the woman who had my heart. Somehow she was even more stunning than she had been when I'd seen her last.

I noticed several sets of eyes watching me. I forced my body to change direction, heading to the bar instead of the stage. Vik told me about his conversation with the bartender, so I knew better than to start asking questions. I needed to get her alone to find out what had happened. I ordered a drink and pulled out my phone. There had to be a place in this bar where I could take Delilah to talk in private. Making sure that my back was toward the wall while I stayed close to the register behind the bar, I pulled up the app on my phone to access the spyware installed in my prosthetic. Within minutes, I had disabled the security system and had access to view all the camera angles in the building.

While I was working, Delilah had left the stage. I scanned the crowd but couldn't find her. We'd come too close to lose her now. I checked the video feeds and located her near the ladies' room. She seemed to be alone, so I headed that way. I spotted her just as she slipped out the back door into the alley. *What is she doing?* I didn't stop to think about it for long, instinctively following her out the door. Darkness enveloped me like an old friend, and my eyes took a moment to adjust. When I spotted her again, she was in an embrace with someone next to the dumpster. It seemed odd, so I moved closer to check it out.

I managed to sneak up right behind her before she realized anyone was there. She turned to face me, blood streaming down her chin. *Vik was right; she's been turned.* Her eyes looked strange, though I couldn't quite place where I'd seen that look before. I didn't have a chance to react before she jumped on me, wrapping her arms around my shoulders and her legs around my waist. My arms went around her automatically. Delilah bent her head and captured my lips with hers. The blood on her mouth tasted strange, but I didn't want to stop kissing her. I could feel her racing heartbeat that matched mine. She laughed against my lips and ground herself against my dick that was now standing at attention. I wanted her so badly but needed to make sure she was okay. I tried to pull back from her to talk, but she pressed herself closer. Her tongue waged war with mine, working me into a frenzy.

My mind was swimming. I thought this was a bad idea, but Delilah slid down my body and unfastened my jeans. Her mouth claimed me in a way that reminded me of our first kiss. That thought brought me back to the present. I grabbed her hands to stop her from finishing her mission to free my erection. I forced her to break contact and look at me.

Her eyes were glazed over, and I knew instantly that something was wrong. "Delilah? Can you understand me?"

She giggled and nodded, refusing to speak.

"Do you know who I am?"

She laughed louder as she shook her head. Delilah had no idea who I was but threw herself at me. This was a problem. I quickly zipped my pants and pulled out my phone. It took Vik less than a single ring to answer.

"Did you find her?" His voice sounded desperate, matching my feelings.

"Yes, but there's a problem. She doesn't know who I am. I think she's been drugged." I wanted to throw her over my shoulder and take her with us. If Vik suggested it, I just might.

"So she's being kept against her will?" I could tell he was struggling to process my discovery.

"I'm not sure. She seemed fine until she fed on a human in the alley. The blood tasted off. I think somehow the person was drugged." I didn't want to give him a play-by-play of what had just happened. "We need to do something because she's not herself."

"Do you think we can take her home with us? I'll get the car." A sigh of relief left my lips as Vik agreed with my idea that she should come with us.

"Hurry, I'll bring her around to the side of the building." She was too high to fight me. Besides, she was still trying to seduce me. "Delilah? Would you like to go for a ride with me?" I knew it was ridiculous to ask, but I would feel better if she agreed.

She growled at me, and for a moment, I was afraid she'd say no. "Mine." Delilah grabbed my arm hard and pulled me to her for another kiss. My heart sang at her claim. Nothing would make me happier than to make her remember everything. Vik pulled up, and I steered her into the back seat beside me. Delilah seemed unaware of what was happening, but she had claimed me. I justified kidnapping her because she admitted we were supposed to be together.

CHAPTER 11

Delilah

WHEN THE HOT BLONDE guy interrupted my feeding, I couldn't stop myself from attacking him. I had wanted to fight but ended up kissing him instead. I had no idea who he was, or did I? There was something familiar about his kisses. I wished that I could remember who I used to be. I felt like everything I was doing was out of character but had nothing to base it on. Declan would probably be pissed when he found out that I left with another guy. I would deal with that tomorrow. Something was wrong with me. My head was spinning, and I felt woozy. If I concentrated hard enough, I could remember that the feeling hit me after I'd bitten the human.

I hadn't planned to leave with another guy. I was planning to seduce Declan, not someone else. I opened my mouth to ask about calling Dec but couldn't quite form the words. What had made me claim this new guy? Why would I think he was mine? Did I know him from before? That was the only thing that made sense. How else would he know my name? Oh, no. He's not safe with me. I'm a vampire. What happens when the blood lust hits again, and I bite him? I started to freak out and grabbed the door handle. The dark-haired hottie that was driving us noticed. "Delilah, you don't want to do that while the car is moving. It's okay. You're safe here with us." His voice was soothing and familiar too. Maybe I did know them. Since I couldn't form words, I leaned back against the seat and closed my eyes.

"Vik, do you think she's going to be okay?" I heard the guy sitting next to me ask. So dark-haired hottie was Vik. I hoped that I would remember that when I could talk again.

"I don't know, Eli. She seems disoriented. I thought she was going to jump out of the car. The only time I've seen someone this messed up was when they'd used Powder." I had no idea what Powder was, but it didn't sound good. At least now I had names for both guys. It would make explaining the situation to Declan easier. I hoped that Vik and Eli were decent people. And I hoped that I didn't kill either of them. I wanted to ask how they knew me, but I couldn't talk.

I couldn't figure out exactly what had happened at the club. Declan had to step away to take a phone call. After that, the human man walked up and started talking to me. He had offered me a taste of his blood then led me into the alley. It seemed strange to me, but Declan had been taking care of my every need, so I figured he'd arranged it. I assumed that Dec hadn't wanted to leave me alone since I still couldn't remember much.

I leaned there against the back of the car seat, running through the few things I did remember. Wait. My eyes shot open, and I sat forward to look into the rearview mirror. I knew those eyes. I turned to the man sitting next to me and stared at him in disbelief. I knew his eyes as well. How? I had dreamed of both of them. More than that, I had dreamed of being intimate with both of them at different times. Oh, no. This could be bad. I opened my mouth to speak, "I...need...Declan." I managed to croak, my voice no more than a harsh whisper.

"Is Declan the man you were at the club with?" Eli grabbed my arms to hold me up as I slumped back again. I tried to speak but couldn't get words out again. I nodded. "Has he been taking care of you?" The concern in his voice almost broke me. I nodded again, feeling the tears spilling from my eyes.

"Do you think we should call him?" Vik asked from the driver's seat. Eli looked concerned, and I nodded again. I desperately wanted Dec to come and make all of this make sense. He could bring Steph, and she could fix me. I wasn't a fan of being high the first time I had tried it in high school, and this wasn't much different. Wait—I remembered something. Maybe this situation wasn't as bad as I'd thought. I still couldn't form coherent sentences, but at least I was remembering.

"I don't know. I think we need to get her sobered up and find out if she really does remember us first." Eli glanced at me sideways as he spoke, as if he was concerned that I would get upset. I wasn't happy that they didn't want to call Declan for me, but until I could talk, I couldn't do anything about it. I also didn't have Dec's number. I wondered if he knew these two guys. A sense of dread washed over me at the prospect that these were his enemies and my life was in danger now.

I stared out the window as the car flew through the city. The buildings zipped past so quickly that my head spun even more. I tried to focus on Eli inside the car again, but everything went black, and I slumped over onto his lap.

When I opened my eyes again, I was lying in a massive bed with the softest blanket over me. I sat up and rubbed my eyes, looking around the room. "This isn't home. Where am I?" My words came out as a whisper, and panic crept in the back of my brain. I pushed the blanket off me, wincing at the pain the movement caused. How much did I have to drink last night? My head throbbed when I sat up, and I noticed that I was no longer wearing the dress I'd so carefully picked out to drive Declan crazy. I was wearing an oversized Metallica t-shirt and a pair of boxer briefs. Someone had changed me, or had I done it myself?

The sudden urge to pee came over me, and I jumped out of bed. I didn't care whose clothes I was wearing; I refused to wet myself. I stumbled to the door and cracked it open to find a hallway. Since there were two other doors in the room, I figured a bathroom was attached. I tiptoed across the floor and opened the next door to find a deluxe bathroom. After relieving myself, I decided to check out the closet before finding out who I had gone home with. I wanted to be wearing more than underwear and a t-shirt in case I had to fight or run.

The closet was huge. It was larger than my room growing up. Uncle Vinny had tried, but he just wasn't good at worrying about our home. The bar and his shady deals were his priority. *Wait, that was another memory. I had an uncle. I wonder why I don't remember my parents.* I found men's clothes on one side of the closet, similar to what I woke up in. On the other, women's clothes that looked like they were my size. I found a set of drawers with bras and panties in them, then grabbed a pair of jeans and a sweater. It was unreal that everything fit perfectly and seemed to be what I liked. I wondered if I'd been here before. Something about this place gave me major deja vu vibes.

I dressed quickly then crept slowly out the door. I had no idea what to expect.

CHAPTER 12

Declan

I STEPPED AWAY FROM her for a second. And for what? So James could whine about his latest conquest rejecting him. My brother drove me crazy. I should have ignored the call. Why had I been so stupid? I should have had someone keep an eye on her while I was gone. I'd spent the next three hours looking for her before one of the bar patrons spoke up and said she'd left with another guy through the back door. Did she remember something? I didn't own her—there was no reason to explain my feeling that she was in trouble. It didn't sit right, though, her leaving without a word.

I forced a description out of the patron, but even with that, no one knew the guy. He had never been to the club before.

Of course, I would have tried to stop her. Maybe that's why she didn't tell me. That had to be it. I had no leads, no way to find her. I didn't even know her last name. To be fair, she didn't know it either. I thought we had a connection, but maybe I was wrong. I headed home to mope about it. I missed her already.

Steph called me before I made it home. I nearly didn't answer. "Yeah, what is it?" I couldn't pretend that I cared.

"Wow, really? I call you to tell you that I may have a lead on your missing girl, and that's how you answer the phone? See if I do you any favors in the future." She growled right back at me. I had to admit that I deserved it.

"What? How? Tell me, Steph," I demanded. I knew that all she had to do was hang up, and I would never get the intel out of her. I took a deep breath and rephrased my demand. "Please, Stephanie. I am sorry for snapping at you. Will you tell me what you discovered?"

She laughed—a hearty belly laugh—then responded, "That's better. You remember that guy who was asking questions the other night? Someone saw him outside the club tonight."

"And you think he had something to do with Delilah's disappearance? You don't think she went off on her own, do you?" The words came out as a growl. It seemed as if my suspicions might have been warranted after all.

"I don't. I've seen her with you, Dec. She wouldn't leave you without an explanation. Trust me. I've got a couple of guys digging around to see who the punk is so we can locate him. It can't hurt to ask him some questions."

I ran my hand down my face, wiping the tears I didn't realize were there. "Perfect. Keep me updated. And Steph?"

"Yeah, Dec?" Apprehension filled her tone. She was scared of what I would say next. I wondered why.

"Thank you." I disconnected the call, still trying to figure out why Steph would be scared by my response to her call. It seemed odd, but tonight everything did, so I guessed it was somehow connected.

It was hard to admit how attached I already was to Delilah. I knew there was a chance someone out there was going through the same misery I was right now because of her being turned. I needed to find her, and I needed to get her memories back.

I didn't know how to fix Delilah's problem, but I had connections. I could use those to find out who she was and give her family closure. I might even be able to find a way to get her memories back.

I turned my cell over in my hands as I thought. I debated the pros and cons. In the end, there was only one choice to make. I dialed Strain Industries and asked if I could speak with Eli. Of course, his receptionist said he was out for the day, so I requested that he call me back as soon as possible to set up a meeting. If anyone could find out who Delilah was, it was Eli Strain. He had the most intricate tech at his disposal. Once she'd assured me that my message would be delivered with my name and number, I disconnected the call.

I hoped that the next call went better than the last. I dialed the number and waited for voicemail to pick up. It had been way too long; there was no way he would answer my call. Suddenly there was a click, "Hello, Dec. It's about damn time you called."

I nearly cried at the familiar voice. "Kayden, I need your help." I was fully prepared to eat crow for it, too.

"Of course, you do. What have you gotten yourself into this time, Declan?" My best friend's smooth voice was soothing, even if he was irritated.

"It's a long story. There's a girl, and she got shot. I may have turned her to prevent her untimely death." I paused for a moment.

"You what? Dec, this is serious. You know that you can't just turn people whenever you feel like it. That will get the hunters after you for sure."

I nodded, unsure how to respond. I needed a minute to work out how to explain it all without sounding crazy for falling for Delilah so fast.

Kayden broke into my thoughts. "So what happened? Did she go crazy and drain someone?"

"No, she woke up with amnesia. The only thing she remembered was her first name. It's only been a couple of days since I turned her, but she's gone missing now. I need your help to find her before something bad happens. Please." I knew that I sounded like a desperate whack job, but if anyone understood, it would be Kayden.

"Amnesia, huh? Rowan has been working on some experimental treatments. I'll call him if we find her. You know I should tell you to go to hell, right? You don't call; you completely ghost me. Then the second you want something, I'm just supposed to hop to?" Kayden's anger simmered to the top. He was usually very reserved, but something had changed.

"Look, man, I'm sorry. I know it was wrong. I should have been honest with you about being turned in the first place. I wasn't myself. It doesn't make the situation any better, but it's the truth." My voice broke as I tried to apologize. Kayden had been my best friend. We grew up together outside the city.

"I get it; wolves don't like vamps. That's not the point. You were my best friend, my brother. But you did this without hesitation and lied about it. I don't know that I can forgive you for it." Kayden's growl, deep and angry, vibrated my ear.

"I understand. I shouldn't have called. I'll find her on my own." A single tear fell down my cheek, and pain gripped my heart.

"I'll help you find your girl. It sounds like she got caught up in a bad situation that isn't her fault. She shouldn't suffer because of your mistakes. After that, I can't make any promises." Kayden disconnected the call before I could respond. He knew where I was, so it wasn't a big deal. I expected him to be here in a couple of hours, especially if he was gathering a search party. I hated to involve the shifters, but they were the best trackers in the state. If anyone could find Delilah, it was Kayden and his crew.

CHAPTER 13

Delilah

THE HALLWAY WAS LONG and narrow, with several doors on either side. Part of me wanted to check behind each one and see what I was dealing with. Waking up in clothes that weren't my own made me wonder what I'd done. The pain in my head made me wonder about a lot of things. My first concern was finding blood before the thirst got worse. I didn't want to risk hurting anyone. I crept silently to the end of the hallway and looked around the open living area. The enormous room was empty.

A strange feeling of calm washed over me. There was something familiar about this place. Being alone was oddly freeing, and my body relaxed. I took a deep breath and walked into the kitchen. The burning in my throat was getting stronger. I remembered Declan's words of warning that the thirst could take over if I didn't drink blood regularly enough. Somehow I knew that the fridge would be fully stocked.

I pulled out a blood bag and drained it without closing the door. I grabbed another bag and flopped back onto the couch. I took my time with the second bag, slowly inspecting the room around me. I could tell that a man had decorated the room. It lacked a woman's touch. There were no photographs on the walls, nothing to indicate who lived here. It was difficult to tell if anyone lived here. This could have been a hotel suite for all I knew. When I finished the second blood bag, I dropped it in the sink and went searching for something to tame this headache.

How can I have a hangover when I didn't even drink anything last night? Wait. That guy. How stupid can I be? Of course, that guy had somehow drugged me. It was the only thing that made sense. But why? That would mean that either Dec didn't send him or that Dec was trying to drug me. I had no idea what he could gain from that, so I found it hard to believe that Declan could be behind it. Maybe the guy knew me from before, and he had a reason to want me incapacitated. The thoughts invaded my brain as I searched the apartment. I found what I needed in the bathroom, which probably should have been where I started hunting, but my mind was fuzzy. I took medicine and walked back to the living room.

I pieced together bits of memory from the night before. Vik and Eli, those were the guys who'd taken me. That wasn't exactly right. They didn't take me so much as to make sure I was safe. I'd even tried to have sex with Eli, and he'd turned me down because he could tell that I was high. Not many guys would have resisted a willing participant. I wasn't sure how but I knew them. Their eyes were the ones I saw in my dreams. My soul screamed mine every time I saw them. And the way they'd talked when I'd pretended to be passed out made it seem like we'd all been in some sort of relationship together.

Now that my headache was taken care of, I searched for a computer or cell phone to get back home. I stopped suddenly at that thought and dropped to the floor. I didn't have a home. Not one that I knew anyway. I only knew one person and had no idea how to get in touch with him. I couldn't even remember if Declan had given me his last name. My chest tightened, causing my breath to come in gasps as I started to cry. My current situation was hopeless. Even if I left this apartment, I had no idea where I was or how to get back to Declan. Pain stabbed at my heart, and I curled into a ball on the floor of the room I woke in a few hours ago. I failed to stop the sobs that racked my body. Hopelessness took over, and I wondered if I'd ever get to leave.

After a while, I fell asleep. My dreams were confusing and scary, like when I was unconscious and dying. I was lost in the darkness, with flashes of color all around me. I stared out into the black expanse. A flash of color highlighted a doorway a few yards in front of me. I stumbled drunkenly toward it. I should be able to walk fine; I haven't had anything to drink. A few steps more, and I bumped into something. I froze, waiting for the light to come again so I could see what was in front of me. My body trembled, and sweat pooled at the base of my spine.

"Delilah, it's silly to be so scared. You're a vampire now." My voice echoed even though I had whispered the thought. The colored light pulsed again, and I looked down toward my feet. Lying there, in a pool of blood, was the man from the club. His neck was bent at an unnatural angle, and blood dripped from his shoulder. I knew without leaning down that he was dead. Somehow, I knew that I had killed him. My head spun again as it had outside the club before Eli walked up. I turned toward the noise and found myself face to face with Eli.

"Do I know you?" My question came out a breathy whisper. My soul sounded in my head. *Mine.* "What are we to each other?" I stared into his blue eyes, willing him to answer me, but he wouldn't. He reached for me, and I backed up. I wanted answers. I *needed* to know before I let myself fall into his arms. My brain and soul were at odds over my choice. Eli stepped forward, and I retreated again, bumping into something solid. I turned to see Vik standing there, his dark eyes burning through me.

The hunger in his eyes terrified me. I could tell they both wanted me, and a part of me wanted to give in to it. I wanted them both. I heard another noise and turned toward it to find Declan's green eyes on me. I stepped further away from all three of them. I couldn't trust myself to make this decision until I knew who I was—who I am. How could I possibly care so much about three different men? It's not like they would be okay with sharing. I tried to think if I'd ever known anyone in that situation. I mean, sure, they write about it in books, but does it really happen that way?

While I was caught up in my thoughts, staring at the three of them, something brushed against my leg. I looked down to find the dead guy grabbing at my ankle. I screamed and ran for the door. If vampires were real, surely zombies could be a thing too. There was so much I still didn't know. I needed answers. I woke in a cold sweat with tears streaming down my face, staring into piercing blue eyes.

CHAPTER 14

Eli

I found Delilah curled up in the fetal position on the floor of my bedroom. I told Vik we shouldn't have left her alone. He'd wanted to give her some space, so she wasn't scared when she woke up. I went to the office for a while and took care of things that couldn't be rescheduled before dropping him off at Midnight and returning here. I was certain that leaving her alone had been a bad idea from how she was shaking. I could punch him for it later. Right now, Delilah needed me. I noticed that she'd found her clothes and changed. She had also found the blood bags. I wondered how long she'd wandered around the apartment before she came back in here.

I scooped her up and cradled her while walking to the bed. I sat down and held her on my lap. I knew that waking her from whatever nightmare she was having could scare her worse, so it was better if I just held her and waited. I was terrified that she would remember what had happened last night and think I tried to take advantage of her. Of course, I wanted her. I just wanted it to be her decision, not something that happened because she was high. I didn't know if she had gotten high intentionally or if someone had slipped her something.

She woke with a start, gripping my arms tightly. She had been sweating and crying. For a moment, Delilah relaxed when she saw my face. Then terror took over, and she crawled away from me. "Who are you? Why did you bring me here? Where are we?" Her questions came out in a long breath. She panted as she waited for my response.

"It's okay, love. I'm not going to hurt you. I'm Eli—don't you remember me? We're at my home. Vik and I brought you here because you were pretty messed up last night, and we wanted to keep you safe." I tried to keep my words soft-spoken and calm to soothe her.

"Eli. That's right. I heard you two talking last night in the car. You asked me to come home with you. Why would I agree? I don't know you, do I?" The fear in her eyes broke my heart. I wanted to scoop her back into my arms and make it all go away. I realized that the fear was my fault, though. She had no idea who I was, but I had taken her to my home instead of her own. I wasn't sure how much I should tell her.

"Did you wake up with amnesia after you transitioned?"

She nodded, eyeing me cautiously. "How did you know?" Her gaze dipped to her hands that were fidgeting with the blanket.

"Because you don't remember us or this place. Delilah, I promise you, I will not hurt you. You're safe here. You found the clothes in the closet, right?" Her name felt strange on my tongue, but I waited for her to look at me and nod again. "Those are your clothes. You put them in my closet. It's a difficult situation to explain, but we were—are in a relationship, and you lived here part-time before you were kidnapped."

Delilah raised her head and stared at me. "Are you saying that Declan kidnapped me? Why would he do that? He saved my life."

I shrugged. "I don't know that he was involved. I don't know him. I can tell you that Vik and I owe him our lives for saving you. We'd be lost without you. He and I have spent all of our time searching the city for you. We've been lost since you were taken." A tear slid down my cheek, and she hurried over to wipe it away.

"Maybe that's why I felt so drawn to you. If we were together, that would explain it. But what about Vik? You said you both owe Declan. I don't understand." Her nose wrinkled as she tried to figure out what I'd meant.

"It's a complicated situation. You were with Vik and me. I don't want to push too much at you at once. Vik and I both care for you, and you wanted to be with both of us. We agreed to try, and before we could finish remodeling our new home, you were taken." I knew it was a lame explanation, but it was all I could offer her right now. I didn't want to overwhelm Delilah with details about how her family home was destroyed or how her uncle had been killed.

"I'm sorry, this is all just too much. I want to go home now. Please would you just call Declan or take me home?" Delilah sat in my chair next to the bed and pulled her knees up to her chest. She dropped her eyes to the floor, and I was sure she was crying again.

"I know this is all a lot to process. I know Vik was anxious to talk to you without being overwhelming. I'm sorry if I upset you. This is your home; at least it was. If you want to go back to Declan, I'll call him for you." I stood up and walked to the door, trying to mask the pain that was tearing through me. "I can get you a bag to take your clothes. There's no reason you can't have them." I walked out the door before she could see my tears. I leaned against the closed door and pulled out my phone.

My place. Now. She wants to go back to Roarke. My hands shook as I typed the message to Vik and sent it before I could change my mind. It would be easy for us to keep her here.

There was no way Declan Roarke could know that we had her. He might not even be looking for her. I had to talk to Vik and figure out what we needed to do.

On my way. Vik's response was short and to the point. I needed to stall her until he arrived. Maybe the two of us together could convince her to stay. We deserved a chance to make things up to her. If only there was a way for her to remember. While I waited for Vik, I tried to steel myself against the thought that we'd found Delilah only to lose her again.

CHAPTER 15

Declan

It had only been a few hours when I got the call that Kayden and his crew had arrived. I knew the moment they'd entered the building. Wolves had a particular scent that could not be masked from a vampire's heightened senses. It was the reason I'd had Kayden send me the profiles of his team with photos of them in human and wolf form. I had distributed the files to my security and other relevant associates. If anyone else showed up, my team would stop them from entering the property.

"Kayden, thanks for coming so quickly. I appreciate your help with this." I offered my hand, and he hesitated before shaking it.

"As long as she hasn't broken any laws, we'll bring her back to you. But you know that there will be repercussions from an unsanctioned transition. I hope she's worth it." My oldest friend ran his hand through his light brown waves as he sized me up.

"You're worried for nothing. I told you earlier I had to turn her in to save her life. This one is special. Trust me. If there had been time to file the paperwork, I would have." I was certain that Kayden could see my regret all over my face. I knew it was only a matter of time before the hunters got to me, but I was hoping for some leniency because my best friend was their leader. It didn't matter anyway. I knew that I would save Delilah again if I had it to do over. I couldn't help it; something was pulling me to her as if we were meant to be together. Logically, I knew that I couldn't already be in love with her, but my heart disagreed. I just had to find her so I could tell her about it.

"Declan? Did you hear anything I just said?" Kayden broke into my thoughts. I wiped my hands over my face.

"Sorry, got a little distracted there." I shrugged and winked at him.

230

Before he could repeat what I had missed, the phone rang. I answered without hesitation, holding a finger up to Kayden. "Yes, Carol, what is it?"

"You said to let you know if anything strange or out of the ordinary happened." Carol's irritation was obvious.

"What happened?" I asked, making sure to keep my tone even. I knew that showing my frustration with Carol would cause a significant backlash.

"Eli Strain called again, insisting that he and Viktor Maxwell meet with you urgently. He refuses to tell me what it's about. He says it can't wait until next week. You don't have any openings unless you want to do a dinner meeting." She knew that I hated dinner meetings. But if it was that urgent, why not let Strain or Maxwell buy me dinner?

"A dinner meeting is fine, so long as it's on his tab. I'm not dressing up either. What night does he have in mind?" I looked at my calendar as I spoke, realizing that I'd cleared my afternoons and evenings to spend with Delilah.

"Tonight. They've made a reservation at Starlight. You're expected at eight promptly. If that's acceptable, I'll confirm with him." Carol's curt tone told me that I'd better accept without making her go back and negotiate.

"That sounds perfect. Thank you, Carol." I hung up and turned back to Kayden. "Looks like I have dinner plans tonight. You guys can still get started without me, right? I'll be available by cell if you find anything."

Kayden nodded. "From the sound of it, this might be harder than we thought. I was reviewing the file while you were on the phone. You know virtually nothing about this girl. How do you expect us to find her if we don't even know where to look?"

I tossed a shirt at him. "You guys are great trackers. This is something she wore. Use it to sniff her out." Smirking, I turned to leave. I needed to do some research and prepare for dinner, and I had other meetings scheduled for today. The business didn't care that Delilah was missing, even if it was tearing me apart.

Kayden caught the sweatshirt and sniffed deeply. I could have sworn I'd heard him moan at the scent of her. It wasn't possible—he hated vampires. My transformation was the ultimate betrayal to him. So often, I missed my best friend, but there was nothing I could do to change his mind.

A low growl stopped me in my tracks. I turned to see Kayden with his hands fisted at his sides. Rage poured off him.

"We're not your lapdogs, Declan. I agreed to do this as a favor for you. Don't treat this as anything else. You gave up your chance to lead the hunters. It was your choice."

"You think I don't know that? You think I haven't questioned that decision every day since I made it? I was backed up against a wall, and the options were to jump in the flames or surrender. Don't think you know everything, friend. Yeah, I made my choice, but so did you." My fist hit the wall, inches from Kayden's face.

His eyes met mine. "You don't want to start a fight with me. I have the hunters on my side. You won't win."

"If you're not going to help me, then leave. I'm not playing games. I need to find her. That is the only thing I'm focused on right now."

"Fine. We're out." Kayden turned, motioning to his crew to leave. It looked like I would be on my own again for this. It didn't matter. I had to find her. That was all that mattered. Kayden would be pissed for a while; then we'd talk again like nothing happened.

After he left, I screamed and slammed my fist into the wall again. It didn't matter if I left a hundred holes in the drywall; I would be the one to fix it. I needed to get my temper under control. Getting on the hunters' bad side was not in my plan. Now I would have to find Delilah on my own while dodging Kayden's men. I shouldn't have had such a flippant attitude about Kayden's anger. *Shit.* And to top it off, I had to have dinner with the pompous asses who'd been dodging me since I took over this zone.

CHAPTER 16

Vik

"WHAT THE HELL DO you mean, we're having dinner with Declan Roarke? That asshole wouldn't even meet with us when we were searching for Delilah." I screamed at Eli on the phone when he'd called to tell me about dinner at Starlight. He seriously expected me just to hand Delilah back to her captor and pay for dinner simultaneously. What the fuck was wrong with him? "He probably had her the whole time we were searching."

"Vik, calm down. It's a business meeting. A negotiation. Ultimately, it's her choice where she goes and who she's with. I hope to show her how much we care by letting her go. Then maybe she'll be open to getting to know us. When her memory comes back, she'll change her mind and come home." Eli made the whole thing sound easy. He was convinced that Delilah would choose us if she regained her memories. How would we watch her leave us again without tearing this guy apart?

"I'm on my way over now. You and I need to talk about this. It's a bad idea. We need to pack up and go. Morocco is nice this time of year. We can take her there until she remembers everything." I growled, unable to let go of the idea that we were about to lose everything. I just got her back and hadn't even had any time alone with her. It didn't matter to me that Eli said she was conflicted. I was certain I could convince her to stay with us. One way or another.

I walked into Eli's place, expecting to see Delilah in the living room. Instead, I saw a version of Eli I hadn't seen in a long time. "Where is she?" His eyes met mine, and I understood. She had rejected him, maybe both of us. That was why he'd called Declan. I stormed down the hall to his room, where I'd helped him tuck her in before we'd both left her alone. I threw the door open, "What the hell is your problem?" My eyes searched the room for her, finally settling on a small figure curled up next to the closet.

Delilah raised her head, and I saw the tears streaming down her face. My heart crumbled. How could I have objected to Eli's idea when she's in this state? "Myshka? It's okay. Eli and I would never hurt you." I crouched down a few feet from her, so I wasn't as intimidating.

"But you did, both of you. You took me from my home and locked me away here in a place I don't know—alone—while you were out there doing whatever." Sadness laced her words. If my heart hadn't already broken at the sight of her, it would have with that statement.

"I'm sorry you feel that way. We were only trying to keep you safe. Did Eli tell you that he called Declan? We're having dinner with him tonight. All three of us. You can go home with him if you want. We won't stop you." A single tear rolled down my cheek, and before I realized what was happening, Delilah was in my arms. She hugged me tightly with her face pressed against my neck. I gently rubbed her back, giving her what she needed.

"Thank you," she whispered on my skin, her lips touching me with the movement. A soft moan escaped my lips. I wanted to pick her up and show her what she did to me, but I knew this wasn't the time. She wasn't ready to accept us the way she did before. Her touch froze me. I could barely breathe with her so close.

She pulled away from me a moment later, and I didn't stop her. I knew that holding on too tightly would cause us to lose her forever. "Are you okay? Do you need anything? Food, water, blood?" I had never been nurturing, but something about her made me want to be. Kat had been the one to take care of me.

Delilah hugged me again, then shook her head, rubbing against my neck more. I practically purred. Her giggle lightened the mood, and she released me from her hold. "I think I remember you. Not everything, not even good things, but I know you somehow. I should be scared of you, but I'm not."

"You remember?" My eyes widened at her admission. What exactly did she remember? How badly would it influence our chances of winning her back?

"Just bits and pieces. Of Eli too. He was so emotional that I didn't think I could tell him. I'm sorry that I can't be who you want me to be. I'm not sure who she was, or even if I want to be her anymore." Delilah hung her head as if she was waiting for me to blow up.

I lifted her chin to force her to meet my eyes. "I get that, truly. I'm not sure I want to be the man I've been since you were taken from us." I leaned down and gently pressed my lips to hers. "Eli and I just want a chance to show you that we care for you. Even if that involves letting you go back to Declan."

"But why? What's so special about me that all three of you want me? I don't know how I would ever choose." She wasn't lying when she said she didn't remember everything.

"You're what's so special about you. I know it sounds strange, but Eli and I had agreed to share your time and affection. If I'm being honest, I never intended to share you. I had planned to win you over by making him look bad. It didn't work, and you were taken from us. Now I can't imagine not sharing you. It's the only way you can have everything you need." My voice was softer than I'd ever remembered hearing it.

Delilah stared at me for a bit before speaking again. "I have so many questions." I nodded and she continued, "First, what was that you called me, and what does it mean? I heard it in my head before I ever saw you. I know it's nothing bad but can't remember if I ever knew."

"Myshka," I smiled, "means little mouse. It's what I've called you since the day we met." Her eyes lit up and I wondered if that had sparked a memory. I hated prodding at her about it, so I let it go. She raised and pressed her lips to mine. The kiss was gentle and loving; it drove me crazy. I wanted to take things further with everything I was, but I knew she wasn't ready. As a human, she had been more open with Eli. I wondered if this meant that she would be different now. I imagined backing her up against the wall and ripping her clothes off, knowing it was a bad idea. My imagination didn't listen to reason, and my cock jumped at the vision.

Just as I leaned into the kiss, she pulled away. Her demeanor had changed entirely. "Wait, you call me 'little mouse' and I don't mind it? That seems a bit offensive. Was I that weak before?" Anger rolled off her in waves. I had no idea my endearment would set her off this way. The roller coaster of emotions she had me on was too much. I understood that she must feel conflicted, especially if she remembered us.

"I didn't mean to offend you. It's just something that my family has always used as a name for someone they love." I wasn't sure if I was irritated at her or upset that I'd made her mad. The whole situation was ridiculous, and I knew that we should just drop her off to Declan and move on with our lives. "Don't worry; you won't have to hear it anymore. You did ask to go back to your boyfriend, after all." It hurt me to be so cold to her on a deep level, but it was for the best. I stood up and walked out the door, leaving her sitting on the floor alone.

CHAPTER 17

Delilah

I sat there on the floor after Vik left. "What is wrong with me?" I asked myself out loud. I'd gone from crying to kissing Vik to biting his head off within minutes. He was trying to help me. He seemed genuinely upset that I didn't remember everything. As I sat there, holding my knees and rocking, memories flooded my mind. I knew it wasn't everything, but it was more than I'd had a few minutes ago. How could I be so conflicted about this? I knew from what I saw that he and Eli cared about me. But I knew that Declan cared for me too. Would it be too much to ask for the three of them to share time with me?

I thought about it for a while. Could it work? I had no idea. Did I want to try it? Absolutely. I just had to mend fences with Eli and Vik first. I'd been such an ass to them both today. And for what? Because they wanted me to remember things I couldn't. Because they didn't take advantage of me when I was drugged. If I were them, I don't know if I would forgive me. I stood up and walked to the bathroom to wash up. If I was going to beg, I'd do it with a fresh face.

Once I was cleaned up, I walked out of the room with purpose. I would make them talk to me if I had to. I mentally pumped myself up as I stomped toward the living area. Two sets of eyes bore into me when I entered the room. My courage evaporated under their stares. I stopped in the doorway and bit my lip as my eyes found everything to look at besides their handsome faces. They sat together on the oversized sofa.

"Is everything okay, love? I'm sorry, I mean, Delilah," Eli tripped over the question, making it evident that Vik had told him about my response to being called by an endearment. What was wrong with me? Ugh.

I shook my head, fighting against the tears that were threatening to fall again. I hoped that my past self hadn't been this quick to cry. I wanted to think that I was stronger than that. "I wanted to talk to you both," I spoke quietly, knowing that neither of them missed my words with their enhanced hearing.

Vik nodded and gestured to a chair instead of trying to get me to sit next to either of them on the couch. I sniffed and took the seat. They stared at me, waiting to hear what was on my mind. I forced myself to look at them both while I nervously wrung my hands.

"I'm sorry. I was a total bitch to both of you after you've done nothing but try to help me." I refused to look away as each of them processed what I'd said. "I don't remember everything about my past. I am starting to remember things about you both, and it's all just so confusing. I'm trying to process it all." A single tear fell from my eye, and both men looked as if it killed them to hold back from trying to pull me into their arms. I respected the restraint now that I understood more about what it cost them.

"You don't have to apologize to us. We were both out of line to assume that you'd remember us. We didn't even know you'd lost your memory until we found you at the bar. We should be apologizing to you." Eli spoke while Vik looked like he was debating yelling at me again. I deserved it and so much more. I stood up and walked closer to where they sat. I wanted to be close to both of them right now. I reached for Eli's left hand, pulled him to stand next to me, and then turned to Vik, who stood without touching my hand. There was something eerily familiar about his rejection, though I couldn't remember exactly why.

"I can't make any promises. I don't know what we were to each other before. What few memories I have—I'm not that girl anymore. I feel different since the change and not just because I don't remember her." I stretched up and pressed my lips to Eli's. He pulled me to him as if by instinct, then released me a moment later. The guilt on his face tore my heart out. I turned to Vik, who was still scowling at me. "Can't we just take things one step at a time and see what happens?" Hope flickered in his eyes as Eli interlocked his fingers with mine. It was clear whose side he would be on, but Vik may not be so easily convinced. I hated the thought of begging. I took a chance and cupped Vik's cheek with my free hand. When he didn't rip my arm off, I knew there was a chance. I pulled him down so his lips could meet mine. He hesitated at first before growling and taking control.

Eli released my hand. Before I could miss him, he was pressed against my back. My body buzzed at the feeling of being sandwiched between these two gorgeous men. It no longer mattered that they were powerful vampires. I was one of them now. I had nothing more to fear. I lost myself in the sensation of four hands exploring my body while two sets of lips trailed hot kisses across my face and neck. I had no way to know if I had done anything like this in my former life, so this was a new experience for me. It didn't matter who I had been, only who I was becoming now.

Vik claimed me with his lips before turning my face to kiss Eli. I was soaked at the thought of them sharing me. I wondered if they'd been intimate with each other before. There were so many things I didn't know. It should have stopped me, but instead, that feeling urged me to continue finding out. Eli pulled my shirt over my head, kissing my shoulders and down my back while Vik concentrated on my neck and collarbone. I shivered with anticipation before I decided that I needed to touch them as well.

Eli was on his knees behind me, so I focused on Vik first. His lips returned to mine, and I started unbuttoning his shirt. It was taking too long—I wanted him naked—so I grabbed it and tore the remaining buttons, shredding his shirt in the process. He and Eli both laughed at the growl that escaped my lips at the sight of his chiseled chest. I wanted to lick every inch of him. I ran my hands over his bare skin while teasing him with slow kisses. Once he moaned his pleasure, I turned my back to him so I could start stripping Eli.

I grabbed his t-shirt and pulled it over his head. It was easier than tearing it in half with him still on his knees. His chest was every bit as cut as Vik's, but Eli was more tanned. I wondered how a vampire managed to get a tan. Then I dismissed the thought because there were more pressing issues at hand. Vik was grinding on my ass while I stared at Eli. He winked at me, then started trailing kisses just below my bra down to my waistband. I was pinned in place between Eli's tongue and Vik's erection. Eli unfastened my jeans and pulled them off me while Vik lifted me to make it easier. I had expected their skin to be cold, yet heat radiated between the three of us.

I was nearly exposed; the material of the bra and thong I'd selected barely covered me. Eli's breath on my stomach and Vik's lips on my neck resulted in goosebumps spreading across my naked skin. I tangled my fingers in Eli's hair while my free hand tried desperately to get between my body and Vik's. I ended up gripping his pant leg while they focused on me. I had never felt so desired before. Vik held me up while Eli kissed me lower and lower until he was at my apex. Even with the thong, I was wet and ready. I growled in anticipation.

Just as I was about to climax, Eli released me. Vik flipped me around and kissed me again, distracting me from Eli's absence. I moaned in pleasure as our tongues tangled while his hand fisted in my hair. I barely noticed him tearing my thong and bra to remove them. My back warmed again as Eli reappeared behind me. I turned my head and claimed his lips. My hands greedily searched for their cocks. I wanted to show them what they were doing to me. I found both of them completely naked and ready.

I started stroking them, not realizing that they completely stopped everything. "What's wrong?" I asked, freezing in place, a dick in each hand. I looked frantically from Vik to Eli and back again. They seemed to be waiting for something or having a telepathic conversation.

"Is this what you want?" Eli spoke softly, forcing me to look at him.

"We're not going to make you do anything that you don't choose to do." Vik's voice was gruff with need, but he spoke as softly as Eli had.

"Seriously? You think I'd say no to either of you right now?" I gripped them tighter, pulling them both toward me until their faces were mere inches from mine. "You both want me, right?"

Both men nodded without a sound. It was as if they were terrified of scaring me off. I found it hot and annoying.

"Then I guess you'd better convince me to give you both a chance. I suggest you start by giving me as many orgasms as possible." My words sounded strange to my ears but somehow made me feel freer than I had in a while. I closed the distance between my mouth and Vik's, nipping at his bottom lip before I turned to Eli and crushed my mouth to his.

Eli stroked my clit while Vik lubed himself and my ass, then slipped a finger into me. I couldn't believe how hot I thought the whole situation was. I wondered for a moment if I'd been okay with anal before. Did the three of us do this in the past? I'd have to make sure I asked later. I lost that train of thought when Eli held me up while Vik slid inside. Then Eli rubbed his tip against my clit before slipping inside. The pressure from having them both in me at the same time was intense. They fell into a rhythm that had my knees so weak that they had to hold me up.

I could tell that they were both holding back. Neither wanted to get rough with me. It was sweet but so frustrating. Even with the slow pace, I felt like I was being stretched to my limits in the best way. With each orgasm, Vik and Eli tensed. Every time I thought they'd be over the edge, they surprised me. I lost count of how many times I came. By the end, I was begging them to finish with me. "Come with me. I want to feel you both at the same time." Vik growled and Eli moaned. The three of us somehow managed to reach our peaks together. I was sated but still felt like something was missing. Declan.

I wondered if I would be able to convince all three men that I needed them. Eli insisted that I shower alone so we could make it to dinner on time. Vik seemed pissed but didn't argue. I suspected that Eli wanted to talk to him alone before meeting Declan for dinner. I knew that soon they would all press me for a decision that I wasn't ready to make. I stepped into the shower as doubt shadowed me. Had I just made the biggest mistake of my life?

CHAPTER 18

Declan

THE LAST THING I wanted to do was hobnob with the dicks who'd been blowing me off for months. I wanted to be out looking for Delilah. I couldn't focus on anything since she disappeared. I'd been interested in an alliance with Maxwell and Strain when I took over the zone. I knew that I couldn't retain control without solid allies. Maintaining power was essential. Earning respect was vital. Without both, I wouldn't stand a chance of running this zone.

Now that Delilah was missing, I didn't care what happened to my company or myself, for that matter. I knew that if I skipped this dinner, I would regret it. There was nothing left to do but shower and prepare. I needed to read the files I had on each of them again before leaving for the restaurant.

What I wanted was to find Delilah and claim her, like I should have done already. I was trying to keep myself in control because of her amnesia. I was scared to move too quickly in case she already had someone. But the more time I spent with her, the more I wanted to make promises to her, promises that I'd never given to anyone before. In the past, I'd kept myself distanced from any chance of falling in love. Somehow Delilah had changed that. I didn't even realize when things changed. I couldn't hide my feelings anymore. I was determined to find her and tell her exactly how I felt and what I wanted to do to her. Thinking about her was dangerous for many reasons, mainly because I was alone and horny.

I climbed into the shower, standing in the scalding water. I was terrified that something had happened to Delilah, and it froze me to the bone. Thinking about her was enough to thaw me, though. I found myself adjusting the water and stroking myself. The smell of my soap set me off because she had insisted on using it instead of getting her own. There was something about her wanting to smell like me that turned me on. I soaped up and continued to run my hand up and down my shaft, wishing it was my girl taking care of me instead. I wanted her on her knees with my cock in her mouth. That fantasy was enough to finish me. I continued to think about her lush lips wrapped around my dick and I started to get hard again. I didn't have time to indulge again. I pushed the thought away and cleaned up. I needed to get ready for this meeting.

I had no idea what they wanted. I didn't like going into a meeting blind. I preferred to know exactly what my counterpart wanted and have my negotiation strategy in place. If you knew what the other side wanted, it was easier to steer them toward your own goal. I wondered if they would be able to help me search for Delilah. Would it even be worth asking? It didn't matter. I would hear them out, and then I would ask for help. I didn't care if they refused; at least I would know that I'd tried everything to find her.

Kayden's words kept echoing in my mind. He meant what he'd said. He wasn't on my side anymore and wouldn't protect Delilah from the hunters. My best friend had turned into my worst enemy. The hunters had the resources to find Delilah before I could. The punishment for an unsanctioned change was severe but typically fell on the vamp responsible, not the person who got turned. I had to do everything in my power to find her first.

I threw on a button-up shirt and jeans. Starlight was a high-class place, but I still wasn't wearing a suit. I had to dress nicely enough that they would let me in, though. I considered my pitch for creating an alliance as I drove to the restaurant. *But what did they want from me?* I wracked my brain to figure out what either of them could want from me. I came up empty-handed every time. Yeah, people came from across the country to purchase my hand-sculpted wood furniture, but these guys didn't seem the type to care about that.

I walked into Starlight with purpose. "May I help you, sir?" The hostess was a cute petite blond who might have been in her twenties. She was pretty but didn't compare with Delilah.

"I'm here to meet with Mr. Maxwell and Mr. Strain. I was told there was a reservation." I wasn't sure if she believed me or not from the look that she gave me. After picking up the phone on the hostess stand and having a hushed conversation, she hung up and walked over to me.

"Right this way, Mr. Roarke. I'm sorry for the delay in seating you. Your party is waiting." She gestured for me to follow her, then led me to the back of the restaurant, to a private event area. This must be big if they want to ensure we can't be overheard. "Just through there, sir." She opened the door and motioned for me to enter. I nodded my thanks at her and walked through the door before she closed it behind me. The room was dark, with only candlelight. There was a small table on the far side of the room, with three figures seated.

"Declan!" Delilah's squeal caught me off guard as much as her racing across the room to jump into my arms.

"Mo chroí! Are you okay? I've been looking everywhere for you." I pulled her into a tight hug, not giving her a chance to respond. She hugged me back as tightly, and all my stress melted away.

"I'm fine. There was a problem, but Vik and Eli took care of me. As soon as I was able to ask for you, they called and arranged this dinner. And just look at this dress!" She stepped back and twirled, showing off the slinky black dress.

"You look amazing. I'm so relieved that you're not hurt. What kind of problem did you run into? Was it at the club?" I wanted answers, but Delilah shook her head and pulled me over to the table.

"Eli, Vik, this is Declan. Declan, this is Eli, and this is Vik." She introduced them as if they were more than strangers who'd helped her out of a jam. I puzzled over what she wasn't telling me. I guessed that my confusion was written all over my face.

Vik held out a hand as he stood. "Pleased to meet you. I hear you've been taking good care of our girl."

I shook his hand, but words failed me. *Our girl?* What did he mean by that? Before I could come up with a response, Eli stood and shook my hand. "We can't thank you enough for saving her life. I know this is a strange situation. Please, have a seat, and we'll discuss it all over dinner."

My gaze darted from him to Vik, then to Delilah and back. "An explanation would be nice. I feel like I've walked into the middle of the story here." I took the offered seat and smiled when Delilah sat next to me. She scooted her chair closer and held my hand. After what Vik said about her being theirs, I expected one of them to have a problem with her being affectionate toward me. Neither of them seemed to notice. Most vamps were extraordinarily territorial and possessive. It was the reason the city was split into zones.

"I'm sorry. I don't want to be rude here, but I don't understand what's happening. You said they helped you with a problem and you asked them to call me. But you said she's your girl. I'm not trying to step on any toes here, and I'm not a homewrecker, but I'm confused." I figured laying it all out there would be the best start.

Vik scowled but didn't speak. Eli laughed. "Forgive him; he's cranky. It's a long story, but yes, Delilah was in a relationship with both of us before she was kidnapped and shot. From what I can tell, that was when you got involved and turned her to save her life. Her amnesia was a product of the change, and you've been trying to help her remember her life before. Have I got it right so far?" He looked from me to Delilah, who laughed and shrugged.

"It sounds right to me, but I'm the one with amnesia, remember?" Her laugh warmed my heart. I hated seeing her sad because she didn't know who she was. This was a welcome change. I would have given anything to see her smile this way all the time. I wondered what it would cost me. "All I know is that I'm attracted to all three of you, and I don't want to choose."

The three of them looked at me expectantly as if waiting for a response. I had no idea what to say about any of it. When I imagined my life with Delilah, it wasn't exactly like this. I didn't fantasize about sharing her. I knew that people could make that work, but I had no idea if I could be one of them. "I'm guessing the two of you are fine with that?"

Vik started to speak, but Eli stopped him. "I think it should be Delilah's choice. I know that Vik and I care enough about her to do whatever it takes for her to be happy."

"If you'd stop interrupting me, I was going to say the same thing. What Delilah wants, she gets. It's that simple. We'll work out the rest as details later." Vik smiled at her as he spoke before turning and glaring at Eli. They got along well, but there was still some tension. I wondered if it would be possible to share Delilah's time and affection.

"What about jealousy? How do you deal with that?" I couldn't help asking the obvious question first.

"Well, usually the jealous party goes for a run or a workout. Or we have a fistfight about it when she's not around." Eli responded flippantly as if it wasn't a big deal.

"Do you all live together in this situation, or does she have to move between houses every few days? I'm just trying to figure out the logistics of it all and decide if it could actually work." I didn't want to lose her, but I didn't want to be blindsided by something I should have asked about in the first place.

Vik held up a hand. "Lately, we've been moving between places while Midnight is being rebuilt. I've already spoken with the contractor and made adjustments to accommodate you and potentially another. It seems our girl is a collector, after all. Once construction is complete, we will all live in the condo above the bar, Midnight. It's where Delilah grew up; it's her home. So, in the end, we'll all be living with her unless she decides otherwise."

I nodded, trying to process everything. "And this is what you want?" I turned to Delilah and asked her point-blank. From the look on her face, some of what had just been explained was news to her as well.

She wrung her hands and played with strands of her hair, trying to avoid answering. Her cheeks turned pink when she finally made eye contact with me. "I think so. There's still so much I don't remember. I think this could help. But I don't want to lose you, Dec. I want us to do this together." Tears formed in her eyes while she waited for my response.

"If I'm honest, I would do anything for you. It won't be easy to share you with two guys that I just met. We already have issues." I stared at Vik, who was glaring at me. It was as if he was angry that I didn't simply agree and fall in line.

What issues?" Eli asked, sounding genuine in his concern.

"I tried for weeks to set up meetings with both of you to form an alliance. Neither of you would give me the time of day. Every appointment was canceled last minute with little to no warning. A few of them left me sitting in your waiting rooms for an hour before your secretary bothered to tell me you weren't even in the building. So, yeah, we have issues."

CHAPTER 19

Declan

THE LAST THING I wanted to do was hobnob with the dicks who'd been blowing me off for months. I wanted to be out looking for Delilah. I couldn't focus on anything since she disappeared. I'd been interested in an alliance with Maxwell and Strain when I took over the zone. I knew that I couldn't retain control without solid allies. Maintaining power was essential. Earning respect was vital. Without both, I wouldn't stand a chance of running this zone.

Now that Delilah was missing, I didn't care what happened to my company or myself, for that matter. I knew that if I skipped this dinner, I would regret it. There was nothing left to do but shower and prepare. I needed to read the files I had on each of them again before leaving for the restaurant.

What I wanted was to find Delilah and claim her, like I should have done already. I was trying to keep myself in control because of her amnesia. I was scared to move too quickly in case she already had someone. But the more time I spent with her, the more I wanted to make promises to her, promises that I'd never given to anyone before. In the past, I'd kept myself distanced from any chance of falling in love. Somehow Delilah had changed that. I didn't even realize when things changed. I couldn't hide my feelings anymore. I was determined to find her and tell her exactly how I felt and what I wanted to do to her. Thinking about her was dangerous for many reasons, mainly because I was alone and horny.

I climbed into the shower, standing in the scalding water. I was terrified that something had happened to Delilah, and it froze me to the bone. Thinking about her was enough to thaw me, though. I found myself adjusting the water and stroking myself. The smell of my soap set me off because she had insisted on using it instead of getting her own. There was something about her wanting to smell like me that turned me on. I soaped up and continued to run my hand up and down my shaft, wishing it was my girl taking care of me instead. I wanted her on her knees with my cock in her mouth. That fantasy was enough to finish me. I continued to think about her lush lips wrapped around my dick and I started to get hard again. I didn't have time to indulge again. I pushed the thought away and cleaned up. I needed to get ready for this meeting.

I had no idea what they wanted. I didn't like going into a meeting blind. I preferred to know exactly what my counterpart wanted and have my negotiation strategy in place. If you knew what the other side wanted, it was easier to steer them toward your own goal. I wondered if they would be able to help me search for Delilah. Would it even be worth asking? It didn't matter. I would hear them out, and then I would ask for help. I didn't care if they refused; at least I would know that I'd tried everything to find her.

Kayden's words kept echoing in my mind. He meant what he'd said. He wasn't on my side anymore and wouldn't protect Delilah from the hunters. My best friend had turned into my worst enemy. The hunters had the resources to find Delilah before I could. The punishment for an unsanctioned change was severe but typically fell on the vamp responsible, not the person who got turned. I had to do everything in my power to find her first.

I threw on a button-up shirt and jeans. Starlight was a high-class place, but I still wasn't wearing a suit. I had to dress nicely enough that they would let me in, though. I considered my pitch for creating an alliance as I drove to the restaurant. *But what did they want from me?* I wracked my brain to figure out what either of them could want from me. I came up empty-handed every time. Yeah, people came from across the country to purchase my hand-sculpted wood furniture, but these guys didn't seem the type to care about that.

I walked into Starlight with purpose. "May I help you, sir?" The hostess was a cute petite blond who might have been in her twenties. She was pretty but didn't compare with Delilah.

"I'm here to meet with Mr. Maxwell and Mr. Strain. I was told there was a reservation." I wasn't sure if she believed me or not from the look that she gave me. After picking up the phone on the hostess stand and having a hushed conversation, she hung up and walked over to me.

"Right this way, Mr. Roarke. I'm sorry for the delay in seating you. Your party is waiting." She gestured for me to follow her, then led me to the back of the restaurant, to a private event area. This must be big if they want to ensure we can't be overheard. "Just through there, sir." She opened the door and motioned for me to enter. I nodded my thanks at her and walked through the door before she closed it behind me. The room was dark, with only candlelight. There was a small table on the far side of the room, with three figures seated.

"Declan!" Delilah's squeal caught me off guard as much as her racing across the room to jump into my arms.

"Mo chroí! Are you okay? I've been looking everywhere for you." I pulled her into a tight hug, not giving her a chance to respond. She hugged me back as tightly, and all my stress melted away.

"I'm fine. There was a problem, but Vik and Eli took care of me. As soon as I was able to ask for you, they called and arranged this dinner. And just look at this dress!" She stepped back and twirled, showing off the slinky black dress.

"You look amazing. I'm so relieved that you're not hurt. What kind of problem did you run into? Was it at the club?" I wanted answers, but Delilah shook her head and pulled me over to the table.

"Eli, Vik, this is Declan. Declan, this is Eli, and this is Vik." She introduced them as if they were more than strangers who'd helped her out of a jam. I puzzled over what she wasn't telling me. I guessed that my confusion was written all over my face.

Vik held out a hand as he stood. "Pleased to meet you. I hear you've been taking good care of our girl."

I shook his hand, but words failed me. *Our girl?* What did he mean by that? Before I could come up with a response, Eli stood and shook my hand. "We can't thank you enough for saving her life. I know this is a strange situation. Please, have a seat, and we'll discuss it all over dinner."

My gaze darted from him to Vik, then to Delilah and back. "An explanation would be nice. I feel like I've walked into the middle of the story here." I took the offered seat and smiled when Delilah sat next to me. She scooted her chair closer and held my hand. After what Vik said about her being theirs, I expected one of them to have a problem with her being affectionate toward me. Neither of them seemed to notice. Most vamps were extraordinarily territorial and possessive. It was the reason the city was split into zones.

"I'm sorry. I don't want to be rude here, but I don't understand what's happening. You said they helped you with a problem and you asked them to call me. But you said she's your girl. I'm not trying to step on any toes here, and I'm not a homewrecker, but I'm confused." I figured laying it all out there would be the best start.

Vik scowled but didn't speak. Eli laughed. "Forgive him; he's cranky. It's a long story, but yes, Delilah was in a relationship with both of us before she was kidnapped and shot. From what I can tell, that was when you got involved and turned her to save her life. Her amnesia was a product of the change, and you've been trying to help her remember her life before. Have I got it right so far?" He looked from me to Delilah, who laughed and shrugged.

"It sounds right to me, but I'm the one with amnesia, remember?" Her laugh warmed my heart. I hated seeing her sad because she didn't know who she was. This was a welcome change. I would have given anything to see her smile this way all the time. I wondered what it would cost me. "All I know is that I'm attracted to all three of you, and I don't want to choose."

The three of them looked at me expectantly as if waiting for a response. I had no idea what to say about any of it. When I imagined my life with Delilah, it wasn't exactly like this. I didn't fantasize about sharing her. I knew that people could make that work, but I had no idea if I could be one of them. "I'm guessing the two of you are fine with that?"

Vik started to speak, but Eli stopped him. "I think it should be Delilah's choice. I know that Vik and I care enough about her to do whatever it takes for her to be happy."

"If you'd stop interrupting me, I was going to say the same thing. What Delilah wants, she gets. It's that simple. We'll work out the rest as details later." Vik smiled at her as he spoke before turning and glaring at Eli. They got along well, but there was still some tension. I wondered if it would be possible to share Delilah's time and affection.

"What about jealousy? How do you deal with that?" I couldn't help asking the obvious question first.

"Well, usually the jealous party goes for a run or a workout. Or we have a fistfight about it when she's not around." Eli responded flippantly as if it wasn't a big deal.

"Do you all live together in this situation, or does she have to move between houses every few days? I'm just trying to figure out the logistics of it all and decide if it could actually work." I didn't want to lose her, but I didn't want to be blindsided by something I should have asked about in the first place.

Vik held up a hand. "Lately, we've been moving between places while Midnight is being rebuilt. I've already spoken with the contractor and made adjustments to accommodate you and potentially another. It seems our girl is a collector, after all. Once construction is complete, we will all live in the condo above the bar, Midnight. It's where Delilah grew up; it's her home. So, in the end, we'll all be living with her unless she decides otherwise."

I nodded, trying to process everything. "And this is what you want?" I turned to Delilah and asked her point-blank. From the look on her face, some of what had just been explained was news to her as well.

She wrung her hands and played with strands of her hair, trying to avoid answering. Her cheeks turned pink when she finally made eye contact with me. "I think so. There's still so much I don't remember. I think this could help. But I don't want to lose you, Dec. I want us to do this together." Tears formed in her eyes while she waited for my response.

"If I'm honest, I would do anything for you. It won't be easy to share you with two guys that I just met. We already have issues." I stared at Vik, who was glaring at me. It was as if he was angry that I didn't simply agree and fall in line.

"What issues?" Eli asked, sounding genuine in his concern.

"I tried for weeks to set up meetings with both of you to form an alliance. Neither of you would give me the time of day. Every appointment was canceled last minute with little to no warning. A few of them left me sitting in your waiting rooms for an hour before your secretary bothered to tell me you weren't even in the building. So, yeah, we have issues."

CHAPTER 20

Delilah

I couldn't believe the way this day was going. I was on the verge of having everything I wanted or losing someone important. I needed to convince Declan to give this a chance. "Are you willing to give this a shot? I understand you three will have some things to work through. But I really don't want to lose any of you."

I wanted to claim them all right then, openly telling them that my soul was screaming that they belonged to me. Somehow that didn't seem like the right thing to say. I could tell that Declan was intimidated, and I didn't blame him. I was too. It seemed like Vik and Eli had everything planned out for me. But the way they talked, most of it had been my decision.

Hearing Vik talk about rebuilding Midnight triggered something inside me, and I got lost in a memory. My mother had run off again, chasing ghosts—my father, and left me with my uncle. *Uncle Vinny.* Oh, no. The memory of his death flooded me, and I felt strong arms pulling me up as I fell.

"Mo chroí? Are you okay? Is it a memory? Just breathe through it. I'm here." Declan's voice pulled me back into the moment. I blinked tears away and looked up at him.

"Thank you," I whispered, then pressed my lips to his for a sweet kiss. I knew he was uncomfortable because he tensed up. I looked from him to Eli and Vik, who watched as if they had no idea how to help.

"Do you want to talk about it?" Eli asked cautiously.

"We can't help you if you don't tell us what you saw," Vik growled. My memories of him were making more sense all the time. He was cranky most of the time. But I could tell that he sincerely cared about me too.

"I'm sorry," I began, holding a hand up to Dec, who was about to tell me not to apologize. "I remembered Uncle Vinny, and with that, his death." I turned to Eli and took his hand. "Please don't blame yourself. I know you were the reason he was in the hospital, but you didn't kill him. All of that was a lifetime ago, and I think I had already forgiven you for your part in it. I just wasn't ready to remember that all of my family was dead."

Vik growled and Eli pouted. I looked at Declan, and he was making a face too. "You three need to calm down. You know what I meant. Of course, you're my family now. But my uncle was like a father to me. He raised me when my parents left. It hurts to lose your memories only to learn that your dad died a violent death."

"You don't need to worry about us. We don't matter right now. You are what matters. Tell us what you need." Declan looked at Eli while he spoke as if cementing his tentative decision to join our little family. My heart soared.

"Right now, I need dinner. Something decadent and sinful. Then we need to discuss some things related to the four of us living together. Like where, and when, and such."

Vik made a face, and I couldn't help but laugh. This adventure was going to be fun. Vik took care of ordering for everyone while Eli smoothed things over with talk of helping Declan with issues in his area of the city. It was a strange situation, but it seemed like it just might work. Who says you can't have it all?

Our food was a fantastic array of various dishes, some of them made with fresh blood. I never expected to enjoy the fancy food that Vik was so fond of, but I did. The guys worked out the logistics of where we would stay and when. It didn't matter to me as long as I got to spend time with all three of them. If I didn't like something they decided, I'd just change it later. Everything seemed to be going well—Eli kept Vik under control, and Dec wasn't trying to argue about anything. Then it all changed.

"So, what was that problem you guys helped Delilah with?" Dec asked again. Eli and Vik had already avoided that question at least twice since Declan arrived.

"It's not important, Dec. I'm fine, and it's all over with. Don't worry about it." I tried to smooth things over and change the subject. "How amazing is this dessert?"

"It is important, mo chroí because you don't want me to know. Would someone please just tell me what happened? I'm beginning to think it's a bigger deal than you make it out to be." He pressed. I groaned, knowing that this could cause a fight between my guys. I had wanted to keep the whole thing under wraps and forget it ever happened.

"It's really not a big deal. I'm not sure why Delilah didn't want us to tell you. Someone at your club drugged her, and I found her before he took her out. She was given human blood with Powder in it. There was no harm to the human but fatal to her if she'd ingested it all. I came along at the right time to distract her, and Vik helped me bring her home." Eli's explanation was concise and straightforward. I hoped that Declan didn't press for details.

"Drugged? At my club? How? Why? Who would do that?" Declan raised his voice with each question. It was clear that this wasn't going to be swept under the rug.

"Don't worry. We have it handled. Our guys are searching for the source, and it will be dealt with once we have the culprit in our sights." Vik interjected with a smirk. I hated how he loved to push buttons. At one time, I thought it was only with Eli, but now I see it's with anyone he sees as competition or a threat.

"Look, Dec, there's nothing you can do about it. It happened. I'm fine, I promise. While I recovered, Vik and Eli took care of me and were perfect gentlemen. Can we please just let it go?" I hated begging, but I also didn't want to watch the three of them fight. The first time I'd watched Vik remove Eli's hand, and I wasn't about to go through that again.

I found myself staring at Eli. That memory was so real, but he had both hands. Was I going crazy? Did it even happen? Disbelief painted my expression, and I got lost in my memories. I still didn't have enough of myself from before to figure out what was going on.

"Love? Are you okay? You've been staring at me for a while now." Eli's words went right through me. He turned to Vik, "She's having more memories. I guess you were right about bringing her here."

"Myshka? Can you hear me?" Vik knelt in front of my chair and took both my hands in one of his. Then he gently turned me to face him. My eyes were glazed over, and even though I could see what was happening, I couldn't interact. It was like watching myself in a movie.

I had no idea how much time had passed. I felt a cool rag pressed to my face. When I looked around, I wasn't at the restaurant anymore. The room was familiar, but I wasn't sure where I was. I tried to sit up, but a hand pressed against my shoulder and kept me from it. "Take it easy, mo chroí. It was hard enough to get the other two to rest with you zoned out that way. Don't give them a reason not to trust me. I told them I'd make sure you stayed in bed until you felt better."

"What happened?" I turned my head toward Declan and found that he was lying in bed with me. Someone had changed my clothes, and he wasn't wearing any from what I could tell.

"Eli and I changed you out of your dress. No one took advantage of you, I promise. Vik wanted to run down some leads on the person responsible for drugging you. I offered to stay with you so Eli could go with him. I don't think either of them was excited about it, but given that you said you didn't want to lose me, they agreed." His smirk made me smile. I was glad that they'd been able to take care of me without fighting about it.

I rolled over toward Declan and pressed my lips to his. I meant it to be a sweet thank you for making sure I was okay. I wasn't ready for the wave of need that hit me when our lips touched. "Are you going to push me away again because I don't know who I was?" I whispered against his mouth.

Dec's breath hitched. My words caught him off guard. I kissed him again, this time working my tongue into his mouth to dance with his. One of my hands was pinned between us, resting on his naked chest. The other wandered along his back, his arm, his waist. I was wrong about him not wearing anything. He had stripped down to his boxer briefs before climbing into bed with me. I play growled at him as I toyed with the waistband.

"Are you sure this is what you want?" The question was whispered against my skin as I trailed kisses down his neck and chest.

"I want you. Is that a clear enough message?" I breathed against his ear, watching the goosebumps radiate from my words. The moment I said them, he flipped me onto my back and kissed me possessively.

"You're mine," he growled, tearing the buttons from my top as he pulled it open. I couldn't suppress my moan. Declan in control was hot. Maybe having to figure out who I am now wasn't such a bad thing.

Dec pulled the ruined top off me and threw it aside. I hadn't known him for long, but this was the first time I'd seen him act dominating. I wondered if this was how he always was in bed, but the thought escaped me when he leaned down and took my nipple in his mouth. Rational thought melted away, leaving only the sensations of his touch behind. I reached up to run my hands over him. He grabbed my wrists, pulled them over my head, and held me still with one hand as his mouth continued its journey to map every inch of my chest.

"I'm pleasuring you first. You'd better behave, or there will be punishment." He growled. I smirked at him, wondering what kind of punishment he'd come up with if I disobeyed. "You won't like it," he warned, obviously noticing my grin.

"How do you know? Maybe I would," I countered, nipping at his bottom lip when he raised his head to look at me. Passion radiated from him as his eyes bored into my soul. As much as I wanted to be naughty and see what he would do, I wanted to see how he would please me. After staring at each other for a minute, I relented, "Okay, I'll be good."

"That's what I thought," he muttered as he ripped my thong off, and it joined my top on the floor. With my assurance that I'd behave, he abandoned my hands, trusting that I wouldn't touch him. He trailed his hands down my body, caressing every inch between my shoulder and my waist. I tried to raise my hips to lead him where I wanted. The second I moved, I realized it was a mistake. He froze, whipping his gaze to mine. "I warned you," he uttered.

"I didn't do anything," I whimpered. My eyes widened as he moved, and the cool air replaced him against my skin. "Please," I begged.

His glare faded into a smug smile. "You don't like your punishment?" How was I supposed to respond to that?

"No, I don't. Get back over here. I'm cold and lonely." I tried to sound sad, but to me, it sounded desperate. I didn't care as long as he came back and touched me again.

He shook his head, taking another step back. "You have to learn to behave, mo chroí. If I don't teach you, who will?"

I decided that if he could tease me, I could tease him right back. "Well, if you aren't going to take care of me, I'll just do it myself. If you're nice to me, I might let you watch." I trailed a finger down my collarbone, between my breasts, then down my stomach toward my center. Declan's eyes were glued to me.

"What if I don't want to watch? What if I want to take over?" He growled before jumping on me. He pushed my hand out of the way and licked my apex. I couldn't stifle the moan. That was all the encouragement he needed. He sucked my clit in his mouth and teased it with his tongue until I screamed with my orgasm.

Just when I thought he was finished, he slipped a finger inside me and found the perfect spot to rub. He stopped a moment before I climaxed, adjusting our position, so he was above me. The tip of his cock pressed at my opening. I wanted to lift my hips to ease him in, but after what happened the last time I moved, I didn't. He was torturing both of us with his teasing. Declan tried to hold out, but the torture was too much for him. My body begged for him to complete what he'd begun.

When I thought I'd go crazy from being so close to orgasm with no relief in sight, Dec thrust his dick into me. His pace was slow and tantalizing, giving me time to adjust to his girth. If I hadn't been so close to coming, I might have marveled at his control. I concentrated on slowing my release. As if he sensed what I was doing, Declan increased his pace, and I couldn't stop the explosion. I screamed his name as the fireworks went off inside me. He tensed with his release, and I heard him whisper my name before he collapsed on top of me.

A moment later, he rolled onto his back, pulling me on top of him. I leaned down and kissed him. Then I laid my head on his chest and let his heartbeat lull me to sleep. I couldn't remember being this happy ever before.

CHAPTER 21

Eli

I KNEW IT WAS risky leaving Declan alone with Delilah. He could have been planning to whisk her away the second we left. I also knew that whatever she wanted, I would agree with. She made it clear how much he meant to her, and I vowed that I would keep Vik in line so we could make this work. Because of that, I followed Vik and left the two of them alone. It didn't matter to me if she was affectionate with other men, as long as I got to share her time. I knew that my time with her would be later.

Vik had a problem with jealousy and a violent temper, so I agreed to go with him to run down a lead on the drugging. The fact that our positions had flipped didn't escape me. Before we were turned, he'd been the one keeping me from killing someone. Jail wasn't a fun place to be. He reminded me of that on more than one occasion. Unfortunately for us, jail wasn't an option. If a vamp killed someone, we would go on trial. If we were found guilty, the hunters would execute our punishment. There was no life in prison, no opportunity for parole. An unjust death resulted in death.

When Vik told us about the lead, Declan mentioned the hunters in the city. It seemed strange to me that they would be here, but he explained that he'd grown up with one of the guys. He'd called the guy for help to find Delilah. Part of me wondered why he hadn't let them know she'd been found. I understood that Delilah was unsanctioned, and we would need to keep her hidden until Declan could complete the paperwork and pay the fines. To be fair, Vik and I would chip in on the fine part. After all, we'd all be living with Delilah. She would be our responsibility to care for and protect. We would probably end up having to go in front of the Council that controlled the hunters to plead our case.

253

Someone would have to explain that Delilah was dying and there was no other choice. There hadn't been time for paperwork.

I knew it was risky, but I also knew that we would do whatever it took to keep Delilah safe. I didn't want to go up against the Council. If they denied us, they would take Delilah away, or worse, publicly execute her. I knew none of us would be okay with that. All four of us would end up dead in that situation. Vik and I needed to find out who'd drugged Delilah and why. We had a limited amount of time to do it. If we could prove that someone had tried to kill her before the Council called us to face them, we might be able to convince them that Jones had been working with the person responsible. That would prove that her death would have been murder. Most cases where the newly turned was murdered ended up sliding by. The killer would be taken out, and the victim would be free to live their life without worry. That was the best I could hope for right now. Without proof, it would be impossible to convince them, though.

"Eli! Come on, man. We have to get moving. This kid isn't going to hang around forever." Vik's voice snapped me out of my thoughts. I didn't realize we'd made it to the meeting spot. I was so lost in my concerns about Delilah. I shook off the thoughts and got out of the car.

"Who is this kid we're meeting?" I whispered as we crept down the alley. I wasn't sure we could trust Vik's informant. After finding Delilah, I didn't want to chance anything happening to us either. She needed us.

"His name's Trevor. He's related to someone who's in on the Powder operation. He's got some inside info on what's going on." Vik kept his voice low, sauntering toward the dumpster at the back of the alley.

Crouched beside it was a kid. He couldn't have been more than ten if that. This couldn't possibly be our contact. There was no way Vik was going to interrogate a ten-year-old kid, right? I slowed my steps and looked around for someone else in the area. The alley was completely deserted except for the kid and us. Vik slinked in the shadows toward the kid. I stayed within earshot, where I could grab Vik if I needed to, and listened.

"Trevor?" Vik whispered when he was a few feet away from the kid.

He looked up and nodded. "You Viktor?"

Vik nodded in response. "I heard you might have some information about something that happened to my friend." I was impressed that he was being somewhat gentle with the kid.

"First, I need proof of who you are. And your friend too. I can't be too careful here. This is dangerous stuff you're asking about." The kid seemed older than ten with his paranoia.

Vik held out a hand for my ID, then passed it along with his own to the kid for inspection. Trevor looked them over then handed the cards back to Vik, who gave mine back to me. Once they were put away again, the kid started to talk. "My dad got caught up in the Powder operation. You have to understand how bad things were for us. We had nowhere to go. Dad lost his job, Mom is sick, and there are three of us kids. I'm doing the best I can to take care of Mom and the younger two."

"We're not judging your family, Trevor. We just need to know who tried to hurt our friend. I promise no one will hurt your dad, and your family will be rewarded for your help." Vik handed the kid an envelope. I was sure it was stuffed with hundred-dollar bills. It was just like Vik to buy whoever he wanted. There were other options, but of course, he couldn't see them. "This is for you and your family. There's a card with my number on it as well. Your dad can call me to set up a job interview. I'm sure we can find him something better to do. And we'll take care of your mom's medical needs, too, as well as housing for the family. I just need you to tell me what you know, okay?" My jaw dropped. What Vik just offered this kid was precisely what I would have done in his situation. I wouldn't have thought of including an envelope full of cash with the offer, though. I guess I didn't know everything about him after all.

Trevor looked at the cash in the envelope then tucked it into his backpack. "What if they don't let him out?"

Vik's expression softened. "Then we will take care of it. If he wants out of the operation to work for me, I will ensure you all get out of the area safely. No one will harm him. Please, Trevor, I just need to know what you heard."

The kid seemed to mull over what Vik had offered and promised. "Okay. Everyone thinks the Phantoms are run by the guy who runs the Eastside. They're wrong." Trevor gulped as if he was scared to share the next part. "Vampires run the zones. Except for the East. Shifters run it. I know it sounds crazy, but it's true. I've seen them. Men who can turn into wolves. They're the ones running the Phantoms. And that's who's behind the Powder operation. I've heard them talking. The wolves want to hunt down the vampires and kill them all. I don't know why." He started shaking and couldn't continue.

"Trevor, I want to tell you a secret. Can you keep a secret?" Vik leaned a little closer but still just out of reach of the kid. Trevor nodded, blinking back tears. "My friend and I are vampires. I know that shifters are real. And I believe everything you just told me. Thank you. I understand how scary this was for you. Please have your dad call me. I meant what I said. I'll make sure you're safe."

Trevor grinned like a cat who'd caught a canary. You'd think that Vik had promised him the moon. "You guys are vampires? I thought so when you got here. I'm getting better at noticing. Can I go now? I have to get home before Dad does. He'll be mad that I left the little ones alone with Mom. She's supposed to be resting."

Vik nodded, and the kid ran off, tossing his backpack on his shoulders as he jogged. He seemed to know his way around the city. I wondered how many times he'd run through the alleys and what kind of things he'd been forced to do to help his family. Their story was heartbreaking. I wanted to help them. Maybe we'd be able to.

"Well, that's more than we had before, but still not enough," Vik grumbled. He turned and stomped off toward the car. I followed him, considering everything we'd just heard.

"It's a start. Maybe Declan will have some ideas of how to get more information. He has a friend in the hunters, after all. If they're using the Phantoms as a front, maybe we can find out why. There has to be more to it than the shifters want us all dead." I knew that my thoughts made sense, but I also knew that sometimes life didn't make any sense at all. There may not be another reason. I climbed into the car and ran a hand through my hair. Why wasn't anything ever simple?

CHAPTER 22

Viktor

I WAS PISSED THAT our lead didn't pan out but hopeful that I'd be able to help the kid and his family out of a bad situation. It sucked to be backed against the wall and see no other option for survival. Turning to the drug trade was not a good job choice if I had anything to say about it. I wondered if the kid's dad would call me. I couldn't spend time worrying about that right now. I needed to focus on getting more information to protect Delilah. She was the top priority. I would burn the city down if it came to that. I wasn't looking forward to meeting with the Council and pleading our case. I needed to connect Jones to the Powder operation.

Eli was quiet on the way back to his place. We'd regroup there before meeting the others at Declan's place. I wasn't sure how I felt about him yet, but he seemed like a stand-up guy. I'd done a background check the moment Delilah asked for him. There was no way I would turn her over to a maniac. He had a record, but nothing violent. Honestly, I would have been more worried if he'd been completely clean. There's no such thing for a vampire. We all have skeletons in our closets. The only question is, how did they get there? Some men were proud of their past indiscretions. I was not one of them, and neither was Eli.

We promised to take care of Delilah and protect her. After spending so much time searching, it was killing me to be away from her. I wanted nothing more than to stay wrapped up in her arms and never leave her again. Logically, that wasn't possible. I knew Eli felt the same way, and it seemed like Declan did, too, even though he didn't know her as well as we did. Of course, he might know her better than we did with her amnesia. That thought killed me. I hated feeling jealous. No matter how hard I tried, I couldn't push it

257

away. Eli had been helping me work through it but adding another guy wouldn't make it easier. I needed to get myself under control now.

I pulled the car into the garage and parked. "Are you up for sparring? I need to work out some aggression before we go back to Delilah."

Eli raised an eyebrow at me, then shrugged. "I can handle that. We need to talk about all of this anyway." He led the way to the elevator and pushed the basement button. A moment later, we stepped out into the full gym that he'd designed and built under his building. It had every machine imaginable and a climbing wall. What I was interested in was the boxing ring.

Once we'd changed to shorts, Eli led me into the ring. Gloves would have been a good idea, but neither of us ever used them. The point of us sparring was to feel the hits' pain and get it all out of our systems. "So, what do you think about him?" I asked as Eli ducked to avoid my first swing.

"I get a good feeling from him. He wouldn't hurt her. He's still kind of naïve when it comes to business dealing, but we can teach him. I think he was smart to seek an alliance." Eli had always leaned on reading people's emotions.

"I did a background check on him," I said between taking a punch and returning it. "The usual, but nothing violent. I think he's a solid guy. I'm not sure how I feel about sharing our girl with him, though." I hated to admit that, but Eli was the closest thing I'd ever had to a brother.

He nodded, dodging and weaving as I threw punches that just didn't connect. "I understand that feeling. It's not our decision who she loves, though. You have to decide if you can deal with it or not. I'm all in. What Delilah wants; Delilah gets. Right now, she's decided that's the three of us."

"I get that." I finally connected a right hook with his jaw, and the feeling of satisfaction washed over me. "You know I'll do anything she asks. Hell, I don't even like sharing her with you. But she's worth it. I just have to work out how to get through it."

Eli threw a punch and swept my leg at the same time. I had no way to avoid it and hit the mat hard. "Do you need to fight him to make yourself feel better? What are you worried about? She's not going to leave you unless you give her a reason."

I knew he was right. Breathing hard, I stood up. "I guess I'm worried that he can't protect her as well as we can. Maybe a fight is just what I need to assess how much training he needs."

Eli laughed. "Don't tell him that's what you're doing. It won't go over well. Just tell him you like to spar and ask if he's interested. I'm sure he'll be game. I'd give it a day or so, though. You don't want to scare him off."

I agreed with him, so I pondered the best way to convince Declan to fight me while I tried to kick Eli's ass. I landed a few punches, but I wasn't entirely focused. He hit me more than I hit him. I hated to admit that he may have been a better fighter than I was. There was no way I would tell him that. Ever. Once we were worn out from beating on each other, we headed to the showers. I would need a couple of hours of sleep before we met the others.

After showering, I convinced Eli to call Declan and check on Delilah. He put the call on speaker, so I could listen without straining. "Hello?" It was Delilah's voice that came through.

"Hey, love, is everything okay?" Eli asked, wondering why she answered Declan's phone. I raised an eyebrow.

"Yeah, Dec is asleep. I saw that you were calling and figured he wouldn't mind if I answered. Did you find anything out?" Her voice was quiet. I could tell she'd been sleeping when we called.

"A bit," I answered, "but not enough. We're still hunting."

"Oh, it's both of you! Good. I was worried about you. I didn't know what kind of trouble you were going to get into." She chuckled, and the sound made me smile.

"Yeah, we're both here. I think we're going to get some sleep before we head over unless you need us now?" Eli sounded hopeful. Part of me wanted her to need us immediately, too. But it made more sense to rest and recover.

"I'm okay. Dec is taking good care of me. Thank you for understanding that I care about him too. I can't imagine my life without you three. Everything will be perfect once we're all moved in together." Delilah sounded happier than I'd ever heard her.

"We'll see you in a few hours. If you need anything, just call this number. Vik and I will come running." Eli made sure she had his number. We would have to get her a phone. Why hadn't I thought of that sooner? Of course, she'd lost her phone when Jones took her. Otherwise, Declan would have found out about us sooner.

Once he hung up, I used his computer to order a new phone for Delilah. We'd pick it up on our way to see her in a few hours. Eli arranged to have all her info from the old phone transferred to the new one, so it would have everything she needed the moment I handed it to her. Before we turned in for the evening, Eli and I packed a bag for Delilah with her clothes he had in her room. Most of what she'd had at Midnight had been ruined in the last disaster. I couldn't believe that I had initially blamed Eli for blowing up Midnight. It seemed like the hunters had been behind everything in some form or another. I wondered if we would be able to connect Jones to them before the Council got involved.

CHAPTER 23

Declan

DELILAH WAS CURLED UP beside me with my phone lying on the pillow next to her when I woke up. I grabbed it carefully to see if I'd missed anything. Eli had called, and she'd spoken with him. It shouldn't bother me, but I felt a stab of jealousy anyway. I would have to get that under control if this would work. I debated calling him back and opted to shoot a text instead. I didn't want to wake Delilah, or Eli for that matter if he was sleeping. *Is everything okay? Delilah is sleeping, and I saw that you called.* I didn't expect an immediate answer, so the buzz of the phone in my hand made me jump. I glanced at Delilah to find she was still sleeping peacefully.

Didn't learn much, will talk when we get there. Have to stop and pick up D's phone on the way. Need sleep first.

I shot off a quick response to let him know I understood. I hated to leave her alone after everything she'd been through. When I'd found her bleeding out at the deli, I had no idea that she'd been kidnapped and tortured because of who she loved. That was a lot for anyone to go through. Add in the amnesia that only gave her random peeks at what her life had been, and this became a much more sensitive situation.

I needed something to keep my mind off the horrors my girl had seen while staying nearby if she had a nightmare. I grabbed my tablet and settled back into bed with her. I could review and tweak designs while she rested. I was certain Eli would let me know when they were on their way so Delilah could be showered and dressed before they got here. I wasn't sure how they would react to the scent of our night together. Everything had become more complicated in the span of just a few hours.

I opted to check my emails first to see if there had been any requests from my clients. I only had a few big projects going on, and one was nearly finished. Watson had requested changes at every turn, so I held off on finishing the piece. I couldn't blame him. The crib was a gift for his daughter, who made him a grandpa for the first time. Nerves were to be expected. But if he completely changed the theme again, I'd charge him double. Twice was enough for starting over. As expected, there was an email from Watson. *Could you change the inlay on the crib? My daughter would love cherry instead of the walnut we'd agreed upon before.* What an ass! I had special ordered the walnut.

I adjusted the design after sending my reply back with the additional cost and time. The crib was intricately carved with woodland creatures along the bars and a fairy tale scene in the head and footboards. At least he hadn't wanted to change that again. I got lost in my design for a while and didn't notice that Delilah was stirring. I added some finishing touches in the preview image to send to Watson when her hand found me. I jumped at her fingers on my stomach.

"You okay?" She asked with a giggle.

"I was working. You caught me off guard." I admitted freely that I'd been lost in my work. For me, creating with wood was more than work. It was my passion. And I was damn good at it. "I heard you got a call last night."

She smiled and nodded. "Eli called for you, but you were sleeping. I didn't think you'd care if I answered."

"I have nothing to hide. If I did, you wouldn't have the unlock code to my phone." I paused for a moment, unsure if I should tell her about Eli mentioning her phone. "The guys will be here in a while. They needed sleep. He's supposed to let me know when they leave."

"Good. That gives me time to shower and get ready. I'm going to make you all take me shopping today. I need clothes. I should have grabbed some from Eli's. Did you know there was an entire closet full of my stuff at his place?" Delilah's joy was apparent. I wondered if she regretted agreeing to come home with me last night. I was too scared to ask, though.

"Maybe he'll bring you some things. If not, we can always go there and get what you want. Or I'll buy you what you need for here, and you can keep that stuff there. It's up to you. I got the impression that they agree with me—we just want you to be happy."

"I am happy. I can't say that I'll be happier when I remember who I was. The girl I used to be seems to have been through a lot. I honestly am not sure I want to remember those things. I want to go from here and move forward. If I could see the memories and not get caught up in them, that would be okay. It just feels like I can't breathe when one of them takes hold." A single tear fell down her cheek. I wiped it away with my thumb and pressed my lips to hers.

"It's okay. We need to figure out a way for you to let us know that it's happening so we can pull you back from it. The whole thing is going to take time. We all have to be patient and work together." I couldn't believe I was saying that. It was as if we really were a family. Somehow, I felt connected to these guys almost as much as I did to Delilah. I hoped it wasn't a mistake.

"I wish I knew how to explain my feelings. There's this connection to all of you, but with the other two, it's different. There's history, and I don't remember most of it. I'm at a disadvantage with them. But with you, I feel safe. When I was with them, I randomly had those memory flashes. I haven't had one since we left. The things I remember aren't all good, either. Those two have done some nasty things to me and for me." Delilah shivered. I placed my tablet on the nightstand and pulled her into my arms.

"I'm here for you. If you want to tell me about it, I'll listen. If you want me to hate those other guys, I will. Whatever you want. You tell me, and I'll do it." I held her close as if my arms could convince her that my words were true.

"I don't want to feel so confused. I hate that one minute, I want them, and the next, I want to punch them." The battle inside of her showed on her face. I wanted to kiss away her worries. There was no way to do that, though. She had to decide what she wanted, and I had to make sure she got it.

"Let's go get ready for that shopping trip. I have a feeling a little retail therapy is just what the doctor ordered." I kissed her gently and climbed from the bed, holding a hand out for her to join me. She took my hand and followed me to the shower. It would have been easy to make love to her again, but we had company coming, and there would be time for that later. Once we were showered, I found Delilah one of my shirts and a pair of leggings Steph had left for her. Since she felt safe with me, I figured it might help ease her anxiety. We got dressed and enjoyed a blood bag in the kitchen while waiting for the guys to arrive.

CHAPTER 24

Delilah

I WASN'T SURE IF it was the stress of everything going on or the workout I'd had the day before, but I was famished. Declan had to stop me at my third blood bag, or I would have insisted on a fourth. "I'm sorry, it just tastes so good." I hated feeling like I disappointed him. From what Dec had told me earlier, I knew I had to be careful with the blood. If I let myself have too much at once, I could spaz out and kill someone. I didn't want that. I needed to remain in control. I took a minute to breathe while he disposed of the bags. The scent of his shirt helped calm me. Maybe I shouldn't go shopping. I could just get pants and make sure I had to wear the guys' shirts all the time.

I knew it wasn't a great idea. Vik would want to go to another fancy dinner, or Dec would want to go to the club again, or Eli would have something that would mean I needed my own clothes. Part of me just wanted to run away with the three of them and not deal with anything ever again. Given that they had their corporations to run, I knew it was just a fantasy. I wondered what Mom would think if she could see me now. She'd always been so convinced that I'd never really amount to anything because I was so attached to the bar. She might have been right, except that now I had three fabulous, rich, intelligent men who wanted me. Not only that, but they wanted me enough to share me. I realized that her opinion of me was something I didn't remember before.

"Dec! I just had a memory, and I didn't zone out," I exclaimed excitedly.

Declan scooped me up in his arms and twirled me around the kitchen. "That's amazing! I knew you could do it." He set me on my feet and pressed his lips to mine gently. I wrapped my arms around his neck and deepened the kiss. I wanted to drag him back to the bedroom, but I heard the door and knew Eli and Vik were here.

I pulled away from him and ran for the door. "Wait! You don't know who it is," he called after me. I heard his footsteps chasing after me toward the door.

"It's the rest of my guys. I know it," I said over my shoulder as I threw the door open. Eli had just raised his hand to knock. "Get in here. I missed you guys." I dragged Eli in first, grabbed Vik's arm, and pulled him inside the condo. I kissed Vik, then Eli, before turning back to Declan with a smirk. "See, I knew who it was."

"Come in; make yourselves comfortable. Delilah wants to go shopping today. I figured we had some things to talk about first." Dec gestured toward the living room. I watched as my three guys walked to the couch with purpose. Maybe we could postpone shopping and stay in for a while. I couldn't help but imagine being with all of them at once. What would that even be like? I must have been lost in my thoughts because Vik waved his hand in front of my face to get my attention.

"Myshka? Would you like to open your gift now?" He asked as I finally returned to the present moment and sat next to him on the couch.

"You got me a gift? Why?" I asked, then realized that I sounded pretty rude. "Of course, I'll open it now. Thank you!" I took the bag he handed me and carefully pulled out a box. I stared at it, trying to make sense of what had just happened. The package I held had a brand-new phone in it. I tore into the box and pulled out the fully set up phone. It was top of the line and appeared to have everything from my previous life already loaded onto it. I scrolled through the contacts. Uncle Vinny was missing, but Declan was already listed. I didn't recognize most of the names besides my guys, but it felt good to connect to the past. "Thank you. This was so thoughtful. How did you get everything transferred? Did you have my old phone?"

Eli grinned sheepishly. "I guess you don't remember everything. Your phone was lost—destroyed actually—when you were kidnapped. I'm pretty good with technology, though, and was able to get your data back for you." He ran a hand through his hair, and a memory hit me again. In it, Eli was missing the hand that had just combed through his blond waves.

I must have looked confused because suddenly, I had three hunks staring at me like I was going to explode. "Are you okay, mo chroí?" Declan asked quietly. I nodded, then turned to Eli.

"Can I ask you guys about some of these memory flashes? Is that okay? I don't know what's imagination and what's real right now." Vik put an arm around me as I spoke, and Declan took a seat on the floor next to my feet. Eli sat down on the other side of me.

"You can ask us anything, at any time, no matter how ridiculous you think the question is. Nothing is out of bounds, love." Eli assured me, placing the hand in question on my knee. It was definitely real, so the memory had to be wrong.

"I keep seeing things. Weird things." I paused, feeling stupid.

"Like what?" Vik interjected, urging me to continue.

"Like you chopping Eli's hand off. I know, it's dumb. He obviously has his hand. I have no idea where the images came from." I stopped myself from rambling as Vik and Eli broke into laughter. "What's so funny?"

"You're not crazy. It really happened. I'm surprised you remember that over other things." Vik said, rubbing his hand down my arm to calm me down.

"I don't understand. How?" I stared at Eli, trying to figure out what didn't make sense.

He smiled at me. "Don't freak out, okay?" He waited for my nod, then removed his hand from my lap and twisted it off his wrist.

"What the actual fuck?!" I yelled. Declan reached up and pulled me onto his lap. I buried my head against his neck. This was the strangest nightmare I'd ever had.

"It's okay, love. Yes, Vik chopped my hand off. I was pissed at first, but this prosthetic nearly makes up for it. This thing can do some pretty neat stuff." It was as if Eli was trying to convince me that everything was normal.

"So, you're okay? And you guys are friends now? I'm so confused." I replied, not moving from where Dec held me.

He rubbed my back and held me tightly. "That is a little strange, guys," he said. "More than a little, if we're being honest."

Vik leaned closer to me. "I'm sorry, Myshka. It's a long story, but we've moved past it. I hope you can as well. We would love to take you shopping today if you'll let us."

CHAPTER 25

Declan

SOMEHOW, VIK CONVINCED DELILAH that shopping was exactly what she needed to get over her concerns. I hadn't heard about the hand either, and honestly, I was a little scared of these guys. I mean, if one of them randomly starts cutting parts off the other and they magically get past it...that's just strange. I kept my thoughts to myself, deciding to discuss it with Delilah when we had time alone. There was no reason to start a fight right now. There may have been nothing to worry about anyway. They both agreed that it was a long story. One day soon, I would corner one of them and force it out. Until then, I'd see what Delilah thinks in private, and we'd go from there.

I suggested that we head to shops near my home, but Vik disapproved. My side of town wasn't as upscale as he wanted. Of course, he said the same about Eli's zone. None of us wanted to cause issues in another area, so we agreed that a neutral place might be better. There were some upscale stores in the East zone of the city, and as far as we knew, none of us had a connection with the guy who ran things over there. It would be equally uncomfortable for all of us. I got volunteered to drive since I was the only one with an SUV.

I ended up getting rid of the one I'd brought Delilah home in after she'd been shot. It was replaced with a brand-new model. I had expected the heads of Maxwell Industries and Strain Industries to have multiple vehicles at their disposal. It surprised me to find out that Eli had two sports cars and Vik had nothing but a motorcycle at the moment. Everyone climbed into the SUV, and Eli brought up directions to the stores Delilah had chosen. The drive was quiet and tense. I sensed there was a lot that needed to be said, but for some reason, no one was willing to say it.

I had wanted to bring a security detail, but Vik assured me he had it under control. Eli rolled his eyes, and Delilah chuckled as if she remembered how stubborn Vik was from before. "Okay, man, if you're sure you have it. Let's go get our girl set up." We walked into the first store amidst stares from the other customers. It didn't take long for me to realize that Vik's security method involved scaring off the other patrons, so Delilah had the store to herself. I turned to Eli, "You knew this was his plan, didn't you?"

Eli laughed. "I suspected. He's pretty protective of her. Blames himself for the kidnapping since it was his guy who betrayed him."

Vik's hesitation to trust me made more sense given that information. I wouldn't trust me either. Delilah followed Vik around the store, picking out things to try on, while Eli and I followed her. Once all four of us had armfuls of different items, Eli asked an employee for the dressing room. With her reaction, I wasn't sure if he had tipped her really well or if he'd just used compulsion. Either way, she was thrilled to help our girl out.

Vik and Eli dragged three chairs over in front of the dressing room. When the girl unlocked the door, Vik insisted on checking it to ensure there was no way someone could get to Delilah. It was a little over the top, but neither of the ladies seemed to mind, and it made him feel better. With him convinced she was safe, we settled onto the chairs and let her have fun playing dress-up.

Delilah would come out every few outfits and do a slight turn as if she were in a fashion show. The three of us would clap and catcall her no matter how silly she looked. I had a feeling she was testing us because some of the things she danced around in were pretty outrageous, and I couldn't imagine her actually wearing them. She sent Vik for a different size pair of jeans, then asked Eli to grab a different color of a sweater she loved. While they were off hunting for what she'd requested, she asked me to find her a new bra and panty set. I didn't want to leave her unprotected, but it seemed crazy to worry when we were the only ones in the store. After a quick kiss, I went off to find what she'd asked for.

I turned back just in time to see the store employee who'd helped us with the dressing room walking into the tiny room with Delilah. I paused, then shrugged it off. Our girl must have needed some help with zipping something. A nagging feeling started to eat at my insides. I tried to convince myself that I was overreacting. I looked back at the dressing room and decided to go back and see where the girl had gone. She couldn't still be in there with Delilah, could she?

I tapped on the door and waited for a response. I knocked again as Eli and Vik returned with the items they'd been sent for. "Something's wrong," I said and pulled the door off its hinges. I'd pay to replace it later.

My jaw dropped at the scene inside that tiny room. Crimson was splattered across the wall, and Delilah was drinking from the girl. I grabbed her and pulled her away from the human as Eli and Vik did their best to tend to the unconscious girl. My biggest fear had just been realized. Delilah's eyes were glazed over, and she was fighting me to get back to the human she'd nearly drained. How had this happened?

"She's dead. We need to go. Now." Vik's voice snapped me out of my thoughts. There would be no way to cover this up. It would be better for Delilah if we could hide her for a while until the hunters gave up on finding the person responsible. They weren't known for giving up, but it did happen on occasion.

"What about the mess?" I asked, throwing Delilah over my shoulder and running toward my SUV.

"We can't worry about that right now. I can wipe the cameras; then, no one will know we were here. That's the best we're going to get right now. But we have to hurry before someone comes in." Eli's calm had an undertone of panic. I could tell that he wasn't sure what had happened either.

I climbed in the back with Delilah. Vik drove and Eli worked on something on his phone. I assumed that he was working on the surveillance, as he'd explained. Delilah had stopped fighting me and was coming in and out of consciousness. "Was this how she acted the other night when she was drugged?"

Vik looked at me in the mirror. "Shit. You're right. I mean, the other night, she was throwing herself at Eli, but she looked like she does now. Really out of it and not herself."

Someone had managed to drug her and cause her to lose control. When she recovered, she would be so upset with herself for killing that girl. It wasn't her fault, but there would be no way to convince her or the hunters of that. Our situation just went from strange to deadly. I held her in my arms and wished I hadn't pissed Kayden off earlier. He was the only one who might be able to help us now. Vik drove us out of the city while I berated myself for alienating my best friend. I wondered where we would go and how we would hide.

CHAPTER 26

Eli

WIPING THE SURVEILLANCE RECORDINGS at the store had been almost too easy. I knew that we should have destroyed the physical evidence, but there was no time. I wanted nothing more than to go back there and blow the place up. How had someone gotten past the three of us to drug Delilah? Why had the drug made her attack the store employee who'd been helping us?

"I thought you said she'd already fed before we left," I growled at Declan, almost overwhelmed by jealousy that he was the one holding our girl. If we hadn't been in the car, I probably would have attacked him. I could feel my control slipping. I wanted to be the one to take care of her. I knew that wasn't possible right now, though. I was the only one who could handle the tech issues that needed to be dealt with. We needed money and a place to hide.

"She had three bags. That was more than enough for anyone. I guess I should have let her have more. I just didn't want to get her dependent on that much blood. This is my fault." So much for beating him up over it. Declan had already decided to do that himself.

"Look, Dec, it's not your fault. You had no idea that this was going to happen. None of us did. It's probably better that it happened outside of our zones. It'll be harder for someone to pin it on us." I was trying to think logically about the situation. "Everyone needs to turn their phones off or put it in airplane mode. We need to disappear."

My phone rang before I could get a response from the guys, and I had to answer. "Scott." I listened as he questioned me about my cryptic text. "I know. I'll explain it all later. Just get the money, burner phones, and other stuff I asked for together, and I'll let you know where to deliver it." Once he agreed, I disconnected the call. We would probably have to send our phones back with Scott so they couldn't be used to trace us. The burners would have to suffice for communication.

I turned to Vik. "Where are we going?"

"Somewhere safe." He refused to give me anything more than that. I would have to trust him. I settled in and watched the city turn to fields as Dec held an unconscious Delilah, and Vik drove us toward the sunrise.

"How long will we be out? I don't think Delilah has an implant." I turned around in my seat. "Dec, do you have an implant?"

He looked at me and nodded. "Yeah, I have one. I hadn't been able to get one for her yet, though. The SUV's windows in the back are safe. As long as she stays back here, she won't get hurt if the sun comes up before we get there. I don't know how that will work with getting her out, but in here, she's good."

I shot another message to Scott, letting him know to pick up five of the UV blocking implants to bring with him once I let him know where. That way, Delilah would have one, and we'd each have a spare. "I'll take care of it. I won't be able to get it before we get to the safe house, but she'll need it in the future."

We drove for almost an hour before Vik slowed down and turned onto a dirt road. Then we were headed back toward the city by way of the woods. I wasn't sure what his brilliant plan was, but I was getting more irritated at him by the moment. "Vik, seriously, where are we going?"

He looked in the rearview mirror at Dec and Delilah sleeping, then answered quietly. "I have an underground bunker out here in the woods. It's fully stocked. Nobody knows about it. I didn't even tell Jones. So, there's no chance of any problems. We're almost there." His eyes never left the road, but I could tell that he still carried guilt over Jones' betrayal. I knew that if it were me, I would too. There was no good way to convince him that it wasn't his fault.

"Does your bunker have internet access?" It was a long shot, but if I was going to keep working remotely while we were hiding out, I needed to be able to get online.

Vik's laugh was all the answer I needed. Oh, well. It was probably better that way. One of the items I'd asked Scott to grab was a mobile network. It was utterly incognito and could drop a network anywhere I needed, even underground. I'd worked for a decade on that technology before I'd perfected it. My company, much like Vik's, could pretty much run itself while I was gone. I needed internet access to research the Powder operation we'd been looking into. I felt like I was getting close to finding out who was behind it.

Now that we'd found Delilah, I could focus on that mystery without Vik guilting me about giving up. Although, now that we had her, all I wanted to do was protect her and keep her safe. I hoped that doing so would provide for some alone time as well. Since I had no idea what Vik's bunker looked like, I didn't know our privacy situation. We might all have to get really cool with a lot of stuff really fast if we wanted to keep our girl happy. I was confident that there was no way she'd be locked in a confined space with us and not want to be intimate. Hell, we were all in this car and I wanted to climb over the seat and pound her. I didn't care if the other two watched.

Vik pulled the car up to a rock formation in the middle of the forest and put it in park. "Stay in the car," he ordered before he climbed out and walked over to a tree beside the rocks. I watched as he located a panel, and the rocks started to move. He closed the panel and stepped back, climbing back into the driver's seat. "Now we go inside. The doors will automatically close behind us. I've been making sure we weren't followed."

As he parked the car, I turned around to wake Dec. We'd carry Delilah. She needed more time to make sure the drug had worn off. I hoped there were no severe after-effects. I knew how guilty she would feel when she was back to herself, and it broke my heart. Dec climbed from the car and handed Delilah to me. We followed Vik down a hallway to a metal door. He pressed some buttons on a panel and the door creaked open.

"This way," he said, flipping a switch that lit up the other side of the door. "I had hoped to keep this place a secret, but I'm more interested in keeping Delilah safe."

The inside of the bunker was terrific. Everything was up to date but simple. There wasn't a lot of furniture, but there was a large living area, and it appeared to have rooms that branched out in four directions. The kitchen area was attached to the living space. The whole thing looked to be about twice the size of my condo.

CHAPTER 27

Viktor

THE BUNKER WAS PRECISELY as I had left it a month ago. Everything was stocked and clean. I had taken great pains to do all the work myself so no one besides myself would have access. I hated bringing Eli and Declan here. I wanted this to be a secret place where Delilah and I could be alone. Of course, the best-laid plans and all that.

"There are four suites off this area. This one is the largest. Put Delilah on the bed so she can rest." I had hoped to take the biggest room myself, but it seemed more logical to let Delilah have it since one of us would most likely be with her at all times. We had to make sure she was okay. I didn't know if there were lasting effects from whatever drug she'd been given. I watched as Eli tucked her into the bed. Once she was comfortable, the three of us walked back into the living area, leaving her door open.

"We should set some ground rules." I had expected to say the words myself, so it surprised me that Declan had taken the initiative.

I nodded. "What did you have in mind?" I would humor him and see if he had a good plan or not.

Eli spoke up, "I think that Delilah should be allowed to have some time to herself if she wants it. And she should be able to decide who she spends time with and when."

Declan nodded, then added, "I agree with that once she's recovered. Until then, I think we should take turns staying with her. We don't know what she'll feel like when she wakes up. I'd rather one of us was there to calm her down if she's upset."

"I agree with him." I pointed at Dec, and Eli had no choice but to agree. The new guy had a solid plan. If our girl wanted privacy after she woke up, we'd give it to her. Right now, we'd keep a close watch on her. "Do either of you know anything about how to find out what drug was used on her?" I stared at them both expectantly.

Both shook their heads. "Do you have food down here?" Declan asked at the same time Eli spoke.

"I need to know where to tell Scott to meet me. I assume you don't want him to come here."

I laughed at their reaction of speaking over each other. "Yes, there are blood bags in the kitchen," I said to Dec, then turned to Eli. "He can meet you a half-mile from the boulders in the woods. Will you be able to bring the supplies back yourself, or do you need someone to help?"

"I could probably use your help." Eli made it a point to request me. I would have sent Declan. I hated the thought of him being here with our girl by himself. But Eli was good at reading people. If he felt that she was safe, I knew that she would be. I could lock the door to her room from the outside to make sure he stayed out while we were gone, but if she needed something, that could get ugly.

"Send Scott a message and set up a meeting time. These are the coordinates for the clearing past the boulders." I scribbled the numbers on a scrap of paper and shoved it at Eli. "While he's doing that, we should figure out sleeping arrangements. Delilah is in my room, which means I'll be taking the room on the left." I pointed to the room I had selected for myself.

"That's fine; I'm planning to camp out next to Delilah's door until she wakes up. I'll take whatever room you want to put me in. I'm sure it will be the furthest from her anyway." Declan smirked at me knowingly. Good, he knew that I wasn't a fan. That would make things easier.

"Nah, I'm taking the furthest room; you can have the one to the right of D's room. Vik might not trust you, but I do. D says you're important to her. I'm not worried about it." Eli said flippantly while tapping away at his phone. I knew that he wouldn't take it out of airplane mode until he was ready to send the detailed message to Scott. I glared at him for giving his room to Declan. That was not what I had planned.

I needed to check on Mike's progress at Midnight, but I knew that Eli would veto a call or text. I typed up an email and saved it in my drafts. I knew him well enough to know that Eli wouldn't go long without connection, so I would wait and email him when he was set up again. There was probably some new gadget that Scott would bring that would get the internet up and running while hiding our location. Eli was always making useful things like that. I guessed that I would need to find a use for the new guy since both Eli and Delilah had seemed to become attached to him already. I couldn't convince her to get rid of Eli, and with her personality changes, I was sure I would fail in chasing Declan away.

I would just have to learn to share. That didn't mean I had to like it. I finished my email draft and a few others that would need to go to critical members of my company. Then I checked on Delilah. She was still out cold. Her color was returning, and her breathing was steady. Those were good signs that she'd be okay. Now we needed to find out who was responsible for all of this.

"Scott will meet us in an hour. I figured we can head out a little early and scope the area to make sure he's not followed."

"That will also give us a chance to discuss a few things," I responded under my breath, hoping that Declan wasn't paying attention.

"Hey, if you guys want to talk about me, just say so. I can make myself scarce. Or we can have a conversation together like adults." Declan sounded as if he were scolding a naughty child. Something about his tone made me like him just a little better.

"We don't know you, so we don't trust you," I spoke just loud enough for him to hear. It was ridiculous to have this conversation when we all knew how we felt. It was impossible to trust someone you'd just met.

Eli held up his hands. "Wait. That's not entirely true. You saved our girl. I trust you with my life. Just because Vik is feeling bitchy, that doesn't mean we were going to talk about you."

I knew from their expressions that my own had given me away. "Fine. I was going to talk to Eli about you. It's not a crime, you know. This is my bunker, and the two of you come in here like you are the ones who own the place. I don't like it. To be fair, I don't really want any of you here, except Delilah."

"You son of a bitch. Is this how all of us being with Delilah is going to be? If so, I'm out." Declan growled. I glared at him, waiting for the challenge to come. I knew that we would end up fighting. I just thought it would happen after we'd spent more time together.

"Stop. Both of you. This isn't what Delilah wants. And it's not going to help her." Eli stepped between us. He turned to Declan first. "You need to back down. Just because he's being a dick, doesn't mean you have to let him get to you." Then my friend turned on me. "And you. If you don't stop baiting Dec, you're going to have to deal with me. I mean it. This stops now. No more snarky comments, no more veiled threats."

I nodded, stepping forward as if to shake Declan's hand. They were both staring at me with distrust in their eyes. It didn't matter what I did now; it would be the wrong thing. So I took a swing. My fist connected with Declan's jaw before Eli tackled me to the ground.

"What is all this commotion?" A soft voice echoed through the room. I didn't have to look up to know that Delilah was awake and had seen my indiscretion. This was going to be impossible to fix. "What the fuck were you thinking, Viktor? You can't just go around hitting people when they disagree with you. And you can't be cutting off hands for touching me, and you can't order people around. You don't own any of us. Do you understand?" Her words tore through me. It was like having the old Delilah back.

She walked over to Declan, still glaring at me, then pressed her hand to his cheek where my fist had connected. "I'm sorry he's a jerk. He had me thrown in a cage the first time I met him. I promise if you give him time, he'll grow on you." She pressed her lips to his cheek, and I growled.

"As for you, mister, you'd better not let me see this kind of behavior again." Delilah was authoritative and angry. The combination had my dick standing at attention.

CHAPTER 28

Declan

It was a good thing Delilah had come in the room right after Vik sucker punched me. I would have torn him apart. From the look on her face, I was confident that she knew it. She glared at him while she chewed him out about it. When her eyes met mine, I saw the fear she was trying to hide. Eli wrapped his arms around her, pulling her close and whispering in her ear. It was as if he could sense her emotions on a greater level than I could. I stifled a laugh as Vik looked shocked and turned on by her outburst. That guy had issues.

Who was I trying to kid? I would be turned on by Delilah tearing into me, too. That didn't mean that his behavior was justified. Part of me wished they would just challenge me to a fight and get it over with. I knew it was coming. At least with that, I knew I had a chance to impress Delilah. She probably wouldn't want me to kill them, though. Besides, I kind of liked Eli, and I respected how protective Vik was.

After Eli let go of her, Delilah growled at Vik, then walked over and embraced me. I expected a quick hug, but she held on as if her life depended on it. "Are you okay, mo chroí?"

She looked up and cupped my cheek where he'd slugged me. "I'm fine. How's your face?" Delilah stretched up and kissed my cheek gently. It must have been bruised for her to be so worried.

"You tell me; I can't see it," I smirked at her, and she couldn't help but laugh at my joke. I forgot that we weren't alone and leaned down to kiss her. She didn't seem to care and let me work my tongue into her mouth to tangle with hers. I moaned against her lips, and

276

someone cleared their throat. I was sure it was Vik, but it was enough to pull us out of the moment.

"We have to go retrieve the supplies that Scott is bringing. I asked him to drop them by helicopter so he could check out the area and report back to me." Eli turned to Vik. "I know I said I wanted to scope the area out, but I was just going to talk to you about your issue with Dec. Now that all of that is out in the open, there's no reason to hide my reasoning."

"What, you're on his side now?" Vik accused, clearly angry that he'd been chastised like a child. He stomped to his room and slammed the heavy door.

"Vik," Eli called as he started to go after him, but Delilah held up a hand.

"Give him a minute. He needs to work through it on his own. You can take Dec to get the supplies. I can handle Vik if he comes out and wants to fight. I'm not scared of him anymore."

I watched Eli's expression change. He accepted what she'd said with no argument. A moment later, he walked over to the two of us and pressed his lips to hers while she was still in my arms. The whole thing should have been awkward, but somehow, it seemed fitting. After kissing Eli, Delilah turned to me and quickly kissed me.

"Blood bags in the kitchen?" She asked as she walked into the other room and opened the fridge. "Is Scott bringing more?" Delilah swung the door open to show that the fridge was nearly empty. It was clear that Vik had been planning for this place to be just for the two of them. I wondered why he'd put in extra bedrooms.

"Yeah, he was supposed to get me as much of the supplies as he could. Once I have a secure connection, I have to call him and explain what happened. Maybe he can try to keep the hunters off our trail." He spoke to her, then turned to me. "We should go. I don't want to be out there after it gets dark. We don't know the area and could get lost. I'll get the codes from Vik." He walked over to the door Vik had slammed and, instead of knocking, walked right inside. We could hear shouting and a scuffle, but Eli came out unscathed and asked me to follow him.

I hated leaving Delilah alone with the psychopath, but she seemed like she could handle anything right now. I would talk to her later about the drugs. I was sure she would want to know what had happened.

I decided to use this time to bond with Eli since we would be spending time locked in the bunker together. It would help if everyone could find some common ground, besides just Delilah. "So, you're into tech, huh?" It wasn't the best conversation starter, but I was trying.

"Yeah. It's always come easy to me. If it has a chip that controls it, I can build it. What about you? What's your thing?" He asked as we crept through the woods toward the clearing.

"I build things, mostly out of wood. I love to carve intricate designs into solid furniture. There hasn't been time for much since Delilah came into my life, though."

Eli stopped and stared at me. "Do you regret it?"

"Falling for her?" I asked. He nodded, and I continued. "Not even for a second. I know that I barely know her, but I feel like we're meant to be together."

"It was like that for me too. I didn't understand it and tried to take her without asking what she wanted. That was how I lost my hand, and it's the real reason I forgave Vik for it. I hurt her physically and emotionally, and I deserved to be taught a lesson. He protected her. That's why I agreed to share time with him. We have a history from before we met Delilah that isn't pretty. Most of it is behind us now, but it's still there." He looked at the ground as he spoke. I felt terrible for him but understood what he was saying. I would expect one of them to do the same to me if I ever hurt Delilah that way.

"You didn't have to tell me all of that. I appreciate it, though. I've felt like the odd man out since I met up with you guys. Knowing that there's history there eases some of that." It should have seemed strange having a heart-to-heart with an almost stranger in the woods, but Eli was easy to talk to about whatever.

He pointed, and I saw the clearing ahead. "It looks like Scott dropped the container already. It's going to take both of us to carry it back, but I want to check it first." I nodded and approached the clearing with him by my side. I understood his hesitation. We had no way to know if this was the package he'd requested or if this was some sort of trap. If the hunters had already put together what had happened and who was responsible, that would be another level of crazy. I figured we'd have a day or two at least before we had to worry.

Eli opened the container and looked inside, scrutinizing the contents. "It looks like everything is here. Are you ready?" I nodded as he closed the metal box. I stood on the opposite side of him with the box between us. We both lifted it and started walking back toward the bunker when he said. The package was heavier than I had expected, so there wasn't much conversation on the way back. I was surprised that the silence between us was comfortable as if we'd been friends for years. I wondered how hard it would be to change Vik's mind about me. I would have to find a way to prove myself worthy in his eyes.

CHAPTER 29

Delilah

I WATCHED ELI AND Dec leave to get the supplies. I could tell something bad had happened, but no one wanted to tell me. I didn't push for answers. I had hazy memories of the day that seemed like I was watching myself from outside my body. I tried to make sense of it all. I was relieved that Vik didn't come out of his room. It gave me time to think through the memories that had been assaulting me since I woke up.

We were shopping. I had asked the guys to grab different sizes or styles of things I'd already tried on. They insisted that I could have anything I wanted, so I thought I'd test that. We were the only ones in the store, after all. I knew that the girl helping us was human—I could smell it on her. Relief washed over me that I'd had extra blood before we came out. I didn't want to hurt anyone. Dec had warned me about blood lust taking over and how dangerous things could get for a vamp who killed a human.

Oh, no. Did I kill her? The guys walked away, and she came to ask if I needed help. She smelled so good. *"Let me help you zip that dress."* The girl had practically shoved her way into the dressing room. I tried to argue with her, but something happened. White powder? There was so much blood. Too much blood. They ripped the door open, and I was covered in blood. *What did I do?*

Guilt washed over me, and my knees gave out. I was glad that Dec and Eli had left already. I didn't want anyone to see me like this. I killed someone. She'd been a daughter, maybe a mother, or a wife. That was why we were here. Hiding out from those people Dec had warned me about. What had he called them? Searchers or something. Well, they'd be searching for me soon. There was no way to fix what I had done. I was a murderer. I was a monster.

279

I tilted my head back and screamed as the tears took over. Strong arms picked me up before I realized I had collapsed onto the floor. I didn't have to look to know it was Vik. I could smell him. That was a perk of being a vamp. We had heightened senses. "Why didn't you just turn me in?" Tears streamed down my face, and I refused to look him in the eye.

"I love you. I would die before I let anyone hurt you. I will never let them take you." He gently laid me down on his bed, then climbed beside me.

"How could you possibly still love me? I'm a monster." I cried harder while he tried to comfort me.

"Myshka, please look at me." He paused to see if I would. I didn't. "I understand how you're feeling. I know it seems hopeless now, but it will be okay. We've all been there, whether it was accidental or not. You're not a monster. Trust me."

I let him roll me over to face him but refused to make eye contact. He held me close and rubbed my back until the sobs stopped. I wondered what he meant. Had he killed people on purpose? I should have been terrified of him, but I wasn't. My soul called out for him the same as it did for Eli and Dec. "How can you be so sure?"

"Because I am one. You're not like me. And even if you were, I would still love you." His words were sweet and straightforward. He thought himself a monster the same as I did about myself. It must have been a vamp thing. I wondered why they didn't tell me about that part. Did they all see themselves this way?

I wiped my face then sat up on the bed. Vik didn't move. I let him take my hand and play with my fingers. "I don't think you're a monster, either," I whispered.

"Oh, Myshka, but I am." He pulled me down to meet his lips, then flipped me onto my back. The glint in his eyes told me he was still upset about earlier. It was laced with passion, and I liked it. I could feel his erection pressed against my leg, and it made me wet. Our lips met again, and he fought to dominate me. His tongue worked its way into my mouth and stroked mine. His hands caressed me through the pajamas I'd been changed into at some point. I was certain the hazy memories were true, but none of that mattered right now.

Vik ran a finger down my cheek and across my neck. His hand traveled down my collarbone and the front of my top. I didn't realize until he leaned down to take my nipple in his mouth that he'd been unbuttoning the top while he distracted me with his tongue. Moans of pleasure escaped me. I wanted to touch him, but he had my hands pinned with the shirt. He kissed, licked, and sucked all over my breasts before moving down my chest to my stomach. The sensations had me squirming and arching my back, trying to guide him to where I wanted his touch. "Please, Vik," I begged in a whisper.

His fingers barely touched me, grazing over the area where I wanted him the most. "Oh, yes." I sighed, arching my back to try to get more contact. But he pulled his hand back. "You have to be patient, Myshka." Then he chuckled and went back to torturing me with his mouth. I wanted that mouth on me but couldn't get my arms free to take off my pants. I kept trying to use my body to convince him to go lower since my words hadn't worked.

Something must have worked because suddenly, he pulled my pants and panties off and tossed them on the floor. Then he positioned himself between my legs and licked his lips like someone getting ready for a pie-eating contest. I was already slick with need before his tongue touched me. Vik took his time, slowly working his way to my apex. I was panting and writhing by the time he got there. The moment his tongue touched my sensitive nub, I screamed at the sensation. It was as if the anticipation had made the orgasm more intense. I didn't remember ever having a feeling like that before.

He worked me over with his fingers and tongue until I felt like I couldn't take any more. My arms and legs were weak, and my center was throbbing. The look he gave me told me that he knew exactly what he'd done to me. He smirked, "I'm not done with you yet."

Vik climbed on top of me, kissing his way back up to my neck before claiming my lips. I felt his cock rub against my skin as he moved against me. He whispered in my ear, "Do you trust me?" My half-closed eyes shot open. I couldn't have answered that if my life had depended on it. Luckily, he just wanted to reposition me and didn't actually want an answer.

He backed up and grabbed my ankles, pulling me toward him as he kneeled on the bed. With my ankles resting on his shoulders, he rubbed his erection against my slit. I moaned, and he slipped inside. He moved painstakingly slow as if thrusting faster would kill him. I tried to move and adjust the rhythm, but he held my ankles in place and leaned forward so I couldn't. "I can't take it," I breathed.

"Yes, you can. Let go and enjoy yourself." He growled. His tone showed me how difficult this pace was for him to maintain. He wasn't just torturing me. I had to guess that this was what he wanted me to trust him with. So far, he hadn't let me down in the sex department. What's the worst that could happen if I just go with it? Once I relaxed and stopped fighting to go faster, he increased the pace a little. Then a little more, until he was pounding into me, and I was screaming his name.

CHAPTER 30

Declan

ELI AND I HEARD Delilah's screams as soon as we entered the bunker. At first, I thought something was wrong. "We have to help her."

He laughed. "I don't think she needs our help right now. Listen closer. She's not in distress. She's enjoying herself."

"Oh," I said, running a hand through my hair. I'd been on edge for so long I hadn't realized that she was being loud because she was having sex. I simply assumed that she was in trouble. I stopped for a minute and thought about how that made me feel. I knew that she was having sex with Vik. It didn't bother me as much as I thought it should have. Before Delilah, I would have been jealous and possessive. I had no idea what it was about her that made me feel like she had enough love and affection for all three of us.

"It's a hard thing to realize, but you're better off once you do," Eli said from over my shoulder. I jumped, not knowing he'd been standing behind me.

"What's that?" I asked, wondering if he'd somehow read my mind.

"I'm sure you just realized that Delilah has enough love for all of us. It made me crazy jealous the first time she spent time with Vik without me. I ran five miles, swam another ten, and climbed the wall at my gym six times. It didn't help. I ended up getting Scott to spar with me for two hours. I was so distracted that he kicked my ass. That was the only thing that took my mind off of it. I felt better when she texted me the next morning. I was worried she'd pick him."

"That's exactly how I should feel, though. Like I'm on the verge of losing something amazing. But I don't. I feel irritated at Vik for earlier, but not for being with Delilah right now." I wasn't sure if Eli could understand how I felt or if I could even explain it.

"You're a better man than I am, then. I'm glad, though. I kinda like you, and I'd hate for you and Vik to fight all the time. I don't want to have to choose sides." Eli laughed, and play punched my arm. "Let's go take inventory of the supplies while we wait for them to finish up. Then we can all have a drink together."

I nodded and followed him to the metal box we'd carried in. He cracked it open again and started removing items. He pulled out a clipboard with invoice sheets on it and handed it to me. "You count, I record?" He nodded and started stacking things in lines. There were clothes, blood bags, first aid supplies, cases that held money or tech equipment, and food. It seemed like he'd thought of everything.

"I have equipment here to create a secure connection for us to communicate with our people. I'm sure you need to let someone know you'll be out for a while. I have to update Scott, and Vik has to call his secretary." Eli spoke as he carefully checked the cases. The first one he opened was full of cash. I'd never seen that much in person before. The next one held what looked like computer parts. I figured those were for the connection. Once those were checked and recorded, he moved to the blood bags. They were packaged in clear coolers. He counted each bag and the type it was. I carefully recorded every item he listed. We continued this way with everything that had been in the crate.

Delilah and Vik came into the garage area when we were nearly finished. "You don't play around when it comes to supplies," Vik said, taking in the stacks everywhere. "Is it all counted?"

Eli nodded, pointing out the last item that needed to be marked off. "Just finished. I see you two made up. Or rather, we heard when we got back."

Delilah blushed, but Vik looked smug. I understood why after Eli had explained his feelings. Vik must have suffered a similar fate on Eli's first night. I grinned at him like I would have one of my guys when they told of a conquest. He growled and walked away. This was going to be fun. "Sorry about being so loud. I know this is a strange situation." Delilah offered me an apology, understanding that I should be the uncomfortable one.

"Don't apologize. It sounded like you were enjoying yourself. Did you have fun?" I responded, taking her hand and weaving my fingers through hers.

She blushed and nodded. "I did."

"That's all that matters." I kissed her lips lightly before releasing her hand and grabbing one of the cases. I needed to help Eli put the supplies away. Then I could try to get Delilah to spend some time with me if she wasn't busy with him. As long as she kept the smile she had right now, it didn't matter to me who put it there.

Eli got to work setting up the secure internet connection while I put supplies away. Delilah helped me with the food and blood, then Vik showed up to help with the clothes and other things. He didn't have much to say, but it seemed like he was trying to play nice.

"How's your face?" He asked, glancing at Delilah, who was glaring at him. Apparently, she'd told him to mend fences.

"I'm fine. A sucker punch isn't going to get me down. I'm surprised you care. Earlier, you looked like you wanted to kill me." I knew that antagonizing him wasn't a good idea, but I felt like he'd gotten off easy over the attack.

"Look, it's not easy for me to admit when I make a mistake. I shouldn't have hit you. I hope we can work through it." Vik's words sounded a little too scripted. I wondered if they'd discussed the issue before or after having annoyingly loud sex.

"Let's get everything put away so we can have a nice dinner," Eli suggested. I figured that meant he was done with what he needed to do for the secure internet.

"Does this mean we have internet now?" I asked cautiously. I didn't want to sound too interested, but I did need to talk to Steph. There would be questions if I just disappeared without a trace. I didn't need her calling Kayden to start looking for me.

Eli nodded, then picked up a bag of clothes and walked away. Eli and I had already sorted the clothes based on who could wear what. Delilah reached for hers, but I picked it up along with mine. "I've got it, mo chroí." I leaned down and kissed her forehead. I knew that my interaction with Vik made me seem petty and jealous. Right now, I was both. I needed some time alone to find a way to work through it.

I put Delilah's bag of clothes on her bed and took mine into my room. I started putting the items away in the small dresser, carefully folding each one. I would have to pay Eli back for this. Most of mine was plain, but that suited me. Vik's had been the suits he was so fond of, and Eli's had been a mixture of dress clothes and t-shirts. I wondered if Delilah had a preference or even cared what we wore. I wouldn't get a chance to ask her because Eli had already gone into her room after I left. It didn't matter. I needed to cool off. I would have my time with her later. I just needed to convince myself that the three of us were on equal footing here. *But were we, really?* I couldn't help but wonder.

I'd never felt so insecure before in any relationship. I guess this was a brand-new situation. Now I had to decide if I wanted to stay in it or head back to my previous life. Ha! My previous life was so long ago I would never be able to go back.

A human kid so jealous of his wolf best friend that he would actively seek out vampires to turn him—what a joke. I don't know what I would have done if Kayden hadn't stopped me the first time. I would have been sixteen forever. That would have made a lot of things more difficult. I already had some trouble running my zone because I look young. Being ruthless was the only thing that got me by. Now I had to be intelligent and relentless to get what I wanted.

While grumbling to myself, I noticed Eli standing in my doorway, watching. "Hey, man. Did you need something?" I wasn't upset with him, so there was no reason to take it out on him.

"I was hoping you'd take one for the team and help Vik with dinner once you're done here. I'll owe you one. I need to talk to Delilah about some stuff." I had no reason to think he was up to something, so I nodded. If spending time with the guy who hates me was what I had to do to prove that I cared for Delilah, that's what I would do.

<h1 style="text-align:center">CHAPTER 31</h1>

<h2 style="text-align:center">Eli</h2>

I KNEW DECLAN WAS still pissed about Vik punching him, mainly because he didn't get to fight back. At some point, the two of them would fight it out. I just hoped no one got seriously hurt. Neither of them seemed to be the type to pull punches. Pitting two dangerous men against each other was a bad idea. Which meant I would have to run interference as much as possible. I had my clothes tucked away before the others made it back to the living area, so I waited for Delilah. I needed to make sure she was okay. And she deserved to know what had happened, whether the others wanted to tell her or not.

She carefully folded her clothes and selected where to put them as I watched her. I knew that I should say something, but I enjoyed watching. "Are you going to stand there staring at me, or are you coming inside?" The irritation in her voice made me jump.

"Are you okay, love? You sound angry." I stepped forward slowly. I wasn't sure what she was mad about or directed at someone specific.

"I am angry. At all of you. At myself." She paused and looked into my eyes. Tears shone in hers. "I know what happened. I remember. Why didn't you tell me?"

I knew she would be upset. I hadn't expected her to remember on her own. "To be fair, you broke up a fistfight and sent us off to get the supplies right after you woke up." She growled at my words. I knew there was no easy way out of this one. "We were going to tell you. That's actually what I came here for."

I held out a hand, and she took it gingerly, letting me pull her toward me. Once she was in my arms, I held her close. "I know you're upset, and rightly so. What happened was horrible. But you weren't in control. I'm not sure how you were drugged or why. I promise you I will find out who is responsible for this, and they will pay." She relaxed a little and tilted her head up to look at me.

"Why do you guys care so much about me? I'm nothing special." Her words were quiet but doubt permeated them. She was feeling as insecure as we were. It had to be because she still didn't have all of her memories back.

"Do you remember anything about me from before?" I asked, testing the theory.

"A little. I remember you hurting my arm before Vik cut off your hand. I remember you saving me from a mugger, and I remember you cornering me in a small room. I'm not sure where or why." She stared at me, puzzling what I was getting at.

"With those few memories that aren't good, by the way, you've decided that you want me, and you trust me. Why is that?" I wondered what she'd say in response.

"Because my soul swears that you're mine." The words fell from her lips like velvet against my ears. I swept her up into my arms and kissed her with wild abandon. I wanted nothing more than to take her back to my room and show her how special she was. But since a "family" dinner had been my idea, I didn't think Vik and Declan would appreciate it if we ran out on them. It was bad enough I had left them alone in the kitchen, forcing them to work together to cook our food.

"Do you want to help me with something while they make dinner?" I needed to check news feeds and see if we were being hunted or if Vik was utterly paranoid. I didn't want Delilah to know, but she was stronger than we'd thought. I knew she'd be able to handle it.

"Sure. Does it involve taking off our clothes?" She ran her fingers up my chest as she talked, then cupped my jaw and pulled me down to her for another kiss.

"I'm definitely up for that after dinner. Right now, I need to look for some info on the computer. I thought maybe you'd like to help me set up the burner phones while I work." I hated turning down her offer, but knowing how careful we needed to be out here was important. If she didn't want to help, I would have to get Dec to distract her while I got everything done.

She nodded. "I'm going to hold you to that promise." Delilah followed me out to the living area, where I had set up the computers. I figured with four of us here; we would need more than one. I pulled the boxes of phones out of the desk drawer and started opening them. Delilah pulled a chair over next to me.

"So, what do I do?" She asked, picking up one of the phones.

"You're going to make sure each of the four phones has the other three numbers in it. You get to decide who gets which one. Scott decided that having different color cases would be a good idea to help us tell them apart since they're the same phone type. Pick a case for each one, figure out who you want to have each color, then put the numbers in with our names. Easy." I hoped that she didn't think I was giving her grunt work, but the way she smiled when I said she got to choose our colors made me think I'd done something good.

"Got it. Can I have a sheet of paper and a pen to write the colors and numbers on to sort out who gets what and make putting the numbers in easier?"

"Of course. Paper and pens are here." I showed her where they'd been put away, then left her to her task. I needed to get searches up and running. I slid the chair over to one of the computers, leaving a little space between us, so she wasn't right over my shoulder. Then I double-checked the secure connection to ensure the whole thing was operating incognito. Once I was sure we couldn't be traced, I searched news outlets.

It didn't take long to find what I'd been looking for. The news was reporting a suspicious death, but there were no suspects yet. There were very few details released, so I checked several more sources. The vampire network said that the hunters were looking into a human murder, and it was clear that it was the same one the humans were reporting on.

I was worried that someone Vik had scared off would remember us, and the hunters would have their lead. I followed the stories to get updates on my phone when the death was discussed again. After making sure we were safe for now, I composed an email to Scott with instructions about what to tell people regarding my quick disappearance, including a story to leak to the press as well as an official statement that I left town on business. He would know not to use any of it unless someone commented on my absence. They would provide the official apology and statement to current clients, and I would either meet with them via video call or reschedule.

<h1 style="text-align:center">CHAPTER 32</h1>

<h2 style="text-align:center">Delilah</h2>

I KNEW THAT ELI was hiding something when he turned down sex. I could have pushed the issue but decided to wait and see what was happening. I was surprised when he handed me four phones and the cases, telling me to decide who got what. I pretended like it would be a difficult decision, but the colors were pretty much chosen to fit personalities. Vik's case was black, Eli's was blue, Dec's was green, and mine was red. Then it was just a matter of putting a phone into a case and inputting the numbers. I figured there was a way to do it faster. It seemed pretty important to Eli that I sit here and work on it while he moved away and looked at news articles on the computer.

I waited until he wasn't paying attention and started reading over his shoulder. Every time he moved, I made sure I appeared to be working on his request. Of course, I had that done in five minutes, but he didn't need to know that.

I guessed it was good that the police had no leads on the girl I'd drained. They were calling it suspicious. Then Eli switched to another news site that seemed to be geared toward vampires. I had no idea that existed. The hunters were looking for leads in the murder of a human. That can't be good. I would have to ask the guys about the hunters later. Maybe turning myself in wouldn't be so bad. I would probably ask Dec because I didn't want Eli to know that I'd been snooping. I wondered if Eli would trade our after-dinner time with him so I could find out tonight.

Ultimately, who I spent time with was my decision. I knew that I could just say that I wanted to hang out with Declan instead of Eli, but I didn't want to foster any sense of competition in my guys. Vik had enough of that for everyone. I needed to figure out how to get that out of him. He needed to understand that we're a family. Everyone needed to do their part so we could be happy.

"Eli?" I said his name softly to get his attention. When he looked up, I continued. "Would you be upset if I spent time with Declan tonight? He's had a rough day, and I wanted to make it up to him. Vik was a complete ass, and I still ended up having sex with him. Don't get me wrong, it was great; I just feel bad about how he acted toward Dec."

"Oh. Um, sure. I don't mind. I get that you want him to feel accepted. Don't worry about it. I have some work stuff to do anyway." His smile didn't quite reach his eyes, and I felt awful. *But I need this information, and he won't tell me.* I'd just have to make it up to him later.

"Thanks. You're the best!" I gave him a big kiss. Then I picked up his phone and handed it to him. "This one is yours. I'm going to give the others theirs now." I pocketed my phone and grabbed the other two, strolling off toward the expansive kitchen to see what Vik and Dec were getting into. I heard their voices and stopped to listen for a minute.

"All I'm saying is that sucker-punching me doesn't make you look good to her. She doesn't like that kind of douchebag behavior. I appreciate the apology and the offer to train me, but I'm good. If she hadn't stepped in, you might realize that I can defend myself just fine." Declan sounded like he was getting pissed. *Oh, no. This isn't good.*

I rushed into the room, expecting to break up a fight. Instead, they were having a drink while the oven timer was counting down. Neither of them looked angry. It was just a heated conversation. I breathed a sigh of relief. At least there wasn't going to be another fight. I couldn't take that right now. "I have your new phones. Eli says they're untraceable. Can you guess which is which?" I smirked at them, convinced that they'd never be able to crack my system.

"Obviously, the green is mine, and the black is for Satan over here," Declan said with a mischievous grin.

"Your leprechaun is right, though I hate to admit it. Green suits him, and black is my color." What was happening right now? Vik agreed with Declan. This was crazy.

"Okay, you got me. Then tell me what color Eli's is. And what about mine?" I figured I'd have them on this one.

Vik looked at Dec, then back at me. "Yours is red, of course, and Eli's has to be blue."

"How did you know?" I asked, impressed that he'd figured me out so quickly.

"I could lie and say that I just knew, but I saw the cases as they were being put away, and those colors seem to explain themselves," Vik said, staring at me. Declan nodded in agreement.

"Fine, you win. Here." I handed them the phones. Vik opened his and started typing. "Can I borrow Dec for a minute?" Vik nodded without looking up. I grabbed Dec's arm and dragged him out of the room.

"What's wrong?" He asked as soon as we were out of earshot. "Did one of them do something? Do you need me to hurt them?"

I shook my head, laughing. "No, I wanted to see if you would spend time with me tonight after dinner."

"I thought Eli had claimed that time." He responded without looking at me.

"Well, the three of you said it's my choice. I think you need a little extra attention right now. So, Eli was willing to trade for tomorrow night. Unless you don't want to spend time with me...," I dropped the sentence as if I'd had more to say. I knew exactly how to wrap these guys around my little finger. I wondered if I'd been the same person before. I suspected not.

Instead of answering, he leaned down and pressed his lips to mine. As he deepened the kiss, he grabbed my ass and picked me up. I wrapped my legs around his waist and enjoyed the strong arms holding me. I needed this as much as he did. I had no idea how long we were there like that. Someone cleared their throat behind me, and Declan groaned.

"Sorry to interrupt, but dinner is ready." Vik didn't sound happy to have found us in this position. I didn't care much. I was certain that Eli and Dec hadn't liked coming home to hear us going at it earlier either.

"We'll be right there," I responded without moving. I pressed my lips to Dec's again and slid down him while we kissed. "We can pick this up later. I'm starved." The look on his face told me he wasn't sure I was talking about food. To be honest, I was hungry and needed more blood. But more than that, I craved time with him. I wanted him to know that he was mine, and it didn't matter who else I claimed. I would always have time for my guys when they needed me.

"Maybe we should work out a schedule, so it's easier on you." He offered after Vik walked away. I thought about his words while we walked to the dining area I hadn't noticed before. The table would seat six and was set with some beautiful plates.

"Something smells amazing," Eli said as he walked in behind us. I wasn't sure if he was talking about the food or me.

"It's nothing fancy. The new guy wanted comfort food for some reason." Vik growled.

"There's nothing wrong with a roast with potatoes and carrots. Comfort food is perfect for what we're dealing with right now." Declan defended his choice.

CHAPTER 33

Declan

"I think it's lovely," Delilah offered, shutting Vik up before he could complain again. I knew that he would have preferred a five-star meal prepared by a fancy chef, but that wasn't what our girl needed tonight. Most vampires could survive on blood only, but eating food kept the humans from figuring us out, and it still tasted good, so what did it matter?

We settled in and ate, with most of the conversation being small talk. I assumed the guys were trying to find out as much about me as possible. I wasn't about to give them everything, but it didn't hurt to find out about them as well. Information was power, and I wasn't about to give mine away. I traded select info for things I needed to know about them.

"Tell me about before," Delilah said when there was a lull in the conversation. Vik and Eli shared a glance. I wanted to know as badly as she did, but I wasn't sure they would be honest about it. They waited for a beat as if trying to figure out where to start.

"I met you when I purchased your uncle's bar. It was a hostile takeover. Vinny thought he would take my money and keep running Midnight the way he always had. I couldn't allow that." Vik began, but Eli broke in.

"I was relieved to hear you ended the blood slave process. I'd been working for years to find out who was behind it."

Vik nodded and continued, "Your uncle took good care of you, but he was not an honest man. He ran an operation that kidnapped people, mostly young women, and sold them as blood sources in exchange for the protection of their families. My corporation can offer that protection at a much lower cost. And the bar was on its way to being successful again when our issues first began."

"I remember a little of that. You had Uncle Vinny lock me in one of the cages because I tried to free the women. Why would you do that if you were going to let them go anyway?" Delilah asked. It was a good question. He was painting himself to be the hero, but I suspected it was somewhere in the middle.

"I had to break their compulsion first. Vinny had a vampire working with him who convinced those women that they had to give up their lives or sacrifice the lives of their families. One of the few things Eli and I had in common before meeting you was our stance on blood donations. Those donated should be cared for and not abused." His words sounded sincere, but there was something about him that made me believe he was capable of being a monster.

"So, you took over the bar and ended the blood slave process. That's how you met Delilah?" I wanted to push further but decided to start slowly.

Vik nodded. "We were still going to supply blood, just in a more reasonable manner. That meant prices would increase, and vampires would object." He looked at Eli as he spoke. Eli's cheeks turned red.

"I was searching for proof that Vinny was doing something illegal. When I got that bill, I had no idea you'd taken over. I had just made an offer to purchase Midnight a week before. I thought Vinny was trying to squeeze more money out of me." Eli growled at Vik. It was clear that this was a sore spot for them.

"Yes, but you overreacted when you found out that I had taken over."

Eli turned to face Delilah and me. "I kind of lost it when I thought Vinny was trying to screw me over. I came into the bar and had a meltdown. Vik and I ended up fighting. I almost broke your arm, and it cost me my hand. I would happily suffer through it all over again for hurting you." Tears formed in Delilah's eyes. I wondered if it was because he'd hurt her or because he'd had his hand chopped off.

"That's a prosthetic? It looks so real." I interjected. I felt like they were trying to push me out of the conversation, and I couldn't let that happen.

"It is. It's top of the line. There isn't another one just like it. This one was a prototype. It has some *special* abilities built-in. The whole thing is hardwired into my brain. That's how it seems so real. It has wiring that simulates pain sensors to prevent the unit from accidentally getting damaged. I ended up being the first to test it out." He didn't seem angry about the situation. I wasn't sure how that was possible. If a guy cut my hand off, I'd probably kill him. I sure wouldn't share a girl with him. There had to be more to their story than I realized.

"I only remember bits of what you're telling me. But what was I like before? I know I had to have spent time with both of you." Delilah was trying to unlock her past to understand her future better. I could see the determination on her face.

"You were perfect." Vik refused to say anything else about it. Eli nodded. It was clear that they were done discussing it.

Eli stood up and started clearing the table, nodding at Vik. He got up to help. We wouldn't get any more info out of them tonight. Delilah took my hand and pulled me toward my room. I wondered why she didn't want to go to hers, but it was right next to Vik's. Maybe she was trying to be considerate about things.

As soon as the door closed, I pulled her close for a kiss. She let her tongue mingle with mine for a minute, then stepped away. "I want to talk to you about something. But I don't want the others to know."

I was intrigued. "I'm all yours. What's up?"

"I need to know about the hunters. How bad is our situation right now? Will they figure out that I killed that girl? What would happen if I turned myself in?" Delilah had started to ramble, so I pressed my lips to hers again. Once she was relaxed, I let her go and thought about her questions.

"The hunters are a group of shifters who police the vampire population. If they find out that you killed that girl, they will find you. It's just a matter of time. They are very good at what they do. Turning yourself in is not an option. They will kill you. Death is the punishment for killing a human, even if it's an accident." Tears spilled from her eyes at my explanation.

"I don't want to hide. I deserve to be punished for it." I knew that she'd been wrestling with guilt since she remembered. Vik and I had talked about it while making dinner. She'd been upset, and he had distracted her the only way he knew how.

"Please don't think like that. You were drugged. If we can prove it before we come forward, they'll have to go after the person responsible. We just have to lay low until we can find out who is after you."

Delilah gasped. "You think someone is after me?"

I nodded. "This is the second time a human has drugged you. I'm pretty sure someone is out to get you. They either want you on the run or out of the picture. I will look into Eli and Vik to see if it could be related to them. It sucks that you can't remember anything but what they tell you. There's no way to know what they're leaving out."

She looked at me for a moment and scrunched her nose. "I thought I was crazy. I felt like I was getting half the story at dinner. I'm glad you felt it too."

CHAPTER 34

Viktor

THE NEW GUY WAS fishing at dinner. I knew it; Eli knew it. The only thing we didn't know was to what end. What was his end game? I was trying to work through it in my head based on the questions he'd asked while we prepped dinner and while we were eating.

"He just wants to know what he's dealing with. There's nothing suspicious about that. I already ran a full background. He's a decent guy." Eli seemed to read my thoughts. I forgot how good he was with emotions.

"Are you sure that's it? How much is really in a background check? Do you think someone could find all of your secrets with one?" I accused, irritated that he'd interrupted my brooding.

"Yeah, I'm pretty sure someone could run a background check on me and find out exactly who to talk to. Give them a chance, and they'll know everything about me. I'm not worried about it. I don't have secrets." He defended.

"But there are things you hope Delilah doesn't remember, right? He was pushing toward those things. There's no reason for her to think we're monsters before she remembers things on her own." I wasn't going to roll over and play dead where Declan was concerned.

"Not everything has to be a battle, Vik. Just give the guy a chance. It's not worth losing Delilah over." Eli turned and walked away. At least I could go back to brooding. Who did Eli think he was? Trying to make me play nice with the competition wouldn't win points with me. I wondered if he was right. Would Delilah choose him if I forced the issue? Probably, especially since Eli was practically adopting him into the family.

I needed to find out who Declan Roarke was. He was hiding something. I just didn't know what it was yet. I wasn't as skilled as Eli at computer issues, but I knew enough to run a background check of my own. I stomped over to the mini library he'd set up. I was glad Eli situated it so no one could walk up behind me while I searched. I hated being exposed.

Within a few minutes, I had everything readily available about Declan. His social media accounts, credit score, banking information—nothing specific, just estimates of his worth, and a list of relatives and associates. That would probably be a good place to start. Who was he related to? Who did he hang out with?

I checked out his family and came back with nothing. They'd lived outside of the city, near the forest. Nothing unusual there, a lot of people didn't like city life. He'd moved to the city shortly before being turned. He had an affinity for working with wood. He was pretty popular. I checked out some of his work on social media and news reports. There were some very upscale pieces. I was surprised he was able to create them.

After getting distracted for way too long, I started looking into his employees. Stephanie and Matt were pretty straightforward and seemed to be the type of people he hired. I came up empty-handed there, so I moved on to his friends.

This was where it got interesting. There were pictures of him as a teenager hanging out with some guys who looked familiar. I couldn't place them but did a reverse image search and pinpointed exactly where I knew them from. They were hunters. He'd grown up with them. It seemed that his best friend was Kayden Dixon. Imagine that, we're hiding from the hunters with the best friend of their leader. I printed off the info and ran to Eli's room. We needed a plan.

Eli answered the door with a laugh. "Really? What, my background check wasn't enough? You just had to run one of your own, didn't you?"

"You won't be laughing after you read this." I shoved the pages at him and watched as he read. When he finished, I pushed him back and closed his door. "Now, do you believe me that there's something up with him?"

Eli ran a hand through his shaggy blond hair. "I can see how this looks. There has to be an explanation. We should ask him about it instead of jumping to conclusions."

"He's friends with the leader of the hunters. What more do we need to know?" I pressed.

"Yeah, but he cares about Delilah. He's not going to rat her out." Eli started to pace the floor. I could see the wheels turning in his head but had no idea what he was thinking.

"What if he frames us so he can have her to himself?" I knew that I sounded paranoid, and at the moment, I didn't care.

"He wouldn't do that. At least, not to me. I've been nice to him. He might do it to you, though. You should probably be careful." Eli smirked at me, clearly amused with himself.

"Fine, make jokes. When we're all locked up and about to be executed, I'll be sure to say I told you so." I growled. It was clear that I was on my own and wasn't happy about it.

Eli continued to pace the floor, trying to figure something out. "Why didn't he just tell us? That is strange. But we didn't tell him about our past either. We'll ask him about it in the morning. Don't do anything tonight. I mean it, Vik. Delilah will be pissed if you do."

I nodded. He was right. She was very attached to this guy. As much as I wanted to get rid of him, maybe I should talk to him about this. "Fine. If he doesn't give us a good explanation, I'm going to kick his ass." Part of me hoped that he didn't talk. I wanted to beat on him from the moment our girl asked us to call him.

"You need to get a handle on your jealousy. She's not going to put up with it. Just let it go. She wants us all. Do you want to deny our girl what she wants?" Eli's tone had changed. I knew that if I told him how I really felt, we'd end up fighting.

"I would never deny her. You know that." He and I both knew that the words were a lie. If it meant getting my way, I would deny Delilah. Maybe Eli was right; I needed to get the jealousy in check. If she realized how badly it was affecting me, she might decide to leave without me. Losing her again would kill me.

CHAPTER 35

Delilah

I KNEW THAT DECLAN was trying to distract me by kissing me. I could push the issue and make him talk to me more about the hunters. There would be time for that later. As much as I wanted the info, I wanted his hands on me more. I steered him toward the bed. We tumbled onto it because I couldn't see where I was going with my lips on his.

He pulled us toward the center of the bed before I shoved him down and sat on his stomach. I smirked at him when he grabbed for me, and I pushed his hands away. "Not this time. I'm the boss now." He smiled and relaxed, content to let me push him around for a while. I leaned forward and kissed him gently, our lips barely touching.

His groan urged me on. I knew this was torture for him because it was for me too. I wanted to let him take over and move faster, but I also wanted to assert my dominance over him. I needed to know how far I could push him. What would he do for me? I slid my body lower, so I was sitting on his massive erection. I was surprised it hadn't escaped his pants.

"Come on, mo chroí. I can't take it." Declan whispered his need, and I soaked it up.

I shook my head and kissed him again. When his arms came up and wrapped around me, I let him think he'd won. Then I wiggled out of his hold and slid lower on his body. I pulled at the bottom of his shirt until he sat up and let me take it off. He reached for mine, and I shook my head. "Not yet. Lie back and enjoy." I climbed off him and slowly unzipped his jeans, then eased them off him and tossed them on the floor. The desire in his eyes kept me moving. I felt like I needed it to live. I reached for his boxer briefs, and he groaned again. I toyed with his waistband before ripping them off him and sucking his cock into my mouth.

He moaned so loudly that I figured Eli and Vik would hear everything. I continued to play with him, sucking on the tip, then licking down to the base. I was teasing him while turning myself on. If he knew how wet I was getting from this, he'd never want me to stop. I stroked him a few times before taking him into my mouth again, this time deep throating the whole thing. It wasn't easy, but his reaction was well worth it. I sat back, looking at him. It would be easy to keep teasing him, but I wanted him inside me.

"Stay," I ordered as I climbed off the bed. His eyes followed me as I slowly stripped for him. His hand automatically reached for his dick and stroked it while he watched me. Who knew that I would be turned on by that too? I shivered as I stood in front of him in just a bra and thong.

"Mo chroí, you are gorgeous. I need you. This is torture." Declan begged me to come back and satisfy him. I kept eye contact with him as I unfastened my bra and let it drop to the floor with our clothes. Then I turned my back to him, slowly peeled the thong off, and lowered it to the floor. He groaned, and I laughed. I couldn't remember ever feeling this powerful and sexy before. Declan knew exactly what I needed.

I strolled back to the bed, watching him slowly jerk off while he waited for me to come back. "You want some help with that?" I asked, hopping back on the bed and climbing on top of him. He hummed his agreement and helped me line his cock up to my slick opening. I lowered myself onto him slowly, enjoying the torture.

As soon as every inch of him was inside of me, I lifted myself off again, hovering just above him. His breath hitched. I slipped him back in and repeated the process, inch by inch, as slowly as possible. I watched his face and saw the exact moment when his control snapped. He flipped me onto my back and took over, pounding his dick into me harder and faster until I screamed his name. That didn't stop him. He kept up the quick pace while his hand slipped between us to flick my clit. Declan tensed as he prepared to cum. He leaned down and captured my lips with his, blocking my moans.

Spent, he collapsed on top of me before rolling onto his back and pulling me over to lie on his chest. There would be a lot to figure out, but for now, this was enough. As he drifted off to sleep, I couldn't help but try to get more info from him.

"Can you tell me more about the hunters?" I whispered, desperate to know exactly what I was dealing with.

"Kayden won't let them hurt you. He's a good guy. Doesn't matter that he's pissed at me. He's family." Dec's words were a little slurred from sleep, and he spoke quietly.

"Who is Kayden?" Something about that name pulled at me. Did I know him?

"Best friend. Wolf. Leads the hunters. You'll like him." With that, Declan was out cold. I wondered if he would remember this conversation. It would probably be bad for me if he did. I needed to talk to Eli. I knew that he loved to run background checks on everyone, and this wasn't something he should have kept to himself. This could turn my guys against each other. I listened to Dec's heartbeat for a while longer before climbing out of his bed and slipping my panties and one of his shirts on.

I tiptoed out of the room, worried that I would wake him. If I did, I could claim that I needed a drink. He would see right through that lie, though. I hated the thought of lying to any of them. I crept around the room to Eli's door. I heard voices and stopped in my tracks. What was Vik doing in Eli's room? I pressed my ear to the door and listened.

They were arguing about something, but I couldn't quite make out what it was. The doorknob turned, and I ducked around the corner to hide. Without looking back, Vik stomped off in the opposite direction toward his room. Once he slammed his door, I slowly turned the doorknob and entered Eli's room. The door clicked closed behind me, and Eli stomped in from the bathroom. "I told you to leave it be. I will talk to him in the morning."

His eyes got wide when he saw it was me instead of Vik. "Delilah. Is everything okay? I thought you were spending the evening with Declan." Concern was written all over his face. "Did he hurt you?"

I shook my head. "I'm fine, but we need to talk."

"That's never good." Eli gestured to the bed then waited for me to walk over and sit down. "What's on your mind?"

"I asked Dec about the hunters. He didn't want to tell me anything. I know they're dangerous, but I think there's more to it than that. He knows one of them. The leader."

"How did you find out?" Eli's question told me that he already knew.

"You knew?" I asked, glaring at him. "Why didn't you tell me?"

Eli reached out and took my hand in his. "I just found out tonight, after you two went to his room. Vik found the connection. He doesn't trust Dec."

I nodded. "I get that. I think Dec does too. Vik isn't making it easy on him. I don't know what to think. He says that Kayden wouldn't hurt me. But why didn't he tell us that he knew the leader of the hunters?"

"It doesn't look good, for sure, but there has to be a reason he held back on sharing that. Maybe they had a falling out, or they haven't talked in a long time. I think we should give him a chance to explain before we go locking him up and torturing the poor guy." Eli grinned at my look of confusion.

"I never said anything about locking him up or torturing him." I countered before realizing that must have been Vik's idea. "But Vik did."

"Not in so many words, but he does want to beat the details out of him. Let's just get some rest and ask him about it in the morning." Eli pulled the covers down to climb under them. "You're welcome to stay here if you don't want to go back to Declan or to your room."

"Thanks. I think I'll sneak back over. He's already going to be mad that I got the info out of him while he was falling asleep. I don't want him to think I used sex to get intel for you or Vik. Especially if we're asking him about this in the morning." I kissed Eli then left his room.

Vik's door was still closed, as was Declan's. I crept back to Dec's room, watching Vik's door the whole time. If he caught me out here, I'd have to explain what I was doing. I knew he wouldn't believe me if I lied. I got lucky, and he didn't stir. I slowly turned the knob and opened Declan's door. I closed it just as quietly. I breathed a sigh of relief, then turned to slip into the bed.

"I wondered where you went or if you were coming back." The light flicked on, and Declan was sitting up in the bed, staring at the door. Pain shone in his eyes. I had done the one thing I was trying to avoid.

"Sorry. I just needed to ask Eli about something." It wasn't the truth, but it wasn't an outright lie, either.

"Look, I know I'm the new guy and all. If you don't want me here, you just have to tell me. I'll go. And I'll keep your secrets. I do care about you, mo chroí." His words ripped my heart in half. I fought against the tears that were threatening to fall.

"You want to leave?" I took a step forward, but he held up his hand.

"I don't want to get attached if you're just going to throw me away. I know that you're remembering things all the time. How long until you remember that you only want Vik and Eli? What happens then? I'm just being realistic." I couldn't handle him speaking to me this way. It cut deep. I wanted to run away and cry, but I also wanted to run into his arms and show him that none of what he thought was true.

"That's not going to happen. I want all three of you. I care about you, Declan. Please don't do this." The tears I was holding back started to fall.

"I'm tired. You should get some sleep. In your room. Good night." He turned the lamp off and settled under the covers, facing away from me.

CHAPTER 36

Declan

I waited for Delilah to leave before I sat up again and turned on the light. I couldn't believe that she'd used me. I trusted her, and she turned against me for these guys. The worst part was that I was sure they wouldn't let me leave. I would be stuck here until it was safe for her to go back home with them.

I knew that what I said to her wasn't fair. I didn't understand why she went to see Eli right after we had sex. Had I said something in my sleep? I wouldn't know because I couldn't exactly ask her right now. My heart ached when she started to cry. I knew that I had broken hers when I broke my own. It was better this way. She shouldn't have to decide. I was making things easier for her. Vik would be pleased when she told him. Eli might be disappointed, but he would get over it. They'd won.

At this moment, all I wanted was to go home. I needed to find Kayden and apologize. He'd been right. I wanted to use him to find her. I treated him like my own personal search dog. He may not forgive that. I wouldn't blame him if he didn't. I deserved his anger. I would contact him as soon as possible and arrange to pay the fines for unauthorized turning. Then I wouldn't have to worry about Delilah anymore. She would be legal. Eli and Vik could keep her safe from the murder investigation.

There was no way my communications were actually secure. No doubt Eli was recording calls, texts, and emails sent. I still didn't feel safe taking my original phone out of airplane mode. He claimed that the only reason we got to keep them was so we'd have whatever numbers we needed to continue our businesses. I think this was a test to see how long it was until one of us slipped up, and our location was revealed. If the hunters found us here, they would know it was one of us who'd killed that girl.

301

Eli insisted that we needed to find out who'd drugged Delilah. I shouldn't have been worried about it anymore, since I'd ended things with her. I still wanted her to be safe. I just couldn't risk my heart. Not like this. My new phone buzzed. No one outside this bunker had that number, and I hadn't set up call forwarding yet. I debated checking it or waiting until morning. This had been a long day, and I was wiped.

The second buzz decided for me. Curiosity won out, and I picked up the phone. Two text messages. I opened the app to see who they were from.

I'm sorry. I didn't mean to hurt you. I wish you'd let me explain. It's not what you think. Delilah wanted to talk. Of course, she did. I couldn't. I knew that if I did, I would give in, and we'd both end up hurt. I read the second text. *Declan, I love you.* Wow, I hadn't expected that from her. Did she mean it, or was she just trying to manipulate me? I had no way to know, even though the ache in my heart swore it was the truth. A third message came through. *Please can we talk?* I knew that I shouldn't respond. I should put the phone down and go to sleep.

What's there to talk about? How you used me to get intel for your boyfriends? It was cold, but that matched how I felt. If I listened closely, I could hear her crying in her room. Great. How long until Vik came beating my door down? I wasn't looking forward to that. I heard a soft knock. It sounded like it came from Delilah's room. I wanted to check it out but didn't want to face Vik's wrath. He was hateful on a good day.

I could hear voices but couldn't make out what was being said. Sure enough, a moment later, someone was pounding on my door. I climbed out of bed and took my time getting dressed. If I was going to have to fight my way out of here, I'd do it fully clothed. "Give me a minute, would ya?" I growled at the noise.

The response was muffled, and the pounding stopped suddenly. There was a loud crash, and I heard Delilah's door open. She screamed and I ran out of my room, no longer concerned with myself. Eli had Vik pinned to the floor, and they'd destroyed the coffee table in the process. "Stop fighting me or I'll sedate you. I mean it, Vik. You can't just start attacking people because one of us had a disagreement or fight with Delilah. Do you want us to do that to you?"

Vik stopped struggling. He was breathing hard, and his face was red. I wondered what she'd told him. "What's going on here?" I asked, running a hand through my auburn curls.

"I heard her crying and I know you have to be responsible. She refused to tell me why, so I was going to ask you. Then Eli jumped me, and here we are." Vik's voice was gravely and raw with emotion.

I looked from him to Delilah, then from her to Eli. It was obvious from his expression that she'd shared with Eli what had happened with us, but not Vik. I wondered why. "Well, I'm going to sleep now. Good night." I turned to go back into my bedroom. Before I could close the door, Eli stopped me.

"We have some things to talk about, my friend." He said and gestured inside. I opened the door and let him in. He turned and motioned for Delilah to follow. When Vik stepped to the door, Eli blocked him. "You need to get yourself under control. We will fill you in tomorrow. Go to bed." He gently shoved Vik back and shut the door. I waited for him to start trying to rip it off the hinges to get to me. Silence met with my anticipation. Then Vik's door slammed.

"What's this all about?" I asked, pacing away from them.

"Delilah is upset. She said you dumped her. Why would you do that?" Was Eli going to play couple's therapist? This should be good.

"Did she tell you that when she came to your room after fucking me?" I asked callously. It was rude and uncalled for, and I just didn't care.

"No, I heard her leave your room and called her. When she didn't answer, I sent a text and found out what had upset her. I can sense emotions. I know that you love her. Why would you end things with someone that you want to be with?" He pressed. Delilah looked as if she would start crying again.

"I can't handle being used. She slept with me to get information for you. Otherwise, why would she have run to your room as soon as I fell asleep?" I accused. He nodded.

"I get why you'd think that. And in part, you're almost right. She came to me because of something you said when you fell asleep. But I didn't ask her to seduce you and obtain intel. She slept with you because she wanted to. When you started talking about Kayden in your sleep, she came to ask me about who he was." Eli explained calmly. I had expected him to be pissed when he found out that I grew up with Kayden. He didn't look upset or angry. I could feel my heart racing.

"I talked about Kayden? In my sleep? Oh. This is bad. I mean, this looks bad on me." I started, then shut myself up and paced the room. What was I going to say to explain this?

"You grew up with him, right? And you didn't say anything to us because you worried that we'd think you were a spy for the hunters. It's not that hard to figure out. Unless I'm wrong?" Eli raised an eyebrow at me, daring me to give an alternate explanation.

"No, that's exactly why. I don't usually share with anyone that I know him. We used to be best friends. Then I went and got turned. He hasn't had much to do with me since then. Until I called him." I knew that they'd find out about this sooner or later.

CHAPTER 37

Delilah

"Why would you call him?" I asked, butting into the conversation that I'd been witnessing between two of my loves.

"I was searching for you. I thought that he could find you faster than I could. I didn't know that you were with Eli and Vik. I only knew that you'd disappeared. I was desperate. We ended up fighting about everything and he left." I wasn't sure if I could believe him or not. He'd hidden this relationship from us all. What else was he hiding?"I can see how you'd think involving him was a good idea. That's how you found out about the fines, too, isn't it?" Eli pressed. Declan nodded.

"I told him I'd pay them. I don't care what it costs. I'll take care of making Delilah legal. You guys will have to protect her from this murder charge, though. I can't take this anymore." Tears filled his eyes, but he refused to let them fall.

"I don't understand how that means we can't be together. I meant what I said. I love you, Declan. I need you with me. I can't survive without you. What do I have to do to convince you?" I was frustrated with myself and him. There had to be a way to fix this. I knew that Eli wouldn't be here with us if he didn't think we could.

"Look, you can't trust me because of my connection to Kayden and the hunters. I understand that. I would never turn any of you in. Not even Vik. Just let me go home and you can get back to whatever you need to do here." He sounded so determined. I needed to crack the shell he'd put around his emotions.

"You said that I used you. But you were the one that used me. I wasn't the one who slept with you and then told you to leave me alone. That was what you did. I just went and had a conversation with one of my other guys. I'm worried about you. I don't want what

I did to get in the way of your friendship." I tried to sound cold, but it wasn't possible. My heart was breaking because this stubborn man wouldn't listen to reason. I hated him almost as much as I hated myself. "I'm not going to beg you to stay. I can't force you to want me. But I want you, even though I'm severely pissed at you right now."

I turned and walked toward the door. Declan didn't make a move to stop me or say anything. The knob turned in my hand. "I'll come to see you in a minute," Eli whispered, kissing my temple. I nodded and closed the door behind me. I leaned against the door for a moment, but they were speaking too softly for me to understand what was being said. I walked to my room and quietly closed the door behind me. I wasn't sure that I wanted anyone to see me tonight.

Eli was true to his word and entered my room almost immediately after I did. "He's not going anywhere. But he is going to need some time to come to terms with his own emotions."

"How did you convince him to stay?" I was half scared to ask but needed to know. Eli picked me up and carried me to the bed. He climbed into it with me and held me close.

"I told him that he can't leave yet. Vik won't let him, even if he tried. The place is locked down. We'd need the code from Vik to get out, and he's not going to hand that over. That would mean risking you." Eli winked at me.

"So, you lied?" I laughed. He nodded.

"Shh, don't tell him that. He'll come around. Just give him time. A few days, a week. Maybe longer. I can't be sure. But I know he cares about you. We have to give him the time and space to realize it." Eli and I settled in and went to sleep. I was surprised that he didn't try anything. I guess he knew that I needed support instead of sex.

The next few days turned into weeks. Things in the bunker were awkward and painful. I wanted to be close to Declan, but he avoided me as much as he could. If Vik hadn't decided that we all had to eat together, I doubted that I would have seen him at all. Eli watched the news articles and let me know when the hunters announced that they had a suspect in the store clerk's death. He couldn't find out who the suspect was or how close they were to finding them.

When Scott brought the next supply drop, Eli had asked for tabletop games to pass the time. I hadn't been as interested in sex since Declan ended things with me. I knew that both Vik and Eli were getting irritated about it. Not that I didn't have sex with them, because I did. I just couldn't force myself to be in the mood all the time with the pain in my heart. Something was missing. So instead of having sex and spending time alone with my guys, we ended up all playing games together in the living area. Eli and Vik had to make Declan play. He wanted to stay away from all of us, but there weren't many games that could be played with only three people.

One evening, I managed to corner him in the kitchen after Eli and Vik claimed they were going to bed. Declan tried to walk away, but I got in his way. If he wanted to escape, he would have to move me physically. "I've got nothing to say," he offered, trying to move past me. I stood my ground, wrapping my arms around his neck and my legs around his waist.

"That's fine. I have enough to say for both of us." I stared into his eyes, my face an inch from his lips. His tongue shot out and desire filled his eyes. No matter how much he denied it, he wanted me. I closed the distance and pressed my lips to his. For a moment, he gave in and kissed me, letting his tongue tangle with mine.

"Delilah, we can't." He pushed me back without forcing me off. I held on tightly. I wasn't going to let him push me away again.

"Why not? Are you seriously going to tell me that you haven't been sulking around here for weeks with that massive erection, thinking about me?" I knew it wasn't fair, but I didn't care. I was still mad at him for rejecting me. He growled in response before capturing my lips with his again and backing me up against the wall.

"Do you really think this is about me not wanting you? Of course, I want you. I want you so badly that I jerk off every night thinking about your perky tits and tight ass. That's not the point. You can't trust me because of who I know. I'm just making things easier for you." His voice was raspy with need. Declan had grabbed my ass with both hands when he pinned me to the wall.

"Why can't you trust me? You made this decision for me, without giving me a chance to trust you. I never said I couldn't trust you. You said that. I trust you with my life. You are my safe space. Don't you understand that?" He growled impatiently while I was talking and started kissing my neck and shoulder.

"I can't be this close to you and not want you. I need you, mo chroí." He hadn't used that nickname for me since the night he ended things.

CHAPTER 38

Declan

I KNEW THE SECOND Delilah cornered me in the kitchen that I couldn't resist her. I wanted her so badly that I walked around with a constant hard-on. Jerking off didn't help. The damned thing just popped back up. I had her pinned to the wall, kissing her neck while she yelled at me. I wondered briefly why neither of the other guys tried to intervene. Maybe they knew exactly what was going on.

Over the past few weeks, they'd all tried to convince me that I was making a mistake. It was pathetic when even Vik got involved. I wouldn't listen to any of what they said. It wasn't that I didn't hear their arguments, I just couldn't afford to let my guard down. Now in one moment, all of that was undone. My dick was trying to rip through my jeans, and I was certain that all the blood had rushed from my brain.

It didn't help matters that Delilah had started wearing short skirts and crop tops. It was like she was trying to torture me. Once I had her against the wall, I realized that she wasn't wearing any panties. Her delicious pussy was pressed against my jeans. That was why my dick wanted out so badly. I groaned and kissed her again to shut her up.

If she wanted me so badly, I wasn't going to deny her this time. I adjusted her higher to unzip my jeans and ease them off my hips. My cock jumped free, and she slid down onto it. I kept her pressed against the wall as I pounded into her, taking out all my frustration in each thrust. When she started moaning, I caught her lips with mine again. I didn't need Eli or Vik coming in to interrupt us. I needed to fuck some sense into my girl. She needed to understand that I was just trying to protect her.

Delilah gripped my shoulders as I thrusted into her repeatedly. When I finally released her lips, she tipped her head back and growled. "Yes, Declan, yes. Don't stop." I couldn't

307

if I had wanted to. I was riding the high of her scent to my release. She tightened around me with her orgasm, and I lost control. I shot my load inside her and kissed her again.

"That was amazing," I whispered against her ear, lowering her to stand. She grinned at me, then punched my arm. "Ow, what was that for?"

Delilah pulled her skirt down to cover herself while I pulled my jeans up and fastened them. "You were being a dick. Don't ever try to leave me again. You love me. Stop trying to pretend like you don't."

I nodded. "You're right. I got scared and tried to run away. Thanks for not giving up on me." No matter how hard I tried to hide my feelings, the three of them knew. And there was no running from it.

"I'm not going to let you run away. We need you too much." Delilah took my hand in hers and pulled me toward the living area. I shouldn't have been surprised to see Eli and Vik waiting for us, but I was. Why hadn't they tried to stop me from having sex with her?

"Oh, good. You're finally done. Now we can talk about the important stuff." Vik's sarcasm wasn't lost on me. It also confirmed that they were listening. Great.

"The hunters are getting closer to finding Delilah. It looks like they identified her. I'm still not sure how." Eli had been searching news outlets for weeks, tracking every story released through human and vampire media.

"What can I do?" I had a hunch that I was about to be asked to do the impossible. Eli and Vik exchanged a glance, and I knew I was right.

"We need you to call Kayden and find out what they know. We need to figure out a way to throw them off." Eli explained.

"He's not going to talk to me. I won't be able to find anything out for you." I tried to explain several times that my former best friend wouldn't be taking my calls any time soon. None of them seemed to understand.

"Can't you just try?" Delilah asked. I knew the moment she spoke that I would do this. It didn't matter that it was idiotic. No matter how hard I tried to deny it, I was in love with her and would do anything for her.

"Okay. I'll call him. What do you want me to say?" I sighed, feeling defeated. Would my best friend even take my call? I had no idea. I hadn't spoken to him since the night I'd tried to have him search for Delilah. I was a dick that night and he told me as much.

Eli explained what they hoped to learn from the hunters, and I took notes. It would be easier for me to call Kayden without anyone else around. I didn't need Vik losing his temper at something I said and freaking out. Once I had everything written out and Eli checked it, I went into my room and dialed Kayden's number.

The new phone would show up as my actual number, which was something I'd never heard of being possible. But Eli had a ton of tech delivered, and I had no idea what some of it was. The phone rang and I stared at the list of things I was supposed to try to ask.

"It's about time you called to apologize. You were an ass." Kayden's deep timbre vibrated through the speaker.

"I know. And I am sorry. I was so obsessed with that girl that I couldn't think straight." It wasn't a lie. I just left out the fact that I was still just as obsessed with her.

"Did you find her?" There was something in his voice. Did he know?

"Yeah. She had a boyfriend that I didn't know about." I hoped that he would drop this line of questioning.

"Huh. Who is he?" Kayden was fishing.

"I don't know, some rich guy. What are you up to?" I hoped to change the subject and get him to tell me something.

"Manhunt for a killer. Haven't you watched the news lately?" He growled, irritated that I didn't know.

"Nah, I've been out of town for a while. Trying to clear my head and move on from this girl." It was another near lie. Not quite true, not quite false.

"A vamp killed a girl in a store. We're closing in on them."

"Them? So, the vamp had help?" I held my breath while I waited for his response.

"There were at least three of them. Killed the girl and took off. No evidence and no trace. But we found a witness." Kayden sounded impressed with himself for his investigating skill.

"Where'd you find a witness? I thought you said there was no evidence." I had to be very careful how I worded things. I didn't want him to know that I was one of the people he was hunting.

"Some girl saw a couple of guys come into the store with a girl. Said she wouldn't have thought twice about it, but the one guy was a jerk and made everyone leave. Probably pre-meditated."

"Well, it's good you got a lead. I'm gonna have to go. I have some plans to finalize for a client. I'm glad you don't hate me anymore. Talk soon." I hung up the call before he could ask me anything else. A witness was bad.

CHAPTER 39

Delilah

DECLAN'S CALL TO KAYDEN was good because it gave us more info than we had before. It was bad in that we found out there was a witness. "A witness? Someone saw what I did?" Panic had set in and I couldn't focus on the conversation.

Eli grabbed my face and made me look at him. "No. No one saw what you did. I destroyed the camera footage. Someone saw us when we entered the shop. They're saying a gang ran them out. Unless they got a good look, we'll be fine." He pressed his forehead to mine and held me there.

His words did nothing to calm me. I was going to be put to death for murdering that girl. I had no idea why I'd done it. I wasn't that type of person. My deep dark secret was that I enjoyed it. I relished drinking her blood, knowing I was draining her of what she needed to live. I could never tell my guys. They wouldn't understand and I'd be labeled a monster. How could they still love me if they knew the truth?

I reached for Declan's hand while Vik paced the floor. To say I was terrified was an understatement. Part of me wanted to turn myself in because I thought I deserved death for what I did. Another part was excited that I'd gotten away with it so far. Then there was the part of me that was scared. There had to be a way out of this.

"Are we any closer to finding out who drugged her?" Declan asked. I thought he was talking to Eli, but I saw that he had directed it to Vik when I looked up.

He shook his head. "The last lead didn't pan out. A new kingpin took over the city's operation, but no one is talking. I can't find anyone who knows who he is or where he came from."

I backed out of Eli's grip and dropped Dec's hand. "What would a new kingpin want with me? It doesn't make sense."

"Probably just someone trying to get the vamp population thinned out. It happens from time to time. We'll figure it out, love." I wished I felt the same confidence that Eli did.

I stood and started to pace the room, much like Vik had been doing. He stopped and stared at me. "What? You can do it, but I can't?" I snapped. He shrugged and sat down. I felt bad about it immediately. There was no point in apologizing. They all knew how freaked out I was.

"So, we're just supposed to assume that this has nothing to do with Delilah directly, even though someone has drugged her twice? Both times, there was a human used as a delivery system. Both times, the intent seemed to be for her to kill the human. How is that not personal?" Declan spoke as if he were inside my head. I'd had the same thoughts.

"But who would want to hurt her? How would we find out without her memories?" Vik wondered aloud.

Eli's face lit up with an idea. "What if I do a new background search on her? The first one I did when we met. I wasn't looking for anything tied to criminal organizations, just her name and where she lived." He looked at me sheepishly.

"I'm supposed to be weirded out that you researched me, right?" I raised an eyebrow at him. When he nodded, I nodded back and kept pacing. I couldn't care less that he'd done a background check on me when we met. As far as I knew, I had nothing to hide. There was no visible connection from me to the Powder operation. "Are you sure it's not someone who had a beef with Uncle Vinny?" I knew that my uncle was into some shady shit when he was alive. Maybe whoever had killed him wanted revenge for something.

"I'll check him out too. And your parents. That may take more research, though. I couldn't find any record of them when I searched you before." Eli explained, apparently feeling less embarrassed about the situation since I wasn't upset.

"Good. I wish I could jump-start my memories so I could help. They happen so randomly. I don't know much about my past." I was starting to get frustrated. I was certain that the guys could tell. Usually, in this situation, one of them would ask me to spend some time with them while the others worked. They claimed to need me, but I knew it was just a way to distract me from worrying. I could probably count the seconds until someone volunteered. *Three, two, one—*

"Myshka, would you come with me? I think a nap might help your memories." See what I mean?

"Sure, Vik. A nap sounds great." He wasn't fooling anyone. For him, a nap meant mind-blowing sex—the kind where I was screaming his name and the other two were fighting their jealousy. But there was nothing wrong with that. It made Eli and Dec try harder when it was their turn. Besides, I would never intentionally cry out just to see how they'd react. And if Vik knew, he'd never tell. I followed him to his room.

After months of being locked up with my guys, I realized that sex never happened in my space. They always insisted that we go to one of their rooms or use a common space.

I'd been with Vik and Eli in nearly every room but my own while Declan avoided me. "Why don't we ever go to my room?" I asked Vik as he closed the door. I turned around to see him slipping out of his shoes and jacket.

I walked over and started unbuttoning his shirt for him. "We all agreed to respect your space. You should have a room that is just for you." His response was sweet.

"But each of you has slept in my room before. So how does that work?"

He laughed. "The room is yours to do with as you'd like. When you've asked us to stay with you, it was because you were upset and sex wasn't what you'd needed." He grabbed my shirt and pulled it over my head, disconnecting my fingers from the buttons on his shirt. Then he peeled the dress shirt off his shoulders and tossed it to the floor. Vik backed me toward the bed, grabbing for my leggings.

"Hey, I'm trying to have a conversation here." I tried to play mad, but he could see right through me.

"Mm, I know you are. And I'm trying to make love to you. Which would you rather do right now?" His voice against my ear made me damp, and the conversation was forgotten. Vik pressed his lips against mine and eased me back on the bed. He poured his passion into the kiss until I wasn't sure I could ever resist him again. "Did you decide?" I nodded and raised my hips to allow him to remove my leggings and panties while I reached around my back and unfastened my bra.

When I looked at him again, he was naked. I have no idea how he stripped so fast, and I really didn't care. The lack of clothing drew my attention to his massive cock growing just for me. I licked my lips and reached for it, but he stopped me, pushing me back on the bed. Vik kissed me again, first on the lips, then trailed kisses and nips down my chest and stomach. He stopped short of my center. I was already wet and waiting for him.

CHAPTER 40

Declan

WITH EVERYTHING THAT DELILAH had to be upset about, Eli approached Vik and me when she was sleeping. The three of us talked and decided that any time things got a little heated or stressful for her, one of us would take her out of the situation and distract her. No one said with sex, but I was pretty sure that was what both of them had in mind. I wasn't complaining; sex with Delilah was amazing. I just didn't want her to be upset that she got left out of some leg work to clear her name.

To be fair, Kayden hadn't admitted that he knew her name. He didn't tell me much of anything. That was the reason Vik was distracting Delilah right now. I needed to talk to Eli and give him information on how to spy on the hunters. I couldn't believe that neither he nor Vik had someone within the organization anyway. They seemed to have eyes and ears everywhere.

"So, he's going to keep her busy the rest of the night?" I asked, walking over to the computers.

Eli nodded. "That's the plan. Whatever it takes to keep her occupied. He's going to keep her mind off what's going on out here. That's what we all agreed on. Why?"

"Good. I need your help. I think we can get into Kayden's system and find out what he knows, but I have no idea how to do all of that." I explained, pulling a chair out and sitting down.

"That's some major hacking, pal. And it's highly illegal. What makes you think I can do it?" Eli tried to deflect and deny, but I raised an eyebrow.

"Oh. My bad, I thought you were a tech wiz. Delilah and Vik are always going on and on about how Eli's the man for the job if it has to do with a chip or processor. If you can't, it's okay. I'll find another way." I knew that my words had hit home when his face turned red, and he stomped away. I sat there and waited, knowing that he would come back.

Not a minute passed and he was back at the computer next to me. "You're an ass. If you knew that I could do it, why didn't you just say that?"

"I did," I started, pausing to cover my chuckle. "What do you need from me to get access?" I had a little info about Kayden's business and his involvement with the hunters, but not a lot. I hoped that I had enough to help Eli get into the system.

"Ideally, I would want a physical location and IP address. I'm guessing you don't have both of those, though." He turned his attention to the keyboard and started typing faster than my eyes could follow. "Do they have business records kept under the hunters, or do they run it through his company?"

"A little of both, I think. He owns the Dixon Corporation. For a while, the hunters were operating under that. I think the secret stuff is kept somewhere else, though." I watched in fascination as Eli's fingers went to work again, typing in search boxes and coding.

"Okay, I can start with his company and we'll go from there. Luckily, I expected to have to do something like this. I had Scott bring my little helper just in case." Eli pointed at a flash drive that was plugged into the computer. I didn't remember seeing it before. He must have grabbed it when he stormed off. A few more minutes of his speed typing passed and then he looked up at me. "We're in."

"Already? Wow, man, that was fast! I expected it to take way longer." He smirked at me and I knew that he'd probably been researching Kayden and his company since they realized I knew him. "You've been working on this for a while, haven't you?"

Eli laughed. "Yeah, since the connection came out. I figured knowing what we're up against would help. But I'm glad you decided to help. I'll take whatever intel you can give me about how they operate."

I shrugged. "I wasn't a Hunter, just some human kid who followed them around until I figured out how to become as strong and fast as they were. I wasn't exactly included in anything they were doing. I just got good at hiding and tailing them."

"That's the key. You know where they go to train, what they do, how they do it, and basically everything else. I don't think you realize how much you know." Eli's encouragement eased the weight in my chest. Maybe I did know something that would help us figure out what they knew.

"Tell me what you need." Eli and I spent the next two hours researching the hunters and going over what I knew. I hated to admit it, but Eli was right. All those years spent watching my friend while he was training finally paid off. I knew where and how they trained. I knew the procedures for their cases. I even helped figure out what Kayden's password for his email was. Once Eli had access to that, we had everything the hunters had.

"Honestly, they don't have much. A vague description of Vik and Delilah. I'm surprised they don't have anything on either of us." Eli sounded offended that the witness had only noticed the other two.

"Isn't that good, though. They think it's a Bonnie and Clyde thing. The hunters aren't looking for us. We could come out of hiding if we needed to. We'd just have to keep Vik and Delilah separated so no one realized that they were the ones the witness saw." The idea made sense in my head, but Eli's face shot it down instantly.

"We can't do that. We've got people who look similar to us popping up in random places to make it look like we're traveling for business. If we just show up at home, it'll look suspicious." He explained. It made sense, but I hated being caged. This was feeling more and more like a prison sentence all the time.

"I guess I'm just going stir crazy. You're right, we need to stay here and keep Delilah safe. But will we ever be able to go back to our lives?" As important as Delilah was, I missed my friends and my life. I would never put her in danger, though. We would stay hidden as long as it took to clear her name.

"I get it. Trust me, I am too. I hate not being able to go out. And Vik is dying to hit up a fancy restaurant. But we're still coming up empty on who the new kingpin is and what they have against our girl. That has to be the priority."

CHAPTER 41

Eli

WHILE I UNDERSTOOD WHY Declan wanted to get out of here, it wasn't practical. We didn't have enough info from the hunters to ensure they didn't know who Delilah was. I tried a few weeks ago to explain to him the plan Vik and I had in place to make it seem like each of us was in a different location weekly. I thought he'd understood that we'd included him in that too. Once I made sure he knew just how important staying put was, I went to work on breaking into Kayden's files.

Within just a few hours, I knew his full name, address, and all his personal information. I even managed access to his bank account. It didn't do much good since he didn't have any records that helped us. Still, I felt better knowing who I was up against. I didn't want to go up against the hunters without some inside info.

"So this is where they train. Where do they live?" I pointed to the map as I spoke. Declan nodded and pointed to another area near the training grounds.

"Here. Or at least they did when I was there. The community is fairly small. Gunnar Trion was in charge of the Shadowtail Hunters when I was young. From what Kayden told me, Shadowtail was the wolf pack in charge of the area. They were charged with policing the other packs and evolved into wolf hunters instead of just shifters. I didn't understand that part when he tried to explain it."

Dec paused and put his fingers on three other spots near the first one. "As far as I know, there are four packs who live in this area. Sablecrest is here, Crimsonfang over there, Darkmaw—that's Kayden's pack—here, and the one nearest us is Shadowtail. Most of the wolves use the pack name as their surname, but the ones who come into the city regularly have adopted more humanized surnames."

"That's pretty good. All of that can help us if we have to fight. I'm hoping it doesn't come down to that. So, Shadowtail hunts wolves? Is that how the hunters we know came about? Do you know anything about that?" I was fascinated by the hierarchy of wolves and wanted to know more.

"Kind of. The Council approached Shadowtail to hunt down out-of-line vamps. Gunnar turned them down. He swore that he was only going to keep his people in line. A handful of wolves from the other three packs got together and formed a group to help the Council," Declan shrugged.

"Did you get to know any of them besides Kayden?" I felt like I was interrogating him, but Dec seemed happy that he could help.

He shook his head and looked at the floor. "Not really. I was young and tried too hard. They didn't want a human following them around. Red would talk to me, but the others avoided me."

"Who's Red?" Finally, we might be onto something.

"She's Gunnar's daughter. He's grooming her to take over Shadowtail at some point. Or at least he was when we were kids." Dec ran a hand through his hair and groaned. We'd been at this for hours. Luckily, Vik was still keeping Delilah busy.

"Okay, let's take a break. I've got some searches going and could use something to eat. Maybe a walk to clear my head." I could have kept questioning him for hours, but he didn't need to know that. We'd break for a while, then come back at it with clear heads.

Relief washed through Dec. It was strange to feel other people's emotions, but I was good at hiding my reaction. He was getting frustrated with himself for not knowing more. There was really no way he could have known unless he'd joined the hunters. From what he told me, he'd wanted to, but they refused him for not being a wolf. Bastards had no idea what they'd lost out on. He was a good ally.

I grabbed a blood bag and stepped outside in the darkness of the night. The sun would come up soon and I would need to sleep. It wouldn't come easy or last long enough. I'd been running on four hours a day since we got here. If anyone noticed, they weren't saying anything. I finished the bag and tucked it into my pocket to dispose of when I got back from my walk. I was going to do a perimeter check and make sure we were still hidden.

It didn't take me long to figure out I was being tracked. I wasn't sure who it was, but someone was following me. I sniffed at the air slowly. There was no reason to let them know that I knew. Declan. But something else was there too. So, Dec was following me and someone was following him. I ducked around a tree and waited. A moment later, a shadow walked past. I grabbed him and threw him against the tree with my hand covering his mouth.

"Shh. You're being followed. I don't know who else is out there. We have to be quiet and careful. Can't lead them to her." I whispered with my mouth against his ear. He nodded slightly and I removed my hand.

Rustling leaves drew my attention. Dec and I both turned toward the noise. A wolf jumped out of the bushes in front of us with its teeth bared. I could tell from Dec's face that he recognized it. This wasn't just a wolf. It was one of the hunters. But how had they found us? I stepped in front of Declan, and the wolf growled. I growled back. I wasn't going to let this monster take my brother from me.

Declan put his hand on my arm and nodded when I glanced at him. "It's okay, Eli. He won't hurt us." As he spoke, the wolf started to shift, its bones rearranging until a human man stood in front of us. He had shoulder-length brown waves and the most haunting gray eyes I'd ever seen. He was also completely naked.

"Did you think I wouldn't find you?" He snarled at Declan before stomping forward and wrapping his arms around my friend. I stood there in shock. What the fuck was happening here?

"Eli, this is Kayden. Kayden, this is Eli." Dec did a quick introduction then turned back to the naked man. "You hunted me down? Why?"

"You were super cryptic on the phone. You never ask about my investigations. I could smell you in the woods here but couldn't find where you were hiding. Where have you been? Are you in trouble?" He sounded like a worried brother, and the emotions that flooded off him matched that.

"I'm fine. You shouldn't have come. Did you bring the whole team?" Dec was nervous. He didn't want Kayden to figure out that this was where Delilah was.

"No, it's just me. Dec, you're my best friend. I'm not going to let you go through something alone. Who is this guy? Are you being held against your will?" Kayden kept his voice low even though he probably scented that I was a vamp and knew I could hear him. I wanted to see what Dec would do in this situation, so I kept my mouth shut and watched.

"I'm here by choice. It's a long story. I'll tell you eventually, but I need some time to get everything together. Someone is in trouble and it's not their fault. I'm trying to help clear their name." He looked at his friend, clearly expecting this to go south.

Kayden nodded. "Okay. If you need me, you know how to get in touch. I'll leave you to it. Let me know if I can help. If your friend really is innocent, they deserve a chance to prove it. Just be careful, bro. It's getting more dangerous out in the world all the time." He pulled Declan into a hug, then turned and ran off into the woods, shifting as he went. We stood there, watching after him, for a long while.

CHAPTER 42

Viktor

DISTRACTING DELILAH WAS MORE complicated than I thought. I had planned to use sex as a last-ditch effort, not my starting lineup. But here we were, naked and about to get crazy. She was excited, but I could tell she was also pissed about being escorted out while the others were working. I wondered how rough she would get. Usually, things were all sweet and loving, but when Myshka got pissed about something, I ended up being the one to suffer. Maybe I would flip the script tonight and be the one in charge.

I walked over to the closet and opened the door. There was a box inside that had just what we needed in it. She growled at me for leaving her alone, even for a second. "I'm just getting some toys, Myshka. I thought maybe we could play a little tonight."

Anxiety crossed her face for a moment; then, she seemed to accept my idea. "Okay. Nothing too crazy, though." Her cheeks were pink with embarrassment. I would have to spend eternity teaching her that sex toys were nothing to be ashamed of. I carried the box over to the bed, tilting it to spill the contents on the blanket. I had a little bit of everything. I sifted through the items until I found what I was looking for.

Delilah grimaced when I held up restraints and a riding crop. "Seriously?" She laughed. I shrugged and set them to the side. I would use them tonight, even if we didn't start there. I grabbed a vibrator that was shaped like a demon's tail. It was curved to hit her g-spot perfectly and the tip looked similar to an arrowhead. I had a matching butt plug, but I hadn't been able to talk her into that since the night she'd been with Eli and myself together. I held up the wicked vibe and she blushed harder. I knew she loved that one.

"Okay, that's settled. We'll start with this, then move on to that." I held up the vibe when I said this and pointed at the restraints when I said that. She growled at me and I took that as a good sign. I didn't want her to give in if it wasn't something she wanted. I planned to make her beg me for it. I put the other toys away and grabbed a bottle of lube from the nightstand. I knew that the only way I would need it was if she agreed to anal, but it was better to have it handy than to have to stop in the middle of something to get it.

"How do you want me?" Myshka asked, trying to be seductive. If only she knew that I wanted her every possible way, all the time. I would take her any way she would allow.

Instead of answering, I grabbed her ankle and pulled her to me. Her pussy was still just as wet as it had been when I'd walked away. That kinky bitch loved the idea of playing with all my toys. That turned me on even more. My cock was rock hard and if I wasn't careful, I'd be blowing my load before either of us was ready. I took a deep breath and pulled her closer. I wanted to taste her before we got started. When she was close enough, I raised her legs and slipped under them, holding her knees on my shoulders.

I let my tongue tease her clit and her seam until she squirted on my face. Her screams of pleasure would probably plague the unfortunate fellows who'd decided I should be the one to distract her. After another orgasm, I spread her legs apart and turned on the devil's tail. She moaned at the sound and jumped when I touched it to her leg. I slid it up her thigh, over her stomach, and back down her other thigh. Delilah whimpered with need. "Please, Vik."

"Do you want me to tie you up first?" I whispered, leaning close to her ear.

"Yes," she breathed back at me. I turned the vibe off, then I grabbed the restraints and tied her hands to the headboard and her feet to the corners of the footboard. She was spread open for me to feast on any way I'd like.

"You know the drill. If it gets to be too much, use the safe word. Tell me what it is." I demanded, standing over her but not touching her. The first time we'd played with the toys, I made her choose a word to say if she felt overwhelmed. I needed to know that she would use it now if she needed to.

"It's so silly." She started to argue. I raised my eyebrows and took a step away, letting her know without words that if she didn't say it, I wouldn't touch her. "Okay, okay. Banana. There I said it, now get over here and touch me." She'd gone from embarrassed to bossy. I loved it. That was one of the ways I knew things were about to get wild.

I stepped back to the bed and turned the devil's tail on again. Delilah shivered in anticipation. I once again rubbed the vibrator up her thigh, over her stomach, and down her thigh. She whimpered when it came close to her clit but kept moving. "Don't make me beg." The request was whispered. She knew that had been my plan. Her quiet request changed my mind. I rubbed the devil's tail on her clit, and she groaned in pleasure.

Then I pulled it away again. Delilah growled in response. I rubbed the vibrating appendage across her nipples and she stopped. Her back arched as if she could control where I put the toy by moving her body. I shifted it back to her clit and she bucked as another orgasm took over. She was pulling at the ropes as if trying to get free. I half expected her to use the safe word, but she didn't. While she writhed, I slipped the toy inside of her, letting it vibrate against her g-spot for a moment before pulling it out completely and breaking contact. I planned to tease her in the best way possible. Watching her pussy drip and her body writhe nearly did me in.

I rubbed the vibrator against her clit again as I slid my aching dick across her soaked entrance before sliding it in. "Hard and fast?" I asked as I started to pound her. She nodded, moaning at the sensations. The faster I went, the more she fought against the restraints until she had ripped through them and her hands were free. She pushed me back for a second and tore through one of the leg restraints, leaving the other to hold her. Then Delilah flipped over onto her hands and knees, silently begging me to take her from behind.

I handed her the devil's tail and watched while she rubbed it on her clit the way she liked. I gasped when she reached behind her ass and grabbed my cock. She pulled me toward her, using it as a leash. When I was close enough, she guided my engorged member into her pussy again. "Hard and fast," she ordered, picking up the vibe again and placing it where she wanted. I started to fuck her with the rhythm she had requested, moving harder and faster with each thrust. My balls smacked against her clit and the vibrator with each thrust. She screamed my name and I lost control, falling over the edge of bliss with her.

CHAPTER 43

Declan

When Eli was sure that Kayden had left, we continued walking around the perimeter. There was no evidence that any other wolf or vampire had been in the area. I wondered if Kayden had meant what he said about helping me if I called him. "Do you think you can trust him?" Eli seemed to read my mind.

"I want to. He was my best friend for so long. We grew up more like brothers. We called each other's parents 'Mom' and 'Dad' and we were together more than apart. But he's the leader of the hunters now. I honestly don't know. If it were just my life on the line, I would say yes without a doubt. But with Delilah and you guys involved, I can't take that chance." I ran a hand through my hair again, trying to figure out what had brought Kayden to me.

"We'll figure it all out. Don't worry. If you trust him, I trust him." I couldn't express how much Eli's words meant to me. I wanted to tell him that, but I wasn't sure that I even trusted myself. Kayden knew where we were now. Sure, he didn't know that Delilah was with us, and nothing we found on his system showed that he knew who she was. But I wasn't prepared to risk her just because my old friend came back and said it was all going to be okay.

Eli and I walked silently for a while until we made it back to the bunker's entrance. I knew it was well hidden, but the thought of Kayden following us made me paranoid. Vampires had eyesight that rivaled wolves, especially in the dark. And our hearing was just as good. I knew that if he'd followed us, I would know it. I had to believe that. I watched behind us as Eli put the code in to open the door. I was secretly expecting Kayden and his men to jump from the bushes and attack us the whole time. I didn't relax until we were safely inside the bunker with the doors locked again.

"He didn't give us any more than we already knew." I fumed, irritated at myself that I couldn't get Kayden to talk. Eli laughed. "What's so funny?"

"That you think he didn't give us anything. It's right in front of you. He handed us the one thing he cares about more than the hunters." He paused and raised an eyebrow at me. I shrugged, then he finished his thought. "It's you. He came here, hunted you down to make sure you were okay. He told you that if you need him, he'll be there. If that's not a weakness, I don't know what is."

"I'm not going to use him like that." It didn't matter to me that Eli was right. I didn't want him to be. I didn't want to believe that I would betray my friend like that. Inside, I knew I would.

"That's not what I'm saying. Look, I'd be the same way for my sister. She's my weakness. Well, besides Delilah. I'm not saying we use it against him unless he pushes the issue by taking her in. I'm just saying that he did give us new info." He walked over to the computers and checked his searches. Eli insisted that he would find something that would connect the Powder operation to Delilah.

"Any luck?" I asked before heading into the kitchen for a drink. Eli was sitting in the chair when I got back, typing frantically. "Should I take that as a no?" I glanced at the screen while he was typing, but I had no idea what any of it meant.

"Narrowing the search parameters of the program. Nothing concrete yet. I got a list of flunkies that we can capture and interrogate, but nothing on the boss. I need a name. Why can't I find him?" Eli slapped the desk and paced the room. Frustration rolled off him.

"What can we do? You've got searches going. Vik says his men are looking. I don't have anyone qualified to help. I feel like I'm not doing anything here." I knew that my little pity party wasn't exactly warranted, but I couldn't help feeling like I was doing less work than the other two. How would I ever convince Vik that I was good enough if I couldn't help out?

"I have an idea. Take your phone off airplane mode. Kayden already knows where you are. Maybe he'll call you or reach out somehow, and we can get a lead that way." Eli's suggestion was ridiculous, but it might just work.

"Okay. I'll do it. Do you think he'll reach out?" I didn't wait for an answer. I walked to my room and retrieved my phone from the dresser. After switching airplane mode off, I waited a minute to see if anything would happen. Silence.

"Give it time. You just saw him. He may not be back at their base yet. You should get some rest. It's your turn to distract Delilah tomorrow. And you know how that will end up." He smirked at me, then walked back to the computers and sat down again. I glanced back as I walked away and he was typing again but much less frantically. His confidence made me feel like this might actually work out.

I took a quick shower then collapsed naked on the bed. I had almost passed out when my phone made a noise. A new message. But it couldn't be Kayden, right? I reached for the phone and opened the app.

Are you sure that you're okay? I have a bad feeling about you being in trouble. Sure enough, Kayden had texted me. I wondered how I would get him to talk. There was no good way to ask him about anything without showing our hand. That wasn't my decision to make.

I'm fine. Just need to find out who's drugging vamps. Can't get anywhere because I don't have connections. Frustrated that I couldn't help my friend. I hoped that he took that as enough of a response. I wasn't sure I could cover up what we were doing here if he pushed the issue.

Is someone drugging vamps? With what? How do you know this? Level with me, and I might be able to help. Part of me wanted to tell him everything. I could completely unload and work through it with him the way Eli can with Vik. But I knew better. We were on opposite sides here, and there was no way he would go against his Hunter training and regulations to help us.

I know someone who was drugged and did things they wouldn't normally do. I'm trying to find out how and why. It looks like Powder was used, but I have no idea how it's being transmitted. Would that be enough detail, or had I said too much?

Dec, this is some really dangerous stuff. You need to watch your back. I don't want you to get hurt. That drug is no joke. And the guys who make it are not the type of guys you want to mess with. Most of them kill for fun. Promise me you'll be careful, and I'll try to get you a name.

I didn't expect Kayden actually to help me. If he could get us the name of the kingpin, maybe we'd be able to find the connection to Delilah. Then from there, we'd be able to protect her. *Thanks, man. If we could find the kingpin, we'd be able to help my friend out.* I felt like I was riding a thin line between my friend and my love. I didn't want either of them to get hurt. But Kayden could take care of himself. Delilah needed me.

I'm on it. I'll let you know if I find something. Be safe, my friend, I thought to myself. I wanted to text him more but decided it wasn't a good idea.

Part of me wanted to tell Eli, but I figured I'd just have to repeat the whole conversation over breakfast anyway. There was no reason to say it all twice. I might as well wait. I made sure the phone was plugged in, then collapsed on the bed, and passed out.

CHAPTER 44

Delilah

LAST NIGHT, I HADN'T planned to sleep in Vik's room, but his crazy sex wore me out. He was already up and out of the room before I even woke up. Damn them anyway! All of this plotting without me has to stop! I can't live like this. I refuse to be coddled like a child. I threw on my clothes and stomped into the living room to give them a piece of my mind. The room was empty. There's no way they would leave me alone.

I walked to my room to make sure Vik wasn't in there for some reason. It was empty too. "Okay, I guess I'll just make my rounds," I spoke out loud but not to anyone. My voice sounded strange and echoed. Dec's room was empty, as was the kitchen. Eli's and the garage were the only places I hadn't checked. I crept over to Eli's door and turned the knob. The second I pushed the door open, something exploded and threw me across the room. My head was spinning. I brushed my hair out of my face and my hand was coated in blood.

A wave of dizziness came over me as I tried to stand. Fire from the explosion spread from Eli's room toward Vik's across the living area. I shook off nausea and forced my feet toward the garage. I needed to get out of here. I had to find my guys. I tried to scream for them but found that I couldn't speak. I walked cautiously into the garage. The SUV was gone. How was this possible? My guys would never leave me. But somehow, they did. I was alone. Something was wrong here. I couldn't explain it, but this felt wrong.

Before I could step outside, a group of masked men came in and grabbed me. I was gagged, tied up, and thrown in the back of a truck. I tried to fight until one of them hit me with the butt of a gun. It didn't knock me out, but it hurt enough that I stopped fighting. I closed my eyes and waited for whatever was coming next.

"Delilah! Myshka! Wake up!" Vik shook me. I groaned but didn't respond. "Eli! Declan! Something is wrong with her. Hurry!" He shook me again, but I still couldn't respond.

"What happened?" Eli asked as he ran into the room. Declan was close behind him. I could hear their footsteps even though I couldn't see them.

"She was having a nightmare and I tried to wake her. It's not working. What can we do?" He sounded so concerned. I wondered what was going on. It didn't make sense. I imagined them while being transported in the back of the truck. That had to be it. Right? I tried to open my eyes, but they refused to cooperate.

Declan's voice was so close. I thought I could reach out and touch him. "Mo chroí, please wake up. Open your eyes. You're having a bad dream. Just let it go and follow my voice." He spoke so calmly. I wanted to follow him. I nodded and tried again, but my eyes wouldn't open. I groaned again, this time hearing it echo around me.

"That's it, love, keep trying. Follow Dec's voice. Come back to us." Eli's whisper found me next. Wait—was the truck the dream? Is that what they were saying? I shook my head, trying to clear it. The explosion, the fire, the loneliness were all so real. I shivered and kept moving toward where I heard Dec talking to me softly. He was encouraging me to find him. I had to find him. Suddenly I wasn't in the truck anymore. I was in the dark. This was so familiar like I'd been here before.

My legs ached from walking for so long. I wanted to lie down and rest, but Declan kept asking me to find him. I pushed on, trying desperately to figure out where he was. I finally came to a door. I grabbed the handle and ripped it open.

"She opened her eyes! Oh, Myshka, we were so worried! Are you okay?" Vik pulled me into his arms and kissed me hard. Then he passed me to Declan, who kissed me with desperation. Eli had his arms open for me when he was done, and I jumped into them.

"I have no idea what just happened, but that dream was so real. You three abandoned me. I was alone and then some masked guys came and took me." I explained, not wanting to get into the details of it. Eli pulled me close and kissed me. His warm arms held me tightly and I finally felt safe again. "I knew you wouldn't leave me."

"Never." He assured me. Dec and Vik echoed his sentiment. At this point, I realized that every one of my guys was wearing nothing more than a pair of boxer briefs. I had scared them if they didn't even get dressed. They were usually so modest around each other.

"You know, a girl could get used to having three mostly naked men around all the time." I teased. Declan stood up and gyrated his hips at me. Eli bounced me on his lap, rubbing his growing erection on my behind. I turned to Vik, and he just shrugged and shook his head.

"You're impossible. A moment ago, you were unconscious and now you're horny. I can't keep up." Then he laughed and leaned over for a kiss.

"I'm sorry for scaring you all. I don't really know what happened. I'm fine now, I promise. I think I want to take a shower. Alone. Then you can all fill me in on what you've been keeping from me." I slid off Eli's lap and walked to the door, not caring that I just realized I'd been naked this whole time myself. Without stopping at the door, I went to my room and grabbed a sweater and jeans, along with a bra and panty set, tossed it all on the bed, and walked into the bathroom.

The water was hot, stinging my skin. I needed it to wash away the memory of that dream. It felt like so much more than just a dream. Was I seeing what was going to happen? Or was my mind just playing tricks on me because I'm feeling paranoid? I would have to ask the guys about vampire gifts. Could seeing the future be one? Part of me refused to believe it was possible. Another part of me knew that at this point, anything was possible.

I grabbed the clean washcloth hanging in the shower and dumped my favorite soap on it. I scrubbed my skin until I worried that my skin would come off. Then I dropped the rag and started washing my hair. Once scrubbed clean, I slathered on conditioner and combed it through while I daydreamed. What if I could see the future? How would the guys handle that? I wondered about different scenarios until I realized that the water would turn cold soon. I quickly rinsed my hair then turned the water off. I wrapped my hair up in one towel and dried myself off with another. Part of me wished that I'd had one of the guys come shower with me. Eli was good at washing me and drying me. Declan always enjoyed being bossed around by me. I think it would have been more satisfying if Vik had done it. He isn't the sweet type, so he doesn't usually do things like that for me. It might be fun to talk him into it, though. I made a mental note to do just that as I got dressed and combed my hair.

I was shocked that the three of them hadn't tried to come in while I was showering. Those three must be up to something. And I was about to find out just what it was. Or else.

CHAPTER 45

Eli

"I THINK WE SHOULD just tell her everything and let her have a say in how we handle it all." I defended my stance once again. Vik was against telling Delilah anything, and for some strange reason, Declan decided to agree with him.

"She can't handle it all," Vik growled, stepping up to get in my face.

"Delilah can handle anything. But she doesn't need to worry about it all." Dec said quietly. He was anticipating her walking in at any moment. I hoped that she did. I wanted her to know what we were fighting about. At least this fight was mostly civilized. I wasn't going to throw punches to get my way.

"Excuse me. I think I should decide what I can handle. Thank you very much." Delilah stated calmly. I couldn't stop the grin that spread across my face. That was my girl.

"Exactly. So, let's fill her in. It's her life on the line here. We shouldn't get to make her decisions." I spoke with renewed enthusiasm since Delilah had entered the room.

Declan sighed. "Fine. I'll change my vote. We can tell her everything."

"You guys were voting on whether or not you'd tell me what's going on? How dare you!" Delilah's face got red, and I took a couple of steps backward. She was small but scary. I held up my hands in surrender.

"Don't be mad at Eli. He's been dying to tell you everything since we got here. We talked about it, and Vik convinced me that it might be too much for you. I'm sorry I didn't trust you to make this choice." Dec kissed her cheek, braving her wrath to get close enough.

"I refuse to apologize for looking out for your best interests. If you're mad at me, so be it." Vik said, then walked to his room and slammed the door. I guessed that he would pout for a while, then Delilah would smooth things over again.

"That's fine; we don't need him for you to tell me what you've learned." Delilah sat down on the couch and gestured for Dec and me to join her. He sat on one side, and I sat on the other. I could hear Vik grumbling in his room.

Delilah listened carefully as Dec and I filled her in on everything. I explained the web searches and hacking; then he explained Kayden and the hunters. We told her about meeting with him outside and his offer to help. We even told her about Vik setting up lookalikes to pop up randomly so people wouldn't wonder where we were. She nodded along and asked questions when she needed clarification. By the time we were done, Vik had opened the door and leaned on the frame.

"I thought you were against me knowing things." She accused, glaring at him.

He nodded. "I am. I think stress is what caused that nightmare, and I think it's only going to get worse if you know exactly what's going on." He looked as pissed at her as she did at him. I never imagined being concerned for my friend's safety because he made a girl mad. There was something almost feral about the way Delilah was looking at him, though.

"I guess we'll see, won't we? Is there anything that you guys left out?" She directed the first question to Vik and the second to Dec and me. I shook my head, and Dec did too. I thought we'd told her everything. She seemed satisfied with that answer. With one more heated look at Vik, she stormed off into the kitchen. I heard the fridge open and slam. We were nearly out of supplies again. I knew that the blood bags were running out. I had contacted Scott, but he was having trouble filling our order this time. Apparently, he'd garnered some attention with our last supply request.

"Are we almost out of everything?" Delilah called from the kitchen. I grimaced. She wasn't going to like this news.

"We are. Scott is working on it, but he's not sure that he'll be able to get supplies this time. We may have to go out and pick stuff up ourselves." As much as I wanted her to be involved, I didn't want to tell her about this. I was hoping Vik and I could run out without her knowing we were gone. So much for that idea.

"When do we leave?" Delilah asked, walking into the room. I ran a hand over my face and looked at the guys for backup. Dec shrugged.

"You were the one who wanted to tell her everything. How are you planning to deal with this?" Vik snarled from the doorway of his room. I would have punched him in response any other time, but he was right. I was the one who insisted that she should know exactly what was going on.

"Look, I get that you don't want me out there. But I'm not just going to sit here on my ass while you guys take risks. Either we all go, or no one goes. And if Scott can't get the supplies we need, there's really no choice." She flopped down on the couch next to Dec, draping her legs over his.

"Okay, but you have to do what we tell you. Vik and I are more skilled at this type of thing than you are. You have to promise." I insisted. I knew it would do no good. She would do what she wanted, and we'd have to figure out how to keep her safe anyway. This would be so much more stressful than it had to be.

"I promise that as long as all four of us stick together, I will do what you request. I will not follow orders, though. So don't even try it." She crossed her arms over her chest and stared at me. I knew that she'd meant part of that for Vik since he liked to try to order her around.

"Great. We'll get everything ready. We need a list. Can the two of you take care of that while Vik and I tend to the SUV?" I hoped that I could at least have a private conversation with him. But that would involve Delilah cooperating. I wasn't sure that was possible.

"Sure, Dec and I can take care of the list. Come on, let's start in the kitchen." She grabbed his hand and practically pulled him into the kitchen. I didn't speak until I heard the door close behind them.

I walked over to Vik, who made a weird face at me. "What?"

"She knows you wanted to talk to me. You'll pay for that later." He turned and walked into his room, waiting for me to follow.

"What was I supposed to do? I couldn't just tell her that I needed to talk to you. If I had, then she would have insisted on listening in." I defended myself as quietly as I could.

"I'm just warning you. What is it that you need that's so important you're willing to risk her wrath?" He asked as he pulled a new suit out of the closet.

"Do you have guys who can watch our backs out there? The hunters are following mine. That's why Scott can't get the supplies. I don't want to take her out there, but I fucked up. Okay? I admit it. Just help me keep her safe." I growled the words through gritted teeth. I hated admitting that he might be right about anything.

Vik nodded. "I'll make some calls."

CHAPTER 46

Declan

I KNEW ELI'S MISTAKE the moment he made it. Asking our girl to make the shopping list was basically like asking me to take her to the other room and occupy her so he could talk to Vik. And she knew it. I let her drag me into the kitchen, knowing I was about to get yelled at for his mistake. The second the door closed, she looked at me, shrugged, then grabbed a notebook and pen. I thought she was grumbling under her breath, but her back was turned so that I couldn't be sure.

"You're not mad?" I asked quietly. This was dangerous too, but I had to know. I was fairly confident I could redirect her anger to the other two if I had to.

She shrugged again. "Not at you. Besides, we need a list if we're going to get supplies. So we might as well write down what we need."

Her response terrified me. She was clearly pissed but wouldn't take it out on me. I wondered what she had planned for Eli and almost felt sorry for him. We started making a detailed shopping list, starting with blood bags and food, then moving to household supplies and toiletries. By the time she was finished, I felt like she'd calmed down a bit. I was amazed at how she made the entire list without checking the other rooms. I figured she just didn't want to run into Eli right now.

"Look, I know that I can be difficult sometimes. I don't deny that. But hiding things from me is never a good idea. It will always piss me off. And I will always get revenge." She spoke quietly and her words made me wonder who'd hurt her so badly. Did she even know? There were moments when I felt like her human personality showed through, then other times when the vampire was so different. I wondered if she saw it too.

"I understand why you're upset. I wouldn't blame you for it, even if you had taken it out on me. I'm glad you didn't, even though I do deserve some of your anger. I agreed with Vik that we shouldn't tell you what was going on." Damn, Dec, just set yourself up for a kick in the balls; why don't you?

Delilah looked at me for a minute. Then she put the notebook and pen down and walked over to me. As much as I wanted to cringe or cover my junk, I forced myself to stand still. If she attacked me, it would be because of my actions. I wasn't going to try to prevent it. She stopped an inch away from me. "I'm not mad at you. I know you were trying to protect me. I'm mad at Eli for not telling me anyway, even though you two told him not to. I'm mad at him for sending me away so he can have secrets with Vik." There were tears in her eyes as she spoke.

I pulled her into my arms, pressing my lips to hers. She growled and tangled her tongue with mine. After a minute or so, she pulled away. "We need to finish the list." She picked up the discarded notebook and pen before exiting the kitchen. I watched as she entered her bedroom, then I went out into the garage.

"Man, you have to talk to her. She's so upset with you. She feels like you're hiding things again. And since we just cleared the air, that's not a good thing. Go talk to her now." It felt strange giving orders to someone who'd been with Delilah longer than I had, but I didn't care. He needed to think about what was best for her and not about himself. There was no room for selfishness here. Delilah had to be our focus.

Eli looked at me with an eyebrow raised. He glanced at Vik, then walked away without a word. I wondered what I'd interrupted. They had the hood open on my SUV and were hovered over it when I came in. "Come look at this," Vik said, his tone a little softer than usual.

"What am I looking at?" I leaned over and searched where he was pointing. It looked like an engine to me.

"There's a tracker in your car. That's probably how Kayden found you so quickly. He already knew where you were." Vik wasn't accusing me this time. He was just explaining what had happened.

"Son of a bitch. How could he? Are you sure it was him?" I couldn't believe that he'd fooled me with his fake concern. I was convinced that he wanted to help me. I thought he was going to be on our side.

"I can't be, but it doesn't make much sense for it to have been anyone else unless you have some secret enemies out there somewhere. Do you?" He smiled. I couldn't remember Vik ever telling a joke before, much less smiling. Was I in an alternate dimension or something?

"Not that I know of. I didn't think the hunters were really my enemies either until this. Kayden said he wanted to help. I feel stupid for believing him." I was pissed. It was good that bastard wolf wasn't here, or I would show him how I felt about being lied to and used. We'd fought in the past, but nothing like what was coming his way the second I found him.

"Okay, so I'm not usually the one to talk anyone out of violence, but I don't think going after him is a good idea." Vik's brown eyes had softened at my anger. "Besides, I think I have a better one. Let's get the others and discuss it."

"How did you know what I was thinking?" Vik's laugh echoed in the garage. He walked around the SUV and put his arm around my shoulders, turning me back toward the entrance.

"It's written all over your face. I have to be honest; I would never have thought you had it in you. I think I might like you after all." We walked together back into the living area and sat down on the couch. I assumed that we were waiting for Eli to make up with Delilah to discuss Vik's idea about how to handle the tracker.

CHAPTER 47

Eli

My heart jumped when Declan ordered me to make up with Delilah. For a moment, I thought he was going to attack me. I wasn't in the mood to fight anyone, especially after what we'd found on the car. Vik and I did a routine check and discovered someone had put a tracker in the engine compartment. We discussed how to handle it when Dec had come in making demands. He wasn't wrong. I did mess up, and I needed to fix it as quickly as possible. I wasn't keeping secrets and didn't want Delilah to believe that I was.

I tapped on her door gently. I waited a moment, then opened it and poked my head inside. "Delilah? I just want to talk." I scanned the room but didn't see her anywhere. I took a deep breath and walked in, carefully closing the door behind me. I paced the room, looking for her. Where had she gone? I looked under the bed—nothing. It was clear that she wasn't in here. If she wasn't in her bathroom, then she had to have gone somewhere else.

Panic rose in my throat as my imagination took over. There were only so many places she could be. Was it possible for someone to have made it in here right under our noses? Could they have taken her? I would never forgive myself for letting anything happen to her. I headed toward the bathroom door, creeping slowly. I didn't want them to know I was coming for them if someone was here. I opened the door slowly, waiting for someone to attack. The bathroom was as empty as the bedroom. I turned and walked back into the bedroom, dropping to the bed. I needed to get my thoughts together and search the rest of the bunker for her before I alerted the guys.

Before standing up, I was tackled and thrown to the floor. I pushed up with my hands, but I was pinned, and instead of trying to see who had me, I simply fought back. I tossed the attacker off my back and tried to stand up. Once again, I was thrown to the floor and someone was on top of me. I tried to buck them off, but I was flipped over onto my back. Then I finally got a good look at the person who'd attacked me. Delilah was grinning from ear to ear, sitting on my chest.

"See? I can take care of myself." She looked so triumphant that I couldn't argue. I stared at her while I caught my breath. Her laugh made my heart smile.

"I can't believe you overpowered me. That's awesome." I grinned back at her, proud that she was able to defend herself.

"Well, I am still mad at you. You're lucky that all I did was pin you down. I could have kicked your ass." We both knew that was a stretch, but I didn't correct her. I was trying to make up, not get a bigger fight started.

"That's why I'm here. I owe you an apology. A big one. I should have just told you that I needed to talk to Vik. I was worried that you wouldn't let us talk in private. I had a hunch and didn't want to say anything in front of Dec until I knew for sure." I explained.

"Wait, you wanted me to take him out of the room? Not the other way around?" Her eyes went wide at the realization. I nodded, hoping that she wouldn't tell him about this.

"I suspected that Kayden had somehow tracked us here. His showing up was too easy. There's no way he would have found us from a three-minute phone call. But I didn't want to upset Dec about his best friend betraying him if it wasn't true. And I couldn't exactly say any of that in front of him."

Delilah leaned forward and captured my lips with hers. I got caught up in the passion of the kiss and nearly forgot that we all needed to talk about the tracker. My mind emptied as she rubbed herself up and down my body until my dick stood at attention. I wanted to rip her clothes off and fuck her. "Wait. I want to, but we can't do this right now." I groaned at my own words. I never thought I'd be cockblocking myself, but here I was. Delilah's face fell. Her look of disappointment hurt me.

"And just why not?" She sat up and put her hands on her hips, suddenly angry again. I held up my hands in surrender.

"We need a family meeting. There are some things we have to work out about the supply run. I promise you can ravish me later. For now, we need to talk to Vik and Dec. This is something we need to all decide together." I scooped her up in my arms and stood up. She was still pouting but didn't look like she wanted to choke me anymore. Although, that might have been kind of kinky. I'd hold onto that thought until later.

I carried her out to the living area to find Dec and Vik waiting for us. "We thought you guys were in there boning. We've been waiting a while." Vik accused.

"Yeah, well, we weren't. But we were making up. So let's move on to what we need to talk about." I replied, dropping onto a chair with Delilah still wrapped around me. She slid around to face the others.

"Okay, Vik, let's hear this plan of yours." Dec sounded defeated. It was clear that the betrayal from his friend had hurt him. I didn't complain when Delilah climbed off my lap to sit on his. He needed some affection.

"I think we should use the tracker to throw them off. We get Scott to meet us somewhere while we're out, and we trade vehicles. I have an SUV parked in Eli's garage. He can bring that. We can have him check it to ensure it's not bugged first. Then he drives the tracker around, and they can follow him." Vik sounded impressed with his idea.

"But Kayden knows where we're staying." I countered.

"That's why we'll go somewhere else. We'll pack up and take our stuff with us, then Scott can even come back here and stay for a while to throw them off. They'll think we made a supply run, then came back. It'll take them a while to figure it out." He replied.

"Where will we go?" Delilah asked, stroking her fingers through Dec's messy curls. He looked as if he was finally relaxing a little.

"That's a good question. I'm not sure." Finally, something he didn't have an answer to. It was about time.

"We could go back to my condo. I mean, if Scott is going to be here throwing them off, it could work. We get them distracted until we get inside. They can't get to us in my home. Everything is state-of-the-art tech there. But only if we all agree." I offered. I didn't want to force anyone into something they didn't want. Delilah seemed excited, while Dec and Vik looked slightly annoyed.

CHAPTER 48

Delilah

ELI'S IDEA SEEMED PLAUSIBLE. We could get in the condo without anyone knowing if Scott was distracting the hunters. Then Eli could have different employees bringing us what we needed every day, and no one would get suspicious. It would be a lot easier than having someone try to shop for four people for two weeks at a time. We could even order things online and have them delivered. I didn't realize how much I had missed online shopping while we were hiding out here.

"Wouldn't it be better just to have Scott come here? Then we could leave in his car, and yours wouldn't have to move." I thought it was a decent idea, but three growls were the first reaction I got.

Vik shook his head. "It won't work, Myshka. If the hunters have someone watching the place, they'll see him come in and realize what we're doing." He pulled me into his arms and rubbed my back. "I don't particularly want to live at Eli's, but since Midnight isn't completed yet, we don't have much choice. He has the best security system."

"If we go somewhere obscure to meet Scott, we can switch cars without anyone seeing. And since the windows are tinted dark, no one will know who's in which car. Kayden might have both followed." Dec rubbed the back of his neck.

"They won't be able to follow us into the parking garage at my building. It's underground and you can't get in without a badge and retina scan. I'll have to call when we're on our way and let them know I'm bringing someone new." Eli explained, "Otherwise, we won't even get in. They'll treat it as a hostage situation and kill everyone to get me back. I don't exactly want that."

"They'd think the three of us would kidnap you?" I asked, shocked by the thought.

He shook his head. "Just him. You and Vik have already been scanned. I'm not taking any chances with my family. We'll make sure everyone gets in who needs to, and no one who doesn't."

"So, I'm the odd man out, huh?" Dec laughed, "Nah, man, it's okay. I understand that you three were together before. I appreciate you looking out for me."

"What's left to do here?" I needed to do something besides waiting to see if this plan would work. I still had a very bad feeling about it. I wished that I could explain why.

"We need to pack what we want to take with us. But only the essentials. The computers are staying. Just a backpack that we can carry quickly when we switch cars." Eli turned to Vik. "Do you still have those packs we used when we went hiking back in the day? You seem to have the rest of our gear hidden out here." He smirked at the memory.

Vik nodded. "They're in the storage area in the garage. I'll grab them. I think there's only three of them."

"That's okay. I don't have anything of mine here. Unless you guys want me to bring the clothes back with me, Scott could use them if he wanted." Declan offered. My poor, sweet love had been here with me for so long without any of his belongings. It broke my heart. It would be the same way at Eli's unless someone brought him stuff. I would make sure to call Steph myself when we got there to see if she'd mind bringing him a few things from his place.

"Yeah, you and Scott are about the same size. That's a good idea." Eli agreed.

I hated that this situation came up, but being forced to hide was a peek into what living together would be like. It wouldn't be easy to keep three guys in line, but I didn't mind. I knew when it came down to it; they would band together to take care of me. I wanted the fairy tale, though. I knew we'd never have kids and that was okay with me. But I wanted the cute little house with a fenced-in yard. Maybe a big puppy to occupy us. I missed Midnight—what I could remember of it, anyway—but I think being turned made me realize that living above a bar forever wasn't really what I wanted.

Hmm, maybe I should talk to the guys about this. I know that Vik had the bar remodeled and adjusted the plans to accommodate Declan. Maybe we could just stay there part-time and find a house to relax in. I shrugged away the idea when Vik handed me a backpack. I grabbed Declan's hand and pulled him with me to my room to pack. If he wasn't bringing anything, he could keep me company.

"What have you been staring off in space about for the last ten minutes?" He asked after the door closed. I dropped the bag on the floor and walked over to him.

"I was just thinking about how unfair all of this has been on you. Because I lost control—whether it was my fault or not—you had to give up everything. It's not right." I pressed my lips to his gently. "I owe you an apology and a thank you. For everything."

"I think I can come up with a way for you to make it right." He wiggled his eyebrows at me and I laughed. Leave it to him to make my serious confession into a joke.

"I'm being serious. I hate that you had to deal with all of this. The other two seem to be used to this kind of thing, but you are the nicest guy I've ever known." I kissed him chastely again.

"Oh, no. You think I'm a nice guy? Damn. I knew this was too good to be true." He crossed his arms over his chest and pouted.

"What? I don't understand. Being a nice guy is a bad thing?" I raised on my tiptoes and pressed another gentle kiss to his cheek.

"It is. See? You're already treating me differently. How long before you just toss me all the way in the friend zone? I can't take it. It's devastating." His mock horror, and the fact that he started tickling me, had me laughing so hard I was in tears.

"Okay, that was mean. Maybe you're not as nice as I thought." I swatted his hands away so he'd stop tickling me, then grabbed them and pulled him close again. "Or maybe you're just what I need." He leaned down and pressed his lips gently to mine before parting them with his tongue. I wrapped his arms around me, then fisted my hands in his hair. Dec's hands slid down to cup my ass, and I jumped up, forcing him to catch me.

CHAPTER 49

Declan

I KNEW WE HAD some time to kill before meeting Scott, but I hadn't followed Delilah to seduce her. Although, that may have been her plan all along. She was a naughty girl like that. And I couldn't get enough. With everything around us, maybe this release was exactly what we both needed. A moment in time when nothing else mattered. I took this opportunity to give that to her. When she jumped at me, I caught her and carried her to the bed, laying her back gently. I pulled my t-shirt off and climbed on top of her.

I moved slowly, teasing her with my kisses, refusing to rush this. I knew that she needed to forget the world and I was determined to make that happen. I ignored the knock on the door, kissing and caressing Delilah, so she didn't answer either. I didn't expect the door to open and to have an audience. I was so caught up in her lips that I didn't realize what had happened until Vik cleared his throat.

"Go away," I demanded, "unless you're here to help our girl get off. Then get in here and strip." From her response, I could tell she was interested in the idea. I knew that she'd been with Eli and Vik together once but wasn't sure if that was something she wanted to do again. I expected him to close the door and leave. I didn't even look in his direction, keeping my attention focused on Delilah.

The door softly clicked as it closed, and I thought we were alone again. I trailed kisses from Delilah's mouth to her shoulder, ripping her shirt off and tossing it aside. When the bed shifted, I jumped. I'd expected to see Vik with the movement, but Eli surprised me. "I didn't know both of you were at the door." He smirked.

"If you're not into this, love, all you have to do is say so." Eli offered. Delilah's eyes were wide with desire, and she licked her lips. She wasn't going to tell them to leave.

"Exactly. If anything happens that you're not okay with, you just have to tell us to stop. You can use our safeword if you want." Vik chimed in. While they ensured she was okay with them joining, I pulled her jeans off. From how wet she was, I was certain that she wanted this. I wondered why she never said anything. She had to know that we would do anything she wanted.

I mean, here I was in a room with her and two rock-hard cocks in my face. If that didn't tell her everything she needed to know about the four of us, nothing would. While she was preoccupied with their naked bodies, I slipped out of my jeans and boxer briefs then started licking her stomach.

Vik tore her bra off and tossed it aside. Then he and Eli went to work caressing and sucking on her full breasts. I carefully slid her panties off and dropped them on the floor. There was no reason to destroy all of her clothes, even though it would make packing easier. I trailed kisses down her stomach, watching her with the other two. She must have whispered something to Eli that I didn't hear. He repositioned himself above her so she could suck him.

I never thought I'd be turned on by watching my girl give someone else a blow job, but here I was. My dick ached to be where his was. I knew that this arrangement would be all about balance. We would trade around until everyone was satisfied. I nipped at her inner thigh, causing her to moan against his cock. That caused him to moan. The energy was intense.

While she focused on getting Eli off, I focused on distracting her. Vik was licking, sucking, and biting her chest. Once in a while, she would react to something he did, arching her back and giving me better access. I wondered if he was doing it on purpose or just a happy accident. I ran my tongue over her wet center. Eli again echoed her moan. I watched her as I went to work on her clit. Delilah groaned and wiggled until she managed to get her hand around Vik's erection. It was as if she wanted the four of us to come together.

I flicked her sensitive nub with my tongue then slid it inside her. I would never get enough of tasting her. She kept raising her hips to push herself into my face. I knew she wanted more. I kept licking, pushing her toward the edge. A few minutes later, she must have made Eli cum, because he and Vik were trading places. Once again, my dick throbbed, watching her deep throat another cock. I wanted to be inside of her. I wanted to make sure she got off first. I knew she had, but I pushed a little more until she moaned against Vik.

Then I sat up and watched for a minute. Eli's hand took the place of my tongue, keeping our girl wet and ready. I needed to get in the right headspace or this would be over way too fast. There was something so hot about watching them get her off. I scooted forward and both of them helped me lift her hips into position. I inched my hard-on inside of her slowly, her moans setting Vik off. Since everyone else had their turn, it was mine. I slid in and out of Delilah's hot pussy slowly at first. She moaned in pleasure until it was too much and she tried to force me to go faster. Vik and Eli held her down gently to continue my slow torture.

"Declan, I can't take it." She begged me to go faster, to give her that release she craved. Her voice set me off and I started to move faster and harder until she screamed my name. Once I was sure she was done, I let go and found my release.

Eli picked Delilah up and carried her to the shower. Vik and I followed. I'd never showered with a group before, but to be fair, I'd never had sex like we just did either. Once everyone was cleaned up, we collapsed onto Delilah's bed. She sprawled across Eli, while Vik was on one side of her, and I was on the other. "You guys are amazing," Delilah whispered as she fell asleep. We spent the night in her bed, all tangled up together. It should have been weird since we were all naked, but it felt right.

CHAPTER 50

Viktor

I woke in Delilah's bed, with her arm around me, and Eli's leg draped over mine. Last night was an interesting experience. If Delilah hadn't been so tired, I would have suggested that we keep going. We were all exhausted from the stress of our situation. There would be plenty of time for adventurous sex once all of this was settled. I would have been perfectly happy staying right where I was forever. I couldn't remember ever being this satisfied. Even with Kat, things were either great or awful. I never felt this connected to her, even though I loved her, and losing her nearly killed me. Or did kill me, depending on how you looked at it since Kat's death was why I became what I am today.

I hadn't ever regretted being turned. It had been the natural decision after Kat's death. I wanted revenge, and having forever to execute it seemed like the thing to do. I hadn't expected Eli to get turned as well. When he did, I thought we'd fight for eternity. Yet here we were, loving the same woman. Somehow it made perfect sense. Delilah was exactly what we needed, and she showed up at the perfect time.

I would never admit it to Eli, but I missed him. We'd been more than friends. He and I had fought but always made up. We were brothers. And having that back meant more to me than I could ever explain. I owed our girl for that. She fixed our family. I even decided that I liked the new guy. I didn't trust him at first, but his reaction to finding out his friend had betrayed him was exactly what I needed to see. He put Delilah first. That was the most important thing. He even made sure that every one of us got off before he did last night. That wasn't an easy thing to do. I wouldn't tell him, but I was impressed.

Delilah started to stir. My watch was in my room, so I had no idea what time it was, but I knew today would be a long day. There was no reason to start it just yet. I rolled toward her and rubbed her back, lulling her back to sleep. I knew that wouldn't last, but it did buy me enough time to slip away and get dressed. I needed to make some arrangements if we would stay with Eli for a while. I didn't want him to think we weren't going to pull our weight.

And I knew that Declan was missing his studio. I'd seen his work; I had even put my name on a waiting list for one of his creations. Maybe now I wouldn't be waiting so long. It was funny how the universe put people in your path. I worried about how he would handle it if we had to put his wolf friend down. There was a point in time when I would have killed the guy first and asked questions later. Since I met Delilah, that urge for blood has been retreating more and more. People would start accusing me of being whipped if I wasn't careful. Maybe that wouldn't be a horrible thing.

Perhaps there was a way to handle this without bloodshed. I considered all the options while I picked out the perfect suit. I always felt more in control if I was dressed in a suit. It was like my armor. In a button-up shirt and jacket, I could handle anything. Sure, it wasn't the most comfortable thing, but if it worked, I'd stick with it. I kept going over ideas while I carefully buttoned my shirt. Everything was pressed to perfection. There was no way I could pack my suits into a backpack. They'd be ruined. At least none of these had been my favorites.

I silently said goodbye to the designer garments that would be left here for Scott to do with as he pleased. Maybe someday we'd be able to come back for them. It wasn't like I couldn't afford more. I had a closet full of them at Eli's. I'd already replaced my wardrobe twice since I met Delilah. I was beginning to think the girl was a jinx to my wallet. I laughed out loud at the ridiculous thought. It didn't matter if she was. I loved her and would give up everything to protect her.

Once I finished my goodbyes, I walked out into the living room. I decided I would offer Delilah my backpack in addition to hers. She seemed to like the clothes Eli had delivered and shouldn't have to give any of them up if she didn't want to. I would move mountains to make sure she had whatever she wanted. That started with her freedom. I was looking forward to being back in the city. I would be able to slip out and search for the Powder operation in person. I was sure I could find the new kingpin in just a few hours. Once I had him, I'd find out what the guy had against Delilah and fix the problem. I would do whatever it took, even if it went against the new no-killing policy.

I sat down at the computer and typed out a message explaining my idea. I filled out paperwork to have everything arranged. Keeping Delilah safe was the only thing that mattered. This move would end the petty feud that Eli and I had kept going even after we'd agreed to work together. It was time to put all of that behind us. A large merger would take months, if not years, to finish. But starting it was key. My family needed to know where I stood. This would cement that.

When I was finished, I heard the others starting to stir. I walked back into Delilah's room quietly, carrying the backpack with me. I knew she hadn't even started to pack yet, because we'd interrupted her. Declan was awake, but Eli and Delilah were still sleeping soundly. "Do you want to help me pack up her stuff?"

He nodded, climbing from the bed and pulling on his underwear and pants. "You're not taking yours?" I shook my head. He seemed to understand that she was more important. We quietly went to work folding and packing everything but one outfit for Delilah to wear today. I was surprised that it all fit in the two backpacks, but we managed it. Just as we finished, our girl stretched and groaned.

"What are you two doing?" Her words were groggy from sleep.

"Just getting your things together. We left you something to wear." Declan responded before I could. It was probably better coming from him anyway. I seemed to keep putting my foot in my mouth when helping Delilah. She nodded and rolled off Eli's chest. When she did, he growled.

"I was comfy. Where'd everybody go?" he whined playfully, grinning at Delilah's laugh.

"Well, unlike you, we're all up and getting ready to go. Not everyone can be lazy, you know. Some of us have to get things done." I tried to sound angry, but Eli just laughed. Today was going to be a whirlwind, and we needed to prepare.

CHAPTER 51

Delilah

WATCHING MY GUYS JOKE around together first thing in the morning was nice. I hoped that we could be like this forever. But that would mean we had to clear my name first. If the hunters found me before discovering who was trying to get me killed, that would be the end. I was terrified of that outcome but had to pretend that it was all going to be okay. My guys needed me to be confident and fight, not give up and cry.

Every day I remembered something else from before. I was getting better at letting it wash over me without overwhelming me. I remembered the flowers Eli sent me after he hurt my arm. And the way Vik tried to resist me when I found out they were vampires. Each memory made me more conscious of how Declan could feel like an outsider. I tried not to let it show that I was remembering. I didn't want to upset him. He was just as much a part of me as the other two were. It didn't matter to me that we met after. He saved my life, and I fell in love with him.

I hoped that we could get back to normal once we were back in the city. I would still be hiding out until we had the proof that we needed to clear me, but it wouldn't feel so much like hiding. I trusted my guys to figure out who this kingpin guy was and why he was after me. As much as I wanted to do it myself, I knew it was better if I stayed out of sight. We couldn't risk giving the hunters any more ammunition against me.

I knew that once we got moving today, everything would be a blur. I needed to enjoy being outside as much as I could since I had no idea when I would get to do it again. It wasn't fair, but it also wasn't my guys' fault. I refused to act like a spoiled child who didn't get her way, throwing a tantrum because this wasn't what I wanted. Even if I really wanted to. I steeled myself against the feeling of dread that pushed at me. Part of me wanted to stay here, even though I knew it wasn't safe.

Declan was pissed and hurt that his friend would betray him by putting a tracker in his car. That's probably how they figured out what I'd done. If you think about it, tracking your best friend is brilliant, especially after you find out he's turned someone without going through the proper channels. They could kill me for that alone. Dec is sure they won't; he'll just have to pay some huge fine, and I'll have to sign some documents that normally would have been taken care of with my application. I wasn't certain it would be that easy, especially after I lost control and killed a girl.

I still couldn't believe I had killed someone. My heart broke every time I thought about it. I knew it wasn't my fault. The drugs made me more aggressive than usual. I knew I was still responsible. No matter how many times the guys blamed the drug, I knew that a monster was inside of me. When the memory of it came rushing back to me, I realized that I enjoyed draining that girl. I got high on taking her life. It was wrong and horrible, but it was true. I was a monster. My guys didn't have to agree with me. I could never tell them that I enjoyed killing. That had to be my secret. They'd never look at me the same way again if they knew.

I showered and prepared to leave this place behind. I wished that I could leave the sense of dread behind as well. None of them mentioned it if my guys noticed that I was distracted and withdrawn. I felt like we were all balancing on the edge. If we weren't careful, we'd fall and there would be no way to recover. I hated feeling so helpless. I remembered that feeling from when I was human. That day in the park, when a vampire had tried to attack me. If Eli hadn't been there, I probably wouldn't be here now. And all I did was run away. I was nothing but a terrified blood sack back then. I would never go back to that again. I would fight with everything I had to keep my guys safe and protect our family.

We loaded the SUV silently. There wasn't much to pack. Eli had a backpack and I had two. Vik insisted that we take a few blood bags with us, even though there weren't many left here. Scott would be able to get more before he came back here. I hated that he had to interrupt his life for my mistake. If I'd been smarter—less trusting, more focused, something—none of this ever would have happened. Vik suggested that he and I sit in the back because Kayden hadn't seen us. The guys wanted to keep it that way. And that meant letting Vik sit with me and comfort me, even if the other two were better at it.

I didn't think that Vik was bad at being sympathetic; I just felt like he was holding back. I didn't understand why he couldn't just let me in. Had he been that way when I was human too? I didn't have enough memories of him to know for sure. We butted heads, but I felt like a lot of that was intentional. It was easier to be passionate with someone when that feeling was tied to hate than when it was tied to something vulnerable like love. I was nearly certain that no one would understand why I cared so much for him. But I saw inside of him. He was broken and needed me to help him heal. I just had to get it through his thick skull that for him to heal, he had to let me in and stop being an ass.

I was convinced that my guys thought I compared them on all levels. They seemed to compete for attention and to see who could help me with anything and everything. It was cute, but at some point, we'd have to talk about how different each of them is and how that's why I love them. Just because Vik isn't good at comforting doesn't mean he's less important to me. He's just better at choosing a matching outfit, which Dec couldn't do if his life depended on it. I chuckled at the thought, and Vik looked at me. "Something funny you'd like to share, Myshka?"

"I was just thinking about how different you three are. There are things you can do that the other two can't. And they can do things you're not good at. It's like this amazing balancing act. I'm so lucky to have you all." Time to push him out of his comfort zone. I scooted closer, pulling his arm around me to rest his hand on my hip. I leaned into him, snuggling up for the ride. I glanced up and had to hide my smirk at his face. Public affection was not Vik's thing. But that's why he had me. To push him to be better, to be more. Together, we were nearly perfect. I couldn't help feeling that something was still missing, even though I had no idea what it could be. How could I feel lonely when all of this love surrounded me?

Eli looked at me in the mirror, and Dec reached back to hold my hand while I cuddled up with Vik. It was funny how they sensed that I needed reassurance. Eli and I had spoken about his ability, but I couldn't remember Declan saying anything about those skills. I guess he just connected to me on that level. A few minutes later, Vik seemed to relax. For a while, I thought he was asleep. I tilted my head to look up at him and found him staring at me. "What?"

"You're amazing. I don't know if you realize how much you've changed us all. In a good way, of course. We wouldn't survive without you." He leaned down and pressed his lips to mine. I knew he wasn't trying to get things started, especially when the other two would be forced to watch but not participate. The kiss was sweet, and the second it was over, he turned to face the window. Was that a tear in his eye? Did I just get Vik to feel something? It felt like a huge achievement for him to have said something nice.

CHAPTER 52

Eli

I HATED BEING THE one who had to drive, although I understood Vik's point. Kayden didn't know anything about him being at the bunker with us. It made more sense to keep him hidden in the back with Delilah than to have him drive or sit up front with Declan. Not that I minded spending time with Dec; he was cool. I just wanted to be the one taking care of our girl. Vik tended to push her buttons in a bad way, and I didn't want to have to stop the car to beat his ass. I knew it wouldn't come to that because our girl could hold her own. He wouldn't even know what had hit him.

I was amazed at the changes Delilah had gone through in such a short time. The store clerk's death was unfortunate, but the fact it took drugs to make it happen said something about her level of control. Most newly turned vamps would have killed the girl when she came close enough. But not our girl. She was the most restrained vamp I'd ever met. It was amazing, and highly dangerous. Restraint was hard. Once it snapped, she'd take out dozens of people without a second thought. I hoped that we were there to get her settled when it happened. I hated the thought of what that would do to her.

I kept thinking about the nightmares she told us about. She was terrified that she was going to be taken away from us. We had to prevent that. I got lost in my thoughts for a while, then caught her eye in the mirror. Dec looked at me, and I nodded subtly. He reached back and took her hand. He felt it too. Good. She needed more than just me that could read her emotions. I'd been trying to teach Vik, but he just didn't seem able to get it. At least he hadn't made a big deal out of her desire to snuggle.

"So, how big is your penthouse?" Declan asked, trying to keep a conversation going to avoid the silence.

"Big enough. Slightly different setup than the bunker but with more space. Delilah won't have her room anymore, though. I only have three bedrooms. I don't think it'll be a problem, given how last night went." I glanced at him sideways and watched his cheeks turn red. He wasn't as experienced as I had thought. Good. Delilah needed someone to go through the new stuff with her. It would help them bond.

"So, we'll all just share a room? Do you have a bed that big?" He chuckled, looking over his shoulder at our girl again. She had fallen asleep in Vik's lap, and he was carefully brushing her hair with his fingers. The content expression suited him.

"I can have one brought in. Why, do you have one that big?" I realized that we hadn't even considered using his condo. We really didn't even know that much about where he lived. I was dying to go home and just assumed everyone else would go with me. It was the most selfish thing I'd done since I tried to force Delilah to go with me the day we met. I suddenly felt like a complete ass.

"No, but I can build one." I nodded at his offer. That wasn't a bad idea. I wondered how long it would be before she begged us to move out of the city. I knew that all of this was taking a toll. Her eyes no longer held joy when she spoke of the city. I blamed myself. There was no reason to go shopping that day. Vik and I just wanted to make up for not saving her ourselves. It was stupid. She didn't care that Declan was the one who changed her. She belonged to all of us by her admission, and we belonged to her. Guilt tore at my insides.

"That's a great idea. You should get started on plans. I'll get whatever supplies you need. There's an entire floor below the penthouse that we can turn into a studio for you. It'll take a couple of days, but it's something we can do. We need to figure out a central point and buy a huge place to share." There was something surreal about planning a future with my girl and her other guys. It should have been strange or uncomfortable, but it was perfect.

We pulled into the garage without issue. Calling ahead had saved us. My team was ready with the portable scanners and ushered us through immediately. I parked in a dark area, next to the elevator. Scott was there, waiting for us, just as planned. "Don't worry, Boss, I've got this. They'll never suspect it's not you." I wished his confidence was contagious. I wasn't about to count on anything. A strange feeling of dread had taken hold of my gut as we drove. I felt like I was driving us to our doom for some reason.

"I appreciate your hard work, Scott." I shook his hand, then ushered everyone into the elevator. The sooner we were inside with the security system activated, the better. I was more on edge than usual and I didn't know how much of it was me and how much was everyone else's emotions. I needed a shower and a rough fuck. I knew I'd get one but doubted the other was possible. Delilah needed to settle in, not deal with men humping her like horny teenagers.

"Love, you get to decide the sleeping arrangements. Dec is taking your room. Vik and I have our rooms here. You can sleep wherever you want with whomever you want. We all agreed."

She nodded, still holding on to Vik for support. It was obvious that this whole situation had taken a toll on her. He surprised me by not scooping her up and carrying her. I realized he was finally listening to what she wanted. At least he was still willing to adapt and change for her. I opened the door and stepped back so they could all enter. I followed behind and closed the door quietly, turning on the security system.

CHAPTER 53

Delilah

I WALKED INTO THE dark penthouse on Vik's arm, with Dec in front of us, and Eli behind us. I noticed the strange dancing lights in front of us but didn't connect them with anything until it was too late. The red lights were attached to the scopes of high-powered rifles, pointed right at us. Instinctually, I raised my hands in surrender. There would be no fighting here. I wouldn't risk any of my guys that way. "We give up. We'll cooperate. Just don't hurt them." I said, getting onto my knees with my hands still up. I didn't want to give them any excuse to start shooting.

Fear gripped me like a vice. It was written all over Dec's face. Vik looked pissed, and Eli was more confused than anything. How had they gotten past the extra security here? I could see him asking himself. Which of his men had betrayed him? If we survived, heads would roll for this. Logically, it didn't matter how it had happened; the outcome would be the same. I could sense a wide array of emotions coming from each of my guys. Despair was the strongest. I hoped they would follow my lead and cooperate instead of fighting. It would go against every instinct they had. I knew they would do it for me. These three men would do anything for me. I hoped I wasn't leading them to death.

We were cuffed and led back downstairs to an unmarked van with no windows. The men shoved us inside one by one before hooking the cuffs to the seats and closing the door. The ride wasn't long and the van stopped. The men took us out again and escorted us inside a warehouse. If there was a way out of this, we needed to pay attention to everything. I started to get flashes of another warehouse and being kept there. These were different than the usual flashes of memory. There was something more sinister about them. Each time a flash happened, I shivered and the memory threatened to take over, leaving me helpless.

I fought against the sensations as we walked. The men put each of us into a small cage with three feet of space between us. That was the worst thing that had happened so far. I needed my guys close, but they were so far away. I refused to speak unless it was to their leader. Talking to anyone else wouldn't benefit me anyway. These guys were just the muscle, not the brains. They had no control over anything that was happening. They were just here to follow orders. I watched in horror as, one by one, my guys were taken away for questioning. I knew that was code for torture. I wasn't sure what kind of information the hunters thought my guys had.

Eli had been taken first. He was gone for an hour or so and returned with a cut on his cheek and some bruising on his face. If we tried to talk, they would hit the bars or jab poles between them and poke us until we stopped. I desperately wanted to make sure Eli was okay, but there was no way to do that without getting hurt. If these assholes hurt me, it would make my guys fight harder. I had to stay quiet and still. I needed to be the example.

Vik was taken next. He was gone closer to two hours. When he returned, his entire face was bruised and cut up. He also had bloody knuckles. That told me he'd fought them once they were alone. I wanted to call out to him but couldn't. There was nothing I could say to make the situation better anyway. I refused to let the hunters see me cry. I wouldn't have them misconstrue my feelings or twist them into something else.

A tall Hunter with brown wavy hair came to get Declan. They seemed to know each other, which made me think this guy must be Kayden. Maybe that would work in our favor. If he really cared for Dec, maybe he wouldn't hurt him. The minutes after he was escorted away stretched into hours. At some point, I fell asleep.

My dreams were fitful, horrendous things. I watched as my guys were tortured nearly to death. The hunters were distorted and spoke in a strange language. I couldn't understand the questions they asked. When I couldn't answer, they would torture one of my guys. I woke myself screaming at the bloodshed. All I wanted was to take my guys and leave this place. It was clear that was not going to happen.

I looked around for Declan, but he wasn't back yet. What could they be doing to him? Who was behind this? I tried to remember anything that would be useful. I had no idea if I had enemies as a human. Someone had to hate me for this to be happening. I just wished I knew who it was and what I had done to them. Hopelessness was taking over. No matter how hard I fought to stay positive, I couldn't see a happy ending here.

The hunters keeping us were monsters. They visibly enjoyed making us suffer. If we were too calm, they would pound on the cages to get my guys riled up or scare me. Just when I thought Dec was never coming back, two of them dragged him through the doorway. I wasn't even sure it was him at first. "Please, just put him in here with me," I begged. I knew it was a bad idea since it would get me punched and upset my guys. But I didn't care. I needed to be close to Dec and take care of him. The two thugs shared a look, then dragged him over and tossed him into the cage I was in.

I cradled his head and held him, waiting for his supernatural healing to kick in. I knew that it wouldn't take too long for his wounds to heal. Before I had a chance to do anything besides brush his bloody hair off his forehead, one of the hunters stomped over. "You monsters want us to think you actually have feelings." He turned to the guys who were guarding the other cages. "Drag those two over here. Then we won't have to waste our time guarding so many cages. Shove them all in this one."

Eli and Vik were taken out of their cages and forced into mine with Dec and me. There was no room to move, but we were all together. I held Dec's head on my lap. Eli and Vik each took one of his hands. At least now we could whisper to each other. I would know they were as safe as possible for the moment. Maybe I would be able to sleep without the nightmares.

For the first time since we were brought here, I relaxed against the bars and fell asleep holding Dec.

CHAPTER 54

Declan

I WOKE FEELING CRAMPED. Where did all these legs come from? My head was killing me, but I figured that was pretty standard when a wolf throws you around like a rag doll. I made the mistake of challenging Kayden as if that would do any good right now. I knew better. He kept at me until he pushed the right button to piss me off, though. I couldn't stop myself. I opened my eyes to find Delilah staring at me, with Vik and Eli crammed in the small cage too. "What happened?" I whispered.

"They beat you up pretty badly. Delilah convinced them to put you in here with her, then they shoved us in as well," Vik said, barely moving his lips as he spoke. The single guard didn't seem to notice. He was more interested in whatever he was watching on his phone.

"Did Kayden do that to you?" Delilah asked softly. I wanted to lie to her and tell her it was someone else, but I couldn't. I just nodded. I knew it would happen again and again until he got what he wanted. I didn't understand who the hunters were working for. They were supposed to be enforcers for the Council, but this was not how they operated. This was something else.

"There's something strange going on here. This isn't how the hunters should be handling this situation." I fisted my hands in my hair.

"I didn't think this was following procedure," Eli whispered, turning away from us. "This seems more like what a drug operation would do." He had already come to the same conclusion that I had. Whoever was behind the Powder operation they'd been investigating had somehow taken over the Council and the hunters.

"This is bad. If someone has control of the Council and the hunters, there's no telling what's going to happen to us here." I hated to scare Delilah, but she deserved to know we weren't dealing with what we thought.

"So, surrendering was a mistake? I'm so sorry. I was trying to keep you all from getting killed. Now I think I've made things worse." I looked up to see tears streaming from Delilah's eyes. Eli wiped them away. If this cage wasn't so small, I could have pulled her into my arms and held her close to comfort her.

"You did what you thought was best. Don't ever doubt yourself, mo chroí. If it weren't for you, we'd probably all be dead right now. Because we would have fought." She ran her fingers through my hair and I relaxed a little. I knew that she wouldn't be finished with her guilt, but we would help her work through it. She had nothing to feel guilty about. If anything, we failed her.

"What did he ask you?" Vik looked at me, then over at the guard, who was essentially ignoring us.

"Nothing really. He just said some asshole things until he pissed me off and I challenged him. Then he shifted and beat my ass as a wolf." I avoided Delilah's stare. I didn't want her to ask what he'd said to set me off. Delilah didn't need to know that Kayden had threatened to gut her while I watched.

"They were asking me about our inquiries into the Powder operation. I wondered if it was the same line of questioning for everyone," Vik explained.

Eli shook his head. "They asked me about your company's security. It was like they wanted me to break in for something. But they didn't say what. I didn't tell them anything, either."

"Why would they care about Vik's security? Or what you know about some random Powder operation? There's something here we're not connecting." The words were out of my mouth before I realized how stupid they were. Of course, there's something we're not connecting. It's Delilah. Somehow all of this leads back to her. But how? I tuned everything else out for a while and thought about it. That was the only thing that made sense. It didn't even really make sense because we hadn't made the connection yet.

"I'm not sure, but it's all connected. We need to get out of here," Eli said, just as another Hunter joined the first one. They spoke in hushed tones for a minute, then walked over to the cage. I could tell from their faces that one of us was in for it.

When their gazes zeroed in on me, I knew that Kayden wanted another conversation. As much as I wanted to fight, I resisted the urge. One of them grabbed my arm and pulled me from the cage. I looked at Delilah as she put her fingers to her lips. She was terrified for me. I wanted to comfort her, but that would have to wait. I hid my fear, keeping my expression neutral as the guard walked me to the interrogation room I'd been in earlier. I wasn't even sure what day it was or how long we'd been here anymore.

The guy shoved me inside and slammed the door. I tripped over my feet but managed to catch myself instead of falling. Kayden would keep me waiting first, then come in swinging. Whatever it was he wanted to know; he hadn't figured out how to ask me yet. It didn't matter. I wouldn't have told him anything useful anyway. I stretched my cramped muscles while I waited. I was facing the back wall when the door finally opened. I braced myself for an impact that didn't happen. Slowly turning around, my eyes met my friend's.

"What do you want from us?" I asked, knowing he'd never tell me the truth. I watched his expression to see if he would give anything away.

"Why are you protecting the girl?" His voice was low and gravelly. If I didn't know better, I would have sworn he was upset about this.

"Because I love her. She hasn't done anything to warrant this treatment. None of us have. This goes against the Council's rules and you know it. Just tell me what's going on here." I didn't flinch when he stepped forward and swung. I didn't budge when his fist connected with my jaw. I wasn't going to fight my best friend. "Did that make you feel better?" I snarled as I wiped the blood from my lip.

"You think I enjoy this? I have to get answers. Then you all have to stand trial. My best friend is probably going to be put to death for his involvement in all of this, and you think I'm so sadistic that I would relish it?" Anger sharpened his features. I knew he was close to shifting. It was awe-inspiring to watch, but I wasn't looking forward to being a chew toy for his inner beast.

"If I'm your best friend, why can't you just be honest with me?" Kayden swung again, and the punch landed on my temple. "You know I'm not going to tell you anything, no matter how much you hit me." He growled and stalked forward. I was certain this would be my end, but I wasn't about to back down. I would face him head-on. If he was going to kill me, he was going to look in my eyes while he did it.

Kayden stopped when his face was an inch from mine. He growled at me again, then turned and ran off. His lackeys took me back to the cage and locked me inside again. What had that been about? Who was he really working for?

<h1 style="text-align:center">CHAPTER 55</h1>

<h2 style="text-align:center">Viktor</h2>

I'd lost track of how many days we'd been locked up here. Since the second day, the hunters had kept the four of us together, only taking one of us out of the small cage for questioning. That usually involved some torture, though it only appeared to be the case for Eli, Dec, and myself. They hadn't taken Delilah anywhere yet, and she wasn't handcuffed. My suit was filthy and being cramped in here was making me cranky. There wasn't even enough room to take care of our girl. Not to mention the handcuffs binding our hands behind our backs. Even with our enhanced strength, we couldn't break them.

Then it came... the moment I was most afraid of. One of them came to take Delilah to another area for holding. "Can we have a moment to say goodbye?" Eli begged, somehow convincing the guy to let each of us kiss our girl.

"Make it quick." Eli let Dec and I give her affection first. What was he planning? Where were they taking her? I put every emotion, love, fear, hate, into the kiss I gave her. Then I stepped back and watched Dec do the same. Eli kissed her first, then nuzzled her neck. The Hunter grabbed her arm and pulled her from the cage. "All right, that's enough." He snarled.

"Don't worry; you guys are getting split up next. And they won't be giving you time to say goodbye." His laughter echoed through the empty room.

Delilah watched over her shoulder as she was dragged away, tears streaming down her face. I knew it hurt her to keep silent, but we had agreed it would be best if none of us gave anything away. I would have done anything at that moment to fix this for her. It broke me to see her pain. Another guard came a minute or so later and took Dec away. He looked as broken as I felt. There had to be a way to fix this. Dec walked solemnly, like a man heading down the green mile. Would this be the last time I ever saw them?

Eli took this opportunity to motion me closer to him. "This is going to be weird, don't make it weirder by reacting." He whispered. I raised an eyebrow at him. He backed me up against the bars and pressed his lips to mine. I was shocked and opened my mouth to protest, but that invited his tongue in. It tangled with mine for a moment until I felt something small and metallic slide from his tongue underneath mine. The kiss lingered a moment longer as if he was making a promise for the future. I wasn't sure how I felt about it, but I wanted to explore the thought further—after we talked to Delilah about it, of course. My heart, our hearts, centered around her.

When he pulled away, another guard was there to take him from the cage. I wondered if I would be left behind or moved. Given what Eli had just managed, I hoped I could keep up my end of the bargain. I would need to keep the hairpin hidden in my mouth until I had time to use it. A few minutes turned into a few hours. Then I was certain I had my answer. I wasn't going anywhere. I knew that it was dangerous, but I wasn't going to sit here and wait to be taken out for execution. I carefully brought my hands from behind my back to my front, stepping through the cuffs. I waited a while like that to be sure no one was coming to stop me. When no one came, I dropped the hairpin into my palm and started to pick the lock on the cuffs.

First, the left one clicked, then the right. After that, the only thing left to do was pick the cage lock. With the cage opened, I needed to move quickly. I had to find the others and free them. We needed to get out of here and find somewhere safe. I searched in the direction each member of my family had been taken. There were so many doors. Checking them so was going to take forever.

I heard a noise coming down the hall and ducked into an empty room. I leaned my back against the door and listened as someone passed by. They were headed for the cage I'd been in. I had a choice to make, either lay low and hope I could escape later, or do a quick search now. I kicked myself for not looking out the door to see how many people had passed and if they were armed. Before I could make the decision, an alarm pierced the air. They knew I'd escaped. Where could I hide? I glanced around the room but there was no secret hatch or passage. The only option was to hide here or climb up into the heating duct.

It took seconds to scale the shelves and duck inside before I heard the door open. "Clear, check the next one," A voice yelled before the door closed again. I wondered how long it would be before they realized their mistake. Hopefully, by then, I'd be long gone with my family. I couldn't leave without them. I turned around and moved through the vents, searching each room below as I went. I easily found Eli and Declan, but Delilah must have been moved further away. I slid silently through the metal shaft, tracking my love. The alarm had been silenced, but I still heard the footsteps of guards searching for me. I waited until they'd passed by again before I tried to talk to either of the guys.

"Eli, up here." I kept my voice low, knowing that he could hear me anyway. He turned his head from side to side, looking for where my voice had come from. "In the ceiling," I whispered again, and his head jerked up. His eye was black and it looked like his shoulder was dislocated. "I'm working on getting us out of here."

He nodded before lowering his head. "You need to find her. They're planning to execute us all in the morning. I heard them talking when they thought I was knocked out."

"I'm on it. I'll be back as soon as I find her." I knew I needed to act fast; I just wasn't aware of how dire the situation was. I crept through the ductwork, searching for our girl.

I searched for hours and couldn't find her. She must have been in a room without duct access. Would they do that to her? Probably. I stopped when I heard talking. I wasn't close enough to hear everything, but I got enough to understand what was happening.

"You can't protect them," a gruff voice said.

"I just want them to get a fair trial. That's what we're supposed to do." The second voice sounded desperate.

"It doesn't matter that he's your friend. They broke the law and have to be punished." The first voice sounded angry. I wished I could see what was going on down there.

"The Council would never sign off on an execution without a trial. It's never been done before." The second voice said something else, but I couldn't make it out.

A loud bang, a fist hitting the wall maybe, sounded through the ductwork. It echoed around my head. There was more going on here than meets the eye. If the wolves were fighting among themselves, we still had a chance. I needed to find Delilah and get everyone out of here. When I couldn't find her, I headed back to check on the guys. Eli seemed to be sleeping, so I moved silently to the vent over Dec's cell.

"You know we aren't responsible for this. She was drugged and something in it caused the blood lust to take over. I explained it to you before, Kayden. What are you going to do about it?" Dec's emotions poured into his words.

"I'm working on it, okay? It's not as easy as it seems. There are other forces at play here. I haven't been able to get a straight answer. I may not be able to fix this." The wolf growled. I couldn't tell if he was angry with Dec or the situation. But he was the first one who seemed to listen to anything we tried to say.

"You can't let them kill her. We need to find out who's responsible and make them pay." Declan was determined to fight for our girl, even though the situation was pretty hopeless. I needed to find a way out of here, but couldn't stop listening.

"I'm doing everything I can. If I come right out and fight, they'll lock me up too. I won't be of any use to you chained to a wall and dosed with silver."

A shuffling noise had me looking through the vent. Someone had come in, and Kayden left. I tried to follow the sound of their footsteps.

CHAPTER 56

Delilah

EPILOGUE

I LOOKED OVER MY shoulder as I was taken away from my guys. Everything in me wanted to fight. There was no point. The only way the three of them would get out of here alive was if I cooperated. Even if I was put to death for my crime, my guys still had a chance. From what little Eli told me, I knew that the hunters were looking for information. I had no idea what they thought I knew, but I planned to use it to my advantage. I was shoved into an interrogation room and left alone for hours. There was no way to know for sure. Our captors had taken our watches and phones when we'd arrived. I was learning a lot about torture techniques. Sleep deprivation, lack of food or water, the threat of violence—these were all valid ways to get someone to talk. Then there was the actual torture. No one had laid a hand on me, but that didn't mean they wouldn't. It just hadn't happened yet.

I wasn't scared for myself. I was terrified for my guys. I wanted to protect them with everything I had. My imagination raced, trying to figure out what was coming next. I wasn't prepared for Dec's hunk of a friend to walk into the room looking like sex on a stick. His light brown curls were messy as if he'd been running his hands through them. His button-up denim shirt was half unbuttoned, showing an enticing patch of chest hair. And his jeans were tight enough that they left very little to the imagination. He looked disgusted until his gray eyes met mine. That anger melted away and he growled.

I stood my ground and maintained eye contact with him. I wasn't going to cower to him no matter how terrifying he was. Besides, there was something else in his eyes. They looked familiar somehow. I knew I hadn't met him before, so I struggled to figure out why I knew those eyes. It didn't matter. A moment after I noticed them, he was stalking toward me. I didn't have time to react before his hand shot out and grabbed my hair at the base of my neck. I couldn't move if I tried.

Kayden's face was so close to mine that I could feel his breath on my lips. My tongue shot out and across my lips to moisten them. His eyes followed its movement. Desire. That was what I saw in his eyes. It didn't make sense. As hard as he fought to catch us, why would he look at me like that now? I could sense his heart racing, calling to me. My heart beat faster at his attention. My breath caught for a moment when I thought he was going to kiss me. Why was I disappointed that he didn't? Instead, he pulled me closer and whispered in my ear. "Why does he care so much about you?"

"Who?" I asked, my voice barely audible. Was he talking about Declan? Or someone else? Instead of an answer, he shoved me away. My back collided with the wall and I let myself slide down. I sat there staring at him, waiting for some kind of an answer. Instead, he just stared at me, then turned to leave.

As the door closed, I heard someone talking. I rushed over and pressed my ear to the wood. "We're all set for the executions tomorrow. Are you sure about this?" The voice was unfamiliar.

Kayden's response was almost too quick. "We have to be sure. This is what must happen. They broke the laws and have to be punished." A shiver rolled down my spine. They were going to kill us in the morning, and I didn't even get to spend my last night with my guys.

Rest was fitful at best. It was hard to sleep, knowing that we would all die soon. What little sleep I did get was marred by nightmares. I watched my loves being torn apart by wolves, staked through the heart, decapitated, and drained of their life forces. It repeatedly happened until I wasn't sure what was real and what was imagined. I knew that someone was watching me. He probably enjoyed my thrashing and sudden jolts upright in tears. These people were a sadistic bunch.

I settled back on the single blanket thrown at me earlier. I was determined to stay awake. I would not be plagued by those dreams any longer. I would face what was coming with my head held high. Determination had kept me alive this long. It was all I had left. I closed my eyes for a second, only a second.

I awoke with a start at the feeling of strong arms wrapping around me and pulling me close. The smell was familiar but foreign, almost woodsy. My head lay on a hard chest, right over a strong heartbeat that lulled me back to calm. A large hand stroked my hair, carefully picking through the tangles and combing it smooth. It was dark, so all I could see was a silhouette. I knew he wasn't one of my guys even though something about him called to me. For a moment, I felt safe in these arms. A hand gently wiped away my tears and cupped my cheek. "Shh, babe, I'll take care of you." The whisper against my skin was warm. I slept again, deep comfortable sleep, with the strange arms holding me close.

I sat up with a start at a noise down the hall. "One of them's escaped. We have to find him." I scanned the room to find myself alone again. Perhaps it had all been a dream. I may never know. One of my guys had escaped. That was amazing. We had hope again. If one of them was free, he would fight like hell to save us all. I pressed my ear to the door to listen. I hoped someone would say which of my guys it was. Things got eerily quiet again. Footsteps stomped down the hall and I jumped away from the door just before it opened.

"Where is he?" A man growled in my face.

"Who?" I asked, hoping he would tell me what I wanted to know. Instead, he backhanded me across the face and I hit the wall on the side of the room. I had already decided that fighting back wouldn't help, so I prepared for him to hit me again. A low growl got my attention and I looked up to see the man's head fly across the room in the opposite direction. His body fell forward, and I was coated in the spray of his blood. Instinct had my tongue licking the sticky substance from my face. My eyes grew wide with terror. This wasn't done by one of my guys. I backed up into the corner and waited for the beast responsible to kill me next.

"We have to go," a deep voice ordered. I stood in the corner, shaking my head, my body trembling. "Unless you want them all to die, we have to go now." He stepped through the doorway, and I realized that Kayden had saved me. He reached down and pulled me up against him before wiping blood from my mouth. I silently followed him out the door. He held a finger to his lips and motioned for me to stay behind him. We crept through the hallway to a dead end. Kayden reached out to the wall and pressed two spots, making a secret door open. He ushered me inside, then made sure it closed completely behind us.

"The others don't know about these passages. We need to get to the guys before they're executed." He started walking down the dark corridor.

"Wait," I said, not moving. He turned to face me and I continued, "What made you change your mind?"

"I learned who's behind it all. I need your help to get the four of you out of here. Come on." He motioned for me to follow, and this time I did. Once we were all back together, I would finally get the answers I needed. I watched him closely as we walked. I was terrified that this was a trick. Something inside of me told me that he could be trusted.

Kayden stopped and cocked his head to the side, listening. It appeared that his hearing was even better than a vamp's. The ceiling here was low enough that his ear was almost on it. His fist shot up through the drywall and something large fell in front of us. "There's one. Now we have to get to the other two." He pushed me behind him as Vik came up swinging. Kayden took a punch in the face and another in the gut before I realized what had happened.

"Vik! Stop. He's helping us escape. We have to get to Dec and Eli before they're executed." I stepped forward and wrapped my arms around him, brushing dirt from his face. He took a deep breath then pulled me close for a kiss.

"Why are you helping us?" He growled at Kayden. "You're the reason we're in here."

"We'll get to all of that after we get the others. Please, Vik. Just come with us." I wasn't above begging. I could feel Kayden's desperation growing. If he was scared for them, this was serious. We had to go.

"This way," he whispered, leading us down another corridor. I could hear the men outside searching for us. So far, it seemed that Kayden was right about them not knowing these passages were here. I gripped Vik's hand tightly, and we followed Kayden through the darkness. None of us made a sound, stopping to listen every few feet. I had so many questions I wanted to ask, but there wasn't time. He paused next to a door and put his ear against it. Then he eased the door open, pulled something large through, and closed it again. The whole thing took maybe five seconds and didn't make a sound.

"What the fuck just happened?" Declan's voice echoed down the passage. Kayden put his hand over Dec's mouth. My sexy vamp's eyes grew wide at the realization, and he nodded. When Kayden took his hand away, Dec whispered, "We need to hurry. They just took Eli out for execution."

"Fuck." Kayden took off running down a passage, and we all struggled to keep up. This was bad. Panic was setting in. Of course, Eli could take care of himself, but with a death sentence and public execution hanging over his head? I wasn't sure.

I ran into his back when he stopped in front of a small square on the wall. "What's that?" I pointed at the thing and whispered.

"Watch," he said, moving a piece of it and looking out into the room on the other side of the wall. "As I said before, no one knows this is here. If we're lucky, no one knows I'm involved." He stared out the small opening for another moment before turning back to me.

Dec and Vik were standing on either side of me. I could tell they were trying not to panic the same as I was. I wasn't the only one who loved Eli. We had to save him. "What can we do?" Dec asked Kayden.

"You can trust me. Stay in the passages inside the wall. When I give the signal, head east." He pointed in the direction he wanted us to go. "We'll meet you at the exit near where you were brought in." Both Dec and Vik nodded, preparing to follow his directions. I was staring out the opening, searching for Eli. Kayden put his hand on my shoulder and spun me around.

"As for you, stay safe, babe. I meant what I said last night. I will protect you." Before I could react, he pulled me close, and his lips crashed into mine. I was caught off guard for a moment before I sank into the kiss. His woodsy scent filled my nose, and I remembered his words from the night before. I had thought it was a dream. But it was Kayden, protecting me from the horrors of this place. I still didn't understand why. His kiss held promises that scared me. Images flashed before my closed eyes, and my soul screamed at me. *Mine.*

As quickly as the kiss began, Kayden was gone. Vik and Dec stared at me. I blushed and put my fingers over my lips. What had just happened? I shook my head and refocused. We needed to be ready to run.

I turned to the small opening and looked through again. I watched as two hunters brought Eli out. He was shirtless with his hands cuffed behind his back. They shoved him toward a minuscule stage in the middle of the room. It was barely big enough for three people to stand on. There was some sort of podium in its center, with metal rings at the bottom. Thoughts of its purpose rattled me.

Laughter echoed in the room when Eli stumbled and nearly fell. He righted himself and kept walking. The hunters talked, but I couldn't tell what was being said. I searched the room for Kayden but couldn't find him. He needed to hurry. Eli was in danger. My fingers dug into the wall as I leaned closer to get a better look. I felt Vik and Dec wrap their arms around me, preparing to run.

I wasn't leaving without Eli. They were positioning him on the tiny stage. It was getting crowded and was hard to see from where we were. People were pouring in from all directions. The crowd was massive. Were they that interested in watching vampires die? The noise grew until there was no way we would be able to hear Kayden's signal. Dec realized it too and leaned closer to look out. I was terrified that Kayden wouldn't make it on time to save Eli. My head filled with all the unspoken promises that would be broken instantly.

Someone stepped forward and called for the crowd to quiet down. A muffled voice said something, and everyone sat on the floor. We had a clear line of sight to the stage again. Eli was chained to the podium, and I realized my fears were right. They were planning to decapitate him. The person who'd stepped forward was wearing a robe with a hood. Their face was covered, and it was impossible to tell if the figure was male or female. So much for facing your accuser. They called forth another figure, this one all man. He was twice the size of Eli, also shirtless, with bulging muscles in his arms and legs. As he stepped forward, he swung a huge ax onto his shoulder.

The hooded figure spoke to the crowd, but I couldn't make out the words. In an instant, they were on their feet again, cheering. After a few minutes, I gave up on watching. I couldn't see Eli anymore. Declan kept watching, convinced that his friend could save my love. I wasn't sure that I believed anything anymore. This was hopeless.

I couldn't help trying to see what was going on. The monster who had the ax had moved closer to where Eli was. He raised the ax in the air, and the crowd went wild again. I knew he was preparing to kill my sweet vamp. I couldn't watch. Kayden had failed. I turned to Vik and held him close as tears spilled down my cheeks. The room shook as a loud noise filled the air. Dec turned to us and yelled, "That was the signal. We have to go. Now."

"I'm not leaving without Eli," I replied. It didn't matter; Vik scooped me up and ran, carrying me the whole way. I fought against him, desperate to get back to Eli, but Vik didn't relent. He held me tightly and followed Declan until we got to the end of the line. There was nowhere else to go. We were trapped. The passage had started to collapse behind us after the explosion. There was only a six-foot section immediately around us that didn't seem to be affected. Dec couldn't get the door to open. Since there was no way I could go back for Eli, Vik put me down and tried to help him. Neither of them could get it open.

So this was it. This was how I would die. My heart broke for Eli—I should have been the one in that position, not him. Darkness was closing in. I couldn't see anything but Dec and Vik desperately trying to force the door open. There was fresh air seeping in around it, but the air in the passage was filled with debris and dust from whatever had blown up. After a while, my guys were worn out and had to sit down. I sat with them, waiting for the rest of the passage to collapse on us. I had given up. I didn't know how long we'd been here or how long we'd last if the whole thing came down. I closed my eyes and took shallow breaths, just like I heard Vik and Dec doing.

I must have passed out because there was a sliver of light coming from the door when I came to. Someone was forcing it open. Knowing that Eli was probably dead, I couldn't bring myself to fight. I watched as a shadow filled the light. This was it.

BLOOD WAR

VAMPIRES AT MIDNIGHT
BOOK THREE

M.P. STARKWEATHER

CHAPTER 1

Kayden

I SHOULDN'T HAVE KISSED her. I knew it, she knew it. My wolf wanted her but I wasn't in the market for anything serious. Distractions could get me killed out here. I berated myself as I rushed from the hidden corridor out into the crowd. There was no time to argue with myself over it. I had to keep moving. I was cutting it close—too close. The ax was coming down on Eli. There was no other way to save him but to risk losing him. I pulled the small switch from my pocket, popped it open, and pushed the button. An explosion went off right behind the executioner, I think it was Jerry today but that didn't really matter. I had to move. Jerry brought the ax down on Eli's neck as the wall behind him pushed him forward. Panic set in, and I pushed myself to move faster.

As expected, the other wolves scattered in the chaos. Most of them wouldn't bother to stick around when explosions or gunfire were in play. I ran toward the podium, stomping on Jerry's neck to make sure he didn't get up. Eli was down and there was a stream of blood pooling under him. Shit. I grabbed him and dragged his limp body behind some debris for cover. I didn't want anyone to see what I was about to do. I gently cradled his head and cut my arm, forcing the blood into his mouth. He didn't respond. "Come on, man. You can't give up. Don't do this to me." I knew if he didn't survive, Delilah would hate me forever. Hell, she would probably kill me herself.

Eli wouldn't drink, but I could tell the blood was working. The wound was starting to close. I wondered if that would happen if he was already dead. I got my answer a moment later when Eli latched onto my wrist and began to drink. I watched his neck knit back together slowly and stopped him from draining me. "Okay, that's enough. I have to be able to carry you out of here." He looked up at me and nodded slightly. With a sigh of relief, I stood. Cradling him like a baby, I rushed down the hall to the loading dock. I needed to get to Delilah before the other wolves did.

I stopped at the end of the hall, peeking my head around the corner to see if the coast was clear. There were three guys searching the room. I set Eli on his feet and grabbed his shoulders. He looked unsteady. "Can you fight?"

Eli placed his hand over mine and squeezed. His eyes met mine, and I could see the determination. He understood that we needed to fight our way out of here to save Delilah. There was no other way. I would have to trust him to have my back while making sure he didn't get killed.

I nodded and gestured to the room in front of us. "There are three of them. We should be able to sneak in and take them out before they find Delilah and the guys." I pushed the door open silently, keeping an eye on the guy closest to us. I pointed and Eli zipped over to him. The man's head was separated from his body before I knew what had happened. He lowered the head and body to the floor quietly, and we continued stalking our prey.

I reached the second guy before Eli had a chance to run toward him. I grabbed him and lowered his body to the ground. My hand shifted to claws and I tore him open, pulling his intestines out while my other hand was over his mouth. His shocked expression branded itself to my brain. I had betrayed this man's trust. I was an alpha—my job was to protect and lead these men under the guidance of the Council.

When I tore my eyes away from my kill, Eli had caught up to the third man. I watched as he sunk his fangs into the wolf's neck and drained him. That could have easily been me a few minutes ago. Once he was finished, Eli turned to me. He still couldn't speak, but the question was understood. I pointed to what appeared to be an air intake on the wall. He walked over to it and waited for me. I grabbed the metal plate and ripped it off. As the dust settled, I heard Delilah cough. With the light behind us, I knew they wouldn't be able to tell who'd found them. "It's okay, you're safe now."

Delilah tensed, but Dec pushed past her, grabbing her hand and Vik's to pull them out of the tunnel.

Once they were free, Delilah noticed Eli and jumped at him. Jealousy tore through me as her lips met his. She pulled away from him to check for injuries. After inspecting his neck and finding only a shallow cut, she turned to me. I braced for her anger, expecting to take the brunt of it because Eli was injured. Instead, she jumped into my arms and kissed me, pouring her emotions into it until I felt her appreciation. As our tongues tangled, my wolf screamed in my head. Mine.

Declan and Vik both growled at my contact with her. "It was one thing to kiss her when you were running off to die. This is completely unacceptable," Vik snarled. I pulled away from Delilah and squared up with him. If I had to fight for my chance to be with her, I would. An alpha doesn't back down.

While Vik and I were preparing to tear each other apart, Eli stepped between us and put a hand on our chests. His words were barely a whisper, but at least he got something out. "We don't have time to fight each other." It was clear he wanted to say more but couldn't.

Dec stepped up next to him, letting Eli lean on him. "He's right. We need to move. Now." My best friend turned to me then. "How are we getting out of here?"

"I have an SUV outside. It's hidden in the alley just behind the warehouse." I started to lead them outside when Delilah stopped me.

"Won't the other wolves see you?" She was holding back tears and her voice cracked as she spoke.

"I killed anyone who knew me, babe. We need to move fast, but be careful." I led the way to the car, keeping watch all around us. Since my wolf claimed her, the urge to protect Delilah had doubled. I had to keep her safe, no matter what. I wasn't naïve enough to think that I would ever have her all to myself. I knew that any claim on her would include the three men she had already chosen. I just hoped that she would give me a chance to convince her that I would be a good mate. I couldn't bear the thought of being rejected. That drove wolves crazy—most of them ended up shifting permanently and wandering the forest alone. That was not the life I wanted.

I loaded everyone into the car and climbed into the driver's seat. Vik decided to ride shotgun, which left Dec in the back with Delilah and Eli. "I'm not sure where we should go. There is no safe place in the city." I knew it wasn't what they wanted to hear, but I refused to lie to my new family. Whether they accepted me or not, I would protect them.

"Head to my place," Dec replied, before tapping Vik on the shoulder. "Can you have some guys you and Eli trust come hang out for added security?"

"As soon as I have a phone to call from," Vik replied. I pulled mine from my pocket and handed it to him. Everyone was silent as he called and instructed his men, then called someone named Scott and gave him similar instructions.

Eli was resting, with Delilah holding onto him as though he would float away if she let go. His chin was on top of her head and his eyes were closed. I would have sworn he was sleeping except he gave a thumb's up when Vik relayed that both of their security details would meet us at Dec's place. I drove slower than I normally would, trying to avoid anyone noticing us. After a few random turns to make sure we weren't being followed. A van pulled out of a side street behind us. I turned to Vik, "I think we have a tail."

He tensed until he got a good look at the van's driver. "We're okay. That's Scott and some of his men. They'll escort us the rest of the way and make sure none of the hunters follow."

I felt the tension wash out of me as I pulled into the garage at Dec's place.

CHAPTER 2

Delilah

I KEPT PLAYING THAT kiss over and over in my mind. I shouldn't have done it. I knew that. But I was so relieved to see Eli in one piece that I threw myself into Kayden's arms. The moment our lips touched, my soul screamed *mine*! Vik's reaction was what I expected, but Dec growling at his best friend threw me off. Was there something going on with them?

It was impossible to sleep on the way to Dec's building. The air in the SUV was tense with distrust. Vik and Dec were on guard, and even Eli seemed unable to relax. I hated the thought of my guys fighting, but I'd be lying if I said the idea didn't thrill me a little.

Once Eli was able to speak easier, I knew that the others would insist on having a meeting to decide what we would do next. Maybe I could distract him for a bit first though. He needed rest. Kayden carried Eli to the elevator and into Dec's home. It amused me how small he looked compared to the hulking wolf. I would never tell him that, though.

"Eli needs to rest. We all do. I'm going to stay with him and make sure he's okay." I grabbed a couple of blood bags from the fridge, took Eli's hand, and led him to the room Declan had given me when I'd first been turned. It was only a few weeks ago, yet it felt like a lifetime had passed since that day. I closed the door behind us and handed Eli one of the bags.

"I know you're having trouble speaking right now. Give it some time. You'll heal soon." I walked over to the bed and kicked off my shoes. All of our clothes were ruined from the torture we'd endured. I knew that each of my guys had extra and would share with the others. We drank in silence until a knock sounded against the door.

"I brought Eli some clothes. I'm sure you'll both want a shower." I opened the door for Dec, standing there with a stack of clothes. Taking them from him, I leaned forward and pressed my lips to his.

"Thank you. It means a lot to me that you're all taking care of each other." I kissed him again and closed the door, not giving him a chance to respond. Even if they hadn't planned on taking care of Kayden, they would, because I'd just let him know it's what I expected. That meant I could give Eli my full attention.

"How about that shower?" I took the empty bag from him and placed it on the sink along with mine. They would be rinsed and recycled later.

I pulled the ripped and bloody t-shirt over his head. He tore my shirt off and pulled me to him forcefully. His lips claimed mine as if we were long-lost lovers. In a way, we were. "I don't want to hurt you," I whispered against his lips. He groaned and kissed me harder, backing me up against the wall. He nibbled down my neck to my shoulder. Before I realized what he was doing, he shredded my jeans and I was standing naked in front of him.

When I reached for his pants, he shook his head, then pressed his lips to mine again. It felt like he was touching me everywhere at once. I wanted more. His tongue trailed from my neck to the top of my breast, causing waves of sensation to wash over me. I gasped when he took my nipple between his teeth. His fingers danced down my sides to my stomach. I was soaked with anticipation. I wanted him to sink inside of me, but he wasn't ready for that yet. My guys enjoyed teasing me, building up my need until I couldn't take it anymore.

Eli's thumb circled my clit gently, barely touching me. This time, when I reached for him, he didn't stop me. Somehow, he'd managed to get his pants off while I was distracted. I found his cock hard and ready. I stroked it and he froze for a second before dipping two fingers inside me. My breath quickened as his fingers worked in and out of me. He knelt in front of me and hooked my leg on his shoulder. Any concerns I had about Eli not being fully healed were washed away by my orgasm as he licked and sucked on my clit. When I screamed his name, he stood and thrust his cock into me, pinning me to the wall.

I was shocked at his strength, holding me up while pounding into me harder and faster, until I cried out in pleasure. He continued to trail kisses and nips along my neck and shoulder while he fucked me. He thrust into me over and over, his pace increasing into a frenzy. With my back pinned to the wall, he kept one hand on my ass and the other slipped between us to stroke my clit. Another orgasm ripped through me just as Eli crested. After he came, he collapsed on the floor.

"Are you okay?" My brow creased in concern as I leaned over him. I shouldn't have let him take the lead like that. He was still too weak.

"I'm fine, love. Just worn out. Let's have that shower now, shall we?" He held a hand out for me to help him to his feet. After we showered and dressed in clean clothes, Eli wanted to talk to the guys. We walked out to see Vik and Dec hanging out in the living room, already discussing everything. I sat down between them when Eli started to speak.

"We need to talk about the wolf's claim. We all heard it when Delilah kissed him. And we need a plan to hide from the hunters." Eli paced the floor in the living room while the rest of us were seated.

"Where is Kayden, anyway?" I asked, looking around.

"Asleep in my room. He had injuries that he didn't want you to know about. He'll be fine," Dec said quickly, when he saw the concern on my face. "Speed healing, you know," he explained.

"Now stop trying to change the subject," Vik growled.

"Okay. Look, I know it's strange. It doesn't make sense to me either. But we have a bond, just like I do with all of you." I'm begging them to be okay with how I feel. I don't know what I would do if they denied me. My heart knows that they wouldn't, but I can't convince my mind.

"He has a lot to make up for, and not just with you," Declan said the words Vik was thinking. They shared the same angry expression.

Eli was the only one of us who didn't look mad. He frowned at my other lovers. "If there's a bond, we can't break it. That kind of pain could kill her."

"He doesn't deserve her," Vik finally spoke, almost a whisper, laced with violence.

"Then give him a chance to make it right. He saved my life. My head was half removed and he didn't leave me; instead he forced me to drink his blood. Most wolves would have left me to die. He carried me back to you all. If that isn't a man trying to make amends, I don't know what is." Eli paced back and forth while he poured every ounce of passion I'd felt in the bedroom into his speech.

I watched my guys debate the merit of another's claim on their woman. I should have felt like a possession, but I didn't. I knew that each of them only wanted to protect me, even if that meant from the others. When the arguing turned to yelling, I stepped in. "Stop." I held up a hand to get their attention. Once all six eyes were on me, I continued, "Do I get a say in who I am allowed to love?"

Vik and Dec turned red and Eli smirked. "I told you it needed to be her decision." I shook my head at his teasing tone. He'd been the only one to defend my right to choose and to offer Kayden a chance at redemption.

"We're not trying to decide who you love. It's just that he's done a lot to warrant our distrust. Don't you think he needs to pay for that?" Declan's words were quiet. I could feel his pain. This was his best friend we were discussing, after all.

"I don't think he deserves you. I'm thankful that he saved Eli. But no amount of ass-kissing will make me like him right now. It's his fault we were captured and tortured in the first place," Vik hissed the words at me. His anger was palpable; radiating off him in waves.

"I'm not saying that I want to jump right in bed with him. I'm saying that he saved our lives and that he deserves a chance to stick around. If something happens, then it happens. I'm not going to close myself off to the possibility." I stood my ground, refusing to back down. If Dec and Vik were angry with me for my decision, they would have to get over it. Kayden was staying with us for as long as I wanted him around. "You don't have to like it, but you do have to give him a chance. That means no fighting. Please, it would mean a lot to me if you guys were on board."

CHAPTER 3

Eli

I was impressed with how Delilah handled the other guys' reaction to the mate claim by the wolf. I knew that she cared for him before he saved my life. His actions surprised me, though. A wolf doesn't give blood to a vamp. It doesn't happen. Period. We're not mortal enemies or anything, more like disinterested neighbors. As long as we don't break the Council's rules, the wolves leave us alone. And their blood doesn't taste good, so we don't bother them. I meant what I said—the fact that he would go against his instincts to save me for her meant that he was trying to make amends. I felt like he deserved a chance to do just that. If Delilah deemed him worthy, then he would be one of us.

Not long after our debate ended, Kayden strolled into the room. From the glare he directed at Vik and Dec, he'd heard our conversation. When he turned to me, he nodded. Then he walked over to Delilah and pulled her in for a kiss. I couldn't stop the smirk that spread across my face. He was testing them to see their reaction.

Vik's face turned red. Dec's jaw dropped. And I just had to laugh at the whole situation. It was ridiculous for any of us to think we could keep our girl away from anyone she wanted to be with. We'd already learned how to share among the three of us. We were just going to have to deal with one more. Vik needed time to get used to the idea, and Dec would have to talk things out with his bestie.

"Did you guys find anything while Delilah and I were resting?" I asked casually as I sat down and leaned back. Vik rolled his eyes at me while Declan glared at Kayden. The wolf didn't seem to notice.

"Actually, fangs, we did. Dec says you're the hacker, but he let me try anyway. I'm not great, but I do have some skills. The leader of the Powder ring is a guy who calls himself

Ghost. I couldn't find anything else on him, other than stories that prove he's a sick son of a bitch." Kayden walked over to the couch and sat down before pulling Delilah into his lap. I had a front-row seat for the torture Dec and Vik were suffering.

"I'll check it out and see if I can find more on him. Thanks," I offered, trying to prove to the other guys that it was okay to be nice. They didn't look moved by my gesture. I sighed, then grabbed Dec's laptop and started typing. It wasn't as sophisticated as my setup, but it looked to be a secure network.

After only a few keystrokes, I was able to find a little more information than Kayden had. There wasn't much on the man called Ghost, but there was a connection to the Council. I would need to do a deeper background check on each Council member to see if I could find out more. It was going to take time. That was the one thing we didn't have. To be more productive, I needed to set up searches that would run while I was doing other things.

"I don't understand why this guy seems to be coming after Delilah. What's the connection?" I pondered the question aloud while I typed. A knock at the door made everyone jump. Kayden stood behind the door, ready to pounce. Vik grabbed a knife from the kitchen and stood on the opposite side. I set the computer on the table and grabbed Delilah, moving toward the kitchen for some cover. Dec carefully walked over to the door and looked through the peephole. "I'm not sure who it is. Hold tight."

He turned the knob and the door creaked as it opened just enough that Dec could ask who it was without seeing the person on the other side or letting them see him. "Declan Roarke?" As soon as I heard the voice, I knew it was Scott. I watched Vik relax, then whisper to Dec, "It's Scott. Let him in." He waved at Scott and headed back to the couch, where Delilah and I were already waiting. Declan took him at his word and stepped back, blocking Kayden from the visitor.

"Scott, did you bring them?" I didn't even give him a chance to get all the way in the door before I asked about the computers. I had asked him to pick up my laptops and some other supplies I knew we would need.

"Yeah, Boss, I got your computers and the other stuff you asked for is in the van. A couple of the guys who work here are bringing those up after they check everything out." He gave Dec a sideways glance as if he didn't appreciate being questioned by his men.

"You know it's standard procedure. And if it wasn't, we'd still do it. We have to keep her safe," Dec said before flopping on the couch next to Delilah. Scott made a face when Delilah linked her fingers with Dec's while still holding my hand. I wasn't sure if he objected to the procedure or to my girl being affectionate with other men. Either way, it amused me. I kissed Delilah before standing up and taking the bags Scott held.

I went to work setting up the computers while Scott talked with Vik about security at his place and mine. Once the computers were set up, I started a more in-depth search for Ghost and his crew. I wanted to know everything about him. I needed a name. If I could find his name, I would have every detail of his life in a matter of minutes. But unfortunately, all I could immediately find told me that this guy was worse than we thought. There were whispers of him linked to every random killing in the city. It seemed as if he had a hand in all the crimes that had been committed in the past six months, maybe longer.

I was convinced that somehow he'd also infiltrated the Council since the hunters had been sent after Delilah before they knew that she'd been the one to kill that girl. Kayden admitted that they didn't have a name when he'd come to the bunker. They had no idea who was responsible, yet suddenly they were sent after us. There had to be a connection. No one mentioned the girl in any of the interrogations—they didn't ask any of us about it. Everything was about Delilah and why we were looking into the Powder operation.

"It all has to be connected," I muttered as I searched. When I finally looked up, I noticed that Scott had left and the others were no longer crowded around. I figured that one of the guys decided to distract Delilah from her worries. I grabbed a blood bag from the fridge and went back to work. I wanted answers, and I wouldn't give up until I had them. The quiet was peaceful for the first time in days. While we were captives, quiet only happened before they took us to be tortured. A shiver ran down my spine. If I hadn't managed to get that hairpin to Vik, we might not have made it out.

Unbidden, an image took over my mind.

The executioner was standing over me and I was tied up. I could feel my heart race as sweat beaded along my spine. He raised the axe above my head and I knew that I was going to die alone. My only comfort was that Delilah wasn't being forced to watch. The explosion behind me was a relief until the ax swung down. It cut deeper than I will ever admit. At that moment, I surrendered to death. I regretted that I would never see Delilah again. I even regretted that I wouldn't get to follow up on the kiss I shared with Vik. Tears ran down my cheeks as the blood drained from my neck.

My eyes fluttered when strong arms scooped me up and carried me away. I wondered what was happening before I felt the tangy blood start to drip in my mouth. I recognized the smell of it and knew instantly that Kayden had come to help me. I didn't understand why, unless it was because of his connection to Delilah. I had felt it before either of them realized it was there. It hadn't been my place to tell them. I knew they would figure it out in time.

I shook my head to pull myself from the memory, my hand instinctively going to my throat. The injury was healed, but the scars would remain—both physical and emotional. I knew that Kayden saving me was the reason I would accept his mate claim on my love. It didn't matter to me how many lovers she had, as long as I was one of them. I knew that I couldn't live without her. I was once again torn away from my thoughts as Kayden ran into the room.

"Fangs, we're not gonna be safe here. I just got a message from one of my guys who's still loyal. They're coming after us. We have to move." I could see the anxiety bubbling inside him. I knew he was telling the truth. That, on top of everything I'd found about Ghost, told me that he wouldn't relent until he got what he wanted.

Delilah.

CHAPTER 4

Declan

EVEN FROM THE OTHER room, I heard Kayden's hushed words to Eli. I hadn't heard him this terrified since we were kids. I was sure that there was no way he was playing us now. Part of me wanted him to suffer for what he'd done to our girl, but the rest missed my best friend. I was struggling with my feelings even though I knew if it came down to it, I would protect him with my life. He was family.

"Where exactly are we supposed to go? They seem to know every move we make before we make it," I said as I stormed into the room, not caring that they would know I was eavesdropping.

"There's a warehouse on the East side of the city. It's been abandoned for a while. They were renovating it and suddenly stopped. No one has been there in months." Kayden's suggestion had me suspicious. Why would he want us to go back to that side of town? That was where our enemies were.

"What makes you think that'll be safe?" Eli asked what I was thinking. I clenched my fists while I waited for Kayden's carefully thought-out response. He was hiding something again.

"Sometimes it's easier to hide in plain sight," he responded with a shrug. There was more to it than he was telling. I knew it but couldn't prove anything.

"Who owns it?" I snarled at him. I had to push for answers.

"Dixon Corp. Look, Dec, I know you don't trust me, but I'm not setting you guys up. The Council and the hunters don't even know about the warehouse. On paper, Red owns it. I haven't talked to her in months. They won't expect us to go there. At least give me a chance to prove that I'm on your side," Kayden growled at me and walked away. I might have deserved that.

Eli looked at me expectantly. I knew what he was going to ask. "I take it Kayden owns Dixon Corp. And you don't trust him enough to hide out in his place because he could easily hand us over to the hunters. Am I close?"

I nodded and hung my head. "How can you trust him so easily?"

"Why can't you?" he snapped back.

"He locked us up and tortured us. That's unforgivable." I was determined to stand by my opinion. I would not falter in my irritation with Kayden.

"He saved my life when he didn't have to. He killed members of his own pack to protect not only me, but you and the others as well. If that's not a man who's trying to prove he can be trusted, I don't know what it is." Eli stood up and walked away, heading toward Kayden's room. His arguments made sense. Kayden could have just apologized for not being able to save Eli and went on like it never happened. But he didn't.

I spent the next two hours alone, trying to figure out exactly why I was so angry with Kayden. I knew it went deeper than just being captured. He may have been in charge of the hunters, but they still took orders from the Council. Eli had shared what little he'd found on Ghost with us, and I agreed that there had to be a connection between that guy and our girl. We just had to find it.

Packing up was easier this time because we knew what to expect. Our supplies were chosen for usefulness rather than comfort. It was strange to see Vik out of a suit, but even he had made concessions to protect Delilah. We weren't telling anyone where we'd be, so there was no chance of any of our guys being tortured to give us up. They were all going to think we were still here. It was going to be difficult to manage, but Eli thought we could make it work.

Once we were all ready, we drove quickly through the city. The tension in the nondescript white van was heavy. The vehicle looked like any other delivery truck and blended into the city traffic perfectly. If there was a way to get to the warehouse without being spotted, this was it.

The building itself looked exactly like every other abandoned warehouse in this district. There was nothing eye-catching about it. The windows were blacked out and parts of the building itself looked to be crumbling from exposure to the elements. I hated to admit it, but Kayden might have been right about this place. It looked like the perfect place to disappear.

Kayden pulled up to the back of the building and typed something on his phone. The doors of the loading dock swung open and he drove the van inside. Once he parked, we got out and surveyed the inside. It was a simple layout with offices on one side and storage shelves on the other. When I walked over to the windows, I realized that they were actually one-way mirrors. They looked blacked out from outside, but from inside we could see everything.

"What is this place?" Delilah asked in awe. "It's not just an abandoned building. There are too many fancy features in here." My girl was definitely right. This wasn't abandoned. It had been carefully created to look that way. But would Kayden admit that?

"It's a safe house. Red is the only one who knows about it besides us. She doesn't know where it is, only that it exists." Kayden's explanation was simple. I wrestled with my own distrust; I couldn't decide if he was telling the truth or still hiding something. "There are secret tunnels under the offices. There's a bunker down there that we can stay in. It's more protected than up here. We can still come up here during the day, or at night, but I think we should sleep underground."

There it was. I knew he hadn't been completely honest. But it wasn't enough that I should be this angry with him. Eli and Delilah followed Kayden to the offices to check out the bunker. I stayed with Vik. He seemed to be as annoyed as I was.

"You don't have to forgive him. You can hold a grudge forever. It's your choice. But you need to stop trying to turn everyone else against him. Delilah cares for him. She's bonding with him. You can't get between that. I don't like him, but I'm convinced that he won't do anything to hurt her." Vik's words were like a punch to the gut. I stared after him as he walked away to catch up to the others. I guess I was on my own as far as being angry with Kayden. That pissed me off even more.

Reluctantly, I followed the others to the underground space. There were only two bedrooms, so it was obvious we'd have to share or sleep on the concrete floor. Each bedroom was sparsely furnished with a king-sized bed, a small table with two chairs, and a nightstand. There was a bathroom between the two rooms, connecting them. It was small, but nicer than I expected.

I overheard Eli and Vik whispering about which room they would take. That meant I would have to bunk with Kayden; I groaned to myself. Sleeping in the van was more appealing. But one smile from Delilah told me that I couldn't do that. I craved her attention and would do whatever it took to get it. "I guess we're gonna be bunkmates," I said to Kayden, trying to keep my emotions out of my tone. I didn't need to start a fight with him.

"Looks that way. Just don't kill me in my sleep, okay?" My jaw dropped at his words. Did he really think that I could kill him? Delilah laughed at my expression.

"He's kidding. You wouldn't hurt him," she laughed. "I guess you guys are planning on me bouncing between the rooms while we're here?" She tried to act offended by the idea, but the scent of her arousal betrayed her. I fought a growl as Kayden took a deep breath of her. I didn't want him anywhere near my love. I'd have to get over that, or I wouldn't get to spend any time with her either. It was an impossible decision.

"You know that's exactly what's going to happen. You'd never give up time with any of us." Vik's words surprised me. I wondered if Eli had coached him on what to say, or if he'd really had a change of heart.

That night was awkward, sleeping in a king-sized bed with the wolf who had been my best friend for years, while Delilah stayed with Eli and Vik. I was convinced it was intentional, no doubt an attempt to make us talk and force our friendship to mend. I made sure that I was in bed facing the wall before Kayden came into the room. His words were whispered, but he knew I would hear them. "I get that you don't trust me. I hope that my word still means something, though. I'm on your side, Dec."

CHAPTER 5

Vik

THE NEXT FEW WEEKS were uneventful. I watched as Eli and Kayden bonded over their shared love of bomb-building. I had a chance to bond with him over our shared annoyance of Declan's attitude. It seemed strange for me to not be the outcast. Part of me wanted to help him, but the rest was enjoying being included by the others. I figured it couldn't hurt to let him sweat it out a little.

Being cramped in such tight quarters wasn't helping any of us. After a couple of weeks, all four of us guys were at each other's throats more often than not. I felt bad that Delilah had to constantly step between us to break things up. I knew that part of our issue was that we couldn't find anything else on Ghost. We had nothing more than a name and a violent reputation.

The space issue was causing problems in the bedroom too. It was hard to have any alone time with Delilah, since things were split in half. And with us spatting, she wasn't interested in group activities. I didn't blame her. I wasn't interested in being around any of those guys either. Our girl made sure that each of us got to spend time alone with her, even if that didn't always equal sex. As far as I knew, she hadn't done anything with Kayden yet.

Declan made the mistake of asking her about it. Bad for him was good for me. She stormed away from him and found me. I was in the bedroom relaxing while Eli and Kayden did security checks upstairs. Delilah came into the room fuming and in tears, which was a dangerous combination.

"What's wrong, Myshka?" I sat up on the bed and opened my arms for her.

She jumped into my arms and buried her head on my shoulder. I rubbed her back until she had calmed down enough to talk. "Dec is being an ass. He had nerve enough to ask me if I had sex with Kayden. That's none of his business."

"Agreed. He's an ass. What can I do to make it better?" I leaned down and peppered kisses along her neck. She made a noise similar to a purr and fisted her hands in my hair. I laid back on the bed, pulling her on top of me. Delilah straddled me and started unbuttoning my shirt. I sighed when her hands touched my bare chest. Every moment away from her was torture. I relished her touch. I refused to let her take control, though. Once my shirt was out of the way, I flipped her over and settled myself between her thighs.

"Vik!" Her squeal of indignation put a smile on my face. She swatted my arm before she started to laugh.

"Be a good girl and I'll let you come," I offered. Delilah stared daggers at me until I began to touch her. I knew that she liked to be in control, but also that it was nice to let go sometimes. I gave that to her when we were together. Outside of the bedroom, we could butt heads and argue about who was right. Inside, though, I was the boss. She never objected and always walked away satisfied.

I ran my hands over every inch of her body without removing her clothes. She whined and squirmed. I stood up and stepped away. Her growl amused me. "Vik. What the hell?"

I smirked as I stepped out of the rest of my clothes. Then I climbed back on the bed in the exact spot I had retreated from a moment ago. "I told you, if you're good, I'll let you come. If not, I'll be the only one who gets to finish."

"I'll just do it myself," she threatened. Staring at me, she began to unbutton her pants before slipping her hand down them. I grabbed her hand and pulled it over her head.

"No," I said, reaching over her to the restraints I'd attached to the bed earlier. "You do not have permission to touch, my girl. I am in control of your orgasm. Do you understand me?" I slipped her hands into the silk ropes and tightened them just enough to hold her still, but not so much that it would hurt.

With an indignant look, Delilah relented. "Yes, I understand." The irritation on her face didn't reach her eyes. Those were filled with need. She always acted annoyed when I tied her up but never used the safe word that would stop everything. Just to be sure, we went through our usual conversation—I made her tell me the safe word and agree that she would use it if she became overwhelmed or wanted to stop. When I was satisfied that she was ready, I lowered my hard, naked body on top of her and kissed her passionately.

She fought against the restraints, wanting to touch me and trying to get me to touch her. She needed to be distracted, so I would take my time with her. I kissed her again before ripping her shirt and bra to shreds. "Hey, I liked those!" Her objection would have meant more if she wasn't straining toward my hand that hovered just out of reach of her perky breasts. Her frustrated grunts made me even more determined to drag out the play session. I wanted to make her orgasm the most intense she'd ever experienced.

I waited until she stopped fighting before I touched her. I was riding a dangerous line. On one hand, torturing her this way was a huge turn-on for me. On the other, if I wasn't careful, I would finish before I got started. Without touching her skin, I removed her pants and panties. Once her clothes were out of the way, I could see how wet she was. I wanted to see how much more she would take before she begged me to fuck her. I gently touched my nose to the skin of her ankle and slowly moved it from there to her thigh.

Her whimpers set me off and my tongue flicked out just beside her core. I knew that was where she wanted me, but I wasn't ready to relent just yet. I could smell her desire and it made my cock jump. I slowly rubbed circles on her thighs, my hands barely touching her skin. "Vik, please," she begged. I leaned closer and sampled the flavor dripping from her. Delilah gasped at the sudden sensation. I continued to lick and suck her pussy until she screamed my name with her orgasm. Then I thrust into her, leaning over to untie her hands. She matched my rhythm, fast and hard. When she was just about to crest again, I pulled out of her and stopped.

"What the fuck?" Her growl echoed in the small room. I captured her lips with mine and thrust into her again, swallowing her moans of pleasure. I pounded into her until she came again, letting myself go with her. When I collapsed next to her, she laid her head on my chest. "That was amazing," she sighed before passing out. I grabbed a rag from under my pillow and cleaned us both up before closing my eyes and letting sleep take me. I woke when Delilah shifted in her sleep, but instead of getting up, I was content to watch her sleep.

When she woke up, her mood had improved. She stretched her arms over her head and smiled at me. "I want to explore. I'm tired of dealing with all the fighting. The only time you guys are getting along is when you're all separated." I knew that she wanted privacy, but I wasn't about to let her go into the tunnels alone.

"How about a shower first? You go ahead and I'll bring you some clothes in a minute." I waited until she closed the bathroom door before I bolted from the bedroom. I needed to find Declan. Fortunately, he was hanging out in the kitchen, putting supplies away and taking inventory. One of us would be making a supply run soon. For now, I needed him to do me a favor.

"Hey, Dec. I need your help," I said, keeping my voice low. I needed to make sure Delilah didn't hear me. I hated keeping secrets from her again, but my need to protect her outweighed the guilt.

He looked up at me and closed the fridge. "What's up?"

"I need you to follow Delilah while she explores the tunnels. But don't tell her I asked you to do it and don't let her see you." He cocked an eyebrow at me and chuckled. I knew my desperate expression would amuse him, but I really needed his cooperation.

"Why can't you do it?"

I closed my eyes for a moment before I responded. "I have some business calls to make. Please, would you just do this for me—or for her?" He nodded and walked away, no doubt to hide in the tunnels before she got there. I strolled back to my room and delivered Delilah's clothes just as she was finishing her shower. With any luck, she would stay safe and be none the wiser that I had her followed.

CHAPTER 6

Delilah

I sensed Declan as soon as I walked away from Vik. I knew it had been way too easy to convince him to let me explore alone. It didn't matter. I was going to explore and if Dec needed to follow, so be it. I knew that ignoring him may not be easy, but I was determined to try. The tunnels snaked off in multiple directions under the warehouse, creating a maze that seemed to connect to the city. Kayden had compared it to the underground tunnels that were used to help free slaves a long time ago. I wondered if these caverns were used for that same purpose or if there was something he wasn't telling us.

Either way, I wanted to see where they led. It was nice to have a break from the constant tension that surrounded my guys lately. I knew that Dec was responsible for a lot of it. I couldn't bring myself to blame him, though. His issues with Kayden were his own. As much as they needed to talk about it, I wasn't going to be the one to force them. They would have to come to that decision together. I wondered if part of the problem was Kayden's claim on me. Neither of us had acted on it yet, but we both admitted it existed. Could Dec just be jealous of his childhood friend?

I could see pretty well in the dark, but still managed to trip over something and stumble. There was no way to ignore Dec's presence when he gasped at my clumsiness. I sighed and turned to him. "I know you're there. Just come out and walk with me."

"Sorry, I know you wanted privacy. I needed to know you were safe." His eyes mirrored the sincerity in his words.

"And what if I was secretly meeting with Kayden down here?" I knew that baiting him wasn't going to help them get along, but I couldn't resist.

"Oh, I didn't know. I'm sorry. I'll leave you two alone." Disappointment dripped from his words.

I grabbed his arm and pulled him to me before he could run away. "Dec, I was teasing. I'm not meeting anyone. I really just wanted a little while to myself. But please stay." I pressed my lips to his and kissed him tenderly. A moment later, I found myself pressed up against the cool stone wall as he deepened the kiss; his hand fisted in my hair as my tongue played with his. Dec tipped my head back and started to lick and nip at my neck while his hands roamed over me. His touch set me off. My panties were drenched and I was desperate to feel him against me.

Before I could get his pants unzipped, I heard something. "Wait, what's that?" It was a strange buzzing sound. I pulled away from Dec and looked around the corridor. I couldn't see anything out of place. "Do you hear that?" I whispered, grabbing his arm and pressing myself against his side. He nodded. I expected him to lead me back to the bunker, but he started walking toward the noise. After a few more turns, I saw an open space ahead of us. There were tables set up with beakers and other equipment that I had never seen before. People in hazmat suits crossed in front of our vision, not noticing us.

I tugged on Declan's arm, trying to get him to go back the way we'd come, but he shook his head. I knew he wanted to fight these guys, while I just wanted to keep him safe. My heart raced as panic descended upon me. What had possessed me to explore the tunnels? At the moment, I was grateful to have Dec with me. I vowed to thank Vik for making it happen. "Come on, we need to go. We have no idea what they're making," I practically begged him to leave with me.

"All the more reason to check it out," he whispered, pulling me forward with him to get a closer look. The room was dark, so we were able to creep in unseen. Dec dragged me behind a stack of crates and pushed me to my knees. Luckily, it seemed as if we were pretty well hidden for the moment. The room smelled familiar but I couldn't place it. Whatever they were making, I had been around it before. It had a faint honeysuckle scent mixed with something fruity—cherry, maybe. I wasn't sure where I had smelled it before.

Dec motioned for me to stay put before he crawled away. I wanted to watch him but was too scared to move. I waited a minute, then barely poked my head over the crate and looked around the room. Most of the guys in the suits had left. I only saw one of them, and Dec was currently sneaking up behind him. Before the guy even knew what hit him, my love had torn his head from his shoulders. Declan even managed to drop the body gently to the floor. I should have been horrified watching him kill a man but instead, I was excited. It was thrilling that he would do that to protect me.

I stood up from my kneeling position, watching Dec as he inspected the table. When he was finished looking at everything, he pocketed a small bag and jogged toward me. "We need to go," he said quietly as he took my hand and led me from the room.

"What is all that?" I couldn't wait to ask the question that was repeating in my mind. I wanted to tell him about that scent and find out if he knew what it was.

"They were making Powder and it was tainted. It was probably the same stuff you were dosed with at my club." He purposefully stopped himself from mentioning the other place it happened—when I'd killed that girl. So that smell was probably the drugs. That was good information to have. He was right, we needed to move. As we ran down the hall, taking the same turns we'd taken earlier in reverse, it was quiet. The silence was deafening. I didn't remember the corridor being so quiet when we'd come through the first time.

Before I could mention how strange the silence was, someone stepped out of the darkness, blocking our path. Dec and I skidded to a stop a few feet away from the intruder. Scuffling behind us indicated that there were more of them. We were surrounded. A small stone bounced toward us and smoke started to flow out of it. I couldn't see anything through the haze. Someone gripped my arms hard, keeping me in place. I could hear Dec struggling but neither of us said anything. A moment later, I heard him grunt and stop fighting. They must have knocked him out.

The strangers dragged us further into the tunnels, away from the warehouse that contained the bunker we'd been calling home. I silently wished there was a way to let my other guys know what had happened to us. I regretted not completing the mating ritual with Kayden. He and Eli told me that telepathic communication was possible for wolf mates once the bond was in place. I'd been so worried about Declan being upset that I had avoided the one thing that could have saved us from being taken.

I realized that my captors would let me walk almost on my own once they realized that I wasn't going to attempt an escape. With one hand free and both feet on the ground, it was easy to leave a trail for the others to follow. I casually pulled a handful of pins from my hair. I had to space the hairpins out since I had no idea where we were going or how far away it was. I figured that Kayden would get my scent and could follow the trail as long as I dropped one at each intersection to show him which way to go. Between pins, I dragged my feet as much as I could without drawing attention.

The fact that they didn't cover my eyes to keep me from seeing which way we went scared me. That meant they didn't expect me to survive. I wasn't ready to leave my guys yet, but I couldn't fight until I knew Dec was safe. I played the part of a terrified, submissive girl and waited for my chance. The men carried Dec and escorted me through a door into a large chamber. There were two wooden chairs in the center of the room. We were strapped to the chairs before one of the men dumped a bucket of water over Dec to wake him up. He sputtered and choked, then shook his head and searched the room until his eyes landed on me.

"I'm okay," I whispered, relaxing a little since he was conscious again.

"Shut up!" A fist cracked against my jaw, jerking my head to the side. I cried out in pain, and Dec shook his head slightly, telling me to keep it in. These guys wanted a reaction. It would take everything in me to deny them the satisfaction but I would do it for my love.

CHAPTER 7

Declan

I WANTED TO RIP the man apart for touching my girl. No matter how hard I fought against the restraints, I wasn't able to break them. I felt weak and a little lightheaded. Our captor must have drugged us. I tried to let her know that we needed to be quiet. He obviously expected a reaction from both of us. When we refused to give it to him, he walked away. I waited until they were all out of earshot and tried to comfort her. "It's okay. We'll get out of this. Just stay as quiet as possible, no matter what," I said softly, moving my mouth as little as necessary.

I had no idea how long we were tied there before a man with an elaborate mask stomped up to us. The mask resembled a ram's head with curling horns. It covered nearly all of the figure's face. His clothing reminded me of what someone would wear to a masquerade ball. He looked me up and down, snarling. My eyes met his dark brown ones and there was something familiar about them. I couldn't place it, but I felt like I knew this man somehow. After inspecting me, he turned to Delilah and looked at her the same way.

When he spoke, his voice was raspy and pained. "I am Ghost. Allow me to enlighten you on the rules of my home. You will only speak when I allow it. You will respond to any and all of my questions. If I believe you are lying to me, I will kill you. Do you understand?" His gaze moved from Delilah to me and back.

I nodded. "Yes, we understand." Delilah nodded but didn't make a sound. The moment his palm connected with her cheek, I pulled against the restraints. I wanted to remove the appendage and choke him with it. Rage bubbled just below the surface, but he ignored me and focused on her.

"I said, do you understand? Answer me, Delilah." Eli was right. This psycho had been after our girl all along. This wasn't just some random drop of tainted Powder. It was a direct attack. But why?

She nodded again and whispered, "I understand."

A fanatical grin spread across our captor's face. The malice that was in his eyes a moment ago was replaced with mirth. He backed away and stood in front of us as if he were about to perform. "Good. Now, what questions do you have for me? I'm sure you want to know why you're here. I'll wait until you ask before I divulge anything." His demeanor had completely changed. He was nearly giddy, and it was terrifying.

"Why are we here?" I asked, drawing his gaze. The grin dropped away and a frown replaced it. Ghost stomped over to my chair and stared at me intensely. I could hear Delilah's breath hitch when his fist shot out and connected with my eye. Blood dripped slowly into my line of sight.

"I was not speaking to you, vampire. I was speaking to her. I will only answer her questions." He leaned close as he spoke, close enough that I could smell the stale cigarettes and coffee on his breath. I could also tell from his scent that he was human. That wasn't very helpful, but it was something we didn't know before. He glared at me before stepping back and turning to Delilah once more.

I had heard of vamps having a connection to their sire. I sometimes felt like I knew what Delilah was feeling, but wondered if I could push it farther and talk to her telepathically. It was a rare thing and I was certain it wouldn't work. That wouldn't stop me from trying.

Her eyes opened wide and her lower lip trembled. I knew she was terrified. *Ask something. Get him to talk. You can do this.* It didn't matter that she couldn't hear me, I would try to talk her through it anyway.

Dec? Was that really you? I'm going crazy now. How could I possibly hear your voice in my head? A confused look crossed Delilah's face before she focused and steeled herself against the monster standing before us. "Why are we here?"

The maniac stepped forward and for a moment, I thought he was going to strike her the way he had me. Instead, he grabbed her shoulders and gave her a shake. "You're here as my guests." He turned and danced away from her before snapping back to face us again.

Delilah and I shared a look, then she turned her attention back to him. "I'm sorry, do we know each other? You seem really familiar but I can't quite place you." Ghost glared at her and rushed forward. He grabbed her hair, jerking Delilah's head back so he could get closer without kneeling.

"I seem familiar, do I?" His manic smile appeared again and he laughed. It was a terrifying sound, like a cross between a cough and a hyena. His fist shot forward and clocked Delilah in the same spot his palm had been earlier. "Would you like to know why you're my guests?"

I expected Delilah to drop her head, but she faced him, gritted her teeth, and answered, "Yes, please." *That's it, mo chroí, keep him talking. You're doing great.* The slight nod of her head nearly had me convinced that she could hear my thoughts. I didn't have time to consider that before he struck her again, this time splitting her lip. *Don't react. You're so brave. Just hold it in. Don't scream, and don't cry. You can do this. I'm right here with you. I love you.* I wanted nothing more than to pull her into my arms and protect her from this monster. Instead, I was forced to watch as he hit her again and again as he told us his story.

"My father was an asshole who abused my mother and kept her from returning to her family. He beat her daily. When I was big enough for him to hit me without it being fatal, he started beating me too." His fists punctuated his words on Delilah's face, chest, and arms. Dark bruises started to form everywhere his hands had connected with her skin. *I'm so sorry. I wish he would hit me instead.*

Don't say that, Dec. I love you. I only wish I knew why he hates me so much. She could hear me. I was right. At least we had that. I cringed each time Ghost punched and slapped my love. I would kill him for this.

"Once, when I was five, the bitch ran off. She wanted to see her other family. He hunted her down and brought her home. While she was gone, he took his frustration out on me. Two weeks after he returned with my mother, he killed her. Then I was the only one to suffer his abuse. She got what she wanted—her freedom—in the form of death." He continued to punch, slap, and kick Delilah the whole time he spoke.

She never gave him the satisfaction of crying or calling out. I watched as he got more frustrated with each statement he made. I wondered what his story had to do with Delilah. He seemed to be getting tired from swinging. Ghost's breathing was labored, and he was pausing longer between rants. *That's good. He's getting tired. He'll have to stop soon. I'm trying to work out a plan for getting us out of here. Stay strong, mo chroí.*

The only indication that Delilah was being tortured was the change in her breathing. I could tell she was struggling to stay awake. Our advanced healing would work better if she could drink a blood bag and sleep it off. That wasn't an option here, so I would have to keep her awake as much as possible. Every time Ghost hit her, I tried to fight the restraints. I knew that he had to have drugged us in addition to whatever the ropes were coated with. There was no way regular rope would hold a vamp this way.

I'm okay. Everything hurts. I think he cracked a couple of ribs, and my face is broken. It'll heal, right? Her question split my heart in two. It hurt me that she was worried about her appearance after everything this dick was doing.

You'll be perfect as always. It'll just be slower without the proper rest and supplies. I knew that she would understand what supplies I was talking about without saying it. Sometimes talking about the thing you couldn't have made it worse. I didn't want to torture her any more than she'd already suffered.

I hadn't been paying attention and didn't realize Ghost had gone. I looked around the room and didn't see him. Turning away from Delilah, a fist connected with my jaw. Was this guy using brass knuckles? I glanced at Delilah and saw tears in her eyes. *Remember, don't react. No matter what he does, keep your expression neutral. Please don't give him the satisfaction.* I saw her nod slightly as Ghost squared up for another punch. This one got me in the eye, which immediately started to swell shut. From what I'd just experienced, I knew that watching someone you loved being tortured was worse than having it happen to you. I hated that Delilah had to feel that now.

Are you okay? I'm trying so hard to stay quiet. Her words in my head were the sweetest sound I'd ever heard. It gave me something to focus on besides the pain from the guy trying to turn my face into ground meat. When Ghost stepped back and looked at her, I nodded and saw her relax a little.

CHAPTER 8

Kayden

ELI AND I WERE fine-tuning the search for intel on Ghost when my phone went off. With Eli's location blocking software, we hadn't bothered with new phones. Still, it was strange to get a message. No one had contacted me since we took off. I assumed they thought I'd been killed. I opened the video message, and my jaw dropped.

The text that accompanied it was simple. *Isn't that guy your best friend?* I hit play on the video and watched as someone in a goat mask punched Delilah repeatedly while screaming at her about something I couldn't understand. Declan was strapped to a chair next to her, forced to watch. Suddenly the figure turned on him and started pounding. Neither of them made a sound, other than grunts, when the man's fists connected.

"What is that?" The noise from the video got Eli's attention. He stood beside me, and I played the video again. My heart raced. My wolf wanted out. I knew that I would be more beast than man if I shifted. I would hunt down this guy and kill him for what he did to my brother and my girl.

"We have to find them," I growled. Eli placed a hand on my arm before taking the phone from me.

"We do, and we will. Let me see what I can get from the video. There should be a location embedded in the image." He walked back to the computer and hooked the phone up, downloading the video and reviewing it again.

While he worked, I was at war with my wolf. How could Delilah and Dec have been taken? Who was responsible? The masked figure matched some images we'd found of the guy who called himself Ghost. Why was this guy after her? I had so many questions and no answers.

"They're somewhere in the underground tunnels. Based on the GPS stamp on the video, they aren't far from our location. I'll get Vik, and we'll see if we can track them." Eli raced off to find Vik as I stood there, too shocked to move. Our enemy was in the same tunnels we'd been hiding in. How did they get so close without any of us knowing?

"Come on, Kayden, let's go. Do you think you can track her?" Vik shoved me to get my attention. I stared at him without really seeing him. He balled up his hand and punched me, jerking my head to the side. The impact brought me back to the present.

"Ow. What was that for?" I rubbed my jaw. I knew he'd just pulled me back from the edge, but I wasn't ready to admit that to anyone just yet.

"Can you track her, or do we need something that she's worn recently?" he asked again, his tone more panicked this time.

"I know her scent. Tracking her shouldn't be a problem. We need to move." I growled the words at him and raced toward the tunnels. I followed Delilah's fragrance away from our makeshift home. We wound our way further into the maze of tunnels and found an area where there had been a fight of some sort. There was a faint scent in the air that reminded me of the smoke bombs Dec and I used to play with as kids.

"This way." I walked quickly but carefully so I didn't disturb the marks she'd clearly left for us to follow. Every turn was marked by one of her hairpins. *Good girl. Smart to mark the trail so carefully. I'm glad you kept your wits about you.* "They must have knocked Dec out and carried him. It looks like she walked, though. Look at the stumble patterns between the pins. She left us a trail."

Vik carefully picked up each discarded hairpin as if it was a valuable piece of jewelry that Delilah would want to be returned. Eli and I exchanged a look but kept moving. I would buy her a thousand hairpins after this or anything else her heart desired. We slowed down when her tracks were more pronounced. She must have realized they were coming to the end of their journey. I took comfort in the fact that we hadn't found any blood.

"From the smells I'm picking up, this place seems to be crawling with wolves. It'll be easier for me to sneak in and grab Delilah without you two." I didn't want to make this a solo rescue mission but figured it would be safer for everyone if I went in alone. "Once I have her, I can distract the guards, and you guys can grab Dec."

Vik made a face before smoothing out his features and nodding. I knew he didn't like my idea. None of us were getting along with my brother recently due to the bond Delilah and I have. His objections were causing many problems, but he didn't deserve to die. Besides, we knew that our girl would be pissed if we left him behind. I took a few steps back and stripped, leaving my clothes in the hall before shifting into my wolf. I rolled on the dirt floor a little to make myself blend in better.

Eli grabbed the doorknob and turned. We were shocked to find it unlocked. I crept in the door and carefully, padding toward Delilah, glancing at Declan as I walked past him. It was worse than I thought. That video must have been made when the torture was just beginning. Dec was slumped over in the chair. He looked pretty rough. There was no way my brother would be walking out of this on his own. Delilah didn't look much better. This guy would pay for hurting my mate. I would bite him in half.

Looking around the room, I could see that there were no guards. I had an eerie feeling that I was being watched but couldn't tell where the cameras were. I easily chewed through Delilah's ropes binding her hands and feet. It was harder to maneuver her onto my back than I had anticipated. I needed to stay in wolf form for as long as possible, though. Once I had her on my back, I signaled to Eli. I crept toward the door as he and Vik raced forward to get Dec.

Once Eli had helped Vik get Dec, he headed over to help me grab Delilah. Before we could get to her, Vik cried out. We turned to see them on the ground. Eli raced back to see what had happened. "Vik's been stabbed," he whispered before helping Vik up and grabbing Declan.

I kept to the shadows as Eli walked past me, with one arm holding Dec up, and the other around Vik. I started moving toward the door again. There was a noise behind me, metal clanking on metal as if someone had dropped a pipe or a wrench. I turned my head to look, and two guys were trying to sneak up behind me. I carefully slid Delilah to the floor and took a protective stance over her. I growled and bared my teeth at the two men approaching, but neither of them flinched. They kept coming at us, backing me into a corner. I grabbed Delilah by the shirt and dragged her with me. When there was nowhere else to go, I put myself in front of her and tried to fight off the two men.

I clawed and bit at them, but it didn't stop their attack. With us in the corner, I had a better vantage point of the room. I saw the additional guards coming at us before they reached the corner. I couldn't tell how many there were, all I knew was that I was outnumbered. There was little chance of me getting out of here with or without Delilah. And I wasn't about to leave her behind.

I growled as the heavy net was thrown over us, capturing Delilah and myself. The more I fought against the net, the tighter it became. The rope started digging into my fur and compressing my body against Delilah's. Then I felt a sharp pinch on my neck before the world went dark.

I woke sometime later, tied to the same chair Declan had occupied, with Delilah secured to the one next to me. Somehow the drug they'd used to knock me out had forced me to shift. Someone had shown a tiny bit of decency and put a pair of shorts on me before tying me to the chair. It must have been the same person who sent the video to warn me about Dec and Delilah being taken.

I fought against the ropes, feeling them cut against my wrists and ankles. Even with my wolf strength, I couldn't break free. I turned to look at Delilah again. She was slumped to the side, her head resting on her shoulder. I would have feared the worst, but her bruises seemed to be fading, and I could see the slow rise and fall of her chest. I knew that vampires could take a lot of abuse. The only way to kill one was to remove their heart or head. Since she still had both of those, I knew she would eventually heal.

The longer I sat there, helpless and angry, the more I regretted not pushing Delilah to complete the mate bond. If it had already been in place, I would be able to slip into her dreams and talk to her. I would know what she was feeling, and we could share thoughts.

As upset as I was that she had been taken, the reality was that there was no way I could have predicted that she'd be taken. I knew that beating myself up about it was pointless, and instead I needed to focus on getting us out.

CHAPTER 9

Declan

I HAD BEEN NEAR death before, but somehow this was different. It was almost like dreaming as I could see every pivotal moment in my life that had led me to this very spot. My memories played like home movies in my head. I watched as I first met Kayden and we bonded as friends, all the way through to when it all fell apart because I screwed up. I saw myself make the choices that led me to become a vampire.

I followed a younger version of myself as I slowly took over the power in my zone until I was finally in charge. I faced every mistake, every wrong choice, every time I faltered, and failed. Each one of my regrets stood in front of me and looked me in the eye. There was no escape. While I was caught up in my past, my eyes fluttered. I could see movement but couldn't tell exactly what was happening. My head was spinning and I felt weak. Sleep threatened to take me. The voices wouldn't let it.

"Dec, hold on. We've got you." I couldn't place the voice, although it seemed familiar somehow. I bounced between the present and my memories, unsure of what was real and what was imagined. I felt hands on my shoulders and legs. I was being moved somewhere. My body tried to fight. I couldn't leave Delilah, not like this. I bucked and thrashed, although I had no idea if my body actually cooperated. I felt that my arms and legs were freed, but I still couldn't feel them. I was numb and being carried away from my love.

Another voice said, "He's pretty bad off. We should get help." This voice sounded familiar too, but I couldn't figure out who it was. Were they really here to help? Or was this another form of torture by taking me away from Delilah?

The light above changed and I was certain that I'd been taken into another room. The first voice spoke again, "Where is he? I thought he had her." The response was muffled and I heard a door creak. Minutes passed, or hours, I had no way to be sure.

"He's right behind us." Finally, I was able to recognize Vik's voice. It was Eli and Vik who had come to save me. But they should have saved her. She's more important.

I tried to scream but no sound came out. I pushed harder. I needed them to hear me. Muffled groans were all I could muster. "It's okay, Dec. Kayden's got her. He'll be right behind us." Eli's voice registered in my brain and I stopped fighting against his hold. I had to heal so I could go back and end Ghost. My consciousness came and went for a while. It felt like I was being carried again, but I couldn't open my eyes. I knew I had lost too much blood. Ghost was a sick man. I hoped that Delilah was in better shape than I was. I had practically begged him to hit me instead of her. I knew it wouldn't really hurt her less, but it was the only thing I could do to keep him from killing her.

The dreams took me under again and I wasn't sure if any of it was real. I saw Delilah, perfectly healed, walking toward me with a smirk. I knew that look; it was the one that meant I was about to get really lucky. Sex with her was amazing. I couldn't wait to be with her again. There was something wrong with the image—something felt off, as if I was forgetting something important. Oh, I was dreaming; that had to be it. This was just a memory or a fantasy. It wasn't real.

I vaguely heard things happening around me but most of it made no sense. "Oh, no. You didn't say it was this bad," a female voice was nearby.

"Can you patch him up?" Vik, I think, asked. It was strange that he cared if I lived or not. He pretty much hated me.

"It's going to take time and a lot of supplies. Matt, here's a list of what I need. Hurry back with all of it. Get someone to help you if you have to." I knew that voice. Where did I know that voice from?

"I have to start an IV. Bring me the donor bags. This has to be changed every time it runs out until I tell you differently. Understood?" She sounded authoritative. I liked a woman who could take charge.

"We've got it. You tend to his deeper wounds. I can change out the bags when they're empty. Do we have enough supplies here to last until Matt gets back? Should I call Scott?" Eli's second in command had been with us every step of the way here. Just like Steph. Wait—that voice! It was her. I let my mind relax, knowing that my favorite doctor was taking care of me. I trusted her with my life. I stopped listening when they began discussing my injuries. I didn't need to know how bad it was. I was there when it all happened. I would never forget how each blow felt; but the physical pain was nothing compared to the emotional anguish. There was something important I needed to tell the other guys but I couldn't get the words to come out. What was it?

"I have to put him under to stitch him up. He's trying to fight me." Steph's voice permeated my consciousness. Why would I try to fight her? I was trying to tell them about my connection to Delilah; that's what it was. The sire bond gave us the ability to talk telepathically. That thought came and went quickly, as whatever drug Steph used to keep me still, took over and I drifted away. The memories assaulted me again, accompanied by strange fantasies and nightmares. Everything I remembered was twisted into some strange sexual image that included Delilah and random other people. She even showed up in memories from before I knew her. It was getting hard to tell what was real and what was imagined.

An eerie cold set in, chilling me down to my bones. I shivered as I walked down the streets of the city I called home. The images I was seeing turned dark. Everyone I knew was coming after me and I had to run, but I was too weak. They all cornered me in an alley. I trembled as the shadowed figures crept closer to me. Was this what dying felt like?

The last thing I understood was Steph crying out. "There has to be something I missed. He shouldn't be coding. I'm going to have to do exploratory surgery. If I can't find whatever is killing him, we're going to lose him." The fear in her voice was as terrifying as the dark figures who crept ever closer. Steph was talking to someone, giving orders, but she sounded so far away. Her words were jumbled and I didn't know what she was saying. I couldn't reach her. I couldn't get back to Delilah. Darkness enveloped me, swallowing my screams.

Chapter 10

Vik

Eli waited for Kayden and Delilah to return while I helped Steph with Dec. I watched as Declan's body thrashed. He'd begun seizing while Steph was trying to stitch up his wounds. She shouted orders to hand her different instruments and I complied. I realized at that moment that I didn't want him to die, and not just because Delilah cared for him, I had grown fond of him too. He was a part of our family. As I watched Steph work, our mission seemed useless; nothing we did calmed him.

Steph kept trying to figure out where he must be bleeding from, or what Ghost had put in him to cause this reaction, but was having no luck. She gave him a sedative to stop him from hurting himself; finally, after a minute or so, he stopped moving. I wasn't even sure he was still breathing. I let the doctor worry about that while I tried a different approach.

I took a step back and surveyed the situation. Sometimes it helped that I could push my feelings down and be the heartless asshole. What had changed from the moments before? Dec had appeared to be healing slowly. Steph was stitching his wounds. I changed out the blood bag, and he started flailing. "It's the blood! Was this from the supply Matt brought?" I ripped the bag off the stand, tossed it into the sink, and ran for our coolers. I knew that Kayden had hidden part of our supply. I brought back two fresh bags and hooked one up.

Tears fell down her cheeks as she turned away from me. She dropped a small piece of metal onto the tray. "I found this inside of him, but it's too late. He's gone." Steph's quiet admission shattered my heart. How could this have happened? There had to be something we could do.

"I'm not giving up. It won't hurt to let the bag hang. And what about CPR? Are you sure his heart has stopped?" There was no possible way to kill a vamp without taking its head or heart. Neither of those things happened, so he had to recover.

"I've never seen anything like it. His heart is barely beating; once a minute if that. I don't think I can save him," she whispered with her hands over her face. I knew that she felt responsible.

"We have to try," I said, starting compressions. After a moment, Steph took over and we tried for another ten minutes to save him before I heard Eli coming.

"What happened?" Eli raced into the room, frantically searching for whatever had caused this scene.

"Can we test this blood? I think it's tainted," I gestured to the bag in the sink and put my arm around Steph, pulling her away from Dec's body. "You did everything you could. It's up to him now."

Eli nodded and picked up the sample. "I'll get on it and let you know." He strolled out of the room with purpose.

Once Eli left the room, Steph turned to me and buried her face in my chest. I held her while she sobbed, knowing that she would be able to think more clearly after her emotions were spent. I wasn't planning on leaving Declan alone, so I had nothing else to do for the moment. Eli would test the blood and let me know if my suspicion is correct, that it was tainted with the same Powder that had been used on Delilah. Then we would be one step closer to finding out who our mole was.

We knew from the moment we were captured at Eli's that there was one, we just didn't know who they were or which one of us was being betrayed. I reviewed the evidence in my head, not bothering to let Steph know what I was thinking. From her reaction to Dec's state, I was certain she was not the one working against us. But there was no way to know that she wasn't somehow involved—at least not yet. With her tears soaking my shirt, I stared at the unconscious body of my friend, watching him fight for his life.

I fought against the tears that welled up in my eyes. No one knew that I actually cared about him and I preferred to keep it that way. I refused to have the world think I'd gone soft because of my attachment to Delilah. My thoughts circled around until they settled on her; we needed to save her. In order to do that, we would have to figure out why this guy wanted her. I needed Dec to recover so I could question him about what he saw and heard while he was captive.

I knew it was more than that. Declan wasn't just a means to an end, no matter how much I pretended. Looking down, I realized that Steph had cried herself to sleep. I scooped her up, spared a quick glance at Dec, and rushed her into one of the other bedrooms. She needed rest. I paused and wiped the tears from my eyes before going back to my vigil. I was gone for only a moment, fearing the worst if I left him alone. I zipped past Eli, who appeared to be on his way to Dec's room.

Upon my return, I checked and double-checked the IV and the blood bag that was attached to it. He didn't look as pale but was still barely breathing. I was testing the heart monitor when Eli entered the room. "How is he?" His pale blue eyes met mine and he knew before I responded. He crossed the room and pulled me into a hug. It should have been awkward, but we both needed the comfort.

"Not good. He seems to be stable for now. I just don't know if he's going to recover. Did you find anything?" I hoped that my suspicion was right because that would give me a reason to rip someone in half for this. I balled my fists at my sides and stepped away.

"The blood you gave me has the tainted Powder in it. I don't understand how someone tampered with our bags," Eli ran his hands through his hair, never taking his eyes off Dec.

"It wasn't our supply. That blood came from his compound. The guy who came with Steph earlier brought it." The anger in my voice was matched by the murderous glare in Eli's when our eyes met.

"Does she know that's what happened? How many of those bags did he have?" Panic reverberated through Eli as he tried to figure out how to filter the poison from Dec's blood.

I shook my head. "She loves him. It was clear from her reaction when he crashed. They're family. I don't think she even connected it when I asked where that blood bag came from and switched them out." I paced the floor as I spoke, the desire to punch someone barely tethered by what little control I had left. "Kayden's still not back?"

Eli shook his head. "No word yet. We'll keep Steph here, then, in case she's a target too. I hate that we don't know who we can trust anymore." Eli's expression mirrored my own, anguish and fear laced with murder. It wouldn't take much to set either of us off at this point. He stormed out of the room only to return a few minutes later with two laptops. "We can at least do some research while we wait."

I nodded, taking the offered computer. Neither of us would admit just how much things would change if Dec didn't make it. We sat in near silence, each searching for a different piece of the puzzle. Eli ran the financials for all of Declan's employees, trying to find a trail that would expose anyone who was working against us. I spent my time looking for connections between Ghost and Delilah. "It's been a while since we returned. Do you think Kayden got captured?"

"It's possible. We need to figure out who Ghost is so we can take him down. We need a plan before we go back in there." It was clear that Eli was blaming himself. He was right, though, we couldn't just race back into Ghost's hideout.

I lost track of how many hours we sat like that, alternating between our searches and watching Dec. "I think I found something," I said, breaking the silence, and looked from Dec to Eli. He carefully set the computer down and walked over to where I was sitting.

"What is it?" He ran a hand over his face and I noticed that his scruff was turning into a beard. I mirrored his movement over my own face and found it covered with the beginnings of a beard as well.

"I think they may be related somehow. I can't find birth records for her, but there seems to be a connection to Midnight. There are records of an attempted hostile takeover by a man whose last name was Stone. That's her last name, so I did some research into him," I paused and showed him the screen.

Eli took the computer from me and typed something, then read whatever came up in silence for a few minutes.

"It looks like that guy was married and had a son. The wife disappeared, then a few years later, the kid did too. I think you're right; they might be related. The guy and his wife are the right age to be Delilah's parents. I'll start looking more into Vinny and see if I can find a connection there. Great work," Eli patted me on the back and grinned.

"If only that helped us heal him and get her back. I'd even save the wolf if I could," I sighed at the confession.

"I miss them too. We need to know what we're up against and not go off half-cocked," he repeated his statement from earlier. Then Eli walked back over to his seat and picked up his laptop. "We're getting close. We know there's someone inside our circle who's working with them. We know where they're keeping Delilah and Kayden. We'll get them, but Dec has to recover first; we need him with us to go rescue them."

CHAPTER 11

Kayden

A FIST SHOT OUT and my head snapped to the side again. I had lost count of how many times this asshole had punched and kicked me since I woke up. The only positive thing about it was that he was focused on me. That gave Delilah time to heal. She was in pretty bad shape when I came to. I watched her carefully, making sure not to get our captor's attention when I stole glances. Her bruises were fading but her color wasn't coming back. She needed blood. There was only one way I would be able to give her my blood, and it would take careful planning to make it happen.

"Who the fuck are you, anyway?" The hooded man flew into a rage whenever I spoke without permission. It seemed he was a real control freak.

"I am Ghost. You do not have permission to speak. Now I must punish you." Anger pulsed through him, apparent in the way he carried himself. There were very few things he could do to me that would actually risk my death. I was betting that he didn't know that, though. Even if he had the wolves under his control, there were things they would not discuss with anyone. Our weaknesses and strengths were considered sacred secrets by the packs.

The knife came out of nowhere, slicing through the rope binding my wrist at the same time it cut through my skin. "Is that all you've got?" I goaded him into punching me again so I could turn my wrist toward Delilah, spraying her skin with my blood. Shifter healing was faster than vamp, so I knew I didn't have long to get her what she needed. When he stepped away from me again, I quickly turned the blood spray toward him. I needed to buy a little time for her to wake up and get some of my blood in her.

"You nasty mutt. I didn't want to be coated in your disgusting blood. I'll smell like a dog until I take a shower," he huffed and stormed away, leaving my arm free and Delilah coated in my blood.

As soon as he was out of the room, I turned toward her. "Baby, I need you to wake up. You need blood to heal. I did the best I could, but you'll have to lick it off yourself. There was no other way." I stared at her as if I could force her eyes to open. The wait seemed to last forever. I was about to give up when she started to stir.

"What's...smells good," her words were almost imperceptible. Delilah's eyes shot open and she sat up suddenly. "Declan?" Her dark amber eyes met mine. "What happened? Where's Dec?"

"Vik and Eli got him out. I tried to save you and got us both captured. You need to get some of that blood in your system so you can heal. I'm not sure I'll be able to pull that trick again," I explained, running my free hand through my hair to push it out of my face. Delilah's eyes grew wide and I knew that I must look pretty bad, even with the accelerated healing. "It's not as bad as it looks."

"That's good, because it looks awful. What did you do to get beat up so badly? He only tortured Dec when I was awake," she admitted as she started to lick my blood from wherever she could reach. Her moans of pleasure at the taste nearly set me off.

"I goaded him into it. You needed to rest so you could heal. Every time he looked like he was going to wake you up, I smarted off. It wasn't all bad, though. I got you some blood," I grinned at her, warranting a small laugh. It was a beautiful sound and I vowed to make sure I heard it every day once we were out of here.

"Where did he go?" Delilah looked around the room, suddenly terrified. What had this bastard done to her to make her so afraid of him?

"I think he went to shower. He said something about needing to get the dog smell off. I made sure to get blood on him too, so he'd be distracted and leave you alone longer." I fought with the ropes at my other wrist but couldn't get them to budge. There was something strange about this rope; I should have been able to tear through it. I wondered what it was made of that it was able to withstand my wolf strength.

That's it! I'll shift to get out of the restraints! I wasn't sure how I hadn't thought of it before. I concentrated and nothing happened. Whatever drug they'd used to knock me out must have blocked my shifting ability. "I can't shift. They drugged me when we got caught."

"Why would Eli and Vik leave us here?" Concern etched along her features.

"I told them to take Dec and go. He was in really bad shape. Dec was barely hanging on. And I thought we were right behind them," I explained, hoping that she wouldn't hate me for sending them away to save my friend.

She stared at me for a moment, then nodded. "Good. They'll take care of him. We need to break free and get out of here." I was relieved to see her resolve had returned, along with her color. She looked almost healthy now.

"I'm with you, baby, but I'm not sure how to get out of these ropes. I can't break them and can't shift to wiggle out. There has to be a way, though. We'll figure it out." I knew

I shouldn't make promises that I wasn't sure I could keep. All I wanted was to keep her safe. And I would, somehow.

Our conversation was cut short by footsteps. "Oh, good. You're awake. It's time to have some more fun." Unfortunately, his idea of fun didn't line up with mine. I snarled at him, making sure not to pay too much attention to Delilah. I didn't want him to realize that he could use her to hurt me, or vice versa.

He shoved a robed figure toward the center of the room, until they stopped directly in front of us. Ghost made a big show of removing the burlap sack from the man's head. The poor guy was short and stubby. He was balding and pale. The way his eyes darted around the room made me think of a rat in a cage, trying to figure out how to escape. The only interesting thing about him was the amulet that hung from his neck.

I knew this man. He was one of the Council members. Jackson, maybe? I wasn't sure of their names, just that the wolves who joined the hunters reported to the Council. I'd stood in front of him and his partners a few times. His amulet was a blood-red stone, wrapped in leather cording and decorated with silver beads. There were rumors that the amulets held some sort of power, but none of us knew what it was. Why would Ghost have a Council member?

"Now, Council member Jackson, are you going to hand over the amulet?" Ghost spoke, confirming my suspicions of the man's name. Jackson shook his head but didn't say a word. "That's okay, this way will be much more fun." Ghost grabbed the knife he had sliced my arm with earlier and stabbed it into Jackson's chest. The man sputtered and coughed before collapsing to the ground. Then Ghost ripped the necklace from his corpse and put it over his own head.

"I'm sure you're both wondering exactly what that was about. Don't worry, you'll find out soon enough," Ghost's voice was raspy and sent chills up my spine. I didn't have to look to know it had done the same to Delilah. Without another word, he turned and walked away, leaving us to stare at the body lying ten feet from us.

"Why did he do that? He has to have a reason, right? Who the fuck is this guy?" Delilah's words echoed my thoughts.

"I'm not sure, but I think it has something to do with the amulet he took. Each of the Council members wears one. I've heard rumors that they have some sort of magic in them, but I'm not sure what they do," I explained quietly, hoping that our captor wasn't listening to us. I didn't want him to know that I suspected what he was up to.

"Wait, magic is real, too? Does that mean that this guy is some kind of wizard?" Delilah's naivete was shocking, given everything she'd been through lately.

"Yes, magic is real. I don't think Ghost is a wizard, though. He seems like a power-hungry man who is used to taking what he wants." I was baffled that my arm was still free. It was as if he knew that I wouldn't be able to break the other bindings and was flaunting it at me. Perhaps the ropes had been treated with magic to prevent my wolf from shifting and somehow made them unbreakable.

CHAPTER 12

Eli

I LEFT VIK TO watch over Declan while I searched through the records and financials of all of our employees. I needed to find the moles. It was a safe bet that there was more than one within each organization. The key would be to flush them out. I focused on Dec's guys first. Vik suspected Matt, who was Steph's trainee. He was also the newest person at Roarke Inc. I couldn't accuse him without proof, but I could set a trap. Steph had been sleeping for a few hours after being awake for two or three days straight and I had no doubt that she would be out cold for a while longer. I had the perfect idea to find out if he was with us or against us.

I snuck into the room where Steph was sleeping and swiped her phone. I didn't really need an excuse to be in there, since it was the room Vik and I shared, but I moved quickly anyway. After I had the phone in my hand and was on the other side of the door, I breathed a sigh of relief. Now to put my plan into action.

I texted Matt from Steph's phone. *I need your help. Dec took off as soon as he recovered. He found a lead on Ghost. He's supposed to meet someone at Crimson Mist to get a location. I want to follow him and make sure nothing goes wrong. Will you meet me there? And don't tell anyone. There's a spy somewhere and we need to be careful.* I waited a few minutes after I hit send. Would this work?

I'll be there in ten minutes. Matt's response vibrated in my hand. Now I just had to set up the rest of the plan. I dialed on my own phone and waited for Scott to answer.

"Scott, I need you to take a small team to Crimson Mist. Wait in the alley across the street and just observe." I paused for his questions, then responded, "Yes, record everything. Get sound if you can." I didn't wait for confirmation, instead disconnected the call and sat on the couch. I had no doubt that I could trust Scott. I would know soon if the rest of his team was as trustworthy, and if Matt was indeed the inside man who'd tipped Ghost off about our location.

I didn't wait long. Exactly twelve minutes later, my phone rang. "Yeah," I answered, knowing it was Scott calling to give me an update.

"How did you know?" he asked.

"What happened?" I would answer his question when I knew exactly what he thought I knew.

"Hunters raided Crimson Mist. Right after we got here. Our guys caught a rogue vamp hiding in the shadows, too. We're bringing him in for questioning. All I got out of him so far was his name. Matt. But I'm sure you knew that already. I'd love to know how." Scott's voice was laced with curiosity.

I chuckled. "It was a long shot, but I suspected that he'd poisoned Dec. He's probably behind Delilah's poisoning, too. Get what you can from him, then lock him up. We'll deal with him later. If I talk to him right now, I'll kill him."

"Got it, Boss," Scott paused, then said, "Thanks for trusting me."

"I know where you stand." I hung up the phone and went to tell Vik. We'd caught one mole and would have to set up similar operations to make sure there weren't more of them hiding out.

Death hung in the air when I walked into the room. Dec looked the same as he had when I left. Vik was hanging a fresh blood bag. "I'm not sure if he's going to make it. I'm not giving up, but there's been little improvement since you left." His words stabbed me in the heart. I felt his pain as if it were my own. In the past, this would have been enough to send me into a murderous rage, just to stomp down the feelings. I couldn't give in to that feeling again. Delilah wouldn't want that.

"He doesn't look good. Maybe when she wakes up, we can talk about dialysis and if there would be any benefits to it for this. We need to get the toxins out of him," I offered, easing into the reason for my return. "We caught the guy who poisoned the blood. Scott and his team have him."

"Good. They're not going to kill him, right? That will be for us to do once Dec is better." The question wasn't really a question. I nodded to let him know that the kill would be ours. My guys knew better than to ever take matters into their own hands. Scott would do as I asked.

"Have you made any headway with tracking down either Ghost's family or Delilah's parents?" I figured Vik would have said something, but I didn't give him much of a chance when I came into the room. His eyes lit up and he stepped away from Dec to grab his laptop.

"Your news nearly made me forget. I did find something. It's not much, but I searched Vinny's background and found that he had a sister, Sofia Capizzi, who all but disappeared after she finished high school. I think someone scrubbed her. There are no pictures, no documents, nothing after graduation. There are only two pictures of her from when she was a child. And look at this," he said, gesturing to the screen. The woman in the picture looked like a younger version of Delilah.

"That has to be Delilah's mother. Now we just have to track down her father and see if there's a connection to Ghost." I was finally starting to feel optimistic. That feeling didn't last long, as Declan started to seize again. "What's happening? Should I get Steph?"

Vik raced over to him, removing the almost empty blood bag and replacing it with a bag of a clear liquid that I assumed was saline. "It probably wouldn't hurt to go get her. I've had to alternate bags of blood and saline for the last few hours. I thought he was getting better, but this isn't good." Concern laced Vik's voice and I found myself impressed with how determined he was to save the other man. I jogged to the other bedroom to get Steph, hoping that she could help.

"Steph? I'm sorry for bothering you, but Dec is seizing again. Can you come to take a look?" I kept my voice calm but loud enough to wake her if she was still sleeping.

"Hmm? What's going on?" She rubbed her eyes and sat up in the bed. "How did I get in here? Where's Dec?" Her panic crashed into me and I had to hold the wall to get my ability under control.

"You fell asleep, so Vik brought you in here to rest. He's been by Dec's side the whole time, switching between bags of blood and saline. Can you please come and check him out? We're worried." I hated how close I was to begging. I guess Declan meant more to me than I realized, too.

Steph jumped up and followed me to the room Dec was in, too scared to speak. She checked his vitals and read over Vik's notes. Apparently, he'd done a fantastic job as a nurse, noting how much of each blood type he'd used, along with how much saline, and Dec's vitals at each switch. I had no idea that Vik knew so much about taking care of someone. Steph was definitely as impressed as I was.

"This is great. Thank you for keeping such good notes. I'm not sure why he's seizing, though," she admitted, fisting her hands in her hair.

"Well, we have a theory," I began, but Vik cut me off.

"More than a theory—we know it's what happened. Matt spiked the blood bags with poisoned Powder to kill Dec. We need to get it out of his system," he said before returning to the chair he'd all but lived in most of the day.

"Do you have equipment for dialysis? I can't think of anything else that could work," I continued, taking the other seat.

Steph's expression changed from frustrated to pissed. "What do you mean, *Matt* spiked the blood bags? Where is he? I'll tear him apart." I appreciated that she didn't try to defend him or excuse the behavior. She accepted that we had enough proof to make the accusation.

"He's in custody, being interrogated by my guys. Then he's going to be locked up for Dec to deal with once he's healed," I explained.

"Good. Dialysis is definitely an option. Someone will have to run to the hospital and grab the portable machine for me. Can you call Scott? I'll tell him where to go and what to get." I nodded and dialed the phone, explaining to Scott that Steph needed supplies and he was the only one I trusted. I handed the phone to her and motioned for Vik to join me outside the room.

CHAPTER 13

Delilah

"You can't break the ropes either?" I knew that I had already asked Kayden at least three times. I figured that he'd snap at me soon for repeating the same question, but he didn't. He was patient and kind. It was impressive, given that he'd been beaten half to death by a psychopath. He shook his head and scanned the room again. I knew he was looking for a way out. Dec and I had done the same thing when we had been captured.

"They'll come for us," I tried to be positive, even though I was feeling hopeless. "I'm sure of it. We just have to hold out a little while longer." I turned away so Kayden wouldn't see the tears that were about to fall. I knew that my guys loved me, but I wasn't convinced that they would be able to save me from this.

"Hey. Babe, look at me," Kayden commanded before changing his tone. "Delilah, please look at me." I turned back to face him again. "The guys will get us out of here. They have to get Dec patched up first and come up with a better plan. I'm sure they're on it. Don't give up yet." His stormy gray eyes held my gaze. I couldn't look away. It was as if he was pouring his emotions into me through that contact.

I nodded, but before I could say anything else, a slow clap began across the room. Ghost sauntered toward us with a terrifying grin. "How sweet. I'm sure your boy toys will be here soon. Don't worry. I'll make them all feel as welcome as I did the first one and this one. Who knew you were such a slut?"

His words were like a slap in the face. It stung for a moment, but in the grand scheme of things, it didn't matter at all. Why should I care what this creep thought about me? I knew I should keep my mouth shut, but I couldn't help it. "Aww, is someone feeling jealous?" I smirked for added effect, enjoying the way his face scrunched in anger and

411

embarrassment. Ghost ran toward me, throwing his fist out and connecting with my eye. Blood trickled down my face and I could feel the tissue start to swell. It was worth it to get under his skin.

"I am not jealous of you. I would never be jealous of someone so unworthy." He dusted himself off and straightened his robe, making sure his hood stayed in place. Other than the goat/ram mask he wore, the only thing I could see was the stolen amulet. It seemed to glow now, unlike before. I wondered if he had done something to make the magic work for him. The whole concept was new to me, so I wasn't sure how it worked. Once he was calm, Ghost glared at me. "Where were we? Oh, yes. I was telling you about my childhood."

As he spoke, his fists and feet went to work. Every sentence was punctuated by a blow. If he didn't think I was paying attention, he would stop and slap me until I responded the way he wanted. One glance at Kayden and I knew that if he could get free, this man would be dead.

"As I was saying, I remember the night she died." Who was he talking about? I hadn't been listening again. "It was so hot that summer and we didn't have air conditioning. She had promised to come back for me. We were leaving him. That was what she'd told me. Why wouldn't I believe the only person who'd ever stood up for me against him? She had an errand to run, then she would come back for me." His smile was sad as if he had cared for this woman, whoever she was.

"But she lied. She didn't come back. Do you want to know why?" I didn't really care at this point but figured I'd better play along.

"Why didn't she come back?" My tone must have annoyed him because he struck me in the face before grabbing my chin and forcing me to look into his dark eyes.

"Because of you."

Ghost shoved me and turned away. "What did I have to do with it?" I found myself very interested in his story now. In my peripheral vision, I saw Kayden leaning forward to hear the rest as well.

"The bitch was planning to take me to you. But he found out and stopped her. He killed her right in front of me. I watched as he beat her, then let her rest. Each time, she thought he was done and she would survive. She was wrong. Before he knocked out her teeth, she told him she should have stayed with you instead of looking for him." Ghost dropped his head and turned away, obviously in pain from the words.

"Who was she?" The question was out before I could stop myself. I was almost certain I already knew the answer.

Ghost whipped around to face me again with a wicked smile. "Our mother, of course."

"*Our* mother? You're saying that you are my brother. How is that possible?" Another punch to my gut and he started to laugh maniacally.

"She told me stories of you at first, until he made her stop. She wanted us to be a family. He wasn't interested, which was why he left you in the first place. Every time she would run away, he would find her and bring her back. She would abandon me to see you. It was always—*oh, I'll take you next time,* and *soon, my boy, soon.* She lied. She always lied.

So, I told him what she was planning and he killed her." His voice was raspy and held nothing but contempt for the woman who had given us life. Of course, that part hadn't been proven yet. I only had his word for it. The story must have distracted him, because he stopped hitting me and simply stared.

"Who was he?" It didn't matter, except that if I survived this, I would rip him in half for killing my mother and torturing that sad little boy.

"Our father, Aaron Stone. But don't worry. I've already taken care of him as well. I used him to kill her, and to teach me how to be strong. Then when he least expected it, I slit his throat, just like I did to your precious Uncle Vinny. That was a special kill. I modeled it after your lover's preferred method. Did you like that present, dear sister?" The saccharine sweetness in his voice gave me chills. My brother had been the one to kill the man who had raised me.

I took my time processing the new information. If everything Ghost said was true, he had every reason to resent me. But there was no justification for the things he had done or the hatred he felt for me. It wasn't my fault he'd suffered. That blame belonged to our parents. I knew that Mom had chased after my father, but she never told me that she'd found him. I didn't know about the abuse or her attempts to escape it. I glanced at Kayden and found sadness in his eyes. I wasn't sure if it was for me or my brother.

I knew better than to just take Ghost's word for it, but something about his story made sense. I believed him. I wanted to know more but knew that asking was risky. He could decide to kill us or simply torture us more; so I had to be very careful about what I asked and how.

"Brother?" I began, waiting for Ghost to slap or punch me again. When his eyes simply met mine, I continued, "What is your name?"

"No. No, no, no. You will not feel sorry for me. You will absolutely not pity the boy who was abused and watched his mother die." His tone was frantic and I feared I'd made a mistake.

I shook my head, waiting for him to finish his rant. "I don't feel sorry for you. I am sad that you suffered, but look how much stronger it made you. I only wanted to know your name. I didn't know that I had a brother. That is the only thing I'm sorry for. I didn't treat you that way. If I had known about you, I would have protected you." My earnest words upset him and his fist connected with my jaw. I felt the bone crunch as it broke beneath the strike.

Tears flowed down my cheeks as he leaned close and whispered in my ear, "My name is Gerolf, but if you call me that, I will kill your lover." I nodded and closed my eyes, expecting another blow to come. When it didn't, I slowly opened my eyes again. Ghost was gone. I felt Kayden's eyes on me but I refused to face him. I needed some time to heal and figure out what to do about my brother.

CHAPTER 14

Vik

When Scott arrived with the equipment Steph had asked for, I left Dec's side long enough to help carry it in. After that, I learned how to set it up and what we needed to do to make it work. Dialysis for a vampire was a strange process. Dec would need a mix of human and vamp blood. I rolled up my sleeves to donate but Steph stopped me. "I'll have to do a test to see if any of us match," she explained, pulling out needles and vials. She drew some blood from Declan first and tested it to determine the type.

She drew blood from Eli and me, then from herself. Scott refused to leave until he was certain that he wasn't a match. Steph drew his blood and tested it first, making sure to note his blood type. "Sorry, Scott, you can't donate to Dec. I'll keep a record, though, in case this comes up again." He nodded to Eli and walked out the door. Eli stepped out after him and they had a hushed conversation while Steph tested the other blood samples.

"Vik, I appreciate that you want to help him, but you and I don't match either. There is one person who can donate, though. Eli is a match," Steph glanced at him, still talking to Scott outside the door. I knew she was nervous that he wouldn't give blood to help Dec, but I knew Eli better than she did. He would do whatever it took to cure Dec.

Eli walked back into the room. "Scott is taking over the hunt for other moles. Hey, Steph, you look like someone kicked your puppy. Is everything okay?" He could sense her nerves. He'd explained to me how his gifts worked and I knew how difficult it was for him to block strong emotions.

"She found a match," I explained, waiting to see if he would realize it was him.

He cocked an eyebrow and shrugged. "Isn't that a good thing?"

"It's you. Honestly, I was disappointed that it wasn't me. I think Steph is worried that you won't donate." Eli nodded at my words, understanding the emotions that were assaulting him.

"Steph, I'll give as much as I can to make him better. He's part of this family now. We can't lose him. Delilah would kill us if we let anything happen to him," Eli chuckled, obviously imagining Delilah chasing after him. It was an amusing thought, but neither of us wanted to find out how true it was.

Steph calibrated the equipment and took two pints of blood from Eli. "We'll have to run one bag of human, then one bag of vamp. When someone is turned, the proteins in their plasma change. For some reason, it doesn't matter what type of human blood we use, the proteins don't react with it. But with vampire blood, if you don't use the right type, it can kill."

"So, we're going to try swapping out four pints of blood total?" I wished I could give some of mine to make sure there was enough, but I wanted to help, not kill the guy.

She nodded, handing Eli an extra bag of blood. "Drink this. You need to rest for a while. Most donations are one pint, not two. You might feel lightheaded for a bit. It'll pass."

While Steph got the machine started, I took Eli into the other bedroom. We still needed a plan to get Delilah and the wolf back. "What are we going to do?" I asked once he was settled.

"I'm not sure. We need Dec, or we'll never get them back. The two of us can't manage it. We don't know how many guards the guy has. There's so much more that we don't know, but that's the biggest thing." Eli ran his hands through his hair and stared at the wall. I knew he was trying to come up with a plan that would get us in and out without being caught.

"We can bring in all of our guys. We'll just storm the place. That has to work, right?" Desperation was taking hold and I wanted to leave now to get our girl. It was killing me that she wasn't safe. I knew he felt the same, so I didn't push too hard.

Eli turned to look at me. "It won't work. There are too many variables. He'll kill her before we can get to her if we storm the place. That defeats the whole purpose."

"I know, but I can't just sit here knowing that some asshole is torturing her. We need to figure this out," I ranted at him, expecting Eli to get in my face or throw a punch. I was feeling antsy like I needed a fight. I welcomed the thought of fists flying, but it didn't happen.

"It won't do any good and you know it." Eli stared at me with a smirk.

"Yeah, I know, but I can't come up with another way besides storming in," I replied, fisting my hands in my hair.

He shook his head. "Not that. Me punching you won't do any good. I know you're itching to start something. We need to get Dec healed up so we can go after Delilah and Kayden. That has to be the priority."

I knew he was right. "Okay. Did you find anything else on Ghost?" I figured changing the subject was a better idea than pushing back and trying to fight.

"I think so. It looks like he might be Delilah's brother. I still couldn't find any birth certificates for either of them. I did find her parents' marriage certificate and some text messages between Delilah's mom and uncle that sounded like she was pregnant." Eli's words shocked me. Our girl had a brother that no one knew about.

"Are you sure?" I couldn't stop the question from tumbling out. Of course, he wasn't sure. He'd just said there was no actual confirmation, just rumors, and speculation.

"I can have Scott go to the neighborhood where the kid grew up and question people. Other than that, I'm not certain. It feels right, though. That would explain why this guy is targeting her. If he has some sort of twisted vendetta against his family, that could be the reason for all of this." Eli grabbed his laptop and started typing frantically. Then he turned it around, showing me the documents that he'd been searching through. "This is obviously Delilah's mother. They look almost identical. And here's a picture I found of her pregnant but there's no way to tell if this was with Delilah or her brother. His name is Gerolf, and there is nothing actually connecting him to Ghost."

"Hmm. This is a good start. Maybe we can use the family thing against him to get her back. Or at least to distract him long enough for us to break them out." I knew that my suggestion was weak, but I was grasping at straws. I hadn't slept since we got back with Declan. Oh, shit. I needed to get back to him. But figuring this out was important too.

I hated showing weakness. It was my biggest flaw and the reason why so many people thought I was a heartless dick. I made sure to hide any emotion I had and do what needed to be done. I wasn't sure I could keep that wall up anymore; it was getting harder every day to hold it all back. But so far, the feelings hadn't stopped me from being ruthless. Sometimes it was the only way.

I couldn't wait to get my hands around Matt's throat for what he'd done to Dec. I stared into space, imagining ripping him in half and pulling his intestines out to show him before I tore his heart out. Or maybe I would remove limbs first, one by one, while he screamed and begged for his life. His pleas would fall on deaf ears because I had already decided his fate the moment my suspicions were confirmed. Maybe I would string him up and drain his blood, keeping him alive and miserable for decades before I gave him the release of death. There were so many delicious torture options to choose from. Ultimately, we would ask Dec what he wanted to do and go from there. But I would be prepared if he gave me free rein.

I must have started drooling over my torture fantasies because Eli shook me to get my attention. "Vik! Are you okay? You spaced and it freaked me out." His words brought me back to the present.

"Sorry, I was imagining different ways to deal with our traitor. You know how much I enjoy that kind of thing." It was a half-hearted apology, but Eli smiled when I explained what had happened.

"That explains it, then. I knew it had to be either torture or sex that you were fantasizing about. I was hoping for torture actually." His laughter echoed for a moment, sounding more ominous than I think he had intended.

CHAPTER 15

Declan

I DON'T KNOW HOW long I was out before I started to hear voices again. My dreams were crazy. There was no way a man held me captive and tortured me to the edge of death. Even as that thought crossed my mind, I knew it was wrong. I had felt every blow. *And he did worse to Delilah.* That thought pushed me forward, egging me to find a way back to the real world. That was when the voices started again.

If only I could understand everything they were saying. At the very least, I knew they were friendly. I concentrated and picked out each voice that entered the room. I was pretty sure I hadn't been left alone for more than a moment since the last time I heard them. Vik had stayed with me, talking about fighting, not giving up, coming back to the family. Eli had popped in a few times to discuss research and check on my progress. And Steph. She had been there for a long while before she left. When she came back, they talked about something that might help me. Then I was under again.

I tried to will myself to wake up. I could feel that my injuries were healed. Why had they been so desperate to save me? I must have missed something in their conversation. For a while, I had floated on a fluffy cloud of...of what? Why was I floating? That had to be a side effect of nearly dying. No. I wasn't giving up. I would fight my way back to Delilah. She would need me to get through what that monster had done to her.

I forced my eyes to open. Slowly, they cooperated and I was able to see the room I was in. It was the bedroom that I shared with Kayden. That dick hadn't come to see me once while I was hurt. Knowing that stung, but I wouldn't hold it against him any more than anything else he'd done to me lately. I glanced around the room and saw Steph messing with some machine that I was attached to.

"What does that do?" My voice was raspy from not speaking for so long. Steph squealed and jumped before turning to me with tears in her eyes.

"I thought I was going to lose you," she confessed. "I'll get the others and we'll explain everything." She dashed out of the room but was only gone a minute before two large figures followed her back in. Relief washed over Vik and Eli, but I wasn't sure why.

"Where's Kayden? I know he's mad at me, but he could at least show a little concern," I growled the words out and watched as all three expressions changed. Something had happened to him. My scowl melted away. "What happened to him? Is he hurt? Where is he?" The questions were frantic, but the thought of losing my brother hurt more than any real or imagined betrayal that sat between us.

Vik and Eli exchanged a glance before Eli stepped forward. "He was captured when we saved you. The good news is that he's with Delilah; the bad news is that Ghost still has them both."

"We're working on a plan to get them back, but we need you. It's going to take all three of us," Vik added softly. Steph's eyes opened wide as if she'd just had an idea.

"I'm coming with you." She turned to glare at me. "Don't tell me no, and don't try to stop me. I'm going to help you with this."

I nodded. Steph was a force to be reckoned with, and when she put her mind to something, she nearly always got her way. I wouldn't stop her. It appeared that Eli and Vik agreed. "We still need a plan, unless you guys came up with something while I was out." I felt groggy from the anesthesia. There was something important I needed to tell them, but I couldn't quite remember what it was.

"Eli has been working on hacking into their surveillance cameras. I think he's made headway, but we're not in yet. That will help us find the best way in and decide what time will be the easiest." Vik's hand fisted in his hair. I had never seen him this disheveled before. He was always in a suit and always put together. But he'd been wearing Eli's or my clothes since we'd been hiding out, and it looked like he'd given up shaving.

Eli didn't look much better, but his blond beard was less noticeable than Vik's dark one. They both had dark circles under their eyes as if they hadn't slept in a while. I wondered if they had enough blood since they seemed to be running everything through me. Speaking of which, I wanted to know what that was all about. "What is this machine? What happened to me after we got back here? I felt like I was getting better, then suddenly I was floating and heard you guys talking about me dying."

"Vik figured it out. Matt mixed some of the tainted Powder into the blood bags he brought with the supplies to save you. I guess he planned to kill you off. Or maybe it was meant for all of us. Either way, Vik figured it out and saved you." Eli smiled at his old friend while he spoke. I wondered if they realized the kind of love that they had for each other. There would be time for exploring that when we got our girl back. I knew she would love to watch.

"This is a dialysis machine, which just means it filters your blood. It removes the tainted blood, filters it, and replaces it with the cleaned blood, in addition to the blood that Eli donated. So, it wasn't just Vik who saved you. Eli was part of it too. His guys caught Matt;

they're holding him for interrogation and if I understood correctly, you'll decide what happens to him." Steph's voice dropped to a whisper when she spoke of Matt and his betrayal. How could my friend have done this to me?

"How much longer will it take, doc?" I was anxious to get the plan in place and rescue my brother and Delilah. I was feeling stronger than I had in a while. I furrowed my brow in concentration. What was it that I needed to tell them?

"Since you're awake, when this bag is empty, you're free to go. There's no reason we can't start planning now, though. How close are you to getting into the feeds?" Steph directed the question to Eli, who had already grabbed his laptop and started typing.

"I think I've got it. I had to code a program to do it, but I think we're in." He turned the screen around and we watched as Delilah and Kayden had a conversation with Ghost. There was no sound, but it looked like he'd said something that deeply hurt our girl. I would rip the guy in half for that. Then I would tear pieces of him off until there was nothing left.

We stared at the video, trying to make sense of the guards' coming and going. They didn't seem to have a schedule, but that just meant it was randomized. All we had to do was figure out how they did it, and we'd be golden. Vik and Eli tossed ideas back and forth while Steph unhooked me from the machine. I was amazed at the lengths they'd gone to in order to save my life.

Watching the video feed reminded me of the torture I'd suffered, mostly at watching Ghost hurt Delilah. She was so strong; even when things felt hopeless, she'd kept her cool and reminded me that she loved me. *Wait, that was it. Delilah!* "I have an idea. It's going to involve us getting close, but it just might work."

Steph, Eli, and Vik turned and stared at me. "Let's have it," Vik said, sounding more like his usual grumpy self, even though it didn't quite mask the relief that still shined in his eyes.

"When Delilah and I were being tortured, we realized that she and I can communicate telepathically. It has to be something with the sire bond. It may have happened because of the trauma we were dealing with. I'm not sure. But if we can get close, I can have her distract Ghost long enough for us to get in and find them." I watched their faces as I spoke. Fear, disbelief, wonder—each of them held a different expression. "Well? What do you think?"

Vik nodded, saying, "I like it. I think it could work."

"I agree. We need to know more about the guards and their schedules first, but it does seem like the best plan," Eli responded, running a hand over his face. These guys needed to rest before we did any sort of rescuing.

"Let me watch the guards for a while. You guys need to rest," I insisted, reaching for the laptop. "Besides, I can watch from right here, so I won't be overexerting myself." Steph chuckled as I thwarted her objection before it could leave her lips.

"A couple of hours couldn't hurt. You haven't slept at all since we brought him back," Eli turned to Vik, motioning for them to leave my room. I was certain if they crashed, it would be more than a couple of hours.

CHAPTER 16

Eli

AFTER VIK AND I took longer naps than planned, we woke to find Declan writing on the walls of his room with chalk. He had made a chart of the guards' movements, which were more planned out than we thought. What looked random was simply a very specific timetable meant to throw us off. It appeared as if Dec had used his five hours wisely and the plan was all but complete.

"You did all of this while we were asleep?" I marveled at the intricacy of his notes. He'd given the guards names based on their descriptions and had their schedules down to the minute.

"I did, but Steph helped. Sorry that we didn't wake you. Steph told me how you guys took care of me and of her. I just wanted to pay it back a little." His disheveled red hair hung around his face in loose ringlets. Showers were definitely in order for all of us.

"This is fantastic work," Vik praised Dec, and the other man's shock was evident. We were all used to Vik being so hateful that when he was nice, everyone noticed. "What? He did good work. Can't a guy compliment another guy without everyone looking at him like he's grown an extra head?"

"Maybe we wouldn't look at you that way if you didn't act like you hated everyone all the time," I countered. I couldn't help but laugh when Vik stuck his tongue out at me. He'd never done anything so immature before. It was good that he was loosening up a bit.

"I'm not that bad," Vik insisted, turning his gaze toward Dec for confirmation.

"I'm gonna grab a shower while you guys review our plan." Dec ignored Vik's comment, grabbing his clothes and heading into the bathroom. Steph and I both doubled over with laughter.

"It's okay, Vik. I know you mean well. Let's see what Dec figured out and get our plan in place." I walked over to inspect Dec's notes more closely. I read through everything on the walls three times to make sure I understood. Vik took his own notes and made some calculations based on how long it would take us to get there and back.

"If we leave here in three hours, we'll get to their base during one of the guard changes. That will give us a chance to get close enough for Dec to talk to Delilah and have her distract Ghost. We should be able to take out all of the guards before we approach them," Vik explained his idea, showing me the math that backed it up.

"That looks good. The guard change will let us take out two sets of guards before moving on to the next section. Or we could split up and enter from three different spots. That would let us take out even more guards before we hunted down the rest," I suggested, pointing out where on the crude map Dec had scrawled on the opposite wall.

"Perfect. Steph can go with Dec. I know he said he's fine, but confronting your torturer would be hard on anyone." Vik's concern was touching. I'd have to remember to tell Dec about it later.

"Agreed. So, we have three hours to prepare. I'll write it all out for Dec to review. You can start gathering supplies. I'll even let you have the next shower," I offered, not telling him that it was a reward for him showing feelings for Dec.

"Sounds good." He stood and left the room. I wasn't sure what he would decide were necessary supplies, but knowing Vik for as long as I had, he would probably call Scott and ask him to deliver a case of weapons. It should have been strange for my second in command to become his as well, but it worked. Scott was the most loyal employee either of us had.

While Vik was taking care of supplies, I pulled up a blank document and typed out the idea that Vik and I had come up with. Vik would enter from the north, while I approached from the south, leaving the east to Steph and Dec. There wasn't an entrance on the west from what we could tell. Splitting up would allow us to take out more guards more quickly than everyone staying together. I had just finished detailing the plan when Dec came into the room.

"Where did Vik go?" he asked, glancing casually around the room.

With a smirk, I responded, "He's gathering supplies. Give him a break, he's trying." Dec laughed and sat on the bed. I shoved the laptop over to him.

"I know he is. It's just weird. I'll get used to it at some point," he laughed. "What am I looking at?"

"That's our plan. Your notes were amazing. I can't believe you figured out their schedule so precisely. We're going to leave in about two and a half hours. I have to find Vik and take over his job so he can shower." I stood up to leave, but Dec held up a hand.

"Thank you. I need to thank you both, but I don't know how. You didn't have to save me, but you did. Each of you gave a piece of yourself to do it, and I won't forget that." The sincerity of his words pressed against my heart. I knew he meant every word.

"Don't worry about it. We're family. It's what we do," I said casually before strolling out of the room. I was glad that he'd had that conversation with me. Despite his recent softening towards Dec, Vik might not have been so receptive.

I found Vik huddled up with Scott, packing small bags with weapons for each of us to carry. "Hey, Scott. Vik, you're up. I'll take over here. Scott can fill me in," I nudged Vik to get him to move.

"Yes, mother. I'm going, stop shoving," he teased as he walked away. Scott looked at me as if he wanted to say something.

"What is it?" There was no point in beating around the bush, I had always offered him the opportunity to speak freely with me. He never pulled punches and told it exactly like it was.

"I'm worried about you guys going in there alone. The plan seems solid, but I don't like it. I want to go. I can bring a few guys with me," he offered. It wasn't a bad idea.

"I tell you what. I'll compromise a little. We have this all planned to the minute. Gather your guys and wait here. If we don't make it back at the exact time we're supposed to, you come after us. Deal?" I knew he would hate it, but I wasn't going to risk anyone else to save my girl.

"I hate that idea, but it makes sense. Can we wait in the tunnels at least? I'll get the guys. But if you're even ten seconds late, we're moving in. That guy won't know what hit him." Scott's hands fisted at his sides. "He won't get away with this, sir, we'll make sure of it."

I listened as Scott made calls to gather his crew. I knew that his loyalty went further than his paycheck. That was why I had agreed to let his crew wait in the tunnels for us. We'd been together since I'd been turned and I trusted him with my life. He'd never let me down before, and I was certain he wouldn't now. "The guys will be here in just a few minutes. They're stopping to grab a couple of Vik's guys and a few from Dec's place, too. We'll have an army to back you up, Boss."

Scott's declaration changed things. I needed to talk to the others. The plan was changing, but it might just work to our advantage. "I'll be back in a bit. I'm gonna talk to Dec and Vik." I left Scott waiting for his newly formed crew to arrive.

I found Vik and Dec discussing the plan. "I'm making one change to the plan. I think it might give us an advantage." My announcement had them both turning to look at me. I was certain I looked half-crazed. They waited for me to explain without saying anything. "Scott gathered some guys from each of our zones. They want to back us up. I was going to make him wait here and see if we needed backup, but I think the numbers might be in our favor. We can still go in stealthy, having our 'troops' cover the guards while we go after Ghost."

"Are they all willing to risk their lives for us like that?" Dec asked. The concern on both of their faces matched my own. I didn't want to take the chance that any of our guys would get hurt either.

"Apparently, we have no choice. Scott talked to Steph about what was going on and he decided that they were going to help no matter what." When Vik and Dec nodded their agreement, I scrubbed my face with my hands and headed for the shower. We had to get ready. We were about to go to war.

CHAPTER 17

Kayden

I thought for a moment that Delilah was bonding with her brother. At first, she was uncertain that he was telling the truth. I could smell his fear when he told the stories. I knew he was being honest about everything. He hated Delilah because she grew up with the love that he never got. He felt that their mom had been more worried about her than him, and their dad was an abusive loser. Once she realized he wasn't lying, her demeanor changed. I knew she pitied him, even though she swore that wasn't what she felt. I could smell her emotions. If we had completed the mating bond, I would be able to feel them as if they were my own. This was the first moment since I'd been captured that I was relieved we hadn't fully mated.

I wanted her more than I had ever wanted anyone before. I always knew that the pull would be strong if I actually found my fated mate, but after Shannon died, I stopped looking. It wasn't important. We'd been convinced that once I came of age, it would be her that I was meant to be with; I guess we were wrong about that. I found that I was finally at a point where I could remember her without the intense pain. I knew that was partially because of the bond; anything I had ever felt for anyone else was dampened because of how strongly I was drawn to Delilah.

Ghost's fist knocked my head to the side, bringing me out of my memories. He had been docile a few minutes ago when Delilah was trying to connect with him. Then she'd asked for his name and he lost it. He'd started hitting and kicking her until he realized that she wouldn't scream for him. Her strength amazed me. It was hard for me to steel myself against the blows that seemed never-ending. I had no idea how she was holding back her reactions. The only way I could tell that she was upset that he was beating me was the tears that she couldn't stop from falling.

Ghost seemed to revel in her pain; it gave him an added incentive to beat me more. Then suddenly he stopped. My left eye was swollen shut; I had a cut over my right eye. I couldn't tell how many broken bones I had, nor could I count the bruises that seemed to cover my entire body. As a wolf, especially a hunter, I was trained to take this kind of abuse. I would never break, no matter what he did to me. But it was hard to hold back when he started hurting her. I wanted to rip him in half. I didn't care that it was her brother.

"Oh, silly wolf. Are you getting angry? That's cute. Hold onto that feeling. It's only going to get stronger. Just wait until you see what happens next. But first, a test is in order." Ghost hopped up and down clapping like a child as he spoke.

He snapped his fingers and someone approached from behind me. I tensed as soon as I saw the blade. The guy slid it carefully between my skin and the wood of the chair, cutting me free. *What was the endgame here? Didn't he know that I wanted to kill him?* The second I was loose, I jumped from the chair and dashed toward Ghost. He looked at me calmly and said, "Stop." The amulet around his neck glowed, and even though I wanted to tear him apart, I found myself stuck. I couldn't move. *Oh, no.*

"Very good. Yes, this will do nicely. Now for the test." Ghost turned toward Delilah, grinning from ear to ear. "Watch closely, dear sister, your fate shall be revealed."

"You can't make me hurt her. I won't do it," I warned, knowing that I wouldn't be able to stop myself from obeying his commands. I struggled, trying to break free. No matter how hard I tried, I couldn't move anything but my mouth. And yelling at the guy didn't seem to do any good.

"Oh, but I can. Watch," he said slyly, turning away from Delilah and pointing at the guy who had freed me. "Kill him." My eyes opened wide as the command took hold. I tried desperately to resist. I didn't want to kill anyone, much less in front of Delilah.

On their own, my feet started stomping toward the smaller man. When his eyes met mine, I growled, "Run." Even as the word came out of my mouth, my hands gripped his shoulders. He never had a chance. I stood there, holding him against both of our wills. For a moment, I thought I could resist. *I don't have to do this. I can stop myself.* No sooner was the thought in my head than I had ripped the man's arms from his body. Even though he would bleed out, I kept tearing at him. I couldn't stop until his heart stopped beating. The kill command had been so strong that I couldn't refuse.

Tears streamed down my face, mixing with the stranger's blood that coated my skin. I turned to face Delilah, expecting to see fear and disappointment in her eyes. Instead, I saw understanding. She knew that I had tried to fight it. Ghost's demand forced my actions as if a demon had taken over my body. I was still here but had no control. I wanted to run from her, to protect her from the monster I had become. All my years spent as a hunter, and I never realized that I was just a trained dog on a leash. I wondered if they'd used that amulet on me before, making me do things I didn't want to and then somehow erasing the memory.

"That will do nicely. Oh, don't look so upset. We're just getting started, it's not over yet." Ghost walked over to me and reached up to pat my cheek. I wished I could move to bite his hand off. "Now go back to your chair and sit still. I have some preparations to take care of, then I'll be back. Do not get out of the chair until I give you permission."

I growled as I marched back to the chair and sat down. I fought against the compulsion with every fiber of my being, but couldn't stop myself from obeying him. Once he left the room, I was able to relax a little more, but still couldn't leave the chair. I had no idea if the amulet had to be close for its powers to work, or if I would have to do what he said no matter where he went.

I turned to face Delilah. "I'm sorry you had to see that. I tried to fight it, but it was like I had no control over my own body." Tears welled in my eyes again as I silently begged for her forgiveness.

"You have nothing to apologize for, Kayden. I know you would never have done that without the magic forcing it. Please don't turn away from me now. I need your strength to boost mine. I'm not sure how much longer I can take all of this. I just want to go home." Tears streamed down her face as she finally broke down. It was the first time I'd seen her lose her composure since we'd been here. I knew that Ghost had kept her from feeding. Most vamps would have been driven crazy by now.

"Babe, you are stronger than you realize. I couldn't have handled half what you did today. It's okay to take a minute and fall apart. Just know that the second he comes back, you have to be ready to fight. I need to know that you won't give up." My voice caught at the end of my words. The look in her eyes suggested that she understood what I had implied.

"But I can't," she began.

"You have to. Just put your fist through my ribcage and tear out my heart. Don't let me kill you if he commands it. Promise me. Because if you don't, you know they will. I never want to hurt you. I will protect you until my last breath." I knew that my thoughts were too much for her. Asking the girl you were falling in love with to kill you wasn't exactly romantic. But if I killed her, I would never forgive myself. And if the other guys didn't rip my heart out for it, I would do it myself—right after I tore Ghost's head off.

Delilah held back her tears. I knew that she didn't want to hurt me any more than I wanted to hurt her. "I promise, I won't just let you kill me. I'm not sure that I'm strong enough to stop you, though. But I will fight back and I will try to escape. If I have to kill you, I'll try. That's the best I can do."

CHAPTER 18

Delilah

AGREEING TO KILL ONE of the men I wanted to spend the rest of my life with was the hardest thing I'd had to do yet. I knew that there was no way I could overpower Kayden and take him down. But I promised that I would try if it came to my life versus his. I made peace with the fact that I would probably die by his hand. Honestly, I would rather Kayden kill me than Ghost. Or maybe I should just call him Gerolf. That was the name our parents gave him, after all.

It was hard to believe that Mom had kept my little brother a secret. But the more I thought about it, the less surprised I actually was. She wasn't around, and when she was, she was obsessed with my father. *I have to find him, D. I just love him so much.* It was sad what addiction could do to a person. I knew when she had said the words that she really meant he had her drugs. Uncle Vinny knew it too. Pain stabbed my heart at the thought of Gerolf killing my uncle. He would always be *my* uncle, not ours. That bastard didn't deserve him.

Wait, did I actually remember something? The more I thought about it, I realized that most, if not all, of my memories had come back since Gerolf had started torturing me. I knew who I was before Jones shot me, and I knew who I was now. They weren't that different, but my human self was less willing to risk herself for anyone. I was more willing to let someone take care of me back then, whether it was Uncle Vinny or my guys. I remembered Vik and Eli fighting over me before they finally forced me to tell them that I wanted them both. I knew myself, finally.

I wasn't sure if it helped or hurt to find out that my brother was the one who had been drugging me so I would kill. I had known it wasn't my fault, but I would always take

427

responsibility for my actions. I remembered what I did to that girl. I even remembered what she'd said to me just before I did. She insisted on coming into the changing room, saying I would need help with the zipper on that red dress. Then she threw the Powder in my face and said, "Ghost sends his regards." I shook my head and blinked a few times as the drug took hold, then I pounced on her.

I shuddered at the memory, knowing I couldn't focus on that or he would win. We *were* going to escape. Kayden and I would get out of here, whether Vik, Eli and Dec came to get us or not. I wasn't giving up. We just needed a plan.

"Kayden, can you shift at all?" I asked, keeping my head low and speaking quietly. I didn't want to chance anyone who may be watching to realize what I was asking.

"I can try," he replied. "But I can't get out of this chair." I turned my eyes to meet his and saw the moment he realized that I had a plan. The grin that spread across his handsome face matched the one I wore. I watched as he tried to shift, forcing his wolf to the surface. "I can't fully shift."

"Can you get your claws out?" I winked at him, encouraging him to try again.

I watched as he fought with his wolf again, pulling it to the surface, this time focusing on his hands. His fingers swelled and split, leaving beautiful wolf paws where his hands had been. "Perfect. Now all you have to do is cut me free."

"I can't leave this chair. How am I supposed to do that?" He hadn't realized what I had. Ghost told him he couldn't leave the chair, not that the chair had to stay where he'd put it.

"So, bring the chair with you. Cut me free, and we'll take it with us." I wiggled my eyebrows at him, making him chuckle.

"Hmm, that might work." Kayden started to pull on the chair and rock it from side to side. The bolts holding it to the floor gave way, and the chair was free. He grabbed it by the arms, holding the chair to his bottom, and crab-walked toward me.

He silently dropped the chair next to me and sliced through the ropes on my wrists before leaning down to get the ones on my ankles. The second I was free, someone started to slow clap. "Fuck," Kayden whispered. I agreed completely. We watched as Gerolf slowly walked toward us. I knew there was no way we could run with him so close. He would command Kayden to stop, or worse, to kill me on the spot. Kayden and I sat there, waiting to see what was about to happen.

"I should have expected my dear sister to figure out a loophole to my command. It was a good thing I didn't go too far. I guess we'll just move up our timetable. Oh, well. It's not my life that's ending. I wanted to play with my new toy for a while longer, but you've sucked the fun right out of it." He walked closer until he was standing right in front of me. Tremors of fear wracked my body, though I kept my face expressionless.

"What, no snarky comment, sis? I really thought you were smarter than this. Why did she favor you? I mean, sure, you're pretty, but how far can that truly get you in life?" He was baiting me, trying to get a reaction. I forced myself to yawn, declaring my boredom at his antics.

Gerolf leaned close, grabbed my hair, and yanked my head back, exposing my neck to him. He drew a knife from his robe and caressed it against the soft skin, leaving a small trail of blood behind. Kayden growled at him, but couldn't do anything to stop it. I took a deep breath, realizing that it could be my last, and forced my heart to slow down. I wouldn't let him know that he was getting to me if I could help it.

"Don't get worked up, wolf. You're still going to get the kill. Would you care to know how you'll do it?" I watched as fear took over Kayden's features. We both knew this was coming. We just had to find a way to stop it. "I'll take your silence as a yes. You're going to bite her."

I raised an eyebrow at my brother's words and he loosened his grip on my hair. When the knife dropped from my throat, I asked, "You're going to make him eat me? That's sick."

"Not eat you, perv. Bite you. Wow, you really are stupid. Wolf shifter bites are fatal to vampires. Why do you think the wolves are sent to police the fang bangers?" His laughter surrounded me and I felt like I was drowning in it.

One bite would be fatal? I saw the truth written on Kayden's face. How did no one tell me this? As hard as it would be to fight him off as a man, it would be impossible to fight him as a wolf.

"Not so smug now, huh? All right, wolf, shift and bite her." Ghost stepped back to watch the carnage. I decided to make it more difficult on Kayden and started to run. I could hear his bones cracking as his body shifted into the wolf that would bring my demise. I slammed into the door, but it was locked and I couldn't get it to budge. Kayden was slowly stalking me, fighting each step. Maybe I should just let him do it and get it over with. Then Gerolf would let him go. Who was I kidding? My brother wasn't going to let his new toy go. He would keep Kayden as a prisoner and make him kill anyone who stood against him.

I got caught up in my thoughts and forgot that I was running for my life. *Shit, Delilah, pay attention.* I barely moved in time to stop Kayden's teeth from clamping down on my arm. I dodged him three more times, finding each door in the place blocked just like the first. There were no windows, and the doors were all locked. I was doomed. I continued to skirt around Kayden, and I knew I was only able to do so because he was fighting against the command. Sooner or later, we would both get tired, and my end would come.

I thought that maybe Kayden was winning against the magic until Gerolf snuck up behind me and held me still. "Hurry up, wolf. Bite her now." I head-butted him and slipped out of his grip, but he recovered and grabbed me again.

I struggled against his grip, but couldn't break free before Kayden's teeth sunk into the soft skin of my neck. Blood ran down my shirt, hitting the concrete floor just before I did.

CHAPTER 19

Eli

AFTER MY SHOWER, THERE was still almost an hour and a half to kill before go time. I decided to dig further into Gerolf Stone and see if I could connect him to the Powder operation and the Council. I was certain that my suspicions were correct, but there was nothing definitive tying him to either of them. Why couldn't I catch a break with this? I knew he was Ghost but couldn't prove it. I knew that Ghost was behind everything that had happened to Delilah so far, but there was no evidence that Gerolf was involved. How was he this good at hiding in plain sight?

Because no one had ever seen Ghost's face! That was it. I pulled up the surveillance feed from his hideout and checked different angles. If there was another view, I would find it. I needed a shot of his face to connect them. Ten minutes later, my efforts were rewarded. The guy in the goat mask, who Dec said called himself Ghost, walked out of a room and pulled the mask off. I was able to get a shot of his face, although, with the lack of light, it wasn't a great one. I started running it through facial recognition software anyway, hoping for a miracle.

"Guys, I got him. I have all the proof we need to take this fucker down!" I yelled, essentially calling everyone to my location.

"What are you talking about?" Dec walked in first, with Vik trailing behind him. They had been in the other room talking about furnishing Midnight when construction was finished.

"I'm talking about Ghost. I have definitive proof that he is Gerolf Stone. Look," I showed them the screen. I stood up and paced the room. "We can prove that she didn't do any of it. She'll be cleared. He has ties to the Council and the tainted Powder. Now we just have to free her."

"Well, we have a solid plan. Now we just have to execute it." Vik stood as his phone rang, taking the call into the other room.

"This is awesome, Eli. I can't believe you got exactly what we need to get the hunters off Delilah's back," Dec commended me.

"I don't know that it will be so easy. We have the proof, and I will definitely take it to the Council, but it looks like Ghost may have control over them as well. We may be starting a bigger war than we thought. Are we ready for that?" I knew that I would do anything to save Delilah, even go to war with the entire supernatural community. Although it might be easier to just grab Kayden and her, and run.

"If he controls the Council, we're all screwed. Once we get Delilah and Kayden out of his lair, he'll send everything after us. You're right, it'll be an even worse war than we ever expected. We can't let our people get caught up in this." Declan had a good point, but I didn't know how to stop them. Scott and the others were adamant that Delilah was as much their family as we were.

"It'll be okay. We still have a chance. The key will be to either capture him or kill him. You should already know my preference. We just have to get close and move quickly." I ran my hands through my hair, waiting for him to try and talk me out of our plan. He didn't, simply nodded and walked away. I had no doubt he would tell the others what we'd discovered and make sure they understood the risks associated with this rescue mission.

While he took care of that, I went to find Vik. I had to make sure he understood the gravity of the situation. He was still on the phone when I walked up, but I couldn't make out the other side of the conversation.

"I understand. I assure you, she is safe, and you will see her soon. Please just wait there. Yes, you'll be safe. Someone will show you to an unused room that you can stay in until we return. Make yourself at home. I'll have someone bring whatever you need. Thank you for calling me. We'll talk soon." The moment he hung up the phone, I knew there was a problem.

"What is it?" I asked, not giving him a moment to collect his thoughts.

"Delilah's best friend, Anna, just showed up at your place. They called me because she asked for me. She got a letter and is terrified to be alone. The letter was somehow delivered into her locked apartment while she was sleeping. In it was a copy of an arrest warrant for Delilah, with us listed as accomplices. They included pictures of Declan, Kayden, and Delilah after they'd been beaten up. She thought Delilah was dead."

"This is bad. And exactly what I wanted to discuss. He has a hold on the Council, which you already know from the phone call. We have to take him out or we'll never be free." As I spoke, I stared at my chosen brother, watching him process everything that I had told him and that Anna said.

"We're running out of time. I'll reach out to one of the Council members and see if I can get any information. Maybe the corruption isn't as widespread as we thought." With that, he turned and pulled out his phone again. I tried to hear the conversation, but all I got from it was that he was calling a guy named Smith who wasn't able to take his call.

"I understand that he's busy, Patricia, but I need to talk to Smith as soon as possible. It's urgent. Please ask him to call me back. Thanks," he said, disconnecting the call. "Smith will call me back. I'm certain he was there, probably banging some intern."

"Well, until he calls back, we need to finish preparing. I'm making a file of all the evidence we have against Ghost. In the event that we don't make it back here, the file will be made public and everyone will know who is responsible for our disappearances. It will also give humans proof that vampires exist. So, we need to do our best to get back here, or the secret will be out," I said, scrubbing my hands over my face. I didn't want to be the guy who told the world about the monsters under their beds. I wanted to live my life privately, with my family. But if push came to shove, Ghost would get his.

With our plan tweaked once more, we set about finalizing preparations for our rescue mission. I didn't want to set Vik off, but I was concerned that we would be too late. I didn't want to face a life without Delilah. I was certain that none of us wanted to live without her.

While I was double-checking my pack, my phone started going off. The notifications were from different guys I had posted around the city. There were dozens of them, messaging me to tell me that they'd captured some of the hunters who'd been looking for us. I hadn't ordered my people to take hunters down, but maybe that was how we would win this war. If Ghost had the Council in his pocket, he would control the hunters. If we could capture them all and lock them up until we proved Delilah's innocence and ours in connection, that might be enough to ensure that our mission would be successful.

I shot messages back congratulating my guys on good work and encouraging them to keep going. Then I messaged a few of Vik's guys and told them about what my crew was doing. They were more than happy to join. Dec's guys also jumped on the idea as soon as I'd sent the message. Now that all three crews were out hunting the hunters, we could focus on saving Delilah and clearing our names.

An unbidden fantasy crept in, of a day when we could be safe and happy. Delilah was at the center of it, with Kayden, Declan, Vik, and myself taking care of her every need. It didn't take long for the thought to turn sexual. I stood there imagining the slope of her neck, the feel of her bare shoulders beneath my hands, the sound of her moans as we all pleasured her together. Imagining the scene made my cock stiffen, aching to be inside of her. Automatically, my hand reached for it, planning to rub one out before we had to go.

A voice pulled me from the fantasy. "Everyone gather up. We're going over the plan one more time, then we have to go," Declan's voice echoed through the small rooms. With the mood broken, I walked out and joined the others. I would save the naughty thoughts for after we saved our girl. Reality was better than a dream any day.

CHAPTER 20

Kayden

I HOWLED IN PROTEST of what I'd been forced to do. I had promised to protect her, but I was the reason she would die. How did he know about shifter bites being fatal to vamps? That knowledge was hidden from everyone but the pack leaders. I wanted nothing more than to rip Ghost apart for his part in all of this, but his control over me was too powerful. I thrashed in place, trying to get free of the invisible hold he was using to keep me still.

I couldn't even comfort Delilah or try to help. He refused to give me any freedom. I stood there, my heart breaking, as I was forced to watch her body react to my bite. The more I fought against his will, the more I felt the invisible collar tighten. At this point, it was difficult to breathe. I gasped for air while he reveled in finally defeating his enemy. In my mind, I had killed him a thousand times, each one more violent than the last. In reality, I had no recourse but to watch as he taunted my love.

"This could have been so much more fun," he whined. "Why did you have to be such a bitch and ruin it?" he snarled at her, his creepy frown inches from her face. I hated him even more because there would be no way to hunt him down except by scent. I could do it, but if I was dead too, the guys would be at a disadvantage. I knew they were coming. I wished I could find out when and convince Delilah to hold on a while longer. *Where are you guys?* It was hard not to lose hope.

She stared up at Ghost, and the only indication of her pain was the tears in her eyes. She refused to let them fall as if her crying would mean he'd won. My girl would never let this maniac win. I wanted to scoop her up and hold her close to me. But even as the thought crossed my mind, the collar tightened again. The edges of my vision went gray and I knew that I would pass out soon.

Maybe I would get lucky and he would kill me once she was gone. That would be the only way I would find peace after what I had done. I suspected that my death was the furthest thing from his mind, though. He would surely keep me around to do his dirty work. I would be the feared enforcer, who did as his owner commanded, like a good dog. I hated being treated like a dog. It had been that way most of my life. I was fated to be the alpha of my pack, but if I had stayed, I would have been under Gunnar's thumb.

I turned my attention away from old memories and back to Delilah. I had bitten her throat, making it impossible for her to speak. She lay there, bleeding, trying to breathe, while Ghost stood over her, complaining about how she'd stolen everything from him, even the enjoyment of her death. At some point, he must have stopped concentrating on keeping me in place. The invisible collar loosened and I could breathe easier.

With the lack of restraint, my body shifted from wolf to man. Ghost didn't seem to notice. "Stupid bitch. I can't believe how completely inconsiderate you are of other people. I have spent years planning this, for what? Not so you could come in here and ruin it, that's for sure." I crawled across the floor slowly, hoping that he wouldn't realize what I was doing. If there was any chance at all for Delilah to recover from my bite, she needed to drink blood so she could heal. It didn't matter that I had never seen anyone survive, I would do everything I could for her.

I knew I would only have one chance. I moved silently, watching him the whole time. When he stopped pacing, I froze. He wasn't even looking at her anymore, just ranting while he resumed walking back and forth in front of her. He was like a spoiled child who didn't get his way. If I thought I'd be quick enough, I would rush him. I wanted nothing more than to sink my teeth into him and tear his head off. But with the amulet on his side, I knew there was no chance of me taking him by surprise.

My plan was the best option. It meant I had to get to her fast, and I was almost there. When I sat down behind her and pulled her head into my lap, Ghost turned. "Well, this could prove to be entertaining. Are you going to apologize now, wolf? Tell her how sorry you are that I'm such a monster. Go ahead." I fought against the smirk that was trying to spread across my face. He had no clue what I was planning to do.

I leaned down to whisper to Delilah. I knew from his scent that Ghost was human. There was no chance he would be able to hear what our enhanced hearing could. "Babe, I'm gonna open a vein. I need you to drink; as much as you can. It's the only chance for you to heal. Don't worry about taking too much." I knew that she would stop before she got enough, but I didn't want her to be scared of draining me. If it would save her, I would drain every drop of blood that I had, plus all of Ghost's.

I glanced up to see him staring at us. He was trying to hear what I'd said to her, but couldn't. From his expression, he was pissed about it too. I cried out in anguish and leaned over Delilah's body, shifting a single claw to slice my other arm open above her mouth. As soon as my blood started to flow, I pressed my arm against her mouth and felt her trying to drink. My eyes were glued to the bite mark marring her throat. It should be healing already, but nothing was happening. I can't lose her like this, not so soon after I found her. *Please, goddess Luna, don't take her from me yet.* I wasn't sure I even believed in the supposed mother of all wolves, but if praying helped me save Delilah, I was game. If the goddess we'd learned about as children saved my love, I would worship as a true believer. If we survived, so many things would change.

If we got out of here, the first thing I was planning to do was rip the amulets from each Council member's neck. There was no way anyone should have the power to take someone's will away. If I could manage it, I would be the last. But before I could go on a mission to protect all of wolfkind, I had to escape this monster and save Delilah. I don't know what I would do if I was the one to kill her. It would be bad enough to lose her, but knowing that it was me who did it? That would be the worst kind of torture.

"That's enough! Get away from her. This is my revenge plan, and I'm going to enjoy watching my sister die." With his words, the collar tightened again and my body was pulled away from Delilah. I tucked my arm behind my back, waiting for the cut to heal, and hoping Ghost didn't realize what I had done. I was lucky that she had already been covered in blood, otherwise, I'd be done for. He wasn't paying attention to me, though. He was watching Delilah suffer.

"There; now, that's better. I can see your life fading, sister. Oh, yes, this pleases me immensely. I will remember your suffering forever. Once I have all the power I'm searching for, I'll be immortal without being turned into a dog or a biter. Then they'll all bow to me. And I will spend every day reliving this moment." Ghost seemed so pleased with himself. His plan was terrifying, but I knew he'd never get that far. The guys would come at some point, and he would be a dead man, especially if Delilah was already gone. There would be no one to stop them from tearing him into pieces. With any luck, they would do the same to me.

My blood should be healing her. It should have jump-started her vamp abilities. But she looks worse than she did before. Her skin pale and coated in sweat. Her eyes were rimmed with dark circles. Her hair was matted with blood and dirt from the days of torture she'd endured before we had tried to save her; before I bit her. *Come on, Delilah, fight. Don't give up.* I silently begged her not to die. There was nothing else I could do. With Ghost's power holding me in place, I was forced to watch as she slipped away.

CHAPTER 21

Vik

I HAD TO STOP Eli from quadruple-checking our packs, then I had to stop Dec from going over the plan again. We'd been over it at least a dozen times.

There was no reason to stall any longer. I rounded up the troops and sent them ahead of us. We needed them to be in position when we got there.

Scott happily led the silent charge, while Steph insisted that she stay with Dec. I agreed that it was the best option, even though Eli and I were with him. We moved quietly through the tunnels, careful to watch for any indication that Ghost was expecting us.

My senses were heightened with the adrenaline coursing through my veins. I knew that Eli felt the same. Dec was a ball of nervous energy, bouncing with each step as if that would prevent him from focusing on what he'd been through.

Each step brought us closer to Delilah. I couldn't help but wonder if we could actually save her. Eli thought we had the numbers, but none of us was really sure how many wolves were under Ghost's thumb. Kayden might know, but even that was a long shot.

There had been no further communication since he'd been taken. It made me wonder if he wasn't a target as well. A powerful alpha would be quite the trophy; or weapon, if Ghost had a way to control him.

There was still so much we didn't know about this guy. Going in this way made me nervous, but the thought of not going was worse. I kept imagining all the things he might be doing to her. Every thought broke my heart.

I shook myself, I couldn't allow myself to dwell on what might be. I had to focus on saving her. We needed her as much as she needed us.

The tunnel curved ahead of us and the dark turn brought me back to the present. We all knew that it would be faster to speed run, but we were trying to be sneaky and careful. No one needed to take unnecessary risks. Creeping slowly around the corner, we saw some of our troops ahead of us. Scott signaled that they were ready.

Good, everyone was in position. Since Dec had done the calculations, we waited for him to make the call. He knew the precise second we would need to move in order for the plan to go smoothly.

A few moments later, Dec raised his hand above his head and whistled; everyone moved forward. The troops had split into three teams, each taking a different guarded entrance to Ghost's hideout. The four of us hung back, conserving our strength for the rescue part of the mission.

It was hard to sit back and watch as our people fought for us. Scott had been insistent that it was the best way to make sure we could get Kayden and Delilah out. He was right. They were capable of handling themselves and the distraction they provided would be enough to get us in.

The first two teams headed to the further entrances to deal with the guards. I watched as they disappeared around opposite corners as we stayed close to the third group. Each group was composed of ten individuals, with a few from each zone.

Having them split evenly so they were forced to work together was Scott's idea. I had a feeling that we would end up combining the three companies into one after all of this was settled. It made sense to have one person as our second in command. Everyone seemed to be listening to him and taking orders with no issues, so it looked like Scott would be getting a promotion.

My thoughts were interrupted by the scuffle happening just a few feet away. One of our people, I think her name was Amber, got jumped from behind by a guard. Scott ripped the guy off her back and snapped his neck. Amber tied him up since wolf shifters had a habit of not dying when we expected them to. They exchanged an intimate look before jumping back into the battle, fighting back-to-back. *Good for you, Scott!* I thought as I watched them take out the guards.

I winced as he took a punch to the throat and dropped. Eli tried to run forward and I had to hold him back. Scott had assured us that we were to stay out of the fight until we had Delilah and Kayden out of the compound. He'd made me promise to keep Eli back in case of this exact situation. We watched as his guys took out the guard who had knocked him down, then helped him back to his feet. Scott glanced over at us and nodded. "Keep moving, we're nearly in," he whispered, knowing that all of us would hear him.

Declan and Steph led the way, with Eli and me behind. I kept an eye on Scott and his group as we passed, but they had the enemies under control. Once they had captured all the guards at our entrance, Scott led them to the next one to meet up with another group. After they disbursed, I continued to watch our backs. I didn't trust that Ghost wouldn't have extra guards hidden in the tunnels. We made it to the large central chamber with no more interference.

The four of us crept through the door, moving silently to avoid detection. In the middle of the room, Kayden was on his knees. Was he praying? Just out of his reach, Delilah lay crumpled in a heap. I couldn't tell if she was breathing. I whispered to Dec, "Can you sense her?" He paused for a moment, then nodded. She was still alive.

"She's hurt badly, though. I can't get her to respond to me, but I can feel her," he whispered back. It wasn't good, but at least they were both alive. Why hadn't Kayden gone to help her?

"Where is Ghost?" Steph asked, turning to look around the room. I didn't see any sign of him. It didn't make sense that he would just leave Delilah and Kayden here, loose, unless he had some other way of controlling them. I took a cautious step forward, watching Kayden for any sign that Ghost was nearby.

He didn't move. He just stayed there, on his knees, staring at Delilah. When I got close enough, I saw the tears running down his face. I turned back toward the others and found that they were inspecting the room, trusting me to check on our girl. "Kayden, are you okay? Can you tell me what happened?" I asked quietly as I approached Delilah. She was so still, barely breathing. There was so much blood. I looked at him again but he only stared blankly at her.

I dropped to my knees next to her, checking for a pulse. It was weak, but the fact that she had one meant there was a chance for her to heal. She seemed stable, so I left her to deal with the wolf. He was obviously in shock. I stood in front of him, gently took his chin, and forced him to look at me. "Kayden. Focus. What happened?"

His eyes met mine and he started to mutter something quietly. I couldn't understand what he was trying to say. From his expression, I could tell it was bad. I slapped him to break him out of whatever trance held his attention. "My fault. Kill me. Please," he whimpered. Something had definitely happened, but we would have to sort it out when we got out of here.

"Wolf, there's no time for this. I need you to get up. We have to get out of here." He didn't react to my command. I motioned for Dec and Steph to come and get him. "Help him out of here. Eli and I will get Delilah," I said, crouching down to pick her up. I watched as Dec put Kayden's arm around his shoulders and started walking back the way we came.

Eli finished sweeping the room for anything we'd missed, then joined me as I followed the others out. "Scott texted. They've taken out all of the guards, but no one saw Ghost. It looks like he left. How is she?" He held out his arms to take her, and I didn't object. It didn't matter who carried her out as long as we made it somewhere safe. Right now, I had no idea where that would be.

We met up with Scott and all of the troops in the hall. "Ghost is in the wind. We've looked through every room and there's no sign of him."

"We'll find him. Let's get out of here." Half of the troops went in front of us to make sure the way was clear. Scott and the other half stayed behind us. Dec and Steph held Kayden up between them and I walked next to Eli as he carried Delilah.

CHAPTER 22

Declan

DELILAH HAD LOST CONSCIOUSNESS sometime before Vik got to her, but she was alive. If I focused, I could hear the soft thump of her heartbeat. Something was seriously wrong with Kayden, though. He wouldn't talk and was completely out of it. Steph and I carried him through the halls back to our hideout. Once we were inside, Scott and his gang, which was composed of people who worked for Eli, Vik, and myself, got to work collapsing some of the tunnels. That would make the warehouse a safer place to be for now.

We settled Kayden into the bed and let him rest. Maybe after he'd had some sleep, he would be able to tell us what had happened. "Will you sit with him?" I hated to ask Steph to babysit, but I didn't think he should be left alone.

She nodded, "I'll take care of him. You go check on her. If you need me, I'll be there."

I jogged through the connecting bathroom and into the other bedroom. "How is she?" I asked, glancing from Eli to Vik and back again.

"I'm not sure. Physically, she's weak. We need to get her cleaned up so we can see what's wrong," Eli said, heading into the bathroom to get some wet and dry towels. He came back with one for each of us, and we went to work washing the blood from our girl. I climbed onto the bed and carefully lifted her head and shoulders into my lap.

The evidence that she'd been tortured was fading. She must have fed at some point. I didn't think that Ghost would let her have blood, so Kayden must have found a way to give her his blood somehow. I let my thoughts wander as we carefully wiped the towels against her skin, as if we could remove the memory of what she'd been through just by cleaning the dirt and blood away.

Eli focused on her left side while Vik focused on her right side. That left me with her head, neck, and shoulders. I started at the top of her head, cleaning her hair and face first. When I got to her neck, I froze. There was a scar; it was fading, but it was there. He'd bitten her. That was why he seemed so broken right now. Without a word to the others, I slid from under Delilah and raced to where Kayden was resting. Steph had cleaned him up and dressed him.

I grabbed him by the shirt and pulled him up to face me. "How could you? I thought you cared for her. Was it all a lie?" I paused to give him a chance to defend himself.

Kayden stared blankly into my eyes. I could see the tears he refused to shed. Guilt burned in his stormy eyes. "Just kill me. I deserve it," he whispered, closing his eyes and lilting his head to offer his neck.

"Kayden, tell me what happened. Now," I demanded, shaking him to get his focus back on me. He shook his head and dropped his eyes from mine.

"Doesn't matter. I bit her; that's all you need to know," his voice cracked at the admission. No matter what I did, he would not look at me. He refused to talk about it. We both knew what a wolf shifter bite meant for a vampire. I wasn't sure how I would protect him when the others found out. Delilah wasn't injured, she was dying. And there was no cure.

Sure, sometimes humans could survive a bite, some even gained the ability to shift. But a vamp? Never. "That was why you gave her your blood, wasn't it?" I accused, knowing already the truth of my words.

He nodded, still staring at the floor. It was as if he wanted to die; he expected to be killed for what he'd done. But why had he done it? How had Ghost forced him to hurt Delilah? I needed answers and he wasn't giving any. I dropped him to the bed and stormed back to Delilah. If I couldn't get the truth from Kayden, I would have to find a way to get it from her.

Eli and Vik both turned to stare at me, standing in the doorway, as I tried to figure out how to tell them. Tears filled my eyes. I couldn't find the words. Vik cocked his brow at me, his silent question evident. I forced the words out, pulling them from deep inside. "He bit her."

"What?" Vik asked, staring at me with his cold dark eyes.

"Why?" Eli asked at the same time, disbelief crossing his face. I shook my head and shrugged. Then I walked over to Delilah and brushed her hair from her neck to show them her scar from the bite. It was still fading slowly, which seemed odd, but it was there.

"He won't tell me, but he's begging for death. He knows that it's a death sentence for her. I need to know why he did it before I can grant his wish. I know him. He would never hurt someone intentionally, especially someone he cared about." I hated that I was defending the man I had campaigned so hard against before Delilah was taken. But ultimately, he was my best friend and I knew there was more to the story than we were getting.

"With Delilah unconscious and Kayden not talking, how do we find out what happened?" Eli asked, maintaining an air of curiosity instead of rage. The look on Vik's face was terrifying and I knew he wanted to give Kayden the death he felt was deserved. At least Eli would help me find the answers first.

"I think I can communicate with her. It's easier when she's awake, but I might be able to connect now. It's risky, though. There's a chance it will mess one of us up." I had no idea if it would work, but tried to make myself sound more confident in my idea.

"Then do it," Vik growled, standing up and walking toward me. "What can I do to help?" His voice softened and I realized that his rage wasn't necessarily pointed at Kayden.

"Don't kill him until we know if he meant to do it," I requested, knowing it was too much to ask. He nodded and I thought I saw tears in his eyes. He walked back to Delilah, planted a kiss on her forehead, then left. Emotions seemed to be his weakness.

"He'll be okay. Vik won't go after him unless we have proof. He's not the monster everyone thinks." Eli's defense of his friend reminded me of myself with Kayden. I hated that either of us had to be in this position. "Now, tell me what you need."

I shook my head and shrugged. "I'm not sure. I don't even know if this will work. I'm going to try holding her hand and talking to her. Hopefully, that will get me into her head." I climbed onto the bed next to her and carefully took Delilah's hand into my own. I leaned back and closed my eyes.

I reached out with my mind, searching for Delilah. "Where are you?" I wasn't sure if I said the words out loud or just in my mind. It didn't matter. If I could connect, she would hear me. I visualized myself walking through fog, searching for traces of her light. I followed a spark, calling for her until I came face to face with Delilah.

"What are you doing here? Did something happen?" she asked frantically. I pulled her into my arms and held her tightly. "Are we dead?"

I could hear the fear in her voice. I wanted to tell her that everything would be okay, but I couldn't force the lie from my lips. I kissed her gently, knowing it wasn't real, even though it felt as if she was standing in front of me. "I need to know what happened with Kayden. He won't say anything besides that he bit you," I pressed, avoiding her questions.

"He did bite me. But he fought against it. I almost felt his pain when the command took over him."

"Why did he bite you? What do you mean, 'the command?'" I needed to find out what had happened so I could find a way to fix it. Delilah held on to me as if her life depended on it. I wished it were that simple.

"Ghost has an amulet that he took from a Council member after killing him; it allows him to control Kayden. He couldn't refuse any command. He tried, though. He even found a way to give me blood to help me heal. Am I dying?" Her amber eyes searched mine, waiting for my answer. "How are you here?"

"Our bond is allowing me to connect with you. I don't know what's going to happen. We're trying to find a solution." The words felt like a lie, but I knew that we wouldn't give up on her, not now, not ever.

CHAPTER 23

Eli

I STOOD THERE, WATCHING as Dec tried to mentally connect with Delilah. I couldn't tell if it was working but didn't want to interrupt him if it was. I felt helpless. I couldn't save Delilah, I couldn't help Dec, I couldn't make Vik or Kayden feel less guilty about what had happened. I had this feral need to hunt down Ghost and take my frustrations out on him. But I knew that this would have to wait. We had to find a way to save Delilah.

I left the room for only a moment, just long enough to get my computer. When I returned, Delilah was curled up in Declan's arms as if they were simply sleeping. How I wished that were true. But wishes weren't going to save us now. I needed to do something, so I turned to what I know best, technology and research. I scoured the web, digging for any indication that Delilah could recover from a wolf shifter bite. After hours of reading, I came across mention of one other person who had survived a bite after being turned. *So there was a chance!* I tried not to get my hopes up, knowing how devastating it would be if she died anyway.

I took notes on the story and set my sights on finding this person. If I could figure out what they'd done differently from everyone else in this situation, I could fix this. I glanced up to see Dec and Delilah start thrashing on the bed. Research would have to wait. I yelled for Steph and raced over to keep them from smacking into anything. She was in the room immediately. "What happened?"

"They were fine, and suddenly this was happening. I don't know," I admitted.

"Why is Dec unconscious? Did something happen?" It was then that I realized he hadn't shared his plan with anyone but myself and Vik.

442

"He was trying to connect to her through the sire bond. Dec thought he could hold her and somehow get through, even though she wasn't awake. It seemed to be working, then they started seizing." I wasn't sure if there was anything we could do. He'd said it was a risky idea.

"Hold Delilah against you; don't let her hurt herself. I'll see if I can wake Dec up. This was stupid; you should have talked him out of it. There was no evidence that it would work," she growled at me, then turned her attention to him. "You son of a bitch, don't give up on me yet. I need to yell at you for this one." Steph proceeded to pull a syringe from her jacket and prepare to give the liquid to Dec.

"What is that?" I asked before I realized that she couldn't hear me. She was too focused on saving Dec. There was love between them, even if it wasn't the same as what he had with Delilah. Steph was his family. I had known that it was a bad idea, but I'd let him do it anyway. There would be no safe place to hide if he didn't survive.

I held Delilah as still as I could, pressing her against my chest as she thrashed. I rubbed my hand up and down her back. "Shh, love, it's okay. I've got you. Just hold on. We're working on finding a cure." My words seemed to calm her. She still shuddered against me, but it wasn't as violent as it had been.

I watched as Dec slowly came back to us. His eyes were wild when they opened. "Delilah? Where did you go?" he called for her and I stepped forward, climbing onto the bed next to him with her still caged in my arms.

"She's right here. It's okay. You're fine and she's calming down now. Take a breath, then you can tell us what happened." I kept my tone soft and calm, even though I was dying to know what had happened between them. It was obvious that he had been able to get through to her.

He sat up and took a deep breath, rubbing his hands over his face. Then he looked from Steph's angry scowl to my curious amusement. I couldn't help it; Steph was hilarious when she was angry, just like a tiny chihuahua who was about to bite your ankles off. "Thank you," he said to her before turning his attention back to me. "I talked to her. Ghost has a way to control Kayden; possibly other wolves too. He bit her, but it was because Ghost made him do it. Her soul seems fine, but she knows that something is wrong."

My face fell for a moment, then I remembered what I'd found. "There is a chance to save her. I found something." I let him take Delilah from me, then I moved to grab my laptop and showed him what I'd uncovered. "If I can find this person, they might know what we can do to save her. As for Kayden, I don't think Ghost's control is permanent. He's been himself since we left the lair."

It was a long shot, but there was no other choice. We had to try. I wasn't ready to give up on our girl. Maybe it was selfish, but we needed her to keep us together. There was no telling what kind of darkness would be unleashed if we lost her. Everyone already thought Vik was a monster. I couldn't imagine what would be said about the rest of us. That kind of loss can break a man.

"Can you find them? Before it's too late, I mean," Dec asked. I wish I was more certain, but it was the only shot we had.

"I hope so. I was just starting to search for contact info when you two started seizing. I'll get back to it now that you're awake and she's calmed down. We're not giving up," I insisted, turning my attention back to the computer and searched. I would locate this person. I would talk to them before it was too late. I made a silent promise to Delilah. After hours of searching, I was no closer to finding the person we needed than I had been when I found the story of their survival.

"I'm hitting dead ends left and right here. I'm going to talk to Kayden. Maybe he knows something, even if he doesn't realize it." I walked out of the room, leaving Dec to take care of Delilah. I found Kayden staring out one of the big windows on the ground floor of the warehouse.

"Kayden, we need to talk," I began, grabbing his shoulder to make him face me. He turned hesitantly, staring blankly. His pain was overwhelming and I had to take a step backward so I could bolster my mental defenses.

"What's there to talk about? Just kill me and get it over with," he insisted before turning away. I spun him back around and planted my fist in the center of his face, feeling the satisfying crunch of his nose.

"Stop feeling sorry for yourself and help me save her," I growled. He blinked, then shook his head, as if he'd just realized what I had said. "You're obviously not under his control anymore. Snap out of it and help me!"

"You think we can save her? How?" his voice finally held something other than guilt. Then his eyes dropped, "You know?"

I nodded and put my hand on his shoulder. "Dec talked to her. We can get into that later, but right now I need to find the one person who has survived this before." I pulled my phone out and showed him the article I'd found. He squinted at it, then zoomed in on the picture.

"That's not possible," he stammered. I took the phone back from him and stared at the picture. I hadn't paid close attention to it before. The girl was beautiful, but I had no clue who she was.

"Who is she?" I asked.

"It's Red, but that story was written before she was born. It can't be her," he insisted. I handed him the phone.

"Call her. We need to talk," I ordered, waiting for him to snap out of it and do what needed to be done. He nodded and dialed the phone. When he spoke, it wasn't to Red, but to someone else—he'd called Grammy. After a short conversation, he disconnected the call.

"Grammy is on her way. The picture isn't Red. From the date on the article, it has to be Grammy. There's no other explanation. I have so many questions, and no answers. I feel so lost," he admitted, falling into my arms. I felt bad for him. I couldn't imagine being forced to hurt Delilah. The guilt from that would be overwhelming. I hugged the hulking beast as he held onto me and cried like a child who had lost everything.

I had Scott keep an eye out for Grammy. He escorted her into the warehouse and brought her directly to us. After brief introductions, she looked at me and frowned. "So, you know," she said simply.

I nodded, "Don't worry, your secret is safe with us. We need your help to save our girl." Grammy looked me up and down, then turned her attention to Kayden.

"I'll do what I can, but there are no guarantees. Even if she survives, she may not be able to control herself."

Chapter 24

Delilah

KAYDEN'S BITE HAD AFFECTED me in strange ways. My body went numb and I collapsed. I vaguely remembered hearing Ghost gloating about killing me. Then Kayden was standing over me, feeding me blood. Somehow Ghost ripped him away from me, then disappeared. I wasn't sure where he went. I could sense Kayden close to me, but I couldn't reach him. I knew that I was on the verge of passing out, or maybe I did. By this point, I really didn't know what was happening.

What felt like minutes or hours later, I thought I heard Vik, then sensed Dec, but the dreams were messing with my memory. Did I really hear him, or was it my mind playing a trick on me? Strong arms picked me up and I was being carried away. I had no idea where I was going or who was taking me. I could only hope it was my guys. No matter how hard I tried, I couldn't open my eyes. I felt so weak.

The next thing I remembered was something soft under me. I relaxed when I sensed Declan nearby. There was no reason to fight if he was with me. I let the darkness take me under. When I gave in and stopped fighting it, I felt like the inky depths weren't trying to kill me. Something else was happening. What was it? I had no idea.

Flashes of memories assaulted me. They moved so quickly that I couldn't tell if they were mine or someone else's. Some things looked familiar, but others were so foreign. Suddenly Dec was standing in front of me. How was this possible? A wave of relief washed over me with his closeness. I held onto him as if he was the only thing that could save me. He asked about Kayden and what had happened. *Don't blame him, he didn't want to do it.* From Dec's face, I knew it was bad.

The moment we touched, invisible forces started pulling me away. I tried to hold on tighter, but it did no good. He was ripped away from me without even a moment to say goodbye. And this felt like goodbye. Dec was gone; everyone was gone. I was alone. Flames erupted around me, burning me without even touching my skin. The pain was excruciating. I screamed, even though no one could hear me.

After what felt like an eternity, I heard Eli's voice. He wanted me to hold on. They hadn't left me after all; I still had a chance. I felt my body relax against something familiar. Eli must have picked me up. Just as I got used to his warmth, he was gone. But somehow I knew he wasn't leaving me this time. He was fighting to get me back. I heard Dec's soft voice in my ear, begging me to come back to him. I did my best to do as he asked, knowing that I didn't have full control of myself in this hellish situation.

Cold hands were on my head when I finally managed to open my eyes. I was sweating; the room was so warm. It was too warm. I hadn't been this warm since I'd transformed into a vamp. Something was wrong. My eyes opened wide, staring into a kind face. She was old, with long gray hair braided and slung over her shoulder. It hung nearly to her waist. The old woman looked short, but it was hard to tell at this angle. Her smile was sweet, like someone's grandmother. When she spoke, her voice was gruff and didn't match her appearance. "She's awake. I need you boys to give her a kiss and get out of here. I have to explain things to her and you won't understand. I'll call you back when she's ready." This grandmother was obviously not scared of my vampires. She spoke to them as if they were children who needed authority. If I had the strength, I would have chuckled because she wasn't wrong.

Vik kissed my left cheek, Eli kissed my right, then Dec kissed my forehead. "Kayden?" I whispered, wondering where he was. Grandmother shooed my guys out of the room, everyone having ignored my question. She closed the door and turned back to me.

"You can call me Grammy. I'm here to help. I've been in your place before, a long time ago. I survived, so I think you can too. Don't worry about Kayden, the boys will take care of him. You'll see him soon." Her husky, yet sweet voice was comforting. I felt as if I was floating somewhere outside of my body, making me wonder if Steph had given me something for the pain. The burning had subsided for the moment.

"Grammy, I'm Delilah. What's happening to me?" The words were hard to articulate; my tongue felt heavy and the room spun. I felt as if I was on the verge of passing out again.

"Well, Delilah, if I have any say in it, you're about to get a lot better. I have to warn you, it's going to hurt so much worse before that, though. I've barricaded the doors, and your boys know that they can't interfere. If you're strong enough, you'll survive. And I think you're plenty strong." She paused and looked me over as if she was trying to convince herself that her words were true.

She pulled a small box from her pocket and began preparing what looked like herbal tea. "This has to brew for a few minutes, then you need to drink it all. It tastes like ass, but you have to promise that you'll drink every drop. If you don't, the magic won't work."

"Are you a witch?" I wondered aloud. I could tell from her scent that she wasn't human. Somehow I didn't think *witch* was the right term either. There was something wild and almost feral about her, but I couldn't put my finger on it.

She didn't respond right away, busying herself with fluffing my pillows and tidying up the room while the tea brewed. When she turned her attention back to me, I had nearly forgotten my question. "No, dearie, I am not a witch. But one did give me the tea. I'll tell you my story while you drink. First, I need your word that no one outside of this room will ever hear what I'm about to tell you. Unless of course, another happens to be in our unique situation." She stared at me, waiting to see if I would agree to keep her secrets. I nodded emphatically.

Grammy handed me the tea and sat, facing me on the bed. "Okay then, I'll tell you my story. I've lived a long time, child. Many decades ago, I found myself in the company of a shadow dweller. I believe you call them vampires now, like your young men out there. He was a handsome fellow and I fell in love quickly. The problem was that I had been betrothed to another, a wolf shifter of the Shadowtail Clan. My wolf was not just any member of the clan, he was the alpha's son, and an alpha himself. He would be the one to lead the pack once his father passed on." She paused for a moment and stared off into space before turning to me and motioning to the tea.

"Drink it all, child." I nodded and brought the cup to my lips again, determined to drink all of the disgusting liquid. Satisfied that I was following her instructions, she returned to her story.

"Now, my predicament wasn't falling in love with two men; that was perfectly acceptable in my village. The problem was that one was a wolf shifter and the other was a shadow dweller. My men hated each other. If they ran into each other, they would fight. It was horrible."

She stopped again and motioned for me to drink before continuing. "Grant, my wolf, was so jealous of my vampire, Sven, that I felt pressured to choose one or the other. It was impossible. One night, I was taking a walk with Sven. It had been raining. I slipped and fell into the creek. I hit my head on the rocks before Sven could get to me. He did the only thing he could think of to save me. He turned me into what he was—a shadow dweller."

Another pause to make sure I was drinking the foul tea, then Grammy kept talking. "He walked me back to the village, went straight to Grant, and explained the whole thing. Of course, Grant lost his temper and tried to bite Sven. I stepped in the way and his teeth clamped down on my shoulder instead." She pulled her shirt away from her neck and I could see the pale scar left by his teeth. "The elders thought I would die, but a witch from one of the neighboring villages came and brought this tea. This, brewed with the blood of your soul bonds, will transform you. You won't be a vampire or a wolf. You'll be something different, like me."

"Will I shift into a wolf?" I asked, almost dropping the cup from my hand. But Grammy quickly grabbed it and repositioned my hands around it.

"Drink. There's no way to know for sure. When I transformed, I was able to shift between my vampire and wolf forms. It could manifest in you differently. Since Kayden is your mate, along with the three others, I put drops of each of their blood into the tea. You'll want to complete the mating ceremony with him before the next full moon. I can't say what will happen if you don't. This situation is not exactly a regular occurrence."

CHAPTER 25

Vik

I stood outside the door after the old woman closed it. I wanted to insist that at least one of us stay in the room with Delilah. I wasn't sure that I could trust anyone at this point. It didn't matter to me that she was supposedly a hybrid. What good did that do us? There was no guarantee that our girl could survive.

Eli and Dec went to talk to Kayden. I wasn't convinced that the wolf had anything useful to share. I felt that my time was better spent standing guard for Delilah. I could hear parts of the conversation, but not enough to know exactly what was going on. I was tempted to crack the door open so I could hear. Dec and Eli had both threatened me before they walked off.

We had agreed to stay out of the room until Grammy told us it was okay to return. She'd been adamant that we not come inside, no matter what we heard. I didn't like it. I let Eli and Dec speak their agreement and I just stood there. She took my lack of response for compliance. But I would never leave Delilah alone with a stranger and agree to stay away. I had to be able to protect her, especially since I hadn't been able to earlier.

The old woman droned on for a while, telling Delilah some story that I only caught half of. It seemed that she might have been telling the truth about being a hybrid herself. There was no real way to know without seeing her in action, though. It was easy enough to smell the wolf on her, but her claim of being half vamp seemed outrageous. It went against the laws of nature. Who was I kidding? Vampires' existence went against the laws of nature. There was nothing normal about our situation.

Her insistence that magical tea helped her through the transition made me cringe. Magic existed; not openly in the city, but a person could access it for the right price.

I just wasn't convinced that herbal tea could fix the death sentence for a vampire that accompanied a wolf bite. I stood at the door, listening for anything suspicious. I knew that if I busted into the room, everyone would be angry with me. But, I wasn't sure that I cared.

A while later, it got really quiet on the other side of the door. The lack of sound made me nervous. I wanted to go in but held back, hoping for the best. I had a nagging feeling in my gut that something bad was about to happen. Eli would call me paranoid and Delilah would say that I'm always expecting the worst to happen. But if you expect the worst, you can be prepared for it. I knew that I would rip the old woman's heart from her chest if she harmed Delilah.

A scream broke the silence. Eli, Dec, and Kayden were at the door next to me before the second scream came. "She said to stay out no matter what," Eli warned.

"I'm sure Grammy has it under control," Kayden offered with a wince. He turned to Dec, who shrugged.

"I don't like it," I growled. "I want to go in there. Delilah needs us." I stared each of them down, daring them to argue with me about it. When I was convinced that they wouldn't, I placed my hand on the doorknob.

Eli stepped forward, nodding to Dec and Kayden. It seemed as if they had anticipated my desire to disobey the elder wolf. Couldn't they see that I wanted to protect our girl? Why would they want to keep me from doing that? I didn't have time to think about the answer. Kayden grabbed my left arm and Dec grabbed my right. They held me in place while Eli positioned himself between me and the door. No matter how hard I fought against them, I couldn't break free.

The screams continued. I watched as Dec's face paled, knowing that he wanted to break in there just as much as I did. The only reason he wasn't on my side was that I had been a dick to him before. "Eli, she's hurting. She might even be dying. We can't let her suffer alone. We need to get in there."

"What if he's right?" Dec asked, relaxing his grip on my arm. I didn't bother to pull away since he was no longer trying to hold me in place.

Eli grimaced as the screaming got louder. "Then we're dicks for keeping him from going in there. But Grammy said it was going to get worse before it got better. We can't let him bust in there and kill Grammy just because Delilah is in pain."

"Look, I know Grammy. She's pretty intimidating. But I can't see leaving Delilah in there alone while it sounds like she's being tortured. Can't we just go in and let her know we're here for her?" Kayden said, trying to be the voice of reason. "At least you guys could go in. I don't really deserve to be with her anyway."

"Fine, but if Grammy gets mad, I'm going to blame you for this. If she stakes you, that's your fault, not mine." Eli's threat was directed at me, but I knew that he would never let anyone kill me. Maim, sure, but kill? Never.

I nodded in agreement, then Dec and Kayden let go of me. Eli threw himself against the door, busting it open, and the four of us walked inside. Before he had a chance to run, Dec and I grabbed Kayden and forced him through the door behind Eli. We closed and locked the door behind us. Grammy looked up and grunted, "It took you long enough." *That bitch.* It was as if she knew that we would bust in. I glanced at Eli who looked shocked as well. "I thought you boys were smart enough to figure out that sending you out was a test. Of course, she needs you in here with her." The old woman was lucky that we needed her.

Delilah was on the bed, writhing in pain. Between her screams and the faces she was making, it must be excruciating. "What can we do to help her?" I asked, stepping closer to the bed. I wasn't scared now. I knew that Delilah needed us, all of us, and we would do whatever it took to save her.

"Hold her, touch her. Let her know that you're here. She needs the connection so she doesn't lose herself," Grammy's grave words urged us into action. I dropped to my knees next to the bed and grabbed Delilah's hand. Dec knelt by my side and placed his hand on her leg. Eli dragged Kayden to the other side of the bed and laid his hand on her other leg, forcing Kayden to take her hand. Somehow it seemed right to have the wolf closer to her.

Each of us whispered words of comfort and she seemed to calm a little. I watched as the writhing slowed, then stopped. Delilah's eyes closed and she was very still; too still. I wanted to shake her, to sit her up, to do something to make her move. Just when I thought I couldn't take it anymore, she squeezed my hand. I looked up and she was staring right at me. She turned her attention to Dec for a moment, then Eli. After that, she pulled Kayden closer and pressed her lips to his. He tried to pull away, but she moved with him. Dec and I helped her sit up so she could maintain their connection.

He was making it clear that he was uncomfortable, but she refused to let him go. It was as if she needed him more at this moment. Perhaps something inside of her was calling out to his wolf. Kayden tried to back away from her again, but Eli blocked him. Seeing that he couldn't escape his feelings, we watched as he surrendered to them. He pulled Delilah close to his chest, crushing her with his kiss. She moaned in pleasure, causing the rest of us to adjust ourselves.

I had reluctantly accepted their claim on each other before she'd been taken. I knew now that my reluctance had kept them from sealing their bond. It wasn't right for me to stand in the way of what Delilah wanted. I vowed right then that I would never stop her from pursuing whatever, or whoever, her heart desired. So long as she still wanted me, I would be happy to have some of her time and affection.

Their desire hung in the air like a cloud. I knew that we should let them have their moment, but it was as if we were frozen in place. Some unseen force was keeping us close to Delilah. It was as if the universe was deciding if our love was enough to sustain her. My heart skipped a beat while we waited. The agony of it all was terrifying. I wanted to snatch her from his arms and run away with her; to keep her safe from everything. But I knew that I couldn't. It was something we had to do together. We had to protect her, not just me, all of us. We were truly a family now.

CHAPTER 26

Declan

I THOUGHT MY HEART would burst from my chest while Delilah suffered. I expected the pain to ease once she came out of the seizure-filled coma, but I was wrong. The initial sight of her wrapped in Kayden's arms was like being sucker-punched in the heart. I wanted to be the one she latched onto.

Instead, I focused on my breathing, just like I had practiced with her. Once I got my lungs under control, I realized that the pain I felt wasn't because Kayden was kissing Delilah. I was finally letting myself feel the emotions I had blocked when I thought she was going to die.

I still wanted to be the one she was kissing, but I didn't begrudge my brother his chance at her affection. I couldn't let my fear get in the way of her happiness. Kayden and I were like brothers in so many ways. We had been conditioned to compete with each other for everything. I needed to remember that Delilah wasn't one of those prizes. She had enough love for us both, for all of us.

It took me a minute to realize that we were all just standing there staring at Kayden making out with Delilah. I shook my head and turned away to give them a little privacy. Grammy motioned for me to follow her into the other room. I glanced back at the others before I went with her. I figured there would be some kind of catch to whatever she'd done to save Delilah's life.

"You boys will have to look after her. The transition will wear her out quickly. There are no restrictions for her to follow. If she feels well enough to do something, then she should. Just don't let her overdo it. And be prepared," the old woman instructed me as if this were life or death.

"Be prepared for what?" I looked at the closed door behind Grammy, wondering how much things were about to change.

"If the tea does what it's supposed to, she'll recover. She should shift. The first few times will be excruciating if she does. You will all have to help her work through the pain so she doesn't get stuck halfway. And in wolf form, she'll be nearly feral. It'll take time for her to gain control. Don't let Delilah bite any of you when she's the wolf. I can't guarantee how that will turn out." Her words seemed to have an underlying meaning as if she'd been in this exact situation before.

"But she's going to live?" I asked hesitantly. I was terrified to hear the answer. I had so much hope, then I felt as if it could be torn away in an instant.

"I think so. She's strong. But you'll know for sure within the next two days. If she hasn't shifted by then, she may not make it." She turned her back to me and started walking toward the door. "Oh, and Declan?" she called over her shoulder. "Don't forget your promise. This never happened, and I was never here. Or else."

I nodded, then watched her go. It was pretty brave of the old woman to make a threat against the heads of the city, but she didn't seem concerned. To be honest, I may have been a little scared of her. Of course, Kayden and I had grown up with her. She never backed down, and we'd seen her exact revenge more than once. I wasn't about to go against anything she said.

I wondered if I should go back into Delilah's room or just wait out here. It seemed awkward to watch her moment with Kayden. Maybe it would be better if I did something else while they bonded. I decided to grab one of Eli's laptops and see if I could find anything new on Ghost. With a little luck, we'd find out where he had run off to. I wanted to kill him, even if he was Delilah's brother.

The story Kayden had told was crazy, but I could see the truth in it. The fact that he only opened up to me about it made me feel like we'd gone back in time. I hated the way that Shannon had died, and that it tore us apart. I knew he still blamed me. Hell, I blamed myself. I should have been there for her. I was supposed to be there but had decided it was more important to chase after Red. I used to think she broke my heart; though, deep down, I knew it wasn't meant to be. But Kayden had a girl, so I wanted one too.

I shook myself out of my memories and focused on the computer. I needed to find a lead. And we needed a safer place to stay. It wasn't practical to have an army guarding us in an abandoned warehouse. Especially since Ghost knew exactly where we were. I mean, besides the army, there was nothing stopping him from barging in and killing us all. And if he had explosives, the army wouldn't even be a deterrent.

My search ended with a couple of leads that Scott would probably volunteer to run down for us, and a possible condo that just happened to be in the center of the city. Somehow, the building bordered each of our territories but wasn't owned by any of us. Yet. I was certain that Eli would want to do more research before any of us made an offer on it, but that building seemed like the best option for a home base that would encompass all four territories. I knew that technically Ghost ran the East, but that wouldn't stop us from executing a hostile takeover.

I knew that when we discussed this as a war, we were being completely upfront. Taking on Ghost and the Council would be like going to war against a quarter of the city. Even though we held a majority stake, it was going to get bloody. We needed to focus on Delilah, not war. Somehow, we would have to do both. I sent the information about the leads to Scott and asked him to have a couple of guys check them out. I didn't want anyone going after Ghost without us, he knew that, but we needed more information.

Then I bookmarked the property to show Eli when they were done smothering Delilah with their attention. I hated not being in there with her. But I also knew that until I could get my emotions in check, I would be no good to her. I had already fucked everything up so much. I couldn't protect her from being taken and abused by Ghost. I couldn't save her. I didn't deserve her attention. *But if there's a chance that she's going to die, you should be there.* I tried to ignore the little voice in my head. He'd become more negative lately and I fought against it.

I didn't want to pressure Delilah since I knew that I had failed her. I had to prove myself worthy of her before I would let anything happen between us. I walked back to the bedroom to check on her. I told myself that I would wait until the others came out, but I couldn't take it. I had to see her again. I knocked gently on the door and waited. I was surprised when Kayden pulled it open. He jerked his head toward the bed, where Delilah was sleeping.

"We didn't want to leave her alone. I was just about to come and find you," he whispered. I stepped back so he could exit the room. Then I closed the door, leaving Eli and Vik to sit with Delilah while she slept.

"I didn't want to overwhelm her. She's been through a lot." I wondered if he would take me at my word or call me out.

"Vik said that Grammy took you in the hall to talk. What did she say?" Kayden ran his hand through his hair nervously.

"That it would be touchy for the next couple of days. If she shifts, she'll recover. If she doesn't, there's no way to know for sure." I summarized the old wolf's words, purposefully leaving out the threat. Kayden didn't need to know about that right now. He needed time to recover from what he'd been forced to do.

"Then all we can do is wait," he huffed. I knew he was frustrated with the situation. His guilt had to be weighing on him at least as heavily as mine was on me.

"Are you going to try to complete the mating ceremony? Or at least talk about it? It might be just what she needs to help her recover faster," I suggested. I wasn't sure if I was trying to help Delilah or hurt Kayden with my suggestion. If they mated and she died, he would suffer. But if there was a chance that it did help her, wouldn't it be worth a try?

"We're going to discuss it as a family when she wakes up. I'm not pushing anything on her, though." His words sounded like a promise. I hoped that he was able to keep it.

CHAPTER 27

Eli

I watched Delilah attack Kayden, vaguely aware that Dec had left the room. I was so entranced with the heat coming from Delilah that I didn't realize Grammy had left too. I glanced over at Vik and saw that he was just as caught up in watching as I was. Logically, I knew that we should leave. It made sense to give them privacy, but I felt Kayden's need to run. I knew that if Vik and I left the room, he would break our girl's heart.

So we stayed. Vik and I glanced at each other, unsure if we should step back or remain where we had been. Our indecision was answered a moment later. Delilah pulled away from Kayden. "I feel dizzy," she muttered before collapsing in his arms.

I sensed his panic. "She's okay. It was too much excitement. She just needs to rest."

Kayden nodded, carefully lowering her to the bed. He stepped back and watched as Vik tucked her in. "Do you think the tea worked? Will she recover?" His guilt was eating away at him. I had to take a moment and fortify my emotional blocks so I didn't absorb it. Once I stopped his emotions from assaulting me, I was free to think about our next steps.

"I think we'll find out soon," I replied absently. My thoughts had already shifted to finding Ghost and making him pay. I guessed that he didn't care for that answer because he walked across the room and opened the door. Dec was standing there. Vik and I exchanged a look, watching as Kayden and Dec walked away to hopefully clear the air. They'd been at each other's throats for long enough.

"We have to find him," I whispered, knowing that Vik would hear me. I was terrified that Delilah wouldn't actually recover. I knew that we'd all be lost if she died.

"We will. Delilah has to be our priority right now. There will be time to hunt down the bastard once she's better," he replied. I made a face at him.

"This is weird, and I don't like it," I said with a small laugh. "I'm not used to you being the level-headed one." I had pulled Vik back from the edge a few times in our past, but neither of us was ever this calm about someone we cared for getting hurt. I was shocked that he wasn't chomping at the bit to go after the guy.

"Patience. I'm trying something new. Don't worry, we'll get him. No matter how long it takes," he assured me with a grin. I could tell he was coming up with wicked ways to torture Ghost once he was in our custody. I couldn't wait.

"I'm going to check on Dec. I think he's feeling almost as guilty as Kayden over all of this."

Vik nodded and I walked out, closing the door quietly. I wondered if Kayden and Dec had come to blows over their shared guilt; it wouldn't surprise me. It also wouldn't be very productive.

I did everything I could to avoid focusing on the big question. Would Delilah survive? I couldn't even consider the question, much less possible outcomes. I needed to clear my head. But first, I needed to talk to Dec.

I found them both awkwardly sitting on the floor in the warehouse, leaning against an outside wall. Neither of them spoke. I wondered what they were doing up here; the perimeter was surrounded, so there wasn't much risk right now.

"Did you talk to Grammy?" I asked as I approached.

Dec nodded, glancing over at Kayden. It was almost as if he was asking permission to discuss it. Kayden gave a curt nod and lowered his head.

"Grammy said she'll probably recover. We'll know within the next two days. If Delilah shifts into a wolf, she'll definitely recover. If she doesn't, there's a chance that she won't make it."

I could tell from his emotions that he was hiding something, but I wouldn't press him for it right now. There would be time to talk it all through once Delilah had recovered.

I turned to Kayden. "Is there anything we can do to help encourage a shift?"

He raised his head and looked at me, his cheeks turning pink. "If we complete the mate bond, it might push her into it."

"Then we'll try that. Give me a list of what you need and I'll set it up." I'd never been around wolves before, so I really wasn't sure what he would need for the ceremony.

Dec laughed and Kayden's cheeks turned bright red. "Um, Eli, I don't think he needs our help with that part." He waited to see if I would catch on. After a moment, my cheeks matched Kayden's.

"I'm guessing you just have to have sex? I don't know much about wolf traditions. I thought there was a ceremony, like a wedding." I felt naive for the misunderstanding, but neither of them made a big deal of it.

"Yeah. Intercourse seals the deal, so to speak. And I'm not going to push her. If she wants me, fine. But none of you is going to try and guilt her into having sex with me, understood?" Kayden stood up as he spoke, his anger taking control.

Guilt washed over me. How could he think any of us were capable of that? "We would never force her into anything she didn't want to do." I stood my ground, refusing to cower in front of the alpha. I knew he was used to getting his way and being in charge, but that wasn't how we did things here.

"I don't deserve her. I couldn't break his control. I couldn't protect her," Kayden whispered, turning toward the windows.

Before I could respond, gunfire shattered the windows and echoed around us. I tackled Kayden to the ground, relieved that Dec hadn't stood up. It sounded like the shooting had come from a moving vehicle. Scott and his team rushed toward the source.

While they raced after the shooter, I slowly climbed off Kayden. "Are you okay?" I turned from him to Dec so both would answer.

"I'm good; didn't get hit," Dec said from his spot on the floor. Bullet holes peppered the wall next to him, but when he shifted, I could see that there were none behind him. Normal ammunition wouldn't kill a vamp anyway, but it still hurt like hell to get shot. I turned to check Kayden out next.

He looked at me with wide eyes. "What is it? Were you hit?" I asked again.

He glanced at his shoulder, where a red stain was blossoming on his shirt. "I was, but I'm fine. The bullet went straight through. But that's not important. You're glowing, Fangs."

I looked down at my hand. Sure enough, there was a faint red glow under my skin. "This can't be good," I muttered. I started to look myself over for a wound. Before I could find one, the room began to spin. When my legs gave out, both of them caught me.

"We have to get him down to Steph," Dec insisted as they carried me away.

My arms and legs were numb, and the feeling seemed to be spreading. How could I have been shot and not know it? What kind of weapon had this effect on a vamp?

I heard Dec and Kayden talking to me as they walked. I could still feel their arms holding me up between them. "You're gonna be okay, Fangs, just hold on."

"Steph will fix you up, Eli. Stay with us, man." I could hear the panic in his voice even though he tried to hide it. His emotions lined up perfectly with Kayden's. This was bad.

I wasn't sure that I believed either of them. The numb sensation that was spreading across my body felt warm. It was as if my insides were gearing up to combust. The warmth spread and intensified.

I tried to speak but couldn't get the words out. My mouth refused to move, just like the rest of my body. I resorted to making noises to get Kayden and Dec's attention. I needed them to know what was happening.

I realized that I couldn't feel their arms on me anymore. Then my eyes flickered and closed. I thought I was still awake, but I couldn't be sure. I heard voices, but they sounded far away. Something shifted, and I heard a voice loud and clear. "Eli, don't you dare leave me!" *Delilah.*

When did she get here? I left her sleeping with Vik to watch over her. She shouldn't see me like this. After everything she's been through, this is the last thing she needs.

I would hold on for her. Dec was convinced Steph could figure out what had happened. I had to trust that she would get whatever resources and supplies she needed from Scott. I tried to squeeze Delilah's hand, not knowing if she was even holding mine. Nothing I did seemed to get my message across. I refused to give up.

CHAPTER 28

Kayden

As soon as Dec and I carried Eli into the living area of the underground bunker, Steph ran over. I'm not sure how she knew he was in trouble, but it was almost as if she'd been waiting for us. She quickly assessed his condition and noticed my shoulder. "What the hell happened up there? I thought I heard gunfire. I was just heading up to check on you guys." Steph quickly checked the entry and exit wound, then turned to Dec. "Clean his shoulder and bandage it. I'll deal with Eli. Can you tell me what happened to him?"

"He shoved me out of the way and covered me when the shooting started. Obviously, he was a little too slow since we both got hit. I don't think it was the same ammo that hit me. He was asking if we were okay and he started to glow, then he collapsed," I explained as Dec tended to my injury.

Steph checked Eli over, searching for something that would have caused this. "Oh, shit. He was shot. I'm not sure I can get this out. We're going to have to do surgery. Like right now." She turned to me. "I'll give you a list of what I need. Dec will have to help me." Then she ran off to write out the list. I hoped I could find what she needed. I pulled out my phone and shot a quick text to Scott, letting him know that he needed to get back here.

Vik rushed in, carrying Delilah. They had apparently heard our commotion. "What happened? Is he okay? Are you okay?" Panic flashed in Delilah's eyes before Dec stepped over to her. Vik dropped her gently to her feet.

"Just breathe. Steph can fix him. Vik and I will help her. I need you to talk to him, then take care of Kayden. Okay?" He kissed her gently, then pulled her toward Eli.

She knelt down and whispered to him before turning her tear-filled eyes to me. I held out my hand and helped her up. "What about the supplies?" I asked Dec since he'd decided that I needed to distract Delilah. I was convinced that was his plan. They didn't like for her to be in the middle of the chaos.

"Vik and I will take care of it. Just let her take care of you. Talk. Work things out. We've got this," he said before pulling me into a hug. Steph rushed in with her list, and Vik intercepted.

"I'll take that. Scott should be able to get everything you need. Delilah is going to make sure that Kayden rests so he can heal. Dec and I will help you with Eli. Pause and take a breath," Vik spoke softly to Steph, then hugged her. I hadn't seen him act this kind to anyone but Delilah. It was sweet.

"Scott is on his way," I said as I let Delilah drag me toward the bedroom. I wondered if she would talk to me about what we'd been through, or if we would just stare at each other. She closed and locked the door behind us. I wondered if it was to keep the others out or to keep us in.

"We need to talk," Delilah blurted. My heart raced. This was it; she was going to reject me. I deserved it for not being able to protect her. I sat down on the bed and waited. "I know you feel like you failed me."

"I did. I should have been able to save you from him, not make it worse. I almost killed you." I ran my hand through my hair, pushing the dark strands out of my eyes.

"If that's true, then I failed you too. I should have been able to break us out of there. It goes both ways, Kayden. We're in this together. You can't shut down on me just because something bad happened. Yes, you bit me. But you didn't have a choice. I saw how hard you fought against his command." She walked over and sat next to me on the bed, gently taking my hand in both of hers.

"I will never be able to tell you how sorry I am." There was no way she believed what she'd said, was there? Did she really think there was nothing for me to feel sorry for?

Delilah pushed me back toward the headboard. I didn't resist. She straddled me, leaning down to kiss me. I didn't deserve her affection, but I couldn't pretend like I didn't want it. I poured my emotions into that kiss, showing her how much I cared for and cherished her. By the time she broke contact, my dick was standing at attention, and Delilah was sitting right on top of it.

I groaned, wanting desperately to adjust myself. She never gave me the chance. "We should talk about it, though." Since there was no blood in my brain, I had no idea what she was talking about.

"What?" I stared at her dumbly, waiting for an explanation. She ground herself against my throbbing cock. Then she bit my lower lip and kissed me again.

"Completing the bond. Grammy and I talked about what happened to me, and how the bond can help. But I don't want you to think that's the only reason." Delilah grabbed my face in her hands and forced me to look at her. "I want you, Kayden. And I've already claimed you in every possible way, except physical. So what's stopping you?"

I shivered at the matter-of-fact way she proposed that we cement our bond. I wanted her so badly that I could barely breathe. But I didn't think I deserved her. How could she want me after I almost killed her? "I, I don't know. I feel like you should be more upset with me."

"So, if I was mad at you, you'd be trying to get me naked? Okay, I'll play along." Her expression went from playful to angry, and I wondered if it was playing or not. "Dammit, Kayden. I'm so mad at you for biting me. I don't know if I'll ever forgive you." She relaxed her face and searched my eyes. "Was that better?"

"Yes. I mean, no. I, I mean, I don't know. I want you. I just don't want to force this bond on you. It's not like either of us will be able to walk away if you change your mind later." I realized my mistake as soon as I'd said the words.

"So, you don't trust me. Sure, I get it. I'm just fickle little Delilah, I can't possibly know what I want." She stopped talking and glared at me. "Fuck you. I hope you're happy now. You actually managed to piss me off." Delilah stood and walked to the other side of the room.

"I'm sorry. I didn't mean that the way it sounded. I just don't want to force you into something that you'll regret. I do trust you. But you shouldn't trust me." Why was I trying to convince her to reject me? I really did have some issues. I briefly wondered if Rowan could fit me in for a session. Surely, he would be able to figure out why I'm trying to sabotage myself.

That seemed to make things worse. *Shit.* "I shouldn't trust you. Why not? Because you risked your life trying to save me, not once, but twice? Or because you weren't afraid to tell me that I was your soul mate?" Delilah stomped up to me, squaring up as if she was going to deck me. I deserved it. "You did everything you could to keep Ghost's attention off me and on you. Did you think I was too dumb to notice that? You went against your pack to save me from the hunters. Does that not matter?"

I could handle her anger, but the tears in her eyes shattered my heart. "I'm sorry. Please, babe, can we talk about this? I only wanted to make sure it was what you really wanted. I was trying to give you a chance to decide for yourself."

"I did decide for myself. You saw their reaction to you when I claimed you. None of them were happy about it. But not one of them tried to talk me out of it. Not even Dec; he just wanted you to grovel first. Only *you* have tried to talk me out of falling for you. Why? Why wouldn't you want someone to love you?" Tears started to fall, but I knew it was a combination of hurt and anger. I had fucked this up pretty well.

"Shit, babe. I'm sorry. What can I do to make it right? I was so terrified that you were going to reject me that I tried to do it for you. Please, just tell me what to do." I would beg her until she caved. Then I would spend the rest of my life making it all up to her.

CHAPTER 29

Delilah

"You can start by not treating me like I'm fragile and as if I can't make my own decisions," I growled. Kayden was really pissing me off. How dare he try to force me to reject him! I'd never been so turned on while being angry before, and I had lived with Vik, so that said something. My whole body was buzzing. I couldn't tell if it was the attraction or the anger.

"I know you're not fragile. And I'm trying to let you make this decision. I just want you to be sure," he defended his stance once more. This argument was getting nowhere.

"Do you want me?" I was going to make this easy for him, and with a little luck, get exactly what I wanted out of it. I smirked.

Kayden ran his hand through his hair again, fisting it into a ponytail at the nape of his neck. "Of course, I want you."

"Good." I jumped at him, forcing Kayden to either catch me or let me fall. At this point, I wasn't really sure which he would choose. He faltered for a second then wrapped his arms around my ass. I hooked my feet together at his back, trapping him to me. I pressed my warm center against his stomach and he groaned. His hair had fallen over his face at the sudden movement, so I took my time combing each piece out of my way before I claimed his lips.

When he winced, I remembered that he'd just been shot. "I'm so sorry, are you okay?" I tried to get down, but he held me still.

"I'm fine. But if you want to stop, I understand." His voice was so sad, even while laced with need.

I could see now that I would be the one claiming him. He would certainly reciprocate in the future, but for now, this was up to me. I kissed him hard and deep, forcing his mouth open with my tongue. I wasn't used to being dominant, but my anger took over. Kayden would do as he was told, and he would like it, I thought as our tongues tangled. I knew there were things we should discuss first, especially if I was going to get rough, but this time it was just going to be us. I could be wild, and if he couldn't handle it, he would have to let me know somehow. I couldn't help but think about Vik's insistence that I have a safe word just in case.

"Here's what's about to happen," I began, "You're going to do as I say. If anything is too much or crosses a line, you're going to use my safe word. Understood?" I rubbed myself against him as I spoke.

He nodded; his eyes glazed over with lust. "What's the word?" From the look on his face, he may have been knee-deep in his own fantasies at this point.

I kissed him again, knowing that this particular word could kill the mood. I refused to let that happen. "Bananas," I said simply and continued to kiss him. Kayden chuckled against my lips, then adjusted me so I could feel how excited he was. It appeared that 'bananas' hadn't had the effect I'd expected.

"Bed," I ordered. He carried me over and carefully lowered me onto the bed, making sure that I rubbed every bit of skin on his stomach and crotch on my way down. I shivered but stifled the noises I wanted to make. It would be difficult to remain in charge if I started whimpering. "Clothes off." Now I understood why Vik usually gave short commands. It was easier to maintain the dominating persona that way. I had no idea if I could follow through with this, but I was determined to have my way with Kayden.

"Am I allowed to talk?" His question pulled me out of my thoughts. I nodded. "You smell amazing. I want to taste you." Kayden's words sent another shiver down my spine. He stripped and towered over me, peeling off my shirt and leggings. His eyes widened at the sight of the matching lace I'd worn for him. Once I woke from Grammy's tea, I knew I would chase him down to seal our bond. I had chosen the least attractive shirt and pants to pair with the sexiest bra and thong I could find.

"Do you like it?" I asked, trying to sound coy. Somehow, my voice sounded insecure and needy. So much for holding on to dominance. I managed to keep my laugh to myself, though.

"I do. But I'll have to buy you a new set," he growled. I furrowed my brow in confusion just before he held up a finger that shifted into a claw. Then he tore my undergarments in half and threw them across the room. "I know you said I would do as I'm told, and I will, but I can't resist you. I'm going to taste you now." I nodded, unable to find my voice.

Kayden gently pushed me back on the bed and climbed over me. He hadn't touched me yet, but I knew I was dripping for him. His cock rested against my thigh as he leaned down and kissed me again. This kiss was different. It wasn't rushed or forceful. It was sensual and sweet, taking my breath away. I relaxed, deciding to let him take over.

I enjoyed the sensations as he slowly kissed his way from my jaw to my stomach, avoiding my breasts. Then he worked his way back up, stopping to pull a nipple into his mouth. I gasped when he bit it, then kept sucking. I ran my fingers through his hair and across his shoulders, digging them in when he started to trail kisses from my chest to my stomach. He stopped just above my apex. "I feel like I've waited forever for this," he whispered against my skin. Goosebumps spread everywhere his breath touched.

Kayden kissed my thigh, nipping as he got closer to my wet center. The moment his tongue touched my clit, I saw stars. My orgasm tore through me, determined to wreck me in a good way. He didn't stop, instead he began using his fingers to tease my dripping entrance. His tongue lapped at my wetness, then focused on my clit again while he slid two fingers inside of me and curled them against my g-spot. I jerked up and raked my nails down his back, leaving red streaks.

He groaned and pulled back. "You taste even better than you smell." My cheeks flushed and he chuckled. Kayden wiped his face with his hand, then climbed up to kiss me again. I'd never been a fan of kissing a guy after he'd gone down on me, but with him, it was hot. His scent mingled with mine as he lined the tip of his cock up with my entrance. His eyes met mine and the question was clear. He silently asked again if I was sure. In response, I grabbed his ass and pulled him into me.

I gasped at the sensation. I had been prepared to stretch for him, but I didn't realize how much girthier he was than my other guys. At my response, he froze. "Don't stop," I begged. Kayden smiled and slowly worked his dick in and out until I moaned in response. As he thrust in deeper and faster, his feral need matching my own, another sensation started to build. It was unlike anything I'd ever felt.

Warmth filled me up, starting where our bodies connected and spreading to every inch of me. The feeling was strange but familiar. I closed my eyes and let it take over as I felt my orgasm slowly build. I moaned and hummed my pleasure, focusing only on how good everything felt.

She's so perfect. I don't deserve her. But she feels so good. My eyes opened in shock. I searched Kayden's face, realizing that the words had been in his voice, but he hadn't said them.

How is that possible? I thought, watching his face. Surprise froze him in place. *You heard that?* I asked in my head. He nodded, a sly smile erupting across his face.

It's the bond. We'll be connected like this forever. He explained without speaking. I returned his smile and he started to thrust again, edging me toward bliss. There were a million thoughts running through my mind, but if he could hear them, he didn't show it. Instead, he made it his mission to push it all away and bring my pleasure to the front again.

Kayden reached between us to stroke my clit as he pounded into me. I raised my hips in time with his movements, forcing him deeper. I let go of any thoughts and rode the wave through my orgasm. As he climaxed, Kayden cried out my name at the same time I whispered his. I sighed when he collapsed on top of me. He quickly rolled to the side so he wasn't squishing me. *That was amazing,* I thought.

You are amazing, babe. I smiled at his words inside my head and dozed off beside him as the adrenaline rush wore off.

Chapter 30

Declan

Vik called Scott and gave him the list of supplies that Steph had requested. While he handled that, I helped Steph strip Eli and try to locate the wound. We removed his pants and shirt, leaving only his boxer briefs. He had to have been shot with some kind of radioactive projectile or something. Neither of us had ever seen a reaction like this before. In addition to the soft red glow, now there were dark red marks appearing on his skin. They branched out, similar to how a lightning strike scars a human, or how a tree's branches grow.

"Can we trace these back to the point of impact?" I asked Steph, pointing out the marks spreading across his abdomen and chest.

She nodded and we turned him over, following the most pronounced marks back to a single point on his back. "There's something in here." The wound had closed up, likely due to the speed of vamp healing. But the projectile remained. "We need to get it out."

"What is it? I've never seen a reaction like this." I helped Steph turn Eli over completely so he lay on his stomach. The angry red branches were thicker on his back, thinning as they spread away from the entry point.

"I don't know." Steph had blood bags ready and carefully placed an IV into Eli's wrist. If he lost too much blood, we could hook the bags up and do a transfusion. Then we cleaned ourselves as much as possible since there was no way to sanitize everything. I pulled on gloves and set up the scalpels and sutures. We weren't sure exactly what we'd find once she cut into him. Eli's skin was paler than it had been earlier but still glowed as the branching red marks continued spreading.

467

Yelling from the bedroom caught our attention. I started to walk toward the sound, needing to make sure Delilah was okay. Steph stopped me. "Let them work it out. If they have to yell to do it, stay out of it. The bond between a wolf and his mate is not something you want to be in the middle of. Trust me."

I wondered how she knew more about wolf bonds than I did, but I didn't push the issue. I turned back to our patient just as the door opened.

Vik rushed in with the supplies Scott had gathered. "Just set that stuff over there. I'm going to try this without setting up the machines. Hopefully, it's an easy extraction." Vik didn't argue with Steph's orders, placing the bags on the floor where she had indicated, then washing his hands and putting on gloves too. We would do whatever she told us to save our friend.

Steph's hands shook when she picked up the scalpel. She took a deep breath, then started an incision next to the spot where the projectile had entered Eli's back. As soon as she cut through the skin, he started to thrash, splattering blood on all three of us. "Hold him down," she ordered, backing up so we could get a grip on him. Then she climbed onto the cot with him, straddling his legs to hold them still.

Vik and I held Eli down while Steph opened his back enough to see what he'd been shot with. "I can see it. I need the tweezers. I might be able to extract it." I risked letting go with one hand to give her what she'd requested. Eli jerked, but Vik was able to hold him still enough that Steph didn't get thrown off. Once I had a grip on his shoulder, Vik released him to grab a bunch of gauze to soak up the blood that was running down Eli's back.

His blood was darker and thicker than it should have been, almost black. The dark liquid moved slowly as if it was creeping away; an inky blob crawling toward us. I shivered and tightened my grip on him while Vik cleaned the mess and Steph tried to grab the bullet. She cursed as she missed it several times before finally clamping down on it. She pulled and twisted, fighting it out of the incision.

As she pulled the projectile out, I noticed that the red color from the branching marks drew back toward the incision. Once the bullet was free of my friend, the red marks had all faded to a light pink color and the glow of his skin started to fade. Vik held out a jar for Steph to drop the item into so she could clean and close up Eli's incision.

With the offending object out of his body, Eli stopped thrashing. He lay still and I was able to let go of his shoulders to help Steph with her work. While we finished stitching Eli, Vik stared at the jar. The projectile was glowing the same red color that Eli had emanated. "What is it?" I asked, washing my hands before walking over to look inside the jar.

"It looks like a regular bullet, but bigger and it glows. There has to be something tech about it. Leave it to Eli to get shot with the tech bullet so he can't tell us what it is." Vik shrugged and handed me the jar. I gave the item a once over, but couldn't tell any more than he'd already noted.

Vik helped Steph turn Eli onto his back and covered him with a blanket. I wondered how long he would sleep. We had done everything we could to help him and now we had to wait. I was so sick of waiting. There had to be more we could do. I looked at my phone and saw a text from Scott. He wanted to know how Eli was. *The weird bullet is out. He's sleeping. Seems to be doing better. I'll let you know when he wakes.* It didn't seem like enough, but it was all I could offer him.

We're chasing down leads for the shooting. Call or text if you guys need anything, or if he wakes up. I figured that Scott would go back to his search for the people responsible. His affection for Eli was apparent. They'd taken care of each other for decades. They reminded me of how Steph and I were.

Steph looked at Eli, then turned her attention to me. "That would have been easier if we'd had those machines set up. I think he'll recover, though."

"Do you think we should have waited and set them up before we operated?" I had thought getting the object out of him was an emergency, but maybe I misunderstood. Before she could answer, Eli started to stir.

"What happened? Where am I?" Eli jolted upright on the cot. Steph and Vik jumped, while I nearly dropped the jar with the projectile in it.

"Shit, man. You scared us. Take it easy. We'll explain everything, just relax." I coaxed him to lean back against the pillows, so he was propped up instead of lying flat or sitting straight up. "You got shot; with this." I held the jar up for him to see. "Steph extracted it, but none of us know what it is." He reached for the jar and took it with surprisingly steady hands.

It seemed that the effects of the bullet were only there when it was in him. Once it was removed, he was fine. His face was still pale, but he looked awake and ready to fight. "Hmm. I've never seen anything like it before," he admitted, turning the jar around to look at as much of it as he could. Then he opened the jar and dumped the bullet into his hand.

"Wait!" Steph cautioned, but it was too late. We all braced for something to happen, but Eli simply held the projectile and turned it over in his hand.

"I think it's okay, as long as it isn't inside someone. It looks like it runs on the electricity inside the body. I need to take it apart and run some tests." He dropped the bullet back into the jar and set it down before trying to get to his feet. Eli stood, wobbled, and fell back onto the cot. It buckled under his weight and he hit the floor. "Ow," he grunted.

Vik chuckled. "Woah, speed racer. Take it easy. You don't have to show us up."

Then we rushed over to help him to his feet. We put his arms over our shoulders and carried him to the couch, carefully placing the jar on the table. When he was settled, I grabbed his laptop and brought it to him. "I need some tools and a tray to take this thing apart." Thankfully, Eli had accepted that he wouldn't be able to get them himself.

Vik went to the desk and grabbed a small tool kit, then on his way back, he picked up the tray that we'd used to spread the surgery implements on. "Will these work?" he asked, offering the items to his friend. Eli nodded, taking the tray from Vik first and setting it on the table, then the tool kit which he carefully opened and selected what he needed. We all seemed to disappear as he began inspecting the small bullet for a way to take it apart.

CHAPTER 31

Eli

I FLEXED MY FINGERS and picked up the flat head screwdriver. There were no visible screws on the bullet, so it had to have been pressed together. I wished that I had some clue what this thing was or where it was made. I worked the end of the screwdriver into the seam, trying to force the sides apart. It didn't work. In the most comical way possible, I ended up shooting the damned thing across the room, where Dec caught it.

"Sorry," I said when I retrieved it from him. "There has to be a way to get it to open up." I just couldn't figure it out.

"So, think outside the box. If you can't pry it open, is there a way to trigger it to open?" I grabbed Dec's face and kissed him. He looked shocked and took a step back.

"You're a genius. I have an idea." I wanted to run off to try my idea, but I was still feeling weak. I walked slowly, turning to see that he was following me. From the way his cheeks turned pink when I looked at him, I could tell things were going to be awkward between us for a bit. Oh, well. You only live once. I grabbed items as I passed them, handing some to Dec when my hands got full, and slowly climbed the stairs to the warehouse.

"Where are we going?" Dec finally asked, curiosity winning over embarrassment.

"Over here. If this blows up, I want to have something to hide behind." I kept walking, leading him to a far corner of the building, away from our supplies. I wasn't kidding when I said this could blow up. I was setting everything up when Vik appeared out of nowhere.

"What are you doing?" He picked up items and inspected them as if he could figure out what I was thinking.

"Well, I'm going to see if I can convince this bullet to fall apart. Stand back," I ordered them both, then turned back to what I was doing. I opened the jar with the bullet in

470

it and poured some vinegar in it. If I did this right, there would be no way it could explode. I hadn't really messed with chemical compounds for years, so I wasn't sure I remembered what I could and couldn't mix. I dumped some hydrogen peroxide into the jar and stepped away from it. I shoved Vik and Dec behind the crates a few feet away from my experiment.

They both looked confused, so I took pity on them. "I'm making an acid that corrodes soft metals. Unless it's made of something pretty strong, the bullet will at least break open. Or that's my plan anyway. Stay here. I have to neutralize the reaction." I stepped out from behind the crates and walked quickly over to the jar. The acid was bubbling out of the opening and onto the concrete. I picked up the baking soda and dumped the box into the jar, sprinkling some around it and on the outside of the jar as well. Then I rejoined the guys to wait for it to cancel out the acid.

"You think that will work?" Vik asked. I shrugged. I had no idea if it would, but it was something to try. I couldn't stand giving up.

"It was worth a shot. Even if it doesn't work, it'll give us some answers." I wasn't sure if I was trying to convince him or myself. I would be pretty pissed if this did nothing.

"Your jar is shaking," Dec interrupted before ducking behind the crates and pulling both of us down with him. "You weren't kidding about an explosion being possible. How are you going to explain that to Delilah? She's going to be terrified if she hears it."

"Give it a minute," I insisted. I didn't think it would explode; I hoped I was right. A couple of minutes later, I was satisfied that it wasn't going to blow me up. I walked over and dumped the foamy liquid, pulling out two pieces of the bullet. "Bingo." I wiped the pieces off, examining the insides of it. There was a tiny sim card, and what looked like a small white rock inside one half of the projectile. It almost looked like a chunk of the tainted Powder we'd found. I needed to get it under the microscope and make sure.

The guys followed me back downstairs and watched as I confirmed my fears. Somehow the bullet had imitated a lightning strike but used the rock of Powder to immobilize me. "Well, we know who was behind the attack now. We just have to find him."

Dec looked at me and raised an eyebrow. "That's not news. We knew that Ghost was behind the attack when it happened."

"But now we have proof. And we know what kind of weapons he has. We can find a way to block them and fight back." I knew it wasn't the best news, but it was all I had. I had already started working on an antidote for the tainted Powder's effects, but didn't have everything I needed. After analyzing the material a second time, I realized that Steph had already asked for most of the ingredients, so it was faster than if I had to gather everything myself.

"Everything comes back to this Powder operation. What's his endgame? If everything he's done is to get back at Delilah for having the life that he thinks he deserved, how does poisoning a drug that's designed specifically for vamps help him?" Declan's question made perfect sense. I just wished that I had the answer.

"We may never know," I said, knowing it was a cop-out. "But if we can find him, we can try to torture it out of him."

Vik looked at Dec. "Are you sure he didn't say anything while he was torturing you and Delilah?"

Declan shook his head. "Not that I remember. I may have missed it. The pain of watching her suffer was worse than when he started on me. I don't remember much of what he said." Vik and I both winced at his explanation. I don't think either of us had considered how it would feel to watch our girl go through that. Every one of us would have to make it up to her. She didn't deserve any of this, especially from her family.

"We need to find the bastard. What if we set a trap?" Vik suggested, scrubbing his hand over the scruff that had been ignored since Delilah was taken the first time. Even Dec had let his beard grow the past few weeks. I wasn't sure if that was because we didn't have access to our homes, or if it was a conscious choice. I shook my head, dismissing the random thoughts that had been trying to distract me.

"What did you have in mind?" I started mixing the chemicals and medications to create the antidote while we talked. Steph agreed to help me figure out dosing and delivery, so she was working on that.

"Clearly, he thought Delilah was going to die from Kayden's bite. What if he found out that she didn't?" Bitterness wove through the words.

"Won't that put her in more danger? Especially since we don't know if she's going to be okay?" Declan asked, running his fingers through his near shoulder-length red curls.

"It could, you're right. But I don't see any other way. He's obsessed with her and making her pay. If he thinks that she survived his murder attempt, he might just get sloppy and give us a chance to take him down. It might be worth the risk." I hated to admit it, but I agreed with Vik. His idea might be the best way to finally catch Ghost and lock him away. The only way to know would be to try it.

"We can't make this decision without her. If we're going to use Delilah as bait, we have to at least give her some say in it. Don't we?" I loved the way Declan fought for our girl's autonomy.

"Absolutely. As soon as she and Kayden come out of their love nest, we'll discuss it as a family. We can each give her our opinion and see what she thinks. Who knows? She might have a better idea. Let's get this as planned out as we can to pitch it to her." I put the chemicals away and turned to the computer. I wondered if this would be the right time for a slideshow presentation. Of course, that was a ridiculous question. Any time is the right time for a slideshow. Especially one that detailed why the idea was our best option. Vik chuckled at me as I started creating the slides, complete with graphs and figures.

Dec opted for a notepad to jot down his reasons why we needed an alternative plan. I didn't blame him, but unless he came up with something awesome, I didn't see another way out of this.

CHAPTER 32

Vik

I HELPED ELI CAREFULLY craft his presentation. I agreed that it needed to be as detailed as possible to convince Delilah that it was the only option. I watched Dec with amusement as he tried to formulate a counter-argument. I hated the idea of using her as bait, but I was also practical enough to know that it was the only way to draw him out. We'd been searching for him for so long with no viable leads. Every time we got close; he went further underground. It was disheartening. All I wanted was to hold Delilah and show her how much I loved her.

But my desires would have to wait. She needed to bond with the wolf if she was going to have a chance to survive the bite. And we all wanted that. I wanted this to be over with so badly. If I could hunt him down on my own and rip him to shreds, I would. But I knew it wasn't practical. We needed to do this as a group, as a family. It was the only way that we would all feel like we deserved her.

I had to channel my emotionless side to work out the details of the plan with Eli. I'd wanted to take the words back the moment they left my mouth. But Eli had agreed it was the best option, so there was no way to take it back. We had to figure out the best way to protect her while still making it look like she was vulnerable.

"The location has to be central to all of our resources, or we won't be able to protect her." Eli wanted to take Delilah out of the city for this. "If we're leaving the city, we might as well try to find someone who can pass for her and leave Delilah out of it." I knew I was being an ass, and I didn't care. This plan had to be perfect or it wouldn't work.

473

Eli raised an eyebrow at me. "We agreed that using her as bait was the best idea, we're not going to try to fool him with a look alike. We didn't agree to let Ghost destroy the city to get to her."

"We could do it. There are plenty of women in the city that look enough like her." I was afraid that Eli would push the issue until we ended up fighting.

"If you don't like my idea, draw up your own. I'll finish this. It's her decision anyway," Eli growled. It was clear he wasn't going to change the plan no matter how I tried to convince him.

I stomped off to grab a blood bag. None of us had been eating the way we should, and being in cramped quarters while hungry always set me off. Maybe that was Ghost's plan, to have us kill each other instead of him doing it. If he really believed that Delilah was dead, wouldn't he be leaving us alone?

"There has to be more to his plan than just killing Delilah. Otherwise, he wouldn't be shooting up our hideout. I just don't want her caught in the middle," Eli had spoken the words I was thinking. It should have been strange, but we had a connection. More often than not, he and I knew what the other was thinking.

"If Delilah doesn't want to be part of the plan, we'll work with someone who looks like her. I think you're right; there's more to it than just her. He wants to take out all vamps. I don't think it's a trauma thing. I think he wants power and sees us as a threat." I voiced my thoughts aloud, shivering at how on-the-nose they felt. Eli nodded as I spoke.

"So, we give him what he wants. We'll set it up as if we want to meet with him to surrender. We'll give him Delilah if he'll let us leave the city and not chase after us. Is that what you're thinking?" Dec had apparently abandoned his counter argument and joined our conversation.

"Exactly. We make him think he's won. We finally see that he's right; she's to blame for everything. It'll take some acting on our part, especially for Kayden, since the wolf bond will make denying her impossible. Wait—that's it. We give him both of them. But first, we have to find a way to block the amulet so he can't actually control Kayden." My plan seemed easy enough. Would Delilah and Kayden agree? We continued to write every detail into the document. The only way to win this would be to kill Ghost.

Would Delilah agree to let us kill her brother? Would any of us be able to do it anyway if she refused? I steeled myself against the possibility that I would have to be the one to break her heart. Eli would get caught up in her emotions, Kayden wouldn't be able to get past the bond, and Declan would never be able to do something that could hurt her so badly. That left me. I wanted nothing more than to protect Delilah, no matter the cost.

I stepped away from my brothers as they worked out the minor details—when, where—and pulled up some documents on my phone. If I was facing this possibility, I would make sure everything was in order first. Especially if there was no other way to take him out than to sacrifice myself. I tapped the screen, adding clauses to my will, then emailed it to my lawyer. I knew that I would have to sneak away to speak with him directly, but that could wait until things were settled here. There would be a very specific set of circumstances to trigger the changes in my will.

I shook the thoughts from my head as I joined the others. Eli would have to find a way to contact Ghost. The rest of the plan would depend on how long that took. I wasn't looking forward to presenting our plan to our girl. I had a feeling that she would either freak out or decide it wasn't enough. I knew that she wanted to protect us as badly as I wanted to protect her.

I didn't have time to worry about it, because the bedroom door opened and Kayden strolled out with Delilah behind him. Both looked more rested than they had in a while. The smell of sex followed them, indicating that they had indeed cemented the bond. We froze, stopping all conversation and her cheeks turned pink. "Are you feeling better?" I asked, hoping to make an awkward situation less so.

She nodded, smiling over her shoulder at Kayden. "I'm starved." Dec jumped up from the couch and jogged to the small kitchenette to make her something to eat.

"Wolf food or vamp food?" he asked with a chuckle.

Delilah laughed, "Both." It wasn't odd that she wanted human food, all vamps could eat it and enjoy it. We just usually added uncooked blood to it for sustenance. Kayden gave her a kiss and headed to help Dec, no doubt he was famished as well. "So, who's gonna tell me what you're plotting?"

I choked on a laugh and Eli replied, "We were working on a presentation of sorts. We may have found a way to flush Ghost out and bring him to us."

"You want to use me as bait, huh?" And just like that, the wind was ripped from our sails. She didn't look pissed, though, so there was still a chance.

"Yes. It's a bit more complicated than that, thus the presentation. Essentially you would be the bait to draw him out. Then we would unload on him and take him out." I explained the plan as simply as possible. If she agreed to it, we'd give her the details. If not, there was no reason to share the rest.

"And by 'take him out,' you mean that you want to kill my brother. Right?" Her face was impossible to read at the moment, but with the way Eli tensed, I was convinced that she wasn't happy about it. Was her reaction because I wanted to kill her brother, or because she wanted to kill him herself?

"Yes. It's the only way to be sure that we'll be free of him," I began, pausing to pull her into my arms. She was stiff but didn't resist. "The decision is yours. If you listen to the presentation and hate the plan, we won't do it. If you like it but want to change things, that's fine too. Everything that happens on our end will be your call." I hated lying to her, but I wasn't about to tell her that I would kill her brother no matter what she said.

"I'll listen to your plan. I'm not committing to anything until I've heard every detail. And if I don't like something, I will change it. This is a lot to be hit with while I'm still recovering." Her admission had Eli grabbing her from my arms and pulling her down on the couch next to him. She snuggled into him as Dec and Kayden returned with food for all of us. Dec took the seat next to Delilah on the couch. Kayden seemed content to sit on the floor in front of him to be near her. I pulled a folding chair over and prepared to explain the plan.

CHAPTER 33

Delilah

I couldn't believe what I was hearing. My guys, the ones who were supposed to love and protect me, wanted to use me as bait to draw out my insane, homicidal brother. What were they thinking? He'd almost killed me the last time. And to include Kayden in that? There was no way. "No. It's not happening. End of story. Find another way." I hopped up from the couch and began to pace. I needed an outlet for my anger before I exploded.

Kayden stepped in front of me, blocking my way. "Babe, you have to breathe. It's not good to get this upset. You could lose control." Why did it matter? It wasn't like I could really kill any of them. Oh, the bite. If everything Grammy told me was true, I might actually be able to kill them accidentally. He was right, I needed to calm down.

I jumped into his arms and he began to pace for me. It was kind of weird being this connected to him when I didn't have the same thing with the others. I didn't want any of them to feel less important to me. I loved them all the same, even if they couldn't feel my emotions or read my mind.

"Okay, let's all take a breath. Stop and think for a minute. What part of the plan is the problem?" Of course, Vik wanted to find a way to make his plan work. It killed me how he could flip that switch and not feel anything. None of the rest of us could.

"All of it. I refuse to put Kayden in that position. I will not let Ghost use him like that again," I fumed. "If you want to use me as bait, fine. I'll go and Ghost can do whatever he wants to me, but you're not doing that to him." I hugged Kayden tighter when I spoke. "I wouldn't ask any of you to go through that again, so how can you ask him?"

Dec stood up and walked over to us. He wrapped his arms around both of us from my back, sandwiching me to Kayden. Mmm, I could definitely get used to this. "That was my biggest objection too. But what if that's the only way the plan will work?" he whispered softly against my back.

I sighed, feeling defeated. The whole time they were explaining the plan, Declan seemed to be on my side. Now he was arguing for me to go along with it, no matter how I felt. "I don't know. I hate the plan. All of it. There has to be another way."

Kayden rubbed his hand up and down my back, trying to soothe me. "What if there's not?"

"You too? Really?" I jumped out of his arms, knocking Dec out of my way. "I can't believe you want to do this. After what he did to you. I just, I, I don't know." Had someone turned the heat up? I wiped the sweat from my eyes and kept pacing. I felt like a trapped animal; terrified and feral.

"It's okay, love. We'll be there the whole time. Us, Scott, Steph, and the whole crew. We won't let Ghost do anything to either of you," Eli assured me. The only part of the plan I liked was that we would have backup. I just couldn't agree to put Kayden in that position again, even if he claimed to be okay with it. They didn't watch him go through it the way I did. They couldn't feel his emotions like I could.

"I'm sorry. I can't. There has to be another way. Why is it so hot in here?" The room started to spin and I heard my guys freak out.

"Get a cold rag," Dec ordered, catching me before my head could hit the floor. I couldn't focus to see who he was talking to.

"Dec, you need to get back," Kayden growled. What was he doing? There was no reason Dec couldn't hold me. "It's happening."

"Are you sure?" Eli asked just before I saw his face. Suddenly they were all standing over me. It was strange, but so much lately was.

"Yeah, I'm sure. Just get back. Stay out of her way," Kayden told the guys. Then he turned back to me, his face filling my vision. "Babe, this is going to hurt. Don't fight it. I promise it's going to be okay. I'm right here with you." He disappeared, so I turned my head to find him. *You can't tell someone you'll be there and then vanish.* I thought. His chuckle was the only indication that he'd heard me.

My eyes settled on his, and I realized why he'd backed up. He was blocking the other three from me. Because if I shifted, I could hurt them. I nodded at him to let him know that I understood before I realized that I could have just thought it. *It hurts.*

I know, mo chroí, but you can do this. Declan's voice filtered through my mind. I nearly forgot that he could hear me too. I turned and looked at each of my guys before scrambling further away. I couldn't risk losing control. I had to give Kayden room to stop me. I didn't get to decide if I was far enough away because the pain took over.

I felt like I was on fire. Sweat poured off me; my insides were burning. That was painful enough without the crunching of my bones as they broke and reshaped. I felt my clothes rip to shreds and fall away. I had watched Kayden shift before, but I had no idea he went through this pain every time. *It only hurts the first few times, then you learn how to relax and let it happen. Don't fight it, babe.* I heard his voice in my head and tears streamed down my face. The pain was excruciating, but I had to try to listen to his advice.

I took a couple of ragged breaths, trying to calm myself. I felt the prickle of fur sprouting through my skin as the bones reshaped and snapped in place. It seemed like the transition took an eternity. I stared down at the large, black paws under me. *Holy shit, I'm a wolf.* I tried to breathe, but just the idea that I'd shifted caused my heart to race. I was immersed in a panic attack like never before. What if I couldn't shift back? What if I hurt someone?

Babe, it's okay. Deep breath in, that's it. And let it out. Good. You're okay. I'm going to approach you now, okay? Kayden's voice melted through my defenses. I nodded but wasn't sure if he would understand. He walked over slowly, waiting to see if I was going to bite him, I guess. I tried to sit, but my tail got in the way. I decided to lay down instead. I didn't want to attack him, but wasn't sure what might set me off.

My anxiety eased the moment his hands were in my fur. *I had fur. That was the strangest thing I've ever thought.* He laughed at my thoughts but didn't share them with the other guys. I turned to look at them, expecting to see fear. They all looked like they were resisting the urge to pet me like I was a stray dog. It was sweet but annoying. I was a ferocious wolf. They should have been scared. I was.

Would you like to see yourself? Dec's voice was soft and sweet. I realized that he could hear my thoughts too. Or could he, now that I was a wolf? *Yes, mo chroí, I can still hear you. You're still you, even in this form.* I stood up, making Kayden take a step back. Then I walked over to Dec. Or I tried to. Walking on four legs wasn't easy. It took a minute to figure it out. I stumbled a little before finally getting my paws to work the way they were supposed to.

How am I going to see myself? I tipped my head sideways at him, stopping a few feet away. I didn't want to risk accidentally hurting any of them. I guess the fact that I wasn't snarling had put them at ease. Before he could respond, Eli and Vik lunged at me, holding me down and petting me. I wished I could say it made me angry, but it felt so good. I actually smiled at them and let my tongue hang out the side of my mouth when I rolled onto my back. I definitely understood dogs' obsession with belly rubs. They were the best. Dec squatted in front of me and smiled, then held out his hand for my paw. I placed my right paw in his hand, then rolled back on my stomach, raised up, and licked him.

He play growled at me and I ran away from him. He chased me for a minute, then decided it wasn't worth the effort. *There's a mirror in the bathroom. You can see how beautiful you are if you want.* It seemed strange to me that he thought I was beautiful in this form. I wasn't sure that I wanted to see, but I felt like I needed to know. I followed him into the bathroom, knowing that I would pay for the full-face lick later.

CHAPTER 34

Kayden

DELILAH'S DELIGHT AT SEEING herself as a nearly solid black wolf was palpable, I didn't have to tell the others how she felt. It seemed that she could still communicate with Dec while in wolf form, and Eli was able to read her emotions as he always could. The only one who struggled was Vik, but he wasn't scared of not knowing. I wondered if there was a way to share part of the bond with him. Maybe I would call Grammy and see. I didn't like any of us being at a disadvantage.

For now, we were all content with watching Delilah as she pranced in front of the mirror. Her wolf was spectacular. She was solid black with a single gray stripe that started between her eyes and ran down her face, widening to encompass her muzzle, widened more at her chest and disappeared at her belly. It would be a stark contrast to my chestnut brown wolf. I couldn't wait to go for a run with her. I wondered briefly what order she would manifest as, then laughed the thought off. Bitten wolves typically manifested as the wolf type most close to their personalities. For Delilah, she would be an omega. They were rare, and the one wolf who could go toe to toe with an alpha and have a chance to win. They were also the ones who cared for everyone and made sure pack life was fair.

I wondered if I would get the chance to teach her about pack life. It was clear that we'd be staying in the city since her vampire lovers wouldn't survive in the pack territory for long. I decided to make it a point to show her how things were done where I'm from, even if we didn't go back there. As far as we had known, hybrids were a myth. Then we learned Grammy's secret. Each of us had sworn to keep it. I had no idea growing up that she was a hybrid. She hid her vamp side well. I wondered if her family knew, or if it made them different.

I was ripped from my thoughts by Vik's hand on my arm. "Is she okay? Will it hurt her to stay in that form for so long?" His concern was touching.

"It shouldn't hurt her. Most wolves shift for long periods of time the first few times. It takes a while to get used to walking on four legs and dealing with the tail. Give her a little while longer, then I'll talk her through shifting back. My first time, I stayed in wolf form for three days. My mother refused to let me in the house because I had rolled in the mud. It was hilarious."

How long do I have to stay like this? Her question was filled with panic. She had heard my story and feared the worst.

As long as you want, babe. When you're ready, I'll help you shift back. I tried to make my voice as comforting as possible. I didn't need her freaking out and biting one of the guys.

"Guys? Can we give Delilah some space? I think she's almost ready to shift back, but she's starting to panic about it. I need to calm her down in order to walk her through it." I thought the others would leave but instead they simply took a few steps back from our girl.

"We need to know how to help her too," Eli reasoned. He was right. They each needed to know how to calm her down and talk her through a shift. I would have to do this the unbonded way.

I nodded. *Babe, I'm going to talk you through the shift so the other guys can hear, okay?* I waited for her nod to begin. "Take a deep breath to start. Relax your muscles. That's it, good." I could feel the tension and fear slipping away as she focused on my voice.

"Now concentrate on the shift. You're a wolf, but you want to be human. Remember the process, but reverse it. Yes, it will hurt, but not as much as it did the first time." Nothing about this situation was normal, so I hoped I wasn't giving her bad information. I knew that the process should be the same, but I had no idea how much it would hurt her.

Delilah did as I asked, pulling the shift forward. It happened slowly and almost in reverse of how she'd shifted into the wolf. Her fur receded while her bones cracked and reformed. Claws and paws turned into hands and feet. Her arms and legs straightened back out. Her muzzle changed into her face, which was contorted in pain. My heart hurt at her suffering, but at least this wasn't torture.

When she was almost completely shifted, Steph walked into the doorway. "What's going on?" Her presence startled Delilah and caused her to change back. It happened quickly this time, and she didn't seem to suffer. She was on guard, growling at the intrusion.

"Delilah shifted and we were trying to help her come back. She was almost done when you scared her into the wolf again." Vik's assessment was as good as I could have given. Sometimes I envied him the ability to say whatever the fuck he wanted without worrying about hurting someone's feelings.

"Oh, I'm sorry. I'll be out here if you need me," Steph said, excusing herself to the other room. I knew that she hadn't meant to scare Delilah, but now I had to calm her down again. This would be easier if I could shift and talk her through it over the bond. But the others wanted to know how to help, so I would try to honor their wishes.

"One more time, babe. You can do this. Focus and breathe. Pull your human form to the front and make the wolf recede." I waited a moment while she was slowing her breathing. *You can do this.* She nodded and I knew she would try again.

Delilah concentrated for a few minutes, but nothing happened. *Why isn't it working?* She asked, getting impatient. I needed to find a way to relax her and convince her to shift back. Then I had an idea.

I turned to Eli, Dec, and Vik. "Take off your clothes." I walked over and closed the bathroom door, locking it to make sure that Steph didn't come back in. Then I started to strip, thinking about the amazing time I'd had with Delilah sealing our bond. My cock hardened, and she noticed. "It's working, come on guys, don't be shy."

Dec rolled his eyes and stripped. Eli and Vik shared a glance, then decided it couldn't hurt. Within a matter of minutes, Delilah had four naked men standing in front of her. "If you shift, you can shower with whoever you want," I taunted. At this point, a quick glance around the room told me that any of us would be interested in that idea.

So, your plan was to get me horny so I would shift? Delilah's voice was soft with laughter. Her wolf growled as the shift started. It was quicker this time and didn't seem to hurt her as much. Once she was human again, she fell into my arms. I knew that the four of us naked would be enough to convince her human side to come out. I also knew that she would be too worn out from the back and forth of it to do anything about it.

"I wasn't kidding about the shower, but now I think it should be a nice, soothing bath. Which one of us will it be?" I asked, expecting her to choose Eli or Dec because they were so much better at taking care of her. She looked at me and grinned.

"You're going to make me choose? That's so mean!" she pouted. I had to admit, she made a good point. None of us had made her choose before. But the tub wouldn't hold all of us.

"Just until we find a bigger tub. Until then, we can rotate if you want." The idea seemed ridiculous to me, but Delilah seemed to like it. Her smile lit up the room.

"Deal," she said. Dec and Eli had already begun to get towels and all the amenities she could want, while Vik started filling the tub. It seemed they sensed her response before she gave it. I may have been wrong about Vik being at a disadvantage after all. I scooped her up and carried our girl over to the mountain of bubbles on top of the steaming water. I kissed her gently before setting her down in the tub. "Get in," she demanded with a pout. I wondered if she knew that was all it took to get her way. I slid into the lavender-scented water next to her, my body immediately relaxing with the warmth of it.

CHAPTER 35

Eli

THE FLOWERY SCENT OF lavender filled the room, indicating that Dec had used too much bubble bath. Delilah's arousal mingled with it until the air was almost suffocating. None of us complained; we were all ready and willing to drown in our girl. Her desire seemed to be contagious, as the four of us were hard and ready.

Kayden settled into the tub with her. She insisted on washing him, even if he objected. While she took care of him, the rest of us decided that we would clean her up. Declan started by wetting her hair, then massaging shampoo into it. Vik and I grabbed washcloths and began to scrub her body. I washed her back while Vik got her front. It was difficult to stay out of each other's way, but we did the best we could. Delilah's moans of pleasure made it all worthwhile.

I made a mental note to have a new tub installed that would hold all five of us. If this was going to be a regular occurrence, we would need to be comfortable. Not that we minded a little discomfort while caring for our girl, but if we were designing a new place or upgrading existing ones, we might as well get what we wanted. Dec had mentioned a property that was central to all four zones. It would be perfect once we took care of Ghost and set Kayden up to run the East.

Delilah washed Kayden's hair while Dec finished rinsing hers. He had applied conditioner and combed it through while she washed Kayden's body. The whole process was so sensual that I knew I wasn't the only one who had a raging erection.

"Tell us what you want," Vik encouraged as he rubbed the soft cloth against Delilah's nipples. It seemed that consent was something that turned him on. He was adamant that she be the one to decide where this would go from here. I was certain that we all felt that way about her.

She dipped her head back and groaned. "I want all of you." Her reply sent goosebumps down my spine. My cock jumped at her words and she smiled seductively. Dec brought towels over to wrap Delilah in and for Kayden to dry off with. The room was filled with the smell of our lust and panted breaths. I was pretty sure that Delilah's only experience with multiple men had been when she was with Vik and me.

I wondered exactly how this would work. We hadn't discussed boundaries or anything like that. I knew that Delilah had a safe word that she used with Vik, but wasn't sure this would be appropriate to discuss. I didn't need Vik getting pissed and storming out because our girl had shared that detail with me. So, I kept my mouth shut and waited to see what happened next. While I was lost in my thoughts, Dec and Vik had dried Delilah off and brushed her dark hair.

Things started slowly, with Dec grabbing lotion to rub on Delilah. He passed the bottle around so each of us could have some. We took our time massaging the softly scented cream into her skin. Her quiet moans were the only indication that she hadn't fallen asleep.

With her basic needs taken care of, I decided to move things along. I trailed my fingers from Delilah's neck down her chest, barely grazing her nipple. Her eyes shot open and met mine, filled with need. Vik caught her lips with his as I slowly moved my hand lower.

The smell of desire couldn't be masked by the lavender of the bath or the soft floral of the lotion. By the time my fingers reached her center, my brothers were all pressed against our girl. Delilah tried to pay attention to all of us at once, which only led to her teasing us in the best way. While she worked her way from one cock to the next, I slipped a finger inside of her and rubbed her clit with my thumb.

Vik moved from kissing her to biting and sucking on one of her nipples. Declan kissed her breathless, while Kayden played with the other nipple. The noises she made worked the four of us into a frenzy. Once she was dripping, I slipped inside of her. I kept my pace slow and torturous. Delilah's concentration wavered and her hands that had been stroking Vik and Kayden stilled. Both of them growled in protest, and she tried to focus on pleasing them.

"Use your words, Myshka," Vik ordered Delilah to voice her needs and desires. I wondered if he was that way when they were alone.

She threw her head back, breathing hard. "More. Give me more." At her request, Dec grabbed a bottle of lube and began to tease her ass while I maintained the slow pace of my thrusts. Delilah looked from one face to the next until she settled on Vik. "I want to taste you." Kayden threw a towel down on the floor and I pulled Delilah down on top of me without breaking contact.

As she straddled me, Dec had lubed up and was gently fingering her ass, matching my pace. Vik knelt down beside my head and Delilah grabbed him. She stroked him from base to tip, then licked him the same way before sucking him into her mouth. The moment Vik was in her mouth, Dec entered her ass. The three of us thrust into her carefully, trying to figure out the best pace. Even though she was pinned in place, Delilah tried to move her hips to get us to go faster.

Once we settled into a rhythm, Dec thrust in when I pulled out and Delilah deep throated Vik every time Dec's balls touched mine. The whole thing should have been awkward, but it was just hot. With our pace even, Delilah reached for Kayden. He knelt on the opposite side of me from where Vik was. Then Delilah started alternating cocks in her mouth. Watching her suck them all the way down got to me, and I started to thrust faster. Dec matched my pace, making sure to add more lube to keep from hurting our girl.

Delilah's moans were cut off by the dick in her mouth, but there was nothing about them that said she was hurting. Kayden and Vik played with her breasts while she sucked the two of them off. Dec and I kept pounding into her, harder and faster, over and over, until she arched up and screamed our names. That act sent us both over the edge, making us come at the same time. "More," she growled, obviously not done with us yet. Dec and I backed off to give Kayden and Vik room to please our girl.

For a moment, no one was touching Delilah. It was clear from her expression that she didn't like that. "Kayden, here." She pointed to her pussy, then turned to look at Vik. "You, here." She pointed at her ass. Her commanding them like that was enough to make my dick hard again. I glanced over and noticed it had the same effect on Dec. We quickly washed off at the tub and rejoined the fun.

I walked over just in time to watch Delilah slide onto Kayden. Dec took the spot Vik had been in. I stood back and watched for a minute as Vik slathered lube on himself and Delilah before slipping two fingers in her ass. She arched her back, then lay on Kayden's chest so Vik could enter her. I was impressed that they worked together almost as well as Dec and I had. Delilah gasped at the sensations, before reaching for Dec's hard-on. She stroked him, then started swirling her tongue around his cock. A thought occurred to me and I knelt down beside Kayden opposite of Dec.

I met Kayden's eyes and asked, "Do you trust me?" He gave me a confused look but nodded. "This will either be really awkward or feel really good." I tapped a button on my prosthetic hand and it started to vibrate. I slipped my hand between Kayden and Delilah, finding her sensitive nub. He groaned and she cried out. I tapped another button and the vibration pattern changed.

"Oh, Eli, why didn't you get that out sooner?" Delilah asked, breathless. She hummed her approval as she ground into Kayden and Vik. They had both picked up their pace. I hadn't realized how powerful the vibration setting was until now. The look on Vik's face told me that he could feel it too.

"That thing is pretty intense," Vik commented. Kayden hadn't said anything, but with the way he bit his lip, I thought he was preoccupied trying not to come yet. Delilah stroked Dec as Kayden and Vik started to pound into her harder. I wondered if it was the influence of the vibrating hand, or if the need to climax was taking over. Delilah called out their names as her orgasm overtook her, and after a few more thrusts, all three of the other men finished. I switched off the vibration and joined the cuddle pile in the middle of the bathroom floor.

CHAPTER 36

Declan

THE GROUP SEX WAS almost more than I had bargained for. It was scorching. I never expected to enjoy watching another guy fuck my woman, but there was something about this situation that was just right. There was no jealousy, no competition. Everything was about giving Delilah what she needed.

After snuggling for a little while, I scooped Delilah up and carried her to the shower. It wasn't big enough for all of us, but we'd just learned that we were good at sharing. Kayden joined us and Delilah insisted on cleaning us up. When she was done, she let us wash her, then insisted that Eli and Vik needed some attention. We left the shower, taking the towels they held out and let them get in with our girl. I was surprised that the shower didn't turn into round two, but everyone was clearly wiped out from the experience. Once we were all cleaned up, we left the bathroom to snuggle on the bed. It was barely big enough for all of us, so we were all piled on top of each other.

None of us bothered with clothes, because Delilah asked us not to. It was amazing the things we would do for her. Honestly, I would have been willing to do whatever she wanted. If she had asked me to fuck one of the other guys, I wouldn't have hesitated. I doubted Vik or Kayden would have been comfortable with it, but I thought Eli would have been game.

I probably shouldn't have been letting these thoughts run rampant while the five of us were snuggled so closely together; especially since we were all still naked. I couldn't help feeling a little embarrassed when my dick got hard again. I tried to angle it away from the others and hide it under Delilah. I wasn't necessarily embarrassed that I was attracted to Eli, but I didn't exactly want to have that conversation with the group at this exact moment. It would be awkward and uncomfortable with Kayden and Vik in the room. What if Eli wasn't interested? What if the other two wanted to know why I wasn't attracted to either of them? Kayden was easy enough to explain, as we had grown up together, but Vik?

He had those dark, brooding brown eyes. Sure, he was handsome, but his attitude was shit. Add to it that he had openly threatened me several times, and I just wasn't interested. I didn't want to start that argument, so I would think about other things until the idea passed. Delilah needed to rest so we could shift our focus to hunting down Ghost. It didn't matter to me that he was her brother, the man needed to be captured. I wanted to kill him, but I wasn't sure how she felt about that. I would never do anything to hurt her, so if she wanted him alive, he'd be kept alive.

That thought was enough to take care of my boner; murder was not a turn-on for me. I glanced around the room, realizing it had gotten really quiet. Everyone else was sleeping or acting the part. I settled in and dozed off for a while.

I woke in a dark tunnel, searching for something. I felt anxious as if I had to find it, whatever it was. *What am I doing here?* I had to find it; no, I had to find her. *Delilah?* But we'd already rescued her. How could she be missing again? None of this made sense. I kept moving through the tunnel, moving faster with each turn. Before I knew it, I was running, chasing the unknown.

The darkness closed in on me, stealing my sight. I could no longer tell which way to go. I stopped, frozen to the floor. "Delilah!" I called to her, hoping she could tell me which way to go. My voice echoed down the hall, but there was no response. I had no idea what direction I was heading, or where I had just come from. Panic began to set in. The air was heavy and it was hard to breathe. I knew that it wouldn't kill me, but with all the new discoveries of ways our kind could perish, I wasn't sure of that.

Footsteps rushed toward me, thundering in my ears. *Would I be trampled?* I tried again to gain my bearings. I needed to get out of the way of whatever was heading for me. I closed my eyes—they weren't doing me any good anyway—and stepped to the side, feeling for the cold stone wall. Once my hands hit the rough bricks, I pressed my body against them and waited, hoping I'd chosen the right direction to avoid what was coming. I felt something solid brush against me and I pressed myself closer to the wall.

The entity stopped moving, seeming to turn around as if it was looking for something. I held my breath and waited to be devoured. It brushed against me again, sniffing all around. Then suddenly, it raced off. I debated following it, but still couldn't see. I didn't know what I was up against and didn't want to run into it. Instead, I stood there, flat against the wall. I realized that with my ear pressed against the wall, I could hear something on the other side. It spurred something inside of me and I dug my fingers into the wall, trying to rip bricks out.

It was an impossible task, but my fingers didn't stop. Digging, ripping, tearing into the bricks until one finally came loose. I pulled it free and started on another. I kept at it until I had made a small hole in the wall. A little beam of light streamed through the opening. I could see something on the other side, but the hole wasn't big enough to tell exactly what it was. I pulled and tugged at bricks, dropping them behind me as I worked, making the hole bigger until it was large enough for me to squeeze through.

I forced myself into the opening, pushing and pulling to get to the other side. I had no idea if it would be safer there than where I was; I only knew that there was some light on this side. I fought my way through, squinting at the light as I got to my feet. Looking around the room, I noticed four posts, one in each corner, with something tied to each of them. I crept toward the closest corner, my eyes whipping around the room to make sure it was safe.

Once I was in front of a pole, I gasped. Tied to it, unconscious, was Eli. I fought with the ropes, tearing through them to get him down. His chest barely moved, just enough to let me know he was still breathing. I lowered him to the ground and stood, searching the room with my eyes. I was certain I knew what I would find when I inspected each of the other poles.

Laughter echoed through the room as I quietly walked to the next corner. Someone was watching, enjoying this torture. I knew instantly who was responsible. *Ghost.* He would pay. First, I had to free my family. Kayden was tied up on the next post I checked. It took a few minutes longer to destroy the ropes holding him, but I lowered him to the ground, leaning him against the wood. I had to take a break before I threw Kayden's arm around my shoulder and dragged him over to Eli. After propping them up next to each other, I crossed the room carefully to the next body.

Vik was tied exactly as the other two had been. I couldn't help the disappointment that washed over me. I'd wanted to find Delilah next and make sure she was okay. I shook the thought away. Vik was family too, even if he wanted me dead more often than not. I freed him as I had the other two, then dragged him back to them. Once I made sure the three of them were as comfortable as possible, I worked my way around the room to the last pillar.

I had expected to find Delilah tied in the same way as the others. What I hadn't expected was to see myself tied to the wooden pole, unconscious and barely breathing like my brothers. I tore through the ropes and lowered the body, coming face to face with myself. It was a strange feeling, to see myself from the outside. One minute I was staring curiously at my own face, then next, the body disintegrated. As it turned to dust in my arms, I turned back to where I had left the others. I ran across the room, trying to get to them before anything could happen.

I was too late. By the time I crossed the room, they were nothing but piles of dust. I dropped to my knees and cried out in anguish. I had lost everything.

CHAPTER 37

Vik

I WOKE UP WITH a start, sitting straight up in bed. There was nothing quite like a fist to the face to start your day. It took me a moment to realize that it wasn't an intentional fist. Dec was thrashing around, obviously having some kind of nightmare. How he hadn't woken everyone was beyond me.

I carefully moved beside him, pinning him down the best I could. Then I started to stroke his hair and whisper to him. "Shh, it's okay. You're safe. Just relax." I watched the others to make sure they weren't stirring. The last thing I needed was for anyone to think I'd gone soft.

As much as I pretended to detest him, Dec had a special place in my heart. He had saved Delilah's life, after all. I mean, initially, I was jealous about having to share her, but I was already sharing with Eli. Besides, how could I tell her no when I saw how happy each of the guys make her? It's not like I've gotten any less attention. I just don't want them to think I'm weak. So, I'll keep the walls up and act like I'm annoyed at them all. Admittedly, sometimes it's not an act.

It should have been awkward pressing my naked body up against another man's, but it really wasn't. It wasn't like I wanted him; I just didn't mind that we were both naked. He wasn't my type. Honestly, neither was Eli. If I were to be with a man, it would be someone like Kayden. He wouldn't get all sappy and emotional about it. The moment I realized my dick was getting hard, I had to push those thoughts away. It was one thing to be pressed up against another man to calm him from a nightmare; it was something else entirely to rub my erection on him.

Filing those thoughts to explore later, I turned my attention back to Dec. He had stopped thrashing but was whimpering now. I brushed the hair from his sweat-coated forehead and continued to whisper soothingly. For a moment I wondered if I should wake him. Before I could decide, his eyes shot open, wildly searching the room. Delilah hadn't been asleep long enough, so I threw him over my shoulder and rushed us into the opposite bedroom. If the look in his eyes was any indication, he had no idea where he was anyway.

I gently lowered him to his feet and took a cautious step back. "Declan, are you okay?" He stared at me, his expression blank and not seeing. It looked like I was going to have to do something to snap him out of whatever trance this was. He blinked and shook his head as soon as my palm made contact with his cheek.

"What the fuck?" Dec gripped my arms as I held him up. "Where am I?"

"You're safe. We're in the other bedroom. I didn't want you to wake the others." His expression was a mix of confusion and concern. "Are you okay?"

Dec looked around the room and nodded slowly. "It was a dream. I can't believe it was a dream." He squeezed my arms harder before he let go and pulled me into a hug. "I'm so glad it was only a dream. I thought I'd lost you all."

"That must have been one hell of a dream if you're hugging me," I laughed. He flinched at my words but didn't let go. This was bigger than I had realized. I was relieved that I'd had enough sense to get him away from everyone else.

"I need to see them, then I'll be able to talk about it," he whispered against my chest, his face buried there as if to hide from what had scared him. I rubbed my hand down his back and eased him away from me before leading him back to the room where our family slept. I cracked the door open a little so he could see inside. He watched them for a few minutes, then turned back to me. "Okay, I think I can tell you."

I followed him back to the empty room we'd just been in. He sat on the bed, clearly waiting for me to join him. I sat, then he began his story. "I was lost in the tunnels; something was chasing me. It was big and warm. I couldn't see anything. Somehow, I broke through a wall; I think I heard a noise. I thought I'd found you all." He stopped talking and jumped to his feet, suddenly needing to move.

"I climbed through the wall and saw four posts with people tied to them. I untied Eli, Kayden, and you then went for Delilah. But it wasn't her. It was me. As soon as I cut myself down, I disintegrated. Then you all did too. I couldn't find her; I couldn't save her. We were just gone." I could hear the panic in his voice as he paced back and forth, trying to work through the nightmare.

"It must have seemed so real. I can't imagine experiencing that. It should help to know it was only a dream." I wasn't good at being comforting, and I knew it. I was tempted to wake Delilah; she would know what to say to calm Dec.

"I thought it was real. At first, it seemed off, I'm not sure how to explain it, just off somehow. Then everything felt so real. I felt myself turn to dust, then ran for you guys. I held it in my hands. I felt it." He stared off into space as he spoke, clearly caught up in the realism of the images. "What does it mean?" He didn't seem upset that I wasn't good at this. It was kind of nice to have this moment with him away from the others.

"I don't know. Maybe it's just a manifestation of your fears. You're afraid of losing yourself; you're afraid of losing us. I'm not a shrink, but that's how it seems to me." I shrugged, hoping that he didn't want me to analyze his dream further. I was better at getting information from people who didn't want to talk than figuring out what symbolism meant.

Luckily, I didn't have to play dream analyst as Eli walked into the room before Dec could comment. "What's wrong?" He looked from Dec to me and back again. I raised my eyebrows, letting Dec explain. He went through the dream once again, detailing the emotions and sights. Eli nodded, not interrupting or responding until Dec was finished.

"That's definitely a nightmare. I'm sorry, man. I can imagine how badly that fucked with your head." Dec seemed to relax with Eli's words. I knew that someone else would be better at comforting him. "But how did you end up over here with him?" Eli turned to me.

"I'm not a total ass. He was having a nightmare and I didn't want everyone to be disturbed. I brought him over here and we talked it through," I grumbled my response at him, detesting the fact that everyone thought I was so heartless.

Dec put his hand on my shoulder. "Don't worry, I won't tell anyone you were nice to me. It'll be our little secret." He chuckled but his offer to keep my secret actually made me feel better.

"I'll hold you to that. I can't have people thinking I'm weak. I won't be able to protect the family if everyone challenges me at once." Vampire politics had been increasingly violent lately; it was getting harder to hold onto a territory. We needed all the power we could get.

Eli laughed before turning back to Dec. "Are you okay? Is there anything we can do?" He knew that even though it was a dream, it might make Dec feel better to know that we were willing to help. I kicked myself mentally for not thinking of that.

Dec shook his head. "I just have to let it go. It was a dream. It didn't actually happen. I think I'll go shower and get dressed before Delilah and Kayden wake up." At this point, I remembered that the three of us were standing around talking while we were completely naked. The thought amused me, but I kept it to myself. Dec walked away, leaving Eli staring at me.

"What?" I snapped, knowing exactly why he was staring at me. No doubt he was going to get emotional and sappy at me over trying to help Dec.

"He's growing on you. I knew you didn't actually hate him. It's nice to see you being kind for a change, that's all." Eli's response irritated me. It didn't matter that he knew I wasn't as scary as I pretended to be. It just annoyed me that he felt the need to call me out on it. His smug smirk grated at me and he knew it.

CHAPTER 38

Delilah

I WOKE TO FIND the bed cold, except where Kayden still lay beside me with his legs over mine. I wondered how long we'd been sleeping. My mind replayed yesterday's events and I was thankful that the others had let me rest. There was no way to know when I would get to sleep this peacefully again. We had to step up our efforts to find my brother.

It was strange to think of Gerolf, or Ghost, as my brother. I'd never even known he existed. I wondered why I'd never been able to convince Mom to stay when she'd come to visit. And I'd overheard her arguing with Uncle Vinny on several occasions, though I was too young to understand what they'd been arguing about. My heart stung at the thought of him, my dear uncle. He'd been far from perfect, but he'd always done his best to keep me safe. He didn't deserve what Gerolf had done to him. Don't worry, Uncle Vinny, I'll take care of it. I would avenge my uncle, and my mother, by taking out my brother. The thought stabbed at my brain.

I hated that he was my brother, my blood. I was angry that my mother didn't bother to tell me about him. Or that she'd pretended to search for my father when she knew exactly where he was. I knew that I should talk to someone about everything, but I didn't want to voice any of it yet. I was still sorting out my feelings. *You know I'm here if you ever want to talk about it, babe.* Kayden's voice flowed into my head even though his eyes remained closed. It seemed that I needed to work on keeping my thoughts to myself, too.

I'm okay. I don't want to talk about it yet. But thanks. I tried not to sound angry, though I was convinced he knew I would be at the intrusion. At the same time, I knew that he didn't mean anything by it. He was getting used to the mate bond the same as I was. I brushed his dark waves from his face, tracing his jaw with my finger. *It's too bad I can't communicate with all of you this way.*

Kayden stirred, fluttering his eyes open and adjusting to the little bit of light in the room. "There might be a way. I can talk to Eli about it if you want."

I raised an eyebrow at him. "How?" I'd never heard of such a thing before, but I didn't know about the mate bond or sire bond before I'd become in a position to have them work for me.

"I read something about an implant; I think Eli's company makes it. Or they're developing it now. They're actually working with a friend of mine. He's a psychologist, and he's brilliant. If you decide you want to talk to someone that's not us, he'd be great." Kayden's suggestion stung as if he wanted me to go to someone else with my problems. I knew that he'd meant it for my comfort; it might be easier to talk to someone who couldn't hear my thoughts.

"I'll keep that in mind about your friend. What kind of an implant is it? I've never heard of that. Do you think it would work?" I didn't figure he'd have the answers but I couldn't help asking.

Kayden shrugged, shifting in the bed to lay next to me. "From what I read, it's a tiny chip that goes near or at the base of your skull. Somehow it allows you to communicate with other people who have chips connected. I didn't really understand how it worked, but the idea was fascinating. I'm better with engines than with electronics. We can ask Eli."

I nodded but made no move to get out of the bed. I knew that we should get up, shower, and get on with the day, but I wasn't ready for that yet. Knowing that the moment my feet hit the floor, I would have to begin the hunt for my brother, then decide if I was willing to kill him, was too much for me. I couldn't make that decision right now. I needed more time. Finding him wouldn't be instant, but I just couldn't do it yet.

"We will. I just need to block it all out a little while longer." From the look on Kayden's face, he'd been hearing my thoughts and understood. I couldn't be angry with him, I wasn't sure how to block my thoughts from him or his from me, so it was unfair to expect him to do it.

I know it's a tough decision. No one expects you to be okay with killing him. But it's your choice what happens to him once we catch him. You know we all want to rip him to pieces for what he's done to you. Kayden focused on the wall, not looking at me while he pushed the thoughts at me. I wiped a tear from my eye and turned to him.

I turned his face toward mine and pressed my lips to his, using that sensation to push away any thoughts of Gerolf and what would have to be done. He wrapped his arms around me and teased his tongue between my lips. I knew that if we stayed here like this, we'd end up making love again. That would be a lovely way to push the bad thoughts away too. Kayden deepened the kiss, and I started to feel warm all over.

The heat intensified until I had to push him away. I gasped for breath, unable to speak. I felt like my skin was on fire. He took one look at me, then rushed to the doors and locked them. I didn't understand what was happening. *It's okay, just relax. Don't fight it. The shift will hurt more if you fight it.* Of course, I was going to shift right now.

Why was this happening at the most inconvenient time? I hadn't even thought about not having control over it. I panted, trying to listen to his words. I didn't want the pain I'd felt yesterday to ever happen again. I was terrified that I would hurt one of my guys when I shifted. I needed to control it. I couldn't let myself shift when it would put them in danger. I had to stop those thoughts. Panic was taking hold. I couldn't even focus on Kayden's voice in my head.

"Babe, you have to breathe. It's okay. You won't hurt anyone. I'm right here with you," Kayden had his hands on my face, making me look at him. I took a deep breath, letting his words wash over me.

I forced myself to calm down, thinking about how the others were safe, and I couldn't hurt Kayden because he was a wolf too. I concentrated on his voice and let the shift take me. My bones cracked and reformed. Fur sprouted all over me. My nose elongated into a snout and my ears shifted and grew. I watched as my hands morphed into paws. I marveled at how this time it didn't hurt as badly as it had the first time. How could I have doubted Kayden? I felt silly for panicking over this.

I was surprised that I felt more myself this time. I could sense my animal instincts, but I knew that I was still me. I wasn't going to attack anyone. When the transition was completed, I stared at Kayden for a moment, then turned a circle on the bed before lying back down. It should have been strange, but it felt right. This was what I was meant to be. Shifting wore me out, and I fell asleep almost instantly.

I woke alone, with the door open. I could hear voices in the other room but couldn't make out what was being said. I stretched, forgetting for a moment that I was still a wolf. It took a minute for the shock to wear off, then I yawned and padded into the other room. I knew that I would be able to communicate with at least one of my guys. I thought that I could talk to Dec, too, but wasn't sure if I remembered that right.

"If you have the technology, why won't you let her have it?" Kayden seemed to be arguing with Eli about something.

"Because it's not been tested. I'm not going to put something like that in her brain without testing it first. I can rush the process, but I will not compromise on the safety checks. Besides, you and Dec wouldn't need one but Vik and I would. Let me make sure it's safe first." I loved the way Eli always stood his ground, even if it made one of the others angry.

"What have we here?" Vik asked, running a hand down the fur on my back. I growled at him, then jumped up and licked his face.

CHAPTER 39

Vik

It looked as if Kayden and Eli would come to blows over their argument when I noticed Delilah padding in from the bedroom. I hadn't expected her to pounce on me and start licking my face. I just wanted to let them know they had an audience. I agreed with them both. If there was a way for me to communicate with Delilah telepathically, I wanted it. But I didn't want to put something into her brain that wasn't tested and proven safe. Eli would fast-track the process, speeding up the testing, and we would have a safe, competent product within a few weeks.

In the meantime, I had to get Delilah to stop licking me so we could discuss our next steps. Scott had informed us of a potential lead, and I wanted to follow it. Most likely, we would send him out with his team. It ate at me to delegate so much of the violence, but protecting Delilah had to be priority number one. If that meant I had to hide so that she would, that's what I would do.

After she tackled me to the floor, I gently pulled the licking machine close to my chest and held her for a minute. Delilah seemed to understand that I needed that affection and stopped licking me long enough to cuddle. I sat there and held her while Kayden and Eli ignored us completely. I noticed Dec's smirk when I hit the floor. I leaned close and whispered in her ear, "You should get Dec next. He looks like he could use some love." She whimpered in response and darted toward him.

His reaction when she jumped at him was priceless. Dec hadn't been expecting her to attack. I have to give him credit, he caught her, even though it threw his balance off and he landed on the sofa. Delilah licked his face with the same enthusiasm she had attacked mine. I laughed while I pulled myself off the floor. Eli and Kayden still hadn't seemed

494

to notice us. I raised an eyebrow at Dec, and he nodded, understanding my plan. He whispered in Delilah's ear, and she rushed Eli. Kayden jumped out of the way, and she knocked Eli to the floor, licking his face until he started to laugh.

Kayden growled and walked away, no doubt to sulk about being the last to get attention. He would get over it when he realized Delilah would get her way. I knew that Eli would have the chip ready as soon as safely possible. I didn't follow him, instead content to watch our girl calm Eli's temper.

"Okay, okay, I'm better. You can stop now," Eli chuckled as he tried to push Delilah away from his face, where she was still licking frantically.

Declan laughed, "She's enjoying distracting you. Her nap was good and she's restless for some action." He'd obviously been communicating telepathically with her. I felt a familiar twinge of jealousy hit me before it was shoved away by guilt. There was no reason to be jealous of something I wasn't meant to have. Besides, Eli and I would both have the opportunity soon enough.

"We all probably need some exercise. Not that sex isn't exercise, just that there are other forms as well. We need to help Delilah learn how to fight. She needs to be able to use her animal instincts as well as her human ones." I wanted to ask if she'd figured out how to control the shift yet but didn't want to upset her if she hadn't. It had only been a day. I was certain that it took most wolves longer than that to master their shift.

"That's a great idea. Delilah agrees, but she's not sure how to shift back. Should I get Kayden?" Dec asked. I was relieved that he was willing to translate for us when our girl couldn't talk to everyone.

Eli shook his head. "I think we can handle this. Let him cool down." He turned his attention to Delilah, gently grabbing her face in his hands. "You need to breathe and focus. Think about being human-ish, you know what I mean. Remember how it feels to be in that form and will yourself to change."

She tried to shake her head, but Dec leaned down next to her. "I know it's scary, but you have to try. You can do this. We believe in you. The sooner you figure out how to make it happen, the better you'll be able to fight the bastard who did this to you." His words seemed to get through to her. I was glad he'd chosen to speak them out loud instead of keeping them between the two of them.

We watched as Delilah took a deep breath and stepped away from us. She wanted the room to shift without worrying about hurting anyone if she thrashed about with it. The three of us understood and didn't try to get closer, even when she appeared to be seizing. I recognized it as part of the process. She had done that the night before when she'd tried to force the shift. In the end, we had to wait until her wolf was ready to allow the change to happen.

This time was quicker than last, but looked every bit as violent. Her limbs cracked and reformed as the fur retracted. The sound alone was enough to make all of us cringe. I had no idea how she could bear the pain that must accompany it. Once she was in her vamp form again, Dec peeled his shirt off and offered it to her. Delilah grabbed it and put it on, relieved to be covered. Recently our hideout had been overrun with Scott's teams. We had very little privacy except in the bedrooms. It was worth it though, as a trade-off for our safety.

"Thanks. That was so fun. I got all three of you. What's Kayden so mad about?" Delilah laughed and launched herself into Dec's arms for a kiss.

"He's angry with me. You two talked about a telepathic chip implant and he wants me to bypass safety and give it to you, Vik, and myself right now. I feel that safety protocols should be enforced. That means we have to wait." Eli's explanation was short and sweet, unlike the argument that had taken place while Delilah slept.

"Well, he's going to have to get over it. Safety first. Always. I don't want something in my head that hasn't been tested." Delilah combed a hand through her dark waves. "I'll talk to him."

"There's something else," I began, pulling her from Dec's arms for a kiss of my own. She hummed against my lips. "Scott thinks he has a lead on Ghost. If they can capture the guy, they're bringing him here." Her body tensed against me.

"Okay," she responded before pulling away to fall into Eli's arms. I wasn't upset that she wanted to give him affection, but her response to our lead wasn't good. I knew that she would have trouble making the decision to take Ghost out. I hoped that she didn't hate me when I took care of it for her. She snuggled in with Eli on the couch. "I guess we should figure out how to get him to talk. We need to find Ghost so we can end this." Her words were solemn.

"Vik and I figured that we would take care of that part. You don't have to even know what's happening," Eli offered. Delilah stiffened again and pulled away from him. Wrong answer.

"No. I refuse to hide while you guys do everything for me. I will be part of interrogating the prisoner, even if that means torture because I'm not weak, and I'm not innocent. You need to stop treating me as if I'll break. I'm just as capable as you are." The defiance in her tone was hot. My dick jumped at her words. Unfortunately, I would have to settle him down and focus on the task at hand.

"I agree. You two are constantly underestimating our girl. She is the strongest, most fierce woman I've ever met. Especially now." Dec's words had Delilah climbing into his lap and snuggling against him. Of course, he would figure out that always siding with her would get affection as a reward. He hadn't argued against our plan until she expressed her displeasure. That slimy little shit was trying to make us look bad.

"It's a mistake we will try not to make again. Just to be clear, Myshka, we don't think you're weak. There are certain things that our lady should not have to deal with. We were simply trying to take care of you in the only way we can. I hope you'll forgive us." I laced my words with a sweetness that I didn't feel. Annoyance with Dec settled in until I realized that if we did train Delilah, we would have to spar too.

CHAPTER 40

Kayden

ELI PISSED ME OFF with his reasonable argument about safety being important. Of course, safety was important. I didn't want him to put some untested chip in our girl's head. I was certain he was lying to me about it. He had a chip ready. Guys like that always have a prototype ready. Something that's been fully tested and is being held for the right situation. The more he argued, the more convinced I was that he just wanted to take credit for the idea himself. Hell, it hadn't even been *my* idea.

I already had the ability to communicate with our girl without an implant. Why did I actually care so much? *Because if it works, there's a chance all of us could communicate that way. Then no more secrets, no more occupying Delilah while we have sensitive conversations.* Not that I had many secrets left; but then they'd all come out. Except for Shannon. That secret was buried deep.

If Dec ever found out that I was the one who'd tampered with the course and accidentally caused her death, he'd never forgive me. It was easier to let him think that I blamed him instead of telling the truth. I felt guilty because I'd been trying to embarrass him. He'd been training with us for months, and I was worried that he would be better than me and the leaders would decide to let him become one of us. They had actually offered after her death. He would have taken over the alpha spot; the leaders wanted to groom him for it. All I could do to protect my standing was treat my best friend like he'd killed my girlfriend.

I had no clue he would run off and get caught up with vamps. All of this was my fault. But if I had told the truth back then, I never would have met Delilah. I needed to push the lie down and leave it. At least there was no reason to pretend like he'd been the one responsible for Shannon's death anymore. Someday we might talk about it. For now, I would keep my secret.

I paced the warehouse floor as I thought. I wanted to shift and run. I probably should have, but I would have missed Scott and his crew bringing in a prisoner. The guy's arms and legs were tied and he was blindfolded. I wondered where they were going to interrogate him without letting him know where he was. Of course, if they planned to kill him, it didn't matter if he knew where we were. I mean, Ghost already knew where we were. I rubbed the scar on my shoulder where his men had shot me with the fancy new vamp-killing bullets.

"We got one. I think we can make him talk," Scott announced as soon as they were in the building. His men who had stayed behind celebrated with loud yells and cheers. I followed the group to the back of the warehouse. I remembered the office in the back of the building; I would have bet that Scott and his men had soundproofed it for just this occasion. While the crew carried the prisoner into the office, Scott turned to me and asked, "You want me to let the others know?"

"Not yet. I want a minute with him first." My growl may have been angrier than intended, but Scott didn't seem to notice. I was annoyed at myself and planned to take it out on this poor sap who'd managed to get himself captured.

Scott nodded. He and his men stood back and watched as I entered the room. They had the guy draped over a chair. His eyes were still covered. His dark hair was greasy and he smelled like he'd pissed himself. *Nice.* It wouldn't be too hard to break him if they'd scared him that bad already.

"Please, please, don't hurt me," the man whined. I slammed my fist onto the desk behind him and stifled a laugh when he jumped.

"Then talk. I want answers. Now." He jumped again at the tone of my voice, then started to whimper. *Did he just piss himself again?*

"I, I don't know anything." I knew he was lying from the way his lips twitched. No doubt Ghost had threatened his men. This one knew he was dead either way. Even if he didn't talk, Ghost would think he had and kill him. There were two ways I could handle this. I opted for a show of mercy, even though he would get none.

"If you tell me what I want to know, I can protect you. You can come work for us," I lied. He took a deep breath; was he crying? Oh, that smell. He definitely pissed himself again. I wasn't even being scary yet.

"You can protect me?" I knew from that moment that he would tell me anything I wanted to know.

"Of course, I can. If you tell me how to find Ghost, I will protect you," I smirked at the lie. It seemed as if this guy was eager to talk.

"Okay, I'll tell you everything. Just take the blindfold off so I know who I'm talking to." The words were whiney and I momentarily regretted that I wouldn't get to punch him. I pulled the blindfold down, freeing his vision.

"Where is Ghost?" I figured I'd get right to the point.

"Last I heard, he was with your mom," the man smirked, all traces of panic gone from his face and voice. He sat up straighter as if preparing to face me head-on.

Crack. My fist connected with his jaw. "That is your only free pass. Tell me where Ghost is, or this is going to get painful for you," I threatened, secretly relieved that I would get to beat the info out of him after all.

"Fuck you," he countered, spitting at me. I stepped closer and punched him in the gut. He groaned and fell over. I started pacing the room, planning my questions and punches.

"Oh, you'll talk. It's just a matter of how much fun I get to have first." I let myself sound a little unhinged, leaning into the character. Was it a character, or was I really going crazy? I wasn't sure anymore. I just knew that I would find the asshole who made me hurt my girl.

He snorted a laugh at me, and I punched him in the kidney, slipping my fist between his arms and the chair. The man made a pained noise, then fell over again. "Where is Ghost's hideout?" If I couldn't get the guy right now, maybe I could find his house and take care of that first.

He didn't respond, shaking his head. I grabbed his hair and pulled him up, almost taking him out of the chair. "Where is the hideout?" I snarled in his face, letting my teeth shift into fangs. His eyes opened wider and terror crossed his face.

He started to whisper and I had to lean closer to hear him. "In your mom's pussy." He cackled a laugh in my ear and I threw him across the room. One of Scott's guys picked him up and put him back on the chair. His left arm hung awkwardly from the shoulder. I couldn't tell if it was broken or just dislocated. I honestly didn't care.

"You don't want to talk? That's fine. I'm going to start tearing off appendages until you decide to change your mind. Where do you want to start? Fingers, toes? Or should I go straight for the arms and legs?" I sounded like a nut job, but it seemed to get his attention.

The man looked at me, the horror of what I planned to do settling into his features. "I can't talk. He'll kill me. Please, I have a wife and kids. Don't do this." He started to beg, but I wasn't sure if anything he said was true. I decided to use his story to my advantage.

"A wife and kids, huh? I bet you want to keep them safe, don't you? You'd better talk to me, then. I'm your only chance of keeping them alive." I paused, took a deep breath, and stepped closer, crouching to be eye to eye with him. "Help me out here, so I can help you. What's your name?"

"Ted. I'm Ted," he stammered the answer.

"Good. Now, Ted, I need to know where Ghost is. Are you going to tell me, or do I have to find your wife and kids and tell them the bad news?" I glared at him, waiting to see if he would understand what I was saying. Confusion furrowed his brow. This guy was not the smartest I'd come across.

"What bad news?" He had no idea what I was implying. I grabbed him by the throat and squeezed a little, hoping to intimidate him into talking.

"That you're dead," I replied, watching his face fall as understanding washed over him.

CHAPTER 41

Eli

I WALKED IN TO find Kayden about to rip our prisoner's head off. Scott's text had come at the perfect time and I was able to sneak away without Delilah noticing. "It looks like I'm just in time," I announced as I strolled through the door and got between Kayden and the man. He'd already pissed himself, no doubt a combination of both Kayden and Scott's tactics. "I'll take it from here," I dismissed Kayden and turned to the prisoner. "Did you say your name is Ted?"

The man nodded. "Are you gonna let him kill me?" He was shaking, clearly terrified of Kayden. I wondered what I had missed. Scott didn't exactly give me a run-down of the conversation.

"Oh, no. If I decide that you need to die, I'll kill you myself. But we're not there yet. I think you'll want to talk to me. I just need to get some info, then you'll be free to go back to your family." There was no way we would let the man go, but he needed to believe that we would so he would talk. I hoped that Kayden hadn't fucked the whole thing up yet.

Ted nodded. It seemed as if the good cop/bad cop thing might work. "So, Ted, the first thing I need from you is an address." He looked at me as if he didn't understand. "I want you to tell me where your base of operations is. I'm not asking about Ghost or his place. Yet. I'm starting with you. Where is your base?"

He shook his head. "I can't. If I tell you anything, he'll kill me. Besides, there's only one base." His eyes opened wide when he realized his mistake.

"So, there's one base. Then you do know where it is. Unless you want me to unleash my friend here, you need to tell me where it is. I have important business with Ghost, and right now, you're standing in my way." I kept my voice steady, hiding all emotion. I needed him to talk, but I wasn't above torture to make it happen.

"I, I can't. He'll kill me. Please," Ted begged. Then he sobbed.

"Look, Ted. I want to help you, really, I do. But you're not helping me. I can't protect you if I don't know where Ghost is. I need that location." I turned to Kayden, who had calmed down a little and understood what I was doing. "Break his fingers," I ordered.

Kayden nodded and stomped over to the dirty man. He tore through the rope on Ted's arms and held his left hand while Scott tied Ted's right arm to the chair. I stared into Ted's eyes as Kayden snapped his fingers, one by one, ignoring his screams. With all of the fingers on his left hand twisted in different directions, Ted's eyes settled on mine. "Where is Ghost?" I asked again calmly as if I hadn't just told Kayden to torture this man.

Ted shook his head, "I can't." I nodded to Kayden, and he grabbed Ted's right hand. Snap, snap. My eyes never left his. Tears streamed down his face as each finger was bent at a different unnatural angle than the last. Once all ten were done, Kayden tied his left arm to the chair as well.

"If you have nothing useful for us, we have no reason to keep you alive." I turned to Kayden, "Prepare the truck. We'll need to dump the body." He nodded and walked out the door. Scott and I exchanged a glance, then he followed. I knew that Kayden would have questions, but Scott could answer them before I got there.

This would be a mission of endurance, not a sprint. If Ted hadn't talked yet, I would have to stoop to less savory methods. I took out my phone and walked over to him. "You mentioned a family to my friend. I'm going to find them. Then I'm going to kill them. After I show you the video of that, I'm going to kill you." I pulled up an app on the phone and grabbed one of his broken fingers. I scanned the print, then turned and walked away. I would have his identity in a matter of minutes.

Ted was begging to talk before the door closed behind me. "Wait! Don't go; I'll tell you everything! Don't hurt them! Please, come back!"

I would let him stew a while, thinking he'd just signed his family's death warrants. I would never go after someone's wife and children unless I had proof that they were guilty. Ted didn't know that, and I would use that to my advantage.

"How did you convince him to talk? Why aren't we in there right now?" Kayden battered me with questions as soon as I closed the door.

"I'm going to let him sweat while I find out if anything he told you is true." I held up my phone, showing him that the fingerprint was running through the human and vamp systems. The system dinged, notifying me that it was done. "It appears that Ted was mostly honest with you. He has a wife and two kids. They live across the city, inside my zone. It wouldn't be hard to capture and bring them here."

"You're not actually going after the guy's family, right?" I forgot that Kayden didn't know me as well as Scott did.

I laughed. "Of course not. But he doesn't know that. I'm going to make him think we have them. Then he will talk for sure." I turned to Scott, "Send someone to this address to make sure Ghost doesn't have someone on his family. I want them protected."

"Got it, Boss," Scott said before running off to grab a couple of his guys. "Video confirmation?"

I nodded, turning back to Kayden. "We have to show him that we have his family where we want them. Then he can weigh his options and decide if they're worth sacrificing himself for. Because he knows that he's dead either way. If he talks, Ghost will kill him. If he doesn't, we will. At this point, keeping his family safe is the only thing he has going for him."

"Okay. I can see you've done this before." I could tell that Kayden wasn't happy about me taking over his interrogation.

"I have. But it probably wouldn't have worked without what you did before I got here. So when we break him, it will be because we worked together." I didn't mind sharing credit. If Kayden hadn't almost botched the whole thing, I might not have been able to convince Ted to talk.

"So, we just wait for Scott's guy to send the video, and then we go back in?" Kayden shook his head in disbelief. "I can't believe it's that easy. I really thought I was going to have to rip his arms off." He sounded a little disappointed, and that worried me. If he was looking forward to torturing someone, we'd have to be careful. I mean, in war, it was necessary to be ruthless. But there was a difference between ruthless and bloodthirsty. I didn't want to have Kayden break Ted's fingers. It was an unfortunate effect of Ted refusing to be helpful.

"I'm glad you didn't. It's hard for men to talk when they're dead." I walked back to the door of the office and listened. Ted was still screaming, begging me to come back so he could talk. Good. His family was important to him. That was a good thing.

In a matter of minutes, the guy Scott sent out had located Ted's family and secured them. We weren't holding them prisoner, but our guy had taken out the snipers Ghost had stationed nearby. With the video proof that I had his family in my sights, I opened the door and went back into the office. Kayden followed, acting as my muscle. I wanted Ted to think that I wouldn't hurt him myself. I needed him to trust me. He was going to talk.

I have something for you, Ted." Saccharin sweetness dripped from my voice as I held the phone out for him to see.

"No, no, no. Please. You didn't hurt them, did you?" He was worked into a full-blown panic now. "Please, mister, I'll tell you anything you want to know. Don't hurt my kids." I watched his face as he viewed the video. It showed his family—wife cooking dinner, kids playing; then it cut to the snipers who had been trained on the property.

"You know those men, don't you, Ted?" When he nodded, I continued. "I have people in place who can neutralize them if you tell me what I want to know. They'll be safe if you talk."

"Anything. I'll give you anything if you protect them. Where's a map? I'll show you where the base is." Ted's concern for his family was touching. It made me feel bad for what I knew would happen to him. But I would keep my word and protect his wife and kids, so long as the info that he gave me panned out. Kayden brought over a map and untied one of Ted's mangled hands. Ted glanced at the map, then pointed to another abandoned warehouse. According to him, Ghost's base of operations was less than a mile from our current location.

CHAPTER 42

Declan

"I'm sure he wasn't trying to keep you from the interrogation, mo chroí. Eli probably ran up there to stop Kayden from killing the guy. We both know that he would do it if he was left unsupervised." I had been trying to calm Delilah down for twenty minutes. Vik refused to let her rush into the office to find out what Eli and Kayden were doing to the poor man who had been captured.

"I just told you guys that I wanted to be involved, and then he ran off with Kayden to 'take care of things.' It's ridiculous," Delilah ranted. I completely agreed with her, but needed her to understand that it probably wasn't done out of spite.

I had no idea how to defend Eli or Kayden from her claims. I tried everything I could come up with, and nothing worked. "I agree with you. I just want you to understand what they were probably thinking. I honestly believe Kayden would kill someone without a second thought if it meant keeping you safe."

Luckily, they both walked in and she turned on them. "You. You two are in so much trouble. How could you?" Her finger was in Kayden's face and she glared at Eli. Neither of them showed any remorse. I didn't figure they would. But Kayden would feel her anger through the bond. Eli seemed to have some sort of enhanced empathy, so he might know what she felt as well.

"Woah, love. Take a breath. We were coming to get you so we can raid Ghost's base." Eli held up his hands in surrender.

Kayden rolled his eyes. "So, we're supposed to let you do everything now? I doubt you could have made the guy talk any faster than we did."

Damn, Kayden, that was rough. I almost laughed at his comment before I saw the fire in our girl's eyes. That had set her off worse than anything else they had done. I was relieved that her anger was focused on him instead of me. She'd blamed me for them taking off, saying that I had agreed to help them by distracting her. It had taken nearly ten minutes to convince her of my innocence, and I was certain that she only believed me because Vik had actually backed me up.

Delilah growled at him before grabbing him by the shirt and pulling him down to eye level. "No, you're supposed to respect me enough to let me help with things that concern me. You're not going to keep me out of things 'for my own good' or whatever the fuck you guys keep saying to each other to justify it. It's not about the final result. It's about respect. If you don't understand that, you're not the man I thought you were." She slapped him, then walked away, slamming the bedroom door.

"She's pissed," Kayden said, rubbing his jaw. "What the hell?"

I cocked an eyebrow at him and turned to Eli. "You said that you know where the base is? When do we leave?"

"As soon as we get her on board. Which may be a while, since wolf-boy over here likes getting her riled up." Eli smacked Kayden on the back of the head and walked toward the bedroom. He lightly knocked on the door before opening it and walking in. Something thumped against the wall indicating that Delilah wasn't happy to see him.

"Why didn't you tell us when Scott got here? Delilah just wants to be part of the process. You don't know what she's capable of until you give her a chance." I felt a little silly scolding Kayden like a naughty child, but it matched how he was acting.

"Why do I have to report everything to you all? Is there some unspoken hierarchy here that I'm supposed to adhere to? I can't make any decisions without asking permission first? That's ridiculous," Kayden fumed.

"And that's exactly how Delilah feels. But in addition to that, four guys insist on trying to keep things from you because they think it'll be too much? She's got every right to be angry. You need to apologize. You're not the only one, either. I have a feeling Eli is doing just that right now." I pointed at the bedroom door, where a couple more thumps sounded against the wall before the screaming quieted down.

"I won't apologize for getting results. We got the location of that dickhead. We should be moving on that instead of trying to soothe the little princess. It's not my fault she got her feelings hurt. That's just more proof that she shouldn't be part of this. We should just protect her." Kayden couldn't possibly believe that, could he? Surely, he wasn't that dense.

"It's your ass on the line. Rejection from her will hurt even more now that you've bonded. You know that. Why are you still trying to push her away?" I knew there was more to his attitude than he was letting on. He was hiding something.

I knew that being tortured had lasting effects. I was having nightmares and struggling with my anger, but it seemed like Kayden's was worse. I wondered if it had anything to do with how Ghost had taken control of him with that amulet.

"It's nothing. I'm going to help the guys load up supplies. Let me know when you're ready to roll out." He stormed off before I could reply. He passed Vik and gave him a shove. I was shocked that Vik took it and walked away. I'd expected the vamp to lay into the wolf.

"What the fuck is his problem?" Vik asked me, brows furrowed.

"He was a dick to our girl and decided that he doesn't have to apologize. Eli too, but he's in there with her right now. She threw stuff at him," I chuckled.

"They should have let her in at the beginning of the interrogation. Then when things got more intense, she could have decided if she wanted to stay or not. It's really not that difficult," he sighed.

I nodded in agreement. "How long before the crew has everything loaded? Kayden was going to help. He's anxious to get moving. I am too, but I want her on board."

Vik examined his hands carefully. "It won't be long now. I need something from you, though. A favor. And you can't tell anyone." His face scrunched in annoyance at the word *favor*. What could he possibly need from me?

"What is it?" I locked my eyes on his, waiting to see what was so important that he needed my help with it. And what was so secret that I couldn't tell the others. I wasn't sure how I felt about being asked to keep secrets. After all, that was what Delilah blew up about a few minutes ago. She wanted us to be honest with her.

"When we find him, she's going to decide on mercy. We can't let that happen. I need you to distract her while I take care of him," he whispered.

"You want me to occupy her so you can kill him when she tells us that she doesn't want him dead. That's your plan?" I kept my voice low because I didn't want Delilah to hear what Vik was suggesting. "You know that is a horrible idea. She'll never forgive you."

"But she'll be safe," he justified his idea with her safety. He was right, but it wasn't our decision to make.

"You can't decide this for her. I can't help you hurt her like this. It has to be her decision. If she wants you to do it, fine. But if she tells us not to kill him, I can't be part of it." I hated to let him down or give him more reason to hate me, but I refused to be part of breaking our girl's heart. Not like this.

"Does that mean you're going to tell her?" His tone sharpened, cutting the air around me. Vik balled his fists at his sides, waiting for me to admit that I'll betray him for wanting to betray her.

I took a long moment to consider my answer. Then I shook my head. "It's not my place to tell her any more than it's your place to decide if her brother lives or dies. I won't tell her, but I am asking you to respect her decision." I braced for the punch I expected, only to have Vik throw his arms around me, pulling me into a hug. It was only slightly awkward, and I wasn't sure if it meant that he didn't hate me anymore or if I still needed to watch my back.

"I don't agree with you, but I respect your reasoning. I'll consider your position, but I can't guarantee that I'll change my mind when the time comes. We both know it's the best decision." His insistence that he was right drove me crazy. Of course, Delilah *would* be better off if Ghost was dead. She'd be better off if she had never met her nut job brother. But she had met him, and I refused to be part of deciding to kill him if that wasn't what she wanted. I would have to find a way to convince Vik that I was right.

CHAPTER 43

Delilah

ARGUING WITH DEC ABOUT Eli and Kayden leaving me out of interrogating the man they'd caught got me nowhere. I knew he could see my point, but even if he agreed, he would always try to get me to see the other side. Then Kayden had to smart off. I hadn't meant to slap him, but I refused to apologize. He owed me an apology, not the other way around. I didn't regret slamming the door either. I was so tired of being treated as if I were fragile. I wasn't going to break just because I saw something violent. None of my guys knew about my dark side. Out of all of them, Kayden should have known. The mate bond gave him more access.

I stewed in my anger, pacing the bedroom floor. Then Eli knocked and poked his head in. "Hey, love. Can we talk?" I threw a shoe at him but missed, hitting the wall just next to his head. He jumped but didn't leave.

"I don't want to talk to you right now," I snarled, my eyes searching the room for something else to throw. I had to give him credit, he didn't try to approach me. Eli opted to stay close to the door; I assumed it was for a quick exit. The man was smart. I wish I understood why he kept acting so stupid.

"I know, love, but we need to talk it out so we can go before Ghost finds out that we've found him. Please," he pleaded with me. The second shoe hit the wall a little further away. I hadn't even tried to hit him with it. I wasn't ready to forgive him just because we were on a time crunch.

"Then go. It's not like I'll have any say in what you all do anyway. Every time you agree to include me, you find a way around it. 'Oh, you were busy,' or 'Well, he needed you.' I'm sick of it." I picked up a book that Vik had been reading and chucked it next.

"I understand how you feel. I promise that wasn't my intent. Scott texted me that Kayden was about to kill our only lead. I couldn't let that happen. We needed the guy alive. I'm sorry, I should have thought about bringing you with me." His explanation was logical, and I hated him for it. I didn't want logic right now, I wanted someone to understand my anger. I wanted justification.

"I don't think you understand anything," I ranted, throwing my hands in the air and pacing the floor. I had to keep myself from getting too worked up, or Eli would have a wolf to deal with instead of a pissed-off vamp.

He must have decided that he'd given me too much space because he walked toward me with his hands up in surrender. I backed up, but he kept coming, walking me back until I was against the wall with his hands on either side of me, caging me in. His lips captured mine in a passionate kiss. I could feel his irritation and I knew he could sense my anger. "I understand more than you realize," he whispered against my lips.

I felt my body relax against him. "Just because I kiss you, don't think you're forgiven. I'm still pissed." I knew that he would talk me into forgiving him, I just wasn't ready to admit that I may have overreacted yet. I might decide to not admit it, and hold onto being angry until he and Kayden had groveled enough.

"What if I just keep kissing you?" He pressed his lips to mine again, this time using his tongue to tease mine apart. When I relaxed into the kiss, he pulled back a little and trailed his lips along my neck to my collarbone.

"I'm not giving up on this. I'm mad. No matter what you do right now, I'm still going to be mad. You guys are going to have to prove that you're changing. No more words. Actions." I tried to sound stern, but by the time I got to the end of what I was saying, it came out all breathless and needy. Damn Eli and his mouth for making me lose composure.

I grabbed his face with both hands and lifted it so we were at eye level again. "I mean it. I want to be included in the things that directly affect me."

He nodded. "I know. I promise that I'll try to do better. Are you ready to go after Ghost, or should I distract you more?"

I shook my head and laughed. "As much as I want you to distract me, we have to deal with him. I have some tough decisions to make, but I want to feel like they'll be respected if I do. I need to know that you guys are all going to listen to what *I* want, not just do whatever *you* want." I wiped a tear from my eye. I'd been trying so hard to block out what would have to come next that the moment I thought about facing my brother again, the tears came out of nowhere.

"I'll prove it. None of us will do anything that you're not okay with. You just have to tell us what you want to happen, and who you want to do it. Okay?" He sounded so sincere; I wanted to believe him, but there was a nagging fear that things would go off-script the second we were all together. I nodded anyway and pulled him close for a hug before pushing him away so I could retrieve my shoes.

Eli gave me a couple of minutes to calm my racing heart, then we went to find the others. No one was in the living area; they must have all been up in the warehouse getting supplies ready. We climbed the stairs silently. I wished we were going home. I wanted nothing more than to go back to Midnight and pretend as if none of this had ever happened. At this point, I'd all but given up on that dream.

Once we were in the warehouse, Eli was called away to discuss something tech-related. I got stopped by Scott who slipped a bullet-proof tactical vest on me. "Is this really necessary? I doubt Gerolf is going to shoot me. He likes things more hands-on."

"I get that, but the guys felt like it was the least we could do. It has a bunch of fun toys in it too. So, it's not just for protection. Look at all of those pockets!" I had to laugh because Scott was right. Girls like pockets, and I was no exception. These were loaded with knives, small explosives that could be thrown, and a few other goodies that I wasn't really sure what they were. I figured if I got in a tough situation, I'd find out.

"Fine, the pockets are pretty cool," I admitted, laughing again at Scott's 'I know, right?' comment. I was glad that we'd got to know each other a little during the time I'd spent being forced into hiding. He was a good guy. I'd have to make sure Eli gave him a raise or something.

I watched the people that were helping us. I knew that each of them was employed by one of my guys. I also knew that none of them were here just to help their boss, they were here because they considered my guys, and me, their family. Every one of them volunteered because they care about one or more of my guys, or me, and they wanted to do whatever they could to help defeat Ghost and his terrorist Powder operation. Yeah, drug ops weren't usually considered terrorist organizations, but when the whole thing was designed to destroy an entire population of people, I figured we could make an exception. Each of these people had a family to protect; they all had lives outside of this battle, beyond this war. I hated that this had come to war, but my brother had pushed too far.

My guys would not stop until he was dead. I knew that decision would be made for me. I didn't want to kill Gerolf, but there really was no other way. Eli had said that any of them would do what I asked. Would they let my brother live after what he'd done? I didn't think so. Could I ask them to? There was a part of me that wanted to. I wanted to believe that I could make him see that he was wrong and that he would change. But deep down I knew better. A man like that never changes. He would have to die. But who could I ask to do it? Eli would, but would it torture him to feel my brother's emotions as he died? Declan would if I asked him to, but I knew it would torture him at night. It would have to be Kayden or Vik. But I couldn't ask either of them to do that. Even if they didn't admit it, they would suffer for it. It had to be me. Was I strong enough?

CHAPTER 44

Vik

I was disappointed that Dec refused to help me take care of our girl's problem but relieved when he said he wouldn't rat me out to her. It seemed as if he was determined to win my respect even if he wouldn't bow to my desires. I knew that just asking him to keep something like this from her was a mistake. When she found out, and she would, he would be in nearly as much trouble as me. Perhaps the wolf would have been a better choice of partner for this. Too late to change my mind now.

We climbed into our vehicles and drove to the location Eli had obtained from the prisoner. The only reason the man was still alive was on the off chance he'd given us bad intel. I knew that Eli would kill him for lying. I would have killed his family, but it appeared Eli and I had different torture styles. Morality didn't matter in war. My brothers needed to learn that or this would be over before it even started. Ghost had declared war on vamps when he started producing and distributing the tainted Powder. There weren't many vamps who actually used drugs, so he'd stooped to other methods for getting it to us.

I was still pissed that he'd drugged two different humans in an attempt to get Delilah to kill someone. The fact that the second one worked didn't matter. I would have killed him for trying. Add to that he'd kidnapped her and tortured her—he was a dead man either way. I secretly hoped that she wanted me to kill him. Delilah had the most innocent heart of anyone I'd ever known, so I didn't expect that to be her decision. I would take care of her, no matter what. She would be safe.

I had called for reinforcements while Eli and Delilah were arguing and making up. Dec told me it was ridiculous to get so many people involved, but the only way to win a war was to have more men. I think he was just angry because Steph had insisted on coming with us. She rode with Scott—those two seemed to be fast friends. We'd split the recruits up into the four vehicles.

I had planned for one of us to be in each, but Delilah insisted that the five of us stay together. I was a little surprised since she was still pissed at Kayden and irritated with Eli. But what Delilah wants, Delilah gets—provided we can make it happen.

The dark SUVs parked about a block away from the warehouse that was our target. The easiest solution would have been simply to blow the building up. Eli vetoed that idea because there was no way to know if Ghost would be inside, or if he had hostages. We weren't trying to kill innocent people. He also pointed out that it was Delilah's decision what happened to her brother. Everyone climbed from the vehicles and crept toward the building as a unit.

Something felt off about the whole thing. It was too quiet. "This isn't right. We need to go back," Dec voiced my thoughts. I was relieved that someone else felt it too.

Kayden shook his head. "This is the only chance we have to take him by surprise. We're going in." Eli nodded in agreement. It seemed that the lines had been drawn and sides were chosen.

"I agree with Dec. Something's off about this. We should regroup and figure out what it is," I insisted. Delilah looked between the four of us, trying to decide how she felt. "Don't listen to any of us, Myshka. How does it *feel* to you?"

She stepped between Dec and myself, a hand on each arm. "I feel it too, but if we have the chance to catch Gerolf off guard, shouldn't we push ahead?" Dec and I exchanged a look.

"Okay, mo chroí, if you think we should go ahead, we will." He spoke for both of us, a decision made with a look. That connection was nice, even if I felt we were signing our own death warrants.

Kayden had decided that he would lead the way. We all fell in line behind him, keeping Delilah protected between us. I couldn't shake the eerie feeling that something bad was about to happen. A glance at Dec showed that he felt the same. We entered the building at the same time as the other three teams our army had split into.

The entrance was deserted. "Shouldn't there be a guard at least?" Dec asked. I suppressed a shiver that ran down my spine. Kayden glared at him and motioned for us to be quiet and kept moving forward. Reluctantly, we followed. I noticed that Eli's expression nearly mirrored Declan's now. He was feeling it too.

We explored three more empty rooms before anyone dared to speak again. "Maybe Vik and Dec were right. Doesn't it seem odd that the place is cleared out? What if this is a trap?" Eli voiced his concern.

Kayden growled. "We're here. We might as well clear the place before we run back to our base. There might be a clue about where Ghost is."

We all looked at Delilah, who glanced nervously between us. "I don't know. Would it hurt to check the place out more?" Her uncertainty made me want to scoop her up and run away. But we'd agreed to let her decide what we would do.

I nodded. "Okay, but let's get this done quickly. I don't like the feel of this place." The others seemed to agree. Kayden huffed and turned to lead us through another room. We were closing in on the center of the warehouse. So far, this one had been set up more like a professional building. The rooms we had searched were offices. We had yet to come across the factory floor, which I assumed would be in the center of it all. I'd expected to find a hub of Powder manufacturing.

What we'd found instead was much more disturbing. The room at the very center of the building was an open floor, set up like a manufacturing plant but smaller. The disturbing part wasn't what was there. It was what was missing. There were no machines at all. The room was cleaner than any we'd been through. No trash, no residue, no dust. It was as if the cleaning crew had just finished with it.

I didn't see the tripwire before Kayden hit it. The explosion was instantaneous, and there was no time to run. Bricks and wood shot at us as we dove to get out of the way. I smelled the fire before I saw it. Dust coated the air, hanging heavy over us. I pushed myself up, remembering when Midnight had exploded with me inside of it. Panic gripped me at the memory of being trapped. I had to get out of here.

I found Dec first, pinned under a wooden beam that had fallen from the ceiling. The rafter lay across his stomach. "Are you hurt?" He shook his head. The weight of the beam kept him from being able to talk. He pushed against it as I pulled until he was free. "Delilah?" My voice was raspy from the dust. He shook his head. "Split up and search. Meet back here." I looked up to make sure more of the roof wasn't going to collapse on us. It seemed as if we were clear for the moment. He nodded and went left while I went right.

I heard Dec's shout a moment later. "I've got Eli, and I can see Kayden. Both look okay, considering." I didn't bother to respond, instead focusing on finding our girl. She'd been on my right, so it made sense that she would have gone this way. I sifted through the rubble, finding nothing.

"Delilah?" I called out quietly as I searched. I heard some bricks fall a few feet away and headed in that direction. I found her caught under a pile of debris, trying to dig her way out. "I'm here, hold on, I'll get you out."

"What happened?" She seemed dazed and I wondered if she'd been hit in the head. I pulled her free and examined her for injuries. The only blood on her was from her wrist which was bent at an unnatural angle. "Ow, that hurts," she cried when I touched her hand.

"I need to set it before it heals. Otherwise, Steph will have to break it again later." I picked up a small chunk of wood and handed it to her. "Bite down on this. It's gonna hurt." She did as I asked, and I snapped her wrist back into place. Delilah didn't scream, which I had expected, but she did sway a little. I wrapped my arms around her, scooped her up, and headed back to meet Dec.

CHAPTER 45

Eli

DEC DUG ME OUT from under the portion of the roof that had collapsed on me when the bomb went off. Then I helped him get Kayden, who'd been knocked out by something. We couldn't tell if it had been the force of the explosion or debris that hit him. He'd been the only one of us so far that hadn't been pinned under something. I had broken my shoulder and my foot, and Dec looked to have some broken ribs, but Kayden only had the head injury. His breathing was fine and I didn't feel any broken bones, so Dec and I opted to carry him out.

"We're supposed to meet Vik here," Dec said, stopping where Vik had pulled him free. "I hope he found her. She has to be okay." I knew that he wanted to say *I told you so* because it's what I would want in this situation if I were him. We should have listened to him and Vik when they'd said something was wrong. I had been caught up in following Delilah's desires, and she must have gotten caught up in Kayden's need for revenge.

"Next time, if even one of us has a bad feeling, we're going to abort," I assured him, shifting Kayden's weight to get a better grip on him. He groaned at the movement but still appeared to be unconscious.

"Is he okay?" Vik asked, carrying Delilah. He nodded at Kayden, still held between Dec and myself. "Our girl is okay, just a broken wrist that I already set. She's a little woozy from the pain."

"We think he'll be fine. He got knocked out," I explained. "Let's get out of here. We need to check on the rest of the team." Vik led the way, refusing to let Delilah even try to walk. Dec and I carried Kayden and followed. Once we were outside, some of Scott's team rushed up and took Kayden from us.

"Take him to the SUVs. Make sure to check them for explosives before you start the engines. We've underestimated this guy too many times. Let's not make that mistake again." I let Vik give orders because I knew he needed that, especially after he'd tried to warn us about what we were walking into.

"Where's Scott?" I asked, scanning the area for my second. "Is he okay?" A few of his crew had stayed with us as an escort back to the SUVs. One of them nodded, but no one spoke. "What happened?"

"His arm got torn up pretty bad. The lady doc is taking care of him. She says he'll be fine, but her face disagrees with her words." It was clear the guy didn't want to tell me what had happened but knew that I could force it out of him.

"If Steph says he'll be okay, then he will be. She's the best doctor I've met. Stay focused on our surroundings and let's get out of here." I gave the order, then started walking toward where we'd parked. Our group didn't get more than ten feet away from the building when all four of our vehicles pulled up. I braced to fight, thinking that the others had been overtaken.

A tinted window lowered on the first SUV and Scott leaned out. "Get in; we don't have much time. Third one's open for you. It looks like he's sent a clean-up crew. We've got Kayden." We hurried to get inside the third SUV, where there was room for the four of us. Kayden had been put in the vehicle with Scott because Steph was there. Tires squealed as we pulled away. The four vehicles went in four different directions. I knew it was so we would have a better chance of evading anyone attempting to follow us.

The SUV with Scott, Kayden, and Steph headed for the medical center on the Western edge of the city. Steph would have the equipment and supplies there that she needed to care for the injured. The next one went toward the North, heading toward Vik's holdings. The third one, that we were in, turned to the East and drove toward the warehouse that had been our hideout. The fourth SUV would head toward my building. We would each take a different route through the city and meet up at the medical center.

We drove past Kayden's warehouse slowly, watching it burn. I wondered if anyone had made it out before it was torched. Ted had set us up. I should have known that Ghost would be a step ahead of us. I'd been smug and thought we had it all figured out. It was a stupid mistake that had cost us. But it was one I wouldn't make again.

I turned my focus to the others. "How many broken ribs?" Dec held up four fingers and grimaced. "My foot and shoulder are too. Steph is gonna have to re-break them because they're already healing. Vik?"

He shook his head. "I'm fine. Scrapes and bruises, I think."

"How did he set us up like this?" Dec asked when the driver turned away from the burning building. He'd turned around in his seat to face the back of the car.

"I don't know, but he's going to pay. I just got Delilah to sleep. She needs to rest. Her wrist had a compound break. She may be in shock from the injury. This is just another thing that he's responsible for." Vik was right. This was Ghost's fault and he would have to pay.

"Agreed, but we can't go off half-cocked. We have to come up with a better plan and we have to find him. How are we going to do that?" I asked, pulling Delilah's feet into my legs so she could lay down fully across both of our laps. She sighed but didn't wake up. I could have planned it all out myself, but I discovered that I wanted their input. We worked better as a team.

"Can we track him by his finances? Or his license? I don't know; something has to be traceable, right?" Declan suggested, staring at Delilah as she slept.

"I can get a search running with all of those as soon as we're someplace safe. If he's trying to stay off the grid, it's likely that he won't have anything in his name anymore. There are still options for searches that will detect that, too. We're not defeated yet," I assured him. His idea was a good place to start. I didn't want to tell him that I'd already planned to search for those things. I would let him think it had been his idea.

"What are you thinking, Vik?" Dec turned his attention to the brooding vamp who hadn't said much the past few minutes. I was certain he was coming up with his own plan, but whether or not he would share it remained to be seen.

"Just trying to piece it all together. Ghost knew where we were the whole time. He had guys shoot the place up." He paused, then continued. "Then we manage to snag one of his guys. After a little mild torture and some threats to his family, he talks. But Ghost knew he would, so we got what he wanted us to get. It was a set-up, obviously, but why? Why not just wait until we were sleeping and sneak in to take us out? It doesn't make sense."

"You're right. There must be something else in play here. Because sneaking in would have been more effective. He had no way to force us into the building. I wonder if that was just a backup plan in case we caught one of his guys." I paused. "You know, have it all set up to blow up, but it's abandoned. That's the address they're told to give if they get tortured." It made sense, but there was still something that bothered me about it. I just couldn't put my finger on what it was.

"Do you think he's trying to herd us into a certain area so he can ambush us?" Dec seemed to have been considering that for a while before he spoke.

Vik and I exchanged a look. "It's possible. But where is he trying to force us to go? He attacked at your place, my place, and Kayden's warehouse. The only other place in the city that we haven't been to is Vik's and that's only because it's still under construction."

"That's definitely something to keep in mind, though. If he is trying to push us toward a certain area, we should fight against it. We need to face him on our own terms." Vik's insistence was contagious. I nodded. We needed to finish this on our turf and under our terms. We couldn't let Ghost push us around or we would lose everything.

CHAPTER 46

Kayden

I woke in the backseat of a vehicle, with Scott next to me. "Where are we?" I tried to sit up, but Scott rested his hand on my leg and shook his head.

"On our way to the med center. We're being followed, so it's going to take a while. Stay down," he ordered. I should have been offended that he'd ordered me around like I was one of his men, but I was more concerned that we were being followed and that Delilah and the other guys weren't with us.

"Where is everyone?" I asked, trying to see the other seats in the vehicle without getting up. It was impossible to tell who else was here. I could only see Scott and the driver.

Steph leaned around the passenger seat and looked at me. "Delilah, Vik, Dec, and Eli are with Joe. He'll bring them to the med center when it's safe. You're with us because you took a pretty bad blow to the head and were unconscious for a while."

At least she would tell me what was going on. "What happened?" I raised my head but it started to spin, so I laid it back on the seat and stared at the ceiling.

"Well, Vik and Dec tried to call the whole thing off, but you insisted that we all go in. No big deal, I agreed with you. Unfortunately, the place was rigged to blow upon entry to the central room. You tripped the explosion. Or at least, that's what Dec said." Scott's explanation had jump started my memories. I nodded slowly, remembering the moment my leg hit the tripwire.

"It's my fault. Damn. Casualties?" I hoped Scott would say that everyone made it out okay even though I'd been selfish and insisted that we clear the place. I should have been more careful.

517

"We're not sure. A few I think, but I won't have an exact number until we go back and recover the bodies." He said it so nonchalantly that he could have been talking about running to the store for a dozen eggs.

"You're going back there? That's insane. What if there's another bomb?" I felt panic taking hold of my lungs as the air got heavy. I guess the experience had shaken me more than I realized.

He patted my leg. "It'll be okay. My team will have full riot gear and we'll be protected. We have bomb scanners that we can take. We would have had them today, but you guys were in too much of a hurry to let me get what we needed."

I closed my eyes and listened to him scold me. I deserved it. I should have waited. We should have planned better. If only we'd sent a small team in to check things out, we might have avoided losing anyone. But no, I refused to listen. Oh, shit. If I had listened to Dec and Vik when they tried to stop me from leading us in there, none of this would have happened. "It's my fault." It didn't matter what Steph and Scott said, I knew that the deaths that happened today were on my head. I was to blame for it all. I was the one who'd refused to listen to reason. I had intimidated Delilah into agreeing with me, even if I hadn't meant to.

It would take a long time for me to make up for it, but I was determined to try. I would start by getting a list of names of those lost and make amends with their families. It wouldn't be easy, but I didn't deserve easy. My head throbbed but I couldn't tell if it was from my injuries or from the guilt eating at me. Either way, it felt better to lay back on the seat and keep my eyes closed.

I felt the SUV stop but didn't bother to move. If they would let me, I would stay in the car until Delilah came. Then I would beg her to forgive me for being so stupid. I didn't deserve her, yet somehow, she had chosen me. Maybe it would be easier to believe that fate had put us together. Then it wouldn't be her poor choices that had damned her to have a mate like me.

"We're at the med center, Kayden. I'm going to get Scott inside, then I'll come back for you. Stay here," Steph ordered. What kind of alpha gets ordered around by everyone below him? *The kind who fucks up and gets people killed,* I reminded myself. I nodded in agreement, letting her know that I wouldn't try to move on my own. I lay there, waiting, berating myself for being such a horrible alpha and person. I almost missed the footsteps coming toward the car from the opposite direction Steph and Scott had gone in. I peeked up in time to see our driver sneaking back to the car.

Sitting up with a wince, I startled the guy as he climbed into the driver's seat. "What are you doing?" I grabbed him, holding his arms so he couldn't take the vehicle out of gear. He was pinned and couldn't fight back.

"I'm just following orders. Ghost wants his pet back. I'm supposed to deliver you to him." The man struggled against my grip and nearly got free. I had to get out of here before I ended up Ghost's prisoner again. I pulled roughly on his arms, knocking his head against the headrest. But he didn't stop struggling. There was one chance this would work. Was it worth the risk? If I timed my next move wrong, I would end up under Ghost's control once more. There was no telling what he would make me do if that happened. Unsure if I was making the right decision, I released his left arm and ripped the headrest off the seat. Then I grabbed his arm again, pinning him back to the seat.

"What are you doing? Let me go. I have to deliver you to him by midnight." This guy was an idiot if he thought I was just going to cooperate in my own kidnapping. I pushed him forward, slamming his head into the steering wheel and horn before pulling him back. His head collided with my own. I saw stars, but he stopped fighting. I'd managed to knock him out without taking myself down. I reached up and took the keys from the ignition, then tore out the passenger seat belt to tie the guy up.

Just as I was finishing up the knot, Steph popped the passenger door open. "What the hell are you doing, Kayden? You can't just tie people up."

"This asshole just tried to kidnap me and take me back to Ghost. I managed to fight him off and knock him out, but Scott will want to question him. Sorry for messing up your SUV." I climbed out and walked into the building, leaving Steph staring at the unconscious man. Scott was sitting on a cot just past the waiting area. I stopped on my way to the bathroom.

"You have at least one mole. That's why our efforts today were wasted. I left him with Steph in the car." I walked away without waiting for a response. From the slamming of the door behind me, I figured he'd run out to help her with the guy. My head was spinning too much to care.

I walked into the bathroom, closed the door, and sank to the floor. The cool tile felt good against my skin. I figured I probably had a concussion and should stay awake if I could. But it was getting harder to keep my eyes open. I wanted to rest, to let it all fade away, even knowing that was the easy way out. I didn't deserve the easy way out. I deserved to suffer for what I'd done. So, I fought against nausea that began to rise. I sat there, forcing the bile down, taking deep breaths, until I felt like I could stand. I pulled myself up at the sink. The cold water felt good against my fingers, even better on my face.

Once I felt steadier on my feet and was certain I wouldn't be sick, I walked out of the bathroom. An orderly was waiting with a wheelchair. "Steph wants me to take you to radiology." I nodded and sat in the chair. I knew that I should have been more skeptical with what had happened in the SUV, but felt I could probably fight this kid off if I had to. He pushed the chair to the door marked Radiology, hit a button on the wall, and pushed me through the door as it opened automatically. I let myself relax when I saw Steph waiting inside.

"Scott had Jeff locked up. He's starting interviews now to see if there was anyone else involved. Let's get you fixed up so you can go be intimidating and help him."

"Sounds good to me," I laughed. Steph helped me lay on the table and set everything up for the tests she wanted to run.

CHAPTER 47

Declan

ONCE WE WERE CONVINCED that no one was following us, we headed to the medical center. There had been no update about Kayden or Scott yet, and I could tell Eli and Vik were getting worried. If Kayden didn't wake up, there was no way to know how that would affect Delilah. I hoped that we wouldn't find out.

Thankfully, she continued to sleep on Vik and Eli's laps until we pulled into the garage. "Where are we?" she murmured sleepily. I turned around and smiled at her, but the guys wouldn't let her sit up yet.

"We're going to get you checked out," Vik told her softly. She sighed and let him pull her up to sit on his lap. I climbed out of the SUV and opened the door, offering to take her. Vik reluctantly handed her over. Delilah wrapped herself around me and I carried her inside without waiting for anyone else.

"Where's Kayden?" she asked against my neck. I enjoyed carrying her and wished she would let me do it more often. I hated that it was something that only happened when she was hurt.

"He's inside with Steph. Something hit him in the head and she needed to check him out. You'll see him in just a bit," I answered, hoping that I wasn't lying about the severity of his injuries. I stopped at the desk and waved down an orderly. "Where's Steph?"

"She has the wolf in radiology. She had to do an MRI." The response was curt and the guy walked away without waiting to see if I had more questions.

"Hmm, looks like we're heading to find them." I turned and walked down the hall to the door. I tapped lightly and waited for Steph to respond. With her okay, I carried Delilah

520

inside and set her down in a chair next to the machine Kayden was lying next to. "Have you checked him out? Any news?"

Steph eyed me, looking for injuries before turning to Delilah. "He'll be fine. Where are you hurt?" She took Delilah's offered wrist and examined it. "Let's check it out." She moved Delilah to the machine and took some pictures, then pulled them up on the screen hanging on the wall. "Someone set this for you?"

"Vik did," she whispered as if she was scared something was wrong.

"He did a good job. It's nearly healed. There will be a small scar along the break, but no reason to do anything else for it." She turned back to me, watching intently. "What hurts?"

"Four cracked ribs, nearly healed by now. Eli's worse. You're gonna have to re-break his shoulder and foot." It was almost evil the way her face lit up at my words. She was the only person I knew who enjoyed re-breaking bones to set them.

"Where is he?" I pointed toward the reception desk since the guys didn't know the place as well as I did. I was pretty sure they would wait there for someone to get them. "I'm on it." Steph practically ran from the room, letting the door slam behind her.

Delilah got up when Steph left and walked over to Kayden. "Are you okay?" she asked in a whisper. When he nodded, she punched him in the gut. "Don't you ever scare me like that again!" Then she leaned down and kissed him.

After a moment, the door opened again and Vik came in. "Steph wants the room for Eli. She needs to hurt him." He chuckled, amused by the thought. These guys were kind of sadistic.

Delilah and I helped Kayden to his feet and followed Vik to the room Steph had ready for us all. It was the biggest room she had and there were five cots prepared. She must have thought all of us had been injured worse than we were. Or she had the room ready before we even left. Either way, I could tell it relaxed Delilah that we wouldn't be separated.

It was quiet for a long while, the four of us sitting there, waiting for Eli to get back. I didn't comment on Delilah's thoughts because I wasn't sure they were meant for me. I tried to stay out of her head unless she specifically intended for me to hear something. I knew it was harder for her and Kayden because of their bond. She was focused on questions she wanted to ask and what we needed to do next.

The door opened and Eli was wheeled in. His arm was in a sling and his foot had a boot on. "It's not as bad as it looks," he said to Delilah when her eyes got wide. "I'll be healed in a couple of hours. Steph is going to have someone bring us some blood and food." He thanked the nurse who had wheeled him in, and she left.

"Can we talk?" Delilah asked, looking at each of us. I knew this would be about her thoughts, so I nodded.

"Of course, babe, whatever you want," Kayden said, looking as if he expected to get punched again. I didn't blame him for that. It would be easy to say everything today was his fault. He was pushy and cranky until he'd gotten his way. But that wouldn't be fair. We could have argued with him. The blame lay with all of us equally. I could tell from his expression that he didn't think so.

"Do we have any way to find him?" She looked at Eli as she spoke. He pulled out his phone and started typing something, then nodded. "I don't want him to get away with this."

"We'll find him, Myshka. Don't worry." It was adorable when Vik tried to be comforting. It came across as completely condescending, but Delilah seemed to understand that he was trying. He'd definitely improved in the past few days.

"I've got searches up and running. If nothing else, I'll exhaust every avenue I have. Then we'll know what won't work." Eli turned to Kayden. "Steph said you had an interesting run-in when you guys got here."

Kayden grimaced. He hadn't been planning to tell us whatever Eli was hinting at. What was his problem? He seemed to always be keeping secrets. "There was a mole. He wanted to take me to Ghost. Said the guy wants his *pet* back."

I had almost forgotten about the mind control necklace the asshole had used on Kayden to make him bite Delilah. "How are we going to deal with that?"

"I'm going to kill him, that's how," Kayden growled. Delilah flinched at his tone. He'd completely dismissed her feelings about her brother.

"You won't get close enough. If he still has a way to control you, he'll stop you. Then you'll be working for him. How's that gonna make you feel?" Eli snarled. It was clear he wasn't okay with Kayden's attitude either.

"It's not going to happen." Kayden crossed his arms and pouted. Leave it to him to act like a child after threatening to kill someone.

I pulled Delilah into my arms. "No one is going to do anything that you don't want to happen. If you say not to hurt Ghost, we won't. Don't let him convince you otherwise." She nodded and laid her head on my shoulder. I noticed that Vik was the only one who didn't comment on Kayden's plan. It was clear that he was still planning to end Delilah's brother no matter what she said about it.

He looked at me, waiting to see if I was planning to keep my word. I wouldn't be the one to tell Delilah that he was going to betray her. I'd given my word and I wasn't about to go back on that. I wished that I could make him tell her, or at least convince him to let it be Delilah's decision.

She pulled back a little and looked at me. "We can't let him have Kayden. We have to stop him." Was she saying she wanted him dead? Or did she just want him captured? I looked at Vik; he'd noticed her words too. I pulled her back into my arms and held her, then cocked an eyebrow at him where she couldn't see. He picked up on my cue.

"Myshka, what are you saying? If you want us to let you make the decision, you have to tell us what you want us to do," he explained. We all stared at her, waiting to see how she would respond.

"Of course, I don't *want* to kill him. He's my brother, right? I should want to save him. I should insist that no one harms him. But I won't. I can't lie about it. I want him dead. He deserves it after everything he's done to all of us." When she finished speaking, she hid her face in my neck again.

Vik and I exchanged a look, then I looked at Kayden and Eli. Would she change her mind when it came time to deal with Ghost? Or would she be okay with letting us take him out? I figured that we'd find out soon enough.

CHAPTER 48

Kayden

Vik forced Delilah to admit out loud the dilemma she'd been wrestling with all day. My heart hurt when she said the words. I had planned to kill Ghost anyway, but the pain that tore through her with those words was torture all over again. That pain had me rethinking my original plan. It seemed that she'd forgotten about our bond. I could feel the hesitation that she felt. I knew that she wanted to be the one to take him out, but that she felt guilty about it.

"We can take care of it for you. You don't have to be the one who kills him. We're not as fragile as you think." As soon as I said the words, I knew it had been a mistake. I should have talked to her in private. Her face turned red and everyone stared at her. Everyone but Declan, who turned to glare at me. Apparently, he'd known about her thoughts too. Great, just one more fuck up to add to my list. I could not seem to get things right with this girl.

"You invaded my thoughts?" she accused. I shrugged. I had no way to deny what she knew, just like she couldn't deny what I'd picked up from her.

"It's not like I did it on purpose. You aren't very good at blocking them from me. It's the bond. I pretty much hear all of your thoughts as long as you're in range." Another glare from Dec. Wow, I just seemed to keep stepping in it tonight.

"Well, I'll be sure to stay out of your range from now on." She turned to Dec, obviously realizing that he could hear her thoughts as well. "Did you know?"

He nodded, then tried to defend himself. "But I didn't say anything because it wasn't my info to spill. If you had wanted us to know, you would have said something. I wasn't being nosey either. You kind of projected it all at me earlier."

I expected her to punch him, or at least yell at him the way she had me. I mean, he did the same thing I did. My jaw dropped when she wrapped her arms around him and pulled him to her for a kiss. "What the hell? He did the same thing I did, but I got yelled at and he gets kissed. Thanks for letting me know where I stand." I stormed out without waiting for her response.

I shouldn't have been pissed, because I knew she wasn't really mad that I knew what she was thinking. She was mad because I told everyone. But I needed some space to figure out how I was going to make everything up to her. And I wasn't ready to admit that to anyone else yet. Plus I was pissed about failing her. So many failures. How could I fix that?

I was also terrified when Jeff had tried to take me back to Ghost. I hated how easily Ghost had controlled me. I couldn't figure out how the amulet worked; I was missing something. I twisted my wolf head ring while I paced the hallway of the med center. I'd headed further in because I knew if Dec came after me, he would expect me to go outside. Normally I would have taken off outside, shifted, and ran for an hour or so.

If I was being honest with myself, I'd been feeling off since Ghost tortured us. Something about him taking over my freewill broke me. It was like I couldn't be myself anymore. I'd been violated so deeply that I couldn't even talk about it. I mean, if Delilah knew how badly that had messed me up, she wouldn't possibly want to be with me anymore. So, I put up mental blocks to keep her out. When that didn't seem to be enough, I started snapping at everyone.

I didn't realize I'd started crying until tears dripped on my hand. This guy had gotten in my head. I was terrified that I would hurt the people I love. I couldn't let that happen. I'd even briefly considered just offing myself so he couldn't use me again. But that would hurt Dec and Delilah. I couldn't do that to them. I had to find a way to kill Ghost so I could be free of his control. Sometimes I felt like he was still in my brain, urging me to do things that I didn't want to do. I heard his voice in my dreams, telling me to bite her. I relived that moment over and over, both asleep and in my waking hours.

I knew I was being ridiculous. I should just go back and tell them. We could talk about it as a family and work through it. As scary as it would be, I decided that's what I'd do. I turned around and started walking back toward the room I'd stormed out of.

But then the air got thick and my feet felt heavy. It was like walking through mud. My head spun and the voices started again. *You will obey me, wolf.*

"No, you can't control me," I said the words, but my body stopped when the voice commanded it. *Shit, Ghost was here. I had to warn the others.*

Now, now. Is that any way to welcome your master? You will not tell anyone that I'm here. You will do exactly as I command. I hated his voice in my head. I couldn't fight him. The magic was too potent; it wrapped around me like a blanket.

"Kayden? Come on, man. Don't be this way. D's not even that mad at you. Where'd you go?" Declan's voice echoed down the hall. I thought maybe he would go back if I didn't answer.

Turn around, Dec. Go back. I silently urged my best friend to run away from me. *Please don't do this.* I resorted to begging Ghost to let me go. I knew he wouldn't.

I can't let you go until she's dead. I would have been long gone by now, but my spies let me know that you saved her somehow. She has to die. If that means I take all of you out, that's what I'll do. His voice was low and gravelly in my head. A shiver ran down my spine.

I kept trying to free myself from the unseen force that held me hostage inside of my own body. My efforts were useless. I could no more break his control than I could turn into a bird and fly away. I was powerless to stop Ghost from using me to exact his revenge. I wondered if I would even be able to tell them it wasn't me, or if I would be forced to kill them while they thought I was betraying them.

Dec's footsteps retreated; thankfully he'd decided that I wasn't down this hall. I had dodged a bullet there. I was certain if he'd walked up to me, Ghost would have forced me to kill him. There had to be something I'd missed when Eli and I had gone over everything. Ghost killed the Council member, then took his necklace. The amulet glowed, and he suddenly had control of me. How many times had the Council used that same magic to force the wolves to do things we didn't want to? Had they used it to convince us that we agreed with their decisions? What if I hadn't had free will at all for the entire time that I'd been with them? I couldn't bear to entertain those thoughts, especially if Ghost was about to make me kill my family. I had to break free.

Find them. I want her brought to me. Then I'll have you gut her so I can be sure she dies this time. I made sure to shield my thoughts and try to keep any advantage we might have secret. I stood there, not moving, trying to resist his command. I held out for a solid five minutes before my feet started to move on their own, carrying me back to the room where I had left everyone I loved.

A couple of turns later, I managed to stop again. I gripped onto a door frame this time, trying to last more than five minutes. I held out for almost ten minutes this time. Then my feet were moving again, carrying me toward my destiny. I would kill the ones I loved, then Ghost would keep me as a pet. I knew that even if Delilah and the others were gone, he would never let me go. The only way I would ever be free again would be if I died or if he found a stronger wolf to control.

I willed my feet to listen to me one more time and forced myself to walk past the room that held my family. I had to get as far away from them as I could. If only there were a cage I could lock myself in, that would be perfect. My steps were slow, each one more difficult than the last. I forced one foot, then the other, to go out the front door. I walked as far from the building as I could, trying to escape his control.

CHAPTER 49

Vik

"I SHOULD GO AFTER him," Dec said when Kayden stormed off. Delilah slipped out of his arms and sat down, crossing her arms over her chest, obviously not planning to chase him down.

Eli stopped him. "Give him some time."

I nodded in agreement before I turned to Delilah, prepared to play devil's advocate. "You were a little hard on him, don't you think?"

She glared at me. "He violated my trust."

"I'm not saying that he should have shared your thoughts with all of us. He shouldn't have. You should have. But getting that mad at him because neither of you knows how to control your bond seems a little ridiculous."

I braced for the slap before she shot out of the chair and her hand made contact with my cheek. I knew that my words would piss her off. I absently rubbed the spot and stared at her. "Do you think that proves your point or mine?"

She glared at me, and I glared back at her. The room was suddenly tense; the air seemed to thicken. Anger rippled between us, a nearly palpable force. Wilting under my stare, she turned her back on me, deciding to ignore what I'd said.

"Forget giving him time; I'm going to find Kayden," Dec announced before strolling out the door. Eli looked at us, then turned and followed him. It was obvious to them that Delilah and I needed a moment for a private conversation. As soon as the door closed, I turned my attention back to her.

"You can pout if you want. It doesn't change my opinion. If you're angry and need an outlet, I can take it." My quiet offer had her turning to face me. I watched as she wiped the tears from her eyes.

"Don't you think I've already beaten myself up about it? I know that I overreacted. I can't change that now. I just felt so violated," she sobbed. Her anger dissolved into regret. Mine eased as well, knowing the reasons behind hers. I should have realized why she'd been so upset with Kayden.

I pulled her into my arms, her head resting against my chest. We stood there like that, my hand smoothing her hair while she cried it out. Her arms snaked around my back while she'd finished. She kept her head down because she was embarrassed. Probably more so because I'd called her out in front of the others.

"He'll understand if you just talk to him. A bond like that is new territory for you both. You have to figure it out together."

She finally raised her head and met my eyes. "It scares me. I want to have that kind of bond with all of you, but I'm terrified that you'll see something in my head that will chase you away."

"Nothing could chase us away from you, Myshka. We're all obsessed with you. There's so damned much love in this family that it nearly chokes me to death sometimes. And you're the center of it all," I whispered, unsure if I was scared of her reaction or of someone hearing me.

"How can you know that?" Her voice wavered. I could hear her tears starting again. For a moment, I could almost feel her fear. It mirrored my own. After all, that was why I'd hidden my plans from her.

"Because it's the same thing we're all afraid of. That you'll see the darkness in us and end things. Every one of us has that part of ourselves that we're scared to show to anyone." I took her hand and lifted her chin so our eyes met. "I know I look like I have it all together, but on the inside, I'm just as scared and insecure as you are."

"Really? You're not just saying that?" Delilah eyed me suspiciously as if she didn't trust what I was saying. I leaned down and kissed her, pouring every emotion I had into it. If my words couldn't convince her, maybe my lips could. A crash sounded in the hallway, pulling our attention away from each other.

Before I could react, the door opened and Eli poked his head inside. "Come on, we have to move. Ghost's men are here." He ushered us out the door and down the hall. "Dec is going to meet us in surgery. It's the most secure room here and actually has a weapons closet. We couldn't find Kayden." We followed him, careful to watch our surroundings.

"Where did they come from?" I asked as we ducked around a corner. I could hear gunfire in the distance and wondered if it was our people or Ghost's.

"I don't know. Everything was fine, then suddenly the place was surrounded. It was like they came from everywhere at once. I couldn't tell how many he had," Eli replied before easing a door open and peeking inside. "This way." He led us through a locker room that must have been connected to the surgery suite. Once we were inside, he had me help barricade the door so no one could follow us.

I wondered why we were running instead of fighting. We would come up with a plan when we got everyone together. Delilah hadn't said a word as we wound our way through the halls or when we got to the room Eli had deemed safe. I looked at her, terror in her eyes and ask, "What's wrong?"

"He has Kayden. I can't reach him. I can talk to Dec, but with Kayden, it's jumbled nonsense. The only thing that makes sense is if Ghost has him. We have to save him. Dec is on his way now." Her words came out all at once, rambling like someone who was in shock. Could Ghost really have captured Kayden? That would explain why Eli and Dec hadn't been able to find him. How was Ghost able to get the drop on us again?

I hated that the guy was always a step ahead. We needed to catch a break or we would never win this. Every scenario I came up with had already been dashed away. We hadn't even had time to find a way to block Ghost's mind control over Kayden. Now it might be too late. I felt helpless and useless. I hated myself for not being able to find a way out of this. I had to protect my family. To do that, Ghost had to die.

"Where are the weapons? I thought Steph had some hidden here." I looked from Delilah to Eli, knowing that they wouldn't have the answer.

Dec came in from the opposite side of the room, barricading doors as he moved. "This isn't going to hold for long. I was hoping we'd have more time before this happened. Shit," he ranted, then pulled Delilah in for a hug.

"Did you find him?" she asked, holding Dec tightly for a moment, then moving into Eli's arms. She needed our reassurance that we'd keep her safe. Dec shook his head, running his hand through his hair. He walked over to a panel on the wall and opened a secret compartment. It was outfitted to hold weapons, but was empty.

We were cornered, being hunted by Ghost's men, and we were separated. It was disheartening, but we had to keep fighting. We needed a plan—to rescue Kayden, and to take Ghost out of the picture for good. I paced back and forth, trying to come up with something useful. A moment later, Dec started pacing in the opposite direction, passing me as we wore a path on the carpet.

"Are you sure that Kayden's been compromised?" Dec asked even though Delilah had mentioned it before he arrived. She nodded, obviously not upset that he was discussing her thoughts. Time changes everything, I suppose.

"He's not answering. It's almost like there's interference when I try to talk to him. This is the first time it's been like that. Usually, the connection is crystal clear, to the point that we don't know it's there sometimes," she said, hanging her head at the end, realizing that she'd admitted to everyone that I'd been right earlier. That didn't seem to matter anymore, though.

"Then we need to find him so we can get him back," Eli offered, letting go of Delilah to join Dec and me in our pacing. She walked over to stand in the center of the three of us while we walked back and forth.

Banging on the door of the locker room told us we were no longer alone. Was our company friend or foe? From the sound of it, we'd find out soon enough. The banging got louder, and a crunching joined it. Whoever it was, they were breaking down the door. "We need to move," Dec said, grabbing Delilah's hand and pulling her toward the entrance he'd used. Eli and I helped him move the equipment he'd blocked the door with, and we slipped out the door just as we heard footsteps rushing into the room behind us.

The four of us ran down the hall, turning left and right at random, trying to outrun the people who were chasing us. I kicked myself for leaving my weapons in the car. We would need to find some soon. I knew that we couldn't run forever. We needed to fight.

CHAPTER 50

Delilah

WE RACED DOWN HALLWAYS until suddenly Vik yelled at us. "Wait! We can't keep running. We're going to have to fight." He was right. Running wasn't getting us anywhere. But fighting my brother's lackeys wouldn't help us either.

"We have to find Gerolf. That's the only way to end this," I insisted, fur rippling across my arms before it disappeared. I was doing everything I could to remain calm so I didn't randomly shift. That was all I needed, to lose control and turn into a form I wasn't used to. I wished we'd had more time. My guys were going to help me learn to fight in my animal form. There just wasn't time; all of this happened way too fast.

"How do we find him?" Eli asked. "Also, can we talk about this while we move to a more strategic location?" He started ushering us toward the emergency department. It was a smart idea, because there would be plenty of things to use as weapons there, plus we'd be able to bandage any wounds we got while fighting.

We didn't make it. A group of people ambushed us when we were one hall away. The six of them pounced like they had been expecting us. The four of us weren't about to give up. Eli ripped a man in half, tearing through his waist. Declan snapped another's neck before grabbing another by the leg and slamming his head into the wall. Vik fought two at once, throwing punches and dancing around them. He was clearly playing with them but they didn't seem to see it.

That left the last one for me. I squared up with the man who was nearly double my size. He smirked at me and made some snide comment about enjoying this. I nodded and motioned for him to come at me. He must not have known that I was a vamp, because he seemed surprised at how fast I could move. He swung his fists at me and I slipped behind him before they could make contact. His face was priceless when I zipped back around and sucker-punched him before kicking him in the balls. Before I could finish him off, Eli and Dec each grabbed an arm and tore his arms off. He fell to the ground screaming.

I surveyed the damage my guys had done. There were body parts strewn along the hallway, and every bit of white tile was tinged crimson. I nodded, impressed that they'd made quick work of those thugs. "You did good, mo chroí," Dec complimented me before trying to wipe some of the blood off me. I laughed and pulled him in for a kiss. I took a moment to show my appreciation to all three of them with kisses, then we started moving again.

"I have an idea," I started, "but you're not gonna like it." The three of them looked at me. Vik cocked an eyebrow. Dec frowned. But Eli grinned at me as if he already knew what I was planning. I couldn't help but think that should have been Declan, but his frown was because he actually knew. "We're gonna let Ghost catch me."

"No. Absolutely not," Eli's grin fell away. "That was not what I expected you to say." I wondered what he'd been thinking, but didn't ask. We could talk about that later. For now, we needed to set up my plan.

"You can't possibly want to give yourself up to him," Dec argued. Vik didn't say anything, and I wasn't sure if he agreed with them or me.

"Just hear me out. We let him catch me, then when he thinks he's got me, I shift and eat his face. It's a fool-proof plan." I tried to sound more confident than I felt. My heart hurt at the thought of killing Gerolf, even if he was a sadistic bastard. I knew it was the only way, though. He had to die or we would never truly be free.

"As much as I like that plan, I don't know if you'll be able to pull it off. What if his amulet gives him control over you as well as Kayden?" Vik's concern stopped me. I hadn't thought about that. But I didn't have any other options.

"It's the only way. Please, I need you guys to help me. I can't do it on my own," I begged. "We have to save Kayden." I turned my head, looking at each of them pleadingly. I needed this to work because I had to save my wolf. We needed him.

Declan's eyes met mine. I knew the minute he changed his mind. He sighed, "Fine, but we're going to take him out before he has a chance to do anything to you." Vik and Eli stared at him, clearly surprised that I'd convinced him so easily. I raised my eyebrows at them, and after a tense moment, they both shrugged.

I couldn't believe I'd won. I made the three of them bend to my will. I felt powerful for a moment until I realized what I'd convinced them to do. What if this was a mistake? What if Ghost took control of me like he had Kayden? I shook the thoughts away; I couldn't afford to let anxiety take hold now. We had to move forward. "First, we have to find Kayden. He will lead us to Ghost. Then we let him think he's got me. When he goes for the kill, I'll take him out. If he manages to get control of me, one of you will have to kill him." My voice hitched at the end of my statement. I didn't want any of my guys to be the one to take Gerolf out. I wanted it to be me. But if I was compromised, they would have to.

"What are we supposed to do if he does get control of you? He'll make you attack us. He'll make Kayden attack us," Eli reasoned.

"We'll just have to find a way to stop them without hurting them," Dec insisted. He really was on my side. I couldn't help but fall a little more in love with each of them for the way they were handling this. My life was a crazy mess, with my brother trying to kill me, yet here they were, doing whatever they could to keep me safe.

"Can you track Kayden from the static?" Vik asked, tilting his head curiously. "I know you can't talk to him, but do you think you can narrow down his location?"

I hadn't thought about trying that. I made a face, then closed my eyes. I focused on Kayden and our bond. I felt the tug of it, pulling me toward him, but the static was interfering. I focused on the static and took a few steps to see how it reacted. I felt it fade a little. I stopped and turned in the opposite direction, taking a few steps. The static felt stronger, and along with it, I felt the tug of my bond with Kayden. "I've got him. This way," I said, not bothering to wait for them to catch up.

I walked toward Kayden, adjusting direction every time the static feeling eased. By the time I could see him, the static feeling was so strong that I dropped my hold on the connection. "He's over there." I stopped and crouched down, whispering to the guys. I knew it was pointless. If I could find Kayden, he could find me. No doubt he knew exactly where I was right now. I watched as he sniffed at the air, turning around as if he was searching for something. His eyes opened wide and he tipped his head back, releasing a crazed howl. I wasn't sure if he was calling to me or begging me to run away.

"Are you ready?" I asked. At their nods, I stood up and stepped toward Kayden. "Kayden, I need you to take me to Gerolf. I need to talk to my brother."

Kayden's face contorted in pain. He looked at me, tears streaming down his face. "Run away." The words were a whisper and it looked like the effort pained him. It seemed that my dear brother was controlling more than just his actions. He wouldn't even let my love talk to me. He would pay for this, all of it.

"It's okay, Kayden. Please, just take me to him. I promise, it'll be fine." I kept my voice low, pushing every bit of confidence that I didn't feel into the words. I had to believe it would be okay. I had to know that we'd make it through this. I couldn't let fear take over.

His eyes met mine. Kayden seemed to understand that I had something in mind. "Okay," he said a little louder this time. It was as if he could speak to me as long as it was something in line with his master's desires. He started walking slowly, and I followed, knowing that Vik, Eli, and Dec were right behind us, backing me up.

CHAPTER 51

Vik

I HATED DELILAH'S PLAN, but she was right. It was the only way to get to Ghost. Part of her plan was us keeping our distance while she faced him. She'd wanted to go by herself, but none of us would agree to that. I wasn't sure how Delilah facing her tormentor would go. None of us wanted to let her do this on her own. We would offer whatever support we could while staying close enough to fight if it came to that.

When we found Kayden, I realized that she'd been right about him too; he was under her brother's control. He acted strange when she approached him, almost like he wanted to run. Was he keeping his distance to protect her?

We followed Delilah, who followed Kayden, who reluctantly led us. It was obvious from his demeanor that he didn't want to take us to his master. He didn't seem to want to be anywhere near any of us. I was certain he was trying to protect us all, even if he didn't have control of himself.

How was Ghost able to hold Kayden's mind only when they were near each other? From what they'd told me, the amulet's reach was only a few yards. That didn't sound like magic to me. What was the connection?

My mind toyed with ideas. Their description of how Ghost had taken control seemed strange. Then it hit me. I turned to Eli. "What if the amulet isn't magic? What if it's tech?"

"Then Kayden would have to have something that connects to it on him or it wouldn't work," Eli whispered back. "It's possible, but what does the amulet connect to?"

We walked in silence, pondering Eli's question. It was a puzzle and we were struggling to find the missing piece. A hand grabbed my arm and I stopped walking, turning to see what he wanted.

534

Dec's face lit up. "I know what it is. When he started with the Council, they gave him that wolf head ring that he never takes off. That has to be the connection."

"Perfect. Now we just have to figure out how to get it off of him. That should be easy, right?" I laughed at the idea. Kayden was by far the biggest of the four of us. It wouldn't be easy to beat him in a fight, much less to sneak his ring away from him. We continued following our girl, determined to find a way to protect her.

We would have to tell Delilah about our idea. Dec could do that without speaking, from where we were, so he was the best choice to do it. "Dec, you need to explain this to her. Maybe she'll have an idea of how to distract him and get the ring," I whispered. Kayden had slowed down, indicating that we were nearing our destination.

How had our lives come to this? None of us had been interested in fighting a war. But this man, this human, decided to find a way to take out all vampires. His plan was simple enough, and had he left Delilah out of it, he might have been successful. That was his mistake; him going after her was the reason we were all here. It was the reason we would fight. And we would win. She would be kept safe.

"I told her. She thinks it's too risky for us to get close. He's on edge about something. If she gets an opening, she'll try to take it from him. But she wants us to stay back," Dec explained his telepathic conversation with our girl, relaying her desires.

"Does she really think that we're gonna let her do everything for us?" Eli asked, keeping his voice low. His eyes were trained on the back of Kayden's head, watching for any indication that Delilah was in danger.

"We have to for now. It's the only way Ghost will let her get close. Why do you think his men stopped following us once we found Kayden? He thinks he's won. She has him exactly where she wants him, I hope," I reason, motioning for them to get down when Kayden looks behind them.

I'm certain he knows we're here. I think it's why he walked so slowly toward this building. We'd walked around the back of the medical center and now stood in front of the storage building that sat alone in the field.

His eyes met mine, pleading. I knew what he was asking without words. I nodded. He shared a pained smile. If he hurt Delilah, I would kill him. It's the assurance he wanted. For a brief moment, I felt his pain at being forced to betray his family. I knew that it killed him to not have control. He and I were the same in that respect. We had to be in control.

We watched in silence as Delilah said something that pulled his attention away from us. She took both of his hands in hers. I watched her finger the ring, no doubt testing it to see how hard it would be to remove. His expression relaxed for a moment, then tightened in pain. I couldn't tell if it was her words that had hurt him, or if Ghost had yanked the leash again.

Dec perked up. "She says the ring is loose. She could take it from him now. But she's worried that her brother will know and use that knowledge to escape. So, one of us will have to take care of Kayden while she's dealing with Ghost."

Eli rubbed his hands over his face. "Did she call him that?"

"What?" Dec looked confused.

"Did she call him Ghost?" Eli asked more clearly.

Dec shook his head. She hadn't referred to her brother as Ghost in a while. It had been Gerolf as if she was trying to remind herself that he was human and not the monster we all made him out to be. She knew the truth, even if she wanted to hide it. At that moment, I knew that she wouldn't kill him. If she couldn't refer to him as his alter-ego, she wouldn't be able to separate herself from her emotions long enough to take him out.

"We will be forced to step in. Otherwise, he will kill her. We have to kill him first," I replied.

"But we promised her that it would be her decision," Eli reminded me.

"I know that, but I'm not going to stand here and watch while he destroys the woman I love," I growled.

"Can't we come up with another option?" Eli asked, still trying to force me to respect Delilah's wishes. I couldn't make him understand that it wasn't about respect. I just wanted to keep her safe.

Dec lit up again with another idea. "What if we take him to the Council? If we can stop him, they'll have to listen to us. Because even if we defeat him, Delilah will still be a fugitive. If we deliver Ghost to them, we can exchange him for her freedom."

I smiled at him. It was an honest, genuine smile. He'd had a brilliant idea. It just might work. It would appease Delilah and the Council both. Justice would be served and none of us would bear the blame for whatever they did to punish him.

"It's perfect. Should we tell her about the new plan? Then she won't have to stress over whether she can take him out or not," Eli suggested. He'd been quiet for the past few minutes, as if trying to figure out a puzzle. "Dec, explain things to our girl. Vik, we need to get that ring. I think I have a way to do it."

I should have been concerned when Eli detailed his plan, but instead, I was impressed. He wanted me to sneak up behind the wolf while he came at Kayden from the front. If I could hold his arms, Eli could take the ring. With any luck, that would break Ghost's control.

Dec didn't bother to tell our girl about that part of the plan, though. She would think it was too dangerous. Besides, we needed the element of surprise to make it work. We would go the moment Ghost showed himself.

We stayed there, crouched behind the sparse bushes, knowing that Kayden could see us. He didn't make a move to stop us, so we weren't concerned. It didn't matter that he knew we were there.

It would have been better if we could have hidden from Ghost, but there was no way. He's been stalking all of us for so long now. I didn't even know how long he'd been following us. From what Scott had told Eli, there were several of our people who had been compromised over the last few weeks. We would deal with that after we took Ghost out. For now, all we could do was wait and hope we didn't miss our chance at him.

CHAPTER 52

Eli

We waited; I'm not sure how long. Kayden growled and said something to Delilah. They'd been keeping their voices low enough that we couldn't hear them. I knew that Delilah was trying to help him fight the commands he was being given. She knew that we thought the ring was connected to the amulet, but there hadn't been a good chance for her to take it from him yet. We didn't want Ghost to know what we were planning before he was within our grasp.

Waiting was hard. There was nothing to do but think. I couldn't stop myself from thinking about all of the ways this could go wrong. I hated my brain for showing me every possible scenario where we would lose to this psychopath. I knew that I was feeling anxious, but it was enhanced by the anxiety of everyone around me. I was convinced that I could feel it coming from Delilah and Kayden as well.

Delilah tensed at something Kayden said. Is she okay? I wished that I had the connection with her that she had with Kayden and Declan. Maybe I should have agreed to test the implant on us. I just couldn't see putting something in her head that hadn't been fully tested.

I appreciate that, but I don't understand how you're in my head. Delilah's voice, loud and clear, sounded in my head. I'd never heard of something like this happening before. To be fair, I'd never seen a vamp survive a wolf bite either, much less turn into a hybrid.

You can hear me? I asked tentatively, waiting to see if she responded. I had expected words, but instead, she looked at me across the grounds and nodded.

"Vik, can you talk to Delilah?" I turned to him, puzzled.

"You want me to walk over there and talk to her? That'll ruin the plan. What's going on?" He looked me up and down, trying to figure out what I was getting at.

"I want you to think something at her. Ask her to do something. See if she responds," I instructed, watching him curiously. Would he think I'd gone crazy? I wasn't so sure that I hadn't. I stared at his face, scrunched up in concentration, not looking at Delilah.

She waved both arms over her head as if she was signaling an airplane. Then she stopped and refocused on Kayden. He seemed to be asking her what she was doing. I hoped she avoided telling him.

Don't worry, weirdo, I'm not telling him about this. I laughed out loud at the nickname she'd used.

You're the one jumping around waving your arms, but I'm the weirdo?

Vik and I exchanged a look. "How did that work? We don't have the implants. There is no way that we should be able to talk to her like that. Are we losing our minds? Is this some kind of trick Ghost is playing on us?" He looked at me as if I would have the answers.

"I have no idea. But if you can talk to her too, then I don't think we're crazy. It has to have something to do with her hybrid nature and us being her mates. It's some kind of evolution or something," I guessed.

"Guys, something is happening," Dec broke into our conversation. Vik and I looked over to where Kayden and Delilah were standing. We had assumed that he'd been waiting for a signal from Ghost to bring her in. It appeared that signal just happened. They walked toward the building and a door opened.

We rushed ahead, trying to get to the door before it closed. I had expected that Ghost would send out some thugs to fight us in an attempt to keep us away. To my surprise, the men who met us outside the door parted, leaving a path for us that led right to the entrance and inside.

"This way," a man said, gesturing to a hallway on our right. Dec, Vik, and I exchanged glances, silently deciding to follow the guy and find out what was going on. He led us to a large open room. In the center, Ghost stood with Kayden beside him and Delilah in front of him. If he'd been anyone else, I would have thought we were too late. His love of showmanship would give us the chance to save her.

"If you're going to kill me anyway, why not let me say goodbye to Kayden first?" Delilah's words echoed across the room and suddenly I knew what she was planning, even without telepathic communication. I watched as Ghost gestured to Kayden, allowing him to hug Delilah. She grabbed his hand, pulled the ring off, and threw it toward us.

Vik ran to the left, Dec headed to the right, and I rushed straight toward them. I grabbed the ring on my way, putting it in my pocket to keep it from being used again. I watched as Kayden shook his head, trying to figure out what was happening. Then he turned, standing in front of Delilah protectively. *You have to make sure he doesn't kill Ghost. We're going to give him to the Council.* I forced the thoughts toward her, hoping she would agree with our decision.

Ghost's scream rang through the room. "No! You can't do this! He's my pet. I need him." His screams turned to whines as he realized he would have to fight. His men came from everywhere at once. The floor was a free-for-all. I fought my way toward Delilah, glancing over to see that Vik and Dec were doing the same. Delilah was solely focused on her brother. It looked like she was trying to reason with him, but it wasn't working. I couldn't hear what was being said because of the men who were attacking me. I knew that none of us really wanted to hurt innocent people, but these men would not submit.

Vik had already unleashed his dark side, tearing off limbs and heads. I turned to see that Dec was doing the same, making easy work of it. "If you can't beat 'em, join 'em," I said, getting puzzled looks from the men I'd been punching. We had been so focused on not becoming monsters that we'd nearly let these men beat us. I grabbed one by the arm and another by the leg and tossed them as far away from me as I could. I knew they'd be back, but before they made it, I took a head and two legs off the other ones who were attacking me. I used the legs as bats, beating the two I'd thrown when they attacked again.

In a matter of minutes, the three of us were drenched in blood, and Ghost's forces were decimated. Kayden and Delilah had him backed into a corner, trying to capture him. He ducked under Kayden's arm and ran into Delilah's fist. The impact caused his hand to go to his face just before his eyes rolled back in his head. Kayden wrapped his arms around him, holding the man still until the rest of us could get there.

"You guys look disgusting," Delilah quipped with a laugh. She walked over to a window and ripped the shades down, using the cord from them to tie Ghost up. Kayden had taken the amulet from Ghost's neck and tucked it securely in his pocket. I would be asking the Council about that particular item when we visited them to deliver the package.

"Let's secure him and get out of here," I said, wiping as much blood as I could from my skin and clothes. I wanted a hot shower and some time with my girl before we dealt with the Council and Ghost. We carried him away, leaving the mess to be cleaned up later.

"Where are we going?" Dec asked as we climbed into one of the SUVs, securing Ghost between himself and Kayden in the backseat while Delilah sat on Vik's lap in the front and I got behind the wheel.

"I think my place would be the best. Scott has been rounding up the traitors and locking them up here at the med center. It should be safer at my place," I offered. No one objected. We raced off and, in a few minutes, had Ghost settled into a cage in the underground holding area. He was still unconscious, so we had time to clean up before anyone tried to get answers out of him.

I had expected everyone to want their own rooms to shower and rest, so I pointed out which rooms were empty. Though everyone went off to shower alone, we all then reconvened in the living room.

"Which one is yours?" Dec asked, pointing at doors.

"This one," I responded, not sure why it mattered. Two seconds later, he and Kayden were carrying mattresses into my room and Vik was setting up the bedframes to go with them. "What are you guys doing?"

Delilah smiled from ear to ear, turning to me and pulling me into a hug. "I wanted us to all stay together. So, I asked them if they would fix it. I hope that's okay."

"It's perfect, love," I said, leaning down to kiss her.

CHAPTER 53

Declan

At Delilah's request, we had converted Eli's bedroom into a space for us all. We brought two of the king-sized beds from other rooms in, setting them up on either side of his existing bed. At some point, when all of this was over, we would need a custom bed frame and mattress. I started planning it in my head. This would work for now.

Eli had checked on Ghost four times in the last hour. I understood his concern. We were all terrified he would escape before we could deliver him to the Council. Each time he snuck away, I distracted Delilah with some other aspect of making this space homey. We'd just finished putting fresh sheets on all three mattresses when he came back into the room. Vik and Kayden had gone on a supply run, insisting that Eli and I could handle our girl. Delilah didn't seem to mind, but she did threaten to make them sleep outside if they forgot to bring her ice cream.

I couldn't blame her for wanting to celebrate. We had been through hell. But we survived and we would build our lives together from this point on. "Where have you been sneaking off to?" she asked Eli, stepping between him and the door so he couldn't leave. So much for keeping her occupied so she didn't notice he was gone. He shot me a look and I shrugged.

"I went to check on him. I'm sorry, I know that Scott has everything under control. His guys are making sure the traitors don't get out so he can be here. I just had to make sure," Eli explained, not using Ghost's name in case it would upset Delilah. His face scrunched in concern at how she would react.

"Gerolf. You've been running off to check on my brother. Why didn't I realize that?" She threw her arms around him and kissed him hard. Damn, I should have gone to check on our guest. If I had suspected that she would react like that, I might have. I stepped back and let them have their moment. When she backed away, he took her hand.

"I didn't want to upset you by mentioning it. He's secure. Scott hasn't taken his eyes off him for a moment. I tried to talk to him, but he refuses to even look at me." Delilah hung on every word as if she'd been concerned herself. Why hadn't we realized that she might need to see that he's not going anywhere?

"Did you want to go see him?" I asked, unsure if it would upset her.

Delilah took her time to answer, making me nervous that I'd said something wrong. "I think I would. I mean, I know that he's not going anywhere. Scott is very good at his job. But I think I'd like to talk to my brother before we turn him over to the Council." She paused and looked at Eli. "Is our appointment with the Council set?"

"It is. They're expecting us first thing in the morning. I didn't bother to tell them exactly why, just that we had something for them," he replied, running a hand through his hair. The idea of going in front of the Council made me nervous, but I knew it would be the only way to clear Delilah's name and make sure the hunters left her alone.

"Okay. Will you guys stay with me when I talk to him?" Her voice nearly broke when she asked. Eli and I nodded. We would do whatever she wanted. The three of us headed to the elevator and traveled down to the holding cell that Ghost was in.

"What's up, boss? You were just down here," Scott began, then paused when he saw that Delilah and I were with Eli this time.

"Our girl wants to talk to her brother. We're gonna go in with her. You can take a break. We've got this handled," Eli said, effectively dismissing Scott for a while.

He nodded and said, "I'll go grab something to eat."

We stood outside the door for a while. Delilah stared at the two-way mirror in the wall as if she was trying to decide if she really wanted to do this or not. "You don't have to go in. We can go back upstairs and watch a movie or take a bubble bath," I offered. I didn't want to keep her from talking to him, but I wasn't going to force her into anything.

Delilah shook her head, never taking her eyes off of Ghost. "I need to do this. He needs to know that no matter what, it didn't have to come to this." Holy shit. She was going to tell him that they could have worked everything out even after he'd tortured her and tried to kill her.

"You're not thinking about letting him go, are you?" Eli asked, suddenly on edge.

She stared at her brother, taking a long moment before answering. "No. We will give him to the Council and they can punish him however they see fit. Don't worry, I'm not going to cave." She seemed to know what Eli had been thinking. Then I realized that was probably because I was thinking it, too. Or maybe their connection earlier hadn't been a fluke. They had tried a few times since we got back to speak telepathically, but it hadn't worked.

Before either of us could respond, she opened the door and stepped inside, leaving it open for us to follow. Eli and I leaned against the door, giving her space to do what she needed for closure. Ghost's head jerked up and his eyes opened wide at the sight of the three of us standing there. He didn't speak.

"I need to know why you did all of this. Why did you want to destroy vampires?" she asked in a soft voice. He looked at her, refusing to answer. "They could make you talk to me. But you would enjoy that, wouldn't you? Forcing me to stoop to your level would make you feel justified in everything you've done."

His eyes met hers in recognition. He knew that it would only take a word from her for us to attack and tear him to pieces. My fangs clicked into place at the thought. Delilah looked over at me and smirked as if we'd planned it. Eli took one step forward, and Ghost shrank back against the corner he'd been crouched in.

"Why do you care? You've stopped me, haven't you? Your bloodsuckers are safe," he snarled, glaring at Eli but ignoring me.

"Because I don't think any group of people deserve to be massacred just because they exist. You talked a lot about our mother, but I'm not sure that I believe anything you told me. She wasn't distant or hateful when she was around me. But she was in love with our father. If he turned out to be a bad person, I'm sorry for that. I just don't understand what any of that has to do with vampires." Delilah took a step toward him; her expression was cold and detached. I knew that it didn't match her roiling emotions, but I was impressed at how much control she was showing. I pushed my support into her, letting her know how proud I was of her for facing him.

She turned her head slightly to smile at me, and Ghost rushed her. He knocked her into the wall before Eli pinned him to the corner that he'd just been in. I scooped Delilah up and checked her for injuries. "I'm sorry, I didn't mean to distract you." I kissed her forehead and held her close, then we turned our attention to Eli and Ghost.

"Give me one reason not to rip your throat out. I'm sure the Council wouldn't mind if we took care of their issue. They'll probably be just as happy with a dead body as they would with you alive," Eli growled in his face.

Ghost whimpered and tried to get as far away from Eli as he could. It was impossible since Eli was holding him by the throat. He forced the human to look at him as he snarled and his fangs clicked. We watched as Ghost's khaki pants changed color. He'd pissed himself. It became clear that he was terrified of us, which was probably the reason he'd been out to rid the world of vampires. I wondered what had happened to him to cause it.

"Don't, don't hurt me," he whined. Eli stepped back and threw him at the wall. There was a distinct crunch, then the human started to cry. I wasn't sure if it was his leg or his arm that had snapped. I looked down at Delilah who was still cradled in my arms. She was watching the whole thing with silent amazement. I couldn't tell what she was thinking.

"Just leave him. I'm done here," she addressed the comment to Eli, then turned her face toward me. "Will you take me back upstairs?" I nodded and carried her out of the room, not waiting for Eli. He caught up to us just as we entered the elevator.

"Scott has it under control. This will all be over tomorrow." He leaned down and kissed Delilah while I held her. The three of us went straight to the bedroom, and shortly after we climbed into the bed, Delilah was asleep.

CHAPTER 54

Kayden

DELILAH HAD BEEN ASLEEP when Vik and I got back. Eli and Dec met us in the living room and filled us in on what had happened. She was obviously more tormented by what he'd done to us than she let on. I was relieved that she was sleeping. "So, are we all going to sleep in that big bed together?" I asked with a chuckle. I already knew that we would, because it was what she wanted.

The other three nodded. We put the supplies away, then climbed into bed with our girl. It wasn't as strange as I had expected to sleep with everyone in the same place. At least with putting the three beds together, we had enough space for everyone without worrying about getting knocked onto the floor while we slept.

I tossed and turned long after the others had given in to sleep. I went over my speech for the Council in my head, practicing what I would say to them. Since I realized they had been controlling wolves for their purposes, I wanted out. I wouldn't be their guard dog anymore. I'm not sure how I'll make it happen; no one had ever left the hunters. *There's a first time for everything.*

Sleep finally came for me but didn't last long before Dec was shaking me awake. "Come on, man, we have to go," he said. I got up without a word and dressed. We gathered our evidence against Ghost, then Eli and Vik went down to get him. We met them at the SUV where Ghost was not only tied up but also had been knocked out. I wondered if he'd given them trouble or if Eli was still pissed at him for attacking Delilah last night. Either way, it was nice to know he'd be easy to transport. Everyone got in and we drove to the church on the East side of the city.

The guys had decided that I would handle talking to the Council because I had a relationship with them already and knew what to expect. Delilah agreed, which surprised me. She'd been adamant about handling things that concerned her. It was almost as if she was scared of the Council. If she was, it was a good thing. They held her life in their hands. I wasn't looking forward to standing in front of the twelve of them and pleading our case. Eleven. There were eleven now. I shook the memory away. I couldn't afford to get caught up in the past.

Eli and Dec carried Ghost up the steps of the church, following me, while Vik walked behind them with Delilah. The old church had been renovated on the inside and reminded me of a theater. The seats were covered in a rich velvet the color of blood. I suspected it was intentional, to hide any potential spray that could coat the audience at public executions. I stole a glance at Delilah, feeling her nerves mingle with my own. I knew that there was a chance we'd be fighting our way out of here and running for our lives. If the Council didn't see that we'd helped them, they might not dismiss the hit order on Delilah.

I stepped up to the stage where the altar had been when this was a church. It surprised me that no one was out here. Usually, the Council would be waiting when someone arrived. "Hello?" I called out. I wasn't sure if I expected a response or not. A moment later, three wolf shifters came in and approached us.

"Kayden. It's good to see you made it, brother. And you've captured the fugitive. They will be pleased," one of them said. I couldn't remember his name, and since I'd bonded with Delilah, I couldn't hear their thoughts through the pack bond anymore. I had rejected my pack and selected a new one. *This could go bad really quickly.* I hadn't meant to push the thought at Delilah, but her soft gasp told me that I had. I couldn't dwell on that either. I had to focus on what needed to be done.

"I need to talk to them. There have been developments," I said before they could make a move toward Delilah to take her into custody. They looked from me to her and back again.

"Developments?" another asked. *Joe? Steve? Shit, why couldn't I remember their names?* So much had happened that I had no idea who these guys were.

"I'll explain it all to the Council," I insisted, standing straighter and trying to look intimidating. It must have worked, because all three of them backed down. The first one who had spoken nodded and the three of them went back to report. The Council would decide if they needed to talk to me or not, and we would go from there.

"I thought we had an appointment," Delilah whispered when they were gone.

I nodded. "We do, but they can still decide not to see us. They apparently think I'm here to turn you in. That's not gonna happen. We'll fight our way out if we have to."

"That won't be necessary, Kayden." The voice was soft but firm and seemed to come out of nowhere and everywhere at once. "We know that you have new information for us and we are willing to hear you out. There should be no reason to fight today." Three hooded figures wearing black robes stepped from the shadows on the stage. They could have been there the whole time and we wouldn't have noticed.

"Where's the rest of the Council?" I asked, momentarily forgetting that I should have asked permission to speak freely first.

"We are all that remains. The others were killed," a second figure spoke. I couldn't tell which ones these were. They seemed set on keeping their identities hidden. I couldn't blame them. I had only been in one meeting where they were open about showing their faces. I hadn't expected this one to be like that one.

"How?" Eli asked, forgetting that I was supposed to be the one to address the Council. I guessed that it didn't matter now.

"We've been hunted, by a man who calls himself Ghost. The three of us were the only ones to evade him," the third figure spoke and I realized that she was the only female left. The Council had been twelve members, half men, half women. It should have hurt me that they'd been taken out, but since I knew about their use of mind control, I found it hard to care.

I introduced my new family to the Council and we explained everything. The three of them were silent for a while after we finished. I was beginning to think they would decide to take us all into custody and have a mass execution. While we talked, Ghost woke up. He looked around the room and panic showed in his eyes. He knew what would happen to him now that he didn't have control of the wolves.

The three Council members had turned their backs to us, discussing what we had told them. The longer it took, the more I was certain we were in trouble. As I prepared to fight, they turned back to us. The first man spoke again, "Thank you, Kayden, for bringing us the man who hunted our brothers and sisters. We will exact justice on him immediately. As for the girl, we see now that her actions were not her own decision. We will drop the bounty."

"There's one more thing," I began, pausing to make sure they would hear me out.

"You wish to be free of your entanglement with the hunters. It shall be so," the female spoke again. I was shocked that I hadn't even had to ask or explain myself. I wondered if they could see the mate bond through their magic or tech or whatever they used to learn things. It may have been that they didn't want me to mention my issues with their use of mind control while their wolf lackeys were so close.

A gesture from one of the men had the three shifters taking Ghost from us. They dropped him on the stage in front of what was left of the Council. I had expected them to set a trial and follow their procedures. Instead, one of the men pulled Ghost to his knees and got in his face. "Do you have anything to say for yourself?"

Ghost refused to respond, growling at the man. "Very well." The man turned to the other two Council members and nodded. He stepped back and the other man stepped forward. He pulled a sword from his robe. In one smooth motion, the sword sang through the air, slicing through Ghost's neck and severing his head. It fell to the ground with a thunk and blood pooled around the body.

I turned to Delilah, hoping that Vik had been able to turn her away from what had just happened in time. From her expression, I knew that he hadn't. She started to shake, clearly going into shock. "It's over," she whispered. I nodded and pulled her into my arms.

CHAPTER 55

Delilah

EPILOGUE

THINGS MOVED PRETTY FAST after Gerolf had been dealt with. The Council ordered the hunters to take care of the Powder operations in the city, whether they were the ones Gerolf had used to drug me or not. Once they were all shut down and dismantled, vampires were free to live in peace without fear of being drugged and killed.

My guys all worked together on plans for our home. Dec had found a building in the center of the city that was perfect. They all pooled money and purchased it, then had the top floors remodeled into a custom apartment for us to live in. The bottom two floors were converted into a karaoke bar and restaurant. It took months for all of the renovations to be completed. We all stayed at Eli's place until our levels were completed.

Since Midnight had been destroyed and the reconstruction was halted while we dealt with my brother, Vik decided to move Midnight to the new property. He still renovated the old location, but it was being used as free housing for newly turned vamps.

The grand opening for Midnight at its new location was a smashing success. The guys had managed to keep it a secret from me until five minutes before it started. Eli told me we were going out, so I put on the slinky red dress he'd picked out. I fixed my hair in a cute half up do and put on makeup. He wouldn't tell me where we were going, only that he knew I'd want to be dolled up for it. When we stepped out of the elevator doors, my jaw dropped. People from all over the city were in my bar. And it was *my* bar. I cried at how they'd made it look exactly like the bar I had grown up in. The only thing that was missing was Uncle Vinny. More tears came with that thought.

After welcoming everyone, Vik convinced me to sing. I loved it so much. After a few others performed, I made Dec sing with me. The other three had disappeared to avoid it. When we finished, Dec escorted me upstairs to the restaurant. "What's this all about?" I asked, wondering what else they could have planned to surprise me.

"Don't worry about it, just come with me," he'd insisted. I followed, on guard for anything. Kayden had already snuck up behind me three times to 'surprise hump' me. Eli had wanted me to dance, and Vik insisted that we would have dinner together. It was crazy how much I loved being pulled in four different directions. I stepped into the restaurant and stopped dead in my tracks. The restaurant was beautiful. Tears filled my eyes again and I realized just how much had changed since I met Vik and Eli.

"What, no hug?" a familiar voice said in my ear. I spun around and came face to face with my best friend. Guilt tore through me when I realized how long it had been since I had seen her.

"Anna! I'm so sorry. I should have called. Can you ever forgive me?" I grabbed her and pulled her into the tightest hug.

"If you stop squeezing me so hard, I will," she said with a laugh. "I know you've been through a lot. I got a call and a couple of guys met me for coffee. They explained everything. I can't be mad at you. But we definitely need to talk later." Anna winked at me. I knew exactly what she wanted to talk about. She would ask how I went from no guys to four in such a short time. I wouldn't have an answer. My guys tracked down my best friend and made sure she was at our opening. Could they be any more perfect?

The rest of the night was a blur. The food was amazing. I had a blast singing with Anna, and promised to have lunch with her soon to talk. After she left, the restaurant and bar closed. Then my guys and I went upstairs to our new home.

It was amazing how much of themselves they had poured into the new space. In addition to our two levels of living space, Kayden and Eli had the gym set up with the latest equipment. Dec had converted a floor into a wood shop where he could work on furniture and other projects. Eli had a workshop with all of his tech inventions spread everywhere. Vik had a floor dedicated to music, with a piano and an amazing stereo system. They had even built me a recording studio in case I wanted to release my own music. There was also a shop for Kayden to work on cars, but that was in the parking garage next door.

We entered the apartment, walked through the living room, past the kitchen, and climbed the short flight of stairs to the bedroom. They had used an entire floor for it and the bathroom. I had never seen a bed so big before in my life. Dec had built and carved the bedframe himself out of gorgeous walnut wood, and the room was decorated around it. Everything they chose was meant to accent the beautiful showpiece that we would sleep in.

The bathroom was nearly as big as the bedroom. The shower and tub were custom, big enough to hold all five of us at once. Clearly, they had some group activities in mind when they had designed it all. There were even hidden drawers all over the room that held toys and lube just in case we wanted to play. I couldn't believe that the four of them had designed it all by themselves.

When they told me that I didn't get to make any decisions on the new property, I was concerned that I would feel like it wasn't mine. Of course, they realized how I was feeling. Dec and Kayden explained that it was only meant to be a surprise, and if I didn't like anything, they'd change it. The first time I walked through the apartment, I knew that I wouldn't change any of it. They had gotten every detail, down to the paint color, just right. I stood at the enormous window that spanned one wall of the bedroom, staring out at our city.

Since we'd taken care of their problem, the remaining Council members had given Kayden control of the East. With the entire city under their control, my guys were working together to make things better for everyone, human, vamp, and shifter. It was amazing to watch them change the world a little at a time.

Dec came up behind me, putting his arms around my waist and pulling me against him. He leaned down and kissed my neck. I turned in his arms and captured his lips with mine. The kiss was soft and sweet, with a burning need just under the surface. While I kissed him, Kayden had slipped up behind me. I moaned against Dec's lips as Kayden nipped at my neck. Before I knew what was happening, Eli scooped me up and I was tossed onto the bed.

I laughed as my guys competed for my attention, shoving each other out of the way to kiss me or touch me. I knew they were playing. It warmed my heart to see how close they had become over the past few months. We really were a family now. The thought stuck in my head while I watched Eli and Dec gang up on Vik, each grabbing a leg to drag him off the bed. Before they could get to me, Kayden climbed on top of me and pulled the dress down, dropping it on the floor beside Vik. His groan got the other guys' attention. I had opted to go commando under my dress. The sight of me naked had rendered him speechless. I loved that I still had that effect on them all.

I knew that they would stop play-fighting now that I was completely available to them. Kayden ran a hand over my stomach. I shivered at the sensation. I closed my eyes for a moment and felt Eli's hand slide up my right leg while Dec's worked its way up my left. Vik kissed me before moving his attention to my nipples. I couldn't believe how well they all worked together to give me as much pleasure as possible.

They continued to touch, stroke, and lick my skin until I couldn't take any more. I was nearly certain they had worked out a rotation beforehand with how quickly things moved at that point. Eli slid his fingers inside of me while Kayden lubed up and played with my ass. I reached for Dec and Vik, who were both hard and ready too. Once everyone was in place, Kayden entered me from behind, then Eli slowly, torturously, pushed into me. They settled into a rhythm that told me they had definitely planned everything out before. Eli and Kayden thrust into me, over and over, alternating so that I was continuously full until I came, forcing them to explode with me.

Then, far too seamlessly to have been random, Dec took Eli's place and Vik took Kayden's. I decided that I liked it when they planned things out. There was no waiting while they decided who went where; no chance for me to be torn out of the mood because of arguing. Dec slid into me, holding me still while Vik teased me with his tip. I knew he wanted me to beg for it, but I had decided to tease him instead. I ground against Dec until he loosened his grip. Then I stretched my arms behind me to grab Vik's ass with one hand and his cock with the other. I guided him to where I wanted him and pushed him inside of me. They thrust into me again and again until we came together.

I lost myself to the aftershocks of my orgasm, enjoying the bliss of being loved. Life couldn't be any better, but we'd earned it, and I planned to enjoy every last minute of it with the men who devoted everything to me. The city and our future was ours. We've fought hard for it and each other. Eternity together would be utter bliss.

About the Author

M.P. Starkweather is a wife, mother, author, poet, casual online gamer, self-proclaimed fan-girl, and full-time nerd. She writes free-form poetry, paranormal romance, sci-fi romance, reverse harem romance, and is branching out into contemporary romance. In her free time, she enjoys writing, reading, Dungeons & Dragons, table top games with her husband and friends, and playing with her son. M.P. also enjoys tv, movies, and music across various genres.

To get the most up-to-date information about her latest releases and book signings, check out www.mpstarkweather.com or follow her on your favorite social media site.

Also By M.P. Starkweather

Standalones - Contemporary RH OV

Forsaken Omega – free with newsletter signup

Cold Princes

Knot My Valentine
The Pack Next Door – Contemporary RH OV series

Princess or Knot

Fiancée or Knot

Queen or Knot

Christmas or Knot
Standalones – Paranormal RH

The Wayward Girl
Vampires at Midnight - Paranormal RH series
Blood Moon

Blood Lost

Blood War
A Vampires at Midnight and Hunters of the Forest Crossover Novella - Paranormal RH, free with newsletter signup

Blood Wolf
Hunters of the Forest - Paranormal RH series

Wolf Bane

<u>Wolf Caged</u>

<u>Wolf Moon</u>
Forged by Magic - Sci-fi/Fantasy M/F series

<u>Hidden</u>

<u>Betrayed</u>

<u>Saved</u>
Daydreams and Sunsets - a collection of poetry

<u>Daydreams and Sunsets</u>